REINHART'S
WOMEN

NOVELS BY

THOMAS BERGER

The Reinhart Series
Crazy in Berlin (1958)
Reinhart in Love (1962)
Vital Parts (1970)
Reinhart's Women (1981)

Little Big Man (1964)
Killing Time (1967)
Regiment of Women (1973)
Sneaky People (1975)
Who Is Teddy Villanova? (1977)
Arthur Rex (1978)
Neighbors (1980)

REINHART'S WOMEN

A
NOVEL BY
THOMAS BERGER

⏋

DELTA/SEYMOUR LAWRENCE

A DELTA/SEYMOUR LAWRENCE BOOK

Published by
Dell Publishing Co., Inc.
1 Dag Hammarskjold Plaza
New York, New York 10017

An excerpt from this book originally appeared in *Playboy* magazine.

For information address Delacorte Press/Seymour Lawrence,
New York, New York.

Delta ® TM 755118, Dell Publishing Co., Inc.

ISBN: 0-440-57408-0

Reprinted by arrangement with Delacorte Press/Seymour Lawrence
Printed in the United States of America
First Delta printing—October 1982

Library of Congress Cataloging in Publication Data

Berger, Thomas, 1924–
Reinhart's women.

I. Title.
PS3552.E719R4   1982   813'.54   82-10000
ISBN 0-440-57408-0   AACR2

*To Emma Berger Jewett
and in memory of
Joseph F. Jewett III*

REINHART'S
WOMEN

CHAPTER

1

Reinhart was preparing brunch for his daughter and his new girl friend. He and Winona had lived together since his divorce from her mother, ten years before. The friendship with Grace Greenwood was a recent development.

At the moment he was slicing little *lardons* from a stack of bacon strips. Grace was not due for another quarter hour. Winona appeared in the doorway to the kitchen.

"Is this O.K., do you think, Daddy?" She turned sveltely in her figured dress of turquoise, green, and blue. With amber eyes and chestnut hair, and a person that was not less than exquisite in any particular, Winona was as lovely a creature as Reinhart had ever seen, and though she was, technically speaking, but half his creation and took her coloring from the maternal side, in spirit she was nothing like her mother. The nice thing about Winona, as one of her admirers had explained to Reinhart, was that though a beauty she seemed to believe herself unattractive. The combination quite devastated this prosperous young lawyer, who had offered her his heart and his considerable goods of life. Among her other suitors had been an up-and-coming, middle-of-the-road politician and a forty-two-year-old department-store executive who professed to be ready to dump his wife and kids for her hand.

Winona's habitual response to male attentions was first disbelief, then amusement, but with the executive she had been outraged.

"Daddy," she had said through tears of anger, "he's *married*. How can a man be so disgusting?"

"It really turns one's stomach," said arch-hypocrite Reinhart, an old frequenter of whores extramaritally, but then his wife had been a real bitch at the time—indeed at all times. "Of course there may be extenuating circumstances, Winona. He's probably not a criminal, but it's not the worst strategy to consider all men as conscienceless brutes." That he was here being a traitor to his own sex gave Reinhart no qualms: he could not remember the last time a man had done anything for him, anything, that is, that did not militate to the advantage of the giver.

"What," Winona asked now, "is Grace's favorite color?"

Reinhart had finished his neat knifeplay, having transformed a half-pound of slab bacon into an accumulation of little strips measuring half an inch by an inch and a half.

"Favorite color," he said speculatively. "Now, I don't mean to offend you, but that would seem a very female question."

"Daddy," said Winona, "how could you offend me, since I *am* female?" She said this with her habitual sweetness, being incapable of irony.

Reinhart always kept a supply of chicken stock in the fridge, but anxious as he was to make the best impression on Grace Greenwood, he had earlier that morning cut up a three-pound bird, immersed the pieces in water to which he had added a sliced carrot, a diced onion, and a quarter teaspoon of dried thyme, brought it to a boil, and simmered it, partially covered, for an hour and a quarter. Then he removed the flesh, putting it aside for another use, and strained the fragrant liquid, which of course was in itself a bouillon. Only half a cup was needed for the Eggs Meurette.

He turned up the gas under a saucepan full of water: the slab bacon had a good strong, smoky flavor that was first-rate with an American breakfast, hen fruit sunny side up and home fries, or with flapjacks (though little pork sausages had the edge here), but eggs poached in red wine and chicken stock, with mushrooms, had a flavor that obviously would be stained by any hint of smoke, nor would the excessive salt in which bacon is cured be welcome.

The point was that Reinhart was about to blanch the bacon—which Winona brought home, for it was she who supported them while he served as housekeeper.

"Daddy, you're like all men," his daughter told him now. "You never look at anybody." She said this in a tone of affectionate reproach.

"Why, of course I do, Winona. But it *is* more like a woman than a man to notice colors. Whether or not that is based on some biological difference I couldn't say."

"Oh, I think it is," she said with vigor. No unisex theories would be entertained by Winona. Of course Reinhart, at his age, was gratified by his daughter's failure to be up to date. In truth the two of them saw eye to eye on almost everything, with the notable exception of food.

Winona had been a glutton until the last year or so of her teens, stuffing her then-stout person daily with sufficient carbohydrates to sate the Sumo wrestler she was on her way to resembling. But when she reformed, her efforts were not niggardly. In fact, what she had done was simply to reverse the coin and eat hardly enough to sustain life. The doctor assured Reinhart that her about-face was not abnormal in an American adolescent, and further he suggested that Reinhart himself, who had not then seen his own belt buckle in years, might do worse than follow his daughter's lead.

It was at this time that Reinhart had really begun to take a serious interest in food, after having gorged on it mindlessly for half a century. But despite his efforts to prepare such delicious meals that small portions exquisitely flavored would fill the role earlier performed by mountainous servings of sweet-and-salty blandness, he could claim no great success with Winona. Nowadays she simply ate almost nothing at all but wheat germ and yoghurt.

True, his leverage of argument was feeble. The slimmer she became, the more robust her health; whereas as a fatty her colds, laid end to end, had embraced the year, and of the common nonlethal complaints of all the popular organs she had evaded few. But the real clincher, unanswerable, was that Winona's dwindle in girth was accompanied by her gain in height, and by the time she had finished her eighteenth year, which coincided with her completion of the last term of high school, she stood five feet eight and she weighed a hundred twenty, and in no time at all she had become a fashion model and supported her father in a style he had never known! Their apartment, for example, was in a high-rise overlooking the river, five rooms furnished with expensive blond wood and chromium and glass, and Reinhart had a kitchenful of appliances. He supposed that it was in his interest *not* to feed Winona much. Yet cooking was the only thing in life he had ever done well.

Once he had wryly made that point to Winona herself. Her response, truly unexpected, had sent him behind the closed door of the bathroom: for, despite all the feminist propaganda, Reinhart continued to believe it unmanly to weep before others.

"Maybe it is a thing you've done *well*," Winona had said in a solemn, even owlish style, "but what you've done *great* is being my dad."

Imagine having a daughter like that!

"Darling," he said now, "whichever color is Grace's favorite, she's going to fall in love with you. Now, I know that's a man's answer and that you're still going to worry about how you're dressed, because even though you're the leading model in town, you're female, and that means you're more anxious about other women than about men when it comes to your attire."

"I wonder why that is?" Winona asked.

Reinhart placed a dozen and a half of the button mushrooms in a colander and plunged the perforated vessel into a potful of cool water. He lifted it out, dripping, and then plunged it back. He decided to add another half-dozen fungi, did so and rinsed the lot once more, then removed the colander and emptied its burden onto paper towels.

"I suppose it makes sense, all in all," he said to his daughter. "Persons of the opposite sex look at each other with a totally different kind of interest from what they have when they see their own kind. They measure themselves against their fellows—they're in competition, aren't they?"

"Well," Winona said, moueing, "so are male models with us, I can tell you."

Reinhart snorted. "But is that the most manly of professions?" In justice it did occur to him that perhaps keeping house for a young woman, when you were not *that* old, might be seen as a failure of virility—but that the woman was a daughter made, as anyone would agree, a substantive difference.

conscience was clean: he had not stood in her way. Winona really
had no ambition for spectacular success and little attraction to any
way of life that could be called glamorous.

She started away from the kitchen, murmuring, and then she
turned and stepped back. "Dad, I must say you have not said much
about Grace. What's she like? How does she strike you, really?"

Reinhart cocked an eye at his simmering strips of bacon. He
turned to Winona. "I guess you're right. I haven't told you much
about Grace—for any number of reasons. Even after ten years
away from your mother I still feel funny speaking of other women
in front of you. But apart from that—" The subject was important
to Reinhart, but he could not fail in his responsibility to the meal:
again he tossed the mushrooms in their lemon-juice bath. "In
addition," he resumed, "I have all my life generally had difficulty
in telling one female person anything about another. Whether
that's my own foible, or—"

Reinhart cleared his throat. The possibility that he might be
turning into a garrulous old bore suddenly suggested itself to him:
it was not a simple matter to identify oneself with the tedious sort
of old-timer one remembered from one's own youth. Consciousness, however far back it can be remembered, always seems about
the same. It is an effortless thing to recall, across half a century,
one's intent to become a cowboy when one grows up.

"Sorry, dear. I'll make it snappy. To begin with, Grace, while not
being quite as young as you, is even further from being as old as
I. That is, she is not old enough to be your biological mother,
whereas I suppose I *could*, technically speaking, have been her
father, if just barely: she is forty." He frowned in thought. "She's
a nice-looking woman, but what really matters is she's smart. I
don't mean to imply that women aren't usually, but Grace has
made a success in a man's world."

He closed one eye briefly and laughed. "First time we met I took
her for a housewife, and a fairly dowdy and out-of-date one at that.
She was wearing a cardigan and the kind of shoes that years ago
were called 'sensible.' In fact, she was generally reminiscent of an
earlier era, which is why I noticed her in the first place. I've found
myself doing that sort of thing more and more. I suppose it's a sign
of growing senility!"

Winona suddenly excused herself and left the kitchen. But when Reinhart had finished blanching the bacon she was back. She now wore the third outfit he had seen within a quarter hour: a long, long skirt, a puffy sort of blouse, and a kind of bandanna tied around her forehead. He liked this ensemble least of all: it was rather too mannered for his taste, but of course he said something flattering.

Winona thanked him. "But you weren't finished talking about Grace."

He raised his eyebrows. "Grace, you see, is all wool, no nonsense. Fact is, it was *she* who first asked me out. And why not? There we were, in front of the Mexican packaged foods—that's where we met, in the supermarket, as I mentioned earlier. She turned to me, in that cardigan and those sensible shoes. 'Say,' she said, 'do you really buy any of this stuff?' She asked it so aggressively that I thought she might be hostile to it herself. 'Not much,' says I. 'I don't cook in any Hispanic cuisine, though mind you I've nothing against any. I've eaten a taco or two in my time, and once, in that Mexican restaurant in the Wulsin Building downtown, I ate a chicken *mole*, which was fascinating with its peppery chocolate sauce, but—'

" 'I am really interested only in the Pancho Villa line,' she said, and she pointed at the cans bearing that label, which carry a picture of a Mexican bandit or general, Villa himself I suppose, with crossed bandoleers and a saber and two guns. 'I'm one of the guys who distribute that,' she said, 'and what I'm listening for is public reaction. The opinion-testers are more scientific, but I like to get the street-reaction on my own. Now, you look like a normal member of the public. Do you think this picture of a bloodthirsty-looking greaser would encourage you to buy, uh'—she chose a can at random and read the label—'uh, refried beans?'

"That's Grace's style, I'm afraid," said Reinhart. "She'll never get the mealymouthed award." He laughed heartily, though in truth he found that quality the least of Grace's attractions. "It turned out that she was an executive with this food-distributing firm, a vice-president no less. When she found out I did the cooking at my house she wouldn't let me go until I had given her a complete rundown on my choices of brands, the types of food I buy, the type of meal my family prefers, and the rest of it." Reinhart gestured with his wooden spoon. "And that would have been that, I'm sure, had I not mentioned that I had a daughter who happened to be the foremost model in town."

Winona blushed. "Oh, Dad, come on."

Reinhart chuckled happily. "No, I'm afraid I was just a statistic until then. But I didn't mind, dear. I like nothing better than bragging about you. Well, as I told you, that's how it began. That was just two days back. We found ourselves having lunch in that restaurant in the shopping center that used to be Gino's." Reinhart winced at a series of unpleasant memories under the old management. "It's a better place now, with a more expansive though somewhat hokey menu sometimes: pineapple with baked fish, and ginger with anything. Grace had the New York steak, hold the potato, and helped herself only modestly at the salad bar. I ordered the *escalope de veau*—we don't have it here very often because the price of veal is really insane"—not to mention that Winona wouldn't eat it—" and when the orders arrived, the waiter needlessly to say put the cutlets in front of her. . . . They were by the way more Wiener schnitzel than *escalopes,* breaded, for gosh sakes, but not badly, with grated Gruyère and what tasted like a little real Parmesan in the breading . . ."

Winona was wearing a sweetly bored look by now.

"Anyway, we also had a drink before eating: I had the vermouth cassis, and Grace, the Jim Beam and water, and the bartender remembered which was which and kidded us about it. Grace is not so big, you know, in body."

At that point the doorbell sounded. Winona gasped and scampered back to her room. Reinhart had never seen her in such consternation over a visitor: she was not above greeting a gentleman caller in an old wrapper and curlers—in which, needless to say, she still enchanted him.

Reinhart opened the door. This was but the third time he had seen Grace and the first occasion on which he might have called her almost pretty. Something had been done to her hair, and her eyes had been skillfully made up. Though she was wearing a suit, as she had on their second meeting, a dinner date, it now seemed more subtly feminine, somehow: lace blouse underneath, a bit of jewelry, and so on.

Grace was not, as Reinhart had mentioned, a large woman. To shake hands with Reinhart, her forearm was put at a steep angle.

"Welcome to the humble abode, Grace," said her host, with an expansive left wrist.

Grace controlled the shake, irrespective of the remarkable difference in fists, and peering around, she penetrated the living room. "It's hardly humble, Carl," she said in her brisk voice. "But then why should it be?" She suddenly looked vulnerable, an unprecedented and, Reinhart would have said, a most unlikely phase for Grace Greenwood. She continued to walk about in a military stride.

"Won't you sit down?" he asked. "May I give you a drink?"

She produced an abrupt, barking laugh. "Anything that's wet!"

She strode to the windows and laughed again. "There's the river, huh?" But the view was not sufficiently riveting to keep her there for a third second, and she turned and marched to the middle of the room, where presumably she could not be jumped by surprise—so it might have looked to someone who was not aware of Grace's credentials. Reinhart had never known anyone so confident at the core of her being; there was no bluster about Grace, none of the self-doubt usually apparent in some form in the boldest of women, and not one iota of vanity.

Despite her apparent indifference to the choice of potation he remembered how precise Grace had been about her preprandial drinks at their other two social engagements. (At dinner she had specified Johnnie Walker Red, diluted only by a sparkling mineral water called Minnehaha, of which, it turned out, her firm was the local distributor.)

He now poured her what she had drunk at their shopping-center lunch, a Jim Beam with tap water and ice, and was on his way to deliver it when Grace seemed all at once a frozen image in one of those cinematic stop-actions which had become a cliché in recent years, from an actress fixed toothily in mid-laugh to a car forever hurtling from a bluff into the ocean. Grace was arrested in a slight hunch of body and an enigmatic moue.

The fact was that Winona had slunk almost silently into the

room, but if Grace had seen her, it was through the back of her own head, for she, Grace, was still facing Reinhart.

"Aha!" he cried, perhaps too stridently, but he wanted to get beyond this purposelessly awkward moment. "Grace Greenwood, this is my daughter Winona."

But Grace remained in her stasis, facing him. Was she deaf? Or had she actually suffered an attack of paralysis?

Meanwhile Winona continued her sneaky approach, which seemed literally on tiptoe, but this was not the least of her eccentricities. She had changed her attire for the fourth time. She now wore black slacks, a tight black turtleneck shirt, and black shoes with high heels—it was her manner of walking in this awkward footgear that Reinhart saw as tiptoeing. Finally, her hair was pulled severely around the back of her head, where it was presumably gathered into a knot. Her eyes had a suggestion of the mysterious East: they had been slightly almondized by the tension on her skin at the temples.

Reinhart knew he would never understand the mysteries of women's styles of dress. Winona of course would have looked perfect in anything, but why for a spring luncheon she had finally settled on a costume suggestive of a Hollywood gunfighter's, sans only the pancake Stetson, was inexplicable.

At last she, as it were, rounded Grace's corner, for Grace had still not moved, and in a special low voice, one Reinhart had never suspected she could produce, she uttered only one word, "Hello," but put a good deal of force into that word, and having said it, she stepped back one pace, put her hands on her sleek black hips, and stared severely at the other woman.

"Winona," said Reinhart, "this is my new friend, Grace Greenwood."

Grace now emerged from her absolute fixity, but only so far as slow motion would take her. It seemed as though she might actually curtsy, but if so she changed her mind. Instead she glared at Reinhart and then abruptly seized the drink from him, almost spilling some in the swirl.

"Here," she said, in a kind of screech as unprecedented as Winona's baritone, and she thrust the whiskey at Reinhart's daughter.

This was the most remarkable display of something or other that he had ever witnessed, and he was so unsettled by it that he took a largish draft of the bourbon and water, a drink that he would ordinarily have put at the bottom of his list, owing to the cloying, almost confectionary effect it produced on his palate. However, though he winced at the earliest taste, the warm aftereffect now was comforting. He realized that he found Winona's performance to be lacking in graciousness: this was not like her at all.

Alas, it was obvious that she and Grace made a poor mix. He would of course stop seeing Grace, but meanwhile she was his guest and he would feed her.

"Winona," he said with a certain asperity, "I have to go now and work on the meal. Please be hospitable. Oh, Grace, if you don't want the Beam, there's Johnnie Walker Red. I've also got your favorite Minnehaha mineral water."

But Grace seemed not to hear him. As for his daughter, she said obediently, sweetly, returning to the old Winona, "Oh, I sure will, Dad. Grace, won't you sit down, please."

"Where?" asked Grace. She seemed bewildered.

Whatever the state of the world outside, everything made sense when Reinhart was with his pots and pans. With his big chef's knife he minced an onion and then a clove of garlic, and put them in a deep skillet with the blanched bits of bacon: all of these were sautéed together until they turned golden. At that point the half-cup of chicken stock was introduced, and two cups of red wine (a vintage Cabernet Sauvignon from California—not dirt-cheap, but the resulting liquid would become the sauce and must be edible), then salt, pepper, and sugar to taste (lest the reduced wine be too acid), and finally a *bouquet garni:* bay leaf, thyme, parsley, and two cloves, bundled in cheesecloth. He put this concoction on to simmer, and he trimmed the crusts from three square slices of a firm white bread, divided each slice in two, and sautéed the six little rectangles in butter.

Ten minutes had been consumed by these labors. The fragrant, simmering liquid would profit by ten more. He now had a moment in which to check on his guest.

The women were silent when he came into the living room, and they sat as far from each other as the arrangement of furniture would permit.

Grace held a glass full of ice cubes and colorless fluid.

"Um," Reinhart asked of her, "vodka or gin?"

She hastily, even guiltily, took a sip, then elevated the glass in a kind of triumph. "Diet Seven-Up!" she cried. "Delicious!"

"Good God," said Reinhart. "Is that your work, Winona? Here, Grace, let me get you something to *drink*. Winona, how could you?" He went across the room with outstretched hand.

But Grace fended him off, and from his left Winona wailed, "That's what she wanted, Daddy! You just ask her."

Grace shouted desperately, "I *love* it!"

Reinhart decided to give up his mission, whatever the truth of her averment: emotions, even if politely hypocritical, should be discouraged before any kind of meal (with the possible exception of high glee at a ball game, followed by a mustard-drenched hot dog and a paper-cupful of warm beer).

"As long as you're happy," he said, halting. "Winona has a professional reason for her diet, but even so I often don't approve of it. I can't get her to accept the fact that she first began to lose weight on my cuisine, but in a sensible way, and with no loss of nourishment or flavor."

"Please, Carl, say no more on that subject," Grace said. It was almost a command. Good, she was coming back to normal. But no sooner had Reinhart made that observation when Winona spoke up in obvious irritation.

"Daddy has a *very* good point, Grace, and you should listen to him."

Reinhart was amazed by his daughter: where had this forceful style come from?

"Sorry, Carl," said Grace, "I didn't mean to be rude."

"You weren't," Reinhart said firmly. This still wasn't going well, he was sorry to see, despite Grace's heroic efforts to get on with her hostess, absolutely the reverse of what the situation should have been. He was really getting very cross with Winona, and had it not been she who paid the rent, he might have considered sending her to bed! This thought came to him as only in part a jest. Though his daughter supported him in money, he provided her security in every other respect, and he was aware that Winona expected him to wield the domestic authority.

She got his implication now. "You see," she said to Grace in a more decent tone, "what Dad says about food is right, but my trouble is that all I have to do to gain weight is to smell something delicious, I'm sorry to say. Until not too many years ago I was a baby elephant. My brother used to call me that, and 'whale,' and other lovely names."

Grace looked as though she might weep. In twenty minutes Winona had evoked from her a display of feelings that Reinhart had not suspected she had, and not once since the appearance of his daughter had Grace shown that part of her personality that had been salient in his previous meetings with her.

"That was because of the high-carbohydrate junk food you used to gorge on," he now told Winona. He addressed Grace: "And so did I! At the worst point I was almost fifty pounds heavier than I am now, at ten years younger." He expected Grace to show some amazement at this, as people could usually be relied on to do, but she merely smiled vaguely into the middle distance. "Well." He made a gesture. "I'd better get back to my eggs."

No one offered to stop him, and he returned to the kitchen. He tasted the liquid, which had reduced somewhat in the simmering. Despite the sugar it was still slightly tinged with acidity, but this condition would surely be corrected when the cooked mushrooms were added, even though they had themselves been sprinkled with lemon juice: you learned such things with experience. He heated butter and oil in a skillet and quickly sautéed the mushrooms. When that was done, it was time to poach the eggs in the perfumed bath of wine and stock and bacon and onions and garlic.

The *oeufs en meurette* when done were pinkish gray, not in themselves a ravishing display, but they were masked in the velvety, rich brown sauce made from the poaching liquid, thickened and augmented by the mushrooms, and they were mounted on the croutons fried golden in hot butter.

Reinhart had opened a fresh bottle of the same wine that had been used for the poaching, and he had made a simple salad of washed and dried watercress without dressing. To follow was only a sorbet of fresh pears, made of the puréed poached fruit and egg white. Some light sugar wafers. And no more to the brunch but Mocha-Java, with heavy cream: too early in the day for the inky-black infusion of "espresso."

This meal represented Reinhart's ideal of great flavor and no bulk. He was pleased with himself as he carried the *plat de résistance* into the dining ell off the living room. The plates were heating on a Salton hot-tray on the sideboard. He put them in place on the table and poured the wine. There was a dramatic moment at the outset of any meal, just before anyone took the first bite, when the napery was spotless, the cutlery unsullied, the wine gleamed behind crystal, the dishes were at their visual perfection —a good moment, but not the best to Reinhart, who was a cook and not a maître d'hôtel.

No, the best time of all was when the persons for whom he had provided the meal began to eat it! He went around the corner to fetch Winona and Grace.

The door to the hall was open, and the living room was empty.

Before he reached the doorway Winona came through it from the corridor, scowling inscrutably. When she saw her father she lowered her head for an instant, then raised it and said wretchedly, "I guess you're ready to shoot me."

Reinhart did nothing for a moment, and then, sighing, he embraced his daughter and led her to the sofa.

"We're going to have a man-to-girl talk," he said to Winona, who was displaying her old schoolchild sheepishness, her head inclining towards his shoulder. "The fact is, Winona: you've spoiled me rotten!"

From the side of his eye he could detect her flinching smirk. "I mean it! I'm the spoiled one, and I'm responsible for this awful waste of your youth." She made some childish murmur of contentment. God, how hard it was to say this! What dad did not want to keep his daughter home forever?

Reinhart rose and stood before her. "It's simply not right that we each be the only member of the opposite sex that the other has as a friend! I'm not suggesting it's perverted or anything of that sort, but it simply isn't balanced. You know, that's one criterion of a meal: whether it's balanced. Cream soup, stewed chicken, mashed potatoes, cauliflower, and blancmange, however well prepared each by each, would be a white horror in the ensemble!"

"Dad—" Winona began.

"No, Winona, we must face the fact that you're not sixteen any more. You're almost twenty-six. You're not in school. You have a profession, and a very lucrative one, in this town. If you went to New York, or even Chicago, you could be positively rich, I'm sure, modeling for Cover Girl or Clairol Herbal Essence or something on TV for hair or skin or whatnot."

"Daddy—"

"I realize that you felt Grace would alienate my affections towards you." Reinhart took long strides to the windows and back. In the river below were two barges in tandem. He had mostly stayed home for some years: the world outside, especially from the height of this apartment, was more and more a mere picture. Often he even ordered food from a high-priced store with delivery service: Winona could afford it. He had not had a lady friend in time out of mind. And now this!

"Don't think I'm criticizing you, dear," he said, coming back to a position before the couch. He laughed for effect, but the irony was real enough. "How could I, when you pay the rent?"

Winona made an unhappy expression: she hated him to mention that. She disliked his making reference to anything that could be interpreted as being personally negative. In that attitude she was unique in all the family, at least since the passing of his own father years before, and in truth Reinhart had always considered his dad a bit simple-minded. He had always believed that his mother's predominant feeling towards him was contempt, and a final proof was provided from the grave: her will had ignored both himself and his favorite child in favor of his son, Blaine, a fellow with whom Reinhart had seldom seen eye to eye in whichever era.

"Daddy," Winona began once more, "you don't—"

"No," said Reinhart, "of course I'm not angry. But I'm afraid that I feel responsible for what had to be an unpleasant experience for poor Grace. I'm going to have to call her up and apologize, Winona." He smiled at her. "I won't bring any more ladies home from now on, I promise. But I wish you would think about what I said. We both, but you in particular, young as you are, need *some other friends*. And listen here—don't forget that I'll be jealous of your young men! That's only natural, close as we are. Now, shall we eat, before my lovely eggs are completely cold?" He clapped his hands. "Something new for you. I know you don't care much for poached eggs, Winona, but these are pretty special—poached in wine, with mushrooms! I know you'll adore them!"

In truth he was fairly certain she wouldn't like them at all, and had really prepared the dish to impress Grace Greenwood, who would probably not have liked it either, judging from what she had ordered on their two dates at restaurants.

Winona had hung her head during all his comments, raising it only to protest feebly from time to time. But finally she made a great gasp and spoke as loudly as she could in the soft voice in which she had never failed to address him.

"Daddy! You're just going to have to listen to me!"

"O.K.," said Reinhart. "I'm sorry, Winona. I didn't realize—uh, go ahead, please."

She stared at him for a while. Had he not known better, he might have believed her emotion to be self-righteousness: something he had never detected in Winona in all her life.

"Dad, I did not first meet Grace Greenwood in this apartment."

"You didn't?" Reinhart cocked his head. "Huh." Suddenly he had a premonition that he should be seated. He chose a low, overstuffed chair across the coffee table from his daughter, the kind of chair from which, in his heavy days, he would not have been able to rise without heroic effort.

"In fact we've known each other for a while," said Winona.

"Then why," Reinhart asked, pointing, "why then did you ask about her favorite color?" It struck him that his own question was silly.

"Oh, I don't know," Winona answered. "It's the kind of thing you say. The fact is, I know her pretty well, you see."

"I see," said Reinhart.

His daughter grimaced. "But I don't think you do, really. . . . Anyway, that's why we acted so funny."

"Why couldn't you have just admitted that you knew each other? Is there some law against that? Why wouldn't I have been pleased to know it?"

She grinned wildly. "I guess it *was* dumb, but once these things begin, well, you know how it goes, one expects the other will say it, and then neither one does."

Suddenly he thought: Well, what does it matter? He slapped his knees. "Sure you don't want to eat my special eggs? It's a classic dish, you know. I really made an effort."

"God," Winona groaned, "don't make me feel worse." She put her flawless face into her cupped hands.

"I didn't mean that, dear. Everything's got snarled up today! What I meant was, it's O.K. with me that you and Grace already knew each other."

"Oh, Dad . . ." Winona took her hands away from her damask cheeks. It had more than once occurred to Reinhart, looking at her, that his daughter might single-handedly evoke all the clichés that were applied to beauty: peaches & cream, silken, velvet, and so on. "Daddy, it's *how* we've known each other."

Reinhart looked towards the windows and enjoyed the glistening floor between the shag rugs: he had himself put that shine on the parquet with real wax and a rented buffer from the True Value hardware store.

"We've been close friends for a while," Winona went on, biting her underlip. "I didn't quite know how to approach the subject with you, so she had the bright idea of the meeting-you-as-if-by-accident. It seemed a good idea when I heard it, I don't know why now. It was stupid and, worse, dishonest. Not that I'm criticizing her, though: I was a full partner."

"Not that I'm criticizing *you,*" said Reinhart, "but what was all the skulduggery about? Why should I object to your being friends with a bright, successful, and prosperous woman like Grace?"

"Well," said Winona, "there was an idea, you see, of sharing an apartment."

"With Grace?" Reinhart almost shouted. "My gosh. That is some idea. You little matchmaker, you. Were you anticipating that Grace and I would get married, or would it be some up-to-date living in sin?" He was pretending to be in robust good humor while all the time feeling a looseness at the core.

Winona was softly weeping. Reinhart went across to the sofa and held her. "Daddy," she said, "how could I ever leave you?"

"Darling, you won't ever have to."

"Well, that was the reason, anyway."

"The reason for what, darling?" Reinhart's own eyes were moist.

You could not call a life a failure when you had produced a child like this.

"The reason why we broke up, Daddy. Grace says she can't go on unless we live together."

Reinhart nodded. For an instant he held Winona as tightly as before, and then he relaxed his grasp. After a moment he stood up.

He spoke as lovingly as ever. "You wanted me to see that Grace was a fine person. You're certainly right about that, dear. I think the idea was a pretty good one on the part of two very decent women. And listen here, Winona, when you get a good friend in life, you want to hang on to her."

Winona's fine eyes began to widen. "Dad, I hope you're not thinking exclusively of my welfare. You always do that, you know, and I won't put up with any kind of sacrifice on your part. I love you, and I won't have it!"

"Oh, I'm not being excessively noble," said Reinhart. "I think you are so fond of Grace that maybe you'd hate me, without even realizing it, if I came between you."

Her expression was anguished. "Don't say anything like that, ever! Didn't I just send her away?"

"Take my word for it, Winona. I'm a veteran in the contradictory forces of the heart."

Winona began to weep again. "You know, I was telling Grace— it will be much harder with him than if he were the usual bigot. Damn it, Daddy, can't you make it easier by being even a *little* nasty?" She was now grinning slightly through her tears.

"Don't talk like that," Reinhart said furiously. "Talk about not making it easy on somebody!" He cracked his fingers. "Do you know why I'm such a tolerant fellow, Winona? Because I'm too chauvinist, that's why! I come from a generation of men who weren't concerned that much with women. When I was young I was obsessed with whether *I* was *virile* enough. We young men were all like that: it was the constant preoccupation in the Army, for example. Even our humor dealt with it incessantly: *fruit, fairy, swish, pansy, fag,* the words themselves were enough to provoke a guffaw. Then I'll tell you something else: if we did hear of a girl who preferred her own kind, we assumed she was some poor little bitch who had simply never met the right man."

Winona, who had never looked more beautiful, uttered one flat, mirthless sound: "Ha."

"And then," said Reinhart, "when I lived long enough to be absolutely certain of myself, I had become the father of a son, and my great worry in the late Sixties was that your brother might turn qu— gay."

"Blaine?" Winona asked in derisive disbelief.

"Well, he's grown pretty square by now, but in those days he dabbled in all the trendy things, radicalism, et cetera." Reinhart flung up his hands. "But look, you don't want to hear all this patronizing stuff. You stick to your friend, Winona. That's my advice."

She was shaking her head at him. "But, Daddy, what will become of you?"

Smiling with all the saintliness he could contrive, Reinhart did not hear the question. He was wondering how long he could conceal from this precious person, whom he loved with all his heart, that she would be the death of him.

CHAPTER

2

Of course Reinhart soon admitted to himself that he was exaggerating in his inner sense of high tragedy. For one, nobody had expired of shame in a good century. Then, sexual deviation had not been regarded by the enlightened as a disgrace since at least the fifth century B.C. and in our time even the *mobile vulgus* had succumbed to a tolerance of variants. Nowadays Gay Pride spectacles were commonplace in our major cities. (Good heavens, must he someday salute as Winona and Grace Greenwood marched by?) That it would always be a joke with respect to Nature might be considered as certain, but then so too was flying when you weren't born with wings, and eating cooked food and reading by electric light, and in fact, simply reading: no other animals did any of these things. If *Homo sapiens* in general was a pervert under the aspect of eternity, then why jib at a subspecies?

As to Winona in particular (and what did he really care about anyone else?), now at least no man would befoul her! No *other* man, that is, for one *had* used her when she was sixteen, in her most extreme moment of obesity, in fact, when she could not have got a proper date—for some are beasts, and no female person, baby, cripple, or crone, is exempt from their detestable advances! Winona had been illegally invaded only in the statutory sense: the honey-voiced fiend had appealed to her generosity, had not used force. Yet had that experience polluted heterosex for her till the end of time? It was not a question that could be or should be asked of the principal.

The fact remained that Grace Greenwood was in love with his daughter, who, whether or not she reciprocated the emotion, at least was not offended by being the target of the other's passion. So Reinhart would put it with scientific and perhaps legalistic precision. Grace was the elder, a forceful and successful business-woman in what must be a game for high stakes, the competitive, even dog-eat-dog strife of American trade. Whereas Winona was a beautiful object whom others dressed and put in place and com-manded to turn and took pictures of. But then, whether exquisite or obese, Winona had been, since birth, the gentle, passive spirit on whom the dominant imposed their will. Bullied by her brother and habitually disregarded by her mother, Winona only came into her own when under her father's protection.

Reinhart was brooding on these matters as he cleaned up the dining room after the brunch that had never been consummated. Winona had offered to help, but her father advised her to go make peace with Grace.

She winced and hung her head.

A certain faint hope made itself known to him. "You *are* going to make your peace?"

"The problem is how," said his daughter, looking up with a different expression from any he had seen. He might have called it slyness had he not known her so well.

"Well, far be it from me . . . but can't you just give her a call?"

"No," Winona said through a firm set of mouth, "no, I can't."

"I mean when she gets home."

"Take my word for it, Daddy." She wore a strained smirk. "I think I'll go out for a while. I really would insist on helping you with the cleanup if I didn't know you were serious about wanting to do it alone."

This was true enough. Reinhart always felt a need to defend his dining room and kitchen against Winona's fecklessness. Though never meaning less than well, she tended to break plates and glasses, and it was her habit to scrape into the garbage can the contents, however abundant, of any serving bowl or platter: no doubt this suggested an attitude towards the leftovers of a meal of which she had tasted all too little of the original! But she had paid for all of this, china, glassware, and provender, while making little use of any. It seemed only right for Reinhart to continue to the end that which had been exclusively his effort from the outset.

Before she left, Winona of course again changed clothes, now to some apparently routine corduroy jeans (which were however a "designer" pair from which, in the ultimate chic, she had removed the label), a fancy blouse, and high-heeled half-boots. Reinhart was aware that this to him incongruous ensemble was actually a high style of the moment. It was not his business to ask her where she was going, but he now thought of Winona's social life in a new way. Would she sit on some bar stool until picked up by a bull dyke in crew cut and vested suit, chewing on a cigar?

It was a luxury to conjure up such bigoted images in private. He had himself, for a few days, thought of Grace Greenwood as his own girl friend. Of course his criteria for a female companion had altered greatly over the years. That sex no longer took priority among the various possible uses of a lady friend was due partly to his own time of life and partly to that of the culture. A sensitive man nowadays, even if young, did well to hang back—for example, had it not turned out that he was right to do so in this case? But not only because inversion was rife. Women in general had grown assertive, had their own magazines displaying naked men and relating filthy fantasies, took out loans from banks, tried murderers, and performed brain surgery. For ever so long now it would have been simple bad taste to buy a broad a rum-and-Coke, kid her along for a moment or two, and then expect to pry her legs apart immediately thereafter in the back seat of a gas-guzzler. Not that this sequence had been characteristic of his experience even when he was young and lusty. Oh, he might well have bought the drinks, but it was typical of the girls he frequented not to keep their part of the implied bargain. In truth, the one time that he did succeed, his companion had been Genevieve, for whom the parked car was a means to ensnare him for marriage—that being in the remote day when girls had a virtue that could be lost.

Reinhart had had nothing to fear from female "liberation": under the old system women had either disregarded him or run him ragged.

But lesbians were something else again. But what? Not "masculine," really, except for the cigar-sucking character alluded to in his bitter joke, who probably existed only in the imagination. He had seen more than one TV discussion show that dealt with these matters when the subject had come into vogue some years earlier, and while the "gay" men never seemed altogether credible when on such display, the homosexual women were seemingly well balanced and in fact often quite attractive to his eye—though in view of what had happened with Grace, should he not suppose his vision to be faulty, or even corrupt? Was there a name for the kind of pervert who preferred members of the *opposite* sex who were themselves inverts?

By the time he had finished the kitchen cleanup Grace had surely reached home, if indeed that had been her destination. He went to his bedroom, sat down on the bed, and lifted the phone from the adjacent table. He was amazed to discover that without trying he had learned Grace's number by heart. He must have had high hopes of some sort. Imagine being cut out, with a woman, by your own daughter!

He fingered the dial. Before any electronic sound was heard at the other end of the line, Grace answered. The surprise made Reinhart mute for an instant: he could have sworn the bell had not rung. This was not the sort of situation in which he was ever glib. The result was that having impatiently cried "Hello" twice, Grace gasped dramatically and began a monologue in a high, fluttery voice that sounded for all the world as though she were giving a malicious imitation of an adolescent chatterbox.

"I've been naughty! A quart of Pralines 'n' Cream! You called just in time, but I knew you would. You always come riding to the rescue like the U.S. Cavalry, flags flying, swords clinking. Oh, I was joking, you know that. I never mean these things. I just get so *flustered!* Well, I mean, I didn't really know how he'd take it, regardless of what you said. No, I didn't doubt your word, but sometimes the closest person to another doesn't see a certain side. And after all it could be pretty devastating. But he's so *sweet* I could just hug him, but of course I see so much of you in him, though I must say you're not always as good-humored—now don't take offense, you know I'm just teasing. Are you on your way? I lied: I haven't touched the ice cream. I've been waiting for you, but unless you come soon, I can't be held responsible."

Up to this point Reinhart had been paralyzed with embarrassment. He could not of course reveal his identity at this late date, and he doubted that silently hanging up the instrument would be more satisfactory: Grace might believe it was the work of a sullen Winona. He was trying here to put himself vicariously in these roles. As he had told his daughter, he was not a tyro in emotional entanglements, but he had two barriers to cross here: plain sex, of which they belonged to the opposite one, and then the deviation from that. Would it have been easier if *he* were gay as well?

Fortunately Grace gave no indication that she would soon stop talking—she who had always been so terse when knowingly addressing him. But are we not all of us different folks from usual when in the grip of passion? Trying to be fair, Reinhart dredged up some of his own memories, most of them necessarily ancient, but a strange fact was that the more recent events seemed even more remote, e.g., he had had a funny sort of fling in the Sappy Sixties with a freaked-out young girl named Eunice Munsing. He thought he had spotted her at the wheel of a cab the week before, fat face like a red balloon, but that might have been a mirage: for romantic purposes he liked to think of her as deceased. The point was that aesthetics always called for the drawing of the curtain across what other people called love, and perhaps one's own as well, which is why the audience for hard-core pornography must always be a relatively tiny cluster of stoics.

Grace suddenly arrested her breathless rush of nonsense about ice cream and asked: "Should I call your dad and apologize?"

Reinhart thrilled with horror, and then at once, magically, his problem solved itself. Grace answered her own question, and added obsequiously: "Shall I do it now?"

He considered making a falsetto grunt or murmur, but thought better of it and merely lowered the receiver to the bedside table to simulate the sound Winona might have produced in putting down the phone to fetch him.

He walked around the room and stared, for once not vacantly, at a little framed snapshot of himself in uniform, taken next to a pile of rubble in Occupation-era Berlin. He now liked the looks he had had then, though he had not at the time: these transformations in taste occur after one has passed fifty.

He returned to the phone, into which, unconsciously imitating Grace as *he* had known her, he barked: "Yes?"

"Oh, Carl," Grace replied, "Grace Greenwood. I wanted to just say I'm sorry I had to run like that, but I guess Win has explained. It was unavoidable, I assure you, just one of those things, and shouldn't be taken as a reflection on yourself. You're a fine fellow."

Reinhart marveled at her change of tone. Once again she was in total command, without a weakness or a doubt. On the other hand, his own situation, if judged according to relative degrees of power, had changed.

"Well, Grace, I might say the same for you! I just regret that you went without a meal." And he couldn't forbear from adding: "I wanted to introduce you to something you have probably never eaten. A classic, but not too much to take if your tastes are for simpler food. Not *aïoli* or eel with green sauce."

Grace grunted almost rudely. He suspected the regrets were all his own. But she spoke in a bright voice: "Listen, Carl, not even Winnie knows about this. I'm bifurcated like all of us: I really *am* interested in you."

For an instant Reinhart did not attend to her meaning: he was stuck on that "Winnie." If there was one thing that Winona had deplored as a child (along with being hungry) it was hearing a diminutive of her name; not even her brother at his most malicious had easily resorted to this usage.

But then he became aware of a new and even more beastly element in the woman! She was baldly confessing to be *bisexual?* She wanted to take on both father and daughter? Was he expected to be tolerant of this as well?

Fortunately he had lived long enough to know that the best defense against any moral outrage is patience; wait a moment and something will change: the outrage, he who committed it, or, most often, oneself.

Grace laughed curtly. "Head and heart!" she said. "I'm always the businesswoman."

Reinhart chuckled in relief: so that was the bifurcation.

Grace said: "Mind giving me your credentials?"

He cleared his throat. "I'm not sure what you're talking about, Grace."

"This cooking of yours. Where were you trained?"

Could he have heard her correctly? No one *ever* wanted to hear him on his favorite subject!

"Well," said he, swinging himself from a seat to a luxurious full-length stretch on the bed, "I have never taken a lesson in cookery. Years ago, when I was first married and my wife would be under the weather, I'd do a turn in the kitchen and maybe take one of those recipes off a can of something. You know, like the tuna casserole that is sometimes on a noodle box, or vice versa. Then—"

"Carl," Grace interrupted, "my idea was not to take you from grilled cheese to gourmet grub with all the steps between. The point is, you seem pretty knowledgeable about the subject. How?"

"Diligence," said Reinhart, "and caring."

"Come on, Carl," Grace said impatiently, "I'm in earnest: I'll tell you why in a minute, but first I want your story, as precise as you can make it."

Reinhart might have taken umbrage at her manner (where'd she get off, being so high and mighty, *now?*) had the subject not been that which was, after Winona, the dearest to him.

"One improves through trial and error," said he, "but the techniques can be learned easily enough, some of them on the TV cooking shows and others from books, those that take you through a recipe detail by detail, allowing for the pitfalls, like Julia Child's, who is a genius as a teacher, and Michael Field's, and *Gourmet* and other periodicals, including the ladies' magazines that once recommended only the tuna casseroles. Now they'll tell you how to make bouillabaisse and quiche and moussaka."

"Uh-huh," said Grace. "And you've only worked at home? You haven't cooked in a restaurant?"

"Never. I've never even thought of doing any professional work. I really cook for the love of it—and I use the word advisedly. Winona"—for a moment he had forgotten the situation; now he felt strange about pronouncing the name to her *friend*—"my daughter hardly touches her meals." Though apparently she gorged on high-calorie ice cream with her *friend*.

"Carl, none of that serves my point," Grace said rudely. "I'm not interested in the personal here, but rather in the public. You know

Epicon, my firm. We're expanding in the gourmet area. It's my theory that we're missing some big bucks unless we reach the people who eat fancy food. This is no small market. One way to escape the label of 'just a housewife,' which is about as popular nowadays as yellow fever, is to be at least a gourmet cook. Not to mention the growing number of guys like yourself who stay home . and fix meals for the breadwinner. Isn't it true that though men were traditionally supposed to be meat-and-potato eaters exclusively, still, when they cook, they often make Cordon Bleu dishes?" She answered herself: "You know they do."

"So I've heard," said Reinhart, "but I'm no authority: I don't get around much any more, frankly."

"And that's another thing, Carl. I think you *should* get out of that apartment more often." Grace became positively avuncular. He could imagine her winking and digging him with her elbow, were he near enough. "Be better for Winnie, take my word for it."

What Reinhart found most outrageous here was that she would use his interest in cooking to promote her selfish plans to lure away his daughter.

"Grace," he nevertheless said with control, "you might be interested to know that I'm not standing in the way of your friendship with Winona. I gave her that assurance, and I believe she's now working on her decision."

Grace breathed quickly. "That's just the point, Carl. Let's talk turkey: if Win moves in with me, where does that leave you? You told me you haven't had a business in some years, or a job."

It was really majestic of him still not to lose his balance: perhaps the years had seasoned him. Apparently he *had* made these confessions to Grace on their two dates, and why not? He had trusted her to make the right interpretation: that only now, at long last, could he claim to be successful in life, now that he had withdrawn from the hurly-burly to make a home for his daughter. Was he not indeed an exemplification of the new kind of man made possible by the liberation of women? He had told his story in pride!

"By your account I sound suspiciously like a bum," he said, with more wryness than reproach. "There are still some women who call themselves housewives, or rather the more honorific-sounding 'homemaker,' and I'm sure they would insist that what we do is

self-respecting, gratifying, and all the rest. True, it's not the construction of the Golden Gate Bridge or a part of the aerospace
program, but—"

"Come on, Carl," said Grace, jollying him in a coarse fashion,
"self-pity's not your game, old boy!"

What a grating woman! Why could not Winona have chosen. . . ?
But at fifty-four he should be done with asking questions of Fate,
whose answers were always implicit in the status quo.

"The fact is that for many years it was my only game," said he,
"but you're right about the 'old boy.' "

Grace said: "You're jumping the gun by a long shot in this day
and age. But I didn't want to talk about dreary matters, believe
me! Everything's going to work out beautifully. Now here's my
proposition." In a supreme effort towards charm, which with men
anyway would not seem to be easily available to her, Grace said:
"And if you don't take it, I'll spit in your eye." Trouble was, she
sounded as if she well might.

"You may fire when ready, Gridley," said Reinhart, reverting to
a time even before his own for this quotation, a favorite of his
father's, who however always corrupted it in one way or another
and sometimes combined it with "the whites of their eyes."

"I don't know whether you've noticed," said Grace, "the existing gourmet shelves in your typical supermarket don't get much
traffic, and in fact in some stores are downright seedy-looking. Also
they're usually poked away in some remote corner, where they're
an easy prey to shoplifters. Products not swiped are there for
months. And this in the face of the greater-than-ever interest in
the aforementioned gourmet cooking. Why?"

At this talk of food Reinhart forgot his resentment. In fact he had
something ardent by way of an answer. "Yes, I have noticed that,
Grace. And I'll tell you why that department is usually neglected
by the public: it usually offers an eccentric choice of products,
which are furthermore, some of them, not at all serious: things like
cocktail franks and those dreary Japanese smoked oysters."

"No," Grace stated firmly, "you're wrong, Carl. The reason
these things don't move—and they are fine products, don't knock
them!—the simple reason is that the public is not aware of their
use."

"That's not true at all," said Reinhart. With anyone else he would have felt he was being rude, but obviously Grace was immune. "A lot of that stuff is absolute crap! Why buy ready-made sauces, like hollandaise and béarnaise, when they're inferior yet expensive as hell, and when furthermore they're quite easy to prepare from fresh materials? And don't tell me nobody knows about the gourmet shelf, with its lousy liver pâté and orange caviar and dip-mixes, because throughout my married years, which ended more than ten years ago, I was served them whenever we went to any neighborhood party."

"You're showing strong feelings, Carl," Grace pointed out. "Do you realize that you're coming alive?"

"Of course," said Reinhart, "but it's nothing new. You know I'm interested in food and cooking."

"O.K.!" she cried merrily. "I'm not debating with you, pal. I want to hire you."

"Hire me?"

"You heard it!" said Grace. "Let me sketch it out. I'm convinced that all it would take to get some real action with the gourmet products would be to highlight them with personal demonstrations. Picture this, Carl: you're in professional apron and big white hat, stainless-steel table on wheels, with whatever implements, gadgets, you need, hot plates, et cetera, preparing dishes that would make use of the products we distribute. Huh?"

"You're not joking, are you, Grace?"

She spoke in brisk reproach: "Carl, I wouldn't have time."

"But, Grace, couldn't it be that the gourmet line is doing badly because of the recession and inflation?" It had been ever so long since Reinhart had had to think about business, and considering his own lack of success at what in a more gracious time was called "trade," he did not miss it. Yet an archaic sense of what was quintessentially patriotic in his place and time—he had been one year old when Cal Coolidge said "The business of America is business"—impelled him to put this question.

But Grace had no sentimental reluctance to put him in his place. "Carl," she said, "don't worry your little head about such matters. They're *my* responsibility. Just stick to your cooking."

Reinhart supposed wryly that he should feel as insulted as women of yore had felt when so disposed of by men—or, to be precise, as militant female publicists insisted that women had felt (his own mild-mannered father had habitually done this to Reinhart's iron-fisted Maw, and she was wont publicly to applaud him for it)—but at his age it was simpler to admit the truth than to uphold principles for which one had no genuine instinct. And truly, Reinhart had always hated and feared the process of buying and selling. When he was young he told himself that this dread was due to his being a poet, but by early middle age he had had to recognize that his collected verse had yet to be written, whereas he had tried several business ventures (gas station bypassed by a new superhighway, movie house when TV came in strong, etc., not to mention involvements in various schemes with arrant charlatans) all of which had failed: in balance he could have been called, and certainly was by his wife and mother, a complete flop. At which point he came to keep house for Winona and was saved!

He was now talking to the woman who threatened his sole achievement. Why was he not more resentful? Because he had always known it would come. The irony was that he had assumed he would be deposed eventually by a conventional figure like a husband.

"This is so sudden," he said now. "I really do have to think it over. . . . I say this without animosity to you, Grace: Winona and I have had a nice life together. I suppose having just me as an intimate hasn't been sufficient for her, and that's understandable. I'm after all in my mid-fifties. I want you to know that I have always urged her to get out and circulate—and when she told me, a while ago, about you, I was taken by surprise, I'll admit. But I'm proud to say I was consistent: I told her one should stick with a good friend."

"That would be like you," Grace said, and he was touched.

"Thanks. But as to my going back into the world, that'll take some deliberation."

Grace spoke in the tone of a football coach: tough-but-for-the-players'-good: "Dammit, Carl, you're not an old man. As President you'd be a youngster. There's more than time enough to make your mark. This could be but the first step! How's anyone to know of your culinary prowess if you hide your light under a casserole?" She made a flat chuckle.

He laughed for another reason. "Do you realize that you have

never even as yet *looked* at anything I've cooked? Let alone tasted
it?"

Grace grew solemn. Obviously she was here enunciating one of
the tenets of her faith. "I know real quality when I see a person,
Carl. After all, did I not pick Winona?"

Assuming that her question had a sexual reference, he was re-
pelled. Yet how could he protest without supplying an implication
that would be unfavorable to his daughter?

In fact he had again misjudged Grace, who proceeded to reveal
that her meaning had been exclusively professional. "Did I not see
her in the ads for Herk's knitted ensembles and know she'd be
perfect for our instant-cocktail mixes?"

Herkimer's was the big downtown department store. Winona
modeled for their newspaper ads and for the special sales that
were hawked on television. Indeed her married suitor was a Herkimer executive.

"She's worked for you?" Immediately he felt better. The image
of Winona's being picked up in a lesbian bar (if, to be sure, there
was such a thing: his fantasies were necessarily based on what he
knew about male homosexuals, nor was that much) had been persistent and repulsive.

"You didn't see the ads?" Grace asked with synthetic incredulity. "The concept was an innovation of mine. That sort of
product is ordinarily only advertised nationally, with everything
handled in New York, of course. There's not a big market in instant mixes and never could be. So why then, you ask, do I throw
away our good money on local newspaper ads? I even wanted to
do TV spots, but on that I was voted down by my colleagues, who
are all *male*, by the way."

Reinhart refused to feel guilty about that. "I gather you are
preparing to announce a sudden burst of sales, a big run on instant
cocktails."

"No sirree!" Grace cried in triumph. "During that campaign
sales were no higher than ever. There's no reason to believe a
single extra can was sold by those ads, featuring your exquisite
daughter against the background of the best local country clubs,
Wynhurst and Checkhaven, and the Silver Huntsman Restaurant
in Stricksville. Carl, are you telling me you didn't see those ads?"

"For some reason Winona didn't show them to me. And I seldom see the papers of my own volition: I had been pretty well burned out so far as news goes when Vietnam and Watergate were done. But I'll say this, Grace, if I do happen to come across a newspaper, I give most of my attention to the food advertisements, you'll be pleased to hear."

"Be that as it may," said she, "you haven't asked me why I am so pleased at losing a fair amount of money on an apparently useless project. Here's why: because it put Epicon on the map." She made a sound that effectively constituted a verbal wink. "That it did the same for me is just between us." Again that sound: a kind of *chock*.

"Grace, am I correct in assuming that your company name is made up of the first two syllables of 'epicure' and the first of 'connoisseur'?"

"Carl, are you following my story?" Grace asked disapprovingly. "You're really not picking up on my points. That's hardly encouraging if we're going to work together."

"I don't think we *are* going to, Grace, with all respect." He had suddenly arrived at that decision: her world, perhaps as much in its business phase as in its private character, was utterly alien to him. "But look here, I'm grateful to you for thinking of me!" He thanked her again and hung up. He would not go so far as to say anything about seeing her around with Winona.

He switched on the television set that had its home on his dresser top and identified the intense green image of the typical Sunday-afternoon golf tournament. The competitors in this one were female, all of them with exceptionally sturdy calves, thighs, and behinds. Reinhart found most of them vaguely attractive, however. They looked like good sports and seemed feminine enough all the same, and he was comforted by the sight of their solid upholstery and, on the average, seasoned age, as opposed to the sinewy striplings of swimming competitions and gymnastics.

. . . Ah, Mildred Donleavy, her pleasant plump face shadowed by the bill of her white cap, was plotting the likely route of her putt. Her sandy hair was gathered into a neat bun; just above her waist bulged a roll, a little bolster, of flesh.

A telephone rang and, startled by the jangle, Mildred missed her putt. There should be a rule against phones on golf courses! But when the second ring came, Reinhart identified it as issuing from the instrument at his elbow.

"Dad, I trust I haven't woken you up."

It was his son. As usual Reinhart believed he detected an implicit criticism. But for many years now he had held his own against Blaine, who had undergone a total transformation since the late 1960s, in which era he had been an exceptionally obnoxious member of the "youth movement" or "counterculture" so beloved and encouraged by journalists and other rabble-rousers. Within a decade Blaine had become precisely what in his early twenties he had professed to despise most. He was now a stockbroker, with wife, two children, expensive suburban house with swimming pool, more than one gas-gluttonous car, and all the rest. He was also a regular churchgoer. His wife, first-named Mercer, came from a "good" local family.

"What's your pleasure?" he now asked Blaine.

"Listen, Dad," Blaine began angrily, and then he blurted: "Damn it all. I can't talk about this on the telephone!" Suddenly he seemed on the point of tears.

Reinhart had never liked Blaine, but if called upon he was capable of loving him, and almost everyone in distress evokes sympathy at the outset.

"Well, then, why not come over here?" he asked his son. "If it's confidential we'll have total privacy. Your sister's out for the afternoon."

"Damn her," said Blaine.

For a moment Reinhart was not sure he meant Winona, whom Blaine had habitually ignored all his life except to jeer at in her time of obesity. But the doubt was soon dispelled.

"She's just been here," Blaine said, his voice contorted with loathing. "I threw her out. I don't want my children contaminated. Dirty little bitch. Goddamned filthy little pervert."

It took all of Reinhart's strength to keep control at this point. He said sharply: "Don't speak like that about your sister, Blaine. I won't tolerate it, I warn you. But if you'd like to talk rationally—"

"I won't come there," Blaine said. He seemed to choke back a sob, but whether it was genuine or merely for effect Reinhart could not say. Blaine had a histrionic streak, derived undoubtedly from the maternal side.

"I could come to you," Reinhart told him, but with a hint of doubt. Blaine had never shown him an excess of hospitality. There were scorching days on which a dip in the pool might have been refreshing: his son had yet to issue an invitation however informal. Indeed in the several years Blaine had occupied the house, Reinhart had penetrated the front hallway but once. The holiday get-togethers had taken place at Winona's apartment and in fact were confined to the lesser, secular fetes such as Lincoln's Birthday and Labor Day. On the religious holidays Blaine consorted with his in-laws, the Seatons, to whom he had always been careful to deny his father access.

And even at this apparent extremity Blaine was none too hospitable.

"When you get here, pull down the road a little way, will you? Past the driveway, please?"

"Shall I wear a disguise?"

Blaine said: "Try to understand for once in your life, please."

Perhaps he had a point. Reinhart did have a certain guilt about his part in Blaine's upbringing. Nor did he believe that an association with the "better" people of a town was necessarily contemptible. Blaine had already, at the tender age of thirty-two, made a conspicuous success, and it would have been difficult to prove that his father had helped him in any way.

And finally Reinhart had to admit that Blaine's outburst against Winona had enunciated a feeling he had himself secretly entertained but lacked the courage to reveal even to the mirror.

"O.K., son," he said. "But the only thing is, your sister's taken her car. I'll be coming by bus. What's the nearest stop to you?"

Blaine returned to his old character. "You don't even have an automobile of your own?" He sighed in contempt. "Look, stay there. I'll drive over. I'll be grateful to you if you'll wait in the lobby."

"I'll teeter on the curb," said Reinhart, "and try not to fall into the gutter."

CHAPTER
3

Reinhart had forgotten to ask Blaine for sufficient time in which to brood over his costume. If he took it now, he ran the risk of making his son indignantly wait at the curb. On the other hand, Blaine was easily offended by his father's attire. Perfectly decent trousers and a sports shirt should be acceptable for a Sunday in late March unless one expected to call upon the royal couple at Monaco, one would think, but Blaine had austere standards. For one, he deplored an open shirt collar on a man older than, say, forty. He had a point, of course: the neck begins early to deteriorate aesthetically and is at best not one of the glories of the human physique. But as it happened Reinhart's Adam's-apple was as yet not a pendulous eyesore, and anyway he had the illusion of being strangled unless the pulse at the base of his throat had unobstructed access to the air.

His trousers were gray, his shirt a subdued plaid in shades of red. Surely a navy blazer would do on a Sunday afternoon: that was the point that should be remembered.

But when the cream-colored Lincoln glided to the curb and the power window effortlessly lowered itself and his son's face was seen, Reinhart could read immediately in the language of corner-of-eye, texture-of-lip, and angle-of-chin the message that once again he had failed to measure up.

But this expression was the work of an instant. Once it had been registered by its target, Blaine exchanged it for the mask of tragedy, a set of feature which did not well accord with his physiognomy, which was by nature of a peevish cast and more appropriate to one of Molière's disagreeable characters than to a Sophoclean hero.

Reinhart hopped in. "What kind of mileage do you get from this heap?"

"Whatever," Blaine impatiently responded, tramping the accelerator while his father was still sinking through the deep-padded leather of the seat. Blaine had once been obsessed with world affairs—in his own warped fashion, of course, holding Amerika responsible for all the horrors of history—but nowadays it was almost impossible to catch him in any reference, however subtle, to the kinds of things that were international preoccupations. The oil shortage, for example.

To confirm his sense of his son, Reinhart now asked: "Think there'll be a fuel crisis by summer?"

"How convenient that you don't have a car," said Blaine, swinging his own around the corner.

"Of course, what I wanted there was your opinion."

"Dad, I'm afraid that to make ends meet nowadays I have to charge a client for that service. It's all I have to sell, you know, and I have two children to support."

Sometimes it seemed to Reinhart that Blaine felt obliged to prove he was literally a son of a bitch. Apropos of which Blaine now said: "What this would do to Mother, I almost can't bear to think about!"

"That I don't have a car?"

"Oh, for God's sake," Blaine cried. "At such times I know what she went through." He flashed a hateful glance at his father. "I'm talking about that degenerate sister of mine! How can you be so tolerant? That filthy little scum, to think I grew up alongside her!"

Reinhart spoke in an even tone. "I told you I won't listen to that kind of abuse. Winona's your own flesh and blood, and furthermore she's a fine woman."

Blaine's features suggested that they would have been coloring with anger under normal circumstances, but he still retained a good deal of the tan he had got in the Caribbean in the early part of the month, and therefore the effect of rising blood was lost.

"Of course *you* would defend her," he said, steering the car up the ramp of an expressway. "I expected that."

And for Reinhart's part he had expected Blaine to have that very expectation. Next Blaine would graciously point out that his father was his sister's helpless dependent. But why then had he come now to seek him out?

"I have the unmistakable feeling," said Reinhart, "that this discussion is only going to make things worse." They were in the high-speed lane at the moment, else he would have asked to be let out at the nearest corner. He wondered at Blaine's choice of a place to talk. The normal thing would have been to find a back street in some quiet district, not to join a clamorous rush of vehicles heading upstate. But any thought of Blaine's characteristics inevitably reminded Reinhart of the boy's childhood: they had never been pals.

But his son now surprised him. "I knew you'd defend her," he repeated, keeping his eyes on the road. He drove as efficiently as he did everything else. "Not because you think it's a great thing that she's queer—I haven't forgotten your diatribes in the Sixties when, naturally, you used to accuse *me!* And not even because she's your sole support, so far as I know—*that* would make sense. I wouldn't fault you for that."

Reinhart realized from the last statement that Blaine was speaking the truth here, from the heart: his son condemned nothing done for a financial advantage, nor did Blaine recognize as serious any motive that did not have monetary gain as its goal. For example, he would have taken an altogether different approach to the matter at hand had Grace been *paying* Winona to be her friend: his concern then would have been only whether the fee was generous enough. . . . So much for Reinhart's cynical exaggerations: the solemn fact here was that Blaine was really not talking about Winona at all, and neither was he speaking about money.

"The truth is," he said, his mouth set, his hands clenched on the steering wheel, "that you have simply always hated me since the time I was born."

Reinhart made no immediate answer. He looked away from Blaine and watched the blacktop rush beneath them.

"Among my other naïveties," he said at last, "was the idea that one's paternal job is over when the children reach their majority, that from that point on things are equal for a couple of decades, and then with old age the father becomes the child. When the circle is complete, the curtain is lowered, if you'll permit the mixed figures of speech."

"That's it, Dad," said Blaine, "play with words. I wouldn't recognize you as my father if you didn't do that sooner or later. I'd think you were an impostor."

Now Reinhart looked at him. "But what you don't seem to realize is that real feelings exist all the same. Words really do stand for something, after all, but maybe it's not always what you expect. . . . I'm embarrassed now, Blaine, if you want a confession. You've hit me dead-center. You're not quite correct, but you're not altogether wrong, and that's what defies my powers at the moment." He had the bizarre sense that he might burst out here, not in a sob but, terribly, in a guffaw—but with the significance of a sob: somehow even in projection he could not play it straight with Blaine.

"Since at the moment I can't really deal with it, let's go back a bit to what led to this moment," he said finally. "Winona came to see you a while ago?"

Blaine grimaced and hit the wheel with his palm. "It's rich, isn't it? We've never been close in all our lives. She's certainly the last person on earth *I'd* confide in, and as for her, I imagine she makes a good income from that posing, but what does she do with it? Has she ever come to me? You'd think, having her only brother in the field, she might want some help with investments . . . ah, well, the devil with that. . . . So she shows up at my house on a Sunday afternoon. We have people coming for a buffet later on. The caterers are there—" He broke off in disgust, as if his sister's arrival in itself constituted a shameful spectacle for which he would be despised by his temporary servants.

Whenever Reinhart was on the verge of feeling some sympathy for Blaine, his son immediately relieved him of that obligation.

Blaine resumed: "Luckily the children were upstairs—"

Now Reinhart could not keep silent. "What does that mean, 'luckily'?"

Blaine shot his jaw towards the windshield. "I could just puke! The vicious little . . ." He nobly raised his chin. "So she asks to speak to me privately, and we go into the den, and she tells me she is thinking of moving in with some roommate, which would leave Daddy all alone in the present apartment, and she would continue paying the rent, of course, but wouldn't he be lonely? What was my opinion?"

Blaine flashed his lights to notify the economy car just ahead that he required the road just beyond it, and it obediently moved to the right.

"Well," said he, "I told her straightaway that she could forget about trying to foist the problems onto me, that she might think we had lots of extra room, but we most assuredly do not. We have hardly enough for our own household as it is, and then of course we must entertain people, and we have family responsibilities. Mercer's family is accustomed to having a number of houses at their disposal, if, say, the Boston branch comes for a Midwestern visit in force, and then—"

"Blaine, old chap," Reinhart said, "perish the thought! I wouldn't think of imposing upon you." He could have made it a bitter statement, but he did not: the emotion would have been squandered. And of course it was quite fervently true that he would have moved to Skid Row in preference to living once again in proximity to his son, this time with Blaine as head of household.

"At which," said Blaine, ignoring Reinhart's contribution, "the little hypocrite denied that she had meant that at all, that as the other child I was being merely asked for my advice, et cetera, et cetera." He glanced indignantly at Reinhart. "I realize now that my dear sister has always been the most sinister sneak imaginable. I'll tell you frankly that what I said to her was that I have my own responsibilities in life, that I can't assume any more, but I do think the apartment would be a ridiculous burden on her: I'm sure a smaller place somewhere would suit you fine. Even a nice bright room. Why throw all the money away on anything bigger? You can't use it."

Reinhart made what once was called a happy-go-lucky shrug. "Makes sense," he said blithely.

"I'm happy you agree," said Blaine, nodding at the rushing road ahead. "Well, then, I suddenly got suspicious and I said, 'Winona, I hope that what you're contemplating is not living with a man.

I know that's popular nowadays with certain trashy sorts, but the best people still prefer the traditional ways, and my profession, for one, is very sensitive to such matters. Do you think a man would be very keen to let me invest his money if he knew my sister was living with someone who had no legal attachment to her? Suppose she got pregnant, and her roommate ran off in the classic way? Who would be expected to pay the bills? Forgive me for saying, 'Not her father.' "

"Certainly not!" Reinhart agreed with an enthusiasm that even Blaine took brief, frowning notice of before he went on.

" 'Oh,' said she, goddamn her! 'Oh, you've got no worry about that.' And, ass that I was, I fell right into the trap."

Reinhart could now see the essential cause of Blaine's fury: *he* had always been the clever child, Winona the dope and dupe.

"I insisted on my point, you see," said Blaine, spitting his words now. " 'Don't be too arrogant,' I said. 'No means is foolproof. We weren't ready for our second child when Mercer somehow conceived in spite of never having failed to take measures, and I doubt very much whether you, with your woolly mind, dear sister, could be relied on to'—well, so forth and on and on, and of course, malicious as she is, she gave me enough rope." Here Blaine again showed the tragic mask he had worn on his arrival. "When I was finally ready for the kill, she did it!

" 'Don't worry, Blainey,' said she." He spoke in a falsetto impression of his sister's voice: " 'As it happens, my lover is a woman.' "

Reinhart put his hands over his mouth. For him it had been greatly preferable to hear this information from Winona herself. To have it repeated now by another (and by such another) was excessively dispiriting. He came out to swallow some air.

"It *is* unfortunate," he said, "if you want my opinion. I can't deny that. I doubt whether any person of the standard persuasion really thinks it's *preferable* that someone is homosexual—still less a member of his own family. We can accept it, think it's O.K., anybody's right, not a hanging offense, and all that, and even applaud geniuses like Sappho and Michelangelo and Proust, but would you want your sister to be one? Not in the best of all worlds, probably.

"Then if you're a parent, you wonder about your own contribution, by commission or omission." He winced at his son. "But finally you recognize that whatever else it might be, it is a fact. And most things of a sexual nature have developed naturally, however unnatural they might seem to some. That is, people don't just up and decide to deviate from the norm and against their own will, even in our decadent place and time. They would seem to be impelled by some force or another."

"Hah!" savagely cried Blaine. "So are murderers!"

Reinhart smiled at him. "What keeps striking me as ironic is a memory of ten years ago. As usual we were on the wrong side of the fence from each other, but in a decade we seem to have changed sides. More importantly, and with all respect, your position has always been extreme. If I recall, in those days any person who defied the generally accepted standards of conduct, political, moral, or sexual, was a hero to you, whereas you were ready to shoot anyone identified as conventional. Now sexual inversion is criminally loathsome?"

One thing that was perhaps to be admired about Blaine: despite his emotion his control of the car was flawless. By now, by virtue of the expressway, they were clearing the outermost suburbs of the city, where there had still been fields when Reinhart came home from the War—more than thirty years before. Certain events seemed to remain in an eternal only-yesterday. To wear the clothes of a bygone era was to be in historic costume: pegged pants and padded shoulders were quaintly incredible, but it was still very real to remember the girl who broke one's heart when one was so dressed.

Blaine answered loftily: "I think my gradual change of opinion has made sense. 'Show me a man who's not a radical at twenty, and I'll show you a man with no heart. Show me a man who's still one at forty, and I'll show you a man with no brain.' Or however it goes. I'm not forty, but I am a husband, a father, and I have had a certain success in my profession. I don't want to hit below the belt, but perhaps if I had had—well, no matter."

"I'll go on for you," said Reinhart. "If you had had a father who was like you yourself are now? Well, you did get shortchanged in that way. But consider this: maybe in that event you wouldn't have had the burning desire to make something of yourself; maybe my bad example was as effective as a good one might have been. Think of this: if I were you, *then perhaps you'd be me.* Repulsive thought, eh?" Reinhart was joking bitterly, but speaking for himself, he thought he had got off lucky: there had been a brief period in his life when his goal was to be very like what Blaine was now.

"Look here," Blaine suddenly said in a mercantile sort of voice, "I've come up with a proposition that should put us all in a situation we can live with. Queers are notoriously unreliable. She may assure you that she'll continue to look out for you financially—and sticking up for her as you have, you do have some claim on her good will—but next she'll fall in love with some other female, maybe even a little child. My God, think of that, my sister trailing a Camp Fire Girl into the park!" He made a loathing face. "It's just unthinkable, that dirty, detestable—"

"Hell," said Reinhart, "I wish you wouldn't put me in the position where I have to repeat all that tedious rhetoric of the homosexual apologists: 'alternate life-styles,' et cetera. But I really don't think it's inevitable that a 'gay' person is necessarily an uncontrollable sex fiend merely because he or she prefers his or her own kind."

Blaine showed an odd expression. "I take it you have had a sheltered life in that respect."

Ah, thought Reinhart, you have not, is that it? But he had no wish to explore the subject of Blaine's experience with his fellow man. Reinhart himself had felt the hand of Time upon his shoulder when, some twenty years before, he had sensed that he was at last beyond the range of homosexual solicitation.

"To get back to my proposition," Blaine said. "We've had our differences, you and I, but I have not forgotten that I have an obligation—limited, true enough, but it's there. Also, I'm sure you believe, whether justifiably or not, that you have gotten a dirty deal in life, and maybe you even blame it on me, for all I know."

To this incredible statement Reinhart could only respond: "You?"

"Well, I'm as convenient a scapegoat as any, am I not?" Blaine asked, going into a kind of bass whisper.

There was no reason to take this kind of thing seriously. "I suppose you are, at that," said Reinhart.

The technique proved an effective one for dealing with the most offensive of Blaine's poses. Reinhart must remember that: it frightened Blaine to hear a confirmation of his own exaggerated expression of self-pity.

Blaine hastily said: "I'm willing to let bygones be." He slipped into the righthand lane of the expressway, and Reinhart could see the turn signal blink on the dashboard. Good, they were about to turn around and head back, having accomplished what they usually did with each other: pure and simple nought.

But when Blaine took the next exit and at ramp's end made a choice, he went not south in the direction of urbanity, but rather towards the pastoral north.

"Say," said Reinhart, "aren't we getting pretty far from home for no great purpose?"

"If you'd ever let me explain," Blaine peevishly replied. "I've been trying for the last half-hour to get a word in edgewise. There's a thing our church sponsors—and before you begin to shout me down with atheist opinions, hear me out, please: there are no religious requirements made of anyone."

"When did you ever hear me say a word about atheism?" Reinhart asked in wonderment. His mother used to make such irrelevant charges as a rhetorical device to throw him vis-à-vis off balance.

"So be it," said Blaine. "But knowing how you operate, I'm trying to dispose of all capricious objections beforehand."

"You're taking me to some kind of religious service? I can't say I'm fascinated by the prospect, if that's what you mean. Is this necessary?" A devilish impulse claimed him. "Shall we pray for the salvation of sex deviates?"

Blaine shrank into himself. "Why you fil—" He caught control at the last moment it could still be captured, and coughed violently. "I'm not always prepared for what you call humor, dear Dad," he said in a voice made guttural by resentment, "but *will you let me explain?*"

Reinhart exposed his two palms.

"It's a little Christian community," Blaine said, assuming an expression that suggested sanctity, "on what used to be a farm, what still is a farm, on good, rich Ohio farmland." He showed the kind of smile that is obviously more eloquent to him who produced it than to the innocent bystander. "Clean air, fertile soil, honest labor."

"Are you serious?" Reinhart had never seen his son in this mood, which seemed perilously near the rhapsodic.

"For God's sake, haven't you the remotest shred of decency?" cried Blaine. "Can't you see this isn't easy for me?"

"Sorry," said Reinhart. He tried to contribute to a polite conversation. "It takes a certain kind of person to be a farmer, though, I'm sure. It has never seemed attractive to me."

Blaine suddenly looked too bland to be true. "But have you given it a try? How would you know?" He produced a sly smile. "I thought you always prided yourself on a liberal approach to things."

Reinhart shrugged. "I know enough about my basic tastes. But listen, I'll be glad to buy some home-grown vegetables, if you want to drop in for a minute or two. I just don't want to stay too long, because I have a feeling Winona might get home meanwhile and want to talk." He frowned. "But wait a minute: they wouldn't have fresh produce yet at this time of year. We're just getting into spring." He put the rest of it together, and peered at Blaine. "You're not proposing that I be installed at this farm, are you? Put out to pasture with the other old fogies? . . . Your point is that if Winona ceases to support me, as you fear she might, if as expected she abandons herself utterly to unnatural pursuits, I can't count on you. But I have already accepted that fact. Why elaborate on it?"

Blaine pulled the car onto the shoulder of the road, adjacent to a wire fence. In the middle distance was a group of cows, an animal of which Reinhart could not remember having seen an example at close range since he was a child. In college he had read a passage in Nietzsche casting doubt on the possibility that the beast of the field could ever explain its serenity to a human being. "Tell me why you're happy," says the man. The animal would like to answer, "Because I forget," but the creature forgets even this before it can reply, and the would-be dialogue comes to nothing.

"What concerns me, *Dad*, is that at fifty-four years of age you have no profession, no occupation, no means of support, and no property, and if you would ever have to go it alone, I can't see how you could survive without going on welfare."

Reinhart stretched his long frame. "These land-cruisers really are more comfortable than cars that make sense," said he. "You simply can't get away from that truth. . . . That's not beside the point, Blainey: long before it was fashionable, I hated big cars, probably because I couldn't afford one. But the funny thing now is that, without benefit of a movement, I am liberated from all sorts of restraints, including those I have imposed on myself. It was ridiculous that I lived almost half a century trying to measure up to the principles of other people." He smiled with genuine good feeling. "The fact is that I love to cook, and I am really good at it. I know you don't agree, but the reason for that is, gastronomically speaking, you're naïve. Not wrong, but childish. Your diet consists of essentially one kind of meat and three or four vegetables, whereas almost everything that lives can be eaten by a human being, and in fact *is* eaten somewhere in the world."

Blaine was sneering at the dashboard. "You could be kidding yourself. What does *she* eat of that gourmet stuff? And what else do you do? Mop the floors? Do the laundry?"

"Whatever has to be done. But the cooking is the center of it. I don't suppose I can ever explain to someone like you what that means: you who spurn Bordelaise sauce and drench your steak with A•1."

Blaine said levelly: "But you'll admit that whatever I eat, I buy myself." He sighed, and then pulled the car onto the road and accelerated. "You're not in an independent position. I want you to take a look at this place."

Reinhart could see that Blaine was determined, and he really didn't want to get into a downright quarrel with his son. Therefore he submitted quietly to being driven some few miles farther on and eventually up a dirt road, to a cluster of farmhouse and out-buildings, the former a shabby white and the barn and sheds the traditional faded red. The vehicles in view were routine automobiles, two of them the worse for wear, with dents and rust and jagged antenna-stems. Farm machines and/or beasts of burden were presumably behind closed doors, as was the local humanity. Reinhart remembered it was Sunday, the most inopportune time (for all concerned) to traffic with persons of sincere religious conviction, Christians anyway.

"Perhaps we're intruding."

"Nonsense," said Blaine. He parked his opulent car alongside the rusting heaps and stepped out. The parking place would have been an extravagance of mud if any rain had fallen lately. Fortunately the moment was windless and the dust lay passive. The buildings seen from closer up looked none too sturdy, but the paint was not flaking badly, and the windows of the house were clean, and the roof was still there.

"Your church sponsors this?" Reinhart asked. Obviously they spared great expense. Blaine belonged to a prosperous Episcopalian flock at which the lesser breeds might sneer, with the encouragement of the needle's-eye metaphor, but there seemed no actual law that would forbid a rich man from being devout.

Blaine stepped up to his father and stared defiantly at him. "These folks *are* very religious. *I* don't make fun of them, though I might not agree in all respects."

Reinhart glanced at the farmhouse. No one stirred there. "You're an odd one, Blaine. I'd say this would be one of the last places to find you."

Changes in those close to you are generally phases in a long and slow process, so that at any point the other person seems routine enough. But in his later adolescence Blaine had without warning, almost within a day, become what for simplicity's sake was known, to anyone who was himself not one, as a "hippie." It was hard to remember that when one looked at him today. Even on a Sunday afternoon in early spring he wore an orthodox shirt and a foulard necktie, a gray suit, and black shoes in the old-fashioned wing-tipped style. Like his father he had fair hair, but Reinhart's now was actually longer and lighter, though at one time Blaine had bleached his hair and worn it shoulder-length. Once Reinhart had vengefully crept into his son's room when Blaine was asleep and sheared away his golden locks just below the ears. They had both changed since those days.

"I know you think me the young fogy," Blaine said now, "but you might be surprised to learn that my values have been more or less the same all my life."

"Uh-huh."

"For example," Blaine went on, "I have always had the greatest respect for those with faith."

"You have?" Reinhart asked incredulously.

"Mock me if you will," said his son, staring in defiance, "but that was really what I was groping for in the Sixties, with so little help from you: faith in the essential goodness of humanity. Perhaps we were naïve, but at least we were searching."

Reinhart indicated the porch of the farmhouse, which only now he noticed was sagging ever so slightly. "Shouldn't we proceed with whatever we've come here for?"

Blaine shook his head. "I'm trying to prepare you. These people may have something of merit if you'll just be patient."

"O.K., O.K! Though it does nothing for my patience to stand here in this bleak parking lot." Reinhart walked to the porch and mounted the steps.

Blaine hastened to overtake his father, who perhaps he feared might disgrace him even among down-at-the-heels religious zealots.

While they were still approaching the door it was opened from within by a small woman of indeterminate age, i.e., she might have been anywhere from prematurely seasoned forties to well-preserved sixties. She wore a workman's outfit of blue-denim trousers and jacket and a shirt of chambray.

"High-dee-ho," she said cheerily. "I'm Sister Muriel."

Blaine quickly said: "This is my father, Carl Reinhart."

"God loves you, Carl," said Sister Muriel, but in a lackluster monotone that contrasted with the first phase of her greeting.

Reinhart nodded in neutral courtesy. Time was, he responded to everybody with classic Midwestern amiability, but somewhere along the line he recognized this as either hypocrisy or folly, an invitation to either bores or crooks, and he adopted his current style.

"If you'd like to make your contribution now," said Sister Muriel, "then there won't be any awkwardness inside."

Blaine formed his lips in an *O* even before he patted his pockets.

Again, in the old days Reinhart would guiltily have whipped out his wallet, but now he showed more patience. "Contribution?" he asked. "For what?"

Sister Muriel sighed and looked at the ceiling of the porch. Meanwhile Blaine slipped inside the door. Reinhart then splayed his right hand.

"After you," he said to Sister Muriel.

"Not without a contribution, brother!" she said with force.

But he could no longer so easily be lured into a cul-de-sac. "Heavens above!" he murmured, raising and lowering his hands and eyes, until he had dizzied her. Then he followed his son indoors.

The interior of the house was for some reason darker than it should have been in daytime—and with hardly any furniture, rugs, or curtains to absorb light. Reinhart followed Blaine through several small, dark, empty rooms until they reached the kitchen, which in old-farmhouse style was of a generous size. It was also, uniquely, furnished: a large wooden table and chairs occupied the center of the room, and along the walls were stove and fridge, sink and cabinets.

A few living souls, representing either sex and dressed much like Sister Muriel (who had remained behind as front-door Cerberus), were either in the kitchen proper or on the screened-in porch just beyond. The youngest seemed in late middle age and none was moving with purpose. They ignored the Reinharts.

Blaine went onto the porch, his father following. The old folks there were also oblivious to them, in the usual passive manner and not necessarily as a positive statement of scorn: they ignored one another in the same fashion.

Reinhart opened the screen door that led to the yard, and he and Blaine went out. The yard was a desolate place, as dusty as where they had parked the car, though, according to the indoor precedent, neat by reason of being devoid of objects.

Suddenly a door in the earth was flung open—half of a double-paneled entrance to a cellar, set almost horizontally against the house wall—and a tall, solemn person mounted deliberately to the upper world on the unseen, sunken steps. Whether or not he was being intentionally mythological—Pluto visiting the surface of the earth—it was a dramatic entrance, or, looking at it in another way, exit. That he was of the race called, according to the era, colored, Negro, or black was as always worthy of note as well as being conspicuous.

Not to mention that Reinhart thought he recognized him as the son of his old friend, now deceased, Splendor Mainwaring. When last seen, a decade earlier, Raymond had been involved with a militant group called the Black Assassins and had himself answered to the name Captain Storm. In ten years (if indeed it was he) he had got a bit thinner and his expression was no longer a fixed scowl. He too was dressed in blue denims.

"High-dee-ho," he said to Blaine.

Once again Blaine introduced his father. "Dad, this is Brother Valentine."

"God loves you, Carl," said the black man, and he showed Reinhart a pious smirk. He was not quite so burnished-handsome as he had been when displaying ritualistic malevolence towards those deficient in melanin, but perhaps that was only an effect of age.

Reinhart asked: "Aren't you Raymond Mainwaring?"

"I was once many things," said Brother Valentine, his eyes disappearing behind his upper lids, "rapist, addict, hooligan, blasphemer, traitor, mocker of the right, defamer of the good." His voice swelled with feeling, and for a moment it sounded as if he might produce an outright yodel. But suddenly he spoke in a quiet, level voice: "Praise *Gee*-zuz."

"Well," said Reinhart, at something of a loss for a response (whether to congratulate or commiserate). He decided to ignore the whole business. Instead he said: "I suppose you don't remember me? I was a close friend of your father's."

Brother Valentine had not yet looked directly at Reinhart, and he did not do so at this moment: he stared between the white men, towards the empty yard, beyond which was an empty field. "I hope," he said at last, "you are still a friend of your Father. For He is a friend to you." He managed very clearly to represent the capital letters.

"I hope so," said Reinhart, who had no wish to mock anyone's faith, but "friendship" was hardly the word to characterize adequately his own association with divinity.

"Brother Valentine," Blaine said, "I hope this was a convenient time to come. My father insisted." Alas, Reinhart was too far away to kick him.

Valentine's style seemed by now pretty well confirmed as being one that took as little note of others as it could get away with. Thus he made no answer, direct or implied, to Blaine's false statement, which of course was no less than Blaine deserved.

"I was a fiend incarnate," he cried, his voice swelling again, "a minion of Satan. I even befouled Old Glory. No vileness did I spurn."

Reinhart nodded and walked near Blaine. "Why did you bring me here?"

"Brother Valentine," Blaine said, leaving Reinhart's vicinity, "is it not true that newcomers are welcome to your little flock?"

Valentine narrowed his eyes and dropped the subject of his own evil past. "We erect no artificial barriers. On the other hand, no one has a special privilege. Each must contribute what he can, in the spirit of Christian America. God bless you, brother."

Ten years back, Raymond had been of the "burn, baby, burn" school, but then we all change from time to time according to our challenges and opportunities, and Reinhart did not find him ipso facto a rogue.

"Thank you for your hospitality," he said. "This has been very interesting." He was about to walk away, irrespective of Blaine, when Valentine at last displayed a squint of recognition.

"Brother Reinhart!" cried the black man. "Forgive me. Oh, God love you." He spoke to Blaine: "I used to call this dear man Uncle Carl."

This was utter fantasy. In truth Reinhart had seen nothing of Raymond's father during those years when the boy would have been small enough to attract the avuncular. He had known Splendor just after World War II, and then not again until the man lay dying, twenty years later. At that time Raymond had been altogether hostile to any white man.

Blaine looked sharply at his wristwatch and then gave a too casual glance at his father. "I can see you've lots of old times to exchange. Why don't I just run a couple of errands meanwhile and pick you up on the way back?"

But Reinhart blocked his route of escape. "I wouldn't think of letting you work on the day of rest! Am I right, Brother Valentine?"

The latter gave him a look that was both knowing and wary.

"Quite so, brother, quite so."

Blaine whined sotto voce: "We've got people coming . . ."

Reinhart said to Valentine: "We can't stay long, but since we're here, would you like to give us the tour?"

"No," surprisingly said Splendor's son, "because if you've come through the house, you've seen as much as there is to see. Upstairs are the dormitories, and underneath is a cellar. We haven't been here long enough to do much but clean the living quarters."

"You have me at a disadvantage," said Reinhart. "I don't quite grasp what it is you're doing here."

"This," said Brother Valentine, "is Paradise Farm." He spoke as if the name were familiar to all: if not, it would be the worst of taste to admit one's ignorance of it.

Reinhart offered: "An experiment in communal living?"

Valentine gestured grandly towards the fields. He had a style that rose above the blue denims: ten years of age had given him more force of presence than he had displayed in the SS type of uniform favored by the Black Assassins.

"Waves of purple grain," said he, "soon enough. God will provide an abundant harvest for His chosen people."

Reinhart sucked a tooth. "You're Jews?"

"Metaphorically," said Brother Valentine, "in the sense of the Judaism that is the basis of judiciousness, which leads to good judgment."

"Judge not, lest ye, and so on," said Reinhart, giving back as good as he was being given: Raymond was mocking him now.

Brother Valentine suddenly understood this. "People of weak imagination and feeble drive must be given a mystique," said he, "rather than a rationale that they are incapable of entertaining. Therefore we have certain slogans and *façons de parler*. You will despise them, but be tolerant: they are needed, I assure you."

"Raymond—uh, Brother Valentine," Reinhart said, "you'll forgive me, I'm sure, but needed for what?"

"For God's work," said the black man. "We shall restore and revitalize this fallow farm, and in so doing bring some human souls back from the dead."

Reinhart put his hands in the pockets of his blazer and kicked idly at the dust. "Those souls inside the house?"

"Oh, don't they look like much?" Valentine asked this with sufficient self-righteousness to shame Reinhart.

"No, of course I don't mean that. But aren't they a bit too old to do heavy farm labor? I hasten to say that I would consider myself over the hill for something like that."

"Brother Reinhart," said Valentine, "the people you see in the kitchen at the moment are not my entire flock. The younger folk are out in the fields, at work. Your earlier concern for the day of rest was well voiced, insofar as it concerned the world of routine commerce and excess consumption. But here, at Paradise, we toil only for our daily bread."

Reinhart still could not decide whether the man was sincere or a charlatan, but most enterprises since the Renaissance have necessarily partaken of both the honest and the bogus in equal amounts to preserve the balance known as modern civilization, and a project that managed to do no more than sway, without tipping, could survive at least for a while.

A certain void in the corner of the eye told Reinhart that his son had taken French leave. He excused himself. Trotting around the corner of the house, he saw that Blaine indeed was already behind the wheel of the Continental.

"No, you don't!" He moved himself to block the projected backing-up. At length Blaine climbed out in disgruntlement.

"Stop pretending that I am trying to dump you here. Honestly, Dad."

"Don't worry about it, Blaine. You won't succeed."

Valentine appeared. "Might I urge you to stay for supper?"

"I'm afraid not," said Reinhart, who regretted having to turn the invitation down: the food was certain to be interesting. "My son has an engagement." He looked around. "I assume you have more sleeping accommodations in the barn?"

Brother Valentine inclined his head ever so slightly, perhaps in assent. "I was really hoping you could stay for a meal. We could dine a bit earlier than usual if that's the problem."

Reinhart remembered he had eaten nothing all day since his coffee and toast on arising. The thought of the poached eggs, now chilled, was attractive: he might even take the time to inundate them in aspic, postponing the meal until the shimmering amber jelly was firm, then plunging through it to pierce and release the yolks, a rich, cool, golden cream; this on a bed of Boston lettuce. Followed by what? A chop or cutlet? Hmm . . . Meanwhile he answered Valentine.

"I'm afraid we just can't, but thank you for the invitation. Perhaps another time. I'll be back later on to see how you're doing here. Maybe you'll have some extra garden vegetables to sell?"

Brother Valentine threw back his head. "We'll have fresh eggs," said he, "and frying chickens. Milk warm from the teat, if that's your pleasure, and farm-made cheese, butter from the churn. Bread from our own wheat, ground in our own mill, baked in our ovens. Country hams from our hogs, steaks from our steers, legs of lambs from our own flock, scallopini from our calves. We'll have a lake yonder, stocked with fish. A peach orchard and a vineyard. We'll make beer, cider, and wines. We'll grind and stuff our own sausages, flavored with our own herbs and spices. We'll put up vegetables and make jams, relishes, and chutneys."

Blaine was wrinkling his nose in boredom. Reinhart realized suddenly that his son had probably never really liked food: there were people like that. For himself he could listen for hours to lists of provender. He reluctantly put out his hand.

"It's been a great pleasure to see you again, Raymond. Yours is a wonderful vision. I hope you're able to realize it." He decided to produce a piece of wisdom. "That's the only thing that seems to make sense by now: to *make* something, or anyway try to. I wish you well."

Brother Valentine's face was working in a strange way. Finally he burst out in desperation: "The thing is, I haven't eaten since yesterday. I was wondering whether you might be good for a Big Mac."

"There's a McDonald's close by?" Reinhart could think of no other prompt response: he had been taken utterly by surprise.

"Look," Valentine said, shrugging, "anything'd be O.K. Burger King, Colonel Sanders, Arthur Treacher's Fish and Chips, Dairy Queen . . . they're all within a mile."

"O.K., Blaine?" Reinhart asked. "Can you spare a few minutes for this errand of mercy?" He turned back to Valentine. "I'm sure he can. Come on."

But Raymond né Mainwaring shook his head. "It would make a bad impression if I were seen leaving at this moment, when there's a certain *crise de nerfs* around here. If you could just drop the burgers off on your way back, with perhaps some fries and Cokes and—"

"You don't mean—"

"Well, now, I can't very well eat in front of all this hungry folk, can I?" Raymond asked indignantly.

"So that's food for how many?"

"The young field workers are due back soon." Raymond closed his eyes for calculations. "Say a couple dozen portions of everything, whatever you get."

"I've got about seven dollars," said Reinhart. "About seventy would be required. Blaine, what are you carrying?"

His son snorted. "A dirty handkerchief," he cried, plunged back into the Continental, and started the engine. Reinhart feared that his own body and Valentine's would no longer prove a deterrent to Blaine's callous getaway, and lest they disappear under the wide trunk of the enormous car, which was already vibrating with power under slim restraint, he drew the black man aside. "This is one of those crazy things," he said. "Because we can't afford to feed you all, you all will go hungry. There's some basic flaw in all communal efforts. I wish I had the answer."

Brother Valentine stared at him for a moment. Reinhart would have been at a loss to say what emotion was being felt by the man.

"All right," Splendor's son said finally, turning away. "You'll see: we'll have something fine here."

CHAPTER
4

"Grace? Carl Reinhart."

"Yes, Carl?"

"I'll accept your offer."

"Eight A.M. tomorrow, my office," said Grace. "Know how to get there?" Obviously she wouldn't waste time telling him if he knew already.

"Glenwood, in the industrial park, isn't it? I can find it."

"See you there," said Grace. She seemed especially abrupt even for her. He wondered unhappily if he had called her away from some intimate moment with Winona.

He hung up the pay phone and returned to the car in which Blaine sat impatiently revving the engine.

"I don't regret having gone to the farm," said Reinhart. "Raymond—Brother Valentine—is an enterprising fellow. Seeing him reminded me that I really did consider his father a good friend. I do want to keep in touch. The results will no doubt be disappointing, but I like the idea he is trying to do something on that order."

Blaine said: "Look, if worst comes to worst, I may be able to find something for you at the office. Speaking of blacks, they nowadays won't do custodial work."

"Have I translated that correctly?" Reinhart asked. "You'll put me on as janitor?"

"Dad," Blaine said slowly, turning back to stare briefly into the hub of the steering wheel, "you can't *do* anything. You have no skills." He threw his head back. "God, that's the kind of thing one should be saying to some high-school dropout and not to a man of fifty-four."

"Look, old boy, I have a confession to make," Reinhart said, clapping his son on the shoulder, a blow from which Blaine recoiled slightly, in an instinctive pretense that it was given with malicious intent. This was too quick to be studied. Their basic enmity, at least from Blaine's point of view, was profound. "I've got a job. You don't have to worry about me."

Blaine pulled away from the curb. They were more than halfway home, already in the outskirts of the city, when his father had asked him to stop at the outdoor telephone. "Please," he said, "don't bother to spin fantasies for my sake. Don't waste the effort."

Foolishly, Reinhart was stung by the implication that he was lying. "All right," said he, "you just ask Grace Greenwood. I start tomorrow. I'm going to demonstrate food products."

"You're going to work for Winona's *girl friend?*" Blaine asked incredulously. "You're trading your daughter to an old dyke *for a job?*"

"Remember ten years or so ago, when you were always able to get a rise out of me?" Reinhart asked calmly. "That was the era for that sort of thing, the baiting of the older by the younger. It was especially offensive because people of my generation had always believed they held nothing more sacred than the welfare of their children. To find that the children disagreed with this conviction was devastating. Now we have come to a time when a son can accuse his father of being a pimp for his homosexual daughter—and the father, shameless as he is, fails even to be insulted by the accusation." Reinhart shook his head and spoke really to himself: "Now you can see why I have submerged myself in cooking—food is really kinder than people."

Blaine drove the remaining blocks in silence, chewing his thin underlip. In profile he somewhat resembled his maternal grandfather, Blaine Raven, a penniless snob, a disbarred lawyer, and a man who had never been sober for the last twenty years of life; the day finally came when once too often he fell into bed, lighted cigar in clenched teeth, and burned himself alive. Reinhart's son was not so good-looking as his grandfather. Neither, in all fairness, could he be said to resemble him in much else but snobbery.

Blaine Reinhart, his father had to admit, was far from being all bad. Notwithstanding his "radical" youth he had got good grades in college and had remained to take his degree, which was more than could be said for Reinhart, who had dropped out of school to support his wife, who was pregnant with—Blaine. How strange could be the most banal of life's sequences.

When Blaine pulled up before the apartment house he had obviously come to a decision. Not unkindly in manner, he looked at his father.

"I'm sure you won't believe this, but for years I've actually been your defender against a Certain Person."

"Your mother," Reinhart said.

Blaine blinked gravely. "No sarcasm, please! The point is that in recent years I've got some sense of what a male human being is faced with."

This philosophical temper was a new one for Blaine—at least in his father's experience. He seemed to expect something. Reinhart therefore shrugged inscrutably.

But Blaine made an unpleasant expression and turned his head. "What's the use?"

Reinhart said: "Blaine, will you please go ahead with your statement? I'm not resisting you, believe me."

Blaine peered at his father and said slowly, suspiciously: "Women can't always understand the pressures on us."

"Good heavens," Reinhart said, "you're becoming a chip off the old block—if you'll forgive the insult. But the irony is that times seem to have changed in that regard, too, and I suppose so have I. The female propaganda, like the black and all the others, has got really tedious, and like them all it is at least half lie, but one useful thing to have learned from it, maybe, is that *no one* understands the pressures on *anyone* else, irrespective of sex. Beyond that, I don't want to think again in this lifetime about those psychosocial bromides. Surely this is the most boring era in the history of the race!" He moved to open his side of the car, then turned back. "I couldn't interest you in an exquisite dish of eggs-in-aspic, could I?"

Though distracted, Blaine managed to reject this invitation with a hideous grimace before going on to prove that he would disregard his father's statement as well: "What do they know?"

"Son," said Reinhart, "are you trying to tell me something?"

Blaine instantly drew back, asking coldly: "What does that mean?"

"I don't have a clue," said Reinhart, almost guiltily. "Forgive me. I thought maybe you wanted to talk about something personal."

"If I did," Blaine answered, "I would hardly—"

"To hell with you." Reinhart opened the door. "I'm not going to listen to another insult."

Blaine set a precedent here. He slid to the passenger's side and caught the door as Reinhart flung it to. "Wait a minute, Dad," he cried. "I didn't mean it the way you thought."

Reinhart turned back, but Blaine simply stared at him through the window of the Lincoln as he slowly closed its door.

"Do you have anything more to say at this time, Blaine?" He wondered whether anyone else ever had such a son.

"Why haven't I *ever* been able to talk to you?" This was wailed with no apparent bitterness, simply in helpless incomprehension.

"The answer to that, son," said Reinhart, "was supplied by a Roman named Virgil, if I remember my Comparative Lit: 'There are tears in things.' "

As he expected, the response got them both over a bad moment. Blaine, who in whatever phase despised literature, leaped back to the driver's seat and positively sped away.

Reinhart felt rotten about this, but probably less so than if they had continued to talk. It seemed likely that Blaine had a problem with his wife, but how to deal with him when whatever one said was taken as an attack?

The doorman on this shift was a large middle-aged Negro of a vanishing breed regardless of race: the competent professional servitor. But he had either misidentified Reinhart early on or mocked him, for some reason, in an honorific style.

"Good afternoon, Colonel." The doorman opened one panel of the double glass portal.

"Hi, Andrew. It's a lovely day, isn't it?"

"Clement, Colonel, very clement." Except for the use of the undeserved title, Andrew was a specialist in the *mot juste,* another earmark of the now rare specimen. Brother Valentine's father had been that sort of guy. Reinhart was suddenly the prisoner of an exquisitely painful nostalgia as he traversed the gleaming, arid lobby and entered the stainless-steel cubicle, which presently lifted him to the fourth floor.

He turned his key in the lock and opened the door of the apartment. Ah, Winona was home. Her keys and change purse lay on the little foyer table, and he could smell a flowery scent. Another thing done by cooking was, so to speak, to hone the nose. His daughter stuck to no special perfume for long: she had access to many.

He called her name.

After a long moment her closed bedroom door opened a crack. "Daddy?"

"The very man," said Reinhart. "May I fix us a bite of supper?"

"Gee, I don't think I can eat anything more today." Winona opened the door sufficiently wide to display her head. No doubt she was changing clothes for the nth time. In answer to Reinhart's cluck-cluck of dismay she quickly added: "I ate a while ago. Honestly!"

"O.K. Want to talk?"

Winona let her head sink. "I'm dog-tired at the moment, Dad. Do you mind?"

"Of course not! But I do think you'll be interested: I took the job with Grace."

Something came and went in her eyes. "Oh."

"So everything's O.K. now, dear."

But Winona was not responding in an appropriate way. Reinhart amplified his statement: "I'll have an income, you see." He realized that he had not even asked Grace about the salary. "I'm going back into the world. You don't have to take care of me any more."

Winona looked at him with feeling. She quickly made some manipulations behind the door and emerged, wearing a white terry-cloth bathrobe.

Reinhart said: "Nothing lasts forever, darling. We've had many good years." This was beginning to sound like the divorce-of-still-good-friends, which one heard about from time to time but which was always allegedly corrupted by the greed of the respective lawyers. Reinhart's proper marriage had been sundered under conditions of maximum hatred between the principals.

Winona came to him. "If that means you're leaving, then all right." Her eyes glistened. "But I'm not going anywhere."

Reinhart backed away two steps. "You're not going to be Grace's roommate?" He had a bizarre feeling that he could not identify: a kind of dread, intermixed with pleasure, whereas of course he should simply have been overjoyed.

"That's the last place I'd go!"

"This is none of my business. But do I gather you two have had a disagreement?"

Winona produced a negative expression that, for the first time in Reinhart's experience, suggested her blood-tie to her brother, whom ordinarily she resembled not at all. But then her own basic nature reasserted itself. She smiled the old generous Winona smile.

"It's just personal," she said blithely, and hugged herself with crossed arms. "I'm sure the job offer still stands. She's very reliable in her profession. I'll say that for her."

Reinhart had no experience with quarrels between lovers of the same sex. It was a widespread assumption that male homophiles could be violent in their intramural disagreements, but who had ever known a certified les— That word had not grown easier to use throughout the day, and in fact he could not understand why the persons to whom it applied did not denounce it as abusive.

"Look—" he began, but Winona suddenly flounced past him.

"Maybe I *will* have something to eat!" she cried, and went towards the kitchen.

He suspected that her energy was false, but Winona's deceptions were invariably of kind intent.

They went in tandem as far as the dining room, which, he had forgotten, was still set for the brunch that never took place. He had put away the food, but from the unrewarding task of dealing in cold china and cutlery he had been distracted by the claims of life.

When he saw the table now, he enjoyed a momentary fantasy in which time was reversed and the entire afternoon lay virginally before him: Winona and Grace had never met, the latter was still his "date," his eggs were hot from the simmer.

Winona obviously had her own emotion on seeing three place-settings. She could no longer dissimulate.

"So after. making my decision, I called her up," she said, in a voice so raspy with emotion that Reinhart would not have recognized it on the telephone. "And who answered?" She balled her fists. "Someone else was there already! So much for her friendship! I waited a little too long to come around, obviously, so she made other arrangements!" Winona's face, contorted as it was, had returned to childhood. She had looked like that when given the slip by her friends at the movies: only yesterday to Reinhart. He had supposed the current era an improvement until now.

She would have run from the room had he not seized her.

"Do you know how many reasonable explanations there could be for that?" He pressed her hands in his. "Wrong number, for one."

But for the first time in her life Winona rejected his consoling. "Oh, Daddy," she said, pulling away, "how could you possibly understand? The things are all so different. You've got to keep always ahead. You can't be reasonable and find excuses: you can't even just simply accept apologies. You either run things or are run by them. You can't *ever* be in the wrong."

"And you think that's different? You think you're unique?" He dropped her hands. "Isn't that the way everything works, for everybody?"

"I don't know."

"Yes, you do," Reinhart said. "Every living thing already knows everything it needs to know: how to succeed, how to fail, how to survive, and how to perish. Sometimes we pretend we don't know, but we know all right. The older I get, the more I realize that nothing is a genuine surprise." He squinted at her. "And what was the decision you had made about Grace? Were you going to move in with her or not?"

"Not," Winona said defiantly.

"Well, there you are. Perhaps she anticipated that."

She raised her chin. "Oh, no. Nobody does that to me. They wait, you see. *I* decide what's what."

Reinhart had done his best to postpone the recognition of a much more shocking discovery than that which merely pertained to Winona's sexual character. But he could no longer cope in this situation without admitting that his gentle, sweet, and yielding daughter, the very model of passivity, could be a tyrant to others. It was of course she who had dominated Grace Greenwood, not the reverse. And why not? *She* was the beauty. He could even feel a fatherly pride! *My daughter leads a powerful executive around by the nose—in fact, the same person's my boss. Does it matter that she too is a woman?*

"Of course there's no question now that I'll take the job," he said.

She looked carefully at him. "Dad, I hope you know I wouldn't say this if I thought it wouldn't be good for you: I really want you to take it. And if you think she got the idea to please me or something, you're wrong. She was already looking for somebody who would fill the bill. When she heard about you she was interested, but she was really sold by meeting you and seeing for herself that you have a marvelous personality. You're just the kind of person who can charm the pants off those housewives."

Reinhart felt himself blush. The image was almost indecent for a man of his years—and also exciting, of course. But that his daughter should conjure it up was unsettling, even though she. . . . He asked himself a wretched question: Was she now exempt from the usual rules that governed the association of daughter and father?

"Yes," he said sardonically, "I'm notorious for driving women wild. Your mother could tell you that."

"Oh," said Winona, "by the way, Mother's back in town." She ran her fingers along the lapels of her terry-cloth robe, as if this were information which he could accept casually.

There were days on which one was hit with everything at once.

"Has she got in touch with you?"

"Blaine told me."

"That's more than he told *me*. I spent some of the afternoon with him. I understand you saw him earlier." At her look he said quickly: "I think it's great that you two have got closer!"

"Huh?" The comment seemed to startle her. "Oh, yeah. Well, anyway, I thought I should warn you."

"Thanks," Reinhart said, "it *is* helpful. But you know I can't decently discuss your mother with either you or Blaine. . . ." He went into the kitchen, but turned in the doorway. "If she's 'back in town,' then it's more than a visit?"

"I don't know. That's all he said. We were talking about other subjects."

Reinhart said: "I really shouldn't say much about your brother, either, Winona, but I hope you're not too hurt if he isn't always as sympathetic as he should be."

"Funny you say that now. He's nicer these days than he has ever been in all my life! I don't like to be cynical, but I do wonder if that's because of his trouble."

" 'Trouble'?"

She raised her hands. "I shouldn't have said that. He asked me not to. Gee."

"Better go the rest of the way, dear, as long as I know there's something I'm not supposed to know." Funny the way that sometimes works out: the precise details are often anticlimactic.

"Mercer has left him."

Reinhart repeated this, again with a purpose to get past the worst moment. How much of life passes in this fashion!

"So that's what he meant, poor devil," he said mostly to himself, with reference to Blaine's cryptic remarks about women. "God, how rotten for him." He pulled a chair from the dining-room table and sat down. "Did she take the children?"

"No. She simply took off." Winona shook her head. "He'd die if he thought I told you."

"Yes, and isn't *that* awful?" Reinhart made a doleful sound. "I wish I knew some way to earn his trust, but this has been a lifelong thing. . . . Your mother has come to look after the kids, then? I hope they get fed properly." He was as scrupulous as he could be when speaking of Genevieve in front of Winona; therefore two truths went unuttered. One, Genevieve was responsible for Blaine's distrust of him in the first place; the situation had no hope of being improved if she was nearby to feed her son more poison. Two, Genevieve was an even viler cook, when she deigned to prepare food at all, than his late mother, whose only culinary technique had been frying-to-ash. Indeed, it had been the combination of these two women, between whom he had spent more than four decades, that drove him into the kitchen. "So you saw her then?"

"Mother—or Mercer?"

"The former," said Reinhart. "Had she already arrived at Blaine's house?"

"She was upstairs, I think. She didn't come down. Maybe she didn't know I was there."

"And you didn't go up?"

"No."

Winona had never enunciated her precise feeling towards her mother, but it was unlikely to have been excessively warm: ten years before, she had readily chosen to live with Reinhart.

"I wonder how the shop will run without her." Genevieve was manager of a dress shop in Chicago. Blaine kept him apprised of her career. She had started out, in the late Sixties, in a local boutique. She and Reinhart, Blaine and Winona, had all lived as a family at that time, and it was Genevieve who supported them, Reinhart having lately suffered the last of his failures in business. He also slept alone: Gen's favors went to her boss, one Harlan Flan, a boutique-chain tycoon in his early thirties. When she divorced Reinhart, however, Flan not only failed to marry her: he coldly dumped her altogether. Reinhart had fitted this story together from various bits and surmises, but the pity was that he got no comfort from it—unless indeed the consolation was that he had thereby been proved to be not a spiteful man.

Genevieve had subsequently emigrated to Chicago, where according to Blaine she had made a new and successful life for herself. Unfortunately, the last five years of their life together had been so bitter as to color Reinhart's memory of that earlier time when he at least had been happily married.

But "normal" life was long gone for him; Blaine's was the case at hand.

"You know," he said to Winona, "for him Mercer has always been more than a wife: she's the proof he has bettered himself socially. It gives him a lot of private satisfaction. And no doubt he is helped professionally. His in-laws are all in the financial world."

"I feel sorry for him," Winona said. "When he gets to feeling bad enough to call me for sympathy—"

"It was he who called you?"

"This morning when you were showering, I guess—but as I say, he doesn't want you to know anyhow."

It really was disgusting of Blaine, despite his anguish, to pretend that Winona had sought *him* out to reveal her sexual orientation.

Reinhart decided to be candid about this. "He did say you had been to see him. I was wondering, Winona, why you decided at this time to tell him about your personal life."

She smiled. "I thought it might make him feel better about himself."

Reinhart rubbed his chin. "Better?"

"I've known my brother all my life. It always makes him feel great to think he's got something on you. Besides, what other help could I give him?"

She really was one in a million. "Have I told you lately," said Reinhart, "how much I love you?"

She made a pshawing sort of wave and left the room.

He was about to remove Grace Greenwood's place-setting, at long last, when the telephone rang. There was a wall-mounted apparatus just inside the kitchen door. When Winona was home he never touched the phone unless she was bathing; all calls were for her.

The bell now continued its spasmodic jangle. He came around the corner of the dining ell and shouted her name. No answer. Either she had slipped out or she was distracted in some fashion. He seized the instrument that was on the table near the front door.

For a moment there was no response to his hello. Then the connection was broken without a word. That sort of thing always gave him the willies.

He went to look for Winona. The door to her room was closed again.

He spoke in the hallway. "I think I'll make some fresh tomato soup, dear. Remember how you used to love Campbell's when you were a child?" He had always made the canned version with milk. Winona's practice had been heavily to butter a handful of saltines and press them one by one into the liquid, crushing them with the back of her spoon, until her bowl contained a thick pink mush.

There had been more calories in that dish than she consumed in an entire day now.

She made no answer to his announcement. She had probably gone to bed. It was not a simple matter for him to accept the simple explanation: that she had been unlucky in love.

CHAPTER
5

Reinhart had been outfitted with a long two-tiered white enamel table on wheels. On one level or another were implements of the *batterie de cuisine:* copper chafing dish, virgin pots and pans in bright chrome, a two-ring hot plate, a food processor, a portable mixer, and various smaller tools including that manually operated essential, the long-handled wooden spoon, invented no doubt by the original cave-chef for the stirring of aurochs-tail soup.

This unit was placed in the far northeast corner of the Top Shop supermarket in the Glenwood Mall, in a situation routinely occupied by the rack for day-old bakery products and the bin for damaged canned and boxed goods. The corner was the most remote in the store, the checkouts being diametrically in the ultimate southwest. But the manager, an elongated, even stringy sort of man with a chin that suggested inherent aggrievement, insisted that no other position was available: i.e., the cable that brought power to the electrical devices could here be deployed with least danger to the customers.

But it was obvious that Mr. DePau cared little for the project, which he tolerated only because of Grace Greenwood's arrangements with the higher authority in the headquarters of the Top Shop chain.

"Frankly," he said to Reinhart on the latter's arrival that morning, before the store was open to the public, "the gourmet shelf does not move, and it is my contention that it won't."

"That's why Epicon is trying this angle," said Reinhart. "There *is* a big interest in this country for fine cooking, and—"

"Look here," DePau said impatiently. He led Reinhart to the "gourmet" area, which happened to be nowhere near where the demonstration table was installed, but rather tucked away, all two short shelves of it, in the middle of a duke's-mixture aisle displaying shoe polish, moth balls, clothesline, replacement mopheads, and beer-can openers of the type outmoded by the pull-ring.

DePau pointed at the shelves. "So what do we have here that's edible? Between you and me?" He pointed to a vial of spices. " 'Crab Boil'? And look at what we have to charge for this little can of patty doo faw: the markup's not that much."

Reinhart had to assent. "Nor does that stuff contain any goose liver, though it's called 'Strasbourg.' It's pork liver, as you can read on the can, and it tastes mostly of tin, for my money. You know you can make a marvelous pork-liver *pâté* at home. The labor takes two minutes or so with a food processor or blender, and it's dirt cheap."

DePau's nostrils arched ever higher above his lip. "Sounds really awful!" It could have been predicted that he was one of those people. He was about to stride away, but checked himself. "You're not going to make a bad smell, are you?"

Reinhart gestured. "This is supposed to be 'gourmet' food."

"That's why I asked the question," said DePau. "I'll tell you frankly."

Reinhart smiled. "I think I know what you mean, and you're not wrong. For that matter, nobody's ever *wrong* when it comes to speaking of their tastes in food. That's private business if there ever was any. But life really can be enhanced if one expands one's palate, and then there's always the question of nourishment."

"Can't be much of that in garlic salt," said DePau. He was anxious to get away, and food was not the sort of subject that could be argued about. It was not simply that any strife, however mild, had a negative effect on the appetite. Food was a great positive, yea-saying force, the ultimate source of vitality—until a phase of the cycle was completed and oneself became food for the worms. It is only through food that we survive, and we die when we are fed on too heartily by microbes, or by the crab named cancer who eats us alive. In the emotional realm there is no more eloquent metaphor: lovers feed on one another, and passion is devouring. A philosopher lives on food for thought. One is what one eats, and eats what one is. Jews and Muslims, old adversaries, are old comrades in abstaining from pork, and Christians are exhorted to eat the flesh and blood of their god. Everybody eats to live, but not everyone who lives to eat is a glutton or, still less, overweight. The world's foremost gastronome, M. Robert Courtine, of Paris, France, who eats two multi-course meals per day, with the appropriate wines, is of a modest weight for his height and furthermore has not exceeded it in twenty years.

DePau loped to the end of the aisle and disappeared. Reinhart had no great expectation of making an epicure of the man, but he would have liked to disabuse him of the opinion that the miserable products on these "gourmet" shelves were in any degree whatever gourmet sans inverted commas. But the word itself had long since become flabby and useless for any service: a hot dog became "gourmet" if treated with anything other than mustard, e.g., tartar sauce, and in fact the term was applied in general to the use of any condiment beyond salt, pepper, and the standard American ketchup. On the lowest levels of gastronomic journalism, that printed on the sides of boxes and cans, the addition of Worcestershire sauce was usually sufficient to gourmetize any dish.

Reinhart returned to his portable kitchen. He had yet to don his apron and the billowing chef's hat which Grace Greenwood had insisted he wear. In France a cook worked for years to earn the *toque blanche.* But Reinhart had not forgotten that the members of the American Expeditionary Force were qualified, by the mere fact of their arrival in Europe, to display more decorations than any of their allies who had been fighting for four years. Furthermore the white bonnet had been Grace's only prima facie requirement. He had been on his own as to which of the "gourmet" products distributed by Epicon he would choose for demonstration, and he was not limited to the selection currently offered at the Glenwood Top Shop. There was a much more generous inventory from which he could choose, and supplies of the appropriate products were available from a local warehouse.

After some deliberation Reinhart had chosen crepes Suzette: a name known to all as the quintessence of Gourmetism, a dish that was simplicity itself to prepare, and a demonstration that could be given a dramatic character, for attracting an audience was the purpose of his job. The particular stimulus for his choice was an Epicon-distributed product called Mon Paris Instant Crepe Suzette Mix: a package containing two envelopes, the larger of which held sufficient powder, when added to a cup of milk, to make a dozen six-inch dessert crepes; the orange-colored dust in the smaller envelope when mashed into softened butter became the sauce in which the crepes were to be bathed.

When tested by Reinhart in his home kitchen, the mixture had yielded rubbery pancakes on the one hand, and on the other, a sauce the predominant flavor of which was markedly chemical, though it was obviously intended to be orange. He prepared several batches of crepes and a number of bowls of sauce, each with another variation of the recipe as given—more or less milk, sometimes thinned with water; a greater or lesser proportion of butter in the sauce—but no effort could alter the truth that the product was simply inferior as food and at $4.75 a swindle as an item of trade, since aside from the chemicals the packages contained respectively only flour and sugar.

At an earlier time of life Reinhart would probably have presented these bald facts to the appropriate authority, but he was by now sufficiently seasoned to understand that a person like Grace Greenwood had not attained her success in the food business by a devotion to the principles of either nutrition or serious gastronomy. What he determined to do then was to make his own mixture, from the authentic materials, of course, the juice and peel of fresh oranges, orange liqueur, and cognac.

But was this not as unscrupulous as what he would replace? For the only point of the demonstrations was to sell Epicon products, and in fact he was not to be alone in the public phase of the project, but rather to be accompanied by a pitchwoman named Helen Clayton, who while he cooked would give the spiel and then, after the audience had tasted the product, then and there sell packages of Instant Crepe Suzette Mix from an adjoining table.

The answer to the foregoing question was surely Yes, if having tasted one of Reinhart's authentic crepes, some naïve housewife bought the wretched powdered product and assumed that from it she could reproduce the model. But there was still another way to look at this situation: wasn't it quite as likely that, incensed by the difference between the real and the bogus, she would, in this era of the aggressive consumer, return the mix with a complaint? And could not the result of enough of such incidents be that Epicon would cease to distribute the offending product?

. . . Actually, Reinhart had no serious hope that the right thing would be done by anybody else but himself—which was the real reason why he must prepare good crepes Suzette.

Getting the equipment and supplies together had taken a good week despite Grace's efficiency and authority. The project was the least among her many, Epicon's major business being in popular junk foods with no claim to being gourmet: various sliced or minced-and-reconstituted deep-fried substances, potato, banana, corn, etc.; powdered soups, puddings, dips; aerosol-canned cheese; tinned meat spreads, stuffed olives, pretzels, relishes, crackers, all manner of munchies, yummies, and tummy-stuffers, comprising most of the joke-provender extant in the Western world, made available, presumably, for the people who lived to eat, rather than those who ate to live, for it did not pretend to offer nourishment.

But a more obvious cause of delay was a general disinclination on the part of all male employees beneath the executive level to work with more than a fraction of the dispatch of the typical practitioner, in whichever job, of a decade earlier, the last time Reinhart had exposed himself to anything that could be called business. Furthermore, this persistent delay as practiced by all functionaries was apparently so firmly established by now as to rouse no ire from the victim, evoke no regret from the perpetrator, and indeed not even stir any wonderment. A kind of half-paralysis, with no political significance, seemed to have claimed the American work force. But he had himself been a downright dropout for more than ten years, and it certainly was easier to get back into a system that was forgiving.

Now back at his demonstration-kitchen, Reinhart assembled the raw materials for a batch of crepes sucrées: flour, eggs, butter, sugar. His colleague, Helen Clayton, was once again rearranging her pitchwoman's table. She was a robust woman in what might be as late as her early forties or as early as the late thirties, with sandy-red hair, pale skin, and a self-possessed, even slightly hostile manner.

Earlier in his life this was the type of woman who would have caused him most discomfiture, and perhaps he would naïvely have believed her seemingly otherwise unmotivated resentment to be caused by a lesbian leaning. But now it seemed likely that matters of relative power, not sex, were in question. Which of them was to be boss? It would be difficult for him to reassure her without being despised for his pains.

When Helen had restacked her little boxes of Instant Crepe Suzette Mix he asked: "How should we go about this?"

She raised her eyes but not her face. "Huh?"

"You're the professional at demonstrations, aren't you? I'm a raw recruit." He spoke with a certain breeziness of voice: obsequiousness would not be the note to strike.

She was no warmer as yet. "How long will it take you to make those things?"

"A few minutes, once the batter's ready and the skillet's hot. I mean the crepes themselves. Then to sauce them, only a minute or so more."

Helen winced. "You don't have a stack already made?"

"I thought of doing that," said Reinhart. "But the Suzetting isn't all that much, just swishing them around in the sauce a moment or two and then folding them in quarters. Of course the flaming adds drama. But I thought the demonstration would have more interest if I started from scratch, more or less. Crepe batter has to rest awhile under refrigeration to be at its best: what I will mix here I won't use immediately. What I *will* use I prepared last night at home: it's in the portable fridge there." The latter was the standard plastic-walled device for picnics. Its interior held two gallons of the batter, surrounded by ice cubes. This was enough for two hundred crepes, surely a sufficient number to get them through a routine morning. By the afternoon the batter he had mixed in the demonstration would have rested sufficiently to be used.

"The thing to remember," Helen said, "is that we're here to move the product, not to give free cooking lessons or free food. Be careful about kids: they're a pain in the ass. They'll want sample after sample, and some of the smaller ones might try to help themselves to things they're not supposed to have, and for God's sake don't let anything dangerous get out of your close vicinity: knives and hot things. Keep 'em away from those burners! That's the bad news. But the good news is that if they like a product, kids will make their parents buy it, so you've got to remember that and put up with them. This time of day you'll have the very little tots who pull things off the shelves and screech incessantly. But they like sweet stuff, so make those crepes as sweet as possible, with extra-heavy fillings of jam." Naturally she pronounced the essential word to rhyme with "grape."

He answered in good humor: "These are crepes Suzette, and they aren't made with jam. Most of their flavor comes from the hot sauce that they will be inundated in. It's quite sweet and rich, with lots of sugar, though, and butter and orange juice—"

Helen peered at his work-table, and then at him. "You're not going to use the packaged sauce mix?"

"Uh, no."

Her eyes were fixed on his mouth. Her own lips were threatening to—yes, definitely, to smile. "You've got a lot of nerve."

Now he smiled in return. "You disapprove?"

She laughed outright. "It's not my affair, is it?"

But why was it so funny? Finally he asked.

"I don't know," said Helen. She lifted one of the little boxes of instant mix and snorted. "Have you tried these?"

"Yes."

She protruded her lips and pronounced, silently: *Sh-it?*

He nodded. "I suppose I'm being dishonest—?"

"Not unless we *say* you're using the mix," Helen said quickly. "But look, this can be to our advantage. You show the real way to make the sauce. The crepes will be terrific, and those are the ones they'll taste samples of, right? Then I'll say something like, 'Well, that's the long way. If you want to do it the short way, here's the instant mix!' "

She had lost her coolness. They were co-conspirators now. She was really quite a nice-looking woman, tall and full-bosomed, and not wearing, he was happy to note, a pungent scent which could be deleterious to good cuisine, distracting or confusing the olfactory sense.

"Yes, I guess that's fair enough," said he. "Makes me feel better anyway. I hate to be dishonest about food, but on the other hand I don't like the idea of cooking anything that's lousy, merely so as to be honest."

Helen shrugged and said, with a pout: "I'll tell you, I myself don't care. I like simple food. Anything fancy makes me sick to the stomach."

He raised his hands at the wrists, signifying that he would not have her shot, though privately he believed the statement insensitive in view of his profession; but then it was humanity's way to suspend the rules of courtesy when speaking of food or art.

The big clock over the fresh produce department was not so large that it could be seen across the vast distance that separated him from it, and he wore no watch. Helen, when applied to, told him it was a minute or so to nine. He took the white bonnet from the bottom shelf of his work-table. It was in a collapsed state. He shook it, inflating its flatness. He put on an apron, the strings of which crossed in back and came around to be tied in front.

Helen was looking at him in what appeared to be approval. "Gee," she said. "Remind me to get some recipes from you." Obviously the costume had transformed him in her eyes. He realized that Grace had been right to insist upon his wearing it.

"Do you like to cook?"

"Hate it," said Helen. "That's why I wanted you to show me some shortcuts."

"First one," he replied in good humor, "is to get yourself some Instant Crepe Suzette Mix."

Helen, who was proving an amiable sort, assured him she was earnest about acquiring "kitchen tips."

"Of course we eat a lot of take-out. I can't do this all day and then come home and cook much at night."

"Who's 'we'? You and your husband?"

"Well . . ." Helen leaned towards him as if to share a confidence; he sensed that she might have dug him in the ribs had he been close enough. "You didn't think I was one of *them,* did you?"

"Them?" The question was altogether honest.

Once again she made her lips prominent and silently mouthed a word. It was *lesbian*.

Reinhart averted his face. "No," he said, "certainly not." He had not yet had time to think of this third phase of coping with the problem of Winona: he had first to deal with it himself, then to witness Blaine's reaction, and now finally to deal with the rest of the world.

With unwitting cruelty Helen persisted. "Did you know *she* was? Grace, I mean."

He mumbled: "I guess so. But I don't much care." He tried to keep from sounding the defiant note.

"I've always kept away from them. They make me feel creepy. But Grace is all right to work for. I've done a number of jobs for Epicon, usually through her, and she's always been a perfect lady with me." Helen laughed coarsely. "But, then, I doubt I'm her type. She likes them skinny, and she likes them young."

"Well," Reinhart said, "here come our customers." God had mercifully steered a young mother and a small child to the head of their aisle.

But Helen Clayton still had time for another innocent thrust: "You should see her present *friend*. My God, she's positively beautiful. I've seen her call for Grace after work in her car. I've seen—"

"Madam," Reinhart desperately called to the young woman, though she was still remote and was at the very moment bending low to poke into a frozen-food compartment, "would you like a crepe Suzette?"

Futile as this was practically—the woman could not hear him—it did serve to distract Helen from her previous theme.

She said in an undertone: "That's supposed to be *my* job."

"Sorry," said Reinhart. "I've got beginner's nerves."

"Aw, you'll be just fine." She considered him a buddy now.

The young mother had not heard him, but it could be seen that her little son was attracted by the promise of a novelty, down there in the corner, a man in a marshmallow hat and a red-haired lady, and he trotted their way.

"Hi, little kid," said Helen, when he came near. "Do you like real sweet things like candy and ice cream?"

The child silently thrust his open hand at her.

Reinhart said: "I haven't even sauced any crepes yet!"

Helen ignored him and continued to smile at the little boy. When the mother came along, the child turned to her and made demands. The young woman sighed and groaned. Reaching past a stack of the crepe-mix boxes on Helen's table, she found a jar that Reinhart could not have seen from his angle, unscrewed the top, chose a bright green pellet, and gave it to her child. He was pacified for the moment. His mother shrugged for Helen's benefit, put the jar on her wheeled cart, and pushed on.

"What have you got over there?" Reinhart asked. "Are you selling other things?"

"I took the precaution to get a jar or two of Gourmet Fruit Drops off the gourmet shelf," said Helen. "You always want to have something to use on the real little kids."

Reinhart was impressed by her acumen. "I'm going to take your suggestion and make some finished crepes, in sauce and all ready to eat, so that the customers can taste them right away. Then maybe they'll stay and watch me cook some more from scratch." He looked at Helen, expecting approval.

But she frowned. "Thing is, you'll be giving them the pay before they do the work. That's never a good principle. Think of it. If you got your money in advance, do you think you'd work as hard? Human nature."

"But will they have the patience to stand and watch a demonstration? That young woman just now didn't even glance at my setup."

"Thing is," said Helen, "you've just got to get the feel of the crowd: some will do one thing, some another. I mean, as crowds. Individuals within the crowd are something else: they can usually be ignored, but not always. There might be a troublemaker, for example. But there might also be somebody there you want to play to, like maybe, for you, a good-looking girl. If you can hold her, you get the feeling you can hold anybody, and that's good for the self-confidence. Or maybe you like a different kind of challenge, some sour-looking individual who will be against you by nature, skeptical, you know? That might put you on your best behavior."

No other customers were yet in sight, and in the preceding hour Reinhart had seen hardly any of the supermarket personnel but the manager, DePau. As yet it was an inappropriate place, this isolated corner, to speak of the psychology of crowds.

"I don't think I'm so good at handling people," Reinhart said. "If I have any gift in life whatever, it's for *making* something. I discovered that late enough. I wish I had known it when I was young, but in those days I never showed any inclination to work with my hands. In manual training at school, for example, I couldn't saw a straight line. I never had any talent at art, and with mechanical things I'm at a loss. When I got out of the Army, I just sort of fell into real estate, and from then on it was a series of jobs of different types that dealt with the public. I don't mind admitting I never did well at any of them. Then I took up cooking, just as a practical thing at home: I had to bring up and feed a daughter."

"Listen," said Helen Clayton, speaking with solemn conviction, "being really able to make something is the greatest ability there is, because you've always got that regardless. People come and go, but what do you care? You've always got what you do. You could be alone on the moon."

Again Reinhart wryly scanned the deserted aisle. "There's a somewhat different character to working with food than, say, with wood or precious metals. Cooking is a craft, or perhaps a performing art, but the product that is created is made to be consumed in a unique way: it is taken internally and, if digested, becomes part of the flesh of a living creature. In a sense then, cookery is the *only* truly creative art. But you do need people to eat the resulting product."

But the point seemed lost on Helen, who was very intelligent but whose philosophy was of another character, being tactical rather than strategic, and in fact Reinhart's favorite people had been her sort during what in retrospect now were established as the most happy times of his life, viz., his days in the wartime Army.

Suddenly customers appeared in bulk. A plausible reason for this might be that the crowd had been waiting for the doors to open: admitted together, they had toured the aisles in ensemble and had only now reached the last. But subsequent events of the same sort, at arbitrary times, disqualified the argument. People appeared by ones or en masse, crowds formed or failed to collect, according to some law that could not easily be identified. Reinhart discovered that though the action could be hectic when people appeared in number, it was more satisfying than when persons came by sporadically. Although his private code had always exalted the individual and, as the case might be, dreaded or despised the mob, in a public situation such tastes are a weakness and not a strength.

But the principal difference between this role and all the previous jobs that had pitted him against his fellow man was that for the first time he had a genuine skill to display, and his being in this situation was not still another example of Fate's inclination towards the arbitrary.

As he mixed his batter and poured his crepes one by one and turned them, stacked them when finished between precut squares of waxed paper, meanwhile bathing others in the hot sauce in the chafing dish (a luscious amalgam of sugar, butter, and orange juice, flamed with Grand Marnier and cognac), folding them into triangles, and serving them to the members of his audience on paper plates, with forks of plastic, as he went through this sequence as smoothly as his batter flowed, Reinhart was conscious of a feeling that was unique in his more than half a century of life: for the first time he did not feel as if he were either charlatan or buffoon. Thus, late, but presumably not too, was proved the wisdom of what in his boyhood had been conventional advice but which, alas, he had long ignored: *Learn a trade.*

But when suddenly, as usual for no reason, their corner was devoid of humanity except for Helen and himself, and he had a moment in which to turn to his associate, intending to show an expression in which gratification and exhaustion were compounded (that old face of the happy worker, none too familiar nowadays except on amateurs at charity functions), he saw that Helen did not share in his pleasure.

"Something wrong?"

She indicated the stacks of boxes. "Four sales, Carl."

"Well, it's early yet. Give it time. We seem to be attracting the audience."

Helen came to the kitchen table and spoke earnestly: "For freebies, Carl."

Reinhart looked at her. "I'm doing something wrong again?"

"Will you forgive me for speaking frankly?" asked Helen. But
the question was a genuine courtesy, and she did not offensively
wait for an answer. "This isn't a lunch counter. The customers
aren't paying for their food. You don't have any obligation to feed
as many as you can within a certain time."

"I'm sorry," said he. "I guess I did forget. Stupid of me, but I was
just mindlessly having fun. I realize that's not the point."

Helen had expressive eyes within those pale lashes. "There's no
law against that," said she. "I enjoy what I do, too, most of the time.
Please don't think I'm criticizing."

He realized guiltily that, distracted by his own performance, he
had not even been conscious of what she had done when the
crowd was there, had not so much as heard her spiel.

He scowled now. "Don't be so damned nice, Helen! I told you
I'm a raw beginner at this sort of thing. I really want your suggestions." He scanned the empty aisle, and then lowered the Grand
Marnier bottle to the second shelf of the work-table, where he
tipped its mouth towards a plastic measuring cup and poured out
a drinkable quantity of the orange liqueur. He passed the cup to
Helen, below the level of the table top.

She lifted it to her mouth and threw down its contents as though
they were bar stock, then lowered the glass and said: "I thought
you'd never ask."

Reinhart suppressed a wince. He liked delicacy in a woman.
And Grand Marnier was not appropriately drunk in a rush, as if
it were what his father called a "cordial" and sometimes furtively
tossed off behind the tree on Xmas Eve with other male relatives
whose wives were teetotallers. He now recorked the bottle without having had one himself.

But Helen was pushing the glass across his counter and leering
significantly. He had no choice but to open the bottle and pour
another. She drank.

"It's a hustle," she said, "like everything else." She held the glass
just beneath her full breasts. "If you don't mind my saying so, you
seem a little too anxious to please the public. In business you have
to remember *they are the enemy.*"

Reinhart changed his mind about having a drink, but he chose
the cognac and poured himself a tot. He postponed drinking it,
however, and left it on the lower shelf.

"Huh," he said in response to Helen. "That isn't an easy theory to reconcile with the serving of food. It seems like a contradiction. Can you feed people you hate?"

"Hate?" asked Helen. "Who said hate? I'm not talking about anything nasty. What I mean is that they are what we feed on, like one animal eats another. Does a tiger hate its prey? Maybe 'enemy' is not the right word exactly. It's not that kind of war. I said that because I have a friend who uses the term. He's in carpets."

At that moment a parade of wheeled baskets came around the head of the aisle. "I'll try to remember," Reinhart said. "I mustn't be too eager to hand out free crepes."

"But you don't want to seem stingy either," said Helen, tossing her right earring, a large green ball, with a movement of her head. "A good thing to remember is that we get them to stop by offering something free, but soon as they receive it they don't have any further use for us. In other words, it's in their interest to get the sample as soon as possible and leave, and it's in our interest to make them stay until they hear our pitch. But once they've heard it and either bought the product or not, then it becomes our interest to get rid of them and not give them seconds."

"Did I do that?" Reinhart asked. And he had been so pleased with himself for keeping the crowd in the obscurity of the mass and not identifying individuals!

"Well," Helen said generously, and she even came to touch his forearm, "here comes a new attack. You'll do just fine."

It went without saying that the difficult aspect of any endeavor was the human.

The first basket to arrive was propelled by a very fat young woman. Neither did she have the flawless skin that sometimes accompanies obesity, whether or not as a result of it.

"Can I have another of those crapes?" she asked. "They're the most delicious darn things. . . ."

Which meant she was the kind of customer who should be discouraged. Seconds! But she was also the very sort of person who delighted a cook. She had not been able to resist coming back for more.

Reinhart managed to restrain himself from hastily meeting her wants. "Do you know," he said genially, "these are easily prepared at home." He looked over at Helen, but she was occupied with an older woman who had actually approached her of her own volition.

"You don't mean that lousy mix she's selling!" cried the fat girl, though in good humor. "I notice you don't use it."

Reinhart served her not one but two of the folded crepes and generously spooned sauce upon them. In addition to all else he could still remember his own days of obesity and the concomitant lust for sweets—which like all ardent appetites grew by its own feeding, but what could one do?

"The instant version saves a lot of time," said he, having so to speak bought her attention. "You have to allow for that. Not all that's quick is bad!"

"The trouble is," said the young woman, already putting the soiled paper plate into one of the two ex-oil-drums that served as trashbins (she had virtually inhaled the crepes), "all that makes a crape Soozette worth eating is the flavor of the expensive ingredients: with the brandy and stuff even the mix would taste good, but who can afford them?"

The approaching crowd had suddenly dispersed, or perhaps it had been not so much an actual accumulation of persons as a trick of perspective. He turned to Helen. She too was again free.

From within she pulled her face into an elongation. "All my lady wanted was the way to the toilet. She got nasty when I said they didn't have them in supermarkets." Helen laughed in her hearty style. "Say, Carl, if worse comes to worst, we'll just have to drink up the booze, so the prospects aren't all bad."

He asked her for the time and then he invited her to have lunch with him.

A certain quick transformation could be seen in her eyes. She looked at her watch and said: "Eleven twenty!"

"Can it be?" asked Reinhart. "We haven't done much business, but we've got through the morning."

"I'd like to take you up on the invitation, but I can't."

"Sure," said he. "Some other time."

"I'll make it up to you." She spoke in an intense whisper. It was a strange thing to say, and an odd style of saying it, and whatever the intended significance, Reinhart was all at once aroused. This happened seldom enough to the sedate middle-aged gentleman he had become.

He turned quickly back to his work. The cooked-crepe supply was not especially low—the stack held at least a dozen—but you could never tell when they might get another crowd. He put the iron skillet on a burner of the hot plate and turned up the heat. In his right peripheral field of vision he saw a lone, cartless shopper approach from the top of the aisle.

What precisely did Helen mean? Or did she herself know? He was shocked to find that where women were concerned he had regressed in recent years to the moral condition of his adolescence. Though today's youth, according to certain authorities, reached adulthood with the sophistication of a procurer, in Reinhart's day and place it had been routine enough to arrive at one's full growth without any experience but the autoerotic, and dealing in fantasies was ineffective preparation for so much as conversing with a live female.

"Carl?"

He was being addressed by the person who had come down the aisle without a cart. He had actually recognized her at the instant she had come into sight, and he furthermore had done so from the corner of his eye. But when you had lived with a woman for twenty-two years—that portion of life generally known as the prime, when all the emotions whether loving or hateful were high, and there was a peculiar vitality even to the worst despair, and when at the end she had discarded you brutally—it was no great feat, even a decade later, to see her through the back of your head.

His ex-wife stood across the work-table from him.

He caught himself just as he was about to burn his hand, instead moving it deftly to take a paper plate to the chafing dish and there choosing a hot crepe. He spooned extra sauce upon it and presented it, with plastic fork, to the mother of his children.

"Free sample," he said. *"Bon appétit,* Genevieve."

CHAPTER
6

When Reinhart told himself that he had recognized Genevieve on her first entering the top of the aisle, he was speaking with the habitual lack of precision that characterizes the internal dialogue. Undoubtedly there had been something about the figure and its movements that suggested an unpleasant memory, but it was a severe shock to be actually confronted by his spouse of twenty-two years, his ex of a decade. The presentation of the crepe was an act of the bravado that Genevieve had so often evoked from him in the last catastrophic years of their association.

It was typical of her to ignore the outthrust plate.

"Carl," she said again, and neither time was it a greeting, "we have to talk."

Reinhart continued to hold the crepe towards her. He began again, in the proper style. "Hello, Genevieve. It's been a while. How have you been?"

At least some of his shock was due to her altered appearance. When last encountered—she in her early forties, he in the middle of his fourth decade—Genevieve had been the sort of woman who could be termed "handsome": her features were well cut, with no ragged edges; her eye was clear, her skin uncreased, her hair of a uniform color, her figure as fit as if she were ten years younger. And if one loved her there was no reason to be this objective: she was a damned good-looking woman by any standard and miraculously so as the mother of two children, the elder of whom was in college. Reinhart himself, on the other hand, had been a sorry specimen, more than halfway through his third hundred pounds, spongy-faced, habitually flushed, short of breath, and loose of bridgework in time of crisis (which came with the rising of each sun).

But by now he had no visible paunch, despite the lowering of the chest which is nature's fee for gaining the age of fifty; and if the hue of his hair was no longer youthful, its growth was, miraculously, as dense as it had ever been. He could still, unspectacled, read a menu at less than arm's length, and he had needed no dental work since early in his forties. He believed that he looked his age but could reasonably be termed a healthy specimen of it. He might turn no female heads, but neither would he cause the aversion of faces. In truth, his current appearance might be pretty close to achieving second place on a personal list of his own lifetime images (first being always himself at twenty-one, or at any rate the representation thereof on a snapshot taken at a ruined German monument in Occupation Berlin, among other GIs and Russian soldiers, buddies for then and forever, conquerors of all the evil in the world—for the rest of that week, anyway).

But Genevieve was not simply a faded snapshot of herself of a decade past: she was the worn and cracked photograph of someone else entirely. Reinhart found he could recognize her better from the corner of his eye than straight-on. It would have defied his powers to say in precisely which respect she had *not* changed, e.g., the cartilage in her nose seemed to have undergone a softening; her eyes flickered behind what looked like peepholes cut through inorganic material rather than living skin; her hair was arranged significantly to lower her once high brow; the joints at the under-ear angles of her jaw were almost as evident, and stark as those on the skeleton that had dangled in the biology lab at high school, forty years before. Not to mention that she was very thin in body—and not in Winona's sense, the willed emaciation of chic. Genevieve looked as though she simply had not had enough to eat in recent weeks: her complexion was a mixture of yellow and gray, her posture was none too steady, her clothes were too large.

Reinhart now found himself urging the crepe on her as emergency nourishment, as one would extend warm soup to the starving. And he was joined by an ally.

"Go ahead, ma'am," Helen Clayton said encouragingly, coming towards them. "It's free!"

"Get rid of her," Genevieve told her ex-husband, without so much as a glance at the other woman. "I told you I wanted to talk."

Despite her current disguise, which could have inspired pity, Genevieve's stark spirit was all too familiar.

Reinhart retracted the crepe. He also became conscious of the pan on the hot plate, in which the butter had blackened, but he was not so distracted as to burn himself on its handle. He gathered up a wad of apron and lifted the skillet away.

Helen shrugged in good-natured indifference and turned away. Reinhart saw that she was that salubrious sort of person whom one need not worry about: she did not seek situations in which to find offense. He saw no utility in chiding Genevieve in front of her.

His ex-wife continued to stare at him.

At last he said: "I can't deal with personal matters until I'm off duty."

"What's that supposed to mean?" Genevieve asked, for all the world as if she genuinely did not understand.

"I'm working here. This is a job, to promote the sale of a crepe mix." She frowned. Had she turned mentally incompetent in some fashion? "I'll meet you for lunch if you like."

"Lunch?" Her stare lost coherence. "Oh." She returned her eyes to his. "I'm not looking for a handout."

"You're hardly being offered one," Reinhart answered in a level tone. "I assume you've got something serious to talk about, if you bothered to look me up here. And if so, then lunchtime would seem to be the moment to talk about it, and I at least will be hungry then, having worked all morning."

As if in support of his point, a cluster of shoppers were approaching, and Helen went out to gather them in. Now, incongruously, Reinhart heard her pitch for the first time.

"Have some free crepes," she said, "and learn an easy way to make them at home. Why not? You don't have to buy anything." The words were less eloquent than the spirit in which they were spoken. Helen seemed to have a naturally persuasive manner that came into play in this function. The women rolled their baskets near. Among them was an old gent in a cap of hound's-tooth check, who put his head on the side and squinted suspiciously at Reinhart.

Genevieve became aware, almost fearfully, of the strangers who moved to surround her. "All right," she said, with a suggestion that these people were Reinhart's bullies, summoned to force her to comply with his wishes. "Noon." She filtered through the shopping carts. Reinhart was ignorant of women's fashions—as he was reminded every time he looked at Winona—yet he knew that Genevieve's attire was out of style by some years. In fact, he thought he could remember the coat from 1968.

"What you got here?" asked the old man, peering at the chafing dish. "Swedish meatballs?"

Reinhart served him a crepe Suzette. The old-timer took the entire triangle of it into the back of his mouth and swallowed it whole, as if it were an oyster. He rolled his rheumy eyes into his yellowed forehead, but said nothing. He took a paper napkin from the little stack at the edge of the table, cleansed his plastic spoon on it, and put the spoon into his pocket. "Why not?" he asked Reinhart with a shrug, and left.

But with successive waves of female shoppers Helen Clayton began to do good business. Insofar as Reinhart could spare attention to the matter, he thought he could identify the power of precedent. If one of the earliest arrivals in any cluster bought a packet of crepe mix, some others usually would follow, but if the customer waited until the group thinned out, a trend was unlikely to be set, not only for the obvious reason that fewer persons were there to be influenced, but also because the principle of like-follows-like can only seriously be applied to the mass. Thus an early purchaser could be seen as a leader and those who came next as followers, but the straggler was probably an isolated eccentric.

Of course, as Helen pointed out between sequences, "buy" was not the precise word for what a shopper did in dropping a packet of mix into her basket: she was as yet a great distance from the checkout stations and could, at any point between here and the wire rackfuls of gossip-tabloids, mounted just before the cash registers, discard any item which failed to pass the test of second thought.

Reinhart endeavored to keep himself in a state of commercial distraction, but succeeded only in part.

"I suppose," he said in that same interim, yielding to an irresistible force, "you wonder who that woman is?"

"What woman?" asked Helen.

"You're being too diplomatic." He smiled sadly. "But I appreciate it. She's my ex-wife. I haven't seen her in many years."

Helen shrugged and then smiled in return, but not in reflection of his wryness: she had a remarkably sweet temperament. "Hell, Carl," she said, "what the hell?"

"Yes."

"I mean, I wouldn't worry. If it's done, then it's done. That's the way I always feel." She continued to smile at him.

"Well," he said finally, "I've got my companion for lunch, and I'm not looking forward to the occasion." He rubbed his chin and added, on what was really an innocent impulse: "I'm sorry it won't be with you."

Helen swallowed visibly. Her reply had a certain intensity, an undue earnestness. "I should be able to make it right after work, if that's all right. I can't ever at lunchtime, you see. I'm sorry, but that's a standing arrangement."

Again he was taken by surprise, but he felt he must apologize. "Oh, I didn't mean— That is, your personal business is, uh, your business . . ."

"Listen," said Helen, "I wouldn't say it if I didn't mean it." More shoppers were coming; she turned to deal with them.

Reinhart poured and cooked more crepes, served them to smiling women. This was more attention than he had got from the female population in decades. Things were supposed to be changing in the relations between the sexes, but women still seemed to like being served by a man who specialized in a craft that was routinely their own.

But what did Helen mean? *What* would she "be able to make right after work"? But more importantly, whatever, why was he apprehensive? What a tame old fellow he had become!

Finally the batter he had brought from home was coming to an end, and he was about to ask Helen for the time when he saw Genevieve rounding the corner at the head of the aisle. He served the crepes, of which luckily there were two more to divvy up than the number of customers who awaited them, and then addressed his partner.

"I guess we can break for lunch now? Though, come to think of it, a lot of people who work might do some shopping on their lunch hour, and we'll miss them."

"No," said she. "The kind of people who shop at lunch aren't the kind who'd buy this product, generally speaking. Take my word for it."

"O.K.," said Reinhart. "I will. I always take your word."

Helen rolled her eyes and made a lump in her round cheek. "But don't turn on me when I'm wrong!" This was the kind of affectionate-joking exchange that he was comfortable with. Though he had few personal precedents for it, the movies of his youth and the early TV comedies often depicted men and women who were pals with an undertone of something warmer, which might come to fruition when the girl removed her owlish spectacles or when the man simply opened his eyes: but you, the moviegoer, even as a kid, knew the score all the while. The wit inherent in this situation was far from being inferior.

"Have a nice lunch." He was reluctant to leave her company, especially to join Genevieve. He realized that he was thinking of Helen as his protector!

Genevieve stopped about four feet from the table and waited expressionlessly—which in her current case was actually with an unpleasant expression even when she was not intentionally displaying one: her lower face was strained and pinched and overlooked by nostrils seemingly tensed in reaction to a foul smell. She showed no acknowledgment of his apron and chef's bonnet as he now removed them. In the latter years of their marriage he had assumed he could have come home in a full suit of armor or loincloth and turban without provoking her to make a response.

DePau, the manager, had assigned him a locker in the employees' coatroom at the rear of the store. There had been only one available, and Reinhart and Helen had to share it. Reinhart had felt odd about this on his arrival that morning. Now the intimacy of the narrow metal cabinet, in which his old tweed sports jacket hung against her trenchcoat, was inviting to think about.

"I've got to go back in for a minute, to get my street clothes," he told Genevieve. Her nod was curt, and it seemed bitter as well, but that may have been but the effect of her permanently disagreeable configuration of feature.

Reinhart would have liked to be bolstered by one more encounter with Helen, but when he reached their locker her coat was already gone: she lost no time in getting to her noontime date, which she had furthermore characterized as being habitual. Was she that attached to her husband, or did the brute demand punctuality? No doubt some men were still like that, or more so than ever, now that classic virility was under siege.

On the way back, passing through the storage area, beyond which the trucks were being unloaded, he ran into DePau. The manager looked careworn: he shook his head and hastened on. It was doubtful that he had recognized Reinhart. Reinhart was old enough to remember a time before the supermarket, or at any rate before it was the institution without which most citizens of the republic would presumably starve. So many basic matters had changed during his lifetime. In his boyhood it was not unusual to know people who had no telephone, and a great many persons went without gasoline-driven vehicles: among them milkmen, whose vans were pulled by horses. Patches of dung, flattened and imprinted with tire-treadmarks, were not uncommon features of the roadways. Dogs, who ran free in those days, had an addiction to public excrement ("It's their perfume," said an aged female neighbor), of which horse droppings were fortunately the least offensive.

But reminiscence did not armor him against the prospect of lunching with his ex-wife. Luckily he had permitted Winona to impose upon him a generous loan against his first paycheck and could afford to take Genevieve to one of the better of the several eating places in the mall, i.e., not to a fast-food assembly line, of which the familiar names were present, nor to the Chinese establishment, which appeared to be the standard chop-suey parlor.

On joining Genevieve, he took the initiative. "I was surprised to hear you were even in town." He began to walk up the aisle.

But for a moment she did not move. She squinted at him and asked: "Why did you say that?"

He refused to return to her, but he did slow his pace.

"Because it's what I felt."

"Why 'even'?"

"Excuse me?"

" 'Even in town'?" She scowled. "I didn't come here to be insulted."

This reminded him of his own admonition to Blaine, at the end of their Sunday drive a week earlier. It was becoming a favorite family saying.

"I trust you're not going to keep being so touchy," he told Genevieve. "I meant no insult. By 'even' I meant that I hardly realized you were in town. I didn't anticipate seeing you. It's been a good ten years, hasn't it?"

She merely shrugged. Time was apparently of no importance to her. To Reinhart it was incredible that you could be so intimately associated with someone in one era and meet as distant acquaintances in the next. Human relations remained a good deal less explicable than anything in atomic physics. Certain platitudes had not changed since Homer.

Genevieve's stride had altered since the old days. It was hard not to see it as a trudge.

They turned at the head of the aisle and went along parallel with the endless shelves of products baked from dough and packaged in cellophane.

"I didn't come to talk of old times," said she.

"No," said Reinhart.

And simple and honest as that word was, again she responded defensively. "You're saying I don't have any feelings, is that it?"

Reinhart made no answer until they had gone the entire route to the front doors, which swung open automatically when their weight reached the mats.

Outside, on the concrete ramp, he stopped and said: "Believe me, I'm not trying to needle you in any fashion. I apologize in advance for anything you interpret as a gibe. And that's the last I want to hear of it. It was your idea to look me up, remember. So far as I was concerned, we terminated our association a decade ago."

As he had suspected, this speech, which really should have been considered insulting, was favorably received by her. Mean people are usually deeply gratified when others confirm their ruthless assessment of humanity.

"All right," said Genevieve, trudging on, "that's fair enough. I don't want any special favors. I didn't come for myself."

"I didn't think you did," said Reinhart, stepping onto the blacktop. Across a block of parked cars was the restaurant he thought he'd head for, a place called, merely, "Winston's." He simply liked the name. The façade was mall-banal, and he knew nothing of the cuisine, but at least it was not called by some term which evoked unpleasant gastronomical anticipations (like "Old" something, or any name in the diminutive).

Nor did the place immediately offend upon entrance. They were seated by a young woman who was civil but not falsely enthusiastic; her clothing and style of hair were unobtrusive but attractive; and she was prompt but not breathless. She led them to a table capacious enough for two more persons. The table top, though not made of wood, was at least not of mirror-gloss, and the disposable mats were not imprinted with patriotic lore, maps of the region, or little-known and useless facts intended to entertain. The cutlery was clean and of a goodly heft, and the napkins were of paper but thick and wide.

Reinhart asked Genevieve whether she wanted a drink.

She sat rigid, both forearms pinning down the prone menu. "No," she said. "In fact, I don't really want lunch. I don't want anything from you."

Having taken it all, is what he might have said at some early time, just after the divorce. But the honest fact was that a great deal of their worldly goods in the last years of the marriage had been provided by Gen's effort and not his own: he could admit that now. Not to mention that he had always disliked the house, the neighborhood, and the suburb, which was not altogether the fault of those three entities, as he could also admit now, but the truth was that he had never been unhappy to be done with them all. The further truth might be simply that he was never cut out to be a father or even a husband. But it is not an easy matter to disqualify so much of your life. Being in Genevieve's presence summoned up such basically disagreeable questions.

"And furthermore," she added, "I don't want to drink anything."

He felt a quick flash of rage at this command, but before he acted upon it a reason for restraint appeared with almost the same speed. His balance of spirit was still new enough to wonder at. There were deeply gratifying rewards for living well into middle age.

"A lot has changed, Genevieve, since we last saw each other. I'm no longer a boozer, but neither am I that other monster, the teetotaller. I just don't drink for effect any more."

"Then why drink at all?" she asked in her manner of old, in anticipation of an argument that was not only untenable but ignoble as well.

"To amuse the palate," Reinhart said. "Beyond sheer matters of nourishment, that should always be the purpose of putting anything in the mouth."

"I'll drink a cup of coffee."

"And what will you have to eat?" He opened and scanned his own copy of the menu (which was unsullied by thumbprints, grease spots, or ketchup drippings). Wonder of wonders, there were other foods than shrimp and steak and prime ribs. For example, there was fresh ham. There was meat loaf. There was Irish stew! Reinhart had a good feeling about this place, though of course the only proof would be in the eating. "It's quite an adventurous bill of fare, for this place and time," said he. "If that's real Irish stew, made of lamb, then it'll be a treat. Nor is a really good meat loaf to be dismissed. . . ." He looked at Genevieve over the bill of fare. "You really should eat something."

For the briefest instant she showed a look of vulnerability such as he had never before seen. "Coffee will be fine, Carl," she said, and perhaps it was his imagination, but he detected the hint of a softer note than he had ever known her to sound. One of the alterations in her appearance (now that he was seated across from her in a good light) was her color of hair: it was off, somehow; still brown, but without a glint of life. It occurred to him that without heavy dyeing she might be pure white: that happened to some younger than she. Suddenly, as if warm water had been poured on him from above, he felt flooded with pity.

He leaned forward and asked: "Are you O.K.?"

But she bridled at this. "*I'm* not the problem." She could not resist adding: "I never was."

The waitress came then. Genevieve would not budge from her lonely cup of coffee, but Reinhart had put in a solid morning of labor. He asked whether the stew was of lamb. It was.

"I don't suppose you have Guinness?"

But surely they did. The waitress was a mellow-voiced young woman with neat hair and a clear complexion.

"All right, Gen," he said when they were alone again. "I realize you're showing great patience. . .'. You want to discuss Blaine's problem, I'm sure. I don't know what I can do. He's so touchy with me that I can hardly talk to him. He didn't even want me to know about Mercer's departure."

Genevieve pointed a finger at him. "Don't worry about Blaine," said she. "We'll work that out, he and I. That's no big deal."

The waitress arrived with the cup of coffee.

Reinhart remembered that Genevieve was wont to smoke a cigarette at table, and he dreaded the moment, no doubt imminent, when she would take the pack from her purse. But it did not yet come.

Genevieve pushed the coffee aside without tasting it. "It's your daughter," said she. "My God Almighty, to have something like that in our family. I could just imagine what you'd be saying now if *I* had raised her. But she's lived with *you* during these ten years."

"That's right," said Reinhart, "and I'm very proud of her. She has been a wonderful daughter, and I love and admire her."

Genevieve looked at him for a long time, and then she said: "Blaine told me you were completely brazen about it, and I'll tell you, despite my private opinion of you, I thought he was not being quite fair. 'She supports him,' I said. 'He's not going to openly attack her, even to you—especially to you, given all those years of bad blood.' But I know something about you, Carl, or I thought I did anyway, after more than twenty years of marriage. I know, or thought I knew, that you can't stand sexual perversion. So far as I know, that's your only sacred principle."

Reinhart stared down into the tines of his fork. What was interesting about this accusation was the tiny grain of truth amidst the inert matter. It had never quite been "sacred," nor had it been his "only," but "principle" had a certain justice. Nor was he repudiating it now.

"I'll stick to what I told Blaine. I don't intend to be a spokesman for gay liberation. What I would like most is never to consider the subject. I wish everybody would drop the matter as something to be discussed and go about their business, each in his or her own way. But I know that's hardly likely, at least not for a long time. And of course there's no getting away from the fact that one is more sympathetic—make that *less unsympathetic*—to certain things if they apply to someone close."

Genevieve's face had become ever more masklike. "I always wondered why she wanted to live with you after the divorce, leave her nice home and room and all, her mother and brother. I really resisted accepting the loathsome suspicion that you and—"

"No, Genevieve," Reinhart said with kindly firmness, "no, you don't want to pursue that line, whatever the malice you still have towards me. No, I have never had a sexual connection with my own daughter. I realize that incest is the current fashionable subject with the quacks of popular psychology and the hacks of TV, but Winona and I would never make case studies."

At that point the waitress brought him a mug of almost black liquid, surmounted by a good two inches of yellow foam: they knew how to pour Guinness here! But he could feel with his fingertips that it was much too cold; very chill stout tastes like varnish smells. He put both hands around the mug, to warm it a bit, but it was too cold to grasp for long.

"The fact is," he said to Genevieve, "Winona is doing fine. There's absolutely nothing to talk about with regard to her, unless one wants to praise her for becoming a success. But Blaine *is* in trouble. I don't mean to disparage what you're doing for him: I'm sure that's going to help. But neither would I dismiss his difficulties."

Genevieve breathed with effort and seemed to suppress a cough. "Mercer's just a bit high-strung. I've had some experience in that area. Daddy was apt to go off half-cocked occasionally." She made the kind of crooked smile reserved for lovable rascals.

At Reinhart's most benevolent hour, full of holiday fowl and spirits, he could have elevated Blaine Raven no higher than the level of dirty skunk. Another of television's recent trends, complete with new jargon-term for the actors to mouth in lieu of showing credible emotion, was the theme of the "battered" wife.

Genevieve's mother had been a forerunner in this area of domes-
ticity, but luckily she was able to escape from time to time for a
ride in the flying saucer which landed secretly in a vacant lot near
her home. When, after many years of Raven's disgraces (arrest for
beating up a whore who had been his client, disbarment as an
attorney, bankruptcy, alleged indecent advances towards a black
sailor in the men's toilet of a downtown tavern—in view of his
lifelong record as a bigot this may have been a bum rap, or again
a logical conclusion) and finally his self-incineration while blotto,
when Reinhart's mother-in-law was free at last, she soon died,
whether or not of a broken heart no one could ever know, but
Reinhart thought it likely. One person may be connected to another by bonds which a third person can never understand. He
was himself still attached to Genevieve, but in a fashion he could
not have understood without this meeting. His old fear of her (yes,
always, fear by one name or another) had been replaced by . . .
God, could it only be pity?

"Yes," he said, after a sip of his still-too-cold Guinness. "Well, I
know you'll do whatever you can for Blaine. You've always been
his best friend in the world, and he reciprocates. I wish I had been
on that kind of good terms with my own mother. . . . I wish I could
be closer to Blaine."

The deft waitress brought his Irish stew. The aroma was the sort
that expunges all forebodings. He sat there for a moment while the
fragrant vapors warmed his face.

"Gen, why not order something to eat? If you don't feel so well,
how about some soup? I suspect it'll be homemade and very good
here. Or eggs in some form? Omelet?"

She pulled her black coffee to her and looked bleakly into it. "It's
not healthy to eat when you don't feel hungry," she said, and
added, with a new vulnerability: "Ask anybody."

"Your coffee's probably cold by now," Reinhart said.

She became the old Genevieve for an instant. "You just stuff
your own face. Don't worry about me! I'm doing just fine. If I
wanted to eat I could go to the finest restaurant in town. If you
knew anything about Chicago, I could tell you of the famous places
I dined at there all the time. I knew all the best people, was invited

to the best functions. I wouldn't be back here at all but for the fact that my children need me." She suppressed another cough.

Reinhart was quite guiltlessly hungry, for the best reason in the world, and with unclouded pleasure he forked up a plump piece of meat and put it between his lips. Tender and juicy, exuding the quintessence of lamb, that unique identity which stewing reinforces even as it brings about the penetration of other flavors, the vegetables and herbs; but all the diverse fragrances are finally complementary. And the last condiment, that which made perfection, was supplied by the now cool bitterness of the swarthy stout.

"This Irish stew is really first-rate," said he. "Who would have thought that such a place could be found in a suburban mall?" It would certainly have been nicer to have had lunch with Helen Clayton, or in fact anyone else who would have eaten something, but he had survived the time when he was at the mercy of a table companion. It wasn't as much fun to eat alone as when accompanied, but he managed.

He even told Genevieve: "I doubt your main purpose in looking me up was to talk about Winona." He did not add what he believed to be the truth: that she had no interest whatever in her daughter, irrespective of Winona's sexual arrangements.

"I expected to be insulted," Genevieve said, and took him by surprise when she smiled in a saintly fashion. "And I guess you know it's not easy for me to turn the other cheek, but I'm willing to try, Carl. I understand a lot more than I used to. I got out into the world. I spread my wings."

He continued deliberately to eat the lovely stew. He was soon down to about an inch of stout. Did he dare order a refill? The risk was not that he might defy some diet, but rather that by taking too much of an attractive flavor he would corrupt the entire experience of it. Then, too, this was his first day at a job in more than a decade, and brewed liquids tended to make him sleepy. Therefore he decided to save the last hearty draft of Guinness to follow his final morsel of lamb.

Having made this decision, he turned to the task of fashioning a courteous response to Genevieve.

"Yes, Blaine has kept me informed. I know you did well in Chicago, but it was no surprise."

"What's that mean?" she asked suspiciously. "Are you making fun of me?"

Reinhart wearily shook his head. "You'll simply have to accept literally what I say nowadays. I'm not in the irony game any more, believe me. I'm too old for it. I was not surprised, because I always thought of you as being extremely good at whatever you tried."

She blinked, though whether she had really been appeased was hard to say. She rubbed her hands together. "I doubt you'd include being a wife in your list of my successes."

Reinhart had finished his stew. Now he took the last drink of stout. "I'd be the worst authority on that, considering the kind of husband I was." He thought about what else he might eat or drink. A simple green salad would be welcome.

"Aw," Genevieve said, "you weren't the world's worst."

This was a sufficiently unrepresentative utterance to distract him from his thoughts of food. "Good God, I wasn't? You could have fooled me."

"Now, now," Genevieve said coyly, waggling a finger at him, "you just said you've given up sarcasm." She touched her hair behind an ear. "The thing is, we were so *young*, Carl. So godawful young. We hadn't lived long enough. We left high school and got married, period. There was a great big world out there that we didn't even suspect existed."

How individuals assess their experiences rarely has any universal application, Reinhart had long since noticed. He could have pointed out, speaking for himself, that he had surely been young when he married, but he had also previously been halfway around the globe with the wartime Army: at least he had been made aware that a world existed from as far west as Texas, where he had trained, to as far east as Berlin, where he served on Occupation duty. However, she was right about his having been naïve in emotional matters—but that had still been true in his forties.

"I couldn't talk you into trying a dessert?" he now asked her. "Or a fresh cup of coffee anyway?"

She pushed towards him the cup that had sat neglected at her elbow. "I haven't touched this one. You might as well take it and save on ordering one for yourself."

The suggestion was so squalid that Reinhart could barely restrain himself from doing something rude: recoiling or sneering. He also realized that his revulsion was due at least in part to the thought of drinking from a vessel that had been consigned to her, even though she might not have drunk from it. The woman with whom he had lived twenty-two years, the mother of his children!

Genevieve never failed to bring out the worst in him, whatever the era. Guiltily he was about to take the cup she continued to offer and do something with it—at least knock it over as if by accident—when he was saved by the arrival of the impeccable waitress.

"We could both use hot cups of coffee," he said to the young woman, and was gratified to see the old cup carried away with his plate and glass.

"Just see they don't charge you for two," Genevieve said meanly. She went on: "This isn't much of a place. You have to eat all your meals here?"

It occurred to Reinhart that she had paid no real attention to him since arriving, had asked him nothing about his job, knew nothing of his talent in the kitchen—but then perhaps he was being just as bad in assuming she should be interested in these matters. But why had she looked him up?

"No," he replied patiently. "This is my first time here, and I think the food is very good, to my surprise."

But she continued to shake her head in what she apparently considered a show of pity. "Poor guy. You could use a home."

"I've got a home," he said, with quiet force. "Winona and I have a very nice home."

"Look," Genevieve said relentlessly, "I realize I threaten your ego with my intensity, my independence, but you may not really know yourself as well as you think. It's quite possible that, underneath it all, it's just such a challenge as I provide that you require." She was staring at him through that odd new mask of a face.

"Those years were not all bad, by any means," he said, "and when they weren't good, it was mostly my own fault. Anyway, we learned a lot, didn't we?" What an empty phrase! If life was all learning, then where did you go to put the knowledge into practice? But it was a thing to say.

The waitress came with the cups of coffee and the bill. She was

an attractive person. Time was, when in the company of Genevieve, Reinhart might have desired this young woman, might
even have imagined that her smile had a special, secret meaning
for him alone, that only his wife's presence obstructed him from
making a new friend—but if he returned alone, the girl would not
even be civil! Had he experienced that in reality or fantasy? Or did
it make any difference now?

He tasted the coffee. It was too weak. Winston's did not succeed
in rising above the norm in this case, but they did supply Half 'n'
Half in the thimble-sized container that was difficult to breach
without being splashed. Thin coffee was enriched by the adultera-
tion of cream: his was potable enough after being dosed.

Meanwhile Genevieve suggested by her inactivity that she
would not drink a drop of her current cup. He decided to take the
bull by the horns. The meal was virtually over anyway.

"Have you been getting enough to eat?"

She let a moment pass and then said in coy reproach: "I've been
waiting for a compliment on my slender figure. Don't you think
I'm pretty fantastic for a lady of my age?" She pursed her lips,
leaned forward, and added, sotto voce: "I had a little help with my
face, of course."

Reinhart made a neutral expression, presumably: he could not
have characterized it further without a mirror. He suddenly saw
the light. "You mean plastic surgery?"

"I'd only admit it to you, Carl. Nobody else knows. If I do say
so myself, it looks completely natural."

Poor devil. Reinhart realized that he could probably never be
matter-of-fact with regard to Genevieve: she could not fail, her life
long, to make him unhappy in some way, even if only in compassion.

"Oh, right," he said, "quite right. You've managed to keep your
youth, Gen, but you should be careful not to diet too much. It's not
healthy. I tell that to Winona all the time, but I feel I'm talking into
the wind. But at least she does stoke up on vitamins. I must admit
she's never sick."

This turn of subject met with little favor from his ex-wife. She
sniffed disagreeably before resuming her favorite theme. "I don't
mind saying that I've fought back against adversity and held my

ground. And yet I've never become cynical. Believe me, Carl, despite my sophistication there's still a lot about me that can still remember that young girl who conquered your heart."

For a moment he was nonplused. Had she learned about his 1968 "affair" (such as it was) with Eunice Munsing—and approved? . . . No, she was talking about herself. He should have understood that from the loving intonations.

"I'm sure there is, Genevieve." He picked up the check. The damages were not severe. Winston's was not out to punish its patrons. He was definitely pleased with this restaurant: the tables were now filled, and yet one's comfort was not reduced one whit, the noise had not increased by much, the service had not turned frenzied, the aromas remained fragrant. . . .

"Don't you get it even yet, Carl?"

He was being stared at with increasing intensity. He hated that in the best of times. He pushed his chair back and stood up. The check directed him to pay the cashier.

"Why, sure I do, Gen," he said with all the amiability at his disposal. "You wanted to show me how great you look and how well you're doing. I'm glad you did. We'll do it again some time, now that you're back in the area." He found his money and placed a tip on the table. He was aware that Genevieve had stayed where she was and was making no move to depart. Nevertheless he turned slowly in the direction of the entrance and began, as it were, to mark time.

"Carl."

"I'm afraid I've got to get back to work, if you don't mind. It's my first day on the job. It's very gratifying to me: I'm self-taught as a cook, you know. I've gone quite a ways beyond the meals I used to make when we were all together."

"We could be all together again," said Genevieve in a low, penetrating voice, a kind of stage whisper.

Standing there in a crowded restaurant, he thrilled with horror. But at last he managed to say: "We really must do this soon again."

Now she cried aloud: "You fool, you lovable fool, can't you see what I'm saying?" The polite eaters at the nearest table pretended not to hear.

Reinhart foresaw that her next speech might be at sufficient volume to command the attention of the entire room, unless he could placate her with an immediate response. She was quite capable of shaming him publicly, on his first day of work. He thought of something even worse: she might pursue him into the supermarket itself!

"Come along, Gen," he said, trying for a devil-may-care grin. "Let's take a walk."

Wondrously, this worked. At least she left the table. Now the nearby people decided to abandon their discretion and gawked rudely. Reinhart hoped no one who had seen him cooking crepes would recognize him now. That's the kind of thing you could not control once you went amongst the public. But it bolstered him to think of himself as a celebrity whom everybody was out to get the goods on.

He hastened ahead to the cashier's station, but that woman, as if in league with his ex-wife, found trivial things to occupy her until Genevieve reached his side and even put her hand through the elbow he necessarily crooked while tendering his money. Then, while the cashier was in the very act of counting out his change, her phone rang. Anticipating that he would be harassed by Genevieve while this woman engaged in a lengthy conversation, he found the energy to say impatiently: "Would you mind? I'm in a real hurry."

This was the sort of thing that he could not have succeeded at in the old days, especially when accompanied by the saboteur to whom he was married, but either the times or his style had improved.

"Oh, sure." Without a hint of annoyance the woman let the telephone ring and completed their transaction.

Once they had passed through the door, he tried discreetly to break Genevieve's hold on his forearm, but she only took a firmer purchase with her talons. This was the woman who, ten years before, had derided and demeaned him in all the classic ways and perhaps invented a new one or two. There had been a time when a moment like this could have occurred only in a desperate fantasy. She was abasing herself before him! He should see it as a triumph. But these reversals traditionally fail to happen at the right moment: when your adversary is at last at your mercy, he is no longer the proper object of revenge.

Moving decisively, Reinhart lifted Genevieve's fingers off him.

"I have to say good-bye," he said with the same firmness. "I'm due back at work."

She was leering at him. This could not have been a successful expression even when she was still pretty. Now it was ghastly.

"Hell," she said in a husky low tone, "you got time." She came close and dug at him with an elbow. "Want to go to a motel?"

"No, Gen, not really." He decided, on a whim, to add: "That won't be necessary."

She was still leering, even as he drew her aside so that an oncoming party of four could enter the restaurant—four businessmen, by their look, the kind of fellows Reinhart had in his day tried to resemble. He had exhausted a lot of life to arrive at where he was now.

Genevieve said: "I know I used to be naïve."

Reinhart was reaching the end of his string. "No, you weren't. You were O.K. Now I really *have* to go, Genevieve. But please let me know if there's anything I can do to help Blaine."

But she persisted, horribly: "I've improved, Carl. I really have. I know how to do everything now. I'm not shocked by—"

He felt a sneeze coming on, all at once, and whipped out his handkerchief. No doubt she said something vile during his nasal explosion. Fortunately he had not heard it. He put his handkerchief away.

"I'm sorry, Gen. You see, I've taken a vow of chastity. It's a religious thing."

A piece of rank cowardice, to be sure, but it was the best he could do on short notice, and if he stayed longer in her presence, he might lose all responsibility for his actions.

As he walked away she cried in a voice that sounded as though it might have come from a loudspeaker: "You pansy!"

She was really broadcasting her age: that had been an archaic term for ever so long.

CHAPTER
7

It was not to be believed. No sooner had he gone back into the world than he encountered his old nemesis. Fate always arranged it so that Genevieve was there to hamstring him at the beginning of any race.

He slowed his stride, looking unhappily across the parking lot at the supermarket. He had half a mind not to return: simply to bug off and not be seen again. It would scarcely matter that much to Grace Greenwood. He suddenly convinced himself that this employment could have no possible motive but to please Winona by giving him a sinecure. Blaine had recognized that truth. And even DePau had been quite right: it could not be imagined that the gourmet department would ever come to any good.

What a fool he had been to spend all morning cooking crepes, and in a foolish costume! The result had been that he now felt worse than at any time during the last decade. In his despair he even began to think otherwise of his lunch: had the stew really been all that good? And as to Winston's in general, what did he know after eating only one dish, not even followed by a salad?

The sequence of unhappy thoughts was interrupted when, slowly as he walked, he was almost struck by a car, a white Cadillac that rolled swiftly across the blacktop on the bias, so to speak, in defiance of the painted parking slots. Reinhart was called back to responsibility. He straightened up, looked left and right . . . and heard an ugly cry behind him. It was Genevieve. Had she been shouting all this while, unheard by him in his slough of depression?

". . . warn you, you pervert. I'll tell the world. I'll get you if it's the last thing I do!"

She was not following him. It was far worse: she remained in front of Winston's and raised her voice to a greater volume as he receded from her. Never had he suspected that her vocal cords could be so powerful.

He refused to look about and count the persons who were observing this ugly episode. No doubt there were some, but fortunately at any given time in such a place most people were contained in cars, usually with the radio playing and, according to season, heater humming or air conditioner blowing, deaf to outdoors. Not to mention that few nowadays had the stomach to interfere with a disorderly person: this was even true of policemen, who could be killed, and doctors, who could be sued.

The white Caddy which had passed him earlier on had come to an abrupt stop and was, reverse-gear lights illuminated, backing up at excess speed. This took Reinhart's attention off his old problem and gave him a new worry. But the car stopped just before running him down, and Helen Clayton got out of the passenger's side.

The Cadillac accelerated away. Helen came to Reinhart. Never had he been so glad to see anyone. He wasn't sure what effect this might have on Genevieve. It might even aggravate her problem, but at least he was no longer alone, back to the wall.

"Hi, partner," said Helen, who was a significant presence even upon a flat sweep of blacktop. The belt of her trench coat was loosely tied, and her green scarf flapped in a breeze he had not hitherto noticed. She came to Reinhart and linked her arm with his, but jovially and not in the raptorial fashion of Genevieve.

She cried: "Back to the old assembly line!"

Reinhart decided against immediately looking back to see what effect this would have on his ex-wife. It might be possible to make some distance without Helen's identifying the shouting, hysterical woman as being associated with him, though it was true that she had seen Genevieve in the supermarket.

"Well," he said bluffly, "did you have a nice lunch?"

She elbowed his ribs. "Not really." She made a snorting kind of laugh, which probably was not mirthful, but listening as he was for obstreperousness from the rear, he could not be as precise in his reactions to Helen as he would have liked.

"I see," he said, though of course he did not. He was still tensed for a shot in the back and could not believe that he was no longer under fire. But the fact remained that he heard nothing from Genevieve. "Uh, I had a good meal, or a fine dish anyway, at Winston's. Have you ever been there?"

Helen stopped and turned to him. "She didn't make a scene, I hope."

Reinhart shook his head. "I was hoping you wouldn't notice, Helen. I'm sorry."

"Gosh, Carl, it isn't *your* fault." She took his arm again. "It's just lousy you have to be embarrassed."

Now he took the nerve to look for Genevieve. . . . She was gone. Utterly. She must have parked her car over that way, unless she had gone into one of the shops. Was it beyond her to duck down behind the automobiles and stalk them? Could she have slipped behind the buildings, to circle around and arrange an ambush?

"You know," he told Helen, "this is the first time I've laid eyes on her for ten years. I thought I was done with her forever, and I'm sure that would have been true if she had been successful in Chicago—that's where she's been for some time."

"Bad penny, huh?" They resumed their walk.

"No," said Reinhart, "not really. Genevieve's a capable person. She's quite good at business. It's in her private life that she has difficulties."

"Now, Carl," said Helen, squeezing the arm she held, "let's not hear you speaking without respect for yourself."

"Was I doing that?"

"Why, sure you were!" Helen said with vigor.

He knew no serious reason why he should have found Helen so reassuring, but he did. Perhaps it was a matter of her physical solidity. From time to time, turning to speak to him, she rested her left breast on his arm. Again she was arousing him. Already they seemed not only old friends, but comfortable lovers—if there was such a thing as the latter: you wouldn't know from Reinhart's experience from at least as far back as the end of his Army days. He had not had a girl *friend* since then. He had never been interested in females whom he had not craved. And when sexual desire came into play, matters of relative power soon took precedence over feelings.

Back at work, an hour passed too swiftly to be believed. More persons than Reinhart would have thought shopped for food in the early afternoon, at least on this day. He had almost exhausted the crepe batter made during the morning session when DePau materialized at the table.

"Say," he said, "your boss wants to talk to you."

"On the phone?" Reinhart served hot, sauced, triangulated crepes to three customers. More were waiting. "Could you tell Grace I'll call back when I get a break?" He looked up the aisle. Still more carts were coming his way. "We're on a roll."

There was a spiteful note in the voice of the supermarket manager. "Fella, she wants to talk to you *right now.*" DePau turned and addressed the crowd: "I'm sorry." He waved his arms. "That's all for today. We have to close the stand down now." He moved so as to block their access to the area of the table occupied by the chafing dish.

Reinhart wiped his hands on a towel and removed his chef's bonnet. He intended to complain to Grace about DePau's officious rudeness. Surely, it was his supermarket, or anyway it was managed by him, but he had no call to be so lacking in common courtesy. Besides, another batch of batter had been made just after lunch and put to rest in the portable icebox; it would be almost ready for use now. They weren't closing up! He considered asking those who had been turned away to wait the few moments he would be on the phone. It grieves a cook to deny an eater.

Helen, selling packets of the instant mix, looked over the bent head of a customer and raised her eyebrows at Reinhart.

"All right," said DePau to Helen, and he actually snapped his fingers at her, "let's close up over here too. I'll have somebody take care of your stock."

Helen grimaced. "What?"

"You'll get credit for what you've got coming," DePau said. "Just leave now!" He was clearly in a state of great impatience.

Helen shrugged and, turning from him, tended to something at her table.

"Did you hear me?" DePau's voice rose an octave.

Reinhart had started away, but he lingered when the manager addressed Helen. At this latest piece of outrageousness he could not restrain himself.

"Listen here," he said to DePau, moving towards him. "You keep a civil tongue in your head."

The manager looked as though he might be suffocated by his internal humors. He coughed and spoke in a voice so constricted that much of what he said was unintelligible. "Police . . . publicity . . . sue . . ." Reinhart could distinguish at least these three words, which were menacing in a general way, but nonsensical as to particular application.

"Just calm down," he said, his emotion changing from outrage to a concern for the man's sanity.

But DePau seemed even more highly exercised when this had been said. Reinhart determined to get to the bottom of the matter without further delay.

"All right, let's get to the phone."

DePau twitched his index finger at Helen. "You too."

They all marched through the rear to a bleak room walled in cinder block and containing battered office furniture and a remarkable amount of papers. In one corner a thin, blade-nosed woman was punching at a large calculator.

The manager handed Reinhart a telephone handset.

"Hello," said Reinhart. "Is this Grace?"

He waited for several moments until she came onto the line.

"Carl, I think we'll wind up the Top Shop demo, O.K.? Take the rest of the day off, and I'll be in touch. Now give me Clayton."

"Grace," he asked, "has something happened?"

"Time to move on, Carl! Now just put Clayton on the line."

Grace really was hard to withstand when she spoke ex cathedra. Reinhart licked his upper lip and gave the phone to Helen.

"Uh-huh, uh-huh. . . . O.K., Grace," Helen said. "Sure." She hung up and said to Reinhart, smiling: "Not a bad deal, Carl. We got the rest of the day off with pay. C'mon, let's get lost."

DePau was hovering near the door. "You can leave by the back."

A plump young woman appeared. She was dressed in the blue smock that constituted the store's livery, and she carried what turned out to be the clothing from the locker that Helen and Reinhart shared.

"Listen here," Reinhart told DePau, "some of that kitchen equipment out there is my personal stuff. I'm going out—"

The supermarket manager put a finger into the air. "All of it," said he, "has already been packed and is on its way to the Epicon office."

They took their outer clothing from the girl, and DePau led them quickly through a dimly lit, windowless storage area, found a door, and opened it.

Reinhart and Helen emerged onto a potholed patch of blacktop on the southern side of the building. Around the corner came an enormous truck, and to avoid being splashed by it from a pool of standing water, they moved along the sheer cinder-block wall to the corner and a vista of the rest of the shopping center.

"Mind telling me the explanation of this strange episode?" Reinhart asked. "Now that we've got a minute? In fact, now that we've got all day?"

She was laughing at him. "You've still got your apron on!" He undid the strings. Helen was getting into her trench coat.

In the same good-humored way she said: "Some woman called up DePau and bad-mouthed us."

"What?" He had balled the apron and taken it in one hand while with the other he helped himself get into one sleeve of his jacket.

"Said we were drinking in public and pawing one another."

Reinhart's jaw ached. After a moment he realized the pain could be relieved by unclenching his teeth.

Helen went on: "Grace, to give her credit, said she didn't believe it, but he complained to her, so what could she do?"

With wincing hang of the head, Reinhart said: "You know who that was, don't you?"

She shrugged generously. "I've got an idea."

"And I was feeling sorry for that bitch." He finally was able to shift hands on the ball of apron and get into the other sleeve of the jacket. "Ten years! I don't see her for ten years, and the first time she shows up . . ."

"Well, hell," said his genial colleague, "look at it this way, Carl. She got us half a day off."

The extraordinary thing was that he did not feel as dispirited as he should have. That he was not utterly devastated by this experience was due only to Helen. It was difficult to feel hopeless in her presence. He smiled at her.

"And anybody but DePau would have ignored it," said she. "But he's always been a dirty creep."

"You've worked there before?"

"Sure," said Helen, "and he's never missed once in sneaking a feel back at the lockers."

"That guy? I'll be damned! And he looks like such a prude. In the old movies a man who looked like that would play a preacher or maybe a mortician." It was amazing: Reinhart couldn't get over the basic fact that he was in a good mood. As they walked slowly towards the parking lot Helen was usually touching him with hip or shoulder. They formed a unit of affection.

"I don't know whether he really thinks we're in cahoots," said she, "but he wants to get back at me. He's not my type." She bumped Reinhart for emphasis.

"Cahoots," he echoed happily. He had a deep attachment to the slang that predated World War II, probably for the simple reason that he himself was of the same vintage, but there had been a geniality to that language and an ebullience, which so far as he could see had been replaced only by grunts of insolence and anxiety: get it on, hang in there, that's a turn-off.

"Should we take both cars?" Helen asked. "Probably simpler to leave one here and pick it up on the way back."

"I don't have a car," said Reinhart. "So that's even simpler. But where are we supposed to be going?"

She swung in against him. "When will we have a better opportunity?"

An erotic interpretation could be made of this, but Reinhart was not yet so old that he had forgotten the frustrated expectations of his youth. In those days, anyway, women conventionally implied much more than they meant to do, and he had been marked for life by such experiences.

Therefore he said, modestly: "We might have a drink." They were now walking among the ranked cars.

"Thing to do," said Helen, letting his arm go and plucking into her strap-hung purse, "is to pick up a bottle." She found some keys and went purposefully to a large, battered, dirty blue automobile parked between two sensible, neat, economical vehicles manufactured by former enemies of the United States. Reinhart had not owned a car in a decade, and he could by now identify few makes. Helen's chariot looked as though it had been designed for the sheer purpose of squandering fuel.

She entered the front seat on her knees and slid over to lift the peg on the passenger's door. The interior of the car was in somewhat better shape than the coachwork. It had a homey feeling, though probably only because it was Helen's. Funny how machines are like that.

Reinhart slipped in. The plastic seat was warm, no doubt from the sun that had penetrated the windshield, though at the moment it was in seclusion behind a barrier of cloud. Helen started the car, making a noise like that of a dishwasher within which a glass has broken, and having driven no more than a hundred yards across the asphalt, she stopped at a liquor store.

Reinhart understood that he was expected to make a purchase. He asked Helen for her choice of beverage, though he was puzzled as to where they were going to drink it: from the bottle, in the car?

"Gee," said Helen, "I'm partial to Scotch, but it's pretty expensive—"

Reinhart raised his hand. "Say no more, my lady. Your needs will be answered." After what should have been a degenerative experience—perhaps his job was gone for good, and would Genevieve stop at that?—he had moved ever closer to exuberance.

He dropped his balled apron on the seat and went into the store and examined the appropriate shelves.

The bulbous man behind the counter said: "Can I help?"

"Just choosing a Scotch," said Reinhart, "for my friend. She thinks it's a good way to kill an afternoon."

"If she's somebody you're out to impress," said the liquor dealer, "may I suggest Chivas?" He turned to the shelves behind him and found a boxed bottle.

"By George," said Reinhart, playing a role for his own delectation, "I think we ought to spare no expense to please the little lady." He withdrew his wallet and paid the bill. He assumed that

Helen would give him a lift home after their drink: he now no longer had bus fare.

"Where do we give this a belt?" he asked her when he regained the car. "We really ought to have glasses and ice." He brandished the bag and could not forbear from gloating: "This is the *crème de la crème.*"

Helen frowned as she started up. "Uh, that's not like cream dee menth, is it? I don't go much for cordials, in general."

He allayed her fears by unbagging, unboxing, and displaying the bottle. "The fact is that I'm not much of a whiskey drinker," he said. "Not nowadays, anyhow. In view of that, I thought only the best would do."

She gave the Scotch a loving smile. "Now you're talkin'." She gunned the car off the blacktop onto the highway. This was a suburban shopping area in which one mall abutted another for what a local promotional effort sought to have called the Miracle Mile, but it consumed even more space than the name asserted. Beyond the malls began a sequence of motels: the notable names were represented, Ramada, Holiday, Best Western, and a far cry they were from the bleak "tourist courts" Reinhart could remember from childhood trips with his parents, when in fact Dad usually decided he could not afford such luxurious accommodations and instead checked them into that even quainter facility of those times, the "tourist home," viz., someone's private house, where Grandma or Sister Sue had to vacate her little bedroom, second floor rear, for the lodging of strangers at one dollar the party, and you had to queue up for a toilet of which the seat never cooled.

But in among the local examples of the famous chains, with the conspicuous landscaping of genuine shrubbery which doggedly persisted in looking like synthetic, the palatial parody of their reception areas, the high marquees celebrating the current gathering of men dressed in polyester—tucked into an interstice, as it were, between two of the gaudies was a simple, almost austere rank of discrete little huts, called, remarkably for this day, Al's Motel.

It was into the forecourt of Al's that Helen easily swung her car. Reinhart honestly believed, by at least 75 percent, that she was stopping there in the performance of some errand.

Helen slowed to a crawl in the approach to the square little building where respects, and a fee, must be paid before access was gained to the cottages behind, but she now said, with evidence of concern: "This is real private, Carl," and pressed her foot down. The car gained speed. They descended a slight elevation and turned in back of the little office building. Helen stopped there. "You can check in through the back door if you want."

Now Reinhart was suddenly soaked to the skin, as it were, with embarrassment, as if God had peeled away the roof of the automobile and poured a bucketful on his head. He sat there grinning as moist heat went everywhere except into his cold toes. As it happened, he had never his life long checked into any public hostelry with a woman who was not his legal spouse, in fact, who was not Genevieve, his only wife. And indeed seldom since their honeymoon had he stayed overnight with her except at their own dwelling. They had rarely traveled in their two decades together. There had never been a sufficiency of money for routine existence, for the two children had arrived in the earliest years (Blaine indeed so soon that Reinhart still might all too easily wonder about the boy's paternity). His extramarital experiences, most of them with professionals, had been in private places, their own apartments or the hotel bedroom which was his first temporary home after the break with Gen.

"Helen," he said, "can't we just be friends for a while? Maybe when we know each other a little better, things will work themselves out."

"Gee, Carl," she said, smiling an insinuation, "I guess I misinterpreted. . . . Uh, well, you're a special kind of guy, you know. It's not easy to figure you out at first."

Reinhart rubbed his chin. "Do you think I'm gay? Is that what you're saying?"

Helen raised her hands. "Listen . . ."

"Well, I'm not." He wondered whether he might have been too defensive.

"It's O.K. by me, whatever," she assured him. No doubt she meant it: generosity seemed a basic trait with her. But it was evident that her disappointment was still greater than her tolerance. She smiled wryly and put her car into reverse.

"Wait a minute." Reinhart had said this on an impulse, surprising himself. "It *would* be a shame to waste a perfectly good afternoon."

But perhaps it was in the interest of pride that Helen continued to back out of the slot down behind the motel office.

"I think the moment has passed, Carl," said she, though in as friendly a manner as ever.

"The idea was terrific. I'm sorry I didn't understand it at first."

Helen was now driving up the ascending slope, towards the highway, the old engine laboring. "I think you were kind of shocked, that's what I think."

"I may have been," Reinhart confessed. "I guess time has caught up, maybe even passed me in some respects, Helen. It's funny when you realize that has happened."

The car had reached the entrance to the highway by now, but Helen stayed where she was even after a gap appeared in the traffic.

"Is that your trouble?" she asked. "Is *that* all?"

Reinhart was actually a bit annoyed by her scoffing, kind as he knew she meant to be. "It's a real thing," he said, "feeling your age. You can't say that time suddenly pulls a trick on you. You've had plenty of warning, God knows, but it seems as if you are suddenly in a different category. I'm actually in better condition now, in every way but chronologically, than I was ten years back. I'm even healthier! I'm not overweight, and I drink very little. My blood pressure's lower, and so on. But I've got *ten years less.*"

"Gosh," Helen said, "I hope *I* didn't make you so morbid. Heck, I've got at least one friend who's older than you, and he still has a lot of fun." She looked at him in what he took to be compassion, and his pride was affected once more.

He said seriously, but with a smile: "Sorry, I really didn't intend to throw myself on your mercy." A thought came to him. He looked back at Al's and saw what he wanted: an outdoor telephone at the corner of the office. "I'm going to use that phone. You want to stay here or back up?"

She did the latter, and he got out and went to the booth.

He dialed his home number and waited until it rang uselessly a dozen times. He remembered that Winona had a modeling assignment which would occupy her all day. Furthermore, the job was about thirty miles from town, at the warehouse of a furniture firm. No doubt she would be depicted sitting at the foot of one of the beds currently on sale. Reinhart suddenly wondered whether there were men who might find this an erotic image.

He returned to Helen's old car.

She immediately asked: "Is the coast clear?"

"Huh?"

"Didn't you just call home to see if anybody was there?"

Reinhart laughed in admiration and a certain embarrassment. "Woman, you scare me! Can you always read minds?"

Helen joined in the laughter. She started the engine.

Reinhart said: "I've never done this before, but I don't see any real reason why it wouldn't be O.K." In truth, he could see several reasons, foremost among them being that he had always considered the apartment as Winona's, where he was essentially a guest. "See, I live with my daughter. But she'll be working for several hours yet."

"If she's a good girl," said Helen, driving forcefully along the highway, "she won't begrudge her dad doing what comes naturally, I don't think." She operated the car in what not too many years before had been thought a style peculiar to men: wheel in a firm but easy grasp, body comfortably slumped. "Gosh, my dad used to like the girls well enough, the son of a gun. Not that that made me happy when I was a kid! I caught him once kissing some floozy in the garage when we lived over on Elm. They were probably going to do more, but I just blundered in. I was ten or eleven, went to put my bike away . . ." Helen rambled on in this wise. Reinhart found her presence to be very soothing. This was hardly the mood in which he had gone to any other tryst in all his life. But, once again, you change with age. One of the first things to go is the sense of sex as suspenseful.

He gave her directions from time to time, but said little beyond that. She related another anecdote about her father's lighthearted lechery, her mother appearing as only a pale, inconsequential shadow. Still another symptom of Reinhart's growing older, to his own mind, was his recognition of the miracle of descent. It was common enough not to see how X, a beauty, could have been born of ugly Y, or how the genius Bill could be the sire of Bill Jr., the imbecile, or why the Fates would bring a saint from the loins of a criminal. But the fact was that no sons or daughters, spitting images though they might seem to be, resembled their parents in any way but the superficial! This was quite a radical theory, but it was firmly founded on Reinhart's own experience as son and father. Really, the more he thought about the matter, the more he saw that his immediate relatives had always been utter strangers.

When they reached the apartment building he directed Helen to enter the underground garage and find the parking slot that was assigned to Winona.

The elevator could be boarded at the level of the garage, but only after its door was unlocked. Reinhart found the proper key on his ring.

"They've got it all worked out, haven't they?" asked Helen. "The way to do things right, how to lock a place and so on. I'll bet this is an expensive building."

"Do you like that?"

"Are you serious?" she asked, and pulled his face to hers and kissed him.

The experience was unprecedented for Reinhart, so far as he could remember; and try to remember is what he did now, lest he lose his bearings utterly. Men of his age and situation were not routinely embraced in elevators. In emotional moments he took comfort in the crafting of general rules, while knowing, all the while, that the only truth is particular.

The door slid away, and they deboarded at the fourth floor. Reinhart was in an equilibrium between wanting vainly to encounter a recognizable neighbor and hoping to sneak in and out undetected. That is, he had a perfect right to bring a woman home, on the one hand, while on the other furtiveness made for more excitement. Yet Helen was the married one. She seemed to move boldly enough around town. He thought of asking her about this, but decided that it would be bad taste until they knew each other better. Which in turn caused him to reflect that he had never gone this far with any nonprostitute of whom he knew less.

But they were alone in the hallway as he unlocked the apartment door.

"This is real nice," said Helen in the foyer.

"There's a river view," said Reinhart. He helped her out of the trench coat, which he hung over a straightbacked chair. Whenever the need came to dispose of a guest's outer clothing, he was reminded of a deficiency in the apartment: there was no closet near the front door. He and Winona were in their third year of residence and had yet to provide a halltree or row of hooks or whatever. Yet he forgot about the problem as soon as the guest went away. In his uncertainty now he spoke of this banal matter to Helen.

Suddenly he saw that she was now as uneasy as he was, rather, as he had been, for this state is oftentimes relieved when it is seen as shared.

He put his hands around her from the rear and lowered his face into her neck. How long had it been since he had last done that sort of thing? This was much too simple an embrace to try on a whore, and too immodest. The complicated ecstasies can easily be purchased, but nobody sells an honestly warm caress.

She took away his hands, but only to pull him by one of them into the short hallway that obviously led to the bedrooms. Her taking the initiative, in his domicile, excited him. He had always been aroused by sexual rudeness or arrogance on the part of a woman, though in early life he had never understood this.

Until this moment his bedroom had been a monastic cell. He went to the buttons of Helen's blouse, she to his belt buckle. He would have lingered at the task, but she was impatient, and they were both undressed in no time at all.

He thought of something. There was an outside chance that Winona might come home early; accidental events were always possible. He stepped across his bedside rug and began to close the door. He could hear Helen draw the sheets over herself. Her body was as opulent as he had supposed: he was worried about doing justice to it.

Something hard to identify either by outline or movement entered the hallway. A shadow is exceptionally fearsome when one is naked, and for an instant Reinhart shrank back. But then he remembered Helen, whom he was obliged to protect as guest and as woman, and he projected his head through the doorway.

The figure had reached him. It was identifiably human by now, and smaller than he, but bent as he was he looked into its face. It was Mercer, his missing daughter-in-law.

She supported herself with two hands on the doorframe and made a strenuous attempt to speak coherently, but succeeded only in breathing on Reinhart. That such exhaust fumes were not colored blue was a wonder.

"Mercer," said her father-in-law quietly. "You've given us all quite a scare."

"Wwww . . ." said she, and spun suddenly about and staggered back up the hall, turned the corner, and by the sound of it, soon fell.

"I'm sorry," Reinhart said to Helen's face on his pillow. "That's my son's wife. I'll have to do something about her." He opened the closet and took his robe from the hook behind the door.

"Some days," Helen said cheerily, "are like that." She made no move to leave bed.

Reinhart closed the door behind him and went in search of Mercer. He came back immediately.

"Say, Helen," he said, "I'm going to be occupied for quite a while. I guess you're right about it's not being our day."

She climbed out of bed. Helen was really something to see, and she lacked absolutely in false, or perhaps even real, modesty.

"Can't I help?"

"I don't think so," said he. "But thanks."

"Is this an old story?" She began deftly to dress.

"I don't really know. Until now I've been on only the most polite terms with the lady. My son and I aren't the closest of pals. . . . Listen, I really am sorry."

Helen for the first time turned inscrutable. "Better get out there," she said. "Don't worry about me."

It occurred to Reinhart that some member of his family, small as it was, had been available to ruin every effort he had made during the last fortnight.

CHAPTER
8

Mercer had the thin, fine-angled sort of face that was once thought to be aristocratic, especially by those who had been filmgoers in the pre-War era. Whether cut of bone was still a criterion for good birth, or whether indeed there was still something, anywhere in creation, that deserved the designation of high-class, was one of the many matters on which Reinhart lacked authority.

His daughter-in-law was a slender, comely young woman, with good long legs, a flat chest, and skin that seemed always somewhat roughened by the weather. She had exceptionally fine hands, of which Reinhart was aware because in the six years of her marriage to his son his association with her had amounted to little more than a handshake on arrivals and departures. And all too few were even those occasions, owing no doubt to Blaine's disinclination to frequent his father. But though Mercer might not be to blame for a negative situation, neither could she be commended for making the least effort towards the positive. Reinhart would not have been astounded had she failed to recognize him on a public sidewalk.

And even now, as he clasped her naked body to him, they were no more intimate except in the most superficial sense. Mercer in fact was unconscious.

Here he was, alone in a bathroom with an unclad young woman, himself quite stark beneath the terry-cloth robe, of which even the knotted belt had worked loose in his struggles to move her person, which could change in an instant from altogether inert to woodenly rigid, to rubbery elastic, to pluckingly prehensile. . . . He had not performed such a job since delivering his father-in-law from the parking lot of a roadhouse bar many years before. At that time brute force was an available, even a gratifying technique. But you couldn't handle a young wife and mother with the same means that were appropriate to a husky drunk you furthermore detested. Moreover, you weren't getting any younger.

He had stripped and hauled her showerwards because she had vomited all over herself and, alas, not only down her bosom and through her lap and onto her shoes—no, she had also puked onto the predominantly pale-blue couch and the altogether beige rug and rolled over the one and tracked through the other. Even more regrettably, she had been drinking not gin or vodka or Italian vermouth or even dry sherry, but rather a fluid that was, at least when regurgitated, maroon.

He propped her now in the shower stall in his tubless bathroom, and because her knees threatened to buckle, he briefly held the knobby patella of the left one, so discouraging the incipient slump. Her sleek thigh rose above his wrist, her flat belly pressed against his shoulder cap. He could not help noticing when undressing her that her chest was not so flat as when she was clothed. She had indeed a remarkably shapely figure for a mother of two. These observations were not erotic, but rather in the service of a moral inquiry: why would such a young healthy body have nothing better to do on a standard weekday afternoon than fill itself with red wine?

When it seemed as though she might lean there in the tiled corner and not slide away, at least not until he quickly got the water flowing, Reinhart released Mercer's kneecap (surely one of the most discreet below-the-waist points of contact, if contact had to be made, and it did), rose smartly from his bend, and seized the glass knobs that controlled the flow of water to the shower. The mix could be a tricky matter when one sought a compromise between melting iceberg and searing steam. In the strait compartment of tile, the characteristic stench of vomit could not be eluded. His own children had been great pukers when small, and in fact Winona, as might have been expected, was notable at the art or craft, performing it often, at a certain age, in public places: restaurants, movies, and of course on parents' night at school.

"Throwing up" had its endearing side for Reinhart, and washing the puker was to some degree an exercise in nostalgia, for it had usually been he, and not Genevieve, who had handled such emergencies as might soil the handler.

In mixing the waters to achieve a comfortable balance, one could not, when sharing a narrow cubicle with another body, avoid getting soaked. Almost immediately his terry-cloth robe absorbed several pounds of water. He had avoided looking at Mercer's face, because though she had been consistent in keeping her eyes closed thus far, she might at any moment open them up, and her subsequent embarrassment would be a horror to him, for he would have no means of relieving it at this moment. Whereas if he could just get her cleansed, put into a pair of Winona's pajamas, and tucked into bed, the worst of it would be in the past when eventually she came to consciousness.

But to clean her effectively he could hardly keep his face averted. God, there was puke on her fine chin and snot running from her delicate nose. This was, he had to admit, less repulsive on a handsome face than it would have been on someone ugly or old: yet another example of life's inequity. Furthermore, one quick shot from the shower-head and her face was impeccable once more. He seized her, by shoulder and waist, and turned her under the spray of water.

He would have preferred to disregard the matter of soap, in applying which there could be no modesty, but when undressing her he could hardly have ignored certain olfactory suggestions that she had not lately had a good wash.

He lifted her over the curb of the shower stall. She had not yet come to, and he gently toweled her dry. Only a few more yards of thin ice to cross. He dropped the dampened towel and draped her trunk with a dry one. Obviously Winona should not be inconvenienced; he would sleep on the couch tonight. He lifted Mercer again and carried her to his own room. This was a more taxing job than any he had yet performed. He had to swing her this way and that to negotiate two doorways, and even slender young women are much heavier than they look. In the hallway the towel that had covered her slithered to the floor.

Reinhart was now carrying an unconscious, naked woman while

himself wearing a soaking wet bathrobe that gaped open almost to the crotch. What a perfect moment for someone to burst in unannounced. Blaine, for example. Or, far worse, Genevieve! He actually listened in bravado-dread for such an intrusion. *Come on, it's all I need!* But how could they get in? Well, how had Mercer penetrated the locked door? It might well be the kind of day when such things were arranged by the Fates, to whom it meant no more to spring a lock than to whip ex-wives into frenzies of hatred.

So goaded by resentment and self-pity, Reinhart managed to carry the leadenly limp burden to his bed. He covered Mercer with the spare blanket from the closet and then went to Winona's room to fetch night clothes. His daughter's chamber was scarcely uncharted territory. Winona would have hired a maid, but why squander money when he was home all day? He ran the vacuum twice a week, changed linens, and whatnot: little enough.

Winona had been none too neat as a fat girl, but as she turned sleek she became tidier in all respects. Of course, her appearance was her fortune. She could not be seen in clothes that had spent the night on the floor. Her walk-in closet was a rustling, ghostly forest of dry-cleaner's plastic bags. Reinhart had no cause to inspect her more intimate apparel, but when by chance he was present as she opened a drawer, the contents thereof always looked so immaculate that he was once moved to ask whether she wore anything twice. "Oh, gosh, Dad, a few more times than that," she had said solemnly. But not many more, he realized: which explained why when emptying her wastebasket, he always saw tumble forth so many of those little tags and labels, straight pins, and clear plastic.

And yet, and yet . . . you could share a home with somebody, somebody of your own blood, you could sleep in the next room, you could vacuum their quarters and empty their waste can, and yet be utterly ignorant of an essential feature of their life.

Reinhart chose the effective dresser drawer on his first try, merely by application of reason: it was on the last level before the floor. He kept his own nightgear in a similar situation. As he expected, along with several sets of pajamas that had perhaps been laundered once or twice, there were even more pairs yet in their original packages. These were invariably of a hard, flat fabric and in a single and simple color: beige, pale yellow, powder blue, or light green. Winona stayed with the matter-of-fact when it came to bedwear.

Reinhart chose a new pair of blue pajamas for Mercer, shut the drawer, and straightened up, feeling a twinge in the small of his back: that kind of thing was routine when you were older, and often happened for no good reason, i.e., you made no real exertion, whereas you might lift a heavy weight with impunity. One wondered whether Nature was really on the ball at all times.

He walked deliberately to his own room. Now that his daughter-in-law had been washed, it would be even more embarrassing to deal with her bare body.

. . . The aforementioned problem was shown to be an idle worry by his glance towards the bed. The blanket was obviously empty, yet in disbelief he wasted a moment by probing into its rumple. Mercer had gone!

He ran into the hallway, but stopped and turned and came back to explore his small bathroom. He then sprinted into the living room, made the righthand turn, passed the dining table, looked into the kitchen, wheeled about, and dashed back.

It was not out of the question that she could have hidden in a closet and emerged after he had gone by. Therefore he once again searched his own quarters, and because by now she might have gained Winona's suite, he looked into his daughter's bedroom and bath.

It was not until his second trip through the front of the apartment that he noticed the door was ajar. No, it was simply not possible that she had gone out. For one, he had not heard a sound. For another, her wretched, reeking clothes were still on the floor of his bathroom. Persons whom one knows do not go into public stark naked, no matter how drunk. Still, searching the place again would clearly be useless. He would not find her within its walls. Reason must insist that she had gone elsewhere.

There was one hope, not by any means farfetched: perhaps she had attired herself in garments from his closet or dresser.

He opened the front door just enough to allow the thrusting of his head into the corridor. At the very outset of any emergency there is often a moment or two in which to admit doubt that there *is* an impending disaster. Suppose that Mercer, wearing, say, his raincoat, was waiting for the elevator out there. Or, at worst, was so occupied, though jaybird-naked, but no one had seen her yet. On this side of the building most of the tenants were employed persons who did not return until evening. Reinhart was the only live-in housekeeper of the fourth floor East, and though some of his neighbors had visiting maids, these women usually came towards the end of the week. The chances were excellent for evading a scandal.

The only trouble was that Mercer could not be seen. He left the apartment and explored the length of the hallway, turning all corners and going through West after finishing with East. He had of course straightaway checked the indicator lights on the elevators. Neither car had been in use since he left the apartment. Again he had to consider what was left after all the eliminations: in this case, stairways. Hardly anybody used the stairs. If you had to choose an area in which to be disgraceful, there was none more inconspicuous. Despite the twenty-four-hour presence of a doorman and the locking of all exterior entrances, the stairways suggested, by their very nature, crimes against the person. If Mercer had gone by that route, she would be unlikely to meet anyone respectable, and all might still be well—unless of course she had been raped or killed.

Reinhart chose the stairway on his own, east side. There was another on the west, but he must assume that even distraught drunks took the line of least resistance. He descended to the third level. Would she have gone on down directly to the ground, or might she have stopped off at one of the intervening floors? If he examined each floor uselessly, and she meanwhile headed for the bottom, there would be no reaching her before it was too late.

He quickened his stride, but he touched every step, not daring to evoke from the distant past the reckless schoolboy style which consumed two at a time. The possibility of being crippled is something to be taken seriously after a certain age—whichever age one is in when the thought occurs.

At the ground level he went through the door to the lobby. A bald man, carrying an oblong case, was just boarding one of the

elevators. No one else was in evidence but the stately black doorman, who was gazing serenely, hands clasped in the small of his
back, through his portal of plate glass.

"Andrew," asked Reinhart, and though no one else was present
he discreetly lowered his voice, "have you seen a lady pass this
way?"

"A lady, Colonel?"

"Young," said Reinhart, "and perhaps—just a moment! You
must have been on duty when she arrived, else how did she get
in? Did a young woman ask for our apartment earlier today?
Second, did the same young woman leave only a few moments
ago?"

"Well, sir," said Andrew, "I saw no such young woman on her
entrance. She might have arrived while I was on my lunch, at
which time Joe DiLassi from the custodial staff watched the door
for me. Or she could have come in through the garage. But not too
many moments ago I did open the door to let out a young woman
not known to me to be a tenant in this house." Andrew had a rich
bass voice. Reinhart wondered whether the man might have been
a professional singer at one time, but never asked for fear that the
speculation might be true and the career had ended thus.

"Could she have been dressed in what might be men's attire?
Though of course it isn't always easy to make that distinction
nowadays."

"No, Colonel, not this lady."

"I see," said Reinhart, putting his hands in the pockets of the
terry-cloth bathrobe, which no doubt had dripped down four
flights of stairs and across the lobby but had lost scarcely any of the
water it had absorbed in the shower. However, one had been
distracted. *He was barefoot and, under the robe, naked.*

"You must be wondering," he said bluffly to the impassive Andrew, "why I am dressed the way I am."

"No, sir. That's not my proper concern."

Suddenly the correct question occurred to Reinhart: "How was
the woman, the young woman you saw, dressed?"

"She was not really dressed, sir," Andrew replied. "She was
wrapped in a towel."

"And you let her out?"

"Sir," Andrew said, manifestly taken aback, "I don't think I have the right to restrain a citizen if she is going about her business, clothed or not."

"God," grunted Reinhart. Closing his wet robe a bit more snugly (it had worked itself almost open), he strode out to the walk, abrading his soles, and scanned the world in both the directions that Mercer could have taken. Persons in passing cars gaped at him, which was not odd, but some did not, and that was. He saw no daughter-in-law.

He returned, really outraged, now that he thought about Andrew's failure.

"Do you have an outside phone here?" he demanded. "Or do I have to go back to the apartment?"

But at that moment a police car stopped outside, and two officers came from it into the lobby.

"You put in the call?" the first of them asked Reinhart. "Which way'd she go?"

"No, Officer, I put the call in," Andrew said. "She went to the right. You might take a look down by the river. You can get there by going around that way: there's a path."

"Oh, my God," said Reinhart. "The river?"

"You always have to consider that possibility with a demented person," Andrew said.

"He's right about that," said the second officer. The policemen ran out and disappeared down the gentle declivity to the right.

"Thanks, Andrew," said Reinhart, recognizing the doorman as not only an ally, but one possessing authority: a very rare item these days.

"Sir." Andrew touched the brim of his cap.

"This is really terrible," said Reinhart, who suddenly felt the cold of the tiles on which he stood barefoot, despite the worry that should have diverted all his attention. He stepped from one foot to another, several times, as if he rather were treading on embers. "I guess I'd better go back upstairs and get dressed."

"Yes, sir."

"I can't do much good here, in a wet bathrobe." There was every reason for haste, but some inscrutable power of anxiety restrained him. He realized what it was, and he explained to Andrew: "The young woman was not in my apartment for immoral purposes."

"No, sir."

"She's my daughter-in-law. She was ill, sick to her stomach, you see. I was washing her . . ." It wasn't easy to make the situation clear.

"You need not give me any idea of it at all," said Andrew, who was as tall as Reinhart and heavier at the chin and around the waist. An imposing figure of a man; had his gray-green uniform not been unadorned, he might have been taken for some contemporary tyrant of the Third World.

"I know I'm not, but—"

"But thank you, Colonel," said Andrew, who had the kind of voice that invariably sang "Ol' Man River" in Reinhart's boyhood. Such Mohicans were dwindling. "I don't think she would have had time to drown as yet," the kindly doorman added, "if she did go into the river, and very likely she did not."

Reinhart took the elevator and returned to the apartment. He gathered up the clothing that he had doffed in the intention of going to bed with Helen: an eternity of fifteen minutes ago. While dressing, he went through the living room, carefully evading the vomit, and looked out the picture window that gave onto the river. He could see no one that fitted into his disaster: not even the cops.

He had got into his shoes and was headed for the door when Winona entered.

"Good God, Winona, something awful . . ." But she was waving both hands at him.

"They have her," she said. "The ambulance came and took her to Willowdale. I wanted to go along, but she was violently opposed to that, so what could I do?"

He sat down on the straightbacked chair usually employed for the holding of coats.

"Poor Daddy," said Winona, patting his shoulder. "How did you know?" She started into the living room.

"Don't go in there! I haven't had a chance—"

But she had already seen the mess on the couch and rug. She came back. "Poor Daddy, you'd better get to bed."

Reinhart got up. "*I* didn't do that, Winona. That was Mercer. I was cleaning her up and turned my back for a second, and out she ran."

"Mercer?"

"Of course," said Reinhart. "That's how she happened to be down there with her clothes off. They're in my bathroom."

"Oh, God," Winona wailed. "As if Mother's not enough!"

Reinhart squinted at her. "You weren't talking about Mercer just now? You were talking about your mother? Your mother has been taken to Willowdale Hospital?"

"I didn't know about Mercer," said Winona, hanging her head in a way that summoned up memory of her adolescent despair.

"She was so drunk she was out on her feet. She was here when I got home—I suppose you know your mother had me thrown out of the supermarket. When I arrived here, Mercer had already vomited all over. I cleaned her up and put her to bed, but while I was getting out a pair of your PJs to put her into, she sneaked out of the apartment, naked except for a bath towel. She got all the way downstairs and out of the building, but Andrew quite sensibly called the police. They are still looking for her, I guess. I couldn't help because I was soaking wet." He did not find his own story at all credible. "It's my fault, I'm afraid, all of it. I should have kept a closer eye on her."

Winona came and clung to him. "Don't say that, Dad. You did everything right. It's me who's at fault. I gave Mercer my car and the apartment key." She was on the verge of tears. "I've really been ruining your life lately, haven't I?"

Reinhart said: "Don't be silly. . . . I'd better go down and help the police look for the poor thing." Actually he was somewhat out of patience with Winona by now.

She was resisting his effort to go out the door. "See," she said, "Mercer left a call for me at the agency. Because of some equipment trouble we got back from the shoot a lot sooner than expected. I picked her up at a drugstore where she was waiting. She didn't seem drunk at that time, but maybe she was on something. Tranquillizers, maybe?"

"Better get the story later," Reinhart said, firmly detaching his daughter from him. "The poor thing's out there someplace. Why don't you come along and help search?"

The intercom buzzed.

It was Andrew. "Mr. Reinhart?" He had never before used that mode of address, and Reinhart believed, terribly, that it was now the introduction to disaster.

"Yes, Andrew."

"She can't be found in the neighborhood," the doorman said softly. "But the police don't think she came to grief in the river. There are some workmen down there who would have seen her. Perhaps she got into her car. A UPS driver told the officers he saw a naked lady driving a green automobile."

"That's probably it," said Reinhart. "She *had* borrowed my daughter's Cougar, and that's green. Thanks, Andrew." He hung up and told Winona. "In a way we're lucky, I guess, unless she cracks up somewhere. Better in a car than running along the street."

"For Blaine," said Winona. "For us all. But hardly for her."

She had called him back to reason. "You're right, of course. What am I saying? God, when she was in the apartment she was out on her feet. Driving a car! And we don't have any way to look for her now if she took your Cougar. I suppose we should go down to the garage and see whether she *did* take it. But she must have. She arrived in it."

Winona looked up a number in the telephone directory and then dialed it. In a moment she spoke into the instrument: "Listen, I need your car right now. . . . Well, postpone it. . . . Yes, right now." She hung up.

"Who was that?" Reinhart asked. Somehow he did not believe it was Grace.

Winona was moving towards the rear of the apartment. Her answer was curt and given without looking back: "An acquaintance." She went into her bathroom and closed the door.

Reinhart consciously avoided thinking about Genevieve, with whom he had had no connection, domestic or legal, in a decade. Consequently, he had no responsibility towards her. Moreover, she had reappeared in his life only to do him harm. It could be proved, to a neutral observer, that she had always been more enemy than friend. She *belonged* in the bughouse.

He waited until Winona came back from the bathroom. "Listen, dear, when your friend comes with the car, maybe you could go look for Mercer? I'd better go see your mother. After all . . ."

Winona showed a peevish expression. She looked at her watch. "Isn't she here yet?"

"It hasn't been five minutes. Where does she live?" But Winona sniffed at the wall. "Dear," he resumed, with a slight edge, "did you hear me say I think I'd better go to Willowdale and see your mother while you look for Mercer? If you have any idea where to look. And I suppose we'd better tell Blaine. By now it's gone too far."

"Oh, sure, Dad." Winona was a bit sheepish now. But the door-bell sounded at that point and she visibly hardened. These trans-formations amazed her father.

She marched to the door and opened it. There stood a person almost as tall as Reinhart, dressed in a gray sweatsuit and sneakers.

"You took your time."

"Oh, Winona—"

"Let's have those keys," said Winona.

But Reinhart came forward. He saw no reason why he should play his daughter's game (of which he could not understand even the rules) to the neglect of common courtesy.

"Hello. I'm Carl Reinhart, Winona's father. Darned nice of you to come so quickly. We have some family problems."

Winona sullenly backed up and the large young woman (for such she was) entered and, thrusting forth a fist comparable to his own, squeezed Reinhart's hand.

"Edie Mulhouse," said she. "I'm a neighbor."

"Oh, yes." But in point of fact he had never seen or heard of her. Edie had short, pale hair, pale eyelashes, and a scattering of pale freckles. Her build seemed of the sort called rangy, though it was hard to tell precisely in the baggy sweatsuit. But her shoulders were broad, and she looked almost six feet tall.

"I'm on Five West," she said.

"Ah." In a moment Reinhart would be uncomfortable. He was too weary to make polite conversation, and Edie looked as though she wanted to linger.

But Winona stepped into the breach. In a falsely sweet manner, which Reinhart identified as being put on for him and not the

recipient, she said: "Gee, Edie, it's very nice of you to do this." She
reached towards the visitor, who in an almost agonizingly exquisite fashion unfolded her left hand to reveal two car keys on a
plastic tab bearing a heraldic device. Winona snatched the keys in
a style that suggested anything but mercy.

Edie smiled at Reinhart.

"Yes, indeed," he said. "You're very generous."

Edie looked as though she might cry out in glee, but Winona
virtually pushed her towards the door, if not by actual physical
power, then certainly by the brute force of the will.

Edie said: "Garage slot 516W. Keep the car as long as you
w—" At that point the door was closed in her face.

In the current emergency Reinhart did not believe it sensible
to chide anyone for rudeness. "What do you think?" he asked. "I'm
always on shaky ground with Blaine, but shouldn't we give him a
call?"

Winona ran her tongue inside her upper lip. "I guess we don't
have a choice."

Reinhart grasped the phone. "You or me? . . . I'm not trying to
dodge the job, but don't you think it wouldn't be quite as bad if
you . . ."

"Sure, Daddy. Sure." She looked in the little leatherbound private directory for the phone number, then dialed it.

Almost immediately she cried: *"Mercer?"*

Reinhart reached for his chin.

Winona spoke with the faint smile of incredulity. "It's Winona,
Mercer. Are you O.K.? . . . Uh-huh. . . . Uh-huh. Oh, I'm sure. Yeah,
the vase. . . . Yeah, if you want." She covered the mouthpiece and
said to Reinhart: "She says she left the car keys in the blue vase."
He went into the living room to the shelf-and-bar complex and
upturned the vase: a pair of keys joined by a beaded chain fell into
his left palm. He dangled them at Winona as if the whole thing
made perfect sense, but he felt worse in a certain way than when
Mercer had been at large. Perhaps *he* was the lunatic?

He made gestures at his daughter. He feared that she might
simply hang up after exchanging these polite commonplaces.

Winona chuckled into the telephone. "I just thought of something, Mercer. How'd you get home if you left the car keys

here? . . . Oh. . . . Well, I'm glad to hear you're feeling better. . . . Listen, any time!" Despite more violent gestures from her father she did now ring off.

"So that's it?" He looked at the ceiling.

Winona was shaking her head. "She claims she took a cab home."

"Jesus Christ." He strode back and forth. "I don't know what to think. If it weren't for Andrew, I might believe I had a hallucination. How did she sound? She was first sick as hell and then unconscious. That should have some effect on anybody."

"She *sounded* O.K.," said Winona, shrugging and speaking in an adolescent style, which was often characteristic of her response to any questions from her father. "That's what's so *funny.*" Then she peeped at Reinhart in a fashion that could have suggested dubiety.

"You think I imagined all of it?" He was annoyed. "Then look at what I'm going to have to clean up!"

"No, Daddy, of course not."

"You didn't know whether Blaine was there, I guess. I keep thinking of that poor guy."

"He may not be back yet from Willowdale."

"He went along with your mother? Aw, hell . . ." He felt he should sit down; the strain was known. But the couch, and in fact the living room as a whole, was unusable. "Let's go to my room and talk. I've been on my feet a lot today."

In his bedroom he made an ushering gesture at the overstuffed chair in the corner, where, under an old-fashioned bridge lamp (an heirloom from his childhood home, having indeed faithfully provided light since the Depression), he had, ever since moving in, intended to settle down with a good book, but in practice he invariably flopped on the bed and watched television.

The blanket with which he had covered Mercer was in a reassuring heap. Had it been folded and put away, he would have been in trouble. He flipped it aside now and sat on the bed's edge. Winona accepted the chair, but hardly had she sat down in it when she rose, went to the foot of the bed, and found something on the floor.

"Huh." She held up a beige, waferlike object.

"What's that?"

"Pad from a shoe. I guess Mercer's heel was being chafed."

But he hadn't undressed Mercer here: her shoes were in the bathroom, with the rest of her stained attire. Suddenly he remembered Helen, as if from many years before.

"There's a wastebasket over there," he told Winona. "Now we'd better work out a strategy. First, let me tell you about the earlier part of the day." He omitted any mention of Helen except as a vague personage who assisted him in the demonstration. Nor did he chide Winona for telling her mother where to find him—as she undoubtedly had told her. He spoke only of Genevieve's obviously disturbed state at lunch. "I assume the causes had to do with her career in Chicago. When things go well, a person generally doesn't suffer a breakdown." He realized that he sounded insufferably smug. "I'm sorry. I don't know what else to say. In a way I don't want to analyze my precise feelings towards her, and if I did, frankly, I wouldn't want to do it in front of you. A man in my situation has many responsibilities. Some of them even apply to her. I have an obligation to myself. On the other hand, I can't be too critical, if half *your* blood is hers."

Winona was shaking her head. "Mercer can't stand her. That's what set her off."

"Who?"

"I mean, Mother didn't show up because Mercer walked out—like Blaine said. The fact is that Mother came down from Chicago about a week ago and announced she was going to live with them. That's what caused Mercer's trouble."

Reinhart was grinding his teeth. "Still, it was a bizarre response, no? Mercer didn't just leave, period. She must have troubles of her own."

"I don't know much of anything about her," said Winona. "Today was the first time I've ever seen her alone. You know how she's always been at the family get-togethers."

Reinhart felt like getting into bed and pulling the blankets over his head, but he forced himself to stand up now. "What I meant about working out a strategy was how to deal with her after this, and also what we can do about Blaine, with both his women in trouble. Think about that, will you? I'd better get to work on the living room before the stain is permanent."

"I'll help, Dad," said Winona, nobly, and got up. "Tell me what to do."

"Go about your business. This is my affair." He waved a finger at her. "I mean it. I'm a veteran in such matters. A great deal of my Army service was spent on latrine duty. You go and take your bath. By the time you're finished, I'll have cleared the decks." Which would be true, given even his dirty work. Winona's sessions in the bathroom were lengthy, and until she left next morning, she would be seen only in bathrobe and turbaned towel.

But now she said neutrally: "You don't want to hear the details about Mother, I guess."

"If you want to tell them."

"I met Mercer at this drugstore, in some mall over at Elmhurst. I hardly knew what to say, never having exchanged more than ordinary greetings with her. But it turned out O.K. I didn't have to talk. She just wanted someone to listen to her troubles."

"That's often the way, Winona," said her father. "And you make a very sympathetic listener."

"You trained me, Daddy, if so. Remember all the times . . ."

As a young teenager she had often come to Reinhart with her problems. The tenderness of this reminiscence was somewhat limited now by his acceptance of the truth that such confidences were things of the past.

"So Mother shows up there a couple of weeks ago, walking in unannounced so far as Mercer was concerned. But of course it turned out that Blaine simply hadn't told her Mother was coming! Now, Mother needless to say began right away to take over, and to keep the peace Mercer—who's anyway a polite sort of person —wouldn't resist. But Mother simply takes that kind of thing as surrender—"

"Yes, yes," Reinhart said quickly, a sour taste in the back of his throat. No wonder at Mercer's performance in the living room. "We don't have to dwell on that subject." But he couldn't forbear from adding: "I'm the world's foremost authority on it."

"Well, Mercer and Blaine aren't any too intimate on things of this sort, apparently." Here Winona sniffed disdainfully, reminding Reinhart of her immunity to heterosexual failures.

"She made a mistake in letting herself be run out of her own house," he said. "You might say I did the same, ten years ago, but it was mostly your mother's house at the time, and she had lots of justification for her dim view of me in those days."

"Well," said Winona, "I'll tell you what she *says* you're going to do now: get married to her again."

So he was not the only person to whom Genevieve had spoken on that subject: he had not even been the first.

He stood up, leaving the springy side-of-bed without the aid of hands: his legs were not yet finished. "Listen, how about going out to dinner with your old dad? This would seem the night to get out of this place for a change. And I'll even pick up the tab —if you'll lend it to me." He was no longer so sensitive about taking money from his daughter, now that he had worked at least half a day.

"Daddy, *are* you going to remarry Mother?"

"I see the question bothers you. Do you mean you'd like to see us back together after all these years?"

"Oh, God, no," Winona said on one intake of breath.

"Good," said Reinhart. "Because it's not going to happen."

But Winona had more to say, more than she had said or so much as implied on this subject in all her life, but obviously she had been storing up her thoughts. "I hate her, Daddy." She struck both arms of the chair, but the movement was not that of a little girl in tantrum. Nor did Winona, an old addict of tears, look even close to weeping now. Indeed there was a glint of metal in her eye, the like of which Reinhart had seen only in—Genevieve's. It had taken him a quarter of a century to find this lone resemblance between mother and daughter.

"That's your business, Winona. I acknowledge your feeling. If I said anything further it would be offensive to the gods. Now, let's get to our respective tasks and then go out to dinner in what—an hour?"

Winona got up. "Gee, Dad, I wish I had known . . ." She mumbled something.

"You're saying you're engaged."

She blurted: "I have to see Grace."

"Oh. Well, good. Give her my—" Reinhart had started to leave the room, but he stopped now and turned and said to Winona, walking just behind him: "You might ask her whether I've still got my job—and where I should go tomorrow morning, if so."

"Oh," Winona said smugly. "You've got it—if you want it."

"No," Reinhart said. "I don't want it on that basis, Winona."

She almost wailed: "I didn't *mean* anything! I mean, what I meant was, why wouldn't you have the job? Grace is not going to be impressed by what some crazy woman told her. . . . I'm sorry. But you should have seen her."

"Your mother? You were at Blaine's?"

"After what Mercer told me, I really thought I had to speak to him. While I was over there Mother came back from lunch with you. To show you how far gone she is, Daddy—she was raving that you hired some Mafia hit man to murder her."

"Christ Almighty."

"What choice did I have but to call for help?"

"It was you?"

"Do you think Blaine would have had the guts?"

Reinhart shook his head. "Me neither. To have someone committed . . ."

"If someone is being violent? She threw a heavy vase against the wall."

"So they came and put her in a straitjacket or something?"

"No." Winona laughed coarsely. "I called the police. They came and talked to her and to us for a while, and then they called an ambulance. When it came, the attendants gave her a shot of tranquillizer, I guess."

"So the cops were called twice in the same afternoon for members of our family?" Reinhart shrugged. "We're getting to be like the Jukes and the Kallikaks."

"Who?"

"It doesn't matter." He finally left the room, clearing the doorway so that Winona too could emerge.

"Some gangster in a white Cadillac!" she howled.

Reinhart marveled at how a diseased mind could put quotidian phenomena to its own use. Genevieve had seen the car from which Helen Clayton had emerged to join him in the parking lot. He had not really thought much about that episode, but he realized now that he had assumed the driver thereof not to be Helen's husband. She had said she was never free for lunch, and she was hardly a newlywed. Ergo, she met a lover every day at noon and not a spouse. And yet she had enlisted Reinhart as still another alternative!

"But wait a minute," he said now to Winona. "Your mother says both that I am going to remarry her *and* have her killed?"

"She's nuts, isn't she?"

He went to the kitchen to fetch the materials and equipment needed to clean up the living room. For a good many years of his life not only the starring roles, but even all the interesting subsidiary parts, had been played by women.

CHAPTER
9

Blaine called his father on the morning after his mother had been taken to the hospital and his wife had returned home from her escapade.

"We have to talk," were his first words on the telephone, and this morning Reinhart found it easy to forgive his failure, habitual, to offer any kind of greeting.

"Come over here if you want privacy," Reinhart said. "Your sister has gone off to work, and I'm alone. I had a job myself for a day, but already I'm on vacation." He said that as a lightener-of-the-moment, but no sooner was it out when he regretted having given Blaine the opportunity to remember, from back in the bad old days, how often his occupational matters had come to grief.

"That's how it *usually* goes, doesn't it?" Blaine asked. "You haven't changed, and now it's happened, hasn't it? You've finally driven Mother beyond the point of no return."

In another time Reinhart would surely have risen to this bait, but now he maintained self-control. "No, if that were true, you wouldn't be calling me now. I'm not, ten years after the fact, the cause of her troubles, and you know it, Blaine. So let's please have a minimum of horseshit."

The admonition had the desired effect. Blaine was silent for a moment, and then he said, somewhat sullenly but without the accusatory note: "They'll be examining her for a day or so, I guess. But what happens then? Will she be kept in the hospital? What will that cost? But if she comes out, where will she go?"

"That could be a problem. Has she really closed out in Chicago?"

"What's that supposed to mean?"

"Only that she lived there nine–ten years. She must have made friendships, associations, had some kind of home. She wasn't back much to visit here, if ever: am I right?"

"We were always in close touch," said Blaine. "I saw her frequently."

"In Chicago, though, right? What I'm getting at is—"

"I know what you're getting at," said Blaine. "You're telling her to go back to Chicago. You're saying you're washing your hands—"

"No, I'm not saying that, Blaine. Not at all. I'll do what I can to help. But what I *am* saying is that I *shall not live with her again.*"

"Then how *could* you help?" Blaine replied contemptuously.

Perhaps in involuntary resentment, Reinhart asked: "How is Mercer?"

"*Mercer?*" said Blaine. "Why would you ask about *Mercer?*"

"She's my daughter-in-law, I think."

Blaine said loftily: "I try to keep my own family matters from her, frankly. She was raised among a different kind of people."

"And the boys?"

"Don't worry about them. They're being fed."

This struck Reinhart as a bizarre thing to say, but he passed over it. "Look, Blaine, I'd go to see your mother at the hospital, but I suspect it wouldn't help her to recover. I don't intend to give her a home, and I could scarcely contribute financially if I wanted to. And, frankly, I don't think I'd want to. When I was younger I wouldn't have had the nerve to say such a thing, or when even younger, even to think it, but with age one gets morally braver."

"Brave? You call it brave?" Blaine snorted. Reinhart was prepared to hear a vicious attack on himself, and was wondering how much of it he must tolerate. The boy had certainly been under pressure. Perhaps his father could do him some service by sustaining an assault, rolling with the punches.

But Blaine all at once changed his tune. "O.K.," he said explosively, but without apparent rancor. "What I'm really calling for is to invite you and my sister to dinner tonight."

"You're joking," Reinhart said quickly, and then apologized with the same speed. "I didn't mean that. What I do mean is that I accept, thank you. I don't know about Winona, but I'll leave a message with her agency and get back to you when she calls." He added prudently: "If she turns out to be busy, am I still invited?"

"No," said Blaine.

Reinhart found it possible to laugh at this. "We'll be there unless you hear otherwise. What time would that be?"

"Seven," said Blaine. "It shouldn't take long, tell her. Tell her I very much want her to make it."

"Yeah," Reinhart said and hung up. Some invitation! He dialed the agency and left the message. And then he called Grace Greenwood's number, but her secretary told him she was out.

"Will you ask her to give Carl Reinhart a ring?" He still didn't know about the future of his job. Winona had apparently come home the night before, after he was asleep, and then left for work this morning before he got up. She sometimes did this, with the energy of youth. Reinhart lacked in one symptom of age: he was not an early riser.

Before hanging up, he asked and received Helen Clayton's home number.

When Helen answered he said: "Hi. This is—"

"Carl!" said she. "How'd it come out, Carl? I was thinking of calling you, but I didn't want to jeopardize anything."

He told her about Mercer's adventures.

"Well," she said finally, "let's hope that's the last we hear of the problem. It might have been a one-shot, and from now on she'll keep her nose clean. You know, they talk about menopause, but a lot of women have their real trouble when they're younger. Especially nowadays."

"Is that right?" Reinhart continued to find new depths in Helen's sense of things.

"Expectations are greater. That always leads to trouble. Just because people expect more doesn't mean they've got it in them to deliver more."

"I should tell you, Helen," said Reinhart, "I get a lot of comfort in talking with you."

But now she showed her limitation, interpreting his speech in another way.

"Gee, Carl, I wish I could, but I can't today."

For a moment he was utterly perplexed. "Can't what?"

"Meet you anyplace. I told you it's tough for me."

"Sure, Helen. That's O.K. I really enjoy talking to you: that's what I meant."

Helen ignored this sincere statement. "I haven't been able to get through to Grace. We're on her shit list, Carl. You know how dykes are: let them hear about anybody with normal urges and they look down on you."

There had been a time when Reinhart himself would not have found this assertion altogether irresponsible. Perhaps even now he might have his doubts that it could be easily refuted, but . . .

"I think she's just busy," said he. "Grace is a real professional at her job. . . . The thing that hurts is that in attacking me, my ex-wife got you as well. By the way, she didn't settle down. They finally had to commit her."

"Aw," said Helen. "Aw, hell. I'm really sorry, Carl."

"Yeah," Reinhart said. "My own feelings are pretty complex. I hate her guts in one way, and then in another I—well, just in a human way you've got to have some pity. She has this paranoid idea of being persecuted." He snorted. "For example, you know that Cadillac you got out of? She claims that the driver was a Mafioso and that he threatened to kill her."

There was a long silence on Helen's end of the wire. At last she said: "Well, she's out of harm's way now, Carl. She belongs there, I bet. Anyway, the doctors have the problem, not you. You're not still paying her anything, are you?"

"At the time of the divorce I didn't *have* anything. She had previously put the house in her name."

Helen spoke softly through the telephone: "You're a real nice, gentlemanly person, Carl."

"Oh, I guess we're even all in all. I'm not speaking in self-pity."

"I hope I see you again," Helen said, "whether or not we work together."

"Oh, we will!"

"I don't know," said Helen, her voice drifting away.

"Well, I do," he said sharply. "You know, the Top Shop demo wasn't my idea. Grace came to me."

"Uh-huh," Helen said.

"You don't believe me, do you?" he asked, almost aggressively. "I'll tell you this: Grace wants to keep on my good side." He was taken aback by his own recklessness, but was not entirely displeased. It was, after all, a symptom of vigor.

"Gee, Carl," said Helen, "don't go away mad!" She said this with mock petulance and a throaty chuckle. "You've got something on her? It wouldn't be hard to get! Except I don't believe she'd be ashamed. There's a new attitude around, you know. How about having gay teachers in the schools? Would you want a daughter of yours in Grace's clutches?"

Funny how the worst could happen before one knew it—and turn out not to be the worst, after all.

Reinhart was even able to make a joke: "Or vice versa!" And before she could react to this, he said: "I always thought that if I were king, I'd let my subjects be whatever they wanted to be, sexually. But to punish by execution anyone who mentioned *what* he or she was." He cleared his throat. "What I meant was that Grace and I are old acquaintances. She enlisted me for the job because she knows I like to cook and she needed somebody to do that. Don't ask me why she didn't hire a professional chef. But she had to talk me into it. She's not going to deny me now, when I want to continue. I really do enjoy working with you."

An intake of breath was audible from her end of the wire. "Gee, Carl . . . I'll *try* to make it this afternoon. Can I call you someplace?"

"Here, I guess," said Reinhart.

Helen laughed gutturally. Oddly enough, she reminded him of certain guys he had known in the Army, for whom everything had an immediate sexual connotation. It wasn't easy to get on to that style again, more than thirty years later and from a woman— though no doubt it was better.

Towards noon Winona returned his call. He told her of Blaine's invitation.

"Can you make it?"

"Oh, sure."

"He wanted you especially. Frankly, Winona, I must warn you that whenever your brother gets that earnest he undoubtedly wants something. So be prepared. I think it has to do with your mother."

Winona seemed lighthearted enough. "O.K."

"Seven, Blaine said. That'll be all right? You won't be on some overtime assignment?" It occurred to Reinhart for the first time that, in the standard style of the wandering husband (that stock character), Winona might sometimes have pursued romance of a kind while claiming to be held overlong at work. If so, was it not absurd of her? Why should she have needed an excuse?

"I'm taking the day off," she said, "so there's no problem."

"Glad to hear it, dear! You could really use a little vacation."

"The agency's not that understanding," said Winona, "but the heck with them. They can just tell the client I'm sick for a change."

"Damn right," Reinhart agreed. "You have a nice time."

"Wait," said Winona. "Here, Grace wants to speak to you."

Grace came on the wire: "Carl, sorry I haven't been able to get back till now. Everything's cool. We'll have something for you in a day or so. Meanwhile you're on salary, of course. Take care!" She hung up.

Reinhart remained for a while with the receiver in his hand, looking into the vulvalike thicket of lines in the etching that hung over the telephone table. Winona had brought that home one day.

He was chagrined to have so quick an answer to the question he had asked himself. Q. Why had Winona needed to pretend she was working late when in truth she was having fun with her friends? A. Look at her friends!

Hardly had he hung up when the telephone rang again.

"Mr. Reinhart? Edie Mulhouse."

"Oh . . ."

"Remember last night? Winona borrowed my car."

"Oh, sure, Edie. That was very nice of you."

"Uh, was there anything wrong with it, do you know? I noticed it is still in its slot in the garage."

"As a matter of fact," said Reinhart, "as it turned out, Winona didn't have to use it. But you were very kind to lend it, and on such short notice."

"It isn't a very fancy car," said Edie. "She probably didn't want to be seen in it."

"Why," he protested politely, "that isn't so." Large as she was, Edie seemed overfragile of soul. "It's a lovely car, I'm sure, and you're a very generous neighbor. I know that Winona was very grateful. I hope she made that clear."

"She doesn't owe me anything," said Edie. "I admire her a lot."

"She's not all bad," Reinhart said modestly, "if I do say so myself." And then he added soberly: "It's nice to know you, Edie. The only other neighbors I've met in the almost four years we've lived here are just at the end of this floor. You know, I never lived in an apartment till I was middle-aged. I spent all my earlier life in houses in suburban communities where you necessarily were acquainted with everybody else. But there are things to be said for privacy."

"I hope I haven't intruded on yours," said Edie.

Something suddenly occurred to Reinhart. "Winona *did* return the car keys, didn't she? Did you look in your mailbox?" She was silent too long. "Just a moment, please, Edie. Hang on." He put the phone down and went back to Winona's room, where he saw the alien keys as soon as he entered, on her dressing table.

Back at the phone he asked: "The tab is blue plastic, and it has a Chevy crest?"

Edie said in a kind of horror: "I used to have a Vega, but this is a Gremlin. But I kept the same key thing. I guess I should get another. Is that why Winona didn't use the car? Maybe she couldn't find it? She was looking for a Vega? How stupid I am!"

Reinhart was annoyed with Winona, but there was also something regrettable about Edie's self-abasement.

"No, no," he said with a certain harshness. "You're too generous. We somehow slipped up on returning the keys: each thought the other was going to do it, I guess. What's your apartment number? I'll bring them to you right now." He suddenly got a better idea. "What are you doing for lunch?"

"Oh."

"Are you calling from your apartment?" It always took him a

while to remember that most people, even women, worked somewhere outside during the day. But Edie said she was at home. She
stayed noncommittal on the luncheon invitation: Reinhart found
her frustrating, but in a challenging sort of way. He decided simply
to bully her into being his guest, so as to expunge Winona's bad
treatment of her, which seemed to bother him more than it troubled her, to be sure, but that was no excuse.

Edie met him in the garage. She wore jeans and a sweater today
and over them a tweed coat. She was not a bad-looking girl, with
pleasant clean features and very good skin. Something probably
should have been done with her fair hair, which was cut short but,
so far as Reinhart could see, according to no plan. And her expression tended towards the lackluster, though her blue eyes were,
physically speaking, bright enough.

"I didn't realize," Reinhart said by way of greeting, "that when
I got up this morning I'd have a luncheon date with an attractive
young woman." He surrendered the keys.

Edie flinched in response to the compliment. It would not seem
by her manner that she had many such dates. She opened the
passenger's door of the Gremlin for him, held it, closed it. He was
made uncomfortable by this courtesy—as he would not have been,
had not indeed been, when it was done by Grace.

When Edie climbed behind the wheel he said: "Do you know
the Glenwood Mall? There's a nice restaurant there." He realized
that his basic motive for this expedition was actually not to pay
Edie back for her generosity (which gesture thus far seemed only
to make her uncomfortable), but rather to eat another meal at
Winston's—and with, this time, a placid companion.

In contrast to Edie's social manner her style of driving was as
forceful as a trucker's. She was a notable tail-gater, light-jumper,
and a bluffer in turning left at high-traffic intersections, blocking
with her little yellow Gremlin any opposing vehicle, be it city bus
or tractor-trailer. In no time they swung into a parking lot near
Winston's, in fact just facing the place where Genevieve had stood
the day before to abuse him.

Remembering that sorry event caused him to be less quick
about hopping out than was Edie, though true enough they dif-
fered in age and spring of reflex. Whatever his excuse, she had time

to sprint around the rear bumper and to get to his door before he had more than opened its catch.

For quite a few years now he had been the occasional recipient of gallantry from young women, but the irony was evident for both parties when the smaller human being assisted the larger in a physical passage. However, Edie was sufficiently large and sinewy to give Reinhart's spirit a shock as she not only seized and took the door as far away as it would go—for a moment he believed she might tear it off its hinges—but also slipped a large hand under his elbow and exerted enough lift so that if he had not quickly projected himself into the parking lot, he might have gone through the roof.

On the approach to the restaurant, in anticipation of her probable intent to perform another manhandling maneuver at the entrance, Reinhart determined to forestall her: he was after all essentially the weight-lifter he had been as recently as 1941. He slid a hand up her near forearm, hooking elbows. But soon she ripped herself away and positively loped, with great, long, high-arched strides, to the large ornamental bronze opener, a bracket and not a knob, on Winston's portal and pulled it and the door attached, and Reinhart was, or anyway felt as if he were being, scraped into the restaurant on the spatula of her left hand.

The place was jammed today, though the time was pretty much as it had been the day before, when just after twelve a third of the tables had still been vacant. There was a good-sized, more or less unorganized queue at the moment, gathered before a sallow-faced man in his forties. This fellow was being conspicuously incompetent at the job. No doubt the regular hostess was not at hand for some reason, illness or vacation, and the man was on loan, so to speak, from a superior situation: perhaps he was the manager. Therefore he was doing a rotten job so that nobody would take him as naturally a functionary who merely directed diners to tables.

Actually Reinhart and Edie, tall as they stood, were in a commanding position in the crowd, whose mean height was several inches lower, and the temporary maître d' proved to be a snob in such matters.

"Two?" he cried at them, up and over several intervening persons who had been waiting there since before Edie had parked the car. Reinhart considered making some public note of this, for justice's sake, but was soon pleased he had not, for the man's cry proved but the prelude to what was not the extension of a privilege but rather a virtual command. "Wait in the bar!"

Reinhart was none too pleased to obey, but decided that any objection might upset his guest. "Well," he said in a jolly tone, "shall we wet our whistles, Edie?"

She giggled shrilly and made a shivering agitation of her large frame. He had not noticed the bar the day before, but there it was now, in a wing off to the left. He took a deep breath and tensed his ligaments before touching Edie's forearm again, should she take retaliatory action, but he believed, even so, that she could more easily be led by contact than by speech at this point. As it happened she proved docile and almost weightless.

The bar was empty, as Reinhart saw once they got inside it and his eyes made the adjustment to the gloom.

"Have a seat, Edie," he had to say. "What would you like? A glass of white wine?"

The bartender came along. He was a young man with a supply of tawny hair and a brushy mustache that were "styled." He looked silently, gravely at Edie.

Reinhart grew impatient. "I'll have a dry sherry, imported, if you've got one."

The bartender went away.

Reinhart asked her: "Have you ordered?"

She shrugged and said hopelessly: "I'll try." When the bartender returned with the sherry, she leaned towards him: "Got any juice?"

"Tomato," said he. "Orange."

"I guess it's not fresh?"

"No," said the bartender, "that's too much to expect."

"Uh-huh."

Reinhart supposed he should have assumed she would be a teetotaller. "We should have our table before long," he said. "I'm sorry about the delay."

"Oh, that's all right," Edie said expansively. The bartender slid away, giving the illusion he moved on rollers.

"Well," said Reinhart, "so we're neighbors. What do you think of your apartment? Have you lived there long? Which direction do your windows face?"

Edie gave him a long and earnest look. Her eyes were delicate in this attitude, and of a color that might have been seen as pale blue or again as a rich gray.

"You're just doing this to be nice, aren't you?"

He waited a decent moment before responding. Then he said: "If you really believe what you're saying, you're being rude."

"I guess you're right, at that." She began to smile.

"Why don't you have a glass of wine?" he asked. "It's the natural product of the grape, you know. A wonderful food, and an aid to digestion. Would God have made fermentation if He didn't want people to taste its products?"

Edie was now simpering in good spirits. "Oh, Mr. Reinhart," she said, "you certainly enjoy life."

This was a novel observation, but he was flattered. He signaled the barman, who came up with a skating kind of movement. Reinhart understood belatedly that the young man considered himself something of a comedian.

"A glass of white wine for the lady, please."

The bartender said: "I'll go squeeze some white grapes."

"Did you know this?" Reinhart asked Edie when the glass had been brought and put before her. "That most white wine is made from red grapes?"

"I certainly did not." She looked back and forth between her glass and him.

"If they leave the skins in long enough after the juice has been pressed from the fruit, the color goes into the liquid. If they take out the skins right away, the liquid remains clear."

"Gee."

"Enough of that," said Reinhart. "Tell me about yourself."

Edie rolled her eyes. "Oh, gee. I'm twenty-four."

Reinhart said: "A human being changes drastically every couple of years. The earlier in life, the shorter the time span, so that a baby's alterations come with weeks, even days. Then you get past thirty, and while time is of course as inexorable as ever, it is very difficult to measure in a credible way. You don't make higher marks on the doorjamb each birthday." She brought out the teacher in him.

Edie still had not tasted the wine. She put the glass down now to say: "I was relieved when I stopped growing, I'll tell you."

The bartender had scooted up expectantly. Reinhart was low on wine, but he would not reorder if their table was ready. He had to rise and go to the doorway to see what was happening with the queue. There was none at the moment: everybody else had been seated, apparently, for no one but Edie and himself had come to wait in the bar.

Furthermore, yesterday's hostess was back at her post, and her male replacement was nowhere in evidence. The couple sent to the bar had been forgotten. Winston's was falling in Reinhart's estimation.

He went over to the hostess and entered a complaint. The young woman was in a different character from that of yesterday, when she had been so quietly amiable.

"But I've been here all the while," she said coldly. "There isn't any man who ever does this job."

Reinhart slapped his hands together. "Then I guess it was a practical joke." He smiled at the hostess, who did not return the favor. "You were probably seating someone, and while you were gone this guy pretended to take over. I fell for it. Sorry." He felt himself begin to smile. "Actually it was pretty funny, now that I think about it." This was the kind of trick that ten years ago would have made him furious: to be able to laugh freely at it now was to enjoy a luxury.

"Well, I don't think it's humorous," said the hostess. She looked very pale. "I'm going to have to ask you to leave."

Now Reinhart laughed in amazement. "Leave? Because I was duped?"

The young woman trembled. He realized that she was afraid of something. She reached towards the phone on the kind of pulpit that held her equipment. "I'll call the police."

"No, don't do that. I'll leave peacefully, if you want. But first will you please tell me what I'm supposed to have done?"

The hostess kept her hand on the telephone. "The lady with you at lunch yesterday—you don't know that she came back in here later and threatened me?"

"God." He moved towards her, but then caught himself and retreated: it might seem as an attack. "Believe me, I knew nothing about it. How lousy for you! If it's any relief to know, she's in the hospital now. She cracked up suddenly, I guess. It was nothing personal."

The young woman made a silly grimace. "Now I feel worse," said she. "The poor thing. . . . But I tell you, it was pretty scary. And I don't know you at all, do I, sir? She accused me of carrying on with you."

"You smiled as you took us to the table," said Reinhart. "No doubt that's what she was thinking of. It's too bad. I'm very sorry, miss." He shook his head and in so doing caught sight of the impostor who had directed him to wait in the bar. It was with relief that he saw the man jollily eating lunch with three companions: he had considered the possibility that the guy was another deranged soul, with delusions of grandeur.

"I hope she gets better," said the hostess. "I really do. Was that her doctor who picked her up in the white car?"

"When was that?"

"Right after she left here," the young woman said, with raised brow. "The second time. You and she had left, and then she came back to make that threat, and I said I'd have to call the manager if she didn't go away, and then she went outside and this white Cadillac pulled up and she got in."

Reinhart apologized again and walked out the door into the parking lot. He would certainly have some questions for Helen. . . . But he had momentarily forgotten about Edie!

He returned to the bar. "Sorry. I was checking on some private matter." He noticed that she had not yet drunk any of her wine. "Well, shall we have lunch?"

"You'll want to kill me, Mr. Reinhart," Edie said sheepishly, holding up her wrist as if in defense, but she was actually displaying her watch. "But I've got a dentist's appointment in fifteen minutes, and I want to run you home first."

"What a rotten host I've been," said Reinhart. "I'll make it up to you, Edie."

She stood up. "Actually, I've had a wonderful time."

They went out to the car. Edie went to the passenger's door, but Reinhart stopped her.

"I'm not going to need a ride home. I'm going to stay here for a while. I have to get something for my grandsons, whom I am going to see tonight."

"How will you get back?"

"Oh, there's a bus that's near enough." He touched her forearm. "Thanks again for offering to lend us the car last night. I'm afraid we Reinharts haven't done much for you in return, but—"

"That's what you think," said Edie with uncharacteristic pertness. She got into her little yellow car and drove rapidly away.

CHAPTER

10

Parker Raven, age four, Blaine's younger son, opened the door on Reinhart's ring of the bell, but he blocked the entrance with his small body so that his grandfather and aunt could not proceed.

Winona pleaded: "Come on, Parker . . ."

Parker extended his hand. "Let's have your money," said he.

Reinhart gently moved Winona out of his way, and then he lifted Parker from the threshold and, carrying him, entered.

The boy did not resist this action. Instead he chortled and asked: "What you got for me?"

"A punch in the nose," said his grandfather, holding him, as usual marveling silently at what tough stuff a child's body is made of: not only sinew but the flesh is so *hard*.

Winona was digging anxiously into her purse. Reinhart said to her: "Huh-uh. I'll take care of this."

"And what else?" asked Parker. "Come on, Grandpa."

Reinhart had always believed that both boys favored his son in appearance, but in his new awareness of their mother he realized that Parker anyway bore a strong resemblance to Mercer.

"I've got a terrific story for you," he told Parker. "If I told it to you now, then you wouldn't have it for later."

Parker struggled in his grasp, and Reinhart put him down.

"I mean a *thing*," said the boy, "not talk. Come on."

"Well," said Reinhart, "I tried. I don't like to see you being so grasping, but I can remember when I was little I too was a materialist." He took a folded paper bag from the pocket of his raincoat, unfolded it deliberately, and removed from it a blue bandanna. "See this? Every cowboy wears this around his neck at all times. It keeps dust from blowing down his shirt. He can wipe his face with it when he's hot. He can put it across his nose and mouth when he's in a sandstorm." Reinhart demonstrated this use, knotting the bandanna's ends, and then he handed the blue-and-white figured cloth to his grandson. "Oh, this thing's got a hundred and one uses. A bandage if you're hurt. Or you can put your money and other valuable possessions in the middle of it, tie it in a bundle, and hide it—or whatever you want."

Blaine appeared in the entrance hall. He was wearing a cardigan. It had been years now since Reinhart had seen his son in anything but a business suit and tie. In informal garb, with an open-necked shirt, Blaine looked somewhat vulnerable.

"Well, I don't like that," he said peevishly. "Teaching him to be a holdup man."

Reinhart saw that Parker had put the knotted bandanna across his mouth and nose to protect himself from the imaginary sandstorm. The aperture was too generous for his small head, however, and the cloth fell around his neck.

Reinhart's explanation was not received sympathetically by Blaine, who made an even more disagreeable face and then scowled at his sister.

"You know where to put the coats, I hope."

Winona went to help Reinhart take off his outer garment. It was amazing: her brother's ability to make an instant servant of her.

But one guest should not so serve another, and her father fended her off. He removed his outer garment without assistance.

Blaine asked: "When's it supposed to rain?"

"Oh, come on," said Reinhart, "it's perfectly sensible to wear a raincoat as a light topcoat, and you know it." He gave the article in reference to Winona, who took it, along with her own, and went down the hall and opened a closet.

"Do you have to go to the toilet?" asked Blaine.

Parker, pulling at his bandanna, was galloping into the doorway of the living room. But he stopped now to laugh and say: *"Toilet."*

Reinhart could remember from the childhoods of his own offspring as well as his own the special interest invariably evoked by that word. And he remembered another, which he now shouted at his grandson: "Underpants!" Parker naturally was rendered hilarious by this bon mot.

Blaine found nothing amusing in the exchange. "You know," he said bitterly, "you have to finish your first childhood before going into the second."

He marched through the door on the right. He had not invited his father to accompany him, so Reinhart waited until Winona came back. She was dressed in an exceedingly conservative style, by his judgment: dark dress, pearls, little earrings.

He asked her: "Where do we go now?"

She shrugged. "Living room, I guess." She preceded Reinhart through the door on the right.

Parker meanwhile had disappeared, but his shrill voice came from somewhere in hiding: "Hey, Grandpa! *Poopoo* and *doodoo.*"

"No, Parker," said Reinhart, "we've changed the subject." The human animal, from pup to patriarch, was such a bizarre creature. What other breed found its wastes so comic?

They entered a large room full of ponderous, men's-club kind of furniture: at least so it seemed to Reinhart, who had seen that sort of place only in movies and on TV. It seemed incomplete without a bald or white head here and there amidst the dark-green leather chairs, and the mantel cried out for a moose's head, though equipped with the next best decoration, viz., a mountainous landscape within a dark frame inner-edged in gold and illuminated from a tube lamp below. It was indeed the latter which provided the only light in the room at the moment.

Reinhart squinted. He asked Winona: "Do you see your brother anyplace?"

"Not really," said she. "He's probably in the den."

They steered towards the lighted doorway across the room. The den, when reached, proved to be an appropriate neighbor to the living room. Though much narrower, it was furnished with similar leather-covered overstuffs, and the table lamps here, as next door, were four feet high, with husky shafts in old gold. Along one wall were built-in bookshelves.

Reinhart's son sat at the end of the rectangular enclosure, behind the sort of desk that looked as if it were not made for use, being of carved leg and high-polished finish, its flat top a glossy expanse of tooled leather.

"Nice den, Blaine," said his father.

"It's the *library*," said Blaine. As could have been expected, he did not invite them to take seats.

Reinhart looked at the row of titles on the bookshelf near his elbow. They were so uniform and lifeless in gold-stamped leather that for a moment he took them for a Potemkin collection, an unbroken façade of book-spines only, cemented to a solid board, in front of no texts. But he poked the *Iliad*, and it receded.

"I see you've got some good yarns here," he told Blaine. "Did you have these specially bound?"

"Or something," said his son, who reached into a desk drawer and brought out a pad of yellow so-called legal paper. "Now I've made a few preliminary notes . . ." He probed at the pad with a closed silver pen or pencil.

Reinhart plucked a book off the shelf. You didn't often come across volumes bound in real leather nowadays. This one proved to be *The Last Days of Pompeii* and belonged, with the rest—the *Aeneid, Black Beauty*, and so on—to a series entitled The World's Greatest Masterpieces.

"Dad," said Blaine, looking up. "Put that back and pay attention."

"I thought I'd make a pile of books for us to sit on," Reinhart answered. "Here, Winona, lend a hand."

"For God's sake," Blaine said, throwing down his pencil. "Is this the way it's going to go? Winona, get some chairs from the main sitting room."

"No," said Reinhart to his daughter, "I'll get them." He found a couple of straightbacked chairs just inside the big room, one on either side of the door, where presumably the footmen used to sit in the house of Bulwer-Lytton, author of *The Last Days of Pompeii:* Reinhart had some vague recollection of his being a lord.

"Here's the point," Blaine said when his father and sister were seated across the desk from him. "We're going to have to come to some kind of terms about Mother." He sucked his body in slightly and opened the center drawer of the desk and found a pair of eyeglasses within. He unfolded the temple pieces and put on the spectacles. The lenses were undersized. The little glasses looked like something he had retained from his countercultural days, but when he wore them now Blaine seemed to have a foot in middle age.

"Now," he went on, squinting through the small spectacles at the pad before him, "I have sketched out what really seems to me a really fair arrangement, because this is not the kind of thing a family really ought to squabble over." He tapped his silver implement on the pad. "A three-way split is what I've come up with." He looked between Reinhart and Winona and smiled. For a moment his father believed that someone had entered the room behind them, but then his attention was claimed by the import of what Blaine had so easily said.

"A split of what?"

"Why," said Blaine, smiling pseudo-warmly now, but at Winona and not his father, "the expense of treatment and care."

Reinhart was reminded once again of life's tendency regularly to face one with the choice of folly or swinishness. On an impulse he decided not to choose; that is, to say nothing at all—and then he was shamed anyway, because what Blaine proceeded to say was quite true.

Blaine addressed Winona. "Of course you'll want to take Dad's share."

"Oh, sure," she replied immediately.

Reinhart sat forward on his chair. "Now just a minute," he said. "First, *Dad has no share.* Blaine, you'll just have to face the truth: I am not related to your mother. I haven't been for ten years, and I absolutely refuse to accept any obligation with regard to her. True, that's academic in my current situation, but it should certainly apply to Winona's assuming a burden that is supposed to be mine."

"Oh, Daddy," his daughter said in sweet reproach, "you know you don't owe me anything."

Blaine was still smiling, but now with a venomous quality. "I don't see it's your affair, then, *Daddy.* Winona and I agree."

Reinhart put his hands on his knees. "So you pay one third, and she pays two thirds." He looked at his daughter. "I'm not going to let you do it." He pointed his finger at her. "Do you hear me, Winona? I won't stand for it."

Her eyes began to fill with tears.

Now Blaine showed himself enough of a diplomat as to toss his chin in apparent indifference and say: "Well, we've got lots of time to make up our minds. . . . Let's enjoy our get-together!" He started to make a toothy smile but obviously decided that his talent was not up to such an imposture at this moment, and his face returned to its habitual pale length and the expressionless character, presumably a professional tool, that he showed to the world, except when, disdainful of his relatives, he wore a pronounced sneer.

"How's about a glass of sherry, Winona?"

At his sister's refusal Blaine smirked in what seemed, for him, good humor, and Reinhart could not help reflecting that the guest who would most please his son was the stubborn abstainer from everything.

"But she's got one coming," he told Blaine. "So I'll take it."

Blaine now produced a dirty grin, and it occurred to Reinhart that perhaps they could, father and son, someday create a kind of friendship based on cynicism alone.

"O.K., Dad," Blaine said. "Fair enough." He rose, went to one of the doored cabinets beneath the open bookshelves, and brought back a faceted decanter half-full of an amber fluid, and a stemmed receptacle of small capacity: in fact, a liqueur glass. Either the wine was an Olympian elixir, too rich for earthlings to take except by the thimble, or Blaine was being consistent in his meanness.

When Reinhart was a boy, before World War II, the local drugstores had sold pints of fluids called sherry and port, and highschoolers on New Year's Eve would contrive to get a bottle and drink it empty and puke on the sidewalk by midnight. Domestic fortified wines had improved greatly since that era, but Blaine seemed to have acquired, no doubt at great expense for such a rare antique, a store of that peculiar decoction of rubbing alcohol and caramel coloring.

"Mmm," Reinhart murmured after wetting his tongue and grimacing in an effort not to celebrate a nostalgic New Year's on the library rug. But to save face he had to go through with it. "Where's Winona's? I've got another coming, remember?"

"Ah," Blaine answered, actually enjoying this badinage, "you've got hers. I didn't ask *you* to have one, if you'll recall."

"By Godfrey," said Reinhart, "you didn't, for a fact. You son of a gun!" He saw that Blaine was seriously gloating, and realized that they had each won a victory. What was incongruous, however, was that the horrible "sherry" had been served in a glass made of exquisite crystal. He held it to the light of the brass lamp on Blaine's desk and turned it so that the facets could do their work. He saw no reason why he could not occasionally be civil: "This is a fine thing, Blaine."

But Blaine's return broke the mood. "Be careful, for God's sake. Those glasses are very expensive."

He took another glass and poured himself a minimeasure. He went behind his desk.

Winona, sitting on her father's left and slightly behind, had been silent. Reinhart now turned and looked at her.

She thereupon, as though they were in league and this was her cue, asked Blaine: "How's Mercer?"

His answer was bland. "No reason why she need be bothered with this. She doesn't know about Mother, and so far as I'm concerned that's all to the good."

Reinhart had wondered all his life which made the more sense: *Ignorance is bliss,* or *The truth will make you free.* There was something to be said for both. In this case the former was probably to be recommended for all the principals: if Mercer was unaware of Genevieve's current situation, Blaine presumably was still ignorant of Mercer's adventure. At the moment only Reinhart seemed to know everything about everybody. But he was old enough to know as well that the person who occupies such a situation is likely to be the greatest dupe of all, serving as mere audience for all performances.

He now asked: "Where's my other grandson?"

"In his room, I would think," Blaine said impatiently. He sniffed and finished his wine. "Now, if we could just wrap up this matter." He tapped his pad of yellow paper. "Maybe the most practical thing would be to get down to details, the actual dollars and cents involved."

His sister spoke humbly: "Whatever you think, Blainey."

Reinhart said: "Tell me this, Blaine: has any determination been made of your mother's problem? Has there been a diagnosis of any kind?"

Blaine passed a hand across his eyes. "Please," said he, "I'm trying to be understanding, believe me. But how can I see these questions as more than hypocrisy? When any question of money comes up, you say you have no obligation. Then how can you really care? Forget it! I'll carry on as best I can alone."

Winona said: "Well, you know I won't let you do that."

"No, no," Blaine cried, throwing his hand on a diagonal rise. "I've made my mind up now. I apologize for introducing the subject. You're here for pleasure. Let's finish up our wine and then go to the billiards room."

"You have a pool table?" asked Reinhart.

"Doesn't everybody?" Blaine obviously did not enjoy being taken literally in his self-righteous irony.

"All right, Blaine," his father said. "I don't want to be callous. And believe me, I don't wish your mother bad luck of any kind. Furthermore, I do think Winona is right to feel a duty. But I don't want her taken advantage of."

Winona spoke with quiet force. "Daddy, I think this is really my affair, if you don't mind."

And all at once Reinhart was struck by a sense that beyond this point he would be out of order; perhaps he had already crossed the line. In his earlier life he had so often been the fool that in compensation nowadays he was capable of erring in overcaution, excessive shrewdness.

"You're right," he said to his daughter. To Blaine he said: "So, probably, are you. I'll go shoot some pool by myself, if you'll show me where."

"Go out to the entrance hall," said Blaine, "and turn right. The billiards room is downstairs. The door's next to the closet where Winona put the coats."

Reinhart followed these instructions and descended to what persons of a lower social order would probably have called the game room, though, true enough, it contained only a pool table. The multicolored balls were nicely collected into the classic vee on the vibrant green felt, which looked very new. Reinhart had not had a cue in his hands since the Army, and never in his life had he had access to such a glowingly virgin table.

He was choosing a stick from the rack on the wall when a juvenile voice said: "Are you allowed to be down here?"

"Yes," he answered without turning. "I was sent here."

"I don't believe that."

Reinhart turned, stick in hand. It was his elder grandson, age six. "You know, Toby," he said to the boy, who was squinting suspiciously at him, "it would be nice if you greeted a guest in a hospitable way."

"Why?"

"It would be classier. Hospitality is an old tradition in all societies, I think even among cannibals."

"Put that stick back!"

Reinhart took a leaf from Toby's book and asked: "Why?"

"Because it's not yours."

The easiest thing would have been simply to see the child as a monster, and admittedly Reinhart had sometimes given in to that natural identification. But with a little extra effort one could extend the leeway of a six-year-old. He winked at the boy and bent over the pool table again.

"Damn you," said Toby. "I told you to put that stick down."

"Now you're getting nasty," said Reinhart, sighting on the cue ball. "There's a thing you should know about being nasty. You should be big enough or smart enough to get away with it without being treated even more nastily in return. Otherwise you're a fool." He slammed the cue ball, characterless bald eunuch that it was, into the rack of brightly colored spheres. That first impact always made a marvelous sound, and then came the blunt, subsidiary sounds as the balls struck the rubber banks and angled away to collide with one another, and then, in a kind of slow motion, two of them fell into as many pockets. This last seemed a gain, though he could no longer remember how to score any of the various pool games.

"You're in big trouble now," said Toby.

"No, I'm not." Reinhart sank an easy ball: the One, as it happened, which had already been hovering on the very lip of a pocket. "Get yourself a stick, and we'll have a game."

"That's just the point," said the child. "That's *my* stick that you stole."

Reinhart had his doubts about the claim, but he sighed and handed the stick to Toby, who marched across the room and placed it in its slot against the wall.

"You're not going to play?" asked his grandfather.

"And neither are you," Toby said decisively, and he came to the table and leaned across it, with an aim to reach the switch of the big round lamp that hung above. But lacking an inch or so in length of arm, he threw a knee onto the edge of the table and tried to climb up. Reinhart inhibited this effort with a single finger on Toby's shoulder. The boy then turned and punched and kicked at his grandfather but was maintained firmly at arm's length.

Toby eventually exhausted himself, dropped his arms, and stood in silent sullenness.

"Come on," said Reinhart, "why don't we have a game?"

"I don't want any presents from you anyway."

Damn! Reinhart had of course brought a bandanna for Toby as well, but having dealt with Parker alone and gone through the little instruction speech on the uses of the cotton square, he had satisfied his own needs and forgotten the other grandchild.

But it would never do to reveal that to Toby.

"I'll tell you," he said. "I was waiting for you to greet me politely before I gave you what I brought."

"Don't tell me that Parker greeted you politely!"

"I don't know that he did," said Reinhart. "But your brother is a little boy, hardly more than a baby. Whereas you should act like the young gentleman you are. Don't you go to school and everything?" He reached into the pocket of his jacket in which he carried the other bandanna.

Toby scowled at the blue square when it appeared. "Is that your *own* handkerchief? Is it full of snot?"

"Certainly not. Here. It's brand new, you can see that for yourself. I threw the sales slip away, never suspecting I'd need it." He handed the bandanna to Toby and wondered whether he should repeat the how-to-use advice given Parker. You never knew what omissions would be resented by children.

So he began: "A bandanna will save your life in a sandstorm, and—"

"Oh, I know all that junk."

But Reinhart nevertheless suspected that he had been right to give the boy an opportunity to reject him in this wise. "O.K. And you should also know how to say thank you."

"Oh," said Toby, "I don't have to say it to you! My father says he owes you no thanks."

To hear devastating truths from children is both better and worse than to hear them from larger persons. Better, because what can a child really do in the way of damage? Worse, in that one's conscience seems to have taken an exterior form, appearing as a derisive midget.

He laughed loudly while thinking up an effective response. It was not a bad tactic. Toby looked with astonishment at the man who found funny what should be negative news. "He's certainly right about that," Reinhart said at last, laughing more. "He owes me no thanks, because I didn't bring *him* a bandanna!"

It was not yet possible to tell whether Toby bought this. The boy looked confused at the moment. "Well, he says you don't have any money anyhow. Aunt Winona has all the money, and if he wants some, he will have to get it from her."

It would serve no cause to let Toby see his anger. Reinhart coughed, at which the boy shrank away and said: "Don't give me your germs!"

Reinhart said, smiling: "Oh, your dad is a great one for getting money out of people. My gosh, he's quite a guy! Who'd he say that to, your mother?"

"No!" Toby spoke with a child's impatience. "To Grandma."

"That's what I thought."

"Grandma's been taking care of us," said Toby.

"Yes. I know your mother hasn't been feeling well."

"She goes away a lot. I think she drinks."

Reinhart's response was involuntary. "Oh, that happens with a lot of people. It doesn't mean they don't like you." If he had thought about it, the sentiment would never have been voiced, but sometimes the preposterous is just the right note to strike, that which agrees with life's preference for burlesque to the deprivation of melodrama, not to speak of tragedy.

"O.K.," sprightly said Toby, who anyway had not been downcast. Like his brother, he resembled Blaine in configuration of jaw and the spacing of his eyes, but unlike Parker he showed little physical suggestion of his mother, except in coloring. Reinhart saw nothing of himself in either grandchild.

"Do you like your grandmother?"

Toby said: "I'll say this: she certainly knows her own mind."

Reinhart frowned. "What does that mean?"

"I dunno. I heard it on TV." Toby squeezed his bandanna into a ball and put it into the back pocket of his jeans. "Do you think television is a bad influence on children?"

This was the longest conversation Reinhart had ever held with either grandson. Blaine would never have tolerated it had he been present. In a sense the privilege was being bought at Winona's expense.

He answered: "Probably, but if you think about it, what isn't?" He leaned over the table and switched off the lamp that Toby couldn't reach, and they both left the room by the light from the stairway. "I have to go see your father and your aunt now," he said. "But maybe we can do something together sometime and take Parker too. Like going to the circus or the rodeo when it comes to town?" But he had no real hopes of getting Blaine's permission.

Toby asked: "Do you go to bars and take dope and have sex with hookers?"

"Not much," Reinhart answered soberly. "I'm pretty old for that kind of thing."

"Uh-huh," said Toby. "Well, I'll see you, Grandpa." He dashed on ahead, taking the steps in a series of leaps, and soon his lithe body vanished through the doorway to the ground floor.

CHAPTER
11

Reinhart knocked on the doorjamb at the entrance to the library, and entered boldly. He expected some resistance from Blaine, but in point of fact his son smiled at him.

Blaine asked: "How's your game?"

"Huh?" For a moment Reinhart was at a loss with this reference. "Oh. Gosh, I haven't held a cue in years."

"That's a championship slate table," Blaine said genially. "You won't see many of those."

Reinhart looked at Winona with some concern. "How are you, dear?"

She shrugged. "Fine, Daddy."

"We'll have to play sometime," said Blaine, rising from behind his desk. "Unfortunately I don't get much opportunity to use that table myself. No sooner do I pick up the stick when the phone rings." He grinned at the carpet and threw his arm in a sweep at the bookcase. "And those pricelessly bound volumes are waiting for me when I get a moment to relax—if it ever comes."

Reinhart's spirit fell. Blaine seemed in an ebullient mood, which could only mean that he had taken savage advantage of his sister.

"You've got an impressive place here, Blaine," he said. "Young as you are, you've done so well. You're to be congratulated. I'm proud of you."

His son peered suspiciously at him for a moment and then said: "That's true. But I'm not made of money. We all have our responsibilities."

For a moment the two men looked at each other, and then Blaine turned to Winona, who had just risen from her chair, and said: "We must get together more often. Living in the same town, really, why . . ." His voice fell away as he slid towards the door.

It seemed that they were being led out to dinner. Reinhart wondered who had cooked the food. But when they reached the front hall Blaine went to the closet and brought back their coats. Winona got into hers in the same stoical fashion in which she did everything at her brother's house.

Reinhart accepted his raincoat in one hand and asked: "Are we going out to dinner at a restaurant?"

Blaine smiled bleakly. "That's generous of you, Dad, but I'll have to take a raincheck. I'm going out of town in an hour. You see—" He broke off to open the front door and in fact never resumed, but simply showed them out.

"Do you realize," Reinhart asked Winona, in a delayed reaction that had waited until they crunched together through the gravel of the driveway and climbed into her car, "do you understand that we were not given anything to eat?"

"I'm not hungry," she said, turning the key in the ignition.

"Neither am I, but that's not the point." He peered from his window at the house as they passed it, going around the crescent drive. Blaine had turned off the front light before they had reached the driveway, and little illumination came from within. "I'm afraid Blaine has become really an eccentric miser."

Winona braked at the exit onto the road. "His expenses are staggering," she said.

Reinhart thought about this for a while. "I gather that he drove a hard bargain," he said at last.

In silence she turned a corner laboriously. As in so many mundane matters, she was the old-fashioned girl: awkward driver, light eater, self-effacing with her brother, obedient to Dad. "Medical care costs a fortune."

"Maybe your mother just has a temporary problem, what used to be called a nervous breakdown. Years ago those were common, and almost everybody had one at one time or another, and then they'd recover, and nobody thought the worse of them for it, either. On the other hand, real maniacs were confined in institutions and never let out if they were dangerous. Nowadays perfectly normal people are hospitalized and madmen often roam free, murdering people. But what I'm wondering is where was Mercer tonight? Did Blaine have her locked upstairs someplace? He is beginning to live like someone in a gothic novel."

"Oh," Winona said quickly, "she was probably just taking a nap." Suddenly she seemed to have an interest in regarding her brother and his household as routine in all respects.

When they reached their apartment house she turned carefully into the entrance of the underground garage, rolling across the strip of front sidewalk. At the bottom of the descent she stopped before the locked door, and Reinhart claimed the key from her, got out, and unlocked the big portal to the garage, which proceeded to lift itself electrically. The security was efficiently managed in this building, but you could never be too careful: he locked his car door again for the short drive to Winona's slot, and when they came to rest, he surveyed the concrete place through the window. Because of the endless energy crisis, it was lighted none too brightly.

Then he climbed out and pushed down the peg to relock his side of the car. In so doing he happened to glance into the rear of the two-door Cougar. There on the seat, in her green dressing gown, lay Mercer Reinhart. She appeared to be unconscious again.

Winona had closed her own door and started for the elevator. She had been distracted since leaving Blaine.

"Uh, Winona," Reinhart said, in one of those voices in which you hope to be heard by the right person without disturbing the wrong one.

But in her state she failed to hear it, and in fact did not notice that her father had been detained until she almost reached the elevator.

He signaled her to come back. She had the car keys. When she reached him he pointed at the back seat.

"Oh, no!" She unlocked the door. "She's not dead?"

"Not likely," said Reinhart. He drew Winona from the slot and leaned in, pulling the seat-back down. "Mercer?" He was reaching towards her when her eyes glinted in the weak light. "Mercer, are you awake?"

She replied in a murmur: "No, thank you." And turned over on the seat, her face to its back. Folded up as she was, she again reminded him of a child, indeed of Winona, who as a little girl was wont to snooze on the backseat in this fashion and then without warning sit up and be carsick—unless her brother sat alongside, in which case she proved the perfect traveler.

"God," said the grownup Winona, quailing. "I guess I'll get the blame again."

"We've got to get her upstairs," Reinhart said, hoping it would not be necessary for him to do much manhandling, the backseat of a two-door being a bastard of a place from which to take anything the shape of a limp human being. Brooding about that, he suddenly became fed up, and leaned in and shouted: "All right, Mercer, rise and shine! Haul your butt out of there, on the double."

The effect was immediate. His daughter-in-law rolled over, put a foot down, and projected herself out the door as he stepped aside. Her eyes looked perhaps wild, certainly bloodshot, but she stood as if at attention, and retied her sash and smoothed the gown.

"Now, Mercer," Reinhart said firmly, though without the hectoring note, "we're going up to the apartment. Can you walk O.K.?" At least she was shod in thin slippers.

She nodded, making big eyes.

"You're not sick, are you?"

She shook her head.

"All right, Mercer, we're heading for the elevator over there. Let's go. *Hut*, two, three, four . . ."

She seemed a bit rigid but otherwise in serviceable condition. The elevator was coming down when they reached it. In a moment its doors slid away and a brisk young couple emerged. Reinhart did not recognize them, nor apparently did Winona. And anyway they greeted only Mercer, in her dressing gown, and went on into the garage.

Reinhart's little party boarded the elevator. He asked Mercer, "Do you know those people?"

She smiled noncommittally and said: "Aren't they nice?"

Winona stared warily at her sister-in-law from behind the barrier of her father, and when they reached the fourth floor she hastened ahead to unlock the door of the apartment.

"Now, Mercer," said Reinhart when they were inside, "you go and lie down."

He told Winona, "Take her to my room. And listen: please shut the door when you come back."

While the girls were so occupied he went to his bathroom, where the clothing left behind by his daughter-in-law on the previous day now hung along the shower-curtain rod. Reinhart had hand-laundered these garments, including the wash-and-wear slacks, and they were now all dry. He collected them and took them discreetly down the hall to Winona's room, passing the door to his own quarters, where Mercer was in the act of lying down. Did she remember having been there before?

Winona shut the door and joined him. "Here," said he, handing her the clothes. "It all comes out even. She left these behind yesterday."

"What a break," Winona said with quiet emotion. "We can get her fully dressed, anyway. That'll be an improvement." She spoke even more softly: "It won't make *him* think it's so crazy."

Reinhart pulled her into her own room and sat her down on the bed. "You've got some idea of concealing this episode from Blaine?" He turned so that he could keep an eye on the closed door of his bedroom. One did not leave Mercer alone with impunity.

"He doesn't know that she has recently been coming to *me*," Winona said, assuming a hunted look. "Or he'd have mentioned it, you can be sure of that."

Reinhart paced the bedside rug. "Are you referring to the meeting you just had with your brother?" She nodded gloomily. Reinhart brought his two sets of fingers together. The situation was both gross and very delicate. "Let me, uh . . . This may not be any of my business, uh, Winona, but did he talk you out of a sizable sum of money for your mother's medical expenses?"

She raised her head. Despite the sheepish expression she said: "It really isn't any of your business, Daddy."

A rebuff from Winona was so unusual that Reinhart's astonished response took the form of a grin.

"You're quite right when it comes to the figure," he said, looking towards his bedroom door, "but I'm certainly involved in everything else."

"It won't affect the way we live." Her smile was very tender.

Reinhart had not considered that subject in the light of her reconcilation with Grace Greenwood: who would live with whom and where? For so long he and his daughter had lived in eventless serenity—or at any rate, so it had seemed to him. But Winona very likely had had crises and recoveries of which he had known nothing. In the first few months after coming back from the War he had lived at his parents' house: no matter what extravagance he had been involved in when at large, at home he maintained a bland façade; it was no more than good taste.

"Well, look," he said now, "I'm going to have to call Blaine. *I'll* take the responsibility here, if it must be taken, but I won't put up with any of his nonsense. After all, I knew him before he could go to the toilet unassisted."

This was supposed to be a joke, but Winona was not as amused as she might have been.

She winced. "It's different with you, but then, *you're a man.*"

He went to pat the crown of her lowered head, but refrained: that was model's hair. What he really felt like doing was to give Blaine a brutal hiding. Alas, the boy had regularly inspired such feelings in his father from birth onward. That was the pity, and nobody was at fault. It is much easier to understand how the wrong people get married to one another than to recognize that Nature too makes mistakes. That is, it was his emotional error to have married Genevieve, but his connection to Blaine was through the most basic of physical elements, the chromosomes, etc.: this was a dirty trick of God's.

He began: "All my life I've been trying to decide whether spelling things out, telling the whole truth, and so on, really helps, and I have never succeeded."

But Winona looked up at him and said: "You know my brother's style. Mother's gone crazy because of *my* private life."

"He actually said that?"

"What do you think?"

"I think I'd strike him if he were near enough," said Reinhart.

He thought for a moment. "First, I hope you know there's nothing in the accusation. Nobody does anything of that sort because of somebody's, as you say, private life. . . . You know you have always been the most forgiving of women with the menfolk of your family, Winona. I have noticed that you are quite different when among your female friends. And that fascinates me."

He wanted to say more; perhaps he was at last even ready to consider that Winona's generosity towards himself and Blaine might be condescension on her part, a radical idea if seriously entertained by a father. But at this moment the door to his bedroom opened, and Mercer emerged.

When he moved quickly into the hall she smiled and said: "I've had a very nice time. I'm sorry I have to leave so early."

"So am I, Mercer," said Reinhart. "Won't you come back here? Winona wants a word with you." He stepped into his daughter's bedroom. "Get her into the clothes, huh? I'm going to phone Blaine."

Mercer continued to smile in her genteel fashion as she slipped by him in an almost Oriental glide. Reinhart went to the telephone extension in the kitchen and dialed his son's number. There was no response to several rings, and he was about to hang up, assuming that Blaine had gone out to search for Mercer, when the instrument was lifted at the other end.

"Hello," he said. "Blaine?"

"No."

"Parker? Grandpa. I want to speak to your father."

"Give me a dollar," Parker said.

"You get him right now."

"I don't know where he is."

"Parker, I want you to promise me something."

"Huh?"

"When your father comes back, tell him to call me. Can you do that?"

"It would be nice if you tell me what you're going to bring me next time."

"Did you hear me, Parker?"

Someone else came on the line, lifting an extension in silence. Reinhart said: "Blaine. Is that you?"

"No, I *told you* it was Parker."

This was getting nowhere. Reinhart repeated his instructions and hung up.

He left the kitchen and was passing the front door when the nearby phone rang. He shouted to the back bedroom that he would get it, and picked up the instrument.

"Carl, believe it or not, I can make it now if you can."

"Excuse me?" The female voice was familiar, but for the life of him he couldn't immediately identify it.

"I'll explain when I get there."

He suddenly remembered: Helen Clayton. Huh. "Helen, I'm really tied up at the moment."

"Well . . ."

"Really. I've got family problems. You remember yesterday afternoon?"

"Oh. Is she—"

"More or less. But listen, there was something I wanted to ask you about." He cupped his hand around his mouth and both lowered the volume of his voice and increased its intensity, so as to be audible to her but not to the back bedroom. "You know your friend with the white Cadillac?"

"Who?" asked Helen.

"You know, the white car you got out of yesterday after lunch."

"Carl, I told you I wasn't free. Now, you've got no right to be jealous."

"I'm not snooping, believe me, Helen. But a funny thing happened in connection with Genevieve, my ex-wife, you know. It seems she was seen getting into that same car that your friend drives."

Helen was silent for a while. Then she said: "We were trying to help, Carl."

"Help?"

"I saw her there screaming at you in the parking lot, so I mentioned it to my friend. He said he'd have a word with her, and I guess he did. Why? Didn't it work?"

Reinhart was shaking his head. By chance he saw the etching on the wall above the phone but now could not find the configuration of the female sexual part or indeed any other. He asked: "Is your friend in the Mafia?"

Helen chuckled. "Naw, he's Jewish."

"Uh-huh. Well, she seems to have taken him for a gangster."

"I could see that, yeah," said Helen. "Well, O.K.. Does that answer your question?"

"I wonder why she'd get into the car with a strange man, though. Your friend, he wouldn't actually threaten her, would he?"

"What do you mean?"

"Pull a gun or anything?"

Helen thought for a while. "Gee, Carl, I don't know why he would. I couldn't see any reason for it. He's in business, you know."

"Uh-huh."

"Floor coverings."

"Is that right?" She heard the girls coming up the hall. "Well, thanks, Helen. I've got to go now. I'll get back to you."

"I'll try, Carl, but I don't know . . ."

"Sure, Helen."

Mercer came out of the hallway as he hung up, Winona behind her. Blaine's wife wore her clothes of yesterday and carried the folded dressing gown over one arm.

To Reinhart she said: "Winona was just showing me her room. The colors are lovely, and I especially like her choice of fabric for the curtains."

"Uh-huh," said Reinhart, as if he were still speaking with Helen. "How are you feeling, Mercer?"

"Very well, thank you. And you?"

"In the pink," he said.

Winona seemed more hangdog by the moment. Reinhart addressed her with fake verve: "Shall we get the show on the road?"

She handed him the car keys. "Do you mind, Dad?"

"Taking Mercer home?" he cried bluffly. "Is it likely I'd complain about being in the company of a good-looking girl?"

Each of them made some show of mirth. Mercer actually produced a whinnying sound: it was even possible she was genuinely amused.

"Oh, that would be very kind. I'm sorry to put you to this trouble, but . . ."

Reinhart bit his lip. On an impulse he decided to ask, flatly: "How'd you get here, Mercer?"

"It wasn't far."

"You walked from your house?"

"No, just from where my car broke down. . . . Will you excuse me, please?" She pointed down the hall and proceeded in that direction. She went into the nearer bathroom, his own, perhaps familiar to her unconscious memory.

Reinhart shrugged at his daughter and spoke in a low voice. "God Almighty, that's more than drunk. Her mind is gone."

Winona peered down the hall. "She's on something."

"Can that be all, though? Can you get that demented on pills?" His daughter nodded. "You can get anything."

Perhaps Winona was right. Suddenly he wondered whether her own sexuality had been, was being, warped by some chemical means. Was Grace Greenwood slipping something into the Fresca? What a wild hope to have, but perhaps less preposterous than a great many phenomena that were now seen as commonplace. At almost hourly intervals he was reminded of how harmless had been the time of his own youth: the most vicious types of that era would today qualify as the most wholesome of citizens. The young toughs of high-school days freaked out on drugstore wine. Someone's second cousin knew a swing musician who sometimes smoked reefers. The love that dared not speak its name was named only in jest.

"I guess one should hope it's only drugs," said he.

"You know, I was thinking," said Winona, looking down the hall. "Grace has a good friend who's a lady shrink."

No matter how good your intentions, you immediately ask yourself: another one of them? Reinhart cleared his throat, expunging the thought. "You may be right," he said. "It would be up to Blaine, or really, to Mercer herself, if she's capable of making such a decision."

"Some of the worst junkies in this country are young married women with children," Winona said, with a TV reporter's note that deepened her voice at the end of the sentence. She was probably repeating some news item verbatim. Reinhart had heard many to the same effect. "I know you've never cared much for psychiatrists, Dad."

Reinhart felt a surge of affection for her. This was one of the times when, without warning, he thought of her as good old Winona—despite her current chic.

"But then, what do I know?" he asked in good humor. "Aw, it's just that I crossed paths with one or two throughout the years, and of all people I have ever met they seemed to know the least about human beings. But, then, perhaps that's the right idea."

He could see that Winona paid little attention to his speech, for he knew her so well. Then she proceeded to prove again that he knew nothing.

"Dad," she said, coming to stand in front of him and lowering her eyes, as if in a proper form of confession. "She's really good, this doctor. She's not a phony."

He nodded. "I'll take your word for it, dear. You went to her yourself, is that what you're saying?"

"For a while. . . . You're not angry?"

"Winona," said he, "I think I've been a jerk. I never meant to imply that you needed my approval to go to a psychiatrist—or to do anything else. I have seldom been able to remember what a good daughter you've always been—an amiable child, as I believe the term went in a more graceful era. You don't have to share my tastes and opinions, nor apologize when you differ." It was true that he meant this earnestly and that he was being hypocritical as well. What he really wanted was that she naturally and voluntarily agreed with him on all matters. "I take it you were helped."

"Oh, yes." Winona said this fervently. "A lot."

He very much did not want her to spell out how. "That's impressive testimony. You might talk the idea over with Blaine and Mercer—and by the way, isn't she taking a long while?" Luckily there was only a ventilation duct and not a window in Reinhart's bathroom.

He and Winona were at the head of the hall when the door swung open and Mercer emerged. She had freshened her make-up and brushed her hair. She was an authentically good-looking young woman, not beautiful nor pretty, but simply damned well made. When Reinhart saw her in this way he sometimes thought of horses: she might appropriately be holding one by the bridle. Again, there was in her own neck a suggestion of the equine. He could easily be envious of Blaine: this was the kind of girl who would never have been aware of his own existence when he was young. And only yesterday he had stripped her nude and washed off the puke! Today she was revealed as being demented, whether permanently or for the drugged nonce. But there was no getting away from it: she still had genuine class.

"Ready to go?" he asked, jiggling the car keys.

"Oh, if you don't mind," said Mercer, with a dazzling grin that seemed to have no emotion behind it. "I really am in the mood to have some fun. I've been home all day." She turned her smile on Winona. "Want to do a disco?"

Taken by surprise, her sister-in-law opened and closed her mouth in silence.

Reinhart said: "We'd better get you home, Mercer."

"*He* won't let me out."

"You understand, we can't operate in that fashion. We'll help you, but we won't do anything behind Blaine's back. . . . By the way, I just remembered he said he was going somewhere. When will he be back?"

"Who knows?"

"Are you serious?"

Mercer gave him a solemn look. "I think I'll just lie down for a while."

Reinhart said to Winona: "Help her to bed in my room. I'd better go over and bring the boys back here."

CHAPTER

12

"Carl, you're booked tomorrow on the *Eye Opener Show,* Channel Five, to go on right after the seven forty-five headlines. Know the show?"

Grace Greenwood was on the telephone. Reinhart seldom watched TV before late afternoon at the earliest, but he was aware in a general way of the programs offered.

"That's the local one, isn't it?" Then he was belatedly struck by the meaning of the announcement that had preceded her question. "What do you mean, I'm booked?"

"I've got you a three-minute spot. What can you cook in that time? It should be something highly visual."

He repeated his question. "I don't understand."

Grace chuckled with the sound of crumpling paper. She was in a capital mood, for some reason. "It all started with the cathode-ray tube, I think. Get the rest of the explanation at the public library!"

"I'm sorry, Grace. I don't know whether Winona mentioned that we have some difficulty et cetera in the family. It takes all my attention at the moment."

"Carl, I'm *trying* to help," cried Grace. "This might well lead to something, and it's only three minutes. My God, do a Hamburg Hawaiian or something."

In spite of himself he asked with horrified fascination: "Is that with pineapple and coconut?"

"Who knows?" said Grace. "I just made it up. But that's the idea:

something colorful, inventive. Lots of people watch that show, and everybody's interested in unusual cooking nowadays."

In fact, Reinhart knew nobody at the moment who was even interested much in plain eating, but it was true that he got no further than his troubled family these days.

"Tomorrow? God, Grace, I wish you'd asked me first." Still, he could feel the faint stirrings of a vanity that had been so long quiescent, as was only appropriate in a man of his years and history. "Television! I don't know that I'd have the nerve."

"Well, just watch some of it and you'll get plenty!" said Grace. "Wear your big white hat and apron, and half the battle's won. I promised you'd be there at five thirty for make-up." She gave him the address of the studios.

"I don't want to be crude, Grace, but is this for free?"

"Certainly not, Carl. Epicon gets a plug for providing you and the products you use. You're still working for us. Bye."

He hung up, nodding wryly to himself. He still didn't know what his fee or salary amounted to, and he was embarrassed to reflect that he could never bring himself to ask.

It was eleven A.M., and he wore the clothes of yesterday, for the reason that Mercer was still in his bedroom, presumably asleep. And presumably Blaine had not yet got home to find Reinhart's note on the whereabouts of his wife and children. The boys had been put in Winona's room. Reinhart had slept on the living-room couch (which was *still* not quite dry from the scrubbing), and his daughter had gone to—where else?—Grace Greenwood's.

In the midst of all this he was supposed to go on television and cook something in a hundred eighty seconds?

He heard stirrings behind the door of his bedroom. He had talked with Grace on the extension near the front door.

Mercer opened the door and came out, rubbing her eyes. She wore a pair of Winona's pajamas, though not in the blue that Reinhart had chosen for her the day before, but in pink, and a borrowed robe.

"Good morning," said he, out by the phone, and she turned her head towards him as if in fright.

"Oh. Hi."

"Winona came and took the boys off to their respective schools,"

Reinhart said. "We saw no reason to wake you up. Was that O.K.?" Toby went to a private academy of some sort, and Parker to a "play school." Winona had arranged the night before to collect them next morning, and so she had done.

"That was a good idea," Mercer said dully.

But nobody should be kept standing in front of a bathroom when they first arise! Reinhart waved at her. "Go ahead. I'll fix breakfast. Do you have any preferences? Or phobias, for that matter?" If Winona ate anything at all before leaving in the morning, it was likely to be something bleak, like wheat germ and skim milk. Of course she had a horror of eggs. "How does French toast strike you?"

"Oh," said Mercer, smiling vacantly, "anything, anything at all."

Reinhart was sorry to hear that unreliable phrase, but he went to the kitchen and broke an egg into a shallow bowl and agitated it with a whisk. For the boys he had made one-eyed sailors, i.e., slices of bread in each of which, in a central hole, an egg was fried. These had even made a hit with Blaine when he was little: Reinhart could number such successes on one hand without exhausting the supply of fingers.

His version of French toast called for a topping of sautéed apples. He had a few red Delicious in a wire basket: they were in decline, but after the peeling and reaming and trimming of discolorations they yielded enough slices to cover two pieces of toast. He cooked them in butter until they were translucent, and then, turning up the heat, and keeping the apples in motion with a spatula, made them golden.

He could still hear the shower, which was just behind the kitchen wall, and was beginning to feel some apprehension—given the fact that the bather was his daughter-in-law—when at last the water was turned off. He stepped into the dining area, which was glowing and warm from the bright sunshine this morning, and had just pulled one of the chairs from the table, expecting something of a wait if Mercer was finishing up in the bathroom only now—when that person came around the corner.

Her hair was wrapped in a damp towel, and she wore his own terry-cloth robe, which he had left that morning, after his own shower, on the back of the bathroom door. She was barefoot and dripping. Apparently she had not dried herself before simply climbing into the robe.

The whole procedure seemed to have its feckless side, but she was a guest.

He held the chair for her. "Here you go, Mercer! The sun's so nice here, I'll set a place at the table." He himself generally breakfasted off the kitchen counter, perched on a stool of appropriate height.

It occurred to him that she might want to lend a hand in the place-setting, but she made no such offer. He got out one of the better, gold-edged plates from the low cabinet against the wall and the requisite cutlery from the set of silver purchased by Winona in an extravagant moment and rarely used since. And a good napkin, of the snowy kind.

"Now," said he, as she leaned aside so that he could arrange these things before her, "what's lacking is a single rose, in a crystal bud vase."

Her face was as handsome as ever under the towel, but Reinhart really didn't like to see a wet towel at table, not to mention his bathrobe, which had never dried from yesterday's soaking and was furthermore too large for her in an unattractive way: absent was the charm of the spunky but modest girl, a standard role in pre-War films, who, overtaken by rain and darkness, ended up, in all innocence, wearing the hero's oversized nightclothes, though he would not kiss her until they were engaged.

Mercer said: "Oh, don't go to any trouble. I just have black coffee in the morning. You wouldn't have any cigarettes around? I ran out."

"No. Neither of us smokes." He went into the kitchen.

She persisted. "There's not a machine down in the lobby?"

He came to the door. "Not that I know of." Actually, there was such a device, he now remembered, in the rear of the basement, outside the laundry room, but he had no intention of revealing its existence until breakfast was over. He turned up the heat under the teakettle, which was already full and warm, and took the canister of coffee beans from the refrigerator. For his standard lone breakfasts he was not wont to fresh-grind Mocha-Java, but this was an occasion.

The kettle, warmer than one had thought, was already beginning its whistle. Before he had switched off the burner Mercer was in the doorway, china cup, sans saucer, dangling from a hooked finger.

"Got to have my coffee quick as I can!" she said, with smirking affection for her own foible. "Where's the jar? I'll fix it myself."

"I was just about to grind some coffee." He showed her the open canister.

She scowled into it. "Is that coffee?"

"That's how it starts," said Reinhart. "Then it's ground." He poured beans into the blender. "This is one way to do it, but there are hand-turned grinders and also little electric ones." He pushed the button that caused the blades to whirl. "That should do it." He took the top off the blender jar and displayed the contents.

Mercer shook her head dubiously.

"You see," Reinhart said, "when you buy coffee in a can, the grinding has already been done."

"I've never made it except with powder," said she. "I guess I never have thought about anything but instant."

"Well, why don't you go out and sit at the table? It'll take just a moment for the coffee to drip through. Meanwhile I've got half a grapefruit here." He opened the fridge. "I'll just put some honey on it."

"What I generally do is take a cup of coffee with me to the bathroom while I dry and brush my hair."

Reinhart patted her damp shoulder. "I want you to eat this breakfast, Mercer. It'll do you a world of good, believe me."

He heated the milk and made *café au lait* for her. The slices of apple were arranged in orderly overlap atop the French toast, dusted with cinnamon and anointed with maple syrup. In accompaniment were three slices of bacon, cut from the chunk by Reinhart's own keen knife and thus not quite regular but thick enough to proclaim their substance, of a robust but natural hue and rendered absolutely of fat.

Mercer ate a respectable amount from this plate, to her own announced surprise. Reinhart was enormously pleased to have cooked something that someone ate, and for the second time this morning, the boys having polished off their own breakfasts.

After tidying things up, he poured himself a cup of coffee and went out to join her. But she was leaving the table as he arrived.

"That was terrific," she said, not looking at him and his coffee. "I'm going to get dressed." And away, around the corner, she strode.

Of course he felt let down. There was now no sense in sitting there to drink his coffee, with no company but her dirty implements of eating. He cleared the table and went back to the kitchen.

An hour later Mercer was still shuttling regularly between his bedroom and his bath, effectively continuing to deny him access to either: which meant not only that he couldn't brush his teeth, a function he was psychologically unable to perform until he had been up for several hours, but also that he had not had a change of clothing for more than a day. The older he got, the nicer his ways: even as late as the War years he might still display a teenager's indifference to the freshness of his underwear, but nowadays, in an essentially sedentary existence, day-old drawers and T-shirt seemed lined with grit, and the thought of his feet in yesterday's socks was loathsome to him.

It occurred to him that he might take this opportunity to clean Winona's room, which no doubt would need some attention after the night spent there by the boys. But here again he was obstructed: this time because of modesty. Just as he arrived at the head of the hall on his first attempt, Mercer passed from bedroom to bathroom, still wearing the robe, but the belt had been unfastened and the garment swung open. Of course he had seen her in the altogether the day before, but now she was conscious—if you could call it that: she was oblivious to him.

He turned and went back to the other end of the apartment. The sun continued to show itself genially, after a procession of gray days had crawled through the no-man's-land between winter and spring. Reinhart was often indifferent to nonextreme weather, but a walk in the warm light, going down towards the river, might be just the ticket this morning, and he believed he should take Mercer along. She seemed all right thus far, even boringly so, occupied with the routine of getting into the day, but he did not like the idea of leaving her alone.

After allowing more than enough time for her to clothe herself, he tried again to penetrate the hallway, but again he was obstructed, at least theoretically, by his daughter-in-law, who was in the act of going from bathroom to bedroom. Now the robe was missing, and though she was not in the altogether, she was hardly overdressed, wearing, as she did, only two pieces of flimsy underwear. For Reinhart this was no more erotic than his cleaning her of vomit the day before, but much more embarrassing. And this time she not only noticed him, but spoke, though did not, thank God, stop.

"You didn't find any cigarettes, by chance?"

She was inside the bedroom by the time he answered. "I'll tell you, I'll go down and see if I can find a machine. Maybe there's one in the rear of the building." He had not forgotten the risk in leaving her alone, but had begun to feel a desperate need to escape until she was clothed. What bothered him, as always, was not really Mercer, nor himself, but his son. The classical theories of the emotions were usually fixed on the guilt felt by the child towards the father. Reinhart had felt little of this that had not been artificially stimulated by the trend of the times, but absolutely genuine was the wretchedness evoked in his soul by any thought of Blaine. He assumed that were Blaine to come here now and find Mercer in a state of undress, his son would believe him a degenerate—and perhaps be justified in so doing.

He took the elevator to the ground floor and went through the corridor that led to the laundry room. He found the machine, had the right combination of coins with which to feed it, worked the appropriate button, and received the package of cigarettes: a brand chosen solely for its silver wrapper. This took no time at all, and he returned hastily to the apartment. Mercer had the capacity to make him anxious by either her presence or the threat of her absence.

But she was there when he got back, and, thank God, fully covered at last—if only in the dressing gown she had worn when lying on the backseat of Winona's car the evening before.

"Say, Mercer," Reinhart said. "It's a nice morning. How about us taking a walk down to the river?"

She was standing in the doorway of his bedroom. "Oh, I think I'm just going to stay here and watch television."

Of course this meant the set atop his dresser. His private quarters were apparently to remain off-limits to him so long as she stayed in the apartment.

He shrugged. "Then do you mind if I get some things of mine from the closet?"

She gave him a vague look which he interpreted as acquiescence, but preceded him into the room. He had hoped for some privacy as he rooted through his supply of clean underwear.

The room itself was in remarkable disorder. How one slender young woman alone could have so twisted the bedclothes, distributed the pillows so widely (one under the chair, the other on the floor beneath the window), and have been so profligate with towels (one underneath the bed, another on the window sill, and still another draped over the little wastebasket), was beyond him.

He opened a dresser drawer and took what he had come for. Mercer stood in front of his closet, and did not move away when he approached. It dawned upon him that she seemed lacking utterly in a sense of existence other than her own, either had no natural radar or disregarded it. Another oddity was that, having made so much of her need for a cigarette, when presented with a supply, she failed to extract one and light it up. In fact, she had dropped the unopened pack into the frozen maelstrom of bedding.

"Excuse me," Reinhart said at last, and sharply. "I want to get into the closet."

She moued and moved aside. He opened the door and took out a pair of trousers and a clean shirt, both on hangers.

He remembered that she was more to be pitied, etc., and said, "Go ahead, put on the TV. But I don't know that at this time of day there's much but reruns of comedies from the early Sixties."

"I like the game shows," said Mercer. She acted on his suggestion, and when an image appeared on the screen she increased the volume of the sound, even though a strident commercial was being broadcast at the moment, with a jangling musical accompaniment. That the product being hawked was a deodorant spray for the private parts of women was so preposterous and ugly a state of affairs as to be answered only with a jolly chuckle from Reinhart. But despite the noise, or perhaps because of it, Mercer seemed oblivious.

He tried once more and now had to shout: "You might keep it in mind, taking a walk. I'd like one, myself. It really is a fine sunny day. . . . I just got a bright idea: we might have a picnic on the riverbank. Not baloney sandwiches, either. I'll make something more serious, a quiche or salade Niçoise. An iced bottle of, uh"—he caught himself—"mineral water."

Mercer smiled sweetly and nodded at him, though he believed it doubtful that she had listened. Without straightening the tangle of bedclothes, she flopped herself down upon them, shoulders against the headboard, and stared dully at the television screen.

Jesus Christ. He left with his change of clothes and went across to his bathroom—compared to which the bedroom had been neat. More discarded towels, it went without saying. Unfortunately, though smaller than Winona's, his was the one with the linen closet, from which Mercer had helped herself as if it were a giant box of Kleenex.

He gave himself an electric shave and washed his face in his hands—the supply of washcloths, too, had vanished—and let the air dry his cheeks. In fresh attire he gathered up the bathroom laundry and added it to that from the built-in hamper, filling a pillowcase and a half. The sound of the TV across the hall was especially oppressive when the musical commercials came on.

He had intended, while gathering up the towels Mercer had strewn around the bedroom, firmly to turn down the volume, but while crossing the hall had second thoughts about such rudeness. The poor thing . . .

"Say, Mercer, do you mind—" he began as he entered the room. But he addressed an empty bed. She was gone again.

Looking on the bright side, at least she was respectably covered. Her dressing gown lay in the overstuffed chair, and her street clothes were gone. Reinhart decided not to pursue her. Were he to admit to the truth, he might even allow himself to be relieved by her departure. His first move was to shut off the television. The room stank of smoke: she had finally opened the pack and, the ashtray told him, already had smoked about a third of each of three cigarettes. He opened the window and carried the trayful of butts across to the toilet.

After putting the room in order, he dreaded what he might find

in Winona's suite, used by the sons of such a mother, but the
marvelous surprise, in both bedroom and bath, was the general
neatness. The boys had even pulled the bedclothes into shape (a
bit crudely, but good God!) and hung up their washcloths and
towels (after using them!) in a splendid try at military precision.
Their toothbrushes were not in a perfect arrangement on the curb
of the washstand, nor had the cap been replaced on the tube, but
their grandfather himself was wont often to commit these very
misdemeanors.

Indeed, this evidence that the boys were already, and untypi-
cally at their tender ages, responsible beings somehow made Reinhart feel better about Blaine's family, wretched as were its adult
prospects.

CHAPTER
13

At the television studio everyone encountered by Reinhart was young, slender, dressed in jeans, and quick-moving. They were also, all of them, unfailingly civil. When he realized that he was actually going to appear on TV that morning, he had dosed his coffee with brandy, but he remained anxious. The studio people needed him two hours before he was scheduled to face the cameras, which meant he had had to arise at four-thirty, after getting almost no sleep. The fact was that Mercer had, perhaps unfortunately, not gone on another binge, but rather had returned to her own house by cab and come back to the apartment in her own car, filled with suitcases containing clothing for herself and the boys. Reinhart had therefore spent another night on the living-room couch, and by the looks of things he could expect to remain there until Blaine turned up.

He had not been able even to close his eyes before three A.M. For one, his daughter-in-law seemed to be making a heroic effort to stay on the wagon. This was certainly laudable, but resulted, inconveniently, in her drinking vast quantities of noninebriating liquids such as coffee, tea, milk, and the root beer which Reinhart had provided for his grandchildren: in fact, anything but water, which she could have obtained from the nearby bathroom. All else was to be found only in the kitchen, to reach which the living room must be crossed.

For another, she habitually operated the TV set at too high a volume for anyone of his age to sleep under the same roof, even though the bedroom door was closed. And when he finally registered a gentle complaint, she was too contrite and turned off the set altogether—to put it on again half an hour later, when she no doubt assumed he would be asleep at last. But of course it took that long to get used to the silence, and no sooner had he done so than the noise began once more.

At the studio he was seated in a corridor through which many people walked briskly. Finally one of them, a young woman of characterless brunette good looks, stopped and introduced herself as Jane.

She consulted a piece of paper affixed to a clipboard. "You're the chef, O.K.? We'll get you into make-up in a few minutes, O.K.? You want to check your pots 'n' pans 'n' stuff?"

He followed her, around little clusters of people and lights and cameras and cables, onto what was obviously a corner of the set.

"You've got a whole kitchen here." It looked like a permanent installation and had everything one would need, within two walls without a ceiling.

"We do a cooking segment of some kind every day," said Jane. "Sometimes we just dye Easter eggs or make Play-Doh from flour and salt."

Reinhart opened the copper-colored refrigerator. Just inside, on gleaming chromium-wire shelves, was a large glass bowl filled with eggs and a generous chunk of butter on a plate of glass. A glass canister bore a solid white label, imprinted in large black letters: GRATED CHEESE.

"Everything there?" asked Jane. He had ordered these omelet-making materials the day before.

"Except salt and pepper," said Reinhart. "I gather they'll be over here." He turned to the free-standing counter that would face the camera. He had not seen much of this show, but he had watched other programs on which cooking was done. Ah, yes: electric burners were built into the top of the counter, and a ceramic jug stood nearby, holding spatulas, big forks, etc., and salt and pepper were alongside in large white shakers, again labeled in black.

"Oh, and the skillet. I was going to bring mine, which is seasoned, but my boss insisted on one that her company is apparently thinking of putting on the market, in a new line of cooking utensils."

"Grace Greenwood," said Jane. "Yeah, she sent over some special stuff." She poked amongst the open shelves below the countertop, on the left of the burners. "Take a look. It should all be here."

Reinhart bent and found a skillet, a lightweight stainless-steel job with a thin wash of copper on the outside bottom. "This is it?" He winced. "I'm going to have to be very careful to keep from burning the omelet. This is trash."

Jane put one finger on the nosepiece of her glasses—which until now Reinhart had not noticed. "If it does burn, then just don't turn it over on camera, O.K.?" She sniffed. "Don't panic: this is the magic of video, remember."

Some young man shouted her name, and she went away. Reinhart looked about: everything seemed a good deal smaller than anything he had ever seen on the screen. For some reason he thought he might have been more at ease had things been larger. He was suddenly jumping with nerves.

Jane returned and took him into a room where he sat in a kind of barber's chair and was made up by a deft, laconic young man. When the job was finished, he ducked into a booth in the men's room and drank some cognac from the half-pint in his pocket.

The well-known movie star Jack Buxton was urinating in one of the stalls as Reinhart emerged. Apparently they were to be fellow guests on the show.

Jane came from nowhere when Reinhart left the lavatory and led him back to a chair in the corridor.

"Sorry we don't have a real Green Room," she said.

"Wasn't that Jack Buxton I saw in the men's room?"

"He's plugging his show." Jane consulted her clipboard. "You go on the air at seven forty-seven, but we'll do a run-through in about five minutes from now, so you'll have your moves down pat. This is live, you know. We can't do retakes." She left the area.

And here came Jack Buxton. Reinhart seldom went to the movies nowadays, and he hadn't seen a performance of Buxton's in— God, could it be that long?

"Hi," said the actor, flopping his large, heavy body into the chair next to Reinhart's.

"Hi," said Reinhart. "This is quite a pleasure for me. I've always enjoyed your pictures."

Buxton's face, perhaps owing to its familiarity, seemed enormous. He grinned at Reinhart. "Thanks, pal, I needed that. Listen"—he dug into an inside pocket of his Glen-plaid jacket and withdrew a leather-covered notepad—"I'll send an autographed picture to your kids, if you give me the names and address."

"My kids are grown up," said Reinhart. Buxton's long lip drooped. It was true he looked a good deal older than when Reinhart had last seen him. "But I'd like one for myself." This lie failed to cheer up the actor by much, but he pretended to take the name and address.

Reinhart asked: "Are you in a new picture?"

Buxton inhaled. "I'm considering some scripts," said he. "But I'm in town here to do *Song of Norway.*" He put his notebook away and adjusted his jacket. Like Reinhart he was wearing face make-up that made the skin look beige. The heavy pouches under his eyes and the deep lines flanking his mouth could be seen all too clearly at close range but probably would be diminished on their voyage through the camera.

"Oh," said Reinhart, "I'll have to see it." If memory served, the vehicle was a musical: he hadn't been aware that Buxton sang. The actor was best known for his war films.

"It'll be my pleasure," Buxton said, cheering up now, and he reached into his pocket and withdrew a pair of tickets. "These are for the show only. Dinner's separate, I'm afraid, but . . ."

Reinhart accepted the tickets with thanks. He joked: "I wouldn't expect you to pay for the food I ate before going to the show!"

Buxton frowned. "It's the dinner theater. That's what I meant. It's no comedown either. That's the latest thing. I don't mind it at all."

But clearly he felt humiliated at the thought of people digesting their steaks while he performed. For his own part Reinhart was only now remembering that he had never really liked Buxton as an actor—or at any rate, he had not found Buxton's roles sympathetic: there was always a resentful streak in the character, of whom one expected the worst, owing to the cocky, smart-ass personality he displayed at the outset. But then he came though courageously in the pinch, kept the plane aloft though badly wounded, or fell on the grenade, saving his comrades.

Buxton was still worrying. "I started out on the Broadway stage," said he. "I was trained for musical comedy, long before I went to Tinsel Town."

So they really said that. "I'll bet you're good," said Reinhart. "I look forward to the show."

Buxton leaned over. He had maintained his familiar widow's peak of yore, and the scalp looked genuine, but why a professional would have his hair dyed matte black, leaving sparkling white sideburns, was not self-evident.

"Say," he said, "you wouldn't know where a man could get a drink?" His breath smelled of mint Life Saver.

"Well, now . . ." Reinhart reached into his pocket for the half-pint of brandy.

But Buxton said: "Not here."

They got up and were heading for the men's room when Jane came along and carried Reinhart away.

"We'll do the omelet run-through," said she, and when they had left Buxton behind she said: "It's Has-Been City around here lots of mornings. Watch yourself with that one: he'll hit you up for a loan."

Reinhart felt he owed Buxton some loyalty, the actor having embodied the old-fashioned virtues until both he and they went out of fashion, to be replaced by nothing and nobody worth mentioning. "I always liked him in the movies."

"He was through before my time," said Jane in her brisk way.

Time was all. Twenty years earlier some Jane might have seen Buxton as a rung on her own climb to success.

They were in the kitchen now. Reinhart practiced the movements he would make on camera. Taking the eggs and butter from the refrigerator to the counter consumed too much of his allotted three minutes. On the other hand, as Jane pointed out, too much premeditation would diminish the dramatic effect. The eggs, for example, should remain whole, to be broken on camera.

"Debbie will ad lib something about making the perfect omelet," said Jane. "O.K., that's your cue to answer. You say, 'Well, Debbie, first you break the eggs.' Don't, for God's sake, tell the old

Hungarian-omelet joke—you know, 'First you steal two eggs'—
we'll get too much bad mail. Everybody takes everything personally."

Debbie was the "co-host" of the program, with a man named
Shep Cunningham. Meeting her backstage apparently violated
some show-biz rule, and having rarely tuned in to Channel Five
at this hour, Reinhart had little sense of the woman. Cunningham,
however, had formerly been anchorman on the *Six O'Clock News:*
his amiable, insensitive face above a wide-bladed tie and even
wider lapels was remembered. But Reinhart was to have no direct
connection with him whatever this morning.

"For all the woman's movement," said Jane, "anything in the
kitchen this time of day is always played to the ladies." She looked
up at one of the clocks that were mounted overhead at frequent
intervals throughout the studio. Monitor TV sets were everywhere, as well. Someone was speaking through a public-address
system: it was like the voice of God, and hence quite startling
when it uttered foul language.

Jane said: "You'd better put on the chef's hat and apron."

Reinhart was getting into the spirit of the place. "Oh, God," he
said, with real despair, "I forgot to bring them!"

Jane shook her head. "Your office sent them over." She led
Reinhart to a little dressing room, where he found the cook's
costume and donned it. The *toque* was pristine, but the apron was
imprinted, over the region of the heart, with the logo of Grace
Greenwood's firm: the name EPICON printed in the form of a
croissant. This was something new.

Jane came along just as he emerged: she apparently had a sixth
sense about these matters, for he was certain she had not been
lingering there. Again she took him to the chairs in the corridor.
Buxton was missing.

Jane said: "O.K., it's just waiting now. You can watch the monitor." She pointed to one high on the wall across from him. "I'll
have somebody bring you coffee, O.K.?"

A young man brought the coffee. As discreetly as he could,
Reinhart dosed it with brandy. He had had the sense to buy expensive cognac: cheaper stuff was hardly drinkable in the best of
times, but with morning coffee it would erode the stomach.

The monitor was showing a rerun of an ancient situation comedy, in which the adult male characters all wore crew cuts and suits a size too small, and all the children were well behaved and everybody did absurd but decent things. The sound was turned down to a murmur, and when the old show gave way to the seven o'clock news report, the volume came up to a level of command and the backstage noise died away.

International crises were routine this morning and given little more than noncommittal platitudes by the newscaster, an attractive fair-haired woman who used the intonations of a man. Locally a citizen had handcuffed himself to a light-pole at a downtown intersection as a protest, but against what had not yet been established, and opening the cuffs had thus far been beyond the powers of the police, who believed them of foreign origin.

Then, to the strains of a lilting musical theme, the *Eye Opener Show* came on. There was Shep Cunningham, between his desk and a photomural of the cityscape. Reinhart saw and heard him on the monitor screen, though presumably the man himself was just a partition away.

After a greeting and an observation on the rainy weather, Shep said: "But enough of this nonsense. Let's get to the beauty part. Here's Debbie Howland." The camera panned to his left, the curtains there parted, and out came a very winsome young woman with dark red hair and a jersey dress in lime green. She had an ebullient stride.

"Good morning, Shep," said Debbie, taking a seat next to her partner.

Shep winked at the camera and said: "Notice *I* don't get to walk across the set. Maybe if I lost ten pounds?" He grinned and shrugged and said: "Tell us who we'll meet today, Deb—or should that be 'whom'?"

Debbie smiled into the camera. "Shep, when you think of that classic quality known as Hollywood there are a few names that embody it in themselves alone: personalities like the Duke and the never-to-be-forgotten Bogie, and likewise with our guest this morning, Mister Hollywood himself, Jack Buxton."

"Oh, wow," said Shep. "I want to ask him how he feels about our new pals the Chinese Communists—after fighting them so many times in Korean War films."

Reinhart suspected this reference was not authentic: in his own memories Buxton was always involved cinematically with World War II Germans. Indeed, if memory served, at least once he had played a Nazi.

Debbie went on: "And then our own Bobby Allen, Man in the Street, live out there in the pouring rain, will get an answer to today's question—hey, Shep, it's not about sex for a change—"

Shep groaned. "That's bad news."

"C'mon, now, this is important: 'Nuclear Power—Love It or Leave It?' "

"That *is* important," said Shep. "I was kidding."

"And then," Debbie said, "a French chef will show us how to make the perfect omelet in a minute. Sound good?"

"Mouth's watering already," said Shep. "My beautiful wife Judy's on a diet kick. I don't know, maybe I'm weird, but alfalfa sprouts on low-fat cottage cheese is not my idea of breakfast."

"Come *on,*" said Debbie.

"Washed down with herb tea."

"Come *on.* You're kidding."

"Yes, I am," said Shep. "Incidentally, that's the same thing my wife said the last time I tried to get friendly with her."

Debbie rolled her eyes. "Oh-oh. I think it's time to hear from our first sponsor."

Under his apron Reinhart tipped the cognac bottle into the now empty Styrofoam cup. It was just as well that Buxton had not reappeared: the cook would not have been keen on sharing his supply of Dutch courage. He was himself no professional performer, and the nearer he got to going on camera, the more he realized how crazy he had been to let Grace do this to him. For God's sake, he wasn't even a professional chef.

Anxiety makes the time fly. Suddenly Jane came and led him onto the TV kitchen, holding a finger to her lips, so that he couldn't ask questions. But he looked up and saw a clock, and already it registered 7:35—and then without warning was at a quarter to eight and a voice was reading brief headlines from the news, and then, in an instant, a red light glowed from the darkness before him and Reinhart was on the air! Or so the sequence seemed.

Across the room, though actually very close to him, Shep Cunningham sat at the desk, and Debbie was just entering the kitchen. Reinhart had been deaf to the preliminary comments, and for a moment he had the terrified feeling that she might be coming to expose him as a fraud.

But she was smiling. *"Is* there a secret to omelet-making, Chef?"

Reinhart was amazed to hear a deep, mellow baritone voice emerge from his chest, as if he were lip-synching to a record made by someone else. "I suppose it could be called that, Debbie, but it's not the kind of secret that would interest a Russian spy."

Debbie giggled dutifully here. Luckily he overcame an impulse to build a large comic structure on the feeble piling of this witticism.

Quite soberly he said: "It's simply speed. The egg, once out of its shell—which has been called nature's perfect container incidentally—the naked egg is a very sensitive substance." He was aware that persons out there, off camera, were gesturing at him, and now Debbie stepped lightly on his foot. Of course, he must begin to break eggs!

Amazingly enough, everything he needed was at hand—and his hand was sure, in fact even defter than when he was alone in his own kitchen. In one movement he seemed simultaneously to have not only cracked two shells but opened them and drained them of their contents. His flying fork whipped the yolks and whites into a uniform cream. Meanwhile the butter was melting in the skillet.

He was speaking authoritatively. "Speed's the secret, but we don't break the fifty-five-mile limit: we let the butter reach the frothing point. Meanwhile, we've got our filling ready. In this case it's Swiss cheese, for that simplest of dishes, a plain cheese omelet. But if it's properly made, there's nothing better, and nothing more elegant."

"Or more nutritious," said Debbie, nodding vigorously. "Gee, Chef, I can't wait."

"Just about time . . . We've got our cheese all grated already—and may I strongly recommend that you always grate your own cheese from a fresh piece: you can do that in a blender or a food processor, if it's too much work for you by hand. In this case the cheese is simple Swiss, but an even more delicious filling would be Swiss mixed with a bit of Parmesan." A moment earlier he had put two tablespoonfuls of the cheese from the canister into a shallow bowl. "Ah, there we go, just as the frothing begins to subside and before it turns color, the eggs go in quickly, quickly, and you keep stirring them, stir, stir, as they begin to thicken and curds appear . . . and *now* the cheese goes in, all at once!"

He emptied the contents of the bowl onto the mass of eggs, lifted the skillet from the burner, inserted the fork under the near edge of what was already an omelet, folded one half across the other, and slid the finished product onto a china plate.

"My goodness," said Debbie, "you don't even cook the top side? That must be my trouble, why my omelets are so dry. I always turn 'em over." She accepted the dish from him, and holding it high, raised a fork in her other hand.

"Yes, the top becomes the inside of the omelet, and you want that moist," Reinhart said. "And you must remember that whenever uncooked eggs are around heat, something's going on. The hot omelet continues to cook for a while after you take it from the pan. That's happening right now, in fact, Debbie."

"Mmm, oh, golly," said she, making rapid eyeball movements as she tasted a modicum of egg from the end of her fork. "Hey. Say. Oh-oh, Shep, we've got a winner, and don't think you're getting any of it." Shep in fact was not behind his desk or anywhere in sight, so far as Reinhart could see. Debbie waved her fork and looked into the camera. "Well, now you know how to do it like an expert." She turned back to Reinhart. "Thank you, Chef—who appeared here courtesy of the Epicon Company. Back to you, Shep."

And just like that, Reinhart was off and Shep, back at the desk, was on, and reading a list of local announcements: fund-raising charity dinners, Shriner circus, and the like. Debbie put down her plate and disappeared behind the set. For a moment Reinhart was desolated: not only was his performance over, but functionaries kept hauling equipment past him as if he did not exist and he stood in what seemed evening, for the glare of the lights was gone.

But then the estimable Jane was at his elbow, steering him out. When they reached the outer corridor she said: "You were dynamite, Carl. Thanks a lot."

"Thank *you*, Jane. Do I go back to Make-up to get cleaned up?"

The light had gone from her eye with her thank-you. Already she looked at him as if he were a stranger. "You can take it off with soap and water." She pointed to the men's room and went away.

So much for show business. Reinhart shrugged and laughed for his own benefit. He went through the door into the lavatory, which was deserted. He had always assumed the performers had a private washroom of some kind, but perhaps that was true only at the big network studios in New York and Chicago. This place was clean enough, with dispenser of liquid soap and a wall-hung paper-towel device. He began to run a bowlful of warm water, but turned the faucet off abruptly.

He had heard a muffled sound: it had been barely audible, but there was sufficient of it to raise the hair on the back of the neck, though he could not have said precisely why: something instinctively dreadful.

He went back to the toilet booths. In one of them a human being was obviously sagging in a terrible way: trousered knees could be seen on the tiles below the door. Nothing else was visible. Again the gasping sound.

The stall was locked from within, and furthermore it would open the wrong way, given the interior obstruction. Reinhart climbed on the seat of the toilet next door and leaned over the partition.

Jack Buxton was kneeling on the floor, clawing the bleak metal wall. He had gone bald in back, just down from the crown of his head: a large hairpiece had become dislodged in his writhings. Trousers and underpants were halfway down his thighs. He had apparently been sitting on the can when the attack came.

His large torso filled the short space between the bowl and the door. There would be no sense in Reinhart's trying to climb down to join him.

Reinhart ran out into the corridor and stopped a young man wearing outsized eyeglasses.

"Jack Buxton is dying in there!"

"Who?"

"There's a man in the toilet, having a heart attack, by the looks of it," said Reinhart. "Show me where to call an ambulance."

For an instant the young man resisted the thought, suggesting by his set of nose that he might respond sardonically, but then he took a chance and said: "There's a house doctor. I'll get him." He went rapidly down the corridor.

Reinhart was trying to decide whether to go back inside. Would his presence, though practically useless, be of some remote human comfort to Buxton? He decided to guard the door until the doctor arrived. Those who might come to use the facilities should be warned.

Of course the waiting seemed endless. Considerable traffic passed him, but none brought the physician. He kept reminding himself that in such a state a second's duration was tenfold, and avoided watching the clock. But when he could no longer forbear, he looked at the dial and saw that he had indeed waited a good ten minutes.

At that point Jane came walking rapidly by, studying her clip-board. She would not have seen him had he not called out.

She stared without expression, perhaps without recognition.

"Goddammit," he cried, "Jack Buxton is having a heart attack in there! Get a doctor!"

His alarm caused some visible consternation among the back-stage studio folk. Persons passing in the vicinity looked at him in fear and repugnance, and a young man came running to scowl at Jane and say: "Get him *out* of here. You can *hear* that on the set." He resembled the guy who had gone, presumably, to fetch the doctor, but Reinhart couldn't be sure—else he'd have hit him in the mouth.

Jane was staring at Reinhart. "Buxton's supposed to go on at eight nineteen."

Reinhart put his face into hers. This time he spoke almost softly: "You fucking idiot: *I said he's dying in the toilet.* Go get help!"

Her immediate reaction was odd: a wide, even warm smile, and for a moment he considered putting his hands towards her throat, but then she whirled and moved smartly away, and now it was no time before a bushy-haired youth in jeans and denim jacket, but carrying the familiar black bag, arrived and identified himself as Dr. Tytell.

Buxton was still living when, with the help of a skinny, nimble member of the staff, the door was unlatched and the actor was examined, there on the tile floor. And he was yet alive, if barely, when the ambulance took him away.

Jane came along as Reinhart stood watching the attendants wheel the stretcher down the hall, and seeing her, he said: "Sorry I had to be nasty before. It was nothing personal."

She made no acknowledgment of the apology, but stared intently at him and said: "Carl, can you fill another ten minutes? All we've got is still only eggs and butter, but there must be lots of tricks you can show with those."

It was Reinhart's turn to smile nonsensically, but even as he did it he understood that, as with Jane on learning of Buxton's heart attack, it was momentary fear. And yet not half an hour ago he had wanted only to continue performing forever!

"Let me think," he said, doing anything but. The effect of the cognac had been dissipated by now.

Jane looked at him for an instant and then left quickly. He sat down on the chair in the corridor. The threat of another performance was warring with the reverberations of the experience with poor Buxton: perhaps it would be resolved by his own heart attack.

But suddenly before him, in all the radiance of her bright hair, dress, and make-up, was Debbie Howland.

She took the chair previously occupied briefly by Buxton, leaned over to touch Reinhart's forearm, and said: "Carl, poor Jack's accident has left us with a great big hole from eight thirty-three till the quarter-of-nine headlines. We've got a couple of commercial breaks and a public-service announcement during that period, so call it eight and a half minutes for you to fill. Can you do it? I know you can. Got a cookbook you want to plug? It doesn't have to be new. Or restaurant or whatever?"

Jane had been wise to fetch Debbie. This appeal was as from one professional performer to another, and Reinhart took heart from it.

"Sure," said he, with confidence, "sure, Debbie. Glad to help out."

She flung her head back, but not one strand of hair seemed to stir. "Oh, godamighty, what a superloverly sweetheart you are!" She leaped up and strode presumably towards the set.

Another repetition of the uneventful news came at eight thirty, and then, after a commercial or two and an exhortation from the Coast Guard, Shep returned to say: "Debbie's hungry again. She can eat all day long, and her waistline just keeps getting smaller. Me, I chew a leaf of lettuce and gain ten pounds. It ain't fair. Let's see what's happening in the kitchen this time."

And Reinhart was on again!

"We're back again with Chef Carl Reinhart," Debbie said into the camera, "for more with eggs. I guess they're one of the most versatile foods around, wouldn't you say, Chef?"

This was actually true enough. "Yes, Debbie," Reinhart smilingly replied in his on-camera voice and manner, which though not studied was markedly different from his style in real life. "You will never run out of ways to cook eggs, and then if you think of all the dishes of which eggs form a part you have a whole menu, because eggs can be the star, as in a big beautiful golden puffy soufflé, or a co-star, as with ham or bacon, a supporting player, as in crepes, and finally, a modest bit performer or even an extra, when, say, a raw egg is mixed with ground beef to make a delicious hamburger."

"Well," said Debbie, "is the trick with eggs always speed, as it was with that scrumptious omelet you made earlier?"

"Not always. With a soufflé of course you might say it's patience!"

Debbie chuckled. "I know we don't have time to make a soufflé this morning, but the next time you come back I wish you'd show us that trick. I guess that's one of the toughest dishes for the home cook to learn, isn't it?"

Reinhart smiled with mixed authority and sympathy. "You know, Debbie, a lot of people believe that, but it isn't at all true. It's just one of the many things in life that are mostly bluff."

"Like early-morning television," cried Debbie. Giggling and addressing the again-empty desk, she added: "Right, Shep?"

"I can't believe that," graciously said the cook, "but with a soufflé all you have to understand is the basic principle: air. Somebody way back in history discovered that if you take the white of an egg from the yolk you can whip it so full of air that it becomes a kind of solid matter, while remaining feather-light. What a wonderful discovery! And a whipped white is pretty strong, too. It will hold in suspension any number of fillings and flavorings: shrimp, asparagus tips, and even eggs themselves, whole poached eggs. That makes a fabulous soufflé, incidentally. You dig down through the fluffy stuff and suddenly come upon a gem of a poached egg. It's like a treasure hunt."

Debbie laughed happily. "I can see you love your work—and by the way, that's essential in cooking, isn't it? Love, I mean."

"It doesn't hurt," said Reinhart. "But I wouldn't want to discourage the people who don't have a natural inclination. You *don't* have to be passionately interested in cuisine to do a commendable job at the stove. I say that because I think there are a lot of people, women especially, who have found it necessary to cook for others and think they have no talent. Even if you can't cook well, even if you hate the idea, you may be in a position where you have to do it—and I assure you that there are scores and scores of wonderful dishes you can make easily."

"Easy for you, anyway," said Debbie. She was looking into the camera. "We'll be back, but now this."

Reinhart waited until the red light went off the camera pointed at them and then saw by the monitor of the wall that a commercial had come onto the screen.

Debbie asked: "What should I say you're going to cook now, or are you?"

"Poached eggs." He took a pot from the shelf below the counter and went to the sink behind him. "Does this work?" He turned the cold-water faucet, and, by George, it did, but he got a better idea and ran the hot water. The commercials were still on the screen when he came back with the water. He sprinkled a bit of salt into the pot before closing it with the lid and placing it on a lighted burner of the electric stove.

Debbie said vivaciously: "Do you know, something I enjoy eating but never have been able to cook right is a poached egg. Can you help me out with that problem, Carl?"

They were of course on the air again. He had to fill some moments before the water came to a boil.

"There are various kinds of gadgets that will do the job," he said. "Have you seen the little pots that have a metal insert with depressions, little wells that take one egg each? You boil water underneath them, and the steam comes up to cook the eggs. But in this case the eggs are steamed and not poached. There is a difference. The classic poached egg is cooked directly in the water and is lovely and tender and always better than anything prepared with a gadget." He reached into the jug which held the variety of tools for cooking, and removed a soup ladle.

"But *how*," Debbie asked in a tone of mock despair, "*how* can we keep the egg from just busting all over the place when you take its shell off and drop it in boiling water?" She mugged at the camera.

Speaking of boiling, his potful of water had begun already to show wisps of steam around its lid.

"Well, first, you don't want a violent boil: just kind of firm and medium, a little higher than a simmer, but not a storm. Next you take your soup ladle and rub or melt a bit of butter in its bowl." He demonstrated this piece of business. "Now, when the bottom of the ladle-bowl is covered with a thin layer of butter, you break an egg into it. . . . This is easy to do if you can break a shell with one hand. If you can't do that, simply prop the ladle up inside an empty pot."

"Gee, you think of everything," said Debbie. "That's how you can tell a Cordon Bloo cook."

"The egg's in the buttered ladle," said Reinhart, speaking of the self-evident, but then perhaps there were TV sets with murky pictures and elsewhere busy housewives were listening as they worked, backs to their sets. "You lower the ladle into the boiling water . . ."

Debbie gasped in enlightenment.

"A white film of coagulation forms around the egg, where it touches the ladle. Now, you gently and smoothly tip up the ladle so that the egg slides free into the water."

"Ooo, but look—"

"That's O.K.," said Reinhart. "Don't worry about the ragged streamers of white that blow around in the water. Also, a bit of the coagulated film remains in the dipper." He grinned. "You rise above such things. Seriously, you see that within a second or two the egg is shaping firmly up. Later we'll trim off the ragged edges —which you always get, no matter the method, unless of course you use a gadget. Meanwhile you quickly add another egg in the same fashion, and so on. If you have more than three or four, you might keep an eye on the order of insertion: the earlier will be done sooner than the later. But for the first few the difference in time will be so little as to be meaningless."

"Well, you could knock me over with a basting brush," said Debby, leering into the pot, then at Reinhart, and finally at the unseen audience. "This man is a marvel. By gosh, if those eggs aren't forming beautifully. I always end up with strings of scrambled *boiled* eggs. That ain't to be recommended, friends. . . . We're going away for a few moments. When we come back, Chef Reinhart will tell us what to do with the eggs now we know how to poach them to perfection."

When they were off Debbie leaned into Reinhart and whispered: "Just terrific, Carl. You're saving our asses."

He wondered briefly what had happened to poor old Buxton—who himself would understand, in the tradition of show business, why any more concern must wait until the performance was over.

He asked his partner: "How much more time do we have to fill?"

"Forty-five seconds."

Could that be true? He confirmed it by the wall clock. Where had the time gone? He could continue for hours!

When they, or the audience, had "returned" (from wherever whoever had been, and whatever was real) Debbie said: "O.K., Chef Reinhart. You were going to tell us how to use our poached eggs."

"I should say first, Debbie, that *I* cook them by instinct, but I'd really advise the use of a timer: about four minutes should do the trick. Ours here haven't been on quite that long yet. But to answer your question: a poached egg goes with almost anything: on top of asparagus or puréed spinach. Or cold, in aspic, as an hors d'oeuvre. Covered with caviar—lumpfish, not the expensive kind. And above all in the ever-popular eggs Benedict: a toasted round of bread or muffin, a slice of ham, a poached egg, and over it all a thick, creamy, lemony hollandaise sauce—which by the way is childishly easy to make—"

"You're killing me!" wailed Debbie. "You know that. Because we're out of time, and I'm dying of hungerrrr! But can you come back sometime soon?" She gestured at him. "Chef Carl Reinhart, courtesy of the Epicon Company, distributors of gourmet foods and their new line of copper-clad cookware. Thanks, Chef. Now back to Shep."

When they were "off," Debbie squeezed his forearm. "Thanks, pal." She walked briskly away, behind the set.

On camera Shep was reading the news headlines. Jane came to conduct Reinhart off.

When they had reached the corridor she said: "You were fabulous, Carl. We're grateful a whole bunch."

Reinhart asked: "Have you checked with the hospital?"

"Huh-uh."

"I'm thinking of Jack Buxton," he said. "It was pretty shocking to find him like that, in the men's room. I wonder whether he pulled through."

Jane looked at him with solemn eyes. "Carl, I'll call right now."

"That'd be nice of you."

"We owe you one."

When she was gone it occurred to him that he could himself have placed the call to the hospital: in other words, his self-righteousness should be restrained.

For the first time since he had put them on, he remembered that he was wearing the apron and chef's bonnet—had indeed been wearing them when finding Buxton in the toilet—and now took them off at last. Once he was out of costume he was more resigned to being off the set. But, God, he enjoyed performing!

When Jane returned she was carrying the jacket to his suit and his raincoat. She helped him into these and then said: "He bought the farm."

"Huh?"

"Buxton. He didn't make it. He died in the ambulance."

"Aw," said Reinhart. "Aw, the poor bastard."

Jane nodded in a noncommittal fashion.

"See," Reinhart said defiantly, "I remember him when he was Hollywood's most notorious ladies' man. The fact is—it just comes back to me—he was in court from time to time for sexual things: paternity suits and charges of statutory rape. He had a taste for sixteen-year-olds. My God, that was before World War Two. It's a good forty years ago. He must have been about seventy now."

"Well," said Jane, "I've got to get back to work. Bye, Carl. Hope you're on again soon."

"Uh," said he, "you know what I forgot? To turn off those poached eggs."

"They're in the garbage long since," said Jane. "Don't worry."

Reinhart left the studio reflecting on mortality, but when he reached the parking lot where he had left Winona's borrowed car, the attendant, a young black man with a marked limp, said: "You're that cook I just saw on TV."

Reinhart could see the little set, through the open door of the shack where the attendant sat between arrivals and departures. Debbie was back on the screen. It was hard to believe he had just left her company. He realized that he had never got around to washing off his make-up.

"I knew you right away," said the attendant. "That's what TV gives you: a high recognition potential." He went, with a jouncing stride that defied his limp, to fetch the car.

Reinhart suddenly understood that as a celebrity he would be expected to tip generously.

CHAPTER
14

Reinhart wanted to watch the *Six O'Clock News,* though he would have to disturb Helen Clayton to reach the set: she was lying heavily against him. Which was by no means unpleasant, but he believed he owed it to the memory of Jack Buxton to see the actor's videobituary.

When he was younger he would have probably succeeded both in missing the news and offending his partner. But for every year past fifty, perhaps in compensation for the weakening of the physical powers, one has more emotional self-reliance.

"Helen," he said, patting her bare shoulder, "I want to turn on the TV."

She groaned. "That's flattering." But she grinned then and rolled away.

Reaching from the bed, Reinhart found his boxer shorts amidst the clothing on a nearby chair, and he got into them while in the act of leaving the horizontal position. He was still deft at that trick, though he was practicing it for the first time in a while. He did not like to climb from bed with a woman and walk across the room, displaying his bare behind to her: it was his foible.

"No," he said to Helen, "I just want to see what they have to say about Jack Buxton's death."

"Jack Buxton died?" she asked, with what appeared to be deep feeling.

"You remember him?"

"I was wild about him as a kid."

"He was older than that," said Reinhart. "His era was during and even before the War."

"He was still plenty big, late Forties, early Fifties. Hey, you just trying to find out my age?"

Reinhart snorted and said: "I trust Al's TV set works."

They had finally made it to Al's Motel. Reinhart had told her about his television appearance but had said nothing about Buxton's death: the two experiences had nothing in common, were actually at odds.

The picture came on, big, beautiful, and in vibrant color. Actually the set looked brand new. But the plumbing seemed to date from the pre-Buxton age: the toilet had an incessant hiss, and the rusty stall shower was surely Navy surplus (perhaps ex-dreadnought, conflict of 1917–18).

The news was already under way. The story from the early-morning report had since reached what probably would be its conclusion: the man who had manacled himself to the lamppost at a downtown intersection had been freed by a young boy who owned a similar set of toy handcuffs and thus was privy to the secret of their springing. The episode was revealed to have had no ideological reference: two friends had bet on the outcome of a basketball game; he who lost must so exhibit himself.

"Honestly," Helen said from bed, holding the sheet up across half her large bosom, "some people are so childish."

Reinhart felt a draft on his bare back. He returned to bed and pulled his part of the sheet up. It was quite warm under there, no doubt because of the heat exuded by Helen's substantial body.

"Here." Helen handed him a motel tumbler that clinked with ice.

He smelled carefully at its brim to determine whether it was the one with plain soda. Helen had brought along the Chivas purchased the day before. She had mixed her own with Sprite.

On the screen at the moment was the two-man team that held down the desk on the news: one of them a lively fop and the other a kindly, folksy sort.

It was the former who said: "And now for today's Short Takes. *Bread:* local bakery drivers on strike. *Lead:* it's in the paint that flakes off public-school walls, says PTA leader. *Fed:* -up, says Oak

Hills bus driver, who lets off passengers, then sends vehicle into the river. *Dead:* former Hollywood great Jack Buxton, at the age of seventy-two." Without prelude a commercial began to unfold.

"Jesus," Reinhart said, swallowing Scotch-and-soda, "that's all?"

"I guess he wasn't that big any more," said Helen.

Affectionate soul, she had moved over to touch him again with the entire length of her body, and he could not remember when whiskey had tasted so delicious. Reinhart had an unalloyed sense of well-being. He was alive and Buxton was dead. Well, *he* was guiltless, had done what he could to save the actor's life. Still, it made a man wonder.

"Honey," Helen said, stirring. "Put down the drink."

"I'd better turn off the TV." He would have got out of bed had she permitted.

"Why? Let 'em watch!" She had a laugh that he was always pleased to hear. She also had a capacity that could not be believed, considering that she also had a husband and a regular lover.

"Today's Feature Close-Up," said the less dapper of the two newsmen on the screen, "by Field Reporter Molly Moffitt."

"That noise really does distract me," Reinhart said. "I better switch it off." He started to get up. He had to feel whether he was still wearing his underpants.

A beautiful young black woman came onto the television screen. Behind her was a familiar-looking farmhouse, beyond which stood a recognizable barn.

"We're here at Paradise Farm," said the young woman into her little club of a microphone. "What's Paradise Farm? That's what we asked its founder and spiritual leader, Brother Valentine."

Raymond Mainwaring appeared in close-up. "Paradise Farm is first of all an idea," said he. "On the surface it might be perceived as an experiment in communal living, and to be sure, it *is* that, but—"

"Carl," Helen said.

"Excuse me, Helen, I know that fellow."

"You know everybody on the news tonight." She spoke with some annoyance.

Raymond had continued: ". . . combining in one effort all the various needs: clean living, nourishing food, brotherhood, security, and a relationship with the Higher Power, whatever you choose to call Him or It: God, Allah, the Great Spirit, or the vision of pantheism."

"Could God be a woman?" asked Molly Moffitt, in close-up. She had a flawless face, the color of coffee heavily creamed.

"I don't see why not," said Brother Valentine.

"And how would you describe your own posture?" Molly asked, in her accentless voice. "Are you priest, preacher, rabbi, monk—?"

"I'm but a servant," said Raymond. "I'm the least of the least."

Molly interrupted him by merely moving the mike to her own lips. She seemed never for an instant to forget that she possessed that power. "You're not saying you're an Uncle Tom?"

Raymond scowled at her. "I don't dignify such terms by even acknowledging that they exist. I've got important things to do, missions to carry out . . ." He was getting the wind up, in a quiet, intense way.

"Carl," said Helen to Reinhart's back: he was sitting on the edge of the bed.

Raymond was continuing: ". . . better to do than *talk about pigment!*"

Molly Moffitt was absolutely unfazed by his passion. She said: "But were you not a militant in the Sixties? A leader of a group called the Black Assassins? Did you not advocate the use of force and violence against the white power-structure? Did you not come pretty close to asking for a racial war?"

Raymond closed his eyes as the microphone came back to him. "All memory of the past was expunged as of that moment at which I was reborn: ten twenty-seven A.M., on April third, nineteen seventy-five."

Molly Moffitt reclaimed the mike. "But just what is it you do here, Brother Valentine? Is this really a farm? I mean, do you grow things? Do you raise livestock?"

Raymond nodded gravely. "Indeed it is a farm, and we are farmers. We are dairymen too, and carpenters, painters, roofers, whatever we need to be. We shall, with God's help, be self-sustaining."

"Utopian, is that it?" asked Molly. "What kind of people are here?" She addressed this question to the television audience. "What manner of person seeks this refuge? Let's go inside the house."

The scene changed. Reinhart saw the empty ground-floor rooms he had himself walked through ten days before.

An unseen Molly demanded: "Why is there no furniture here? Is that because of some religious belief?"

The camera came around in front of Raymond for his answer: "At the moment we do not possess any furniture for these rooms. We're rich only in faith."

Behind Reinhart, Helen groaned. "Come on, Carl, that's one of those stupid documentaries. What do you want to watch that for?"

"I told you, I know that guy. In fact, I visited that farm recently."

"Looks like one of those cults," said Helen. "I don't know what a man like you would want with that kind of thing."

"*I* wouldn't," said he. "My son was curious and—"

Molly, Raymond, and the camera now reached the big old farmhouse kitchen, where it looked as if the same people seen by Reinhart were still in place along the counters or at the table.

Helen said to Reinhart's spine: "Your friend is pretty stuck on himself, isn't he? That's no criticism, but . . ."

"He's stuck on something," said Reinhart. "I'm not sure what. He interests me. I knew his father, who was a great idealist and would have liked Jack Buxton's films, for example."

The camera had followed Molly and Raymond out the back door. They proceeded towards the barn.

"What are the criteria for acceptance here?" Molly was asking, and before Brother Valentine could answer she amplified her question: "I guess what I'm trying to do is find out what makes this community tick in an overall way. In other words, have you collected together for a religious purpose, primarily, or is it ecology, or are you, Brother Valentine, AKA Captain Storm, AKA Raymond Mainwaring still, underneath it all, a political animal?"

Molly stopped at the door of the barn. "Or," she asked blandly, "or are you, as some have charged, in it just for the bucks?" She looked into the camera. "A provocative question, a provocative man! Brother Valentine, the spokesman for the communal project called Paradise Farm. Watch tomorrow evening for his answer to this question and for the conclusion of our report. This is Molly Moffitt for the Channel Five news team."

The picture switched back to the pair at the desk in the studio.

"She's part white, don't you think?" asked Helen.

Reinhart said: "Um. I suspect from her remarks that Paradise Farm has been the subject of a muckraking investigation of the kind that has become fashionable in recent years. Probably one of the newspapers, with nothing better to do. Poor Raymond. Though of course for all I know he *is* a crook." He realized he was talking to himself. He extinguished the TV set and went to do his best to answer Helen's remarkable need, unprecedented in his memory. She really deserved a stripling, not a graybeard.

When they had concluded their commerce, she abruptly hopped from bed, plunged in and out of the quaint rusty cubicle that stood for a shower, toweled, dressed, and picked up her purse from the rickety table near the door.

Reinhart was both relieved and slightly hurt to have witnessed the foregoing sequence. "You're on your way now, I take it?"

"Got to," said Helen. "It's almost suppertime."

"Gee, past it! You'd better have a good excuse."

"Don't have to go far," said she, putting the bottle of Scotch into the pocket of her trench coat, where it bulged conspicuously. "Everything's O.K." She went to the door. "So I'll call you, Carl, huh?"

"I'm certainly glad you did today," Reinhart said, stretching down to his toes. He still lay supine in bed, under the sheet. "Your call came at just the right time. I was feeling a letdown after my TV appearance. It's really an odd experience: there you are, before thousands of people one moment, and the next you're all alone. I thought I did a pretty fair job, if I do say so myself, and Debbie and the studio people seemed to also, but then you go home to complete silence." But once again he was thinking of himself. "Thanks, Helen, you're really a nice person. . . . Say, don't I get a good-bye kiss?"

Helen kissed him and while so doing ran her hand down his body. It did not escape his notice that until only recently her performance would have been seen as infringing on the masculine, whereas his own . . . After she left, he rose and before the mirror performed various body-builder's poses: face overlooking distended biceps, forearm, wrist, and hand in the swan's-neck formation; then the full-front wedge, with prominent deltoids; then the hands joined at the crotch, trapezius muscles sloping between shoulder and neck. By God, he still was far from being a wreck. In high school and the early time in college, pre-Army, Reinhart had religiously used the products of the York Barbell Co., York, Pa., and for several years his principal heroes had been not of the tribe of Jack Buxton, but rather the extraordinarily swollen men depicted in the York weight-lifting magazine, *Strength and Health,* fellows who had to turn sideways to penetrate the standard doorway. His fifty-four-year-old body had not altogether forgotten this period of its history, and one already had had, after all, a few years in which to practice stoicism with regard to the relentless degeneration in muscle tone. And Helen had commended him as lover. No doubt she was merely being polite, but what the hell, it was anyhow nice to hear.

He unflexed as he felt the first suspicions of a crick-in-the-neck. The fact was that no middle-aged body, not even one well maintained, could do better than just get by. There *were* laws that could not be abrogated by state of mind.

Checking out formally at Al's was not done. One merely walked away, leaving the key in the door. Nor had Reinhart himself checked in. Helen had performed that task for him. That she was obviously a habitué of the motel did not bother him any more than, presumably, it bothered Al, if indeed there was one. Helen was a fine figure of a woman: he was not required to assess her beyond that point.

After taking an inordinately lengthy shower for such wretched facilities—indeed, the hot water ran out before long, and finally even the cold dwindled to a staccato drip—Reinhart drove home in Winona's Cougar, which had been his all day, and which in fact would be his so long as she stayed with Grace, who had an extra vehicle. It occurred to her father that it had been Blaine, really, who managed things in such a fashion that Winona had finally been *obliged* to move in with her lover, an action which until now she had been reluctant either to take or to forget about.

Where *was* Blaine? And what of Mercer and the boys? How long could they continue to live at the apartment—by which question Reinhart actually meant: how long could *he* stand it? Because, by all appearances, *they* were coping very well. . . . Yet he had been on TV for almost ten minutes that morning, and later on Helen Clayton, his junior by a dozen or fifteen years, had praised his performance in bed!

Therefore it was in a hearty, Elizabethan mood that he drove home, and with ebullience that he opened the apartment door to join his grandfamily, whom he had by no means neglected to go and roll in lust with a doxy. Far from it! He had that afternoon roasted a lovely plump chicken, with butter and thyme in its cavity and bastings on the quarter-hours, and made a potato salad with a vinaigrette of olive oil and shallots. Remembering his own childhood, he believed that what had pleased him most when eating elsewhere than at his own home had not merely been the dessert as simple sweet course, but rather as an entertaining, even surprising event, e.g., when the ice cream was dosed for once not with Hershey's chocolate syrup but with jam made from green-gage plums or pulverized hard candy, or the Jell-O came to the table as turned out of a ring mold, the central well filled with high-peaked whipped cream and surmounted by a maraschino cherry. (These events had never taken place at his own home: his mother disapproved of such caprices.)

Therefore he had applied thought to the dessert he would leave for the boys and of course for Mercer too, if applicable. It must be something that, like the chicken, could be eaten cold to advantage. He decided upon a splendid *dacquoise*, in which layers of meringue alternated with a filling compounded of butter, sugar, and almond extract, and the whole structure was eventually shrouded in sweetened whipped cream and dusted with powdered almonds. There was no mammal who could turn away from such a confection until it had been devoured: one could stand on that truth.

He prepared as well a platter of choice crudités: bright cherry tomatoes, sticks of jade pepper, serene cucumber, stanch celery, and romaine allowed to stay in the long whole leaf. (As a boy he had hated salads made from iceberg lettuce, a gnarled and ugly plant that seemed to be made solely for packaging. And what fun it would have been to choose the raw elements and eat them from the fingers.)

All these lovely things he had left in the fridge, wrapped and in fact identified by Scotch-taped label, and on the kitchen counter lay a prominent notice addressed to whom it concerned among his guests (for either of the boys might be treated as being at least as responsible as their mother): the menu was printed in capitals, for the convenience of those who could read at all, big or small, in the order in which the dishes should be attacked, which was optional, but it was required that each of them know that the chef left his best wishes for a good appetite and, it went without saying, his affection.

Now nobody was home when he got there, and when he went into the kitchen and saw that aside from the filthy coffee cup on the counter, three cigarette butts in its saucer, there were no dirty dishes in evidence, he understood, before opening the refrigerator, that his guests had not touched the supper he had provided, for not only was Mercer incapable of washing a plate, she could not manage even to scrape one, still less insert it into the dishwasher below this very counter.

Reinhart discarded the butts in the pedal can and rinsed the heeltaps of powdered coffee from the cup. It was not until he opened the otherwise unused dishwasher that he saw the note, which was impaled on one of the little plastic-covered fence-palings around the wire tray designed to support glassware during the commotion of the wash.

Went out for burgurs.

M

The only thing that really annoyed him, he told himself, was the misspelling. How could anyone who lived in this culture make such an error? Jesus Chryst!

Cold roast chicken being one of the glories of the world, Reinhart ate his supper in good appetite. There was a virtue in dining alone. In Mercer's presence he would have felt obliged to wash down his food with the homogenized milk he had laid in for the children. As it was, he could dig out of the broom closet the crisp little Chenin Blanc and quaff it in good conscience.

"Hi," said Mercer, in the doorway of the kitchen.

"Mercer! I didn't hear you come in: I was thinking." In the grip of his old-fashioned, instinctive manners Reinhart left his stool. His daughter-in-law was both female and his guest. "May I get you anything? Coffee? Hey, where are the boys? Is it too late for them to have some of the meringue-and-whipped-cream cake I made?"

"Gee," said Mercer, "they really stuffed themselves at Burger City. You know how kids are: eating makes them sleepy. They went right to bed." She lowered her chin and up across her thick eyebrows gave him a long look of the sort that signals its maker's preoccupation with another subject than that under discussion.

Reinhart asked: "Do you want to talk to me about something, Mercer? Let me get you a chair." He did as promised, from the dining room. The kitchen was equipped only with the one stool, which, after he had seated her, he regained.

Mercer proceeded to sit there in silence. She was the sort who could persist in that sort of thing without apparent discomfort, but Reinhart was surely not. Nor did he even feel he could properly finish his wine. Unfortunately he had not got in one last swallow before she appeared, for he had had one coming for quite a while and had been prolonging the suspense: a little funny thing he had been doing with favorite foods and beverages since childhood.

Finally he rose and Saran Wrapped what was left of the chicken. The roast bird also gave him a pretext to say something pertinent as well as morally neutral: "Still a lot of chicken left, if you want a snack later. Remember it's high in protein and low in calories, especially if you don't eat the skin." He shrugged and put fowl and plate into the fridge.

"I was thinking," Mercer began at last. She vigorously rubbed an index finger beneath her nose.

Reinhart took his stool once more, but by the time he had sat down she had again established silence.

When he was certain of this, he said: "What were you thinking?"

She looked up. "Huh? . . . Oh . . . well, I don't even know if I could say it to anyone else."

"Why, sure you could, Mercer," said he. "If you wanted to, that is."

Suddenly she grinned. In such an expression her nobility of feature disappeared entirely. A grin for her was a grotesque disguise. Furthermore it was utterly mirthless. Reinhart suddenly felt like slapping her face, to bring her out of it.

But instead he said: "Or then don't tell it, if it's embarrassing." He eyed the wine bottle longingly when she turned her head away, but then plugged it with the cork and pushed it out of their lines of vision. There was still a good solid mouthful of it in the glass. What would be better, to let it sit there quietly or to empty it in the sink?

She stopped grinning at last and said: "The thing is, my parents always wanted me to have a profession. I mean, it was me who wanted to get married and have children."

"Uh-huh." She had taken him by surprise, but he thought quickly. "You mean, it was a switch, given your place and time."

"That's right!" Mercer said brightly. "Another funny thing is that I got really good grades in college, in the tough stuff like math and science. You can ask Blaine."

"I wouldn't call that funny," said Reinhart. "I'd call it impressive. Blaine, you know, was a brilliant student, but I think he did least well in math."

"I remember!" Mercer cried. She seemed happily nostalgic. "I really hated him then."

"That's right. You *did* know each other in college."

"Well, I knew who *he* was, but he never noticed me."

"He was probably too busy with his political protests and so on," said Reinhart.

"I hated all that," said Mercer.

So had Reinhart, but he was actually embarrassed to remember that period, from which nobody, of whatever stripe, emerged victorious. Suddenly defiant, he seized his wineglass and emptied it into his throat, then put it in the dishwasher.

This event had no discernible effect on Mercer. Now that he thought about it, she had been in residence for twenty-four hours and had spent at least part of that time alone in the apartment, and though he had concealed his few bottles of alcoholic beverages, she could easily have purchased her own. But he had seen no evidence of that. Nor had she acted as if drunk or drugged.

Mercer was shaking her head. She addressed the black-and-white vinyl tiles of the floor. "I should have gone into computers."

Reinhart sat down again. "Excuse me?"

"Or something," said Mercer. "But you see, it never occurred to me that you could think you were cut out for something naturally and then discover that you weren't. That doesn't seem to make sense, but actually it's true."

"That's right," said Reinhart. "It's the damnedest thing, isn't it?" For the first time he actually felt an affinity with his daughter-in-law. "I know just what you mean! For about twenty years I thought I was supposed to be a businessman. Isn't everybody? You know. That everything I tried ended in failure made no useful impression on me: I always assumed that I hadn't yet found the right business. I was in my late forties before I discovered the truth."

"But," said Mercer, "I was designed by Nature to be a mother, and if you bear young, then it's certainly your job to care for them. No matter what they say, that's obviously the way things were designed. And if you're taking care of your children, you can't go out and chop down trees and find food and do a man's work. No matter what they say."

"Mercer," said her father-in-law, "I'm going to make some coffee. I hope you'll join me in having some." He put on the water. "I take it that by 'they' you refer to the people whose profession it is to harangue the populace in the interest of various causes that will obviously benefit the haranguers but be of dubious service to those listening."

Mercer made a wry mouth. "Funny, isn't it? He was a war-protester in college. But he told me once that secretly he would have liked nothing better than to be a fighter pilot or hero at hand-to-hand combat."

"Blaine? I'll be damned." Did one's son inherit, along with certain physical traits, one's own fantasies as well?

The water was boiling. He had intended to make powdered coffee, but it was just as easy to grind some real beans and put the product into the four-cup filter pot and fill the top with water. He went to the dining-room china cabinet and brought back a pair of demitasses and the sugar bowl.

Mercer accepted the cup but spurned the sugar.

She rolled her eyes. "Let's face it, we belonged to the wrong generation."

"But then again," said Reinhart, "who hasn't?" But this was polite hypocrisy: there had been nothing wrong with his.

CHAPTER
15

Next morning after breakfast and the wait for the bathroom Reinhart eventually got himself cleaned and shaved and put together, and he left the apartment, intending to shop for food.

But while he was in the garage, unlocking the door to Winona's car, he was hailed from across the way.

"Oh . . . good morning, Edie!" For it was that tall young woman, at the door of her own automobile. He found himself pleased to see her. It had been years since he had known someone so slightly as to forget her when she was not present and yet feel a mild gratification when encountering her by chance.

He closed the Cougar's door and went towards Edie. For a moment she looked as if, in a kind of panic, she might dive into her car and flee—never had he known a shyer person—but he slowed down, grinned less broadly, and looked not directly at her but just beyond, and she was able to hold her ground.

"Well," he said, "well, well." He decided to seize her hand and shake it, being certain that once contact had been made she would lose a good deal of her nervousness. This proved true.

She showed him owlish eyes. "Well . . . how is Winona?"

"She's fine," he said. "If you haven't seen her for a day or so, it's because she's staying with a friend."

Edie nodded vigorously. She was dressed in a beige cardigan, plain white blouse, and, he noticed, not jeans but what resembled the so-called sun-tan pants that were the summertime uniform of the U.S. Army in World War II. He always imagined that he could smell soap when near her.

"She must," said Edie, "have lots of friends."

"Enough, I suppose."

Edie looked unhappy, and he immediately regretted having told her: after all, she was a defenseless creature.

"Speaking of friendships," he said quickly, "we've also got a lunch to make up for. How about today?"

In answer she heaved a great sigh. Reinhart had never seen anyone do that at such a point, but he found it strangely attractive. Or perhaps it was strange that he found it attractive, for it might be taken as merely a helpless acquiescence to fate.

"O.K." He beckoned and almost bowed. Something about Edie caused him often to come close to doing a parody of an old-fashioned gentleman. "Shall we step over to my car? Or rather Winona's, which I have the use of at the moment."

But suddenly she became defiant. "No, at least I can provide the transportation." She marched around to the passenger's door of her Gremlin, unlocked and opened it.

Reinhart didn't mind being chauffeured. Now that he operated an automobile only sporadically—Winona generally drove her own car—he found that he no longer had the old ease that had once characterized his technique of driving, and the traffic seemed heavier and more uncompromising, despite the "fuel crisis," which should in reason have had another effect. But then one's sense of anything is highly colored by one's age.

Having pulled out of the garage, up the inclined driveway, and stopped at its intersection with sidewalk and street, she turned questioningly to Reinhart.

"Take a left."

She accelerated away. He noticed that she tended to take him literally, in her need to comply, but he had lived long enough not to confuse this with obsequiousness: there are people who perform this way because of a serious outlook based inconspicuously on self-respect.

When they had reached a street important enough to have traffic lights he asked: "What kind of food would you like to eat?"

"Oh, anything, really." She was stealing little glances at him. She shook her head at the dashboard and swallowed with apparent difficulty. "Uh," she said, "what's it like, being on TV?"

Reinhart smiled expansively before he realized that he was doing so. When it did occur to him, he frowned: vanity in a man of his age was an embarrassment. "You saw me?"

"Oh, sure." She now gave him a smile that could be called dazzling. Her teeth were slightly larger than average and absolutely perfect. "You were just terrific!"

"Thank you," said Reinhart, crossing his ankles the other way. "Thank you very much."

"Imagine that," Edie said, "cooking like that. What a terrific thing!"

"You're being generous."

"Oh, I think it's really great. But it's hard to understand how Winona stays so slender, with you in the kitchen!"

"That's simple," Reinhart said. "She hardly ever eats anything I make!" He worried that he sounded indignant, and added: "Makes sense, of course, for a model. I'm not complaining. I cook in the spirit of scientific inquiry. I'm fascinated by what happens to flavors and textures when food is prepared in certain ways. But of course I myself like to eat. What I cook never goes to waste."

"I'm certainly never going to miss that show from now on," Edie said.

"Actually," said Reinhart, "I was just making that one appearance on the program. I gather they have all sorts of guest cooks. I do some things for this food company, you see, to promote their products, and they booked me on the show." He was reminded that Grace Greenwood had yet to be heard from on the subject of his performance. She had not even had the courtesy to return his call.

Edie stopped the car at a red light. They were now in an old-fashioned suburban shopping area, which, unlike the malls, had not been constructed for the role but had simply grown into it over the years and now was congested and somewhat down-at-heel and gave Reinhart the familiar feelings of nostalgia and despondency.

"See that delicatessen?" he asked, pointing. "My uncle took me in there once in 1936 or 7. We were coming back from a ball game.

I had a cold roast-pork sandwich, heavily salted, on homemade bread. The proprietor was a Swiss. His wife made all the baked goods, and he made his own horseradish and sausages and of course all the cooked meats. Funny how I still remember that, though in more than forty years I've never been back."

"Do you want to try it now?" Edie asked eagerly. "We could get something there for lunch." She had a dreamy smile for the deli; she was probably sharing in his nostalgia.

"No," he said decisively. "I'll tell you why. It's unlikely that the Swiss would still be there, and I really don't want my memories polluted by the sight of what it may have become. But the idea of getting some takeout food is a great one on a day like this. We'll pick up—not here, but in the next bunch of shops we come to—some cheese and decent crusty bread, if it can be found, and wine, and have a picnic. There are various parks to choose from, or we could just drive out into the country somewhere."

He found Edie's presence much more satisfying than that of any other female person he knew at this time, which might not be saying much had he not been able to include Helen Clayton, who was enthusiastically heterosexual.

Edie made an odd shrugging movement and hunched farther forward over the steering wheel. "I think a picnic would be great."

"Hey." He pointed to the shopping mall that was coming up ahead, the signs for its principal enterprises towering on great standards which rose from the flatness of a former meadow: BOGAN'S . . . TOP SHOP . . . KIBORWORLD. "Pull in at the Top Shop, and we'll take on some provisions."

"O.K.!" Edie made her agreement an ebullient little event. She slid the Gremlin into a parking space on the asphalt plain, and they entered this branch of the Top Shop, an even larger example than the one in which Reinhart had cooked crepes Suzette.

They went through the automatic doors and once inside stopped and looked at each other with affectionate smiles. Hers was only slightly below the level of his. He had not known so large a female person since he was in the Army. But unlike Edie, Veronica Leary, his friend in the Nurse Corps, had been a great beauty. Of course he himself had been but twenty-one years of age at that time.

"Well," he said finally, breaking the deadlock of genial silence, "shall we go see whether they have any edible cheese?"

They loped in step for a while and with a purposeful air, but had no reason to suppose they were nearing the dairy section. There was here the kind of vastness on which progress had no effect, as when one drove towards a distant mountain: for every step they took, the farthermost wall receded in the same degree.

But at last they reached the long, open, refrigerated trough that held the various products which took their origins from the milch cow, and Reinhart was about to sift through the packaged cheeses in search of one that would bear being eaten, when, down at the bottom of the aisle, he saw a familiar figure.

It was Helen Clayton, at work alone. She stood before a metallic table which held paper-platefuls of cubed cheese. There were two kinds, bright orange and off-white, and in each cube was an embedded toothpick. Helen extended a plate to anyone who passed her.

Each saw the other at the same moment. Helen's greeting was to elevate her paper plate. Reinhart's wave was a kind of salute.

"Would you be offended if I talked to that woman down there?" he asked Edie. "She's a business associate."

Edie simpered at the extraordinary suggestion that anything would offend her.

"I just want to say a word to her about business," he nevertheless found himself explaining almost guiltily. "It would be boring for you. Look through these cheeses and choose something you like."

Helen greeted him breezily when he reached her table. "Hi, there!" She thrust the paper plate at two female shoppers in turn. Then there was a lull in the traffic. She put down the selection of samples and gave him a more personal grin. "Whatcha doin' in this neck of the woods? Grace send you to check up on me?"

"Pure accident," said Reinhart. "Just was passing by and dropped in to pick up a few things. Speaking of Grace, she hasn't been in touch since I did the TV thing. I thought it was successful, if I do say so myself, and the television people seemed to like it. They said something about inviting me back. But Grace hasn't even returned my call."

Helen made a slow wink. "She's having love problems, I believe.

I didn't get this assignment from her. I hear she's been out sick for a while."

Reinhart felt an involuntary wave of revulsion. He simply couldn't help it: Nature did assert itself from time to time. "Oh. Well, that's the way it happens, I guess."

"Yeah," Helen said with a wry mouth. "You can't have your cake and eat it too."

In desperation he reached for a sample of cheese: an orange-colored piece was closest. He clasped the cube behind his front teeth and slid out the toothpick.

"This has no taste at all," he wonderingly told Helen while chewing. "Why are you giving out samples of it?"

She shrugged. "It's new, I think. I haven't tasted it. I'm watching the calories, as usual." She suddenly leered at him, in a discreet but intense way that had almost the intimacy of a touch. "I'm off when the cheese is gone. That'll be any minute by the looks of it." She opened her lips and closed them silently, moistly, warmly.

"Uh," Reinhart replied, "I can't make it today. Uh . . ." For some reason he was at a loss for a feasible excuse.

"Look, honey," Helen said, changing into a pal, "I know you're with your daughter. What I meant was, only if you were going to be free a little later."

Now Reinhart moved quickly, without reflection, to consolidate this fraudulent, fortuitous gain: Helen had actually seen Winona once, calling for Grace, but didn't know she was his daughter. Let it go at that! And it was even better if she believed that he was Edie's parent. But what would happen when Helen found out? That was the kind of thing Reinhart would have found inhibiting as a very young man, but he had since learned that a good many claims in life are never put to the test, and from those that are, often enough, truth still does not issue, and finally in the rare event that it does, even rarer is to find the mortal to whom it matters.

Anyway, he and Helen, though colleagues of a kind and certainly lovers in the physical sense, would quite likely never really know each other at all well.

"Yes," he said now to his friend, "ordinarily I don't get to see that much of her at this time of day. We thought we'd get something for a picnic."

Helen looked up the aisle. "I'd know her if you weren't anywhere around. She's a chip off your block, that's for sure. Doesn't look anything like the ex-wife."

Reinhart stepped out of the way so that she could offer the cheese to several women who appeared, distractedly pushing their carts. Two of them spurned the offer, but one, a jolly, fortyish person, took a cube in an excessively dainty fashion, fingers fanned. After an instant he understood that she did this in an intentional burlesque of gentility.

After taking a nibble, she asked Helen, in good humor: "Why are you giving this away? Because you can't sell it? It's *terrible.*"

"It's a cheese-industry promotion," said Helen. "To get people to eat more cheese. There were several other kinds when I started, blue and Swiss and so on, and flavored spreads, onion, mustard, port wine, but they're gone by now. There were also some brochures that gave various recipes for dishes made with cheese—soufflés, casseroles, and the rest—but people have taken them all by now. One thing, though, never did show up: I was supposed to have some standing posters for this table. I don't know what became of them! You run into that a lot these days."

"Gee," said the woman, depositing her toothpick at the end of the table. She looked quizzically at Reinhart. "You'd think they'd give out better cheese if they want you to buy some. Put the best foot forward, you know?" She rolled her cart away.

"I'll be seeing you, Helen," said Reinhart.

"I'll give you a call tomorrow," said Helen. "It can't hurt."

Edie seemed in a standing coma as he approached her, but eventually she saw him and smiled.

"Did you see any cheese you liked?"

"I wasn't sure what kind you'd want."

"What about yourself? Don't you like cheese?"

"It's just that I don't *know* what cheese to get!" Her tone was that of authentic distress.

He had been unknowingly inconsiderate. "Well, it doesn't matter. Suddenly I've lost interest in cheese. Let's attack the subject from a new angle. Tell me what would be a typical lunch for you."

"A hot dog," said Edie. "Or a hamburger, unless it would be a pizza."

"Let's go to the car," he said, "and drive someplace in the country and get a hot dog. This place is depressing me."

When they reached the car, she gave the keys to him. "Please drive where you want."

Reinhart unlocked the passenger's door and held it open for her entrance. Then he went around to the driver's side. Edie was looking at him when he inserted himself behind the wheel. He did not of course need to push back the seat.

She said: "I'm sorry I couldn't choose a cheese."

"You're a real criminal," said Reinhart, winking at her.

"Are you angry?"

"You betcha." He touched the back of her near hand, and started the engine.

She did not speak again until they were on the motorway. "I've met some nice people in our building—at the mailboxes and around. I met Winona!"

"That's a pretty nice building," said Reinhart. "We've always liked it."

Edie asked anxiously: "Is your apartment satisfactory?"

"It's quite nice. It's my favorite of all the places I've ever lived in."

"Good," she said. "Because if anything's wrong I wish you'd let me know."

"With the apartment?"

"My father owns the building."

"I see," said Reinhart, speeding up to the fifty-five mark on the dial. "That's right, now that I think of it, there's that sign on the front corner of the building, isn't there? 'The Mulhouse Corporation.' That's your father?"

"I guess so," Edie said, flinching.

"Nothing wrong with that. I've seen the name on quite a few buildings around town. Your father must own a good portion of this city." Furthermore, Mr. Mulhouse was probably no older than he, perhaps even younger.

Edie said fearfully: "I just have a studio apartment. I'm not taking up any extra space that should go to couples with families."

Reinhart smiled at her. "You're too apologetic, Edie. You don't have to ask the world's permission for everything! Did anyone ask you whether you wanted to be born?"

He grinned at her. She was apparently a real-life example of the poor little rich girl, but in the course of life, he had become aware, it is routine to encounter at least one example of every legendary type.

CHAPTER
16

Reinhart had been driving for some time as it were unconsciously. An exit sign was coming up.

"Look where we are already: Brockville. We'd better get off here if we're ever going to get anything to eat."

He sent the little car down the ramp, at the bottom of which was a blacktopped county road.

Soon they were entering Brockville. Reinhart could not remember having visited this community, though it was not an uncommon name in his personal gazetteer. Now and again throughout the years "Brockville" would be pronounced by someone as being a point in space from which something else could be measured. "Worthing? Oh, that's on out north of Brockville." The town itself, into which within a moment or two they had penetrated to the heart, had a business district one block in length and occupied really less than that measurement of distance would imply, for on only one side of the street were there any establishments of "business," if a café-restaurant and a little delicatessen, both of them of the seedy if not flyblown character, could be said to have a serious association with the term.

Brockville was the kind of place in which at noon you could park at the curb directly in front of the only restaurant in town.

Reinhart shifted into neutral and switched off the ignition. "Shall we try this place? If it looks too bad inside, we can just have a cup of coffee and leave. It has been my experience to be horribly disappointed in life when I've looked for anything quaint."

He had meant that in ironic jest, but Edie said soberly: "I don't think I've ever looked for anything of that kind, unless I just don't know what it is."

They left the car. Reinhart noted with approval that the façade of the place had not yet suffered the hand of the routine renovator who applies solid siding or wooden shingles, leaving only a tiny window displaying a neon beer-sign and a framed liquor license. No, the Center Café had the big plate-glass front window of yore, though seeing clearly through it was another matter.

They entered. If the population of Brockville was at lunch, it obviously ate at home, for few representatives were currently in the only eatery. Of the three options, far-left counter, central tables, far-right booths, only the first-named was in use: three men, spaced intermittently, sat at the counter, but only one of them seemed honestly a diner: that is, only he had a plate before him. Another simply sucked at what looked to be a stark coffee cup. The third man partook of nothing at the moment, though it was possible he had already fed. He was dressed in dark-green work clothes, shirt & pants, and he talked with, or rather listened to, the proprietress, a blousy, voluble, spirited woman of about Reinhart's age.

She shouted at him and Edie: "Take a booth, kids." Reinhart waved at her, and she refined the invitation: "Take *any* booth."

"Who knows what we're in for?" Reinhart muttered as they went along the far-right aisle. There had been a time in life when he would have chosen the farthest booth, and another when the nearest would have been most attractive to him, and again there had been eras for the nearest-but-one and the next-to-the-last. No doubt a man's philosophy could be measured in hashhouse seating arrangements.

He said now to Edie: "Let's boldly take the one in the middle. We've got nothing to hide." But once again his little witticism was accepted almost dolefully by her.

By the time they had, leggy persons that they were, inserted themselves at their respective sides of the table—though there was plenty of room here, Reinhart always felt a certain emotional pressure when bending to penetrate a booth—the woman said good-bye, with a jovially rude sound, to the man in the green uniform, and crossed the room. She seemed more loose of flesh than actually fat, but it was hard to tell. She was wearing a kind of smock, in pale orange; it was clean enough. She had small and blue but warm eyes.

"Well, sir," said she, including Edie in the address, her little eyes swiveling, "what can I do for you today?"

"What's the specialty of the house?" asked Reinhart.

The woman winked at Edie, jerking an elbow in Reinhart's direction. "There's a brave man." She turned to him. "Sure you wanna know?"

Reinhart said: "I live dangerously." He winked at her. "Does a fellow have a choice in Brockville?"

"Say." The woman put her hands on her hips. "You serious? The shopping center's got 'em all: the Colonel, King of Burgers, Chinky Chow Mein . . ."

"Well, lucky for us, we missed all of that," said Reinhart. "We're from the city, and are trying to get away from all the known junk."

"O.K.," the woman said robustly. "I sure hope your will is in order! I don't have a long menu, because I don't have many customers for any meal after breakfast, and in fact I don't stay open very long for supper. But I'm here as of four thirty A.M., and I get enough business from the truckers to keep my head above water. I'll tell you what I've got all day, every day: I've got eggs any style. I've got ham and cheese sandwiches. I've got hamburger of course. I've got chili con carne. And then I always have a daily special. Today it's red-flannel hash."

"The hash sounds terrific," said Reinhart, "but I think I'll try the chili if it's homemade."

The woman shrugged. "It is."

"Edie, what do you think?"

Edie said: "Oh."

"Two chilis, then," cried the woman in her energetic way.

Reinhart liked her a lot, though he feared the worst with reference to her cuisine, suspecting her of carelessness.

"Say," he said, "I don't suppose you sell beer?"

She bent and pressed her midsection against the edge of the table. "Hon, I'm going to take a chance you're not a state inspector. I don't have a license, but I'll be glad to step over to the store and bring you back some brew. They keep it ice-cold."

"Sounds good to me," said Reinhart. The woman went away. He noticed that she wore sneakers. He spoke to Edie: "Seems to be a little place that time forgot. At least, the old part of Brockville. No doubt the shopping mall's in the new part. Did you notice those houses on the opposite side of the street? Imagine that in the middle of a business district these days, little houses with porches. At least one is equipped with a swing that hangs from chains. I can remember when those were routine on front porches, and the people who wanted to be up-to-date replaced the old swings with a sofalike thing that rested on the floor and was called a 'glider.' "

Edie gave him a long, intense, probably worshipful stare.

"Of course," he added, "that was during the Depression, and one had to have money to buy a glider. There were men, neighbors of ours, who had been out of work for years, and there was a form of welfare then called 'relief,' but some people were too proud to take it. Another word from those days was 'prosperity,' but that didn't really come until the war. A good many people had to be killed, in other words, before others had a good life in the material sense." He picked up the nearby salt shaker. Its chromium top was shining; its contents were as loose as dry sand. "This place is cleaner inside than it looks from out. Also the woman seems to be here alone, and she trusts the two guys at the counter, and of course us, not to open the cash register while she's over at the beer store. You don't see that kind of faith every day."

Whenever he looked at her Edie's eyes were fastened so intently on him that he could not bear to meet them, for fear that his own would water in sympathy.

It was with relief that he saw the woman returning with the beer. She carried a whole six-pack but went first to the counter and took two bottles from their slots in the carrier. She brought these to the booth, along with two squat water tumblers.

"Sorry I don't have any nice glasses," said she. "But the beer is cold. I brought the whole six-pack to be on the safe side, but you don't have to pay for what you don't drink. Now's the time to put the cuffs on me if you are state inspectors." She put down the bottles and thrust her wrists at Reinhart.

"Thanks for not getting cans," said he, "and in fact for getting the beer in the first place."

"I'm just trying to soften you up for the food." She laughed widely but silently. "It isn't much of a risk. My old man's the Brockville chief of police, which is more of a job than you might think if you've only seen this part of town. The new part's where the shopping center is. We live in back of it, in a new ranchhouse. The café's got sentimental value for me. My folks used to run it when I was a kid, and I grew up in the apartment upstairs. I don't make enough nowadays to hardly pay the expenses, but it's a good hobby for me." She withdrew her hand from a pocket in the apron and produced an old-fashioned bottle-opener made from one continuous piece of brass wire. Reinhart could not remember having seen one of those in forty years.

After she had poured a glass for each of them and gone to fetch the food, he raised his tumbler at Edie and took a swallow. It was a local brand and, thank God, one that chose to be yeastily flavorful rather than insipidly "light."

Edie gave him a strained smile and with a sudden effort picked up her own glass and drank deeply from it. She swallowed with a wince.

The woman arrived with two heaped plates.

"What's this?" Reinhart asked admiringly. He had expected the kind of chili that contains at least as many kidney beans by weight as beef, ground beef—but the plate before him held a lovely dark-chocolate-colored and chunky stew, with meat that looked tender enough to embrace the tines before they could pierce it, and the fragrance that rose from the sauce, which was so thick that a spoon thrust into it and raised would not have dripped, was almost of cinnamon.

"This is the real Tex-Mex McCoy, isn't it?"

"I learned how to make that down in the Panhandle," said the woman, "when my husband was in the service. That's pinto beans and rice underneath the meat."

Reinhart dug in. "By George," said he, after having chewed and swallowed a specimen forkful. "Marvelous. What all's in it? Chili powder, garlic, what else? Bay leaf? But something else. What am I missing: cinnamon, ginger?"

She rolled her small eyes and sucked the air from her cheeks. "Well, sir," said she, laughing slyly. "That's my secret weapon."

Edie spoke up: "Do you know who you're talking to? The TV Chef, that's who!"

Reinhart protested. "Come on, Edie."

"TV?" asked the woman. "You're not kidding?"

"Aw, well . . ."

"Cumin and oregano."

"Is that right?" Reinhart repeated the names of the spices, and he tasted the chili again. "You know, these pinto beans and rice, what could be a better complement to the chili? This is an excellent dish, Mrs. . . ."

"Huffman, Mrs. Gerald T., but you can call me Marge. When are you on television? I don't want to miss it."

Reinhart introduced himself and Edie. "I'm not appearing on a regular schedule at the moment. But I'll tell you something that's more important right now. I have a connection with a food company, a firm that sells specialty products. At the moment it's mostly that fake gourmet stuff: instant sauces, canned liverwurst *pâté*, et cetera. How about my selling them on your chili? What about a deal in which they make it up in bulk according to your recipe and can it?"

Marge looked as if she were in pain. She squinted as though she were about to weep.

Edie said again: "Do you realize he has the power to do this? He's on *television*."

Reinhart reached across the booth and took Edie's wrist in his fingers. "She knows," he said.

"God Almighty," said Marge. "Who ever thought something like this would happen to me?"

"I don't want to get your hopes too high," Reinhart said quickly. He should have said that earlier. "I can't guarantee they'll want to handle it. All I can do is to take the chili to them. I'm just sort of a consultant." Or whatever you could call a man whose daughter was the lover of a female executive, a man who had been given some make-work but no money, a man who—"But listen," he said aggressively, "I'm going to tell them they had *better* take it unless they want me to go to their competition." This was more than bravado; he had a certain feeling of strength: was cumin an aphrodisiac of power?

Marge went to the refrigerator back of the counter and returned with two more bottles of beer, though Reinhart had as yet drunk only half the first bottle. However, he noted with surprise that Edie had finished her own and was now diligently applying herself to the second, though her chili had scarcely been touched.

Marge said: "Listen here. This is all on me." She raised her eyebrows without increasing the size of her eyes.

"No, certainly not," said Reinhart. "We might be confidence men who go about getting free meals. People may be trustworthy in Brockville, but you should be aware of how they are in the outside world, Marge." He raised his elbow. "If this chili idea catches on, it'll probably ruin your serenity."

Marge shrugged joyfully. "I'll take that chance."

The final coffee-drinker pushed his cup away and rose from the stool at the counter. He stepped behind the cash register, pushed a button, and made some transaction in the drawer that shot out.

"I wouldn't mind having a place like this myself," Reinhart said. "Gosh, a customer makes his own change."

Marge asked solemnly: "You serious? Are you in the market for a restaurant?"

"Probably not." He smiled rhetorically at Edie, who was finishing her second beer already. He wondered whether he should worry. "I'm an amateur cook, you see, and I guess I sometimes think of having a place where I could show off my talents."

Marge straightened up and put her hands in the pockets of her smock. "It hasn't always been so quiet here. When my folks ran it, years ago, they used to do a lot of business. One time in the Thirties a couple of fellows came in and ate a real nice lunch: breaded veal cutlet, mashed potatoes, peas 'n' carrots, stewed tomatoes, and fresh peach pie à la mode for dessert. Used to have more of a menu those days. Anyway, after they paid up and left, my dad said, 'Know who that was? That was John Dillinger and Homer Van Meter.' I wasn't there at the time. I was in school. I suppose it could have been them. Dad always insisted on it and would rattle off what they ate."

Reinhart asked Edie: "Do you recognize those names? They were famous bank robbers of those days. Real celebrities of the Midwest. Household words. When Dillinger was killed by the FBI in an alleyway next to a movie theater in Chicago, newsboys came out from the city to sell extras on the residential streets of the suburb where I lived. Do you even know what an 'extra' is?"

Edie was smiling at him. She made no verbal response.

To Marge, Reinhart said: "Could have been them. They certainly came through this part of the country. Probably was them." Dillinger had supplied to the region its only color, so far as was known: it seemed reasonable enough to claim it whenever feasible.

"About that chili recipe," Marge said. "Do you want me to give it to you now, or do you want me to make up a take-out order to bring back to the city with you?"

Reinhart drank some beer. "I think I'd rather bring somebody out here from the city to taste the product on the spot. They might get some ideas for packaging it when they see your restaurant. Does that overhead fan work? This is a great-looking place. That's a real vintage Coke sign, isn't it?" He referred to a framed rectangle of metal against the back wall, with "Coca-Cola" in bas-relief script. "You see reproductions of stuff like that on sale in shops that cater to young people."

Marge nodded. "We're rough and ready but real," said she, chuckling. "How about calling it John Dillinger's Chili?"

"With a tommy gun on the label," said Reinhart.

After more of this badinage Marge went away to let them eat their meal. When Reinhart finally poured the remainder of the first bottle of beer into his glass and reached for the second, he saw three empty bottles: four, counting the one he had just drained. Edie had her glass to her lips at the moment. She peered strangely at him over the rim. Had she drunk three bottles of beer?

Before long Marge was back. "How about more chili?"

"No, thanks," said Reinhart. "This was quite a generous portion, and it's just right. I don't want to dull my taste by eating too much. This flavor's like a rich perfume."

Edie spoke up. "He's an authority. He's a television chef." She emptied her current glass.

"I'll get the rest of the beer," said Marge, and set off.

But Reinhart called her back. "We have to be on our way, Marge. I mean it about exploring the possibility of marketing the chili. I'll be in touch soon. Write down your phone number for me, and I'll give you mine." Marge went to fetch writing materials. Reinhart said to Edie: "I wish you'd eat some of your food. If you're not used to drinking, that's too much beer on an empty stomach."

She wrinkled her nose and looked as though she might whine, but then straightened up on the seat and stoically forked up chili, pinto beans, rice.

Marge arrived with a piece of brown paper bearing her name and phone number, followed by a dash and the word "chili." Reinhart tore a strip from the bottom of the paper and wrote upon it his name and Winona's number.

"I really have to warn you again," said he, "that I can't promise anything. But we'll give it a try. And at the least I'll be back to eat your chili myself and will recommend it to others."

"On TV?" said Marge. "I guess this is certainly one of the most important days of my life."

Reinhart feared that irrespective of his warnings she would encourage her hopes to go as far as they could, and he remembered only now that on his first meeting with Grace Greenwood in the supermarket, her position on the Pancho Villa line of Mex-Tex canned goods, distributed by her own firm, had been none too enthusiastic.

Edie was undoubtedly feeling the effects of the alcohol. When they got into the car she lowered her head until her chin touched the base of her neck and said nothing as Reinhart drove back to the motorway and entered it pointing south.

Owning a restaurant! What a crazy fantasy. Nevertheless he entertained it for some miles before noticing that Edie had awakened.

He glanced at her and said: "Are you O.K.?"

"I'm just fine," she said coolly.

They exchanged no further speech during the remainder of the homeward drive. The beer had apparently extinguished such light as Edie had, and Reinhart had really never quite known what to talk to her about: his intent from the first had been merely to be kind.

CHAPTER
17

When Reinhart returned from his country outing his grandsons were home alone. They were peacefully occupied, Toby in the hallway with a fleet of miniature cars and Parker on the floor of Winona's bedroom, working in a child's inept fashion with a pair of those blunt-bladed scissors made for small people.

Toby pushed one of the tiny vehicles up the alleyway of bare wood between the wall and the hall runner. He defied custom by not simulating the sound of an engine.

Reinhart asked: "That wouldn't be a Rolls-Royce, would it?"

"Why do you ask?"

"You're not making any engine noise. They used to say about a Rolls-Royce that it ran so quietly the only sound you heard was the ticking of the dashboard clock."

"Ticking?" asked Toby. "Was there a bomb in it?"

Reinhart thought for a moment. "Clocks used to tick. That was before they were digital."

"I can tell time on the ones with hands!" Toby announced with pride. "We learned that in school."

The telephone rang. He answered the one beside the door.

"Carl?" It was Helen Clayton. "I thought you'd want to know why Grace Greenwood has been out of touch. It seems she made a suicide attempt yesterday."

"Oh?"

"Lovers' quarrel! Can you imagine that? She got this girl to move in with her, you know, after working on her for weeks. Just like it was a *guy* and a girl. And they didn't get along, so this girl was going to walk out on her, and Grace took an overdose of sleeping tablets. Of course she claims it was by accident: it was dark, and she got the wrong bottle or something. What surprised me though is that it was Grace who did this and not the other dyke. Grace is always the boss."

"Not in this situation," said Reinhart.

"Excuse me?"

He said: "I guess even authoritative people have someone who knows their number."

"Dykes!" said Helen. "God in heaven. I guess fags have got nothing on them." She said this with a hint of female pride, the old-fashioned kind that predated the recent phase of feminine activism: the sort that had been characteristic of his mother, a roughhewn woman who despised the aims of femlib as being degenerative of the authority she had acquired singlehanded.

"I guess they're all human," said Reinhart, but without piety. He got a grip on himself. "Thanks, Helen. I *am* interested in that information."

"I've got my own source," said she.

"No doubt male?"

"Now, now," Helen said. "Do I ask you to explain everything?"

"I'd be glad to."

"I'll bet," said Helen. She seemed to think his life more enterprising than it was.

"Maybe we can get together again soon."

"Let me call you about that," said Helen. "Al has to go in the hospital for another operation. That means I'll have to spend a lot more time at the motel office."

"Al's Motel?"

"Didn't I mention it? Al's my husband. He's been disabled for a while and in a wheelchair, but he can run the office when he's not in the hospital."

"I'm sorry to hear about his trouble," Reinhart said. He cupped his hand around the mouthpiece, so that Toby, up the hall, would not hear him. "Do you mind my asking? Did Al know we were there the other day?" Helen couldn't understand his whisper, and he had to repeat the question in a somewhat louder voice.

She answered: "He knew *I* was there. I don't think he saw you. I didn't tell him your name, Carl, if that's what's worrying you. I'm not a pervert."

"I hope things work out for him at the hospital," said Reinhart, with real feeling.

He had just hung up and was starting for the kitchen when Winona came in. His instantaneous emotion, which came and went like a flash of light, so swift it might have been imagined, was one of repugnance. In guilty compensation he went to her, seized, and hugged her.

She seemed ill at ease with him. Her trunk was rigid.

"Dad," she said. "How are you?"

"I'm fine, Winona. How are *you?*"

"I'm all right," she said defiantly, almost angrily. She went into the living room and dropped with a funny shoulder movement onto the sofa, as if she were a little girl again.

Reinhart followed her. She was wearing a long skirt. He liked that. He was bored with those eternal jeans.

"Daddy," she said, "Mother's been in touch with me. It seems she's out of the hospital. She claims there was nothing wrong with her at all, that there was no reason for me to call the police, that there was no reason for the police to call the ambulance, and so on down the line, and she intends to sue everybody involved."

"How much more money does she want you to give her? Do you have anything left after paying Blaine for her supposed treatment?" Reinhart ground his teeth.

"Ah, well . . ."

At just that moment the doorbell rang, with a marked effect on Winona. Reinhart was annoyed to be interrupted just as he was about to talk turkey with her.

When he opened the door, he saw Genevieve, showing what he knew from experience as, by intention anyway, a sweet smile.

"Hi, Carl." She had undergone an alteration in appearance: something, some neatening, by cut or comb, had been done to her hair. She also seemed to be better dressed, or perhaps it was merely that today she was not wearing that old green coat. All in all, it was an improvement.

Reinhart blocked the doorway with his large body. "Just what can I do for you, Genevieve?"

She continued to grin. "You're not going to ask about my trouble the other day, the emergency trip to the hospital, et cetera?"

"No," said Reinhart. "I don't have the slightest interest in it."

In what would seem an instant of genuine admiration, Genevieve said: "Carl, if you had always been the mean son of a bitch you've turned into in your old age, I'd probably have stuck by you."

"Thank God, then, my change came too late." Reinhart sighed to dramatize his sense of tragedy averted, but in point of fact he too now grinned. Bantering with Gen was a sadomasochistic entertainment, but sometimes even yet he could remember when they had been, though for all too short a term, comrades.

"Are you going to invite me in?"

"Why should I?"

"For old times' sake." Her morale had been raised by something or other—perhaps the commotion she had caused last Monday. At any rate she did not hint at the beseeching note, alternating with the spiteful, culminating in the vicious, which had characterized her style at the shopping mall.

Reinhart stepped out into the corridor, closing the door behind him. "This is Winona's apartment and not mine, and in fact she's here at the moment. She just told me you had an idea of suing all the poor devils who responded to your fake emergency the other day, including her! I recognize that threat to be as false as your breakdown itself, and I warn you if you say anything to make her feel bad, you will be given a ride out the door on the toe of my shoe."

Genevieve raised her hands and said: "O.K., O.K.!"

Reinhart sighed again and ushered her through the door.

"Winona!" he called in warning when he reached the entrance hall. "It's your mother."

He gestured towards the living room, then stepped ahead of Genevieve and led her in.

Winona, however, came from the bedroom hallway, behind them. "Mother," she said.

Genevieve now wore the kind of curled lip that she wished, but not ardently, to be taken as a polite smile. For a while she ignored her daughter absolutely and instead surveyed the room.

It had dawned upon Reinhart shortly after setting up his domestic partnership with Winona years before, when she was still a teenager, that his daughter had a taste in furnishings and their arrangement that was markedly superior to that of her mother— though indeed he recognized his own gifts in that area as being minor: he could not, for example, have said why a chair bought by Winona invariably had a unique agreement with the situation in which she deployed it, or how her hand, to all appearances even careless, could throw a bouquet of flowers into a vase, touch them here and there, and place the vessel at just the precise convergence of all reasonable sightlines in the room and furthermore in that corner which most profited from new color.

Whereas Genevieve's sense of decor, if it could even be so termed, was unfailingly pedestrian. Indeed, very much like Reinhart's own, it seemed to him in all frankness, and that would have been quite O.K. had not the woman, sporadically throughout their years together, been vociferously interested in interior decoration and aggressively vain about each of her successive versions of the living room, imposing them on their neighbors (envious wives, indifferent hubbies) at lavish holiday open houses, which added even more to the bills Reinhart had to pay from the proceeds of whichever will-o'-the-wisp he was chasing at the moment in "business."

His ex-wife now completed the circuit of eye and at last brought her vision to bear on her daughter.

"Oh, Winona," she said, the name shading away in a fervent sigh. "Oh." She threw a loose wrist towards the nearest wall, presumably to indicate just everything. "It's certainly *you*, every inch of it."

"Thank you," said Winona, who, Reinhart could have sworn, was turning pigeon-toed and concave-chested before his eyes.

His command applied to them both: "Sit down."

But Genevieve, as he might have known, turned suddenly and walked to the windows at the far end of the room, those which overlooked the river. For an instant he couldn't remember whom this action reminded him of, and then he could: Grace Greenwood. But one thing about Gen: she had never seemed dykey. You could say that for her.

Reinhart suddenly remembered the children.

"Where'd the boys go?"

"To take a nap," said Winona. "They were all tuckered out."

Reinhart asked: "What did that cost you?"

Genevieve whirled suddenly and came back. She pointed a finger at Reinhart. "The security in this building leaves something to be desired. I walked right in past Stepin Fetchit. I could have been a criminal."

"He could see you were harmless," said Reinhart, knowing she would hate to hear that.

Genevieve exposed her front teeth in a snarl, but it was a parody, and she seemingly remained in her good mood. "I suppose you're wondering why I came here?" She took a seat at the other end of the couch from Winona and leaned back against the cushions. "Call it pride."

"Pride?" Reinhart hospitably gave her the expected cue: she was after all a guest in this house.

"I didn't handle myself too well the last time you saw me." She stared at him. "But who among us is always at the top of his form?" Her grin turned dirty. "I can mention certain episodes that would scarcely be flattering to you!" And for only the second time since entering did she look at Winona. "And you too, God knows. Don't get me started."

"Genevieve." Reinhart spoke in quiet menace.

"O.K.! O.K.!" She crossed her legs and leaned forward over her knees. "I came to say good-bye."

This time it was Winona who did the courteous thing. "Where are you headed, Mother?"

"*California,*" Genevieve said decisively, slapping her top knee as she leaned back. "I should have done that long ago, but the time never seemed ripe. But now's the moment. Oh, I know it."

Reinhart stood up. "I'm sorry, Genevieve. Where are my manners? Would you like a cup of coffee or a drink?"

"Carl, did you hear me? I'm getting out of your hair for good." Genevieve spoke vivaciously, uncrossing and spreading her legs in an almost indecent movement even though she was wearing slacks. "I'm remarrying."

Winona stood up. "If you'll both excuse me . . ."

"No, Winona, I won't," said Reinhart. "I have some things to talk over with you when your mother leaves."

His daughter sat down.

His ex-wife shrugged and said: "I can take a hint. I just wanted you to know that I'm riding high again."

Reinhart stood up. "So it would seem, Genevieve. No doubt your prospective husband is a wealthy and powerful business- or professional man."

"You don't believe me, do you, Carl?"

Reinhart said sincerely: "I shouldn't have said that, Genevieve. I apologize. The fact is that it's none of my business."

She rose from the couch. "You tell her she can come home now."

"You mean Mercer?"

"Yeah, the society girl." Genevieve snorted and turned to her daughter. "Good-bye, Winona. Be sure to let me know when *you* meet Mister Right. I'll come back for the wedding with bells on!"

Reinhart snapped his fingers. "I'll bet you're going to San Francisco. Isn't that where your pansy brother Kenworthy has lived for years?"

Genevieve looked stoically at the floor, then flung her head up sharply. This had been a gesture of her father's. "I know you think you've given me a devastating shot," she said. "But I didn't come over here for petty bickering." She put her hands on her hips. "Let me put it to you straight: I *have* got an opportunity out there, but I'll admit I'm strapped at this moment. I need the price of the fare —one-way only, I assure you."

Winona went to the sideboard and opened the drawer in which she kept the big flat checkbook used to pay the household bills.

"That's to Los Angeles," Genevieve said. "And better add enough for cab fare. That airport is supposed to be miles from town."

Reinhart said: "Just a minute, Winona." He asked Genevieve: "She just the other night gave Blaine a sizable sum that was supposed to be spent on you. Is that all gone already?"

"Oh, God, Daddy," wailed Winona. "Let's not have a scene." She opened the checkbook and groped in the drawer for a pen.

"I'm just trying to establish the truth," said Reinhart.

Genevieve said: "It seems to me that's your lifelong complaint. It ought to begin to occur to you that life is just a collection of stories from all points of self-interest."

Winona ripped the check from the book, folded it in two, and gave it to her mother.

Genevieve said defiantly to Reinhart: "You expect me to unfold it and examine it, don't you? You haven't ever thought I had any class."

This was a phony attack. From the first it had been Genevieve who was the snob.

"If you say so," was the best he could come up with. Besides, he was longing for her departure.

She stood up. "Well, now you can all rest easy. I'm leaving for good. You won't see me again."

"Mother . . ." Winona murmured feebly.

"Good-bye, Genevieve," said Reinhart. Staring at her, he began to walk towards the door.

His ex-wife looked stubborn for a moment, but then she shrugged and followed him. At the door she took a kind of stand.

"I caught you on TV, Carl. You have a lot of nerve, I'll say that for you."

Reinhart opened the door.

"If you could of found that kind of gall years ago you might have made something of yourself. What a con artist you are! Remember Claude Humbold? He couldn't hold a candle to you. Cooking! What do you know about food aside from being a glutton?"

As real-estate salesman for Humbold just after the War, Reinhart had met Gen for the first time. She was Claude's secretary.

She went on now: "And that boogie-woogie bugle boy, Splendor Mainwaring. The two of you were inseparable. Frankly I always thought you were a couple of qu—" Without looking back she called: "Oops, sorry, Winona."

Reinhart took her by the shoulders and steered her firmly out into the corridor.

She made no resistance, but when he took his hands off her, she said: "What would happen if I screamed bloody murder? You know you can't push women around any more."

"I'm sure that Winona would cancel payment on the check. For another, I've got a lot of friends in this building, including the owner's daughter."

Genevieve's transitions were breathtaking. She went from the onset of rage through a crooked, perhaps crazed simper, into a broad grin. She threw her open hand at Reinhart. "Congratulations, Carl! Put 'er there!"

He didn't understand this, but he shook with her anyway. "I hope things work out for you in California." He suddenly remembered how frail her shoulders had felt under his fingers. "If they let you out of the hospital you must be in good health."

"I'm all right. I've got plenty of steam left. I just need a break."

"And you've got one waiting in California, right?"

"That's right." Her eyes darkened with suspicion. "Don't you worry about me, fella. Maybe I'll take a leaf from your book and try television. At least I wouldn't be any worse than you. And that's the TV capital of the country, not a tank town like this." She winked at him. "A TV chef, huh? I'll bet you think you're King Shit."

"You have a way with words," said Reinhart. Nevertheless he walked her down to the elevator. He suddenly felt reluctant to let her go. "Hey, Gen," he said, "remember Jack Buxton, the actor? Didn't we see him together lots, in the old days, in the old movies?"

"He kicked off yesterday. Good riddance. He was always a real scumbag. I happen to know, through some friends who are high in Chicago law-enforcement circles, that Buxton was arrested once for molesting an underaged boy, but the charges were dropped because the kid's family didn't want the publicity of a trial."

"Buxton?"

Genevieve wore her tough-guy grin. She spoke in fake sympathy. "Aw, and he was one your idols too, wasn't he?" She shook her head. "My, my. I wonder what that says about you."

"For once, can't you put aside that malicious crap?" he asked. "I saw the man die, yesterday at the TV station. I was the last person to talk with him while he was still conscious. It's really strange to remember that I started seeing him in movies when I was still a boy in high school, forty years ago, and then through the

War. I even saw him at the Onkel-Tom-Kino, a German movie-house in Berlin! And then in the early Fifties, remember, before we got our first television, we'd go to the Regal on Friday nights? After we did have the set of course, we watched all his old films from the Forties and Fifties. I think that by that time his career had faded . . ."

"Jesus Christ," Genevieve said in contempt, *"who cares?* He was a forgotten ham actor and also a pervert, his pictures were stupid garbage, and if he suddenly dropped dead, it was probably as a result of an overdose of drugs."

"I wasn't really thinking of him personally. I was thinking really of the recent past in what?—entertainment, publicity, or whatever: that funny illusionary plane of existence which one is in when watching TV or movies, where a Jack Buxton is a recognizable figure. It's a shock to have it proved, and in a brutal way, that there is a real man who has served as a pretext for an image which consists of impulses of light."

Genevieve punched the button for the elevator. The doors opened immediately: the car had been waiting. She said: "You haven't changed. You've never learned: if you're going to be an ass-kisser, then you ought to at least kiss the asses of winners."

She gave him the cocky World War II salute that in fact Buxton had specialized in cinematically. Was this a conscious parody or coincidence?

"Good-bye, Genevieve."

"So long, sucker." She stepped into the elevator and the doors closed behind her.

Reinhart stood in position for a moment. Despite his relief at any departure of hers nowadays, he felt as though it were a historic occasion, marking the end of something that should be ended.

He returned to Winona. Already she seemed distracted by other matters.

"Do you think that Genevieve alone is to be blamed for the trouble between Blaine and Mercer?"

"Well, it's a theory." Winona frowned. "I wonder if the boys are asleep. Because if they aren't, I want to go to my room and get something."

Reinhart spoke from experience. "No, it's the other way around:

you should go in if they *are* napping and stay out if not. Sleeping kids aren't bothered by intrusions, but they tend to obstruct you when awake." Apropos of nothing he asked: "Winona, you know our neighbor Edie Mulhouse, well—"

"That creep. Has she come around looking for me?"

"She's not so bad," said Reinhart, feeling, with this wan defense, like a traitor. "Did you know she's the daughter of the owner?"

"The owner of what?"

"This apartment house. You know, the Mulhouse Corporation."

Winona shrugged indifferently. "If you say so. Excuse me, Daddy, I think I'll just check on the boys, according to your theory." She went down the hall.

Reinhart went to the kitchen. His larder needed replenishment. He began to draw up a grocery list, but heard Winona's good-bye shout from the door. This seemed rude of her. He came out.

"You're not leaving already?"

She put the suitcase down. "I really have to . . . You were sure right about the boys: they didn't even wake up when I got this off the high shelf and dropped it."

"I wish you would ask me to do things like that," Reinhart chided. He looked at the suitcase, and then at her. "Have you made your permanent plans yet? Of course, at the moment Mercer and the boys are still here."

"You mean, will I be coming back?" She smiled in a fashion that was meant to be helpful but looked uneasy. "Gee, Daddy . . ."

"I'm not trying to pry, believe me."

"I know you're not. . . . It's just that . . ."

Reinhart picked up the suitcase. It felt empty, but then women's clothes weighed nothing. "I'll go down to the car with you. By the way, I still have your Cougar. Do you need it?"

Winona shrugged. "Not really, and you do."

As they went along the hall he asked about Grace. "I heard she was under the weather. Is that true? Because I have a couple of matters to discuss with her."

"She's fine," Winona said quickly. "I'll remind her to call you."

"She *is* at home, then? I don't want to disturb her. I can wait till she's back at the office."

"She'll call you," Winona said firmly.

They went silently down in the elevator, and then, past a gravely smiling Andrew, out to the front walk. Winona led her father down the street a way and stopped at a glistening vehicle. Reinhart had not kept up on the latest makes of cars in recent years, but there was no mistaking a Mercedes. This one was colored beige. Winona unlocked the trunk. The interior was a kind of handsome little living room.

"A rich dwarf could make his home in there," he joked as he put the suitcase therein. "Grace just buy this heap? She got rid of her Imperial?"

Winona smirked uncomfortably. "I miss you, Daddy." She kissed his cheek, got into the gleaming car, which was obviously brand new, and drove away.

The telephone was ringing as Reinhart returned to the apartment. He took the instrument just inside the door.

"This is Blaine. Put Mercer on the line."

"Blaine! God Almighty, you had us worried. Where have you been?"

"I asked if Mercer was there." Same old Blaine.

"Well, she and the boys have been staying here, but she's not in at the moment."

"When did she leave? How long has she been gone?"

"That I can't tell you, Blaine. She was here this morning when I left, at about eleven. I got home I guess an hour ago."

"You were out all that time?" Blaine asked in outrage. "Were the boys home alone?"

As usual Reinhart was stung. "For God's sake, you vanish for three days without a trace, abandoning your wife and kids, and then you have the nerve—"

"Are you senile? Vanish? I've been out of town on business, but I've called her every day. I called earlier this afternoon, but nobody answered."

"I was here all last night," said Reinhart. "The phone never rang."

"I talked to her in the afternoon!"

"Where are you now, Blaine?"

"At home. I just got back from Detroit. I took the night plane the other evening after seeing you and Winona."

"Why don't you come over here now? Your life is your own business, but I seem to have become involved in this part of it. I want a better understanding than I have." His son remained silent. "Blaine, did you hear me?"

"All right," Blaine said sullenly. "I'll come."

"All right, then. Maybe Mercer will have returned by that time." But Reinhart spoke this into a dead wire: his son had hung up in his usual graceless style.

Reinhart had not had the heart today to so much as look into the bedroom currently being used by Mercer, and before going out that morning he had shaved, etc., in Winona's bathroom, the one at present assigned to the two small boys, who were neater than their mother.

Now however, distracted, he went for a pee in his own bathroom, with its wastecan overflowing with those female items of volume but no substance, such as wadded Kleenexes, discarded cotton balls, ex-tampon tubes. He washed his hands, planning to carry them wet to the kitchen and dry them on paper towels: none of cloth was available. If Mercer had showered today, she perforce used one from the heap of soaked terry-cloth on the floor between the toilet and the wall—unless of course she simply swathed her wet body in his thirsty-fabric bathrobe, which she had commandeered on arrival and never yet surrendered.

He shook the excess water from his fingers and glanced briefly at his face in the mirror. A note was Scotch-taped to the glass.

> *"Dad"*—
> *I had to go away—can you run boys home—or wait*
> *til B. gets in and hell do it.*
>
> > *sincerly,*
> > M.

When Blaine arrived, a half hour or so later, Reinhart assured him that the boys, still napping, were fine, but that Mercer had not yet returned. Meanwhile they might have a conversation in the living room, over a good stiff drink if Blaine would state his pleasure.

His son stared at him, shrugged, marched in, and took one of the modern chairs that faced the couch. He rejected the repeated offer of a drink. He pointed to the sofa. Reinhart hesitated for a moment, and then, deciding this was hardly the moment to resist Blaine's bullying in meaningless matters, took a seat where directed. (He thought he could see a faint stain on the cushions where Mercer had vomited, but that may have been a trick of light; the beige rug showed a blond patch, which was now more or less covered by the coffee table.)

He opened his mouth to speak, and Blaine said: "No."

"But—"

"No, Dad," Blaine said curtly, "you don't know anything about it."

"I just wanted to say about Mercer—"

"I don't want you to say anything about her," said Blaine. "That's what I mean. You don't know what you would be talking about."

"I'd be the first to admit that," Reinhart said. "I don't claim any powers of analysis. Even at close quarters I've found her an enigma."

"Is that all you were going to say?"

"If," said his father, "that's all you want me to say." He would have to seek another means by which to introduce Mercer's note.

Blaine rubbed the right lobe of his nose with a thumb. As a gesture it was out of character. He sighed, lifted both hands, and brought them down on his thighs. He stood up. "I'd better get the boys."

Reinhart put out an arm. "Could you stay for a meal? You just got back from a trip, and your children haven't eaten since lunch at their schools." He rose. "Let me rustle something up."

"I just can't spare the time. Some people are coming in from out of town. I really must get back—"

"Sit down, Blaine," Reinhart said, gesturing. "I can understand how a man will protect his pride, especially from other members of the family, but there comes a time. . . . I'm hardly in a position to score off you. My failings are public knowledge, and your sister has only recently made her confession, though nowadays her ways would not necessarily be called even a weakness. The point is that no human being is without places of sensitivity."

Blaine's sneering smile was not attractive. "Well, thanks, Dad. When I need some help you can be sure I'll apply to you."

Reinhart drew the note from his pocket and handed it over.

Blaine glanced quickly at the message, balled the paper, and thrust it in the pocket of his pin-striped suit-jacket.

"I'm sorry," said Reinhart.

Blaine arched his eyebrows. "For what?"

"Doesn't that mean she's walking out?"

Blaine shook his head. "Certainly not. She had an appointment, that's all. Probably one of her classes. She takes various courses. She did some modern dance, studied playwriting, even went to a class called 'The Police and the Public,' at the Catholic college over in West Hills. I think it's admirable for a person to explore their potentialities."

"I think I really should tell you," Reinhart said, grimacing, "a couple of times recently Mercer turned up over here, somewhat the worse for wear, as if more than drunk. Does she take any kind of medication?"

Blaine looked at him. "She has a full life. She has lots of her own friends. I say, more power to her." He stood up abruptly, wrinkled his nose, sniffed, and spoke. "I really must leave."

"Your mother was here earlier. She got some more money from Winona. Is she really going to California?"

Blaine nodded briskly. "Of course. If she says so. I have never known Mother not to carry things through."

"Same is true of you, Blaine," said Reinhart. "You actually are quite impressive at it."

Blaine turned and marched back to the bedroom to get his sons. Before long he reappeared, followed by two small stragglers, each of whom carried a Matchbox car. Blaine held the one valise that served both boys: the smaller you are, the lighter your travel. In the pocket on the right round of his little jeans-clad butt Toby carried the bandanna given him by his grandfather. It was too big for the pocket, and most of it dangled. When Reinhart came to say good-bye, he snatched at it.

"Somebody's going to steal your tail," he said.

"No, they're not!" Toby cried in his contrary style, but when Reinhart turned to address Parker he saw, from the side of eye, that the senior grandson was furtively tucking the bandanna in.

"Well, Parker, it's been nice having had you on board," said Reinhart, and did not dwell on the ceremony of parting, for a child of that age is like a cat about such matters and won't meet your eye.

He opened the door and told the boys: "Run down and punch the elevator button. The bottom one."

"I know!" said Toby. He got the jump on his brother, but Parker's flying sneakers were close behind.

"But don't get on the elevator until your father gets there!"

"I know!" said Toby.

Reinhart spoke to Blaine. "I really enjoyed having them. I got to know them a little better. They're nice boys, Blaine. Any time I can serve as baby-sitter . . ."

Blaine looked lofty. "Of course a nanny would be the answer." He did not go so far as to assume a British accent, but still, he was a remarkable fellow.

When they had left Reinhart went to gather up the dirty laundry, stuffing to the limit two pillowcases. He took these down to the basement, filled two washers, dropped into the respective slots the requisite coins, and was on his way back to the apartment, there to wait until it was time to return and transfer the wet wash to the dryers, when he encountered Andrew, the doorman, who was just coming off his shift. He hadn't spoken anything beyond the commonplaces to Andrew since the day that Mercer had left the building clad only in a towel. Reinhart had not seen any great reason to bring the man up to date on the subject of his daughter-in-law. Andrew had no doubt seen worse in his years of service.

"Home to supper," he said now, remembering that he himself was all alone this evening.

"Yes, indeed," Andrew said with obvious satisfaction. "I'll say good evening to you, Colonel."

"Say, Andrew," Reinhart said, turning back after they had passed each other. "It was only today that I discovered that the landlord's daughter lives right here in the building." He laughed lightly at his ignorance.

"I expect you mean Edie Mulhouse," said Andrew. "But she is

Edwin Mulhouse's child. He just works as a bookkeeper for his brother Theodore M., who is the one who has the money."

Reinhart looked up and down the basement corridor, seeing no one. "Edie's a very nice girl, but I don't think she's found herself yet."

The doorman maintained an expression that might be seen as benevolently detached, and Reinhart understood it as the mark of the professional.

"Sorry," he said. "I was just thinking out loud, not asking your opinion of a tenant."

He said good night to Andrew. After two more trips down to the laundry room, one to transfer the clothes to the dryer and the second to fetch the load back home, he fell into the kind of dispirit which sometimes even claims a cook, and he made his own supper childishly on a peanut-butter sandwich and a glass of milk.

He was lonely, but it was at least a relief to have his room back. He made up a fresh bed, and after having taken a leisurely shower and dried himself with a fluffy fragrant towel, he put on the television set and inserted himself between the fresh sheets. If he ever made any money, he wanted to get himself one of those remote-control gadgets. As it was, he did not dare to do more than nap fitfully throughout the evening, for fear he would fall into a sound sleep and stay in it till morning. Yet climbing out of bed and going across to extinguish the set was just enough to keep him awake for any subsequent hour.

When finally he had nevertheless cranked up sufficient courage to undertake the mission, at about one A.M., had already swung his feet down onto the bedside rug, the late-late movie came on, starring Jack Buxton.

CHAPTER
18

Reinhart was half asleep when he answered the phone.

"Carl? You're not still in bed?"

He covered the instrument as he cleared his throat. "In fact I am, Grace." Only in recent years would he have had the nerve to make that sort of admission. When younger he would have denied the charge had it been made at five A.M. He squinted at the electric alarm clock on the bedside table. "It's hardly seven thirty."

He had stayed awake last night for the entire Buxton film, for once not the kind of action movie with which the man was usually associated, but a romantic comedy, probably the only one he ever made. It wasn't bad: a kind of hygienic bedroom-farce-cum-mistaken-identity caper, co-starring a cream-faced, retroussé, wry but cheery young actress (who had never been seen again) and featuring a supporting cast of benevolent zanies, the inordinate Slavic concert pianist, the stuttering maître d'hôtel, the effeminate hotel clerk, and the fluttering middle-aged lady wearing a hat and, for some unexplained reason, speaking in an English accent. Movies were better then.

Grace was saying something. Reinhart came back on the line and overrode her voice. "I'm glad you called finally, Grace. I've been trying to get hold of you for several days. First, the TV show went well, I thought. At least so the studio people told me." She tried to recapture his ear at this point, but he said imperiously: "No. Let me finish. Then I found a little café up in the country that serves an extraordinary chili con carne, homemade, made in fact on the premises. I think that Epicon should maybe consider it as a product to can and sell to the public. It's a different concept of the dish from the other canned versions you can buy—your own Pancho Villa brand, for example. And this is an example of the kind of thing that I think Epicon should try to go in the direction of, whether or not this chili works out: namely, the interesting and, if possible, unique product that would deserve the name of gourmet, instead of the line of more or less fake stuff offered at present."

Grace cried: "Carl! I think you were just pretending to sleep just now, weren't you, you sly dog? You've got the jump on me." But she seemed in a good mood: perhaps Winona had trained her to acquire a taste for a certain amount of bullying from anyone named Reinhart. "Listen for a moment, please! The *Eye Opener* folks are looking for you."

"You mean the TV show?"

"Sure! This is a comedy of errors. You're not listed in the book—"

"That's because of Winona," said Reinhart. "It's her phone, really, not mine."

"And that wouldn't have mattered ordinarily, because they could have called me for the number, but in point of fact I was laid up for a day or so and not in the kind of communication with the office that I usually maintain."

"I hope you have fully recovered," Reinhart said, in a ritualistic expression.

Grace went on: "I had neglected to put your number on my wheel, so my secretary couldn't help—"

"Yes, Grace. Go on." The fact was that his "employment" had been merely her private project, a feature of the cajolery of Winona. "But what did they want?"

"Only to say that you were sensational, old boy!"

"Pardon?"

"You were the hit of the show, Carl, and they got tons of calls and letters asking for more. All raves, buddy."

"Is that right?"

"It's your image, Carl: knowledgeable, but all wool and a yard wide. You're plain folks. You don't talk down to anybody, but you

have your specialty down cold. That's what they're saying over at
Channel Five! See, when it comes to food, everybody's got to eat.
You become too partisan about a certain kind, though, you lose a
lot of people, or if you get too fancy-pants. On the other hand, as
a nation we've passed beyond the simple meat-and-potatoes
phase. Well, that was my idea in bringing your expertise into
Epicon in some way, except that for a little while I couldn't figure
out just the right way to maximize what either one of us, or the
firm, would get from it—"

"Did they, the people at the *Eye Opener Show,* have any plans
to put me on again?"

"That's the whole point, mister! They want to give you a regular
daily spot to cook up something on the air! You're on the threshold
of stardom, Carl. Now here's our idea—mine, just now, but the rest
of the board will go along with me, I can promise you that. To have
our own man on television every day, who would turn that down?"

"You mean Epicon will sponsor me?"

"That's the most popular of the wake-up shows in the local
markets, outdrawing even the network programs of the same
type. They get a damned stiff commercial rate, but hell, you'll use
our food products, clearly marked, and I'm getting us into cookware these days. Did you use that copper-clad fry pan I sent over
to the studio the other day? Unfortunately I couldn't catch the
show."

"That skillet was junk, Grace. The copper's just for aesthetics:
so thin it looks as if applied with a paintbrush. That's the kind of
thing I disapprove of, along with bottled hollandaise sauce." He
got out of bed. "And if I do this show, I won't be bound by an
obligation to use anything Epicon sells. Most of your line is crap,
Grace, whether you know it or not."

"Come on, Carl," said Grace, with no diminution of enthusiasm.
"I don't mean for a minute that you would be standing by with
your finger in your ear while everybody else collected the bucks.
You'd be an integral part of it, on a percentage of the increase in
sales, et cetera. We wouldn't be asking you to do charity work, big
fellow."

Her style was remarkably reminiscent of several male con men
with whom Reinhart had been associated in past commercial ventures; beginning with Claude Humbold the frenetic realtor in

whose office, so many years before, he had met Genevieve. A practice of them all had been to talk money incessantly while never delivering a cent.

"Apparently that's what I've been doing thus far, Grace."

"Now, Carl, you know I've been under the weather. I'm back now and full of beans. You'll be paid well for these one or two little things, of course, but what I'm talking now is big bucks."

"I'll have to speak to the *Eye Opener* people first."

"I think we ought to make our deal before you go to them," Grace said. "I really do, Carl. I don't want to lean on you, but after all it really was me who saw your potential. As I recall, you practically had to be dragged out of your home kitchen. I mean, if you're going to make a *career* of it, don't you think I should get a *little* credit?"

"It's true that at one time I would have thought that way," said Reinhart. "But now I don't." And as if that were not blunt enough, he added: "You've got enough from me. Think about my chili suggestion. I can always take it elsewhere."

Grace whistled low and said: "I'll tell Win she's a chip off the old block. Don't go away mad, Carl. I think we can do business. If you insist, though, call Billy Burchenal at Five. He's the producer of *Eye Opener.* He'll be at his office till noon." She gave the number.

Reinhart took his pajamas off and nakedly crossed the hall to the bathroom, having learned that trick from Mercer. But it *was* one of the advantages in living alone. After showering, he had some coffee and toast. He should have been ravenous the morning after dining on peanut butter, but he was too excited to be hungry.

At last the time reached a decent hour to call Burchenal, he hoped.

The producer answered his own line, perhaps because it was Saturday.

"My name is Carl Reinhart. I was supposed—"

"Carl, hi. You're a hard man to find. Could you possibly zoom over here this morning, say by eleven, and we can get this deal wrapped?"

Reinhart chuckled to relieve his nervousness. "You don't waste time, do you, Mr. Burchenal?"

" 'Burch,' please. Sixth floor, six-oh-two. I'll give your name to Security downstairs." He hung up.

A quarter-hour later Winona called her father.

"Daddy, you're going on TV? Isn't that great?" She giggled.

"It might be," said Reinhart. It helped to have someone else's enthusiasm to play off. "I don't know, though. I'm not a professional cook, let alone a performer." He waited for and got Winona's loving protests. "We'll see. I haven't talked to them yet. I'm going over there this morning."

"That reminds me," said Winona. "This is a thing I know something about. You've got to get yourself an agent to do the negotiating of the deal."

"Oh, yeah?"

"A show-business person, though, not the kind of agency I have, which is for models."

"Shouldn't I wait until I get a little farther along in my career —if in fact I have a TV career?" Yet this talk was thrilling to him.

"Noo," his daughter said forcefully. "*Now* is the time to set the pattern: you wanna talk turkey from the beginning. Otherwise they'll try to screw you."

Reinhart wet his lips. "Really, Winona . . ."

"Sorry, Dad. That just slipped out."

"Huh? Oh. No, I meant, gee, the whole idea of my being a television performer is so startling if I think about it, that I'd probably do it for a while for no payment whatever." He did not add that he had performed a few jobs for Grace in that fashion, including even one TV appearance. "Let me just go and talk to the producer first and hear his proposition. I'll consult with you on the deal I'm offered, I promise."

"Some of the models here have done some acting work. One of them has a small part in *Song of Norway* at the dinner theater in the Lemburg Mall."

"Jack Buxton was in that, wasn't he? The actor who died the other day?"

"Gee, I couldn't say," said Winona.

"Didn't we ever watch him together in old movies on TV when you were a kid?" Reinhart asked, softening in nostalgia. "We had some good times, didn't we, baby? Remember the popcorn I used to rush out to make at commercials? And those enormous Dagwood sandwiches we'd eat?"

Winona took in air. "I can't even listen to that kind of talk without going up one size." She sighed out. "I gave up a lot for my career."

"Is that right? You mean you still have to discipline yourself?" He couldn't believe it; she was sweetly trying to make him feel good. He adored his daughter. He changed the subject. "Don't tell me you are working today too."

"Not me," said she. "Grace went to her office, but I'm still in bed."

He regretted having asked the question, but within a trice recovered when Winona added: "My room is practically soundproof, and anyway you know what a heavy sleeper I am. I didn't hear her go out, but she just called me now with the good news."

"Blaine came over not long after you were here yesterday and got the boys," said Reinhart. "He refuses to acknowledge that anything is wrong with Mercer. What can I do? I don't want to interfere, but I'm worried about the boys' being neglected."

Winona cleared her throat. "I've talked this thing over with Grace." She waited for his objection: he understood that, but none would be forthcoming. Did not Grace by now have the status of an in-law?

"And?"

"First, the shrink I told you about is a prerequisite. Don't blame me, Dad! I didn't say it!"

"Look, Winona, I'm not against anything that works."

"Then Grace thinks she might find something for her at Epicon."

"A job?"

"Maybe part-time anyway."

"You know, that's a damned fine idea," Reinhart said. He saw no reason to add that it would probably be unpaid unless Mercer spoke up. The fact was that he did think it a splendid thing to try on for size: his daughter-in-law *was* a college graduate after all, which was more than he could say for himself. Given a certain kind of employment, she might even learn to spell most common words.

"Do you miss me, Daddy?"

"You know I do. But I also recognize that this is a transitional time, Winona. Besides, we probably know all there is to know about each other at close quarters. Now there's a whole new perspective for us both, looking back and forth across town."

"Who can say where you might be living a year from now if this TV thing pays off as I think it might? Heck, you might be picked up by one of the big networks and go to New York or the Coast."

"I'm trying not to have delusions of grandeur," said her father. "I used to be addicted to such fantasies while not bothering to see whether there was any solid ground beneath me when I came down. No, Winona, I'm the sort of guy who does better by looking at the eggs in hand rather than at the soufflé to come. I'm a cook and not a waiter: I'm better at making things and letting someone else take over from there. I'm going to try to remember that if I do get on TV regularly, and keep from being too much of a ham."

"I beg to differ with you, Dad!" Winona protested. "I think I know something about an allied field. Modeling after all is performing too. You have to have *presence.* You can't think first of what would be your natural good taste. I worry only that you might be too modest!"

"My, oh, my," said Reinhart, "but aren't we anticipating?"

After some endearments he hung up. He had used the phone more in the current week than in the previous twelvemonth. No doubt the practice would continue if he went into show biz. He must cultivate the quick, sure style of Billy Burchenal. . . .

Who, an hour later, turned out to be a tall thin man of indeterminate age: i.e., his tight, curly hair was very light gray, yet his face, with a synthetic-looking orangey tan (but which must have been real, for why would a producer wear make-up?), looked hardly more than thirty-five. He wore a tieless blue shirt with epaulets and sat behind a desk that was strangely, but for two telephones, bare. The blue walls of his office, however, were crowded with certificates: awards apparently, citations of merit for public service, and the like.

"Hope you don't mind ruining your Saturday morning," Burchenal said. "I come in then to get a little work done without being interrupted by *that.*" He pointed at the nearer phone. "Brain-work, I mean. I've been sitting here now trying to come up with a name for your spot, a catchy name for Debbie and Shep to say. You'd be surprised at how effective a name can be. We've always called it the Cook Spot, but that's when it was the guest chefs. We need something to call attention to your unique contribution."

He had neither shaken Reinhart's hand nor asked him to sit down. Burchenal himself was standing behind his desk.

Reinhart said: "You know my real first name is not Carl, but Carlo."

"For God's sake," said Burchenal. "That's perfect: *Chef Carlo Cooks.* What a perfect name! It's foreign, but you're all-American in looks. You won't scare anybody. That's what the viewers loved about you the other day—show you the letters if my secretary were here—you made it clear, and you made it look easy. They thank you for that. They know it isn't really easy, but they are grateful to you for letting them lie to themselves. This can be a big first step for you, Carlo. There's a tremendous turnover here. Faces change week by week. Most of them go on to bigger things. We're monitored incessantly by the big networks. Despite what you might hear, the youngsters are a drug on the market. An older personality, who is furthermore a new face, can attract! There's no doubt about it."

Burchenal's style in person was notably different from his speedy, bare-details manner on the phone. Suddenly he made a humorless smile and flattened both hands on the desk top. "Now what we can pay, with a restricted budget of the kind we have, is —we don't get prime-time commercial money, obviously, and the craft unions are ferocious. I mean, Carlo, you have to revise downward any idea of getting rich that early in the morning." He ran a finger under his nose and looked sternly at Reinhart, this time meeting his eyes, though actually looking through them. "We can pay fifty per spot, and we'll give you a spot every day unless exceptional circumstances arise: you know, like the Pope coming to town and we get him exclusively, or something."

Reinhart grunted.

Burchenal said: "I talked to Greenwood this morning. I'm afraid nowadays you can't get away with the kind of blatant promotion she would like, for example using a lot of things that are boldly labeled with trade names, and if the spot becomes a permanent feature, you'll have to sever your official connection with Epicon: we can leave that in the gray area to begin with. We'll see how things go."

"Then I'll be only trying out at first?"

Burchenal showed his palms. "That's true of everybody, including me. No, I'm *with* you, Carlo, all the way, but think of life: nobody lives forever. That's also true, in condensed form, of television. I think you've got tremendous potential, but I have to be careful. We'll try you for a couple of weeks to start, O.K.?" Now and only now did he sit down.

"My daughter told me to get an agent before I agreed to anything," said Reinhart. He half expected Burchenal to be offended by this statement, and added, apologetically: "She's a professional model."

But the producer nodded in agreement. "That's essential. You also will have to join AFTRA."

"The performers' union? Gosh."

Burchenal stood up again and leaned across the desk to offer a handshake. "I hope to see your man on Monday then. But can I assume meanwhile that we have a deal in spirit?"

Reinhart shook with him.

The producer said: "I've got a personal motive in all this: the lady I live with could use a few cooking lessons. Jesus! She can burn water."

"Then take a turn at the stove yourself," said Reinhart. "You'd probably amaze yourself. It's a thrill when something turns out well."

Burchenal squinted at him. "Cooking as therapy?"

"I don't care much for the term. Having the natural need and the ability to make something doesn't have to be justified. Of all the things that have been said to be exclusively human—thinking, which can't be proved one way or the other; use of tools, but doesn't a simple-minded chicken make a tool of the gravel he takes into his crop?; laughing, but people who have owned pets for many years swear their furry friends can grin at those who can see —of all the activities of human beings, there is one thing that they alone, in all the world, do, and that is: cook the food they eat."

Burchenal said: "Carlo, you're a philosopher."

"Naw," said Reinhart. "I'm better than that! I'm a cook."

Burchenal repeated that he wanted to see Reinhart's agent on Monday and predicted that *Chef Carlo Cooks* would begin a week later.

When Reinhart got back to the apartment house, he stopped off in the lobby to collect the mail, if any. The box yielded a utility bill and a circular announcing the opening of still another supermarket in yet another local shopping mall. In the past he had been wont to study the latter sort of announcement for bargains in short ribs, pork shoulder, Florida grapefruit, etc., and would tear out the redeemable coupons, with an eye to saving a few pennies for Winona—though if she caught him at this practice, she would fondly denounce him for it.

Dammit, he would miss his daughter, with whom he had lived for all her twenty-five years on earth!

He boarded the elevator. As the doors closed he lowered the hand which held the mail, and a blue envelope slipped from a fold in the supermarket circular which had concealed it and fell to the floor of the car. It was addressed to him and its stamp had been cancelled yesterday. But by now the elevator had reached the fourth floor. He went into the apartment, threw the bill and the circular on the telephone table, and, strolling through the living room to the window that looked down on the river, opened the blue envelope with his thumbnail.

> *Dear Mr. Reinhart* [he read],
>
> *First, can you forgive me for not having the courage to make this apology either in person or on the telephone? Notice that I am apologizing for even the manner of my apology, which is a compounding of my habitual style, which is boring even to me, and what must it be to anyone else?*
>
> *I am an utter and contemptible fraud. I am not the daughter of the owner of this house. I work at a dreary job of no distinction, and otherwise I read a lot. I hardly ever drink anything containing alcohol. Therefore it would not be strange that several glasses*

of beer would make me obnoxious. But what is hu-
miliating to remember is that at the time of my
prevarication I had had nothing whatever to drink.

I don't know how to atone for my conduct this
afternoon except by promising to avoid you in fu-
ture. I am not being false when I say you are the
finest man I have ever known and that I shall remain
in your debt.

Yours respectfully,
EDITH MULHOUSE

This was written in black ink on the blue paper, in a fastidious,
yet graceful hand.

Reinhart refolded the letter and put it on the coffee table. He
went to his liquor cabinet. Champagne was the drink of celebration, but he had none at hand. Looking through the bottles, he
came upon the good bourbon he had bought for Grace, which had
gone untouched that day, only two weeks before, when she had
come for brunch. Could anything be more appropriate for him to
drink now than two fingers of Jim Beam? Did he not owe all his
success to his daughter's lover? He brought a tumbler and some
ice from the kitchen.

During Reinhart's lifetime the world had changed so thoroughly
that were a Rip Van Winkle to have awakened after a sleep of any
twenty years he would be able to make use of none of the experiences, convictions, or even faculties in his possession at the moment he shut his eyes.

While sipping the bourbon, slumped on the couch, shoes off and
stockinged feet propped on the coffee table, he began to get hungry, this time for a very particular and celestially simple menu: red
meat, yellow sauce, golden potatoes, green vegetable, red wine.
The best way to get this right was to make it oneself: top round
of beef, sauce béarnaise, julienne potatoes, undercooked green
beans, and as big a Burgundy as you had the money to buy. A
chunk or hunk of meat, to be sliced thin and served in overlapping
strips napped with sauce, and not an individual steak to be attacked whole. But maybe rather Bordelaise sauce? But that would
require shallots, if you could find them, and a marrow bone, and

he had forgotten whether he still had on hand, in the frozen state, a supply of the jellified essence of beef stock called *demi-glacé*, which he liked to use in the brown sauces. The green beans should be left whole except for the tips and plunged into as large a volume of boiling water as could be managed, taken out when still crunchy . . .

He picked up Edie's letter and reread it. Naw: he remembered her in the supermarket. He had better go shopping alone.

CHAPTER
19

Next morning Reinhart felt an urge to acknowledge with grati-
tude that rise in his fortunes that could not be narrowly ascribed
to Grace Greenwood, that part which was divine or at any rate not
rational—for example, Buxton's collapse could not have been fore-
seen—and not belonging to a sensible faith which offered graven
images for this purpose, e.g., a Golden Calf, he turned towards the
humanitarian effort.

Unless crops could be sown and brought to harvest in a fortnight, it was unlikely that Brother Valentine's flock at Paradise
Farm had any more to eat now than when Reinhart and Blaine
had made their visit.

Reinhart now got out the strip of brown paper from his wallet
and dialed the out-of-town number.

"Center Café!"

"Marge? Carl Reinhart—I had your chili the day before yesterday?"

"My God," shouted Marge. "I never thought I'd really hear from
you."

"Here I am. I'm going to be on morning TV starting in a week."

"I'll sure be watching, if you tell me when and where."

"Sure," said Reinhart, "and I'm proceeding with the idea about
marketing the chili. But what I'm calling about at the moment is,
do you suppose you could make up several gallons of the chili by
say eleven this morning? Along with an appropriate amount of the
pinto beans and rice?"

"It's already simmering," said Marge. "Boy, you must *really* like that stuff."

"Oh, the order will be take-out. I guess I'd better organize some big containers. I doubt that you keep any gallon-size on hand, do you?"

"I'll have my husband pick up some at the Kentucky Fried Chicken in the mall."

"The police chief?"

"He'll run them over in the cruiser, so don't you bother."

In the basement garage Reinhart saw Edie's yellow Gremlin in her slot across the way. As it happened, last night he had cooked and eaten his celebratory dinner alone. He had phoned her several times throughout the early evening, but there was no answer. He had an impulse now to slip a friendly note under her windshield wiper, but decided against doing so lest the look of the folded paper, as she approached the car, give her a fright. Complaint? Obscene letter?

When Reinhart arrived in Brockville the main street was somewhat busier than it had been on his earlier visit. Persons were coming and going at the delicatessen, and only one parking space offered itself in front of the Center Café. Four vehicles were at the curb in that block, two of them pickup trucks. Sunday was an active time out here.

Inside the restaurant were six or eight male customers, most of them at the counter, though two heavy-set middle-aged men in suits and ties were having a solemn and what might even be seen as a conspiratorial discussion in the remotest of the booths: a romantic interpretation might present this as skulduggery-hatching by two provincial politicians.

Marge was serving a hot sandwich to a muscular young fellow across the back of whose chino shirt some trade name was embroidered in red.

"Looks good," said Reinhart. "Is that roast pork in its own gravy?"

Marge colored slightly when she saw him. "I got your order all ready to go. All's I have to do is fill the buckets with the chili, which I've kept hot on the stove in back, and I got the rice and beans too."

"I thought you might not be open on Sunday," said Reinhart. "But I see you have quite a good business."

"Oh, sure," Marge replied, wiping her hands on a wet cloth she found beneath the counter. "You'd be surprised how many people work on Sunday. I don't get much of the Sunday-dinner family trade that my folks used to have though. Families now head mostly for the fast-food places."

"But I was thinking about you doing everything here yourself. You're open seven days?"

"Close early on Mondays, though," said Marge. "I guess I'm crazy, but it's been a tradition to keep the Center Café open. Maybe that's gonna change soon, though."

"Hey, Marge," said the recent recipient of the hot sandwich, "when do I get my mashed potatoes and applesauce?"

"Lenny, you're too heavy as it is," said Marge, shrugging an apology to Reinhart. She seized a little bowl and, using a spring-levered ice-cream scoop, filled it with potatoes and then dampened them with more of the gravy, which by its light-brown color suggested it was the real stuff, from an actual pork roast and not a can.

He saw the roast itself, or one of them, on the steam table. "That's fresh ham, isn't it?" he asked Marge.

She was filling another small bowl with what would certainly seem to be, from its spicy fragrance and coarse texture, home-made applesauce. "These bums needn't think they're getting loin for these prices."

Lenny, tucking into his sandwich with a fork, smirked at this jibe. A name was embroidered over his left pocket: interestingly enough, it was not "Lenny," but rather "Bill."

Reinhart said: "They're lucky. Loin doesn't have nearly as much flavor." He followed Marge, on her beckon, through the swinging doors into the large old kitchen: a very clean and even spacious place. A bony man of indeterminate age, aproned and with sleeves rolled high, was washing dishes at some sinks on the far wall. Nearer was an enormous stove in black metal trimmed in shining steel—with none of the white porcelain of home appliances: this was the real thing.

"French chefs call their stove a 'piano,' " said Reinhart. "It must be a thrill to play a tune on that one."

"A lot of folks would think it's plain hard work," said Marge, "but I enjoy feeding people." She seemed a bit melancholy.

"I see you have some help anyway with the dishwashing."

Marge lumped her tongue on one side of her mouth. "We could use a machine. Bob does a good job, though." She paid the compliment in a loud voice. Then, with Bob's back still turned, she pantomimed to Reinhart the lifting of a bottle and the gulping at its throat.

Two capacious steel stockpots sat on the stove top. Marge took one of the candy-striped Kentucky Fried Chicken tubs from a stack on a vintage butcher's block (with side-slots for an assortment of black-handled, gray-bladed knives in all sizes and a surface that remembered a history of the cleaving of bloody meat: things like this were poetry to Reinhart).

"I'll fill the buckets now, if you are in a hurry to get going. Or would you want to try the fresh-ham special first?" Again he saw her color slightly. She was still a bit shy with the big-city big shot she believed him to be.

Someone out at the counter was shouting for her: "Hey, Marge!"

"To hell with them," said she.

"Get out there and take care of your people," said Reinhart. "I can do this. And I really would like to eat here, but I think I'd better get this chili to where I'm taking it, or they won't have it in time for lunch."

By the time he had ladled three buckets full she was back.

She flipped her thumb at the swinging doors. "My husband's back there right now, in the booth, talking with a gentleman who wants to buy this place."

Reinhart put down his ladle. He felt as though personally wounded. "You don't mean it. Not the Center Café?" It was perhaps an absurd excess of emotion with regard to an obscure eatery he had never seen until the day before yesterday. But it was already precious to him.

"Fact is," said Marge, "I've been losing money for some years. If I raise the prices too much I'll lose the customers I've got. But my costs have more than doubled over the past ten years. I'm not getting any younger. Let's face it, the place has only sentimental value for me."

"'Only'?" Reinhart asked indignantly. "What's worth more?"

"Well, I don't mind telling you, I will miss the old joint." Marge wiped her hands on a damp cloth and yelled in the direction of the dishwasher: "Hey, Bob! I can use some glasses."

He turned, showing a nose like a berry, and said: "Sure, Marge." He began to find tumblers in the soapy liquid before him and rinse them with hot water in the adjoining sink.

"What's this guy want to do with it?" Reinhart asked. "Have his own restaurant?"

"Storage space." Marge got a bucket and began to fill it with the pinto beans and rice from the other stockpot. "Cheaper to buy a place like this than to build something or even, would you believe it, cheaper than renting over a couple of years. I got quite a lot of space all told. There's a storeroom out back, and of course the second floor is empty: used to be an apartment where we all lived when I was a kid. He's got a business over at the mall: home improvement, paint and wallboard and stuff, and has to keep a big inventory."

Reinhart had been thinking. He picked up the ladle again and gestured with it. "Marge, you don't know me at all, and if you did, you might not trust me anyway. But do you suppose you could hold off on this sale for just a little while? I'll tell you why: *maybe* I can come up with a better offer. A week from Monday I'm going on TV regularly, with a spot on the early-morning *Eye Opener Show.* I've been in touch with the Epicon Company, where as I told you I'm a consultant, about the idea to market the chili. If I have any kind of success on television, there's no limit to what might be possible. What occurs to me is something along this line: what if I became involved in the Center Café? Maybe buy into it in some fashion? Become your partner, under an arrangement whereby either one could buy out the other if it didn't work?"

For the third time Marge colored slightly. It occurred to Reinhart that she might have a kind of crush on him, she who was so rough-and-ready with her customers. She was probably not used to this sort of attention. She claimed the ladle from him and began to fill more chicken buckets with chili.

"My gosh," she said. "I just don't know what to say."

"If you could just hold off on making a deal with anybody else for a few days." Reinhart gestured. "Some interesting ideas have begun to occur to me. You said your main business was early in the morning. I'll bet you serve really great traditional Midwestern breakfasts: country sausage, farm-fresh eggs, flapjacks, hashbrown potatoes, ham steak . . ."

Marge was nodding shyly. "I serve a nice oatmeal in wintertime, with cream and brown sugar, and usually I get a chance to make my own doughnuts and coffee cake."

Reinhart sighed. "Generally nowadays the last place you can find real food is in the country!" He accepted a filled bucket from her. "What I have in mind is that you would continue to handle the breakfast for the working guys on the early shift, but maybe on Sundays from say about this time of day until three we might do a brunch together. All your great classic dishes, to which might be added an English mixed grill with kidneys, lamb chops, broiled tomato, and so on, and maybe chicken crepes and some form of seafood, say shrimp quiche or individual soufflés. We might attract people up from the city, especially in the oncoming warm months." He took the bucket to a counter and fitted on the cardboard disc that was its top.

"Maybe we could start like that, and if it went over, we might think of doing something ambitious with dinners—again on the weekends, at least at first. We could have an interesting menu. What I'm thinking of is a simple one, with only a few main dishes. Say two really good down-home American classics, country ham and red-eye gravy and deep-dish chicken potpie, and then maybe I could try my hand at a dish or two, maybe veal Orloff or poached fish in season. No doubt one must always offer steak in addition, but that would make only five or six dishes, with a few appropriate opening courses and a dessert or two."

Marge put down the container she had just filled and leaned against a counter. "Whew," said she. "I'm getting a little dizzy. Things had been getting more and more quiet for years, and then all of a sudden this now."

It looked as if between them sufficient food had been tubbed. Reinhart now fitted the rest of the tops on the buckets.

"This is all speculation as yet," he told her. "But I'm not talking completely through my hat. A big executive in the food business is practically a member of my family, and I really am going to start appearing on television. If you could just hold off for a while on the selling of this wonderful place to some guy for a warehouse, maybe I'll be in a position to talk turkey about an arrangement that would work out for us both."

"It's true," said Marge, "that a lot of trade would come to a restaurant operated by a TV chef." She was grinning as if to herself: he could see that he had successfully corrupted her, whether for good or ill. He wondered whether he was himself corrupt in supposing he might get Grace to back him in this venture.

He and Marge proceeded to quarrel about the bill for the chili, he of course wanting to pay and she refusing to accept his money. Bob the dishwasher suddenly stopped his work and slipped through the door to the outside.

"There," said Marge, mock-reproachfully, "you've got Bob all worried. He'll have to take a drink to calm down."

"But for all my talk," said Reinhart, "it might well be that nothing will come of any of these ideas, and until something positive actually happens I want to pay as I go." He gave her the money and then shook her hard, sinewy hand. "I hope we'll be able to call each other partner one of these days."

Marge gave him a crinkly smile. "I'd like that." She steered him to the door through which Bob had slunk, as if it were more convenient to go out past the garbage cans and along the narrow passage between the buildings to reach his car parked at the curb out front. He suspected that for her own reasons she did not want to attract her husband's attention.

"Where does Bob go for a drink on Sunday?" He had half expected to see the dishwasher lurking, with brown-bagged bottle, in the alleyway.

"Over to the cellar of the delicatessen," said Marge. "It's his sister and brother-in-law run the business."

"Everybody's related to one another in a village like this," Reinhart noted admiringly.

When they got to the car, he unlocked the trunk and put the

buckets therein, arranged in a snug fashion so that they would not be likely to overturn.

"Well," said Marge, "I guess there's certainly enough there for anybody to decide whether it's good."

He realized that she assumed he was taking the chili to be tested by the people at Epicon, and he saw no point in disabusing her: explaining would have taken too long.

"On the other matter," said Reinhart. "If you could just—"

"It's my old man who's so all-fired anxious to sell," Marge said. "You know how it is when you're married—I don't see a ring on your finger, but you must have been married once to have a great big fine-looking daughter like the one you brought the other day." She waited for his response.

Reinhart was sure he had given the last name when introducing Edie, but such was the power of the expected.

"Which one was your husband, out there in the booth? I didn't think either one of those fellows was wearing a uniform."

"The fatter one," said Marge. "He won't wear the chief's uniform on Sunday. He's got a lot of niceties like that." It wasn't clear whether she was being ironic.

"I'll be in touch," said Reinhart.

He drove the twenty miles cross-country to Paradise Farm and parked near the barn, as before. From the trunk he took as many buckets as he could carry in one big embrace and walked around to the rear of the house. Distracted by a need not to spill the chili, he did not digest the fact that no other cars were visible on the property, but as he stood on the little step and shouted helplessly at the closed back doors, screen and wooden, he began to wonder whether anybody was there.

Suddenly a known face appeared behind the glass panel and peered disagreeably out at him: it belonged to Brother Valentine, AKA Raymond Mainwaring. After an instant the hostile expression changed to neutrality, and Raymond turned the key in the lock, opened the inner door, then unfastened the latch on the screen door, and pushed it open.

Reinhart by now was in some worry as to the buckets of food, which had begun to feel uncertain in his grasp. He remembered that they had probably not been made waterproof to hold fried chicken. He rushed to the kitchen table.

"This is lunch," he said, freeing himself of the load. "There are a couple more buckets in the car. I'll go get them."

But Raymond lifted a beige palm and spoke wearily. "Too late."

Again Reinhart had been slow to notice a lack. This time it was people who were missing. Aside from Raymond and himself there was no one in the kitchen.

"Do you mean—?"

"That's exactly what I mean," said Raymond. He pulled a chair away from the table and sat down upon it in slow motion. "Paradise Farm is now a community of one."

Reinhart took a chair for himself. His first thought was selfish: all this chili and rice & beans. But then he asked Raymond what had happened.

"I was on television." Raymond wore an expression that probably was a cruel grin, but he didn't have the right face for it; he merely looked puzzled. "I was investigative-reported." His look turned certifiably peevish. "The world has too many people in it whose profession is to interfere with the plans of others."

"That's probably true. . . . What happened, were you accused of something?"

Raymond tightened the flesh around his eyes. "No, *I'm* clean! But to be investigated is to be guilty in the eyes of some people." He pushed out a bitter chin. "They left, all of them. Either on their own or some relative came and hauled them off. All of a sudden Paradise Farm became a potential Guyana and I was working up to be a Reverend Jim Jones."

"I'm really sorry to hear that," Reinhart said. "The farm sounded like a good project to me as you sketched it out." He looked at all the buckets of food. "Well, you and I can have lunch anyway. How about some chili con carne, beans and rice?"

Raymond winced suspiciously at him. "That wouldn't be your idea of darky food?"

"Come on, Raymond, don't be rude. The other day you told me you didn't have anything to eat here. Now I've brought something, and nobody's here to eat it." Reinhart got up from the table and poked into the wall-hung cabinets and counter drawers until he found two plates and two forks. He opened a couple of the buckets and served them each a hearty portion of beans and rice covered with the chunks of beef in their thick sauce.

"Try this." He put a plate in front of Raymond.

The younger man took a morsel of chili on the end of his fork. He made a face after chewing it briefly, but he did not spit it out. "Where'd you get this? It's certainly not very good."

Reinhart ignored the complaint. "Did the young people too leave because of just the TV thing?" he asked, beginning to eat from his own plate. But the chili wasn't as good today; of course it was tepid.

"There actually weren't any young people as yet," said Raymond. "I misrepresented that situation. I was anticipating. I intended to make an appeal to youth, and I assumed that they would answer it. But the fact is that in the short time we had been under way, I could get only older people, retired persons, and widows. That was one of the things that caused a certain suspicion about my motives, I suppose. It was obvious that the older people couldn't do the heavy work of running a farm, especially since most of them were urban types."

"You know what I forgot to bring?" asked Reinhart. "The beer! Though it *is* Sunday. But I've got connections with a little deli and could have bought some under the counter, I bet."

Raymond looked along his dark nose. "I don't use intoxicants," he said disapprovingly.

"Well, for me water just doesn't do the job with something of this persistent a flavor." Nevertheless he got up and searched the cupboards, without any help from his host, until he found a glass. But when he turned the Cold faucet and then, unrealistically, the Hot, nothing came from either.

Raymond at last said dolefully: "There's a well here, with an electric pump. But in fact the power has been turned off owing to failure to pay the last bill."

"Then," Reinhart said, "it's just as well I didn't try to heat this food. Isn't there anything to drink around here?"

Raymond got up. "There's another well outside, with an old hand pump." He rose and led Reinhart out the door, the latter bringing along the glass.

The warm light and gentle breeze were of the kind that could make failure even worse, Reinhart well knew from personal experience: sometimes good weather was a mockery and rain a balm.

Raymond walked straight and rigid in his denim work-clothes. He was as tall as Reinhart, though more slender; taller than his late father. Behind the barn was an ancient rusty horse trough, with a pump at one end. Raymond seized the long iron lever and began to move it up and down.

Reinhart held his glass at the pump's mouth. "Has this thing been used lately?"

"Once for washing a car."

Reinhart decided that further questioning would be offensive, and therefore, when after much squeaking the water suddenly gushed forth in a rust-colored flow that immediately overwhelmed the waiting tumbler and wet his sleeve to the elbow, he turned as if in a certain disorder owing to the flood, and with his back to Raymond, got rid of the glassful without tasting a drop.

"Thanks," said he, coming around after this sequence was at an end. "What's next for you now, Raymond?"

The young man looked expressionlessly at the dripping pump. "That's the obvious question."

"Do you mind my asking, how did you come to be at this farm? Do you own it or what? Granted, it's none of my business."

Raymond answered in a neutral, noncritical fashion: "You're curious about only the financial arrangements? You have no interest in my beliefs?"

"That's not tr—" Reinhart began, but caught himself. "Yes, I suppose it *is* true. It's too important a subject on which to tell diplomatic lies." He was still holding the water glass and was therefore preoccupied physically with it: funny how you can't find a decent way to get rid of certain things at special times. "My idea of such matters is that they are private. I generally feel a certain disdain, perhaps unfairly, when I hear on TV that some celebrity has been 'born again.' But I think what I dislike is not his faith, which is none of my business, but that he is telling the public about it. But that's a Christian obligation, I suppose." He suddenly appealed to Raymond: "Would you mind if I put your glass down here?" He pointed to the base of the pump. "I'll take it back to the kitchen in a moment."

"The fact is," said Raymond, himself preoccupied, "I always believe in what I stand for. I don't repudiate my basic beliefs of a decade ago, which are not really incompatible with what I believe now. But I seem to have a gift for falling in with persons whose motives will not bear scrutiny. For example, certain of my supposed political comrades were common thugs and are today still serving time for criminal acts for which their ideology was a hypocritical mask." He kicked some dirt and stared into the horse trough. "Leave it to me to walk right into what was really another version of the same thing."

"You don't mean some political movement was in back of Paradise Farm?"

"No," said Raymond, shaking his finely made head. "Some financial movement. What I mean by 'same' is in the lack of moral principle. To the people who handled the money Paradise Farm was only a tax write-off."

Reinhart grasped the handle of the pump and gave it a few experimental thrusts and recoveries; already the water had receded too far to be induced so easily to flow again.

Raymond went on: "Of course I was aware of the situation, but I assumed that I would be allowed to develop the project along the lines I explained to you on your earlier visit, successful but losing money for the early years and thus achieving everyone's purpose. But then eventually being able to pay for itself, at which point the original backers would turn it over to us, having accomplished not only their financial purpose but also having done a good deed as Christians or Jews or humanitarian atheists for that matter."

"There was a change of plans?"

"They got cold feet when that investigative reporter, that black girl, began to sniff around."

"Oh, yes. Molly Moffitt of the Channel Five News Team." Reinhart was now one of her colleagues, in a sense. "I've got some connection with that station. Maybe I could help in some way, anyhow find out just what's going on?"

"Too late for that," said Raymond. "Paradise Farm is finished. This place has been sold. Molly told me that. It's sold to some Arabs. And not just this immediate farm, but a great part of surrounding acreage."

Reinhart dry-pumped a few more times. He was dying of thirst, but didn't want to take a chance on rusty water. "Are we going to see people riding through these fields on camels?"

"I doubt that any actual Arab has ever been here," said Raymond. "They have agents who do all this purchasing, and I doubt that they have any immediate purpose for the land. Molly tells me that they simply buy everything they can."

"Speaking of Channel Five," Reinhart said, "what I should have mentioned is that I have a job there, as of Monday a week. You could leave a message for me there. I hope you keep in touch, Raymond."

The young man looked at him. "My father always spoke well of you."

"I wanted to ask, if you don't mind: is your dad's body still frozen?" How bizarre this question would have sounded to a casual passer-by; but Raymond's father, Reinhart's friend Splendor Mainwaring, had been cryogenically embalmed ten years before.

Raymond's expression was for a moment exquisitely sensitive, and then it returned to the stoical. "I couldn't afford myself to keep up those annual maintenance charges. Furthermore, the belief in bodily resurrection is at odds with my faith. Finally, those people who did the freezing inspired little confidence."

Still, there was something unfortunate, something awful, in—what? Burying the body, cremating it, thus ending all hope, quixotic though it might be, that eventual thawing and revival would take place?

"I understand," said Reinhart. "But it depresses me to—"

"Oh." Raymond was suddenly in tune with him. "Yes, of course, the body is still frozen. It is with others at a scientific facility in southern California, where research in cryonics continues."

Reinhart picked up the glass he had put down. "I'll just take this back indoors."

But Raymond took it from him. Without warning he smiled in a smug way. "I can make a better chili than that."

Reinhart smiled. "You can?"

"Surely. With chocolate."

Reinhart raised an eyebrow.

"Unsweetened, of course," said Raymond. "As in *mole poblano.*"

"That's interesting," Reinhart said. "I think chili con carne is supposed to have been invented in Texas, but it was certainly based on Mexican cuisine, so what you're suggesting makes sense."

"Oh, it's not my own fantasy. It's a standard on the menu at the Ten Gallon Hat. I cooked there for three or four years."

"The restaurant downtown? I've never eaten there." Reinhart was excited. "I've got this project in mind, buying an interest in an old existing small-town kind of restaurant in Brockville and keeping the good old stuff on the menu, but adding terrific things from other cuisines, all fine dishes, nothing fake, but very ambitious when we wanted to be. We could in fact do anything we wanted. There's a wonderful woman who owns it; it's been in her family for years. She'd retain half ownership. I'd want her to. I don't know anything about the restaurant business."

Raymond was not being ignited.

Reinhart suspected why. "Oh," he said, "what I meant was, if this thing gets going, would you like to be associated with it?" Raymond looked somewhat aggrieved. "I don't mean to offend you. What I meant was, if you didn't have immediate plans to start another religious colony."

Raymond shrugged. "I'd like to get back to cooking, in fact. I think it's probably the best profession for someone of my personality. But, frankly, what I don't care for is going in to some nice simple little place in the country and transforming it into a chic eatery designed to attract adulterers and sodomites from the city."

"All God's children have to eat," Reinhart said. "Look here: if I'm not able to work something out, this restaurant is going to be sold to some local businessman for storage space—after forty or fifty years of being open seven days a week. Did you ever hear of the gangster John Dillinger? He ate there!"

"Don't tell me," said Raymond, "you want to put a bronze plaque on his booth, and submachine guns will make up a prominent part of the decor?"

"I think you're ribbing me now, Raymond."

The younger man stared at the barn for a moment. "Is this offer in atonement?"

"Atonement?" Reinhart scowled. "What does that mean? Something about your father?"

Raymond turned his head back. "Something to do with your son."

"Well, what?"

"You don't really know that he was one of the backers of Paradise Farm?"

Reinhart shook his head slowly but with weight. "No, certainly not. But he did say, that time we visited, something about his church being a sponsor. Of course, one must understand that Blaine is a fanatical believer in the religion of money." Suddenly he felt defiant, and he stared at Raymond with spirit. "But am I my son's keeper? After all, did he not suggest that I myself move in here?"

Raymond said: "At that time there was really going to be a Paradise Farm. I don't accuse him of deliberate deceit, and it doesn't seem to be the case that he and his partners broke the law."

"It was just a crappy thing to do," Reinhart said. "No, a downright lousy thing to do. But look here, Raymond, maybe we can get this other project going: Paradise Restaurant: the idea, anyhow. I don't think Marge would want to change the existing name, which is classic: the Center Café. Isn't that great?"

CHAPTER
20

When Reinhart returned from the country and saw the little yellow Gremlin still in place he tried to reach Edie by telephone. He tried several times again throughout the succeeding two hours, but there was no answer. He began to worry about her.

He first went down to the lobby mailboxes to find the number of her apartment and then to the fifth floor, West wing. He had rarely been in that section of the building, which, extending really towards the northwest while the river at this point wended southwestwardly, was to some degree the Other Side of the Tracks.

He found 516W and pushed the button. . . . No response. He drummed upon the metal face of the door.

"God *damn* it," cried a petulant voice within.

That certainly did not sound like Edie. Reinhart shrank in embarrassment: he had obviously got the wrong apartment.

But then the door opened and there, in bathrobe and traditionally toweled hair, stood his friend. On seeing him, Edie gasped and actually began to hurl the door shut in his face. It seemed a reflex action. She caught herself, stepped behind the jamb, and bending her body so that Reinhart could see only her towel-framed face, was probably about to apologize.

But he spoke first: "I've been calling you since last night. At first I thought you were out, but your car's been in the garage all day."

She flushed within the environment of white terry cloth. "Maybe something's wrong with my phone."

Reinhart grinned at her. "You sounded pretty rough just now, when you didn't know who was pounding on the door. I think I have just seen your sweet side." She grew pinker. This was the day when he made the girls blush, but he was not complaining. He decided to go for even more color. "You look very pretty in that outfit."

But this seemed a gaffe. She paled quickly. Obviously he was deficient in eloquence when standing in a corridor and addressing this kind of young lady, though he had been telling the truth. She was a nice big pink girl wrapped in white.

But she was saying solemnly: "Last night I wouldn't have been here, because I was at work."

"On Saturday night?" Reinhart nodded to take the harsh edge off his incredulity. "Where do you work, Edie?"

She answered in that ingenuous or ingenuous-seeming style in which a statement is made a question: "A bowling alley?"

Reinhart said: "Look, I'm sorry to have bothered you. I see you're doing your hair or whatever. I just wanted to check on whether you were—"

"You don't believe me, do you?" she suddenly asked boldly. "I work nights as a cashier in a bowling alley. The pay's good, since it's hard to get people, even men, to work at night. That gives me my days to myself. And my hours are the kind you wouldn't know where they went anyway: five to midnight."

Reinhart shifted from one foot to another. "Well, as I say, I was just trying to get in touch to . . ." It seemed bad taste here to mention her apologetic letter, standing in the hallway, speaking to a young woman wrapped, even unto her head, in terry cloth.

Edie said: "I don't work tonight. Sunday and Monday are my weekend."

"Uh-huh."

"Of course, a lot of bowling goes on on both those days, but I've got to get off sometime."

"That's true," said Reinhart. He was beginning to feel stupid, but he was as yet unable to do anything decisive. "Probably you'll be doing a lot of reading, then."

"Pardon?"

"You mentioned you did a lot of reading."

"Oh. Oh, yes, that's true."

"I used to be more of a reader when I was a young fellow," said he. "I got away from it in later years, I don't really quite know why. Unless you count cookbooks." He exposed the palms of both hands. "When you've lived a long time, you find it hard to explain where the years have gone and what you did in them and why and why not."

Edie lifted her shoulders and let them fall, while smiling sympathetically. Winona too was invariably in sympathy with him, but she was his daughter. There were more differences than similarities. He thought here of Winona because he was trying to make some sense of his interest in Edie.

"I'll tell you why I especially wanted to get in touch with you last night: I wanted to invite you to have dinner with me, to celebrate my getting a regular job on TV."

Her reaction to this was to disappear for a moment back of the door, perhaps to collect herself. After all, she had been the only person in his circle of women, other than Genevieve (who had naturally insulted him on the matter), to have watched his triumph in replacing Jack Buxton, or at least to tell him of it.

When she returned to view her eyes were pink. She thrust a hand out of her robe. "Congratulations."

Her fingers were almost as long as his own and her palm almost as broad, but her hand was virtually weightless. The flesh of women is not as dense; in addition Edie was too shy to insinuate the least movement in her hand; it was up to him to do with it as he wished.

He shook it gently and returned it to its owner. "Thanks. I realize now that you wouldn't have been able to accept the dinner invitation anyhow." He supposed he was smiling foolishly. "I hope you enjoy your day off." He began to leave. He could not explain why, more than four decades too late, he was behaving like a schoolboy.

Edie suddenly spoke in a bell-clear voice. "Why don't we have dinner together tonight?"

Reinhart was released from his strange paralysis. He turned back eagerly—and found, or seemed to find, that Edie had embarrassed herself and vanished behind the door.

He addressed the empty space. At his angle he could see nothing significant through it, and he wanted badly to look at the interior of her apartment. But he did not dare to touch the door. "Last night I was going to cook. But maybe you'd rather go out tonight?" He remembered that in the code that obtained in the time of his young manhood it was considered ipso facto illicit for a woman to be alone with a man in *his* home, though for some reason quite O.K. for them to be together, unchaperoned, in hers. But like so many practices that once seemed preposterous, this one, when viewed from afar, could be seen to have had its use: the establishing of probabilities; a girl who visited a man alone would probably "put out," or in any event not be offended by a "proposition."

Edie came back into view, her hands at her towel. "The thing is," she said firmly, "it's my turn to entertain you."

Reinhart looked down at her slippers. They resembled huge bearpaws and were covered with long synthetic fur.

"All right. Thank you. I like your slippers."

"Do you know what they're called? Abominable Snow Shoes. I'm not kidding!" She was laughing with white teeth. She seemed in perfect health, but that was a routine condition with the young.

"Well," Reinhart said, making a type of bowing movement, "I'll see you later, then?"

"Would seven be O.K.?"

"Perfect." He started away, then turned back. "May I bring something? Wine? It's Sunday, but I always have some on hand."

The suggestion seemed to startle her. "Oh, no. No, thank you."

Reinhart went back to his own apartment. He feared her rejection of the offer meant that he would get no wine with dinner, whatever the dinner might be. Edie knew nothing about food and did not herself drink wine. God! It had been years since Reinhart had eaten a meal he had not himself cooked or at least ordered from a restaurant menu. He really dreaded being at the mercy of someone else's table. . . . That was what happened to you as you grew older: your habits became all-important; you could sleep only in your own bed and watch TV only with the sound set at a certain volume. As a boy, when Reinhart had to surrender his room to a relative and sleep on the living-room sofa he was overjoyed with the sheer novelty of it. So had he been hopeful when as young marrieds he and Genevieve went to eat at someone else's house. He could not remember ever before having been invited to dine at the table of a single girl: such an experience, back in his day and milieu, would have been unique.

What time was it now? . . . Only five o'clock? He wasn't cooking this evening. He had *two hours* to get through! He went to the liquor cabinet and poured a generous measure of Scotch, iced and watered it in the kitchen, and took it to the bedroom. He switched on the television set atop the dresser. . . . A sturdy woman wearing a billed cap was bending a putter. Sunday afternoon and ladies' golf, of course!

He reclined on the bed, nape against headboard, Scotch cradled in two hands at his navel. He watched for a while, but the upholstered bodies no longer had their old appeal. He went to the set and roamed the dial. Tennis would hit the spot today, with younger legs under pleated skirts. This was not a concupiscent taste: he was interested in relative levels of vigor.

But no more female athletes of any sort were available at the moment, which belonged, on one channel—indeed, his own Channel Five—to stock cars speeding around an asphalt oval and on another to two undersized Latin American prizefighters who pounded each other furiously without apparent damage to either. On "public" television a hirsute young chap was talking rapidly to a bald-headed middle-aged man about—by gosh, about the upcoming Jack Buxton Film Festival! . . . But apparently it was not to begin for a while. At the moment what one got was a discussion between these two fellows, who werely oddly paired: the hairy youth spoke like a hoodlum, the bald-headed critic was peevishly effeminate. At the moment the latter was saying: ". . . *really* think that's *true?* Oh, come *off* it." To which the former replied: "Chroo? Of cawss! Wadduhyuh think, I'm loying?"

Reinhart discovered that his Johnnie Walker was missing: a ghost had drained the entire glass while his attention was elsewhere. He returned to the bar and got a refill onto the same, or much the same, ice.

He was restless. He showered again and made an entire change of clothing from the skin out, though he had put everything on fresh that morning. He must make arrangements with a profes-

sional laundry to do his work. As a TV personality he could hardly
be seen trundling his wash down to the basement. The job could
alter his life in many ways. He might be recognized on the street.
One of the local papers had a show-biz gossip column. Could he
ever afford to be seen with Helen Clayton? "Which TV chef is
consorting with an invalid's wife?" Your life is not your own when
you get into the public eye.

A good deal, but by no means all, of these reflections were
ironical: it is amusing to mock oneself when things go well. And
when one has waited so long for success that one has forgotten
what is being awaited, there is a limit to the swelling of one's head.
But he *was* impatient for Monday to come, after all these years,
and therefore while waiting first for sufficient time to pass before
he could go down and eat Edie's probably overdone and surely
wineless meal, he drank more Scotch than he should have, certainly more than he would have if he himself had been cooking.
It anesthetizes the palate, you know (he said to himself in the
bathroom mirror), really belongs in the after-dinner range, an
interesting and worthwhile potation, surely, but its place is post-
prandial.

He winked at his large visage and added: "Listen to the epicure,
who was himself reared on well-done meat and vegetables boiled
to death and served dry. Who when in France as a soldier looked
for whores and not meals. . . . Who, hoohoo, is now drunk for the
first time in many years." Not helplessly. His stride was straight
enough, and when speaking to himself at least, he could not hear
that his tongue was getting stuck behind his teeth.

But his emotions were intensified. Suddenly remembering that
he had nothing to take to Edie, who had spurned his offer of wine,
he decided to go out and find a florist who was open. This was not
the kind of shop normally accessible on Sundays, but the alcohol
evoked from Reinhart a stubborn determination to leave no mall
unturned.

This was a splendid aim, but in point of fact the same spirits had
caused his sense of time to be deranged. It was 6:55 when he
looked at the bedside clock. He brushed his teeth once again, put
on his blazer, checked it insofar as he could for lint (but living
alone, one must forget about a certain area in the back of garments

being worn; Grace could now perform inspection service for Winona, he himself had no one), and left the apartment.

Edie was certainly a conveniently placed friend. He would now have been in no mood to visit someone by car.

He reached her door and pushed the buzzer. She was quick to answer this time. No doubt the Scotch had something to do with his vision, but Edie looked even taller than usual. Before crossing the threshold he tried to figure that out and at last saw that she wore high heels.

"I'm sorry to say," he confessed, "I'm empty-handed."

"Good," said Edie, beckoning him into her home. She wore some kind of soft white blouse and an ankle-length figured skirt. This seemed an occasion for her. She was fairer of hair this evening, and her eyes had . . . whatever. More make-up, certainly, but—

"That's what 'karate' means, incidentally," said Reinhart, interrupting his own process of observation. "In Japanese. *Kara*— 'empty.' *Te*—'hand.' " He smiled into Edie's limpid eyes. "A bit of the useless information I've accumulated throughout the many years of my life." For some reason he was delaying a survey of the apartment, staying just inside the door.

"Won't you come down here?" said Edie, who had gone ahead and now spoke from a slightly lower situation. She was in the living room, which like his own was one step down from the level on which one entered.

Reinhart stepped jauntily down to join her. Half the room, that half towards the large window, was a kind of greenhouse full of standing or hanging plants, which seemed to exude freshness and verdant moisture, as the sun radiates warmth and light. Reinhart's sensibility lacked in the horticultural faculty, and he had never before felt this effect from vegetable life. Nor was Winona, though a deft hand with cut flowers, a grower of plants.

"Now I see what's wrong with my apartment," he said. He went to the window, or at any rate as close as permitted, and looked out through the greenery. The view, especially at this fading time of day, was none too vast, being mostly of an angle of the building, with only a glimpse of the river, as if one were looking illicitly through a chink. Yet living among these plants one would feel no deprivation.

"I wish I knew enough about the subject to discuss it with you," said he, "but I don't think I've tried to grow anything, with the exception of lawn-grass some years back, since the scrawny little tree we used to be given annually on Arbor Day at school—which always died. I've thought about starting some herbs in windowsill pots, but I'm still too shy."

Edie invited him to sit down. Comfortable facilities were available: a sofa upholstered in tan-flecked brown, a chair or two, modern but capacious and genial. He chose the couch, where he could expand in any direction. When he sat down, he was looking across at a long low bookcase, pleasantly variegated with spines in various hues. He thought he might ask Edie what she read, but when he looked for her, she was gone . . . but not far. Back of a counter, at the top of the room, was her kitchen.

She soon returned with a glass of sherry. He could not remember that he had been asked, but perhaps he had. She found a little knee-high table at the end of the couch and brought it near him.

"Are you all right?"

"Me?" asked Reinhart. He smiled at her. "Sit down, why don't you?"

She chose the rust-colored chair.

"Come sit on the couch," Reinhart said. "I want to talk to you like a Dutch uncle, as they used to say. . . . And don't worry that simply because I've had a few drinks I will behave improperly. I have always been what the American lower-middle class thinks of as being a 'gentleman,' which is to say, a prude with respectable young ladies."

Edie smirked at this statement, but she did not blush. She sat down on the couch, at just the right distance from him: not so close as to embarrass, not so far away as to offend. But she sat tentatively, towards the edge of the cushion, as if she might rise. She was now wearing an apron, a merry one, in colorful stripes.

"Ah, you're cooking," said he. "Well, I won't detain you."

"And am I nervous!"

"Please don't be." He started to get up. "Why not let me do it?"

"I want to do it myself," Edie said. "I think I *can* do it, and when I invite a guest, I *should* do it."

This was a new aspect of her, or at any rate one he had previously not given her an opportunity to show. Her manner in her

own domicile was very different from that she displayed when
abroad. And how right she was to feel strength here: it was a warm
and wonderful little cave. The rug was the color of peach pre-
serves. In the embrasure of the window a geranium was blooming
redly: one of the few plants in all the world that Reinhart could
identify offhand. A hanging pot was blossoming in white stars. He
still retained the aftertaste of Scotch, which was not altogether
pleasant, yet he was not really sorry he had drunk so much. He felt
in a vulnerable state, but well protected here.

She returned with one little bowl of small, withered black olives,
the sort that are cured in fragrant olive oil, and another filled with
smoky salted almonds.

When she was back in the kitchen Reinhart called up-room:
"Are you going to tell me what the bill of fare is?"

"Maybe I shouldn't, so that if something doesn't turn out well
I can change it!" She looked up from her work, across the counter.
"Are you ready for more wine?"

"Not yet, thanks."

"Isn't it drinkable?"

"It's superb, a lot better than I can usually afford."

Edie came back. Her apron's stripes included Reinhart's favorite combination of turquoise and navy.

"This is just a delightful apartment," he said. "It makes one feel
good just to sit in it."

"It could be bigger. What you see is all there is, except for the
bathroom of course."

"It's just the right size for a person living alone, I'd say." He
finished his wine but held onto the glass lest she take it and leave
for a moment. "Mine will probably be too big now. You see,
Winona has moved out. She's gone to live with a friend, a woman
friend, and it's high time she came out from under my wing, to tell
you the truth, and lived with someone of her own age, more or
less." He looked at Edie with feeling. "I'm misrepresenting that.
I'm acting as if it's Winona who needed me, rather than what is
true, the other way around: she supported me for a good many
years. I kept house, of course, but she was the one with the career."

"I'm sure you were just biding your time," said Edie. She put out her hand for his wine glass.

He surrendered it. He was becoming aware of a sort of motherly force immanent in her. When she returned, he said: "I confess I had a bit to drink before I came up here. I was nervous on general principles, and then I was feeling a funny reaction to getting the new job, a mixture of elation and maybe megalomania and greed —and most of all, disbelief. But then I remember that I did step in to fill the breach left when Buxton had his heart attack: I did it, off the cuff, ad lib! Yet even that gives me mixed feelings. Maybe I've wasted my life. Maybe I should have been a performer of some kind from the beginning, studied acting or even tap dancing or whatnot."

Edie had not sat down this time. She said, in her new maternal style: "I think you're wrong about wanting to be anything other than you've been." She went back to her work without his feeling that she had left him: that was a true art, but apparently unstudied.

"I hope you're aware," he said, "that it's all I can do to stay out of your kitchen, but I know what goes on in mine and how I hate to be watched." There were times when you just had to plunge your hands in to the wrists, so to speak, or retrieve something edible from the floor or scrape off charrings or mask raggednesses with sauce or garnitures. But if the error had been to put too much salt in solution, you might be in real trouble, though you could try boiling a raw potato in the liquid. Over the years one learned a lot of tricks. These would make nice little bits for the show. Already he was thinking professionally.

> Q. *If by accident some hardboiled eggs got mixed up with uncooked ones, how could you distinguish each from each without breaking any?*
> A. *Simply spin each egg on its side. The cooked one will spin in uniform revolutions, whereas the raw egg will wobble erratically.*

Edie came to him. "Dinner is ready."

He got up and said, face to face: "We're about the same height when you wear those shoes."

"What a relief," said she, "to be able to wear heels without making someone feel lousy."

"You mean men? I thought that had changed nowadays."

"You can't change biology," said Edie. "Most men are bigger than most women. If you're not like most people, then you are in a special situation. You can't just say it isn't true."

She led him to the counter between living room and kitchen. Two places had been set there for a meal, with wooden-handled eating utensils of stainless steel and blue bandannas for napkins. Each setting was on its own island of a straw mat, bound in blue fabric. As Reinhart sat down Edie went behind the counter and with a big wood spoon and fork served spaghetti and sauce, already combined, from an earthenware casserole onto painted plates of similar crockery.

Accepting his, Reinhart noted with approval that it had been prewarmed. He asked her if he might at least pour the Valpolicella, which was already uncorked.

"I see you have a glass for yourself."

She put her own plate onto the counter and came around to the eating side and took a stool. She lifted the glass he had just poured.

"I'm all right now," she said. "I'm drinking wine."

"I didn't mean—"

Edie touched her glass to his. "To your health."

It was a fine and simple and unexpected thing to hear.

"To yours, Edie."

The spaghetti sauce proved to be a rich *ragù bolognese,* a far cry from the scarlet acidity of Naples, made from ground beef and pork, bacon, and chicken livers, simmered in beef stock and white wine. Edie had found the recipe in a book.

"Why," said Reinhart, "this is the best thing of its kind. Did you just happen to have all the ingredients on hand?" It was really a rude question, as he recognized when he had put it. But her transformation from the awkward creature she had hitherto been into this gracious hostess, the accomplished cook, the lovely young woman she was at present, could not be taken as a routine event. Perhaps some of it was due to his altered perception, but if he was drunkenly upgrading her now, he had soberly failed to appreciate her previously.

"Let's just say that I was planning something, for sometime," said she.

Reinhart grinned at her over his wine. The Valpolicella was as pretty on the palate as its name was in the ear.

"Edie, all I know of life tells me you cannot always be as sweet as you have thus far been to me, but I'm shamelessly enjoying it at the moment." He went on in what to him was a logical progression: "I have lived with my daughter all her life, and yet I had no inkling of . . . what shall I call it? Her darker side? If by 'darker' what is meant is not evil but a kind of moral toughness. Winona can be, well, rude of course, but beyond that . . . not exactly cruel —though I suppose she could be that, too, outside my experience —but 'forceful' would probably be an accurate word."

Edie had stopped eating to listen even more attentively than usual.

He asked: "You know her only to chat in the lobby?"

Now she seemed guileless again. "I'd seen her pictures a lot. You know how it is when you see a celebrity, you feel you know them."

"It was awfully arrogant of her, though, on the basis of that slight an acquaintance, to want to borrow your car."

"Oh, I don't think so!" She took a sip from her glass. There was that about her mouth which suggested the curve of a stringed musical instrument.

She went behind the counter.

After a while Reinhart said: "You, Miss Mulhouse, are making a spinach salad with a warm dressing of bacon and vinegar." He saw that the minced bacon had previously been rendered of its fat; the skillet was now being reheated on the stove behind her as Edie thin-sliced some plump white mushrooms.

When she took away the dinner plates and served the salad, he said: "The mushrooms are definitely an asset. I have previously known only the purist version: all green, except for the flecks of bacon, though there are those, I believe, who sprinkle on chopped hard-boiled egg, but that is almost entirely an aesthetic effect." He winked at her. "Forgive me for the shop talk."

"Don't stop," said Edie. "I really like to hear it."

"Judging from this meal, in composition and execution, you know quite a bit about food already. It's the kind of simplicity that comes only with gastronomical sophistication. For some reason you were deceiving me, with your talk of living on hot dogs and hamburgers."

Edie stared at him. "I swear that I just got all these things out of a book."

"Nothing wrong with that. It's exactly how I learned to cook seriously."

"But this is the first time for me," she said, with a mixture of shyness and something else, perhaps defiance: as if she were talking of a sexual experience. "I've never really cooked anything before, except maybe a fried egg."

Reinhart nodded sagely. "You see how easy it is."

"Is it really O.K.?" asked Edie. "Or are you just saying that?" She proceeded to give him an intimate feeling by chiding: "You are always being too easy on me."

"Winona says the same thing." Reinhart brought his fingertips together. "Can I help it if I like girls?" Now Edie sighed cryptically. "Look," said he, "the Center Café in Brockville? I was out there again today. It's become an obsession with me to think of acquiring it somehow. It's a fantasy and will probably never come to reality, but I've started anyway to assemble a staff of kindred souls. Would you want to be part of it in some fashion?"

"Me?" Edie drew back on the stool. She seemed genuinely startled.

Reinhart touched the Formica counter with his forefinger. "You're a cashier by trade, are you not? Am I wrong in thinking that if you could practice your profession at a bowling alley, you could do it at a restaurant, where at best the traffic would be lighter? . . . Mind you, this is all theoretical at the moment. I am not even considering how we could earn a profit. Marge has been losing money."

Edie received this information inscrutably and then went around to the kitchen, opened the freezer compartment of the refrigerator, and removed an ice-cube tray. She looked into it and winced, agitated it slightly in her hand, and winced again.

"Something didn't jell?" Reinhart asked.

"Pear sherbet. I'm afraid I flopped at that."

"No, you didn't. It just hasn't had time to freeze. It takes a while." That was the very dessert he had made for the uneaten brunch to which Grace Greenwood had been invited.

"Would you like to have coffee in the living room?"

He was not unhappy to be relieved from sitting on the stool, which was a jolly perch at the outset, but even when younger, with his length of body, he liked at certain points during a meal to lean against the back of a chair.

"I'll pass up the coffee, though, if you don't mind. I have acquired the kind of equilibrium between food and drink that caffeine might unbalance." He went in to the couch. "Why don't you sit down and tell me about yourself?"

Edie took off her apron. In the living room she chose a chair some distance from him. She looked at him and said levelly: "I'm not gay."

Reinhart had not been prepared for this statement. Of an unusually generous supply of possible reactions he chose in effect to shrug it off. "Neither am I." He had brought his glass of wine along, and now he drank some.

Edie said almost fiercely: "I'm not criticizing anyone who is."

"I know you're not," said Reinhart. He raised his glass to her, but lowered it without drinking. "I must tell you, Edie, that I suspect you do everything well, but you pretend to be defenseless. You must be aware that that's an old-fashioned style. It's the one I have always preferred, though having had not only the other kind of mother but also the other kind of wife."

"Sometimes," Edie said, "it seems at first you are making fun of me, but then I realize you're not."

"That's right. I'm not. I don't ever make fun of anybody." He put his glass down and got to his feet. "I think I'll leave now, though it is awfully rude to eat and run. But I'll tell you why I think it's necessary: on the one hand, I think I desire you, but on the other I dislike the *idea* of lasciviousness in a man of my age—if what I feel is that. I have just been separated from a daughter who is only a year older than you. Maybe what I feel is really a simple longing to be in the presence of a young woman to whom I'm closely attached, and since you're not a relative by blood, I crave some other kind of intimacy."

Edie remained seated and looked up at him with deep blue eyes. "Are those good reasons for leaving?"

"Then how about cowardice?" But she laughed at him. "All right, then, I'll just take a nightcap, but first I have to go to my own apartment for a moment. I have to make a phone call. Business. . . ." He put his hand out, and she gave him hers. "Don't go anywhere."

"Not me," said Edie.

He took the stairway down to the fourth floor. Inside the apartment he found he had to look up the number in the public book: Winona had taken the personal directory from the drawer in the telephone table. He wished she had also taken that etching full of hairy lines.

"Grace, Carl Reinhart."

"Aha."

"May I speak to my daughter?"

"She's not here at the moment, Carl."

"Not there?"

"That's right," Grace said tartly. "She went to the movies."

Reinhart looked down into the living room, but the light was too dim to see the little clock above the liquor cabinet. "She's out alone this time of night?"

Grace snorted. "She's with Ray!"

"Ray?"

"My son. He's in from California for spring vacation."

Reinhart had never heard of this person before, but he felt that courtesy required him to fake it. "Oh, yes, *Ray*. He's in the last year of college, isn't he?"

"Last year of law school!" crowed Grace. Her voice had very clearly taken on an unprecedented tone of affection. This too was new to Reinhart. He had never heard her use it with reference to Winona, but there are all forms of human emotion, and he himself had certainly experienced many of them.

He said sincerely: "I'd like to meet him."

"You would?" Grace asked, incredulous for a moment, and then she recovered: "I want you to! Which night's good for dinner? It's on me this time. But you pick the restaurant. You're the expert.

Make it fancy. We've got all kinds of celebrating to do. Did you know that tomorrow I become president of Epicon?"

Reinhart congratulated her. "And I have a new idea I want to talk to you about in the area of food," said he. "How about Tuesday night for dinner?"

"I'd better check with Ray first. He's seeing my ex, his father, one night this week. . . . Good to talk with you, Carl. When should Winnie return the call, tonight still or tomorrow?"

"I'll call her tomorrow," said Reinhart. "It's nothing crucial."

"Sleep tight," said Grace, in what would appear to be a certain affection for *him*. Well, he had never thought her the world's worst.

As he rode the elevator up to Edie's floor Reinhart understood that Winona's absence at this moment was another piece of the good luck he had been enjoying lately. How fatuous had been the impulse to ask her whether she could permit him to have a girl friend younger than herself. Of course she would have refused! Winona was a notorious prig. Who would want any other kind of daughter?

Social Change in Melanesia

Development and History

This book is a companion volume to *An Introduction to the Anthropology of Melanesia* (1998). It gives a clear and absorbing account of social change in Melanesia since the arrival of Europeans, covering the history of the colonial period and the new post-colonial states. Paul Sillitoe deals with economic and technological change, labour migration and urbanisation, and the formation of the modern state, but he also describes the sometimes violent reactions to these dramatic transformations, in the form of cargo cults, secession movements, and insurrections against multinational companies. He discusses contemporary development projects but brings out associated policy dilemmas. He reviews developments that threaten the environment, and implications for local identity, such as a tourist industry that romanticises 'primitive culture'. This fascinating account of social change in the Pacific is addressed to students with little or no background in the region's history and development.

PAUL SILLITOE is Professor of Anthropology at the University of Durham. He has conducted extensive anthropological field research in the Southern Highlands of Papua New Guinea. His books include *Give and Take* (1979), *Roots of the Earth* (1983), *Made in Niugini* (1988), *A Place Against Time* (1996) and *An Introduction to the Anthropology of Melanesia* (1998).

Social Change in Melanesia

Development and History

Paul Sillitoe

Department of Anthropology, University of Durham

CAMBRIDGE
UNIVERSITY PRESS

PUBLISHED BY THE PRESS SYNDICATE OF THE UNIVERSITY OF CAMBRIDGE
The Pitt Building, Trumpington Street, Cambridge CB2 1RP, United Kingdom

CAMBRIDGE UNIVERSITY PRESS
The Edinburgh Building, Cambridge CB2 2RU, UK http://www.cup.cam.ac.uk
40 West 20th Street, New York, NY 10011-4211, USA http://www.cup.org
10 Stamford Road, Oakleigh, Melbourne 3166, Australia

First published 2000

Printed in the United Kingdom at the University Press, Cambridge

Typeset in Plantin 10/12 pt in QuarkXPress™   [SE]

A catalogue record for this book is available from the British Library

ISBN 0 521 77141 2 hardback
ISBN 0 521 77806 9 paperback

For Melanesian friends
coming to terms with a rapidly changing world

Contents

Maps

Figures

Plates

The logo featuring in this book is based on the contemporary steel sculpture on the wall of the Rural Development Bank of Papua New Guinea at Waigani.

Both these white men looked on native life as a mere play of shadows. A play of shadows the dominant race could walk through unaffected and disregard in the pursuit of its incomprehensible aims and needs . . . a barrier against the march of civilisation. The poor folk here did not like it . . . a great step forward, as some people used to call it with mistaken confidence. The advanced foot had been drawn back, but the barricade remains . . . but then it is the product of honest fear – fear of the unknown, of the incomprehensible.

Joseph Conrad, *Victory: An Island Tale*

Preface

Melanesia's peoples evidence a legendary and bewildering variety; several hundred languages, the product of millennia of local differentiation, are spoken in the region today. The indigenous societies are similar, however, in being small-scale and kin-ordered; they are stateless tribal societies in which sociopolitical exchanges of wealth such as pigs figure prominently on occasions such as marriage and death.

This book is an anthropological introduction to the post-contact history of these intriguing societies. An earlier volume, *An Introduction to the Anthropology of Melanesia* (1998), has described the region's traditional cultural orders. Like that book, this one is intended for both those who have some background in anthropology and those with little or no knowledge. Each chapter serves as a vehicle for some contemporary theme, and brief introductory comments on modernisation and dependency, nationhood and cultural identity, participatory development and indigenous knowledge, ethnicity and Orientalism, economic development and urbanisation, millenarian movements and religious change help to set the ethnography in a wider disciplinary context.

Again it also further attempts to dispel misunderstandings that are common about Melanesia and which are voiced regularly in the Western press, for example:

Neighbourhood disputes do not last long in the highlands of Papua New Guinea. If someone irritates you, a local *sanguma*, or hired assassin will kill him or her for the price of a stick of home-grown tobacco. For good measure the victim can also be eaten . . . 'In some cases, people are sacrificing then eating their own children' . . . Despite more than a century of work by Christian missionaries on the margins of this untamed and mountainous country, the old beliefs and superstitions still run deep. 'It is hardly surprising that these people are confused', said one long-term resident. 'They've gone from the Stone Age to helicopters in one generation. Most of them never owned a bicycle before they saw a helicopter.' (*Sunday Telegraph*, 23 August 1998)

In contrast to the earlier volume, however, this book is not solely anthropological. It deals with issues and problems that have traditionally been the concerns of human geography, sociology, development studies and economics. It is in relation to these other disciplines that present-day anthropology is having to establish its identity as ethnographers increasingly find themselves working in rural regions or urban centres where extensive externally influenced social change has occurred and people's lives are markedly different from those of pre-contact times. In these contexts local people frequently experience problems of cultural identity, and similarly anthropology is having to shift its focus. Along with these societies caught up in rapid social change, anthropology is having to ask itself what it is.

The discovery of the Melanesian islands by Europeans set in train a process of rapid social change. The nature of this change is unique to the region; its cultural heritage and history have set it off on its own trajectory; it is not simply repeating the experiences of European societies. Through modern communications, the world's cultures are influencing one another as never before, and at the same time there is increasing concern worldwide for the protection of ethnic and national identities. Throughout Melanesia people point with regret to the loss of their 'ancestors' customs'. The documentation of their cultures is not, from this perspective, a misplaced emphasis or a romantic gesture harking back to some 'primitive' past but something that can be of crucial importance in their search for cultural identity in a rapidly changing world.

A distinctive feature of anthropology is its pursuit of comprehensive coverage (what some writers call holism). It tries to set issues in a broad cultural context and from their consideration postulate generalisations applicable to human social behaviour. Accordingly, its approach to social change is not just a critique of historical narratives but an examination of the social implications of development interventions. Although the predictive record of anthropology and the social sciences generally is not a good one, this active engagement with often intractable problems reflects a tendency not to be satisfied with mere academic debate. Intellectual debate does help, however, to give direction to research intended to inform development interventions. What, for example, is the role of technology versus ideology in social change? Is it technical innovations that lead to new social arrangements, or is it the unending conflict between opposed ideologies founded on differing values and views?

It has recently been suggested that many anthropologists have largely overlooked the history of the region but in fact it is just that reliable historical documentation has only relatively recently become available. There is little evidence of the changes that had occurred before Europeans arrived except for that in oral histories and archaeological finds which remain sparse.

It is estimated that the first human beings arrived in Melanesia 50,000 or more years ago, coming from South-East Asia during the Pleistocene era. We assume that these people lived by hunting and gathering and envisage them slowly spreading into the South-West Pacific moving gradually from the west to the east, occupying the region over several thousands of years. The people who made the pottery now called Lapita ware started arriving, again from South-East Asia, about 4,000 years ago and they are assumed to be of the same stock as those who went on farther east to populate Polynesia. Some writers have tried to divide the population into biological racial types, each corresponding to a different wave of prehistoric migration into the region, but these distinctions are dubious. However different the various racial stocks were originally, they have since interbred extensively. 'Race' as cultural difference or ethnicity is, however, relevant to understanding the region, having recently emerged as an issue with the outside world's intrusion.

No society is static, and documenting the changes that occur is problematical and these problems are increased by the cultural variation found in Melanesia. This variety makes the region interesting for anthropologists but gives further problems in structuring an introductory text. The strategy adopted again is that each chapter takes a topic common to many places throughout the region, such as attitudes to land, and discusses it using one society in particular. As with *An Introduction to the Anthropology of Melanesia*, two concerns guided the choice of material: first, to ensure a good geographical and cultural distribution; and, secondly, to select studies covering the topics in adequate detail. While the region displays startling cultural variety, there are constant underlying themes detectable across it, from labour migration to cargo cults, cashcropping to mineral exploitation, and so on. I use these studies to represent these wider themes in Melanesian society. The choices were difficult, for there are many excellent studies on Melanesia.

I tried to remain true to the ethnographic evidence, although sometimes I offer reinterpretations. Contemporary post-modern criticism suggests that this is inevitable in the interpretation of any ethnographic 'facts'. Anthropological theory contributes to this process. It is now evident with hindsight that anthropological interests and concerns are largely driven by contemporary Western concerns of the moment. The current emphasis on social dynamics and process, the centrality of history and identity issues, all reflect our perception of rapid social change and preoccupation with globalisation, our need to try and account for it. Other topical issues concern sustainable development and conservation of biodiversity, which have come to the fore as the environmental costs of industrial development have become increasingly obvious and urgent.

It is my hope that readers will not only find this book interesting and informative, but also be stimulated by it to read further on this fascinating and relatively little known part of the world. Each chapter therefore concludes with some references for further reading on the topics discussed. The book arises from a series of university lectures and I thank the students who attended them for asking questions and making comments that helped to clarify issues. I also thank the National Research Institute at Waigani in Papua New Guinea and particularly Colin Filer, Head of the Social and Cultural Studies Division, for inviting me to take up a Visiting Professorial Research Fellowship which afforded me the opportunity to revise and add to this manuscript while living in Port Moresby. As always, I thank my wife, Jackie, for reading through the manuscript, helping to ensure that it meets the requirements for an introduction, and improving on my expression besides assisting with countless editorial revisions. Assistance from Durham University Publications Board with meeting the costs of the plates is gratefully acknowledged.

1   Change and development

People in the Southern Highlands of Papua New Guinea tell the following story:

Long ago in the forested mountains of Papua New Guinea lived two brothers, one dark- and one fair-skinned. One day, the fair-skinned one, who was considerably more talented and able than his dark-skinned brother, made a particularly successful hunting trip. Returning with several marsupials, he told his somewhat lazy brother to collect some firewood to heat stones for an earth oven, for they were going to have a feast. Once the oven had been prepared and the eviscerated and singed marsupials were cooking, the fair-skinned man decided to go to a garden some way off to collect greens and other vegetable delicacies to cook and eat with the meat. He was gone a long time. When he returned he found that his brother had opened the oven and eaten all the meat and was sleeping off his gluttonous meal. He was furious; this was the last straw. He told his greedy, stupid and indolent brother that from that day forth he would have to fend for himself, and then he went away. He disappeared, no one knew where, and from that day to this those mountains have been inhabited by dark-skinned people only.

Storytellers today often go on to say that the arrival of Europeans marks the return, after many generations' absence, of the fair-skinned brother's descendants. This book is concerned with the consequences of this 'return'.

Social change

Any society, tribal or modern, is a dynamic entity. Although anthropologists commonly present their work in the form of a synchronic account, they do not intend to imply that the societies they study are static. They work in this way for a variety of intellectual and practical reasons, not the least of which is that it is all many fieldworkers can manage. The societies they study are clearly not stagnant, if only because their membership is constantly changing through births and deaths, and their institutions and arrangements will be continually changing for this and other reasons as well. Some crucial questions are the source of this change, its extent and the speed with which it takes place.

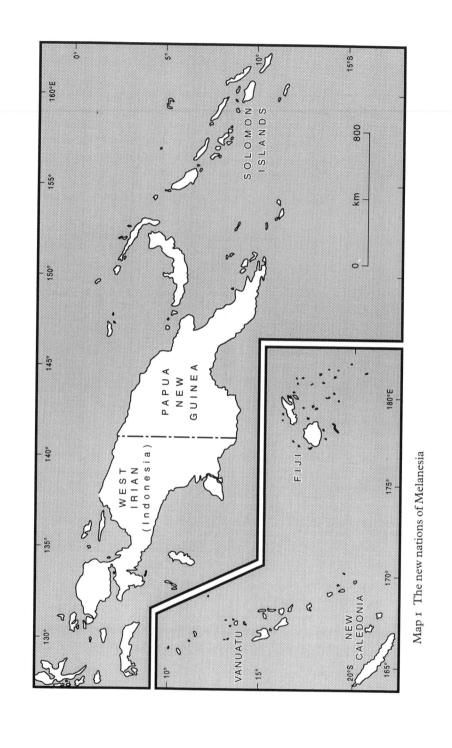

Map 1 The new nations of Melanesia

Plate 1.1 The fair-skinned brother's descendants return: a two-way
radio link established at Lake Kutubu *ca*. 1938.

Change may be internally or externally generated or even imposed. No
group of human beings anywhere is entirely content with its lot; its
members are constantly pressing to improve their social situation. The
changes they effect in the structure of their society, its institutional
arrangements and so on, are usually small in any generation, although
cumulatively they may appear considerable. Whereas generally they are
gradual, constraints may cause pressures to build until they erupt, commonly as revolution. The slower the change in technology, the more
gradual the change in social arrangements. Internally generated change is
rarely disruptive of the established order.

Change of this kind is the concern of evolutionary theory, which postu-
lates that societies, like organisms, evidence lineal change, being subject
to dynamic environmental and sociocultural forces that constantly
promote it. The idea is that this change is advancement. In this respect
evolutionary theory underpins the notion of development, which assumes
the adoption of improved technological procedures and more effective
institutional arrangements. The danger is that this idea of improvement
can lead us to make pejorative judgments about the societies that are tar-
geted by development agencies, thinking of them as a lower order of
humanity.

Plate 1.2 An armed Papuan constable taking manacled prisoners back to stand trial.

Internal forces are rarely solely responsible for change, however, because, leaving aside the problem of distinguishing one society from another, few societies exist in isolation. Besides generating change themselves, societies inevitably adopt practices and objects from their neighbours. Many changes in societies occur as a result of pressures from outside. The critical questions are again the extent and speed of these changes and who is controlling them. In traditional Melanesian cultures it was the people concerned who made these decisions, and the rate at which they adopted traits from their neighbours was gradual and the resulting changes rarely disruptive. It is when one society moves on another and forces it to change that the situation is altered dramatically – the extent and speed of change increase markedly, resulting in social disruption and confusion. This happens only when the invading society is sufficiently powerful to dominate the other which invariably means that it is technologically superior. We recognise here the historically inevitable intrusion of industrial society into the non-industrial cultures of the Pacific, which started with European exploration of the world and has proceeded apace over the past 200 years, leaving very few if any places unaffected. This is the change that is associated with economic development in the Third World.

We can distinguish three aspects of this forced change: technological innovation, social consequences, and indigenous rationalisations. In a broad sense (for these issues inevitably overlap in reality), the following chapters are ordered according to this sequence.

Technological innovation is inevitable given the technical superiority of the industrial world. People with only stone tools are certain to jump at the opportunity of acquiring steel ones once they recognise their superior efficiency, and the same is the case with many other manufactured goods, clothing, processed food, and so on. Those who adopt many of these things do so freely; Melanesians are eager to swap grass skirts for cotton dresses, local vegetables for biscuits, and so on. There is no necessary compulsion at this level, and because there are no checks considerable damage can result – sickness through wearing dirty clothing, malnutrition through a shift to unbalanced processed-food diets, and so on. Where those involved see the technical innovation as having no advantages or as threatening to interfere with their lives, representatives of the powerful industrial world may compel them to accept it – to construct airstrips or roads, for example, or to give up land for plantations or mines.

Technological changes, whether voluntarily or coercively adopted, are certain to have social consequences. Access to manufactured food and clothing will lead to changes in local productive arrangements and possible modifications in the composition and organisation of the social groups involved. Gardening and hunting may decrease, for example, or the cultivation of plants required for apparel may cease, with consequent changes, sometimes extensive, in the cooperative arrangements among those involved. The establishment of a mine or plantation employing considerable numbers of local people, for example, can produce far-reaching social changes in a brief period – a virtual externally generated revolution – and, sometimes nearly as disturbing, can attract migrant labourers from other regions, deserting their homes and families for varying periods in pursuit of work.

In addition to these indirect technologically induced social changes there are others directly imposed by the colonising social order. These usually include, for instance, modifications to the traditional political system, which are particularly disturbing if the dominated polity is stateless as it was everywhere in Melanesia. Pax Europa always involved the imposition of a system of alien law courts to settle disputes, the curtailment of local political autonomy, and the ruthless suppression of 'tribal warfare'. In the Sepik region of New Guinea, for example, patrol officers executed those whom the Supreme Court found guilty of head-hunting by hanging them in public and then cutting up the rope into short lengths for distribution among those present – in the words of one such hangman 'as a reminder of the power of the government and what it could do to people that offended its code' (Bloxham quoted in Nelson 1982:187).

When swift and far-reaching technological and social changes occur, the people caught up in them are often confused, even bewildered and dismayed, but they inevitably try to make some sense of what is happening to them. The myth with which this chapter opened is an example of an attempt to understand such events – to explain them in terms of what is known. Especially in the early stages of contact, before those colonised have been exposed to formal education and come to some understanding of the invading order, these indigenous rationalisations are bounded by traditional knowledge. This knowledge may be inappropriate for making sense of the changes forced on them pell-mell by the outside world.

Attempting to account for the arrival of Europeans with little knowledge of the world beyond the valleys they occupied or the islands and swampy coastline they frequented, Melanesians have no choice but to extend their cultural lore. Because of the inappropriateness of this traditional lore for explaining what is happening, indigenous rationalisations may appear comical in their misconceptions of industrial society, although more often they strike the sensitive as melancholic. Melanesians are individually as intelligent as anyone: it is simply that their cultural heritage equips them only in a limited and seemingly unpragmatic way to explain what happens when the industrial world overturns their lives.

Issues defined

Central to the study of social change in anthropology is the notion of **economic development**. This is a somewhat unfortunate phrase because the word 'development' implies improvement, which is not always the experience of those subjected to it. It customarily refers to a material advancement in people's lifestyles: the introduction of scientific medicine or improvement of medical services (inoculation programmes to control disease or pesticide spraying campaigns to eradicate vectors, the establishment of health centres and so on), the introduction of scientific agricultural knowledge and practices (programmes to introduce new crops or improve strains, to promote soil conservation and the application of fertilisers, and the like) and the establishment of industries and businesses. All of these developments involve new technology and therefore it would be more accurate to speak of technological rather than economic development.

In many regards this development covers the first of the above three aspects of change, namely technological innovation. It is only here that we can legitimately talk of development representing progress, for it is only on a technological level that we can refer to industrial society as more advanced than non-industrial society. Chain saws and tractors can fell timber far more quickly than stone axes, modern drugs cure certain diseases more effectively than ritual, fertilised soils yield considerably more crops than untreated ones, and so on. These are indisputable advances which, if introduced sympathetically with regard to both the cultural and the natural environment, may be welcome. **Modernisation theory** assumes that technological advance and economic growth will proceed when conditions are right and bring material benefits to currently less developed nations. Development is a matter of arranging conditions to promote take-off.

Technological innovation invariably brings in its train other changes that may not be perceived by those caught up in them as desirable or in their interest. We cannot speak of this **social change** – change in the social organisation, economic arrangements, or political ordering of another culture or shifts in the aspirations or ideology of its members – as improvement, for who is to say that one social system or political ideology is better than another except in terms of culturally specific values? There are no absolute grounds on which to make such judgments. Growing more and better crops can be considered progress, but we cannot speak of the breakup of extended families into nuclear units or the demise of totemically organised social groups as good or bad. Indeed, we can turn the tables on ourselves by looking at some Melanesian institutions in the light of our own priorities, for they are often very sound in these terms. If we believe in equality, fairness and individual liberty, for example, the stateless political systems of the region are superior to states in their promotion of these values. Likewise, if we value biodiversity and worry about industrial destruction and pollution of the natural environment, we have to appreciate the tribal land tenure systems of Melanesian societies which, subject to constant renegotiation, repeatedly thwart outsiders' attempts to overexploit natural resources. The disturbance and bewilderment experienced by those concerned when such change occurs swiftly often cause it to be judged undesirable. More than just the social consequences of technological change, social change may include technological innovation and indigenous rationalisations as well. It is a more neutral term than 'economic development', and is the term favoured by anthropologists, who are keenly aware that rapid change cuts both ways.

Anthropologists who become involved in development projects are seen as practising **applied anthropology**, but this is something of a

Plate 1.3 A sign of the globalised times: dancers from Central Province, Papua New Guinea performing at a 1997 cultural show.

contradiction in terms. The only way in which anthropological knowledge can be applied in development contexts is to couple it with a knowledge of some other field such as agriculture, engineering, medicine or economics. Training in one of these vocational areas combined with an anthropological background that fosters awareness of and sympathy for other cultural arrangements is far more likely to promote a sustainable and workable development project than technical expertise alone. Otherwise, anthropologists can only advise on social problems and policies as they think those concerned perceive them, and here they run the risk of indulging in social engineering – interfering in uncalled-for ways in other people's sociocultural arrangements.

Anthropology is not an applied science; it cannot predict outcomes or solve problems. Beyond documenting the traumas of social change, it can only suggest likely outcomes in a general way and recommend policies that may prove less disruptive. The problem is that social disruption is unavoidable, and anthropologists commonly find themselves acting as weak brakes on the development juggernaut. The culturally loaded issues in question, arguments over ideology and belief, become political matters out of any discipline's hands. Nevertheless, the term 'applied anthropology' continues to be used by those who think there are solutions to the

Plate 1.4 Picking tea on a plantation in the Western Highlands
Province, Papua New Guinea.

enormous social problems posed by economic development when
instead they are amenable only to compromise and attempts at concilia-
tion. The idea that social scientists, and anthropologists in particular, can
help move less developed countries relatively painlessly into the industrial world is a dangerous myth, raising people's expectations far beyond
what is practicable and leading to disillusionment and even a sense of
betrayal.

   The people of the world's less technologically developed nations – the
Third World – tend to be materially poor, largely peasants or the urban
dispossessed. The resources of their countries tend to be concentrated in
a few hands while the majority of the population lives in poverty. Political
revolutions will be necessary to effect substantial technological development that will assist the masses. It is manifestly inappropriate to think that
applying anthropology or any other discipline can solve problems of this
order. In Melanesia, with its traditional egalitarian social order, a small
wealthy immigrant community, scarcely developed resources and predominantly tribal population, the issues are of a somewhat different
order, and we can think of the region in some regards as beyond the Third
World. The majority here are materially poor, but exceedingly few live in
poverty, and many lead contented and fulfilled lives according to their

own cultural lights. It is refreshingly different from places like India and South America, and its problems with regard to technological development are its own.

The first phase of the development process experienced by the majority of Third World nations was **colonialism**. When the European powers claimed suzerainty over other regions, the inhabitants of these regions, technically and politically less powerful, were unable to prevent them from exercising it. The European governments subsequently instituted colonial administrations to create the conditions conducive to European settlement and the exploitation of the region's resources. Local populations were enslaved or even systematically slaughtered (as were Aborigines in parts of Australia and as are Indians in parts of Amazonia today). After the unspeakable terrors of the World War II a new spirit entered into international politics – a resolve to give ordinary people, including those in the colonies, a fairer deal. There were also at this time stirrings of militant nationalism as the colonised began to demand their rights. As one colony after another was granted political independence, we entered the post-colonial or neocolonial era. The latter term is used by some writers because few of the nations involved have achieved economic independence; they remain exploited, the colonial powers having created and left in control local elites with a vested interest in seeing that the situation remained unchanged. Today multinational companies exploit their resources to the benefit of the industrial world instead of colonial governments.

This view of the development process is referred to as **dependency theory**. Its argument with modernisation theory reflects in large part our culture's political divide between left- and right-wing philosophies. The dependency interpretation of the international economic and political order is that development aid for the massively underprivileged populations of the Third World is no more than a gesture towards Western electorates' virtually non-existent conscience and that investment in technological development in their regions is largely intended to facilitate exploitation of their resources for the benefit of the industrial world. There is, unfortunately, some truth to this jaundiced view.

Implicit in the foregoing discussion is the idea that development policy and practice operate on two levels: that of national or international debates about priorities and agendas with macro-level development plans; and that of regional or local demands for assistance prompting micro-level development initiatives. At the national or international level, we find large-scale development programmes designed to influence an entire country and its economy. Some examples of nationally planned development are road construction, the establishment of health centres, and so-called green revolutions, which reorder agricultural practices. They are the province of politicians, economists and development planners, working in consultation with specialists from the fields involved (agriculturalists, engineers, and so forth). The policy decisions regarding them rest with the national governments and international agencies involved, which also supervise their formulation and monitor their execution through their bureaucracies.

Nationally and internationally planned developments also have an impact at the regional level. The regional or local level of development concerns direct assistance to small groups of people and the immediate alleviation of poverty. It is at this level that the majority of charities and non-governmental organisations (NGOs) operate. The emphasis is on small-scale projects in specific regions or communities. The impetus for these may be generated locally or result from the efforts of outside bodies which perceive a need in a community and mobilise the capital and skill required to meet it. There has also recently been a significant change of emphasis in development agencies, with the perceived failure of macro-level driven policies to deliver development effectively, towards acknowledging that people at the grass-roots level also have a part to play. This is largely effected through the incorporation of a **participatory** approach into development programmes, which aims explicitly to allow local people more of a voice in planned interventions that affect them.

While some anthropologists contribute as social scientists to the theoretical and philosophical debates about the ideological and global forces behind development, others are involved at the regional level with more immediate problems of assistance to ordinary people. We work traditionally at the grass-roots level, our intensive field research bringing us into intimate contact with particular communities. This involvement centres our concerns on local problems arising from economic development strategies and their amelioration. Some anthropologists go on to generalise from their experiences in a small area to a nation as a whole in an attempt to influence policy, but such generalisation is exceedingly difficult given the small samples upon which it is based. This highlights the limited assistance that anthropology can offer, contributing to Band-aid remedies at the local community level when transplant surgery is demanded at the international one.

FURTHER READING

On social change in Melanesia see:
N. and N. Douglas (eds.) 1989 *Pacific islands yearbook* Sydney: Angus and
     Robertson
I. Hogbin 1970 *Social change* Melbourne: Melbourne University Press

D. King 1998 *A human geography of Papua New Guinea* Bathurst: Crawford House
     Publishing
H. Nelson 1982 *Taim bilong masta* Sydney: Australian Broadcasting Commission
A. B. Robillard (ed.) 1992 *Social change in the Pacific islands* London: Kegan Paul

On anthropology and development see:
M. S. Chaiken and A. K. Fleuret (eds.) 1990 *Social changes and applied anthropol-
     ogy* Boulder: Westview Press
K. Gardener and D. Lewis 1994 *Anthropology and development* London: Pluto
R. D. Grillo and R. L. Stirrat (eds.) 1997 *Discourses of development: anthropological
     perspectives* Oxford: Berg
M. Hobart (ed.) 1993 *An anthropological critique of development* London:
     Routledge
N. Long 1977 *An introduction to the sociology of rural development* London:
     Tavistock
L. Mair 1984 *Anthropology and development* London: Macmillan

On world systems theory see:
I. Wallerstein 1991 *Geopolitics and geoculture: essays on the changing world system*
     Cambridge: Cambridge University Press

2   The arrival of Europeans

Up until the arrival of outsiders in Melanesia there is relatively little reliable evidence about its history beyond what archaeologists are able to surmise from their excavations and the hypotheses of linguists and biological anthropologists regarding the evolution and diffusion of Melanesia's many languages and racial characteristics. The Melanesians themselves, whose cultures were non-literate, had only oral histories – memories of the recent past and mythical narratives like that of the dark- and fair-skinned brothers. While Westerners were willing to give some credence to what people recalled of the recent past and their accounts of what their parents and grandparents told them, they were less sure of the status of mythical accounts, which frequently involved fantastic events beyond our experience such as marsupials giving birth to human beings. Early researchers in the field therefore tended to assume that social change proceeded sufficiently gradually in these contexts that they could write in terms of time frames that overlooked it. Recent critics have accused these ethnographers of pretending to have observed or even inventing pre-contact cultures with their ethnographic present tense (an impossibility of course, the presence of the anthropologist implying contact with the outside world) and overlooking the study of contemporary social events. Whatever the grounds for these criticisms, there is agreement that the synchronic assumption is not valid when we come to consider the rapid change produced by the extended confrontation of tribal society with the industrial outside world. Reliable documentary evidence is now becoming available through which historical developments leading up to the present day may be traced.

To understand contemporary social change it is necessary to set it in its historical context. Not being attuned to the overall situation threatens the viability of many development projects, for history and cultural heritage need to be considered in planning and implementing them. The following historical sketch establishes the all-important diachronic framework for considering social change in Melanesia.

Racism in history

The shallowness and dubiety of the Melanesian historical perspective from a European intellectual viewpoint has resulted in the domination of the region's history by Western accounts, in which Europeans play a central role and Melanesians a largely passive one. This Western domination reflects racist attitudes which have plagued Melanesians' relations with Europeans from the time of first contact to the present. They relate to the 'us' versus 'them' distinction that remains the battleground of many contemporary intellectual skirmishes in anthropology and beyond.

The name of the region itself, which emerged as a historical category in the nineteenth century with discoveries made in the Pacific and which has been legitimated by subsequent use, reflects something of the racist sentiments that informed its definition. The name 'Melanesia', or sometimes 'Black Islands' according to some authorities, refers to the inhabitants' dark skins. Others favour a more colourful denigrating derivation based on the region's early grisly reputation as the home of 'black' customs such as cannibalism, head-hunting, sodomy and sorcery. The Goaribari of the Papuan Gulf achieved notoriety, for example, at the turn of the century for eating the missionary James Chalmers and his party, and as recently as the 1960s the Yali of the central highlands consumed unwelcome missionaries. Another frequently used name in this region for various linguistic, physical and political groupings is 'Papua', which derives from another distinguishing physical trait of the population, coming from the Malay *papuwah*, 'frizzy-haired'. It suggests that it is not only Europeans who have expressed xenophobic sentiments towards Melanesians. Whatever their origins, these labels evidence a certain racially expressed disdain for the inhabitants.

The racist attitudes that have informed the historical record have changed over time. The early explorers, bent on plundering Melanesia of any wealth, considered the inhabitants subhuman and treated them as dangerous beasts. Later explorers, realising that there were only exotic curios to be collected, acknowledged that they were human beings and treated them with more respect. With more extended contact, Europeans continued to think that Melanesians were inferior to them – an attitude reinforced by the intellectual climate of the time, in which Darwinian evolutionary thinking was at its height. The region's colonisers' approaches to its natives ranged from exploiting them as a source of cheap labour to protecting them in their innocence and offering them the benefits of European civilisation, especially Christianity.

The colonial authorities and missionaries walked the narrow path between commitment to civilising the natives and contempt for them for needing it. The assumption was that these tribespeople were unable to manage their own affairs, the irony that they had previously enjoyed thousands of years of independence was lost on the colonisers. This belief was enshrined in items of colonial legislation such as the Native Regulation Ordinance and the Native Labour Ordinances of Papua. Both social and sexual intercourse between the races were legally restricted through instruments such as the White Women's Protection Ordinance. At one time a native had only to approach or address a European woman improperly to face a serious penalty. Melanesians could work in town and go to jail there, but they could not live there. Segregation was enforced, in the interests, it was believed, of both blacks and whites, with the result that Melanesians were forbidden to visit certain places in their own country, such as beaches designated for *mastas* and *misis* (Pidgin for 'white men' and 'white women') only.

The belief that indigenous people were unable to manage their own lives continued to inform colonial administration almost until it ended, reflecting the policy of 'white Australia' with equally disastrous results. It contributed to the failure to prepare people adequately for independence when it finally came, sowing some of the seeds from which today's new nations' troubles have grown. But racial tensions in contemporary Melanesia are surprisingly few, given generations of racial bias, reflecting perhaps the need to assimilate by default citizens from many different cultural backgrounds. Also, for the most part the region's new nations experienced fairly brief periods of colonial rule and never had to resort to violent anti-colonial revolutions to gain their independence as did the people of parts of Asia and Africa, and therefore racial and political attitudes were not fired to the same extent. Among the exceptions is Fiji, where the colonial legacy of South Asian migrant labour has resulted in serious racial tensions. There is antipathy throughout the region to people of Chinese origin and, increasingly, between Melanesians and French settlers in New Caledonia and Indonesian settlers, notably Javanese, in West Irian.

Discovery and early exploration

The first sighting of Melanesia is attributed somewhat doubtfully to the Portuguese navigator d'Abreu, who in 1511, while exploring the Spice Islands (present-day Indonesia), may have sighted the western end of New Guinea. But it was not until 1526 that his fellow countryman Jorge de Meneses is thought, again somewhat uncertainly, to have set foot on the Vogelkop, calling it Ilhas dos Papuas. Although these were the region's first European contacts, they were not its first contacts with the outside

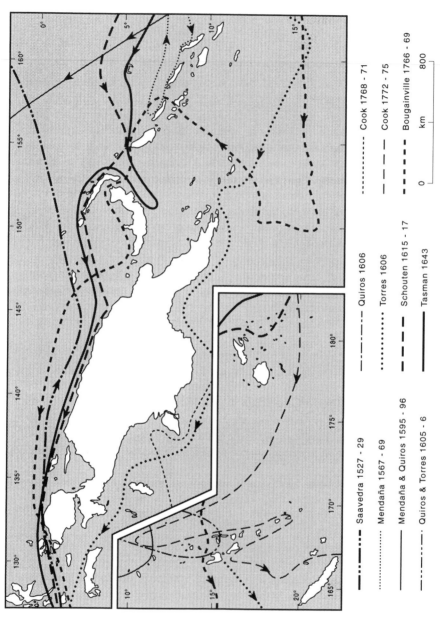

Saavedra 1527 - 29

Mendaña 1567 - 69

Mendaña & Quiros 1595 - 96

Quiros & Torres 1605 - 6

Quiros 1606

Torres 1606

Schouten 1615 - 17

Tasman 1643

Cook 1768 - 71

Cook 1772 - 75

Bougainville 1766 - 69

0   km   800

Map 2 European exploration of the Pacific

world. It was known to Indian and Chinese merchants from ancient times, and the Moluccan sultanates to the west had laid claim to parts of it for centuries, visiting it to trade and exact tribute in mother-of-pearl, bird of paradise skins, and aromatics.

After the hazy initial Portuguese sightings there were various European sightings and landings in the course of the next 300 years. These were initially cartographically confused and imprecise, showing the Melanesian islands and even Australia as one large southern continent, and later voyages rediscovered lands sighted decades and sometimes centuries before. The navigators – Portuguese, Spanish, Dutch and British – came from the Spice Islands in the west and the newly found Americas in the east. The Spaniard Alvaro de Saavedra sailed along the north coast of New Guinea as far as Manus Island in 1528–9 and Inigo Ortez de Retes discovered further smaller islands in the Admiralty group in 1545. It was he who named the large southern landmass Nueva Guinea, after a likeness he perceived in the natives to those living in African Guinea. He also claimed the region, fruitlessly as it turned out, as a Spanish colony; effective annexation was over 300 years away.

The next significant discoveries were made from Peru in 1568 by the Spaniard Àlvaro de Mendaña, who landed on several of the Solomon Islands. He returned to the region in 1595 to establish the first European settlement, but the attempt was abortive and he and many of those with him died. He called the islands the Solomons because they were believed to be the legendary Isles of Solomon, visited by the Incas and the home of unspeakable riches. A popular myth that had exercised European imaginations since ancient times was that of a fabulously rich southern continent awaiting discovery. Antonio Pigafetta who sailed with Ferdinand Magellan, for instance, wrote, 'The King of these heathens, called Raja Papua is exceedingly rich in gold, and lives in the interior of the island' (Gash and Whittaker 1975:10). This fantasy is difficult to sustain after meeting Melanesians, but it was a motive force behind much of the exploration of the South-West Pacific well into the twentieth century. It is noteworthy, particularly from the perspective of dependency theorists of development, that European interest in the region from the earliest contacts was to acquire wealth.

In 1606 Spain sent another expedition, headed by Mendaña's pilot, Pedro Fernandez de Quiros, into the Pacific and this one discovered the New Hebrides. The expedition was split up by strong winds, and the second-in-command Luis Vaez de Torres navigated his vessel to Manila along the south coast of New Guinea, discovering this coastline and the straits that bear his name today. A few months previously a Dutch ship commanded by Willem Jansz had explored the south coast of what is today Irian Jaya as far as Frederik-Hendrik Island. Jansz wrote of the people as 'wild, savage, black and uncivilised', reporting that they had 'murdered several of the ship's hands' (*Pacific Islands Year Book* 1978:236). These comments capture the tenor of many of the early contacts between Melanesians and outsiders, again extending well into the twentieth century; they were violent, bloody and fraught with misunderstanding on both sides. The Melanesians can be warlike and fierce, especially when they feel threatened, and they had every right to feel menaced by these invaders. Searching for wealth, the outsiders considered the natives less than human and treated them accordingly. The reputation of the Black Islanders for violence and sometimes cannibalism became well known and augured tumultuous change.

In 1616 the Dutchman Willem Schouten discovered New Ireland, and in 1643, during his circumnavigation of Australasia, Abel Janszoon Tasman discovered New Britain and was the first to sight some of the smaller Fijian islands. In 1700 Britain entered into Pacific exploration. Although all the major landfalls had unknowingly been made by then, it dispatched the one-time buccaneer William Dampier to the Pacific, where he consolidated the exploration of New Britain (calling it Nova Britannia) and New Ireland (which he thought comprised one landmass) and discovered some smaller islands. It was later in the eighteenth century that several of the hazily identified early discoveries of the Iberian navigators were rediscovered, precisely located and charted. In 1767 Philip Carteret rediscovered parts of the Solomon Islands and established that New Britain and New Ireland were separate islands (naming the latter Nova Hibernia). He also made on New Ireland the first of several void declarations of a British colony in the region. The Frenchman Louis-Antoine de Bougainville was probably the first to sight New Caledonia in 1768, when he rediscovered some of the islands in the New Hebrides and Solomon Islands chains and discovered the large island that bears his name.

It was James Cook, a particularly talented cartographer, who made the first definite sighting and landing on New Caledonia in 1774 and thoroughly explored and charted the New Hebrides, discovering several of the smaller islands and sighting some of those in the Fijian archipelago. These were not his first contributions to European knowledge of the region. He had landed in 1770 on the south coast of New Guinea and charted a passage through the myriad reefs of the Torres Straits. The main islands of Fiji were not discovered until 1789 when William Bligh sighted them from the open boat in which he and some of his crew were cast adrift after the mutiny on the *Bounty*. He explored them on a return voyage in 1792. In the same year the Frenchman Joseph Antoine Bruin d'Entrecasteaux, searching for the lost voyage of Jean François de la Pérouse, discovered the extensive archipelago off the south-east tip of New Guinea, part of which is named after him. He also named several of the islands after members of his crew, among them the Trobriands and Rossel Island.

By the beginning of the nineteenth century the major islands and configuration of Melanesia were known and reasonably accurate charts now replaced the hypothetical maps of the early Iberian and Dutch navigators. Some small islands awaited discovery and exploration, as did the interiors of the larger ones. This process was not completed until the 1930s. The number of ships plying the South Seas now gradually increased, particularly with the establishment of a European colony in Australia and the subsequent fairly rapid settlement of some Europeans on a few of the Pacific islands, notably Fiji and New Caledonia. Up until this time contact between Melanesians and outsiders had been sporadic and brief and often violent. They had sometimes thrown lime at the foreigners (an act believed to placate spirits, which is what some people thought the white-skinned invaders were) and sometimes hurled spears and shot arrows at them. Although doubtless disturbing, these brief encounters effected scarcely any changes in the Melanesians' cultures, doing no more perhaps than confirming their beliefs in a spirit world. In the new era that followed, however, contact was more sustained, although frequently no less bloody, and social change began in earnest.

Consolidation of contact

There were four significant sources of change during the nineteenth century: whalers, traders, blackbirders and missionaries.

Several whaling grounds were found in the South-West Pacific, and the interaction of whalers with the local populations was somewhat similar to that of the explorers, who stopped off occasionally to revictual and for water. They were in these waters for longer periods and in larger numbers, however, and their contacts with the inhabitants were consequently more frequent and sustained. They had little to do with the local populations otherwise, except sometimes to include some of their numbers in their crews, dramatically changing individuals' lives and worldviews.

The traders had more regular and ongoing intercourse with the natives, whose local resources they sought to exploit. They settled on islands to trade for trepang (a Chinese sea-slug delicacy), sandalwood, seashells, pearls, bird of paradise plumes, and so on. Their numbers included deserting and shipwrecked sailors, escaped convicts, beachcombers and other adventurers. In addition to broadening people's horizons, these traders supplied quantities of manufactured goods (clothing, tools, etc.) in exchange for valuable local products. They set in train the technological impetus for change in traditional arrangements, notably in production.

Trade in human beings was organised by the so-called blackbirders. Long after slavery had been abolished in Europe and America it arose in the Pacific, developing to supply the sugarcane and cotton plantations of Queensland and Fiji with cheap labour. Islanders were lured onto vessels with offers of trade and then imprisoned in the holds to be transported to distant plantations where Europeans paid £4-10s to £6-10s per head to cover their passage – thus in their minds not engaging in slave trade, the 'labourers' supposedly being volunteers. The islanders suffered considerably at the hands of their recruiters. There were some gruesome episodes in which those kidnapped fought and tried to escape; on occasion crews fired indiscriminately into holds, subsequently heaving the dead and wounded overboard. Captain G. Palmer of the British Navy, who cruised the islands in 1869 to put down this trade in human beings, gives a graphic account of conditions in his book, *Kidnapping in the South Seas* (1871):

We found . . . a small schooner . . . fitted up precisely like an African slaver . . . [the 100 New Hebrides natives on board] were stark naked, and had not even a mat to lie upon; the shelves were just the same as might be knocked up for a lot of pigs. (p. 108)

numbers of the people had been taken away by the traders . . . in most if not all cases they were seduced on board by false promises of tobacco, etc., and . . . do not understand anything about engagements. (p. 60)

[One native recounted how] when the vessel made her appearance off the island, he went on board to sell mats and fowls, and towards sunset he was told by the white men that as it was late he could sleep on board. There were between sixty and seventy of them, besides fifteen women. They went down into the hold and slept there, but in the morning found the vessel at sea, no land being in sight . . . [they were told] not to be alarmed, as they were only going to another island close to; but they were all brought to Makongai, Fiji. It was not until they arrived there that he was told they were to stop thirty moons to work. (p. 84)

We can see here the genesis of a system of labour recruitment that has continued in modified form up to the present day, whereby people in remote areas are recruited for work on plantations for two years or longer. Today workers volunteer, but previously they were for the most part pressed into labour. Large numbers of those kidnapped never returned home. Some died under the harsh conditions on the plantations, and others became the nucleus of a substantial South Sea islander population

Plate 2.1 Lured on board ships by trade goods, men like these from Marovo Lagoon in New Georgia were transported to work on plantations elsewhere.

in Queensland. The blackbirding episode was a frightening and degrading introduction to the brutal and exploitive aspects of capitalist industrial society and rapidly effected social changes in some islander populations.

Other Europeans fostered change in Melanesian society more peacefully, seeking not to take advantage of the native peoples' relatively defenceless position to exploit their labour but to save their souls. The missionaries contributed significantly to social change, not only undermining traditional beliefs in the supernatural and, with varying success, replacing them with their own beliefs but also promoting various precursors to today's development projects and engaging in programmes of formal education. The latter, in the long term, is among the most potent of all forces of social change. The incursions of missionaries into Melanesian life, like those of traders and blackbirders, did not become significant until the latter half of the nineteenth century. They arrived in Fiji in 1835, the New Hebrides in 1839, New Caledonia in 1840, the Solomon Islands in 1845, and the D'Entrecasteaux Archipelago in 1847. They soon retreated from the latter two places where they suffered heavy losses through sickness and native attacks, and did not return effectively until the 1870s. Whatever we may think of the activities of these early missionaries – perhaps deploring the manner in which they destabilised traditional cultures – we cannot deny their courage and commitment to their cause. The populations they set out to proselytise regularly killed and not infrequently ate them. Of the thirteen Catholics who first landed in the Solomons, for instance, four were killed and a fifth seriously wounded with a spear in his back, and another died of malaria before they moved to the D'Entrecasteaux, from where they retreated after more deaths and appalling hardship.

Colonial annexation

The missionaries and others, notably, people living in Australia, who became aware of the depredations of traders and blackbirders in Melanesia started to voice their concerns and advocate colonial annexation. They argued that European governments should assume responsibility for administration of the region to protect the local population. But the heyday of European colonial expansion was past, and governments were becoming aware of the enormous responsibilities and problems they had assumed overseas and were in no hurry to add to them where they could see no ready and substantial economic return. The mere protection of native peoples from the rapacious advances of their citizens was hardly sufficient inducement. Eventually, however, events in the latter part of the nineteenth century forced the European powers to come to terms over Melanesia and formally establish their spheres of influence.

The forces that finally pushed them to annex parts of the Melanesian region and declare them colonies included an acknowledged moral obligation to protect local populations from marauding blackbirders and their own subjects from the violent assaults and cannibalism of the native people. They also recognised that it was necessary to contain the hegemony of rival European powers in the region, and they saw a chance of organising the large-scale exploitation of tropical products and resources for the benefit of their own economies by supplying the required administrative infrastructure.

The initial pattern of development varied from one colonial area to another and depended markedly on the motives for annexation. The first to declare their interests were the Dutch, who formally claimed sovereignty over the western half of the island of New Guinea in 1828. They had unofficially asserted rights to the region long before this as part of their Spice Island empire, and they proclaimed them formally again later in the nineteenth century when pressed by the British to define precisely the limits of their sprawling colony. The Dutch set the boundary well to the east to protect their trading interests, with a line down the centre of the island of New Guinea corresponding to the 141st meridian. They otherwise had relatively little interest in what to them was a largely inhospitable island and consequently left it virtually alone except for establishing a few small administrative centres on the coast.

The next part of Melanesia to come under formal European sovereignty was New Caledonia, the French raising the tricolour there in 1853 following pressure at home to protect French missionaries from native attack; in 1850 the local inhabitants had killed and eaten the entire crew of a French survey ship. The French also viewed the island as a mercantile base close to developing Australia and as a possible penal settlement. They subsequently transported some 40,000 prisoners to New Caledonia – nearly as many Europeans as the local Melanesian population. This sudden influx of foreigners promoted rapid social change marked by bloody native risings that added to the colony's notoriety as a penal island. Many released prisoners and their descendants remained on the island and, together with other European settlers, engaged in various enterprises, largely depending economically today on the nickel mining industry.

The British were incensed at the French action over New Caledonia, although they did nothing at the time. Twenty years later they became the next European power to annex part of Melanesia, accepting Fiji as a British possession in 1874. The history of the action is involved, Britain having refused two offers of cession in the preceding sixteen years, and having finally capitulated when the numbers of British settlers arriving in Fiji via Australia and New Zealand became too significant to ignore and the blackbirding of labour to work on their plantations a scandal that demanded control. The possibility of British annexation attracted settlers to Fiji to grow cotton following the worldwide shortage caused by the American Civil War. The political order of the indigenous Fijians is a blend of egalitarian Melanesian and hierarchical Polynesian, and at this time one chief claimed suzerainty over a considerable part of the region. He owed a bogus debt to the United States owing to the machinations of a so-called US consul and offered to cede Fiji to Britain if it would settle the matter. Fear that America, if not France or even Germany, would soon act unilaterally was the spur needed to prompt Britain to accept.

In the years following the declaration of colonial status, sugarcane eclipsed cotton as Fiji's principal cash crop, with extensive plantations established for its cultivation, together with coconuts for copra oil production. The British administration, anxious to protect the Fijians and other islanders from overly exploitive conditions, created a labour shortage and authorised the indenture of labourers from India to overcome it. The demographic consequences were similar to those that resulted from migration to New Caledonia: the Indian population approached the local Fijian one in size by the beginning of this century, overtook it in the 1940s, and is considerably higher today. Together with the establishment of the extensive plantations on which they were initially recruited to work, these newcomers have been a force for social change. Their presence has also given rise to considerable racial tension.

The next part of the region to be colonially annexed was that of present-day Papua New Guinea, which the British and German governments divided between them in 1884. Again Britain was reluctant to add the region to the Colonial Office's responsibilities, having rejected several earlier attempts to add it to its dominions – after Philip Carteret in 1767, there was Charles Bamfield Yule in 1846, John Moresby in 1873, and the Queensland government in 1883, all declaring it a British protectorate. It finally announced its intention to establish a protectorate over the southeastern part, subsequently called Papua, following considerable pressure from Australia and New Zealand, which feared that an enemy power (notably Germany, although they watched Russia, France and even Japan warily too) would annex it and threaten them. Despite calls from certain parties in Australia for a programme of European plantation settlement and extensive native labour recruitment, the policy of the British, established firmly under the energetic administration of William MacGregor, the first lieutenant-governor of British New Guinea, was to protect the native population and supervise its gradual advancement. The Australians continued with this policy when they took over responsibility for the colony, calling it the Territory of Papua, in 1906.

This benign colonial policy continued virtually up to independence, becoming entrenched in the territory's administration under the long governorship of Hubert Murray. Nonetheless there was some interference in native life: Murray's (1923:234) view was that 'it is in many cases impossible to keep [certain] native institutions alive. Some of them, of course, are clearly out of the question. Cannibalism, for instance, and headhunting must go, regardless of any social disorganisation that may follow.' In other words, where the administration could achieve effective control on its limited budget, it forced certain social changes. Similarly, the few plantations established and the activities of growing numbers of missionaries effected changes in restricted areas, but relative to the size of the colony there was little economic development. It was probably gold prospecting more than any other activity that led to European intrusion into many Papuans' lives; early administrations expended considerable energy in protecting prospectors in remote regions. This fortune-hunting was responsible for much of the region's exploration, in some senses pushing the understaffed administration forward into new areas. This trend was even more marked in the north-eastern part of present-day Papua New Guinea annexed by Germany, culminating in the 1930s in the penetration by prospectors of the densely settled Highlands of New Guinea.

Following the British declaration of a protectorate, the Germans moved quickly, raising their flag in several places on the north-east coast of New Guinea and the Bismarck Archipelago. They claimed the islands there, such as New Britain and New Ireland, where Britain had annexed the smaller ones of the Massim to the south. For the Germans this was a belated attempt to cash in on the rich pickings of colonialism. Believing that it would foster rapid commercial development, they initially administered the region through a company, but when the company failed to maintain proper control the government took over in 1899. The aim of the Neuguinea Kompagnie was to promote the rapid establishment of extensive plantations of tropical crops. Many Europeans were attracted to the colony to oversee and manage developments, and many died. The Germans viewed the local population as a source of cheap labour and treated it harshly. In some locations, such as the Gazelle Peninsula of New Britain, where soils and other conditions were favourable, they alienated considerable areas of land and established large plantations. Here social change was rapid and disturbing to the local populations. Enormous areas, notably inland, were left untouched even by the many missionaries who also came to the colony.

Plate 2.2 The beginning of an era: on a Motuan beach a native, directed by a Jack Tar, assists in running up the Union Jack, by which Britain proclaimed suzerainty *ca.* 1880s.

The New Hebrides was the next region to be annexed. Here the British and the French, who had substantial numbers of nationals on the islands as planters and missionaries, had been suspiciously watching and diplomatically wrangling with one another for several years. Blackbirding had caused an alarming decline in the local population, and missionaries in particular were calling for their protection; there were tensions over the settlement of released French convicts from New Caledonia in the island chain. Against this background the British and French agreed in 1887 to form a joint naval commission to safeguard the islands' interests, inaugurating what was to prove throughout its nearly 100-year existence a confused colonial rule. The commission was not a success, and fearing German designs on the region the two countries agreed in 1906 to set up a condominium to administer it. About this time large numbers of islander labourers were repatriated from Queensland, their horizons and awareness of the outside world considerably widened. The change they brought to the region augmented the effects of the several expatriate-run copra plantations and associated commercial developments established on the islands in this period.

The final part of Melanesia to be declared a European colony was the

Solomon Islands, over which Britain piecemeal established a protectorate between 1893 and 1900. The principal motive was again to protect the local population from the depredations of labour recruiters. There were only a few European traders in the group at the time, but efforts were soon made to open up the islands commercially and to encourage the establishment of plantations by a few large companies. Combined with the influence of large numbers of labourers returning again from overseas and the earnest proselytisation of missionaries and governmentally enforced pacification and judicial intervention, these set in motion considerable social changes.

Nationalism and independence

It took the two World Wars to fracture the colonial mould of Melanesia. At the outbreak of World War I, the Australians dispatched an expeditionary force to take German New Guinea, which remained under military government until 1920. The German plantations were expropriated and there was a gradual relaxation of their stern conditions of native employment – although not to the point of substituting the 'humanitarian' conditions characteristic of Papua. Both New Guinea and Papua remained administratively independent; indeed, relations between them were akin to those of two foreign countries. Amalgamation was considered but rejected for various reasons: New Guinea was considerably more prosperous than Papua and would have had to support it and thus lose capital for further development; the lingua francas in the two territories were different (Pidgin versus Motu); the administrative structures and laws familiar to native peoples were different and beyond straightforward combination; and the immigrant populations were quite different (predominantly British in Papua, Asian and German in New Guinea).

It took World War II to bring about the unification of the two colonies into the single Territory of Papua and New Guinea. Whereas the first war had barely touched Melanesia (except for the Australian annexation of New Guinea) the second devastated a large part of it. The Japanese invaded and occupied the Bismarck Archipelago, the north coast of New Guinea, and the Solomon Islands in 1942, and these regions witnessed fierce battles as the Allies gradually pushed them back until they were finally repulsed in 1944 (a few pockets of Japanese remained until 1945 and even until the 1960s and 1970s, when Japanese soldiers were found on remote Pacific islands thinking that the war was still going on). The New Hebrides and New Caledonia, although never invaded, became large Allied bases besides supplying considerable numbers of volunteer soldiers.

While the war was a terrifying and painful experience for many Melanesians, it also marked a revolution in their perceptions of the world and their place in it. It kick-started an awareness of nationalism that was to take them from colonialism to independence. The words of John Guise, independent Papua New Guinea's first governor general, intimate the profundity of the change:

I think the attitude of the Australian soldiers, together with American soldiers, made a tremendous impact psychologically. Because here we saw a different type of white people who were friendly, who shared things with us. There was no paternalistic outlook from them, you know. And when the coloured Americans came along, the negroes came along . . . This had a tremendous effect, it made us think that the brown and the black person were just as good as the white people. (quoted in Nelson 1982:173)

Shifts of perspective and awareness of this magnitude promoted rapid social change from within and led inevitably to criticism of the colonial situation. No longer Stone Age 'savages' unaware of what was happening, ripe for labour exploitation or needing protection, Melanesians had learnt, after a fashion, the ways of the world – or at least what they considered their fair place in it – and started to demand, albeit mildly, their rights.

The international community was also now sympathetic to their position; Papua New Guineans, for instance, had earned tremendous respect in Australia and the affectionate appellation of Fuzzy Wuzzy Angels for their bravery in the war, and the public wished to see their position improved. The stage was set for independence; at least the colonial powers admitted for the first time that this was their long-term objective. In the event it was some decades away, although even then sooner than many people had envisaged – indeed, sooner in some cases than was fair to allow the new national governments and their inexperienced bureaucracies to cope with it. Nevertheless, the handing over of power from colonial administrations to national governments was effected with hardly any violence or ill feeling. Melanesians have had little need of freedom fighters: the colonial powers, having experienced these elsewhere in the world, have given back sovereignty to the local populations in most places long before their demands reached this violent stage.

The first colony to become genuinely independent, with a democratically elected government and bureaucracy built up over several years, was Fiji, which became a Commonwealth dominion in 1970. Papua New Guinea followed in 1975 as an independent Commonwealth nation, a status to which it was advanced rapidly, having had its first democratic elections to its House of Assembly only in 1964 and its bureaucracy swiftly localised only a year or two before independence. In 1978 the

Plate 2.3 The end of an era: John Guise, independent Papua New Guinea's first governor general, receives the folded flag of the departing colonial administration at the Independence Day ceremony in 1976.

Solomon Islands too became an independent Commonwealth nation, the culmination of a progressive hand-over of authority and steady establishment of a governmental structure. The New Hebrides became the independent Republic of Vanuatu in 1980, with an untidy transfer of power by the Anglo-French condominium. The two European governments were unable to coordinate their actions and passed authority to a woefully inexperienced indigenous administration. The new government faced threats of secession from some islands, urged on by expatriate planters who fiercely opposed plans to return all land to its traditional owners, that culminated in the quickly subdued so-called 'bow and arrow rebellion' on Espiritu Santo Island.

A considerably more violent move to independence may await New Caledonia, which, still a French overseas territory, is the only remaining European colony in Melanesia. The French maintain that they have no intention of granting independence to the island, with its enormous nickel reserves, but the militant Kanak Independence Front of New Caledonia has other ideas. A similar tense situation exists in the western half of New Guinea, which was the first colony to change hands in the

Plate 2.4 Papua New Guinean carriers in the Wau-Mubo region taking supplies to Allied forces on the front lines in 1943.

post-war years, the Indonesians claiming it in 1963, after the Dutch withdrawal, as a province called Irian Jaya. This was a somewhat bungled affair, the Indonesians occupying it on the historical grounds that Moluccan sultanates had exercised some kind of suzerainty over parts of the region long ago. The country effectively remains a colony, under foreign administration from a Melanesian perspective. The Melanesian population is unhappy with the situation, the resettlement of many Javanese on their land in World Bank-funded transmigration schemes has exacerbated their bitter feelings, and their small liberation army, the OPM (*Organisasi Papua Merdeka*, or Free Papua Movement), regularly harasses the Indonesian administration.

The extent to which these historical events have touched life in Melanesia varies considerably from one part of the region to another, from long-established contact and extensive economic development to life scarcely or only very recently affected by the industrial world. The next chapter looks at contact from the viewpoint of a society which has only recently become caught up in the course of Western history, addressing further the issue with which this one opened – the domination by Europeans of accounts of the region's history. Scholars have recently started to ask what that history looks like from the other side – as experienced by Melanesians caught up in it.

FURTHER READING

On the history of contact in Melanesia see:

H. C. Brookfield 1972 *Colonialism, development, and independence* Cambridge: Cambridge University Press

N. Gash and J. Whittaker 1975 *A pictorial history of New Guinea* Milton (Queensland): Jacaranda Press

J. Griffin, H. Nelson and S. Firth 1979 *Papua New Guinea: a political history* Richmond: Heinemann

K. S. Inglis (ed.) 1969 *The history of Melanesia* 2nd Waigani Seminar, University of Papua New Guinea and Australian National University Research School of Pacific Studies

B. Jinks, P. Biskup and H. Nelson (eds.) 1973 *Readings in New Guinea history* Sydney: Angus and Robertson

L. P. Mair 1948 *Australia in New Guinea* Melbourne: Melbourne University Press

R. J. May (ed.) 1986 *Between two nations: the Indonesia–Papua New Guinea border and West Papua nationalism.* Bathurst: Robert Brown and Associates

D. McInnes 1992 *A tribute to the brave: 1941 to 1945 Papua New Guinea* Port Moresby: South Pacific Post

D. L. Oliver 1961 *The Pacific islands* New York: Doubleday

Pacific Islands year book 1978 Sydney: Angus & Robertson

N. Thomas 1991 *Entangled objects: exchange, material culture and colonialism in the Pacific* Cambridge: Harvard University Press

J. D. Waiko 1991 *A short history of Papua New Guinea* Melbourne: Oxford University Press

E. P. Wolfers 1975 *Race relations and colonial rule in Papua New Guinea* Sydney: Australia and New Zealand Book Co.

Also see:

D. Denoon and M. Meleisa 1997 *The Cambridge history of the Pacific Islanders* Cambridge: Cambridge University Press

H. P. Murray 1923 The population problem in Papua: lack of direct evidence *Proceedings of the Pan-Pacific Science Congress*, vol. 1, pp. 231–40

H. Nelson 1982 *Taim bilong masta* Sydney: Australian Broadcasting Commission

FILMS

OPM (*Organisasi Papua Merdeka*) Irian Jaya Resistance Movement
Yumi yet (PNG Independence) Pacific Video-Cassette Series No. 7
Angels of war Ronin Home Video

3   Another history

The Melanesians' experience of being swept up in the flow of European history was predictably quite different from that conveyed in the preceding catalogue of prominent historical events. Recent attempts to present something of the dark-skinned brother's descendants' experience of contact – to report on local people's perception and interpretation of events as a counterbalance to the European perspective – derive from the post-modernist critique, being attempts to deconstruct earlier accounts in the light of indigenous commentaries. The argument is that when Europeans presume to represent the histories and cultures of others who are foreign and politically weak and hence probably silenced, they create their own version of events and behaviours – one that conforms to their own view of the world.

This critique, which has long existed as an aspect of the critique of ethnocentrism in anthropology, has recently been called Orientalism, following Edward Said's argument that Western intellectuals created the Orient, especially the Near East, as an essentialised category fundamentally different from Europe. The people of the Orient had no voice, and they are now judged by Westerners in terms of this 'textual creation', any action which does not conform to it being labelled aberrant or inauthentic. Orientalism not only promulgates something of a fiction, a distorted, timeless view, but also has a political dimension linked to Western imperialism. It facilitated empire and domination as the powerful metropole's definition of the 'other', by depicting people as simultaneously exotic and fascinating and alien and offensive, in need of civilising. According to Said, 'Orientalism was ultimately a political vision of reality whose structure promoted the difference between the familiar (Europe, the West, "us") and the strange (the Orient, the East, "them")' (1978:43).

The Orientalist critique strikes at the heart of anthropology and history beyond Europe, and it is disturbing in its implication that these disciplines are handmaidens or creations of Western domination and xenophobia. They are unavoidably products of European society and inevitably reflect to some extent its concerns, and it is difficult to conceive of their avoiding the shortcomings identified by the critique, particularly regarding subjectivity – but many would challenge the notion that they connived in the promotion of ethnic aversion and domination rather than intending to foster tolerance through understanding. Both the study of our common human heritage (all of 'us') and the exploration of our various different cultural and historical inheritances ('us' and 'them') are inevitably informed by our conceptions as late-twentieth-century observers bearing a particular culture and its historical tradition. The past is another culture just as much as any contemporary 'exotic' society. The extent to which I can empathise with and understand the worldviews of others is equally questionable whether they are my own Victorian working-class ancestors labouring in unsafe factories and mines or their contemporaries in Oceania suddenly confronted by emissaries of the same capitalist system.

The 'us' and 'them' distinction that is central to the Orientalist critique is in a sense unavoidable because we *are* different; to pretend otherwise is a dangerous academic delusion. We may all increasingly converge and become alike as globalisation proceeds – that is, as world communications promote the adoption of similar Coca-Cola-iconised sociocultural practices and ultimately global history – but we still have different cultural heritages and histories that we are proud to maintain. The challenge is to present these differences with sympathy and with whatever comprehension we can achieve – to promote a better understanding of one another. This is to promote tolerance, even the celebration of ethnicity and one way to achieve this is to allow everyone a say.

The democratisation of representations attempted here is parochial. It concerns accounts of the first time that Europeans penetrated valleys occupied by Wola-speakers in the present-day Southern Highlands Province of Papua New Guinea. This occurred in 1935 when a Papuan colonial government patrol, led by two Europeans, Jack Hides and Jim O'Malley, entered and passed through the region on one of the epic exploratory journeys of that time. The Wola's homeland in the rugged Southern Highlands lies south-west of Mount Giluwe and north-east of Lake Kutubu. They are typical highlanders living in squat houses dispersed along the sides of valleys, where there are large areas of cane grass, the mountains above them being covered with rainforest. Their well-kept gardens are scattered across the landscape. They follow a semi-permanent form of swidden cultivation and subsist on a largely vegetable diet in which sweet potato is the staple. They also raise large numbers of domestic pigs and exchange them and other items of wealth (today largely cash, previously sea shells) with one another in interminable series of transactions that characterise important social events such as marriage and death. These exchanges are sociopolitical in character, maintaining order in their fiercely egalitarian stateless society. The supernatural conceptions of the Wola traditionally centre on beliefs in the ability of ancestor spirits to cause sickness and even death, in forest spirit forces, and in others' abilities to perform sorcery and administer poison. Today many people profess to be Christians, subscribing to markedly millenarian beliefs.

This chapter recounts something of the effect on and the response of the local population to the patrol which, uninvited, forcefully intruded into their lives. Men and women who had witnessed the event described what they remembered of this first contact with emissaries from the outside world. The patrol account quoted here for comparative purposes comes from Hides's book, *Papuan Wonderland*, a popular record of exploration adventure when it was published in 1936, which closely follows the official report submitted to the colonial Papuan authorities. The comparison serves as a stark illustration of the Orientalist critique, showing how people may differ in their recall and interpretation of the same historical events. We can detect here a socioculturally conditioned difference of perspective with a political dimension. Hides portrays the Wola as savage and treacherous warriors to justify their slaying, a view with strong contemporary racial overtones; the patrol officers were only men of their time. Furthermore, as the only voice on events, the report manipulates them to its own political ends, disguising from senior colonial officers the full extent of the violence as reported by the Wola (the killing of people contrasting markedly with the peaceful conduct of subsequent patrols). These criticisms should not prompt us too hastily to condemn the patrol, which showed great courage and fortitude in exploring one of the last unknown regions on earth.

The outside world arrives

When Hides and O'Malley's patrol entered the part of the Waga Valley occupied by the Wola, it threw the local population into turmoil. It was for them a cataclysmic event:

'Oh, there's something coming, something very strange approaching from over there. They say that it is ancestor spirits, arrived to eat us.' That's the kind of thing we said, when we heard about those first whites. Some of us fled in fear, into the forest, while others said they would go and have a look at them.

The patrol was no more comfortable, according to Hides's (1936: 115–16) account:

We went on south-eastwards. We travelled along wide roads with hundreds of natives to watch our passing. Crowds of curious women and old men with sticks

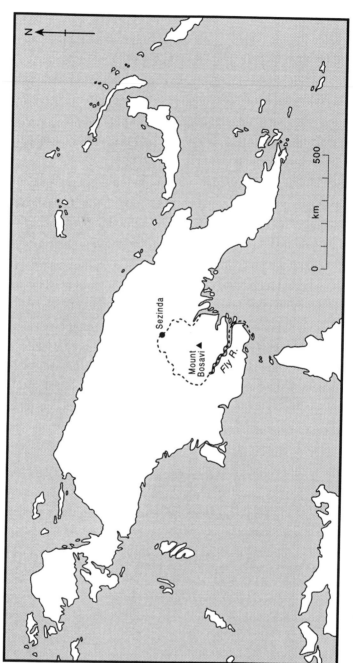

Map 3 Route of the Hides and O'Malley patrol, 1935

stood by the sides of the road, or followed at the rear. Our hats were of great interest to them, and as we walked along O'Malley and I continually raised them for the benefit of the sightseers. We frequently met new people, and always it was the same questioning gesture: 'Where are you going?' And always we waved our arms down the length of this densely populated valley. For five days we travelled through friendly people, but late in the afternoon of the fifth day we arrived among a new section of people. I did not like the shifty looks of some of the men, while an evil-looking chief particularly came under my notice. None of them would answer our appeals for food, and the forced friendliness of this scoundrelly old chief, who thought we concealed pearl shell in the tin box of medicines that we carried, could not be mistaken. With over two hundred men in the park as we made camp that evening, their intention to massacre the whole lot of us with their stone battle-axes, which every man at that time held in his hands, was most obvious.

But the police were kept together, well apart from the natives, and it was this fact, I think, that prevented an attack. This was no illusion. One had only to watch the nervous faces of a hundred men surrounding O'Malley and myself, the fidgeting hands holding the battle-axes, the cunning whispers that were being exchanged, and to see a crowd of about fifty men cunningly trying to surround the police, to realise the seriousness of the position.

'They will find someone to trap some day,' said Emesi. And I believe he is right.

We posted a strong guard that night, and when day-light came we departed from this inhospitable spot without tasting food, to go down to the Waga and cross it. I had hopes of meeting a friendly section of people on the opposite side of the valley.

Before the arrival of the patrol the Wola had been unaware of anything that existed beyond their region; its appearance revolutionised their perception of the universe. Individuals received intelligence of the patrol in different ways. Some maintain that they had some forewarning that something very strange was afoot. According to one man:

Before they arrived, someone came with a piece of tatty cloth and showed us. 'Where did that come from?' we asked. He said it came from some white spirit. Also before they came, people living to the north heard something strange which they thought was a wasp, but it was a plane they saw – something to do with those whites, just before they arrived. So I've heard it said, that they saw it, some months before those whites arrived.

But others disagree. When asked if he had heard such rumours, another man replied:

We said it was like a bird, not a wasp. Anyway, that came after that first patrol had passed through. It was a bird, we said – Oh, high, high up, like a mountain swiftlet.

And several others responded in a similar vein:

We neither heard about nor saw anything. The arrival of those Whites was the first we knew. Those other things came later, didn't they?

Plate 3.1 An early patrol into the Wola region: men come to trade food
at the patrol officers' tent *ca*. 1938.

News of the patrol's approach spread rapidly:

We had gone off to collect screw-pine nuts. We were cooking some when this
woman arrived. She pulled her skirt to one side and revealed herself to us completely. 'Ahh, look at that,' she said, 'some ghosts have come!' We decided that we
should go and have a look.

According to someone else who was present:

What's-his-name's father was so shaken up he fetched along a pig and was going
to kill it [whether because he thought it was the end of the world and so might as
well eat it first or as an offering to protect them from the spirits believed to have
arrived is unclear]. 'Ghosts are coming, quick, let's kill our pigs,' he said.

Some missed seeing the strange visitors. As one man recalled it:

They said, 'There are things coming, making houses and then taking them down
again as they come. They are coming along the path now. They're white-skinned,
with their bodies covered. And there are black men with them too!' We were
frightened that they were going to come over this way and molest us. We hid ourselves, waiting for them. But they never came this way.

Others almost collided with the patrol inadvertently. One woman
recalled:

Plate 3.2 The expressions on the faces of these Wola men are eloquent testimony to their astonishment at the arrival of white-skinned foreigners *ca.* 1938.

I don't know where they had slept or come from. But when my husband and I saw them they had put their 'houses' up. We turned round and hurried back, with the patrol coming behind us.

Others remember their return well:

Suddenly everyone started to yell, 'There are bush spirits coming.' That was the very first time whites came.

Few people have extensive knowledge of the route followed by the patrol, knowing only the paths they followed in their neighbourhood:

We don't know where they originated from. They came 'outside' . . . [i.e., appeared] to the north. They slept, then went on, slept again and moved on. Kept moving. We all scattered from their path in fear. Those men wearing clothes.

Those who approached the patrol did so with apprehension; the experience disturbed them. A woman recalled:

Someone came back who had gone to see them. He came back very frightened. 'Something has come,' he said.

But men urged one another on:

Others came for us to go and see them. They even persuaded us to leave some screw-pine nuts cooking in an earth oven and come . . . A brother of mine came that night and we decided to follow them.

When in the vicinity of the patrol, the men were understandably very cautious:

We didn't go close. We kept our distance, watched from [the cover of] the cane grass, and so on, to see what they were doing. We didn't walk across where they were camped, just up to the edge to have a look and then away again. When they moved they were sandwiched between those whose land they had passed over and those whose land they were approaching. We just looked from one side, not crossing to the other. They separated us. They were in the middle, where they camped.

They had good reason to keep their distance beyond their fear of the strangers as potentially malevolent spirits, for, as one woman explained,

They had killed a man. He was barricading a path with branches – to hide it from the patrol and protect his wife and children, so they wouldn't see it and find them. The path was to his wife's house and gardens [where she and their children were hiding]. It was not the main path followed by the patrol, but off it. One of the black men in the patrol saw him as he passed and hit him with an axe. Just like that, for nothing [some men surmised that he thought the man intended to impede his passage]. I didn't see it, I've only heard about it. I was hiding in the forest.

Nevertheless, there was some interaction of sorts between the patrol and some bold men, much of it puzzling to them:

One of those white men grabbed hold of someone who had gone to see them, grabbed him by the beard and said something to him. We supposed he was telling him not to molest them. He also took two blades of sword grass and tied them together and gave them to him. I think he was trying to tell him something like 'our fathers have never fought'.

According to someone else who witnessed the same or a similar incident:

We were returning from the forest, after collecting and cooking screw-pine nuts, when we met with those whites. One of them took a blade of sword grass and held it up to someone's nose. A taboo gesture, eh? Hands off.

The difficulties of communication were formidable. Some confusion was inevitable and doubtless contributed in considerable measure to the bloody disasters that marked the patrol's passage. As one man explained,

They didn't say anything to us. Who could have understood what they said, anyway? We went in terror, I tell you. They didn't communicate with us. One of the whites had his compass, which he kept looking at, and the patrol followed its own path. It was the first time we had seen them [Europeans], and we went in fear.

Another man's experience was somewhat different:

They indicated to us that they wanted us to show them the path, with their arms –
waving them – no words. We showed them, but we were frightened. And then they
killed some of us. After that we were terrified and ran off in fear. Before that we
weren't so scared; some of us didn't run away in fear. Women and children were
always frightened and kept out of it, at home.

Besides the route, the other urgent matter that prompted the patrol to
try to communicate with the local population was its need to secure food.
In his writing Hides strongly expresses his scorn and dislike of the Wola
for not giving food generously to the hard-pressed patrol. His comments
suggest that there was a food shortage at the time; he reports that people
repeatedly shouted at them '*Nahai*', which means 'There is none'. Not
only was there plenty of food in the gardens at the time however, but
screw-pines were in season and their nuts abundant:

It was a time when we had sweet potato. It was not a time of hunger. And we had
screw-pine nuts too.

Someone wounded by the patrol was suspicious:

There was sweet potato when they came. There was no hunger. If they [Hides and
O'Malley] said so [in their writing] they were lying – to their Masters [i.e., government superiors] to excuse their wrongdoings?

In this event, it is probable that those who shouted '*Nahai*' were trying to
tell the frightening newcomers that whatever they had come searching for
in their region was not to be found there and therefore they should continue on their way.

The patrol secured local produce in a variety of ways. The Wola would
certainly have been more forthcoming if they had been sure of some
material reward, and while the patrol had unfortunately omitted the
highly esteemed seashells from its trade goods, some of the things it had
would have sufficed for them at this first contact (later patrols, fore-
warned of the highlanders' desire for seashells, especially pearl shells, had
few problems securing food). But only rarely did they offer anything:

They tied an axe and a large knife to a dillenia tree to pay for the bags of sweet
potato they had dug up for themselves. They never did that elsewhere, they stole
food.

The theft of food was repeated several times:

They stole and ate everything: taro, bananas, sugar cane, harvesting it for themselves. We were afraid they would kill us. Even pigs, they dispatched them with
their guns.

Others commented:

Who were they going to buy food from? They went in anger. They erected their 'houses', ate, slept and then left . . . they didn't give us anything. We didn't see those things. They didn't buy their sweet potato. After they shot all those men, then perhaps they gave things for food? We don't know, we ran off in terror. They didn't have anything – like pearl shells, axes, or beads – those things the later whites brought with them.

No one could remember the offer, related by Hides (1936:116–19), of beads for some measly sweet potatoes, probably at a place called Huwguwn, or the surprisingly bold action of the young Wola man involved, given the terror everyone felt:

Hooting and yodelling followed us from the park, for the natives had risen early to watch our movements. Just before reaching the river, and while the treacherous natives were in the front and the rear of the party, an old woman surreptitiously came from a house by the side of the road and handed O'Malley and myself a bundle of cooked potatoes. The looks of this old mother showed that she knew how the rest of the people were treating us, and the action moved us both greatly. I placed a string of red beads over her head and we went on.

The road led us to a bridge across the Waga; but it was old and dangerous, and could only take one man at a time. I crossed it with O'Malley and some of the police, and then I sent my companion up the opposite side with four constables to meet the new section of people and see if he could obtain some food from them. We were all starving men, longing for a baked potato or a juicy bundle of broiled spinach.

After O'Malley had gone, I stood firmly by the end of the bridge to see the carriers over; my rifle was loaded, and I would have shot the first native that made an attempt to murder one of my weak and gallant carriers. These despicable people! We had not touched a house or garden, nor harmed dog or man. Why then did they treat us like this? Such were my thoughts as I watched the weak carriers, one by one, climb across that rotten bridge to the jeering and laughing calls of the natives standing by on the opposite bank.

I suppose it was because they saw in our weak and ragged party a small band of meek foreigners who were unarmed and thus easy prey. Our rifles to them were just so many wooden clubs, for not a shot had yet been fired in their country.

But nothing happened at the bridge, and after the last of the carriers had crossed, I followed them with the Sergeant and his police along the road that O'Malley had taken. This road led up a long slope, and on the crown of it we entered another of the parks. There were about four hundred men sitting down in rows close together on one side of it, while our party was resting on the grass lawn opposite them.

O'Malley said there was no food, that the people were unfriendly. I gazed across at those silent, inscrutable faces. Here were bigger and darker-skinned men than those on the opposite side of the valley, and they all wore large pom-poms of cassowary feathers on the tops of their wigs. I could see from the expressions of their faces that they had no intention of being friendly.

I walked slowly over to the group, and pointing to our starving men, made another appeal for food. But they shook their heads and said 'Nahai,' and waved their arms for us to go on. All around us were hundreds of acres of potatoes, and we could have dug a ton of them in half an hour; but I knew that these people were only wanting the slightest excuse to murder us all, and I did not want bloodshed. I held up an axe to them, and explained that I would give it if they allowed us to dig some food. But they just shook their heads and remained silent.

I went back and sat down with O'Malley, to make a cigarette with some tobacco and a dried leaf, and to think over our position. We had no food, no shelter, and only a little trade left; we were now practically walking along with our rifles and the clothes that we stood in. We were dependent entirely upon the hospitality of these people – and they unfriendly. What was I to do? If my carriers did not get food soon, they would be too weak to walk, and then we would be in a worse position.

As I sat there smoking, a young native from the western side of the valley, who had followed us over, and who, I had noticed, was prominent in camp the night previously, came forward to me with a small bag of potatoes. It contained seven. The self-assurance, the smirking, insolent smile on this young man's face, gave me a sick feeling in the stomach. He had not come to trade, but to mock and belittle us in the eyes of this new section of people.

He took the potatoes out with his hand, and placing them on the ground, demanded an axe. All the police were watching intently, as were the people of this new section.

'Wait until there is a Government gaol here,' murmured Dekadua. 'I will not forget your face.'

'Stand by the Taubadas,' I heard Sergeant Orai say, as we sat watching this native.

When he had placed all the potatoes on the ground, the native looked at me questioningly.

I took a good string of beads from my sling bag, got up, and carefully handed them to him.

He took them, but also smilingly started to take back four of the measly potatoes, food that was fit only for pigs. I indicated that he must place all the potatoes on the ground, and when I thought he would not do so, I made him by force. Then he stood back and flung the beads violently in my face, and, turning his back on me, walked over to where all his fellow-men were sitting down. He calmly sat down with them, at the same time making a gesture which obviously said: 'That's the way to treat these people.'

We had stood more than I had thought possible, and I was beginning to fear that the people, believing that we were weak and would offer no resistance, would start kicking us along the roads. So I ordered Dekadua to kick this man out of the park and on to the road that led to whence he came – and Dekadua did it well. He went up to the native.

'Who child are you?' he asked insolently in Motu. And when the native did not answer him, Dekadua pulled him up by the hair and kicked him good and hard right out of the park.

I then explained my action to the assembled crowd. Their faces never moved;

they all remained silent and sitting. And like a little band of outcasts in this forgotten land we went on without guides, and we slept that night in an old park for the second time without food.

It is intriguing to reflect on what the Wola audience made of this harangue in an incomprehensible tongue. Nevertheless, some people gave the patrol food:

People picked and gave the men *Rubus* berries to eat. They had heard that others had done this before along their route, and so did it. They gave them sweet potato and things too. They never gave anything in return. They put up their 'house' and ate and slept. They took food without paying and then left. When we gave them bananas and other food, they didn't give us clothing or any of those other things of yours. We just threw down sweet potatoes, bananas, and firewood and then went off in fear. We didn't know what to expect, it being the first time we had seen Europeans.

In the light of what he considered his kinsmen's generosity, one man asked:

Why did they do it [i.e., attack us]? When they were here we gave them screw pine nuts and sweet potato and bananas. I went and dug some up myself for them. They were wild things. We gave them to them for nothing. They just took them. We were frightened of them and didn't demand anything. If they had been true men they would have left some payment. We just threw the food down and left.

The Wola gave food even though they were aware that the patrol was carrying what to them were quite considerable food supplies:

When we went to see them they had packed up their house and had it in their bags, ready to leave. They had something white, some of which they left behind. Someone picked up some of it. It was like sago starch [flour?].

When people failed to bring the patrol the food it required, its members simply helped themselves to what they needed, often after violent incidents when everyone fled in terror:

They dug it up for themselves. We were frightened of them and kept our distance, especially after they'd killed us, and they got their own food. Bananas, sugarcane – they took for themselves. They went and dug up their own sweet potato from men's gardens and helped themselves to bananas – filled their bags with them. Everyone was frightened and keeping away, not giving them anything.

Non-human newcomers

Seeing the patrol helping itself to food and eating suggested something unexpected about the status of its members. As one man explained:

We saw them helping themselves to sugarcane from gardens as they came, so we supposed they must be true men [real human beings] for they became hungry.

And we thought we would offer them bananas and sweet potato. But they shot us up, and we fled in fear instead.

Another's comments indicated some confusion about what the newcomers were:

We said, 'Those ghosts are wearing "houses", they've put on "sleeves" like we put on arrow points. They're different to us.' But we could see they had bodies. When we heard about them coming, we didn't know what to think. We had a great surprise when we saw them.

A common reaction to the patrol's arrival was suspension of credulity, almost numbing of the faculties:

We said, 'Here comes something we've never seen before, come to see us and go.' Had we seen the like before? No, we'd seen nothing like it. Who was there to tell us who they were or where they'd came from? . . . that white man was tall. I only saw one of them. There were two, eh? The other must have gone on ahead. How should we know where they came from? I didn't think anything about them. Terror, that was all that occupied my mind, and I fled.

Few believed that the patrol was made up of human beings. Their minds turned more readily to spirit explanations. For many people these were the returned spirits of deceased ancestors:

'Ancestor spirits are coming, there are ghosts coming,' we shouted. Then they shot up two communities. Where they went then, I don't know.

Others had more frightening thoughts:

We considered them ghosts come to eat us. [The Wola believe that their ancestors' spirits, and other spirits, are malevolent – that they attack them, causing sickness and death. They refer to their attacks as 'eating,' gnawing at their vital organs to kill them.] We ran off in fear. We said they were ancestor spirits and were frightened, weren't we? They'd come to kill us, and we went in fear. When we heard about them, when we saw them, we were terrified.

Some people even thought that they had identified the spirits of deceased relatives returned:

You know, we said it was Kenay Hond's spirit come back. He was light-skinned and had only recently died. He was tall and pale-skinned, like those first whites. We thought it was him and his father, come back to demand an exchange payment owed them. We said they were ancestral ghosts, come back to eat us.

According to others they were malevolent forest spirits. These grotesque spirits are anthropoid heaps of ambulant vegetation with human-like limbs and features that lurk in remote forest regions and kill and eat the unwary:

We said, 'They're bush spirits coming. Their teeth are black, like cordyline berries. Black, real black, like cordyline fruits, they're coming.'

Some members of the patrol apparently had stained teeth, probably from betel nut chewing, hence this description of them as having blackened teeth like cordyline fruits. Another explanation was that it was the spirit called Sabkabyin, who lives in the sky, and its retinue fallen to earth:

Man-eating things, we said they were. We'd seen nothing like it before. Our fathers, our ancestors hadn't told us about anything like that. 'Sabkabyin is coming,' some said. 'He is crazy and seeking for a path, a way-out.' Lost they were, just wandering around. 'They're white-skinned spirits,' that's what we said. We went in terror. Where they came from, were going to, we had no idea. 'A spirit something is coming.' We fled in fear. Horribly terrified, we all fled, when we went to see them.

Some had high hopes about the Sabkabyin interpretation:

'They're coming, they're coming', someone shouted out. 'It's Sabkabyin dropped from the sky and bringing many pearl shells to share out among us!'

Yet another explanation was that the Europeans were the returning descendants of the fair-skinned brother who features in Wola myth:

We said, 'Look it's the descendants of that fair-skinned brother who lived here long ago but left by jumping down a pothole after a dispute over an earth oven of sweet potatoes with his do-nothing black-skinned brother. Look, it's spirits coming back.' We thought they were long-lost brothers and would have treated them so. We had the same faces and bodies and everything, though they wore clothes. We were excited to think that it was that fair-skinned brother from the pothole come back.

According to some it was expectable:

It was that white brother, who had told the black one to stay and that he'd be back some day. It was him come back, we said.

All this talk of white-skinned spirits led to the coining of an oath used today by speakers wishing to emphasise a point:

We said they were *towmow hundbiy*, pale-skinned ghosts. And since that time, you know, we've used *towmowhundbiy* as an oath we swear. like we say *sezinda* to affirm a pledge.

The latter oath also originated with the penetration of the outside world in the guise of the patrol into Wola lives:

That killing, that massacre, that occurred at Sezinda. Since then, the word *sezinda* has become a strong oath word we swear when angry.

Tragic misunderstandings

The origin of the swear-word *sezinda* is associated with one of the tragic occasions on which the patrol opened fire on the local population. The event poignantly captures the utter confusion that can occur when two alien cultures meet and graphically conveys the terror experienced by these New Guinea highlanders confronted by strange beings:

They came this way, and we proceeded together down into that narrow ravine, where they killed us. Down there in that defile, where the rock face runs along. They followed that path. They went along there, where the rock face closed them in. There were four of us. They shot two of us with their 'arrows.' Nobody fired any arrows or anything. They just suddenly fired – 'pow-pow.' No one drew a bow, not even playfully. When they fired, I fled in terror. I ran up there, to the top of the hill. I had nothing to eat. They shot us all at once, together. We couldn't have retaliated with our bows, even if we had had them; we couldn't fight against that. Their 'bows' and ours weren't the same. They didn't shoot one by one slowly, but all together – 'pow-pow'.

Others' experiences were slightly different:

They went down into the defile at that chestnut-oak tree. They were travelling across. I stood there watching, where Ndikiy's father had tied up some sugarcane. I didn't follow them down there. The two whites and the patrol travelled along, and I traversed the slope higher up until I reached Paziy's house. When I arrived there – wah, something made a loud 'pow-pow' noise. Someone shouted that there was an avalanche, that the cliff was falling down. [The confined space and rock wall must have magnified and echoed the rifle fire considerably, giving this fearsome impression.] Again and again there was this 'pow-pow' sound. I turned my back to it. Just then Lol's father and Hiyt Duwaeb came running up, screaming that they were spirits come to kill and eat us. They shot many of my brothers. Lol's father had been carrying his axe and they had hit its stone head and shattered it into pieces! I was hit in the neck, here.

Another one of the wounded recalled:

We followed on behind them. They came to Korpay [scene of the massacre]. We did nothing down there, but 'pow-pow.' They shot to the front first, and then 'pow-pow', behind and all around. I was hit. I had blood pouring out. I wasn't knocked off my feet. I didn't fall down. I just fled – oh, terror.

Others not present and not so emotionally involved gave more reflective accounts:

As I heard what occurred, people surrounded the patrol, looking at them. And they blocked the path. They were like a garden fence, all around them, and the strangers became worried and feared an attack on them. Then they opened fire with their guns and shot many men. All those men running hither and thither, pushing and shoving, breaking down undergrowth noisily, frightened those whites, I guess. They thought it was an attack. There they were in the middle of all this rumpus, thinking that we intended to wrong them, and 'pow-pow' they opened fire on us. We thought that their guns were 'man-eating' things, belonging to ghosts, and that they were seeking men to eat. Some say a man did something, they say he had a bow and drew it, pulling it in fun and not intending to loose off an arrow. The whites and their carriers saw it, I suppose. What was in his mind, who knows? He was the only person carrying a bow. He came from the other side of Sezinda [where the patrol was heading] to meet the patrol, with a crowd. He had a bow, which the Whites thought, when they saw it, signified we were up to something. He and his relatives have always strongly denied it. There has been some dispute over the business. Those who lost relatives in the attack have demanded reparation payments from his relatives as the cause of the misfortune. They've always denied any responsibility and have never paid over anything, maintaining that the demands are empty, nothing. They killed them for no reason. They were so close to them too. The path was narrow, hemmed in by a cliff on one side and a steep forested slope on the other. In this confined space, with all of us milling around, they became frightened and 'pow-pow' opened fire, for no reason. They did wrong. They should have been friendly with us, not assaulted us like that. We gave them no grounds. We were all coming along the path together.

This line of reasoning is quite plausible. The place where the massacre occurred is confined and narrow, just the sort of location where a nervous European would fear a massed ambush, and Hides, tired and over-wrought, makes it clear that he imagined just such treacherous designs (1936:119–22):

Morning came with a cloudless sky, and the sun over the mountains in the east to make the heavy dew sparkle in the grass of the park. With hungry stomachs life seemed hard indeed. Three men, carrying unstrung bows and bundles of arrows, came in to lead us as we prepared to move off. I asked them again for food, but they explained that we would get it at some place farther on. I knew that they were up to something, but we had nothing else to do but follow them.

We crossed a grass basin covered with snow-white balsam and heliotrope stock – a pretty sight – and followed the guides to some small limestone pinnacles two to three miles distant from the park where we had rested for the night. Through a gap in these pinnacles, and extending south-eastwards, we could see another valley system, a tableland of hollows and mounds, all covered with grass and culti-vations. The three natives pointed to it, and called the country the Wen.

A large crowd of men now began to appear at our rear. Some of them trailed their bows behind them. Whenever they saw us look back, they would drop their weapons and stand with arms akimbo. Others carried their arms covered with green pandanus leaves, or hidden in bundles of sugarcane.

A terrific din of yodelling was going on all the time, in front as well as in the rear; but apart from watching the men carefully, we made no sign.

Climbing to the top of the gap, where one track led up both ways of the saddle, and the other down into the south east, we found about twenty unarmed men ready to receive us. Their friendliness was overdone – obviously forced – but I did all I could to show that we neither feared them nor anything they could do. We fol-lowed closely their every move. I took photographs of them, and explained that our way was down the valley of the Wen; they in turn told me that they were of the Injigale people, and the place where we now stood was called Bangalbe. I knew what they were up to, and I wanted to ask them why they wanted to kill us, and to

Plate 3.3 A homestead above the steep-sided defile at Korpay where Hides was convinced that the Wola intended to attack his patrol.

explain that our rifles were not things to be despised; but some of those smirking, self-possessed faces would have taken a lot of convincing.

While all this was going on, a man appeared on the saddle about twenty yards away above us, and with an impatient, plain gesture told the unarmed natives with us that they were to move the patrol on down the track. With that he disappeared down a side-track, and the men to whom we had been talking now nervously urged us to be on our way. The yodelling on the by tracks had ceased, and we were told there would be no guides, that the people were going back. This was an obvious lie; how cheaply they took us! I turned to Sergeant Orai standing by me. His beard was black and fuzzy, his uniform torn and dirty with a hundred and fifty days of breaking across as many miles of mountains, and in the haggard and worn face of the great Papuan was a grim coolness. I did not speak to him, but he uttered my thoughts.

'It is here that we find it, Taubada,' he said.

I ordered all the police to load their carbines, and getting the carriers bunched closely together, we went down into the timber following the track south-east-wards. Of the four police in front, two watched the right-hand side of the track and two the left side.

We had not gone more than two hundred yards when a terrific din of yodelling arose on all sides of us, and the whole line was attacked. It all happened with remarkable suddenness, but every man was ready for them, and Borege was the only one to take an arrow. I fired in front of me and at the back of me, at men not fifteen feet away, rushing with short stabbing spears. The poor carriers got new strength; they yelled and screamed and threw their steel tomahawks at the attack-ing natives. To give some idea of how these people regarded us, and how closely they attacked, Constable Budua, rushed at close quarters by spearmen, started swinging his rifle instead of firing. He was pulled to the ground, a man with a battle-axe on top of him; and had I not heard Budua's call for help, and seen the incident, he would have been killed by two other natives assisting his assailant. I shot one of them as I rushed to Budua's assistance, and, pulling his assailant off him, after hitting him with the butt of my rifle, allowed him to run off. The strug-gle was over by then; it had only lasted about fifteen seconds. The thunder of the rifles had brought silence in the country around us, and we walked out of the timber into cultivations again.

The Wola deny to a man that they had any treacherous intentions and that they attacked the patrol, making what occurred tragic indeed. All those I spoke to vehemently denied that they or anyone they saw had even carried weapons when they went to see the strange arrivals:

We all went empty-handed. We carried nothing. We said that they were ancestor spirits come, so what do you think we would be doing going off to fight them? Come on! We didn't carry axes or bows. I had my string bag, that was all. We just went to look at them. What are they up to, we wondered?

Hides's description of Wola fighting tactics is strange, too. He refers to many spearmen armed with 'short stabbing spears'. Few Wola possess or fight with spears – their favoured weapon is the bow and arrow – and they have no short stabbing spears, the few spears they own being six or more feet long and hurled in fighting. In ambushes they employ only bows.

One thing in particular which seems to have rattled Hides was the yodelling of the Wola, which he erroneously interpreted as their 'kill call'. What shouting there was expressed high spirits and nervous excitement:

We did hoot and dance a bit before they shot us. But not a sound did we make afterwards. We just fled in terror . . . those of us who were following the patrol, we didn't hoot. It was those leading in front who did that [to warn those ahead of the patrol's approach].

There was nothing aggressive in this:

Who were we going to fight? Anyway we went empty handed. What would we be doing with a bow? We just went to look. No warlike shouting or hooting.

In view of what they think was the unprovoked nature of the patrol's attack, the Wola have subsequently tried to explain to themselves why it occurred. Several have taken up the rumour of the man carrying a bow, even foolhardily stringing it, and so inciting the patrol to open fire on them. Others, present at the massacre, dismiss this as nonsense:

We didn't fight. They killed those men for no reason. We didn't do anything at all. That fellow some say had a bow, I never saw him there. That's empty talk.

According to someone else:

They deceived us. They killed us for no motive. We carried nothing like bows or axes. People did something wrong to them over there, eh? [In the place the patrol had come from, thus provoking the attack on them.] That talk is nonsense. He did nothing. None of us did anything. Why should we have? We were frightened of them. Who was there for them to fight? They just shot us down. We hadn't seen the likes of their 'bows' before. They played us false. We did nothing.

Whatever precipitated the unfortunate shooting, the response of the survivors was predictably panic-stricken flight into hiding:

We fled in terror, up the side of the garden there, towards Sezinda. Some entered Pabol's house nearby. They all piled in and huddled there in fear. Women too, they cowered in their houses, with doors fastened. I hurried on to Sezinda proper. I tore open the door of Pawiyn's father's house and crept in. There was a woman in there who shrieked, 'Who's that coming into my house?' Scared us both. I told her what had happened.

When asked if he thought of taking revenge the speaker looked amazed:

What! Oh no, we were all terrified. Who could have taken revenge against that?

Others agreed with him:

Aaah no, no we couldn't fight back. Terrified we ran off to hide. Who would even go to look at them after that? Panic-stricken they fled away. We hid ourselves in the forest, under rock-faces, curled up in balls. Those strangers we feared would come back to 'eat' us.

The death toll and the numbers seriously wounded were horrendous. In a few moments the patrol had wreaked greater carnage than the Wola could have achieved after weeks of fighting. The lists given by different individuals vary, each forgot some fatalities; some included only those killed instantly and others those who died subsequently of wounds, and all tended to recall only those related to or known to them. Ten names occurred several times in different accounts as among those killed, and a total of eighteen persons were named as wounded. According to one man:

They killed Sol, Obil, Moromol, Wenja Taizom, Haenda Wabuw, Obaynol, Penj's brother – that's seven – and Ezom, Eberol's father (he's the one whose head was blown to pieces), and Hwimb Olnay. That's ten. They killed this many men [holding up all fingers and thumbs]. Many died. Those wounded who survived were Hiyt Duwaeb, Kal Hobor, Periyen's husband Naway, Waendiyaem, Hoboga Waeniym, a woman – who's-it, Haelaim, Hwimb Hiyp, and Waendor. That's another ten. That's twenty altogether, ten killed and ten wounded who didn't die.

The European and Wola accounts of the massacre's aftermath also bear little resemblance to one another and could be taken to describe different events. According to the patrol version (1936:122–3):

Our attackers came to meet us with presents of food. They stood and offered the bunches of bananas and bundles of spinach; but the food was thrown back at them, and I explained that we did not take presents from people who tried to murder us; and further, that when we were ready for the food, we would take it. They stood like down hearted schoolboys, and for all their treachery, my heart went out to them. So that when a little later about twenty venerable old men met us, and with great difficulty and care explained by gestures that this was not the section that had attacked us, I pretended to believe their story. At the same time I told them that we would now take the food we wanted.
Their answering gestures could have been read as: 'Go to it, old man.'
We killed two pigs in a pen nearby, dug what potatoes we wanted, and then handed the old men axes, which they all smilingly accepted. Then with large fires going, and food cooking, we gorged ourselves to contentment. The attitude of these people was extraordinary. Within an hour or so of the attack, fully three hundred men, all of them genuinely friendly, were sitting around the party; and it would have been indelicate, I thought, to have even suggested to them that only a short time before we had been fighting with them. They seemed to treat a fight like a football match. They could be treacherous, but they could also be gentlemen.
That night we slept contentedly in one of their parks, with the natives sleeping in the farmhouses within a hundred yards of the camp, and the next morning at daylight we were on our way following a good road down the western side of the Wen plateau.

According to the Wola, after the shooting members of the patrol emerged from the narrow path and descended on a lonely women's house, where they committed inexcusable and barbaric violence. All women and children were kept away from the strange spirits to protect them, hiding in houses or in the forest:

'They've come to "eat" us,' we said. And so only men remained behind. Women and children we sent off to remote places to hide.

One of the women who were inside the house attacked by the patrol recalled what happened on that horrifying day:

We were sitting indoors, with the door fastened, when they came. All the men had run off in terror. We had heard the 'pow-pow' of them shooting our men. We hadn't any idea what it was. How could we, when we were sitting inside? We wondered what it was. 'Has the rock face fallen?' we asked ourselves. 'Has there been an avalanche of stones?'

We were terrified. After they had killed our men, they came to kill our pigs, and us women and children. They tore open the door of our house and demanded everything. Puliym's mother released the pigs one at a time and drove them out of the door to them waiting outside. They were black-skinned men, policemen. The whites were on the clearing over there. The cloth I saw was black with red – like policemen wore. I saw it around their legs. We didn't see their faces. I didn't get a good look at what they were wearing. When they arrived we were sitting inside with our door securely fastened. They tore the front off the house, attacked it with axes and bush knives. They ripped off the screw-pine bark lining and some of the wall stakes.

They took the pigs, one at a time, and shot them outside. They killed them all, nine pigs. And they were all big ones too, Like this, not small ones. After they killed them, they singed off their bristles, over a fire made from the wood torn off our house. They broke up our house for wood to singe the pigs. Then they butchered them ready to carry off, ready to cook in an earth oven. They lashed the pork on poles with their belts to carry it. After they had killed and prepared the pigs to carry off, they turned on us. They attacked us women. We didn't see well what was going on. We were cowering inside, terrified. They returned and stood there and fired their guns into our house. They shot Hiyt Ibiziym, Hoboga Paeriyn, Bat Maemuw my sister, Ndiy, Maeniy and me. That's six of us. Also my son Maesaep and my daughter Perliyn. We were all hiding in that house. They came right up to the house to shoot into it, and they fired on us. We sat indoors petrified. We didn't cry or anything like that. We just sat.

After they had shot us up, they carried the butchered pigs off to cook. We remained huddled indoors, terrified. All the men had fled. What was to become of us? We didn't do anything. We were so frightened that we were all dizzy and faint. We slumped into a sort of stupefied coma. When we went outside we couldn't walk, but trembled and kept falling over. Who was there to bandage our wounds with moss and leaves? No one bandaged them. We had all been shot and wounded, so there was no one present fit enough to bandage us up. We just slumped indoors. We didn't think anything. All we felt was terror and dizzy. I was sort of senseless.

After mentioning the attack on the women's house, one man remarked with some irony:

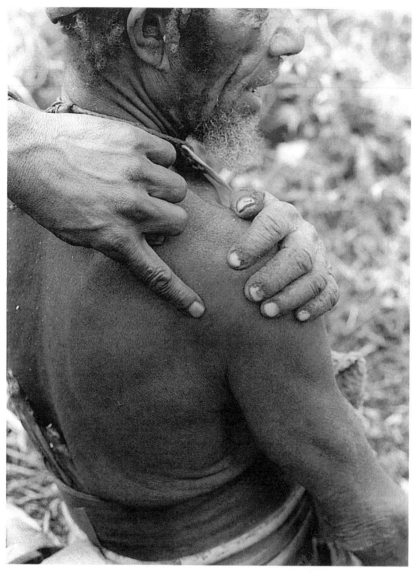

Plate 3.4 Recounting the events of the tragedy nearly fifty years later, Kal Naway shows a bullet-wound scar on his shoulder.

Well they didn't rape any women. That was done by later patrols, when they not only stole our pigs but our women too, and broke into our houses and smashed up our possessions, like our bows and things. They even excreted in our fireplaces.

One of the wounded women – the one who released the pigs – became a celebrity years later:

That Puliym's mother, she received a bullet here, in the temple [and survived]. A bit of it came out of her head by itself [was expelled] years later.

Some of the wounds received were gruesome:

They had shot my cross-cousin Huruwmb, and I went to see him. You could see his liver exposed. They kept sending me to fetch water for him to drink because he was thirsty. Back and forth, I kept going to fetch water for him. He lived in agony for three days. On the fourth day he died. They laid him to rest at a rock face [an exposed burial].

Others went into equally lurid detail:

Kal Aenknais had his thighs and lower torso smashed, completely pulverised here and here. He kept groaning, 'oh, ah.' I saw him. He died later. Wounded in the guts he was. His intestines were punctured. When he was given water to drink, to cool him off, it came spurting out of the holes in his body. Then there was Obil. His eyes were blown clean out of his head. When they landed on the path they wriggled around and around for ages. He died too. And then there was that poor blighter – aah – whose entrails were shot out. His intestines and stomach were blasted right out of his body. Huwlael Tila, he had a bullet go in his throat here and come out there. And Naway was hit here in the shoulder and it too went right through him and out here. They say that the same 'arrow' went through them both. Maendop Wend's father had his hand shot, cleaved in two it was. And Hoboga Waeniym lost an ear.

In several cases there was little that relatives could do except watch the wounded die. Some were more fortunate:

My wound healed itself, with no operation or anything – unlike poor Hiyt Duwaeb.

Others killed pigs in an attempt to facilitate their recovery:

Hoboga Waeniym, he killed a pig in offering [to placate his ancestor spirits]. He was wounded here . . . those wounded, who feared that they might die, decided to kill and eat some of their pigs. They ate them to give them strength, to fortify them in their weakness.

Relatives operated on some poor souls to try to remove bullets:

We operated on Kal Waendiyaem. We cut him with chert blades to remove the 'arrow.' The thing we removed was black with holes in it. It was round [a shotgun pellet?]. We took it from his shoulder, here. It was small and round and pitted with holes. It just went into his flesh, not into any organ or bone. Some men, you know, they say were shot by one bullet – it went through one and into the other.

Following the massacre, there was a funeral the like of which the Wola had never before witnessed:

Tomorrow, the day after, we thought, we'll collect up the corpses. We sat terrified indoors with our doors securely fastened. Some hadn't returned from the forest but sat out cowering under rock outcrops. We collected those who had fallen nearby, but further away we left them. We got them that day and spent the night with the corpses in with us because we feared that those whites would return to eat them. The next day, when we had collected all the corpses we could, we lashed them to poles on that clearing at Sezinda. [The customary way of mourning the dead is to tie them horizontally beneath a pole, suspended at chest height above the ground, and keen over them for a few days before interment.] The clearing was full of poles with corpses tied to them. Like a pig kill! [The analogy here is with the many sides of pork draped in display over the horizontal pole at a pig kill.] We were surrounded by corpses, there was no room left. We gathered them up, one after another. In sorrow, in mourning, many of us killed pigs [as part of the mortuary exchange following death].

After a few days of mourning, relatives disposed of the corpses:

We mourned over them for a few days and then we put them in raised exposed graves. We didn't bury them in the earth. We built platforms at a rock face. Some relatives carried corpses off elsewhere to mourn and bury. Those left at Sezinda we laid out at that rock face.

Not all those killed received a proper funeral:

There was Henep Obaynol. He was completely blasted to pieces. We couldn't pick up his corpse, he was in bits. We left him there on that narrow path. We collected up what we could of his body and deposited it in a crevice of the rock face [bordering the path].

In the meantime the patrol had moved on:

Those whites spent the night at Shobera. Then they went on to Mungtay, and then Meruwt, where they say they killed many more men. They didn't kill any more of us round here.

The last those living in the vicinity of the massacre heard about the patrol involved another shoot-out in which it is said, with some satisfaction, that one of the patrol was killed:

At Meruwt – ooof – there was more violence. Someone there shot one of the patrol through his clothes with a bone-tipped arrow. He hit a black-skinned man. They buried him, they say, in the soil inside their house, and covered over the spot with ash and charcoal like a fireplace. They saw it when they left. After that, where they went, search me!

The experiences of the Wola of first contact with the world outside their valleys were not unusual for Melanesia. The confusion and mayhem they experienced were a common feature of initial meetings between black islanders and white intruders. When industrial nation states confront stone age stateless societies rapid and disturbing change inevitably follows. In extending to 'them' their say about events 'we' gain more insight into these events and the processes that underlie them. Seeking a balance between **our** questions and **their** views, however, we do not speak for them, we inevitably impose ourselves on what we study.

FURTHER READING

B. Connolly and R. Anderson 1987 *First contact* New York: Viking Penguin

D. Denoon and R. Lacey (eds.) 1981 *Oral tradition in Melanesia* Port Moresby: Institute of Papua New Guinea Studies

J. Hides 1936 *Papuan wonderland* Glasgow: Blackie and Son

P. Hope 1979 *Long ago is far away* Canberra: Australian National University Press

R. Keesing and P. Corris 1980 *Lightning meets the west wind* Oxford: Oxford University Press

M. J. Leahy 1994 *Explorations into highland New Guinea 1930–1935* (ed. D. E. Jones) Bathurst: Crawford House Press

E. L. Schieffelin and R. Crittenden (eds.) 1991 *Like people you see in a dream* Stanford: Stanford University Press

J. Sinclair 1969 *The outside man* London: Angus and Robertson

For biographical accounts of contact and change see:

R. M. Keesing (ed.) 1978 *Elota's story* St Lucia: Queensland University Press

A. M. Kiki 1968 *Kiki: ten thousand years in a lifetime* London: Pall Mall

P. Matane 1972 *My childhood in New Guine* Oxford: Oxford University Press

Ongka 1979 *Ongka* (trans. A. Strathern) London: Duckworth

On Orientalism see:

F. Barker (ed.) 1985 *Europe and its other* Colchester: University of Essex Press

J. G. Carrier (ed.) 1992 *History and tradition in Melanesian anthropology* Berkeley: University of California Press

E. W. Said 1978 *Orientalism* New York: Pantheon

N. Thomas 1989 *Out of time: history and evolution in anthropological discourse* Cambridge: Cambridge University Press

E. Wolf 1982 *Europe and the people without history* Berkeley: University of California Press

FILMS

First contact Institute of Papua New Guinea Studies

My father, my country Film Australia, Wide World

4   Technological change and economic growth

Many populations throughout Melanesia began to experience changes in their lives some time before they saw the Europeans who were responsible for them (and occasionally even before they were aware of their existence) as manufactured material objects, new crops, markedly increased numbers of sea shells, and so on, imported elsewhere by the unseen newcomers were disseminated along local trade routes. These indirectly induced changes are instructive with regard to the process of social change because they involve relatively few new elements and their consequences can therefore be more readily perceived. They are directly attributable to technological shifts, and they proceed gradually and on a relatively small scale, the societies concerned adjusting to accommodate them without experiencing disruption. Because this preliminary and short-lived stage of social change can never be observed by outsiders, we are reduced to speculation informed by the comments and remembrances of local people.

In its review of the economic and social consequences of this initial, technologically driven phase of change, this chapter turns to the Siane people of the Eastern Highlands of Papua New Guinea, just west of the present-day township of Goroka. They are typical New Guinea highlanders, shifting cultivators whose staple crop is sweet potato and who raise pigs that serve as wealth, together with other items such as seashells and birds' plumes, in the sociopolitical exchange that features prominently in their social lives. It is through excellence in these that men can achieve the status of 'big men', the nearest position to leader that anyone can aspire to in this stateless and fiercely egalitarian society.

The Siane were unaware of the existence of any world but their own few precipitous valleys until 1933, when the first European explorers, gold prospectors, and government patrol officers reached their region. For the next decade they had little contact with Europeans and this was the period of indirect change. By the early 1950s, when the anthropologist Richard Salisbury lived among them, the Australian administration had established control over them and initiated various development programmes, introducing cash crops and some basic medical services, and considerable numbers of men had been recruited as indentured labourers for coastal plantations. This was the beginning of direct and prolonged contact, and the result is that the Eastern Highlands is one of the most 'developed' regions in the highlands today.

Stone to steel tools

During the indirect contact period, the most important source of change, according to Salisbury, was the arrival of steel axes. These were introduced into the highlands by Europeans at only a few centres initially but were soon dispersed over large areas when people elsewhere learned that they were considerably more efficient than polished stone axes. They reduced the time men had to spend working, releasing them to pursue other activities, and thus engendered social change. (Siane women never possessed or worked with axes.) At first, when they were in limited supply, the steel tools also counted as wealth in sociopolitical exchange, their value increasing with the distance from their European-imported source.

According to Salisbury (1962), relying on the impressions of Siane men, it had previously taken them three to four times longer to complete any task using a stone axe. He estimates that whereas in the stone era men had spent about 80 per cent of their time engaged in subsistence activities, in which axe work featured prominently, the arrival of steel axes had reduced this to 50 per cent. In other words, men had found themselves with 30 per cent more time to spend on other activities (see also Godelier with Garanger 1973). Shifts of this magnitude – what we currently call technological unemployment – are sure to prompt some social changes. But these estimations of the times involved in this technological change are probably too generous.

In a series of experiments in which Wola men worked at different tasks using stone and steel tools to allow comparison of their relative efficacies, steel axes proved 1.5 times faster than stone in garden work and artifact manufacture and 1.2 times faster in firewood collection (Sillitoe 1979). An overall statistic calculated from the data on all the activities in which stone and steel tools were used revealed that steel implements were 1.4 times faster, but this statistic is of little practical use. In the first place, it is not the case that the Wola saved themselves about 25 minutes for every hour they worked with steel tools compared with stone ones. The times for the different activities amalgamated in the statistic are not directly comparable in this way because people worked for different periods of time on the various tasks. They collected firewood daily, cleared a garden perhaps every year or two, built a house every five years or so, and

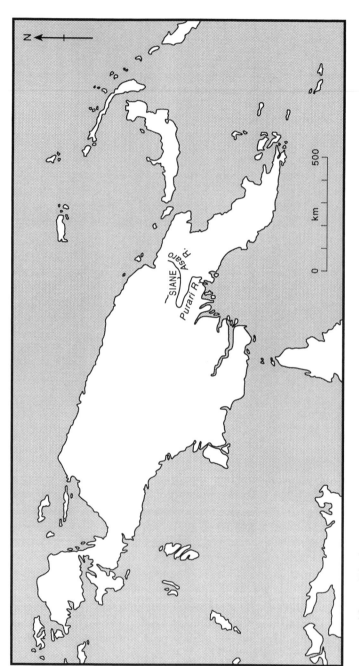

Map 4 The Siane and the Asaro River

made certain artifacts only once in a lifetime and sometimes never. Furthermore, it is not always feasible to make direct comparisons between stone and steel tools. Their use requires different techniques, and their comparative efficacy varies from one task and one material to another. Also, men use steel axes for work not previously attempted with stone, such as felling and splitting enormous hardwood trees. On top of this, time expenditure is an inadequate measure of efficiency: it ignores the more efficient exploitation of the environment and the better-quality work facilitated by steel tools. Indeed the extra time now spent on some tasks to obtain the better finish attainable with steel tools increases the comparative efficacy of stone when measured in terms of time alone.

The arrival of steel tools doubtless led to some changes by shortening the time required to complete various tasks. (The time involved with the Siane could have been greater than with the Wola, for according to Salisbury they were classic shifting cultivators who abandoned plots after a single crop, whereas the Wola cultivate many of their gardens continuously for several years; this would have increased considerably the time the Siane spent clearing new gardens each year and consequently the time-saving impact of steel tools.) Furthermore, it is unlikely that steel tools were the only new things to affect Siane subsistence activities. New crops, and particularly new high-yielding varieties of traditional crops such as sweet potatoes, would have had a significant impact too. These new varieties spread rapidly through the densely settled highlands from community to community, and people experimented with them enthusiastically. They would have reduced the amount of work required to produce the same amounts of food as previously, and here the time saved would have concerned women as well as men, for they were involved in the later stages of cultivation, in which axes were not used. Other manufactured items that would have arrived during the same period could have saved further time, substituting for traditionally made artifacts. These time savings may again have significantly concerned women too, notably when fabricated cloth replaced certain string netted items which women spent substantial periods of time producing.

Whatever the source and scope of the technological changes resulting from indirect contact, it appears that they led to certain time economies – allowing people to achieve their stone age level of production by working fewer hours. How did the Siane use the time they saved? It turned out that it was not to increase their output as the theory of economic development assumes. Uninfluenced at that time by capitalist economic assumptions of growth, improving standards of living, and so on, and lacking an economic system that would have facilitated the distribution of increased surplus at a profit if they had produced it, the Siane were apparently

Plate 4.1 A New Guinea highlander, Ak Lauwiy of the Augu River valley, carrying a polished stone work axe *ca.* 1939.

Plate 4.2 The distribution of pearl shell valuables in the Southern Highlands Province to compensate allies who had lost a relative in a war.

content with their lot. This may be a retrograde response with regard to the promotion of economic advancement, but it is one that suggests the manner in which Melanesians would probably have managed technological change if the industrial world had not intervened directly to supervise its adoption.

Instead of using the time they saved to produce more food and goods, according to Salisbury, the Siane fought more wars and engaged in more sociopolitical exchange. 'Demand for subsistence goods remains stable, and the amount of capital investment *shrinks* to the amount needed to produce the same amount of goods. People try to gain additional power, for which there appears the most elastic demand, either by fighting or by the use of material tokens of prestige' (1962:209). Regarding increased warfare there is little information; presumably the Siane had reasons for fighting beyond a desire to pass the time, and without an investigation of them we cannot know whether or how wars during the indirect-contact period were associated with the arrival of steel tools. Given the evidence from elsewhere in the highlands an increase in sociopolitical exchange seems more probable.

Although the arrival of steel tools, new crop varieties and other manufactured items may have released men and women for indeterminate periods of time from subsistence activities and allowed men to devote more time to exchange, equally important was the import of large quantities of traditional seashell wealth by Europeans to pay local people for produce and services. This wealth, like steel tools, again flowed out from the few centres established by Europeans, moving over considerable distances through numerous transactions. The dispersal of this dramatic increase in the supply of wealth from a few locations led to some intriguing short-term social changes as people adjusted their exchange rates to cope with it. Those near the European centres suddenly found themselves with considerably more valuables than their neighbours to offer in sociopolitical exchange. They were able, for one thing, to afford to have more wives than before, and there was a speculated flow of women towards them until the increased wealth, moving against women and pigs, reached others.

Again, it is not clear why the Siane dramatically increased their exchange activity. They would doubtless have given more things in any payment to absorb the extra valuables, but they would not necessarily have increased the number of transactions in which they engaged, which were linked to births, marriages and deaths. And while some ambitious men may have sought out added opportunities to contribute wealth to exchanges in order to earn respect and big man status, they need not have generated considerable numbers of new exchange events to do so. Furthermore, pigs featured as wealth in the exchange nexus, and Salisbury maintains that the stimulus given to these activities also resulted in an increase in pig production. These animals consumed a considerable proportion of the produce grown in gardens; the Siane only needed to start keeping a few more pigs for men to have been obliged to use the time saved with the arrival of steel axes to clear larger gardens to feed them. It appears that the Siane may have used at least some of the time saved with the arrival of steel tools productively.

Shifts in demand for imports

The significant point in respect of the arrival of steel tools remains that the Siane did not use these technologically induced changes to augment their stock of capital and promote economic growth: 'In stone-using times the capital stocks of the society represented about 12 per cent of one year's income; in steel-using times they have shrunk to about 10 per cent of the national income . . . it is clear that Siane prosperity has not been accompanied by any dramatic *increase* in the rate of capital investment' (Salisbury 1962:146–9). This trend continued into the early period of

direct contact, the Siane displaying little inclination to increase the
material standard of their lives or their subsistence productive capacity,
instead using many changes resulting from the European presence in
what was for them more important social and political activities. Men
were eager to obtain imported objects to give away in exchange, working
to acquire them, and devoting the time saved in the subsistence domain to
earning and manipulating them. These objects were not additional productive or economic capital but social and political assets.

The social pressures on men to behave in this way were immense.
Migrant labourers returning from contracts on coastal plantations were
obliged, for instance, to distribute shares of the money they had earned,
either directly or as material goods, among relatives and friends. If they
refused they would seriously damage both their social relations and their
reputations, for a successful and respected man was one who gave generously of his wealth. This was the road to social and political influence, to
big man status, along which all ambitious men strove to walk as far and as
fast as they could. Hence the desire of men to obtain (and willingness to
labour for) objects to distribute to others rather than to augment their (to
them sufficient) subsistence productive capacity. Whether or not markedly more exchange events occurred, there was considerably more
wealth circulating in them. Each man sought to increase his assets and
strengthen his position and thus contributed to an inflation of the size of
payments. This had the effect, given the even distribution of wealth and
roughly equal opportunities to obtain it in any region, of putting men on a
downward-moving escalator on which they struggled to stay in more or
less the same place.

Left alone, with no outside agency interfering to change values, aspirations and demands, there is no reason a society like that of the Siane
should have moved beyond this stage. Payments would have risen until
certain valuables became too common to be acceptable, and this would
have pulled payments back down to manageable levels. But outside forces
did intervene, and Salisbury maintains that in his dealings with the Siane
(paying them for food and services) there was a shift in preferences from
(1) goods featuring in exchange (e.g., *tambu* shells, beads) to (2) those
regarded as luxuries and used to entertain visitors (e.g., tobacco, salt) to
(3) hard goods of a novel kind, largely consumables (e.g., matches, tinned
meat) and finally to (4) cash. He argues that as demand for each was
satisfied or reached a certain level the Siane started to demand goods in
the next category. In my experience, however, no matter how great the
supply of wealth one individual anthropologist could offer highlanders it
would not come anywhere near satisfying demand, for as individuals they
could not lay their hands on too many valuables. Furthermore, the items

listed under category 1 would scarcely qualify as wealth; rather they are materials for the making of decorative objects such as the headbands worn at sociopolitical exchange events, which are valued but unlike traditional wealth objects have a readily saturatable demand level. Finally it seems probable that throughout Salisbury's brief stay the Siane considered cash, particularly paper money, as transactable wealth. Whatever the reasons for the changes in demand observed, they proceeded in spurts: 'people make extra efforts to meet [expected] standards, but once the standards are met, their demand is saturated until they find new standards towards which to strive and a new package of goods to demand' (1962:181). This assumes that something has happened – some external influence has intervened – to break the traditional cycle. In other words, social conditions and expectations have changed sufficiently for Western-style economic development to proceed but in fits and starts.

Stop-and-go development

Several writers have noted this tendency for economic development to proceed in bursts. The economist E. K. Fisk (1962) has advanced an abstract model to account for it in a Melanesian context. It looks at the phenomenon from the point of view of the linking up of a 'pure subsistence economy' (that is, one like that of the Siane, entirely independent of the outside world) with the international monetary economy and its sophisticated technology, manufactured goods and global market. It assumes, to begin with, that the pure subsistence economies of Melanesia operate below their productive capacity and proposes that by working a little harder, without unduly upsetting their social lives, people could increase their output appreciably with no technological change or need of more resources: 'The level of production is . . . subject to a very definite ceiling, which may be well below their potential capacity to produce, in that when they have produced sufficient of what they know how to produce to meet their immediate needs, there is no point in producing more. The production of a surplus beyond that requirement adds nothing to their satisfactions, present or future' (1962:463). This is evident in the Siane's response to technological advantages resulting from the use of steel axes, in not investing them to build up subsistence productive capital – they had sufficient and saw no point in augmenting it.

The graph of Figure 4.1 shows output at different labour inputs (curve O–T), the demand ceiling set by customary expectations (line D–D), and the labour supply possible given current physical and social constraints (curve E–M–N–P–S). In the traditional pure subsistence economy, level of output is at point A, whereas with the added labour A–P output could

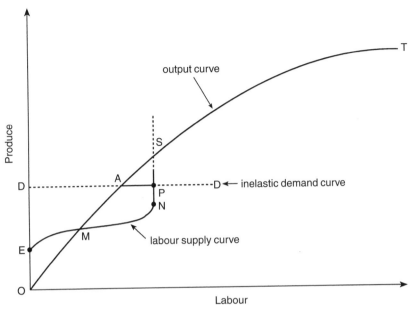

Figure 4.1 Labour and output in a tribal society (after Fisk 1962)

be increased to S, which under traditional conditions would be a useless surplus (below E the population would starve to death and at M would just maintain itself). It should be noted that increases in population will reduce the amount of the potential surplus or even erase it and limited technological change involving relatively small capital outlays (such as supplying steel axes) may increase it although the increase will not be large.

Having established the possibility of surplus within pure subsistence productive groups, Fisk proceeds to investigate avenues for encouraging those involved to exploit it for sale. The level of production in the subsistence situation is 'limited by the internal demand for subsistence products, rather than by the supply of the factors of production. There is therefore a developmental potential concealed within the subsistence sector, in the form of a surplus of available labour and unused productive capacity of the tribal lands, which could be diverted to increase production if the necessary incentive were provided' (1964:156). The incentive here will depend on the effort people have to expend to produce a surplus and earn a monetary reward and the utility to them of the money earned – that is, the opportunity to spend it and their desire for the goods they may obtain. The response to these initiatives, in turn, will be influenced by traditional beliefs and expectations, on the one hand, and the way changes are introduced on the other. Rejection is probable, for changes 'will, in many cases, do violence to the very culture of the society concerned, as well as to its economic organisation, and this will be resisted' (Fisk 1964:158). Culturally inappropriate and unsympathetic handling may well obscure the incentives, and this is where anthropology has a role to play.

This approach to development is informed by modernisation theory, according to which economic development occurs through the application of advanced technology, the commercialisation of subsistence agriculture, the industrialisation of production, and the urbanisation of populations. A well-known advocacy of the approach is W. Rostow's *The Stages of Economic Growth* (1960), which argues that development requires the engineering of the conditions required for economic take-off, including not only technological and economic conditions but also value systems and social institutions. The stimulation of domestic savings, international investment, and development aid initiate the process of modernisation, and expansion occurs through various 'stages of growth'. The modernisation approach is essentially evolutionary, seeing development as a unilinear process. It expects changes in less developed countries to imitate what occurred in the West with the industrial revolution and its aftermath. It assumes the transformation of traditional societies, with appropriate changes in technology and social arrangements, into economically 'advanced' nations. This is depicted from a sociological perspective as involving two processes: structural differentiation, in which traditional institutions change and evolve into more 'modern' specialised and autonomous social entities, and integration, in which these emerging new institutions mesh into a new system (e.g., economic activity is no longer organised by homogeneous families but by heterogeneous firms, wage labour replaces household cooperation, and so on).

Economists concentrate on incentives, looking at, on the one hand, the income people can earn by putting in more work to exploit their potential surplus and, on the other, the usefulness to them of that income. Especially in the initial stages, the income earned per unit of extra labour expended will be low because of problems relating to the processing and marketing of the resulting surplus produce. The people will lack the capital equipment to turn out high-quality produce, to dry copra efficiently, to smoke rubber properly, and so on, and will consequently receive only a small payment for it. In addition many rural areas in Melanesia are remote from outlets for any cash-earning products, and people may face several days' walk or canoe journey to market their poor-quality produce. There is little incentive to produce a surplus and earn a little cash; the effort required is hardly worth the return, and without some outside impetus the situation is unlikely to change. But where is the entrepreneur who will invest in a plant for processing a tiny cash crop, in the hope that the increased returns possible will encourage people to produce more, or build the roads, bulldoze the landing strips, or erect the wharves that might link these remote regions to the market?

A local population may gradually increase its output until it reaches a level at which such scale of investment becomes viable. It is more likely, however, that the government, eager to promote economic development in a region, will finance it at a loss. It may also subsidise the cash returns, giving people an artificially high reward initially for their limited output to stimulate an increase in production or increasing their desire for money by subsidising the supply of goods they can buy with it (although these measures are currently frowned upon by the world's financial institutions). Whatever happens, technological and other developments are irregular occurrences subject to the 'lumpiness' of capital, and 'the increase in the cash return per unit of labour will not occur as a steady response to increasing output, but will occur in sudden discontinuous jumps as certain levels of output are reached at which specific scale-economising services become a paying proposition' (Fisk 1964:164). When a piece of capital equipment arrives in a region and makes it more profitable for people to produce whatever it processes, they are all simultaneously stimulated to work more and increase their output.

A similar situation obtains with regard to the usefulness to people of any money they earn. If they have to walk many miles to the nearest trade store, which is poorly stocked and often lacks the tobacco, tools or clothing they wish to purchase, the incentive to earn money is small and they will be content with their traditional subsistence regime. And, again, who is going to establish a well-stocked store in a low-cash-earning region and put up with an unprofitable turnover indefinitely in the hope of stimulating people into production by the sight and availability of the tempting goods they can buy? When income has gradually crept up to a point where an entrepreneur can expect a certain minimum turnover that will grow and so establishes a retail outlet or when the government intervenes to subsidise the location of a store at a loss to stimulate local cash-earning activity, services in an area markedly increase overnight; where there was previously no store or a small one, a store or a considerably better-stocked one is established.

The graph of Figure 4.2 shows the jumps that occur as economies of scale prompt investments in both productive and distributive develop-

Plate 4.3 Pouring latex into the coagulation tank in a small-scale
rubber plant in the Kokoda district of Papua New Guinea (smoking
racks in rear).

Plate 4.4 A large, well-stocked trade store in Vanimo, West Sepik Province, Papua New Guinea.

ments, allowing people to earn more from their labour and offering them more opportunities to spend the cash they earn. The lines O–C represent different rates of cash return for labour put in (increasing with capital investments); the curves O–U depict the labour supply, which varies depending on the usefulness of money; the heavy dotted zigzag line O–P shows the maximum cash income people will be satisfied to earn at different rates of capital assistance to their labour; and the solid stepped line O–Q shows the labour they think it worthwhile to expend to earn different amounts of cash depending on their opportunities to dispose of it. The steps in the two heavy lines represent the effects of developments of scale, showing them clearly as jumps, from one level to another. When a new piece of processing equipment or cheaper outlet to the market appears, people see a larger profit for themselves and produce more. If an improved source of desired goods and services purchasable with cash is established, up goes production to earn money to buy them. The problem spots are marked with letters S: they are stagnation points which require some external impetus to promote further development; the spots marked with letters G are self-promoting growth points.

It is the stagnation points that give development programmes their

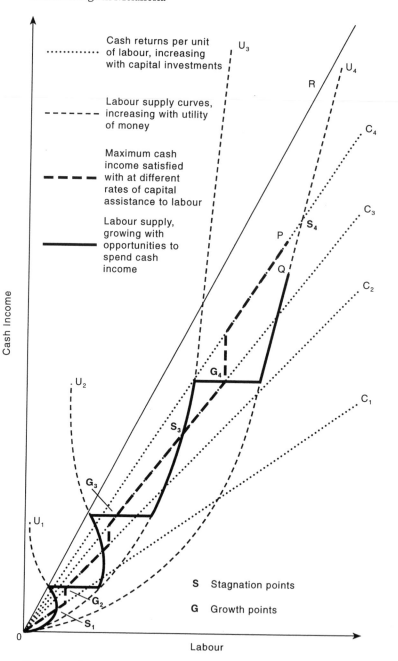

Figure 4.2 Labour and output with capitalistic economic change (after Fisk 1962)

stop-and-go character. A policy of substantial investment by the advanced economy in backward regions is required to break through these rapidly rather than wait indefinitely for local conditions to become favourable. The alternatives are investment through private enterprise or by public intervention and subsidy. Government programmes seem more probable currently, given the political climate in Melanesia and the distrust of foreign-owned private enterprises, but they will depend on substantial development aid from industrial nations. Their success will also depend to a considerable extent on the local response factor.

The assumptions of modernisation are deeply embedded in Western intellectual discourse and condition our expectations of the development process. The approach inevitably informs our view of development, but it needs to be set in an analytical framework that accommodates widely differing cultural and historical circumstances. The cultural and historical traditions of any society influence its acceptance, rejection or modification of outside institutions and arrangements. Two themes appropriate to this run through the modernisation debate. The first seeks to identify cultural practices that act as barriers to development, prompting people to resist incentives. It looks for those social obstacles and conservative attitudes towards change that explain why development initiatives fail. The second addresses the issue of development from the opposite direction and seeks to identify those cultural and social factors that encourage 'modern' socioeconomic institutions to emerge, and facilitate economic take-off. Traditional and modern systems are not necessarily mutually exclusive and need not always be in conflict; some traditional values and ways may be compatible with or even promote development. It is to the responses to change that the coming chapters turn, for it is here that anthropologists can make an important contribution.

FURTHER READING

On the economic and social aspects of the initial indirect stage of social change see:

I. Arnon 1987 *Modernization of agriculture in developing countries* Chichester: Wiley

E. K. Fisk 1962 Planning in a primitive economy: special problems of Papua New Guinea *Economic Record* 38:462–78

E. K. Fisk 1964 Planning in a primitive economy: from pure subsistence to production of a market surplus *Economic Record* 40:156–74

E. K. Fisk 1971 Labour absorption capacity of subsistence agriculture *Economic Record* 47:366–78

M. Godelier with J. Garanger 1973 Stone tools and steel tools among the Baruya of New Guinea *Social Science Information* 18:663–78

R. Salisbury 1962 *From stone to steel* Melbourne: Melbourne University Press

P. Sillitoe 1979 Stone versus steel *Mankind* 12:151–61

W. R. Stent 1984 *The development of a market economy in the Abelam* Boroko: Institute of Applied Social and Economic Research Monograph 20

C. Wharton (ed.) 1969 *Subsistence agriculture and economic development* Chicago: Aldine

On modernisation theories of development see:

D. E. Apter 1987 *Rethinking development: modernization, dependency, and postmodern politics* London: Sage

D. Harrison 1991 *The sociology of modernization and development* London: Routledge

B. Kagarlitsky 1995 *The mirage of modernization* New York: Monthly Review Press

J. Martinussen 1997 *State, society, and market: a guide to competing theories of development* London: Zed Books

A. Y. So 1990 *Social change and development: modernization, dependency, and world-system theories* London: Sage

5   Land rights and community

While it is perfectly legitimate for economists and others to formulate abstract models of development, their sweeping universal assumptions about the issues and problems give their theories limited validity in real-life contexts. They assume that the responses of human beings to changing circumstances will be the same regardless of cultural background; they distort what is likely to happen when change occurs and development plans are put into effect. We should never lose sight of the fact that these issues concern human beings whose cultures and views of life are quite different from ours and whose reaction to changes planned for them, conditioned by these radically different circumstances, are in all probability going to be quite at variance with our expectations.

The failure to accommodate to local people's expectations results time and again in the frustration of imposed development schemes. The incentives identified by the economist in the abstract models described above are certainly significant, for without them economic development as envisaged by Western planners is unlikely to occur. But the responses are equally important, for they too can make or break a scheme. And these responses are those of the human beings concerned: their aspirations and their understanding of what is intended and how it fits in with or challenges their traditional practices, which will lead them variously to embrace or obstruct the plans in question. The carrot-and-stick perspective of modernisation concentrates too exclusively on external forces promoting change and overlooks the internal dynamic. Seen from the inside, things are different. It is not just a case of getting the conditions right for take-off through the appropriate management of incentives; the traditional culture will modify the impact of modernisation.

The modernisation model, with its Western assumptions, can hinder understanding of the processes of social change, which are far more complex than it assumes: different cultural heritages condition responses and developments in quite different ways. Other societies are not going to repeat Western historical experiences, they are embedded in quite different sociohistorical and contemporary circumstances. It is ethnocentric to equate modernity with Western capitalist economies and liberal democracies. The transformations attributed to modernisation pressures involve interactions both within and between traditional economic and sociocultural practices and the new arrangements instituted as change proceeds. 'Modern' ways of doing things do not simply displace pre-existing relationships and values: there is some accommodation between the traditional and the new. The interesting question is how particular societies, such as those of Melanesia, adapt their traditional institutions to changing circumstances and develop new ones.

Land issues

What stirs up Melanesian reactions to economic development perhaps more than any other issue is change that affects their land or their relation to it. One of the few things that characterises nearly all Melanesians is their singular relationship with their land, to which they all possess rights. Since independence it has become one of the features by which they distinguish themselves from other nations and peoples. They might be characterised as nations of landowners. All Melanesians identify strongly with their land and have a marked sense of belonging to a place. Land figures centrally in their lives not merely as a resource exploited to meet subsistence needs but also as something held in sentimental regard, laden with religious and kinship values and embodying spirit forces and kin relations. They value land highly and resent any interference with their rights to it. Land is, however, unavoidably one of the three fundamental factors of market economic production (together with labour and capital), and manipulation of it is inevitably a prominent feature of any development scheme. Attempts to interfere with land rights are a potent source of tension and confusion and have led to the frustration of many development plans.

Governments, colonial and national, may prevent people from using their land by legal fiction sanctioned by their superior force of arms, and grant rights to exploit the areas or 'ownership' of them to outside individuals or companies, either expatriates or nationals from elsewhere. This interference is implied by the recommendation that governments promote the rapid creation of incentives which will involve land grants if they are to encourage the establishment of commercial ventures by private or government-owned enterprise that will draw the local population into the monetary sector. But in general these business ventures are launched not to draw the local population into the cash economy but to produce profits for the companies involved. During the colonial era, large areas were alienated from local populations and offered to planters on easy terms and at low prices. It was the combination of cheap land and readily available cheap local labour that attracted many settlers and companies to Melanesia. The large-scale alienation of land for commercial purposes ceased many years ago, and in some regions such areas have been returned to the local populations. But the annexation of land, notably by governments, continues and remains a sensitive issue throughout Melanesia. While it is perhaps morally more justifiable for the governments of independent nations than for colonial administrations or private enterprise to alienate land with a view to stimulating development for the intended long-term benefit of the local population, the problems involved and the emotions aroused remain the same. No matter what the justification, they are tampering with people's traditional and cherished rights to their land, and frequently they are doing so for investments in which overseas companies have a stake.

The areas involved vary throughout Melanesia, as do the proportions of different kinds of legal title claimed by the new owners, from outright freehold to various lease arrangements. The most severely affected region is New Caledonia where the French colonial administration initially annexed all of the islands, making land grants to settlers and establishing Melanesian reserves; currently some 80 per cent of the islands' total landmass is alienated (although limited land reforms are intended to increase the area of the reserves). About 20 per cent of Vanuatu has been alienated, and half of this land is in French hands. The Fijians had some 17 per cent of their land alienated by the first decade of this century, but subsequent careful protection of native land rights has prevented any increase to this day. Large areas of Papua New Guinea were not discovered and explored until well into the twentieth century, when the days of uncontrolled colonial land speculation and annexation were past, and only about 4.8 per cent of the country has been alienated, almost all of it by the government.

These figures are calculated according to total land area, which given the rugged uncultivable terrain of large parts of Melanesian islands results in an underrepresentation of the effects of land alienation. Land-use experts have estimated, for instance, that some 10 per cent of Papua New Guinea is capable of commercial productive use, and assuming that the land alienated falls into this category, this suggests that nearly 48 per cent of the prime developable land has been taken away from its traditional owners. In Irian Jaya it is estimated that only 3 per cent of the land is favourable for agricultural development, and five-sixths of this is under primary forest; little has so far been alienated. Given Indonesian plans for massive Javanese transmigration into the region, however, this could change.

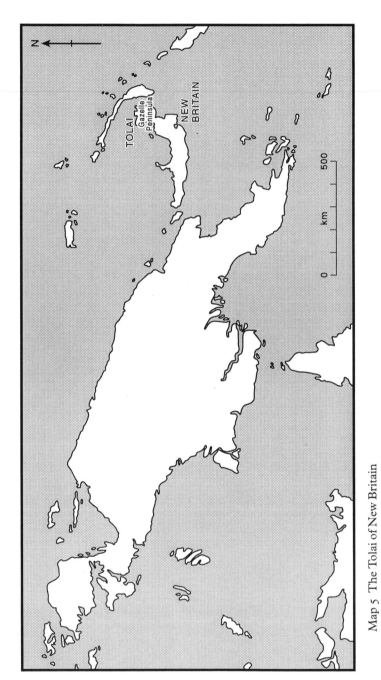

Map 5 The Tolai of New Britain

The situation is not as serious as these figures suggest. Subsistence requirements are not threatened, for Melanesians traditionally cultivate and exploit areas such as steep mountain slopes and sago-bearing swamps which are considered physically unsuitable for economic development. These statistics do, however, indicate that they have lost a considerable proportion of the land judged commercially usable. In many regions, of course, people have only ever had access to less desirable land, which experts consider beyond large-scale economic development. Only the areas best suited to cultivation have attracted those interested in acquiring land in Melanesia, and these are relatively few (for instance, parts of New Britain, the hinterland of Madang, and the Wahgi Valley in the highlands, to name three areas in Papua New Guinea).

One region disrupted particularly seriously by land alienation is the Blanche Bay region of the north-eastern Gazelle Peninsula of New Britain. This area, surrounded by active volcanoes, has fertile soils which yield a high return and invite intensive commercial exploitation. Volcanic eruptions in 1937 and in 1994 blanketed the region with ash and rendered all land uncultivable for a period, causing considerable hardship. The Germans first colonised the area and annexed large areas for plantation development, and the Australians continued this policy, albeit on a reduced scale, with the result that the Tolai people who inhabit the region have only 51.4 per cent of their territory left to them (around one hectare per head) for subsistence and cash-crop cultivation. The Tolai have experienced increasingly acute land pressure for some years with an expanding population, and access to land is the focus of considerable social tension. 'Every fresh approach by the Administration to the Matupi [a local Tolai community] to acquire land for some new purpose has the effect of triggering off acrimonious and bitter quarrels' (Epstein 1969:138). Resentment and discontent are expectable where land has been alienated on this scale, but there is far more to the story than this.

The Tolai raise taro, yams and bananas as subsistence crops and coconut palms and cocoa trees for cash. They also depend heavily on fishing for food, using seine-nets and large basket traps. Many of them work for cash in the town of Rabaul. Descent among the Tolai is reckoned matrilineally, and people live either avunculo-virilocally or patri-virilocally in small hamlets scattered across their matrilineally defined territories. The exchange transaction of *tambu* wealth – lengths of button-sized dog-whelk shell discs in coils upwards of 100 metres long – characterises important social events such as marriage and mortuary rites. The society remains an uncentralised one in which elders have a certain influence; it is a fragmented polity featuring big men. The Tolai are well known for the *tubuan* masked dancers associated with their *dukduk* male cult.

Land tenure

According to the rules of their traditional land tenure systems, Melanesians cannot permanently alienate land to strangers; such action is inconceivable. Consequently, when Europeans paid traditional owners for areas with various trade goods and annexed them, the two parties to these transactions interpreted them differently. The European planters, traders and others thought that they were buying the land in perpetuity, and governments support them in their freehold claims to this day. The natives probably thought that they were allowing these fair-skinned strangers temporary use of the land in return for the goods they offered them; selling it for all time was a totally alien concept to them. Years were to pass before they recognised their error. The local people, while not deliberately duped (for the two parties were ignorant of each other's views), certainly entered into contracts without realising what they were doing, and this ignorance forms the basis of many present-day land claims. The argument put forward by bodies such as the militant Mataungan Association of the Tolai is that the original purchases of land were made under false pretences and are therefore morally wrong if not illegal. They argue legitimately that their ancestors never intended to sell the freehold in their land.

Throughout Melanesia land tenure depends traditionally on kin relations. Individuals do not hold freehold title to any parcels of land, although they will have prior claims to the use of certain defined plots. The rights to exploit any territory rest with groups of kinsfolk, variously defined. Among the Tolai these groups are matrilineal descent groups called *vunatarai*. A Tolai man has prior use rights to garden and house-site land on the territory to which his matrilineage lays claim, but if he does not exercise these rights another member of the matrilineage may, with his permission, do so. If the descendants of someone with prior rights to an area fail to act on them and they are forgotten and no one else has subsequently claimed the area for his descendants, then it reverts to the general matrilineage pool, which any member is free to use and establish rights to. The fact that men may not bother to claim their matrilineal land rights indicates that they can gain access to land in other ways. While the jural rule to which the Tolai subscribe stipulates that men should ideally claim land on their matrilineage's territory, they can also lay claim to the use of land on the territories of other matrilineages to which they are not related matrilineally. The Tolai's preference for patrilocal residence tends to encourage men to cultivate land where their fathers did before them, giving rise to patrilines within matrilineages. Besides this, men can take advantage of their wives' land too, anticipating their sons' establishing legitimate matrilineal claims to it.

Plate 5.1 The land of the Tolai: a view across Blanche Bay towards Rabaul town.

The result of this flexibility is that local landholding Tolai groups are variously composed although structured ideologically according to matrilineal principles. The numerous present-day exceptions will be adjusted in the long term to comply with these, for Tolai's genealogical knowledge, like that of Melanesians generally, is shallow. They forget precise connections after five generations or so and convert patrilineal connections into matrilineal ones. If this process establishes unbroken matrilineal descent connections, the group becomes a pure *vunatarai*. A great deal of Tolai local politics centres on people establishing and justifying their claims to superior matrilineal status over others with male links in their pedigrees and validating their prior jural rights to land when access to it is in dispute. Neither the groups nor the territories to which they lay claim are static, their composition and boundaries are constantly in flux, as one segment after another tries to establish its matrilineal *bona fides* and achieve access to land. They regularly split up as their populations grow.

While this flexibility in composition and flux in constitution give rise to a fascinatingly fluid social order, what is significant is that all Tolai have rights to land in several different locations. They may on occasion dispute the precise nature of these rights and the priority of claims, but no one can be dispossessed. All have equal rights to the same amounts of land, sufficient to ensure their subsistence and, as they view the situation, they hold the land in trust for future generations, using it while they live and passing it on to their descendants when they die.

Plate 5.2 The Tolai depend on the sea as well as the land to supply their livelihood: an outboard-motor-powered outrigger canoe.

Tenure and development

The attitudes of Melanesians to their land – particularly that they cannot own it as individuals but only claim rights to the use of it – are cited as a major hindrance to economic development. Developers' views are often based on quite erroneous assumptions about traditional land tenure systems, with the result that attempts to modify them to promote development tend to exacerbate already difficult situations.

Some development planners maintain, presumably because it is an axiom of our capitalist order, that individual tenure is essential for promoting the incorporation of Melanesians into the industrial monetary economy. They argue that the traditional tenure system militates against people's making the necessary improvements to land – investing the work and the capital required to increase its productivity and integrate it into a cash-crop market. This criticism is based on the assumption that because they themselves would need the security of individual tenure as an incentive for making such investments, so must Melanesian people. A little anthropological knowledge would prevent such damaging ethnocentric judgments. The Tolai can claim as individuals priority rights to parcels of land on the territories of the kin-founded corporations to which they can trace a legitimate relationship, and so long as they maintain these rights by using the land it effectively belongs to them. They have it, if you will, on perpetual lease from their kin-groups. In effect, with regard to expending effort to improve the land there is no practical difference between this and our idea of freehold landownership.

Where the Melanesian land tenure system does differ from the Western one is, of course, in not placing the right to dispose of land in the hands of the individual user. The developers maintain that holding land in this way impedes economic change in that it prevents the use of it as collateral to secure loans. Financial institutions require individual title deeds so that in the event of a default they can seize the land to cover the debt. This problem with indigenous tenure arrangements reveals a genuine and profound difference between traditional Melanesian subsistence orders and capitalist industrial economies, the former depending on a kin-group constitution and kinship obligations and the latter on corporate law and individual contracts. We can anticipate conflict in attempting to change the kin order to comply with the commercial image. Nonetheless, there is no reason why financial institutions in Melanesia should not explore ways of adjusting their rules somewhat to accommodate to the traditional land-tenure system. But the problems are formidable. If they enter into agreements with kin-groups as landholding corporations they will have difficulty identifying those responsible for any arrangements, for the groups have no corporate representatives. There is also the individual nature of actual land use and the difficulty of defining the landholding corporations in the first instance where many people not resident on a territory have rights to its land. The negotiations will prove tortuous, perhaps even impossible for our bureaucratic legal system.

Another oft-cited drawback of the traditional land tenure system is that it results in numerous small holdings. Under this system individuals' plots are dotted about a territory, rather than arranged in contiguous blocks and may even be located in more than one territory. This dispersal of holdings, it is argued, is an impediment to economy-of-scale developments such as mechanisation. Again, there is no reason why individuals could not consolidate their holdings to some extent, swapping plots with one another to acquire sizeable areas, if they could see any point in it. Nevertheless, even if an individual could consolidate a single plot of developable land, the area would still be small from the perspective of economies-of-scale, and by himself he would be unable to raise the necessary capital to finance them. In this event planners are obliged to think in terms of development not by individual entrepreneurs' companies – the basis of capitalist economics – but by cooperatives made up of kin who hold adjacent plots of land. This makes it irrelevant to mechanisation whether individuals hold single large blocks within the area to be developed or several smaller ones dotted about it, following the traditional pattern of land distribution, and the criticism regarding fragmented holdings disappears.

Regardless of these purported shortcomings of traditional land tenure arrangements, in many regions of Melanesia people grow considerable quantities of cash crops on a small scale. The Tolai, for instance, have respectable holdings of coconut palms and cocoa trees. The opportunities for sizeable capital improvements to their small operations are few to non-existent and will remain so whatever their system of land tenure, and therefore it is prudent for them to continue seeking avenues of development founded on their traditional tenure system. Even these small enterprises, however, have interfered with social arrangements in undesirable ways. When people try to adapt their kin orders, as they are frequently reported to do, to accommodate commercial crop production, conflict often results.

The cash crops are frequently perennial tree crops (notably coconut palms, coffee bushes and rubber and cocoa trees), which people are reluctant to plant on any land except that to which they have unchallengeable use rights. The Tolai, for example, are careful to cultivate these on matrilineally claimed land, fearing that elsewhere their rights may be disputed and they may lose their crops. The system is becoming rigid when a degree of fluidity is necessary for its optimum operation. If cash crops

Plate 5.3 A *dukduk* dancer today, captured on a video camera by a tourist at a cultural event.

were annuals, they could be cultivated under the traditional rules of land tenure with no disruption, for they would not entail long-term use of land, but these are the crops that require extensive capital investment to make their cultivation a commercial proposition. The Tolai are finding it increasingly difficult, with perennial cash crops coming on top of the pressures induced by extensive land alienation and an expanding population, to order their landholdings according to traditional rules and are spending ever more time on difficult and divisive disputes over land rights.

These perennial tree crops, which offer one of the few opportunities for many Melanesians to enter the cash economy, also threaten the order of their lives in other ways. The cultivation of these crops removes areas of land from the subsistence pool. So long as people grow cash crops on a small scale the situation is unlikely to become serious, but as the proportion of land put under them increases the amount available for subsistence agriculture diminishes, possibly threatening adequate food supplies, particularly where cash crops are established on the most fertile soils. The earlier annexation of considerable areas of the best arable land by plantations is a further exacerbating factor and, combined with a rapidly growing population, as on the Gazelle Peninsula, could in the future threaten serious food shortages. The attitude of Melanesians to cash and processed food worsens the position further. If they spent what they earned on nutritious foods this would help correct the situation, but they divert considerable sums of cash away from food consumption and spend much of their food budget on processed foods of little nutritional value. They need education on the worth of different foodstuffs if they are to turn from growing most of their food to purchasing it. In regions where cash-cropping is prominent, a careful watch needs to be kept for malnutrition, particularly among young children, who tend to be affected by the shift to a nutritionally poorer diet.

Land and society

Land resources development, if not carefully monitored, may lead to the material impoverishment of a population. It is also certain to give rise to social problems and conflict whatever planning goes into it and if not well thought out may go seriously awry. The attitude of planners to land is worrisome in this respect. Arguing, on questionable grounds, that traditional land tenure hinders economic development, they have devised all manner of strategies to undermine it.

One strategy, for example, favoured by the World Bank (a powerful influence on development in Melanesia, funding many schemes), is the

Plate 5.4 An oil palm plantation on alienated land: a labourer pruning diseased leaves.

'nucleus estate' settlement scheme. Near Cape Hoskins in New Britain, for instance, the administration alienated a sizeable area of underused land and together with a plantation company established a large oil-palm estate with capital facilities and community services. Around the estate were sited numerous small blocks for Papua New Guinean settlers (many resettled from areas of dense population such as the Gazelle Peninsula), who were required to cultivate a certain number of oil-palms and use the plantation's facilities for processing them. The arrangement has solved the problems facing smallholders of access to the capital equipment they require to ensure marketable produce and also facilitated their education through example by the commercial estate but the resettled people are discontented and unhappy away from their homelands.

Another strategy to change customary land tenure practices is to offer people the opportunity to convert their rights into legally registered individual ownership. This has been attempted, for instance, in Papua New Guinea, but the people there have been reluctant to make the change. The land area converted to date amounted to less than 0.2 per cent of all alienated land by the early 1990s.

Land for Melanesians is not merely an economic asset but a fundamental aspect of their social and political organisation, underpinning the continued existence of their local communities. Among the Tolai (Epstein 1969:201):

in so far as the islanders [of Matupit] continue to work their land under traditional rules of tenure they remain involved in an essentially indigenous structure of social relationships, and much of their behaviour is still regulated by the customs and values which define and inform these relationships. Thus where one resides, where and to what extent one can make gardens or grow cash crops, all these depend upon membership of a local descent group, the unit which exercises proprietary rights in land. Such membership is fixed by birth, but continuing claims to land also depend upon recognition of the authority of the elders of the group as well as the fulfilment of one's customary obligations. In these ways land provides an obvious cornerstone of the social system.

Disputes over land rights define Tolai social groups and serve as a forum for their local political interaction. Furthermore, the Matupi Tolai maintain and define their cultural identity as Tolai, preventing their settlement from becoming a mere suburb of the nearby township of Rabaul by continuing to claim land through their kin-groups and cultivating on it both subsistence and cash crops. In short, their land – their attachment to it – holds their community together, and contributes significantly to their integration as a cultural collectivity with similar values and aspirations.

Land occupies a similar place in the constitution of many societies throughout the non-industrial world, and it is clear that meddling with rights to it will upset their very ordering. The jurist H. S. Maine (1871:112) noted this long ago in India: 'the separate, unchangeable, and irremovable family lot in the cultivated area, if it be a step forward in the history of property, is also the point at which the Indian village community is breaking to pieces.' To interfere with customary land tenure – to attempt to individualise rights to land so that it can enter the market and change hands there – is to attack the continued existence of Melanesian social groups and communities. Regarding Tolai land tenure, Epstein (1969:137) points out that 'leases or purchases of land in the modern European sense strike at the very heart of this system, since the effect of disposing of any parcel of land in these ways is to place it under the control of those who do not recognise the customary obligations and traditional encumbrances, and against whom they appear to be unenforceable'.

Melanesians are comfortable with their way of life and value their cultural heritage, and understandably they resist and frustrate ill-conceived attempts to change it, albeit inadvertently, through interference with their land tenure arrangements. Planners should be trying to promote developments with consideration of the traditional context, not assaulting societies and causing their members fear and heartache with unnecessarily disruptive change which they will resist. Who, after all, is this development intended to benefit? At least the early colonials were open in their aims of interfering so as to facilitate their exploitation of Melanesia's economic potential. If today's development mandate is not to be suspected of so-called neocolonialism – of continuing to promote these aims under cover – those involved need to give considerable thought to what they are doing and why.

FURTHER READING

On the Tolai people see:
A. L. Epstein 1969 *Matupit: land, politics and change among the Tolai of New Britain* Canberra: Australian National University Press
T. S. Epstein 1968 *Capitalism, primitive and modern* Canberra: Australian National University Press
A. L. Epstein 1992 *In the midst of life* Berkeley: University of California Press
A. L. Epstein 1998 *Gunantuna: aspects of the person, the self and the individual among the Tolai* Bathurst: Crawford House Publishing
K. Neumann 1992 *Not the way it really was* Honolulu: University of Hawaii Press
R. F. Salisbury 1970 *Vunamami: economic transformation in a traditional society* Melbourne: Melbourne University Press

On land tenure in Melanesia see:
B. Acquaye and R. Crocombe (eds.) 1984 *Land tenure and rural productivity in the Pacific Islands* Rome: FAO

I. Hogbin and P. Lawrence 1967 *Studies in New Guinea land tenure* Sydney: Sydney University Press

J. Knetsch and M. Trebilcock 1981 *Land policy and economic development in Papua New Guinea* Port Moresby: Institute of National Affairs

H. P. Lundsgaarde (ed.) 1974 *Land tenure in Oceania* Honolulu: University of Hawaii Press

D. Morawetz 1967 *Land tenure conversion in the Northern District of Papua* Canberra: Australian National University New Guinea Research Bulletin No. 17

M. Rimoldi 1966 *Land tenure and land use among the Mount-Lamington Orokaiva* Canberra: Australian National University New Guinea Research Bulletin No. 11

M. C. Rodman 1987 *Masters of tradition* Vancouver: University of British Columbia Press

P. Sack (ed.) 1974 *Problems of choice: land in Papua New Guinea's future* Canberra: Australian National University Press

S. R. Simpson, R. L. Hide, A. M. Healy and J. K. Kinyanjui 1971 *Land tenure and economic development* Canberra: Australian National University New Guinea Research Bulletin No. 40

Also see:

H. S. Maine 1871 *Village-communities in the East and West* London: John Murray

R. G. Ward and E. Kingdon (eds.) 1996 *Land, custom and practice in the South Pacific* Cambridge: Cambridge University Press

6   Business big men as entrepreneurs

Not all aspects of traditional Melanesian society conflict with and impede modernisation and development along capitalistic economic lines as customary land tenure arrangements do. Some values and aspirations promote positive responses to changes urged following contact with the industrial world. One cultural feature commonly singled out in this regard is the indigenous system of achieved leadership, the big man syndrome. On the Gazelle Peninsula, for instance, it has been considered 'striking that many of the most prominent men in Tolai communities combine the running of successful business enterprises with the sponsorship of, and full participation in, ceremonies of the traditional kind' (Epstein 1969:250).

According to economists, entrepreneurs are the fourth factor of production; they are the managers who risk capital in new ventures. Some writers, disenchanted with the sweeping generalisations of grand theories of development such as modernisation and dependency, have turned to entrepreneurship as an alternative perspective. The anthropological study of entrepreneurs has sought to identify the social characteristics of those who play a leading part in connecting their local economies with the wider market and to investigate the strategies that these individuals adopt.

The study of these economic brokers considers how they achieve and maintain their positions of economic pre-eminence. Some studies attempt to correlate ideological commitment (e.g., religious sect or political group membership) with entrepreneurial behaviour, seeking to identify the attitudes and values that promote economic success in the tradition of the classic work of Weber on the role of the Protestant values of hard work and thrift in the rise of capitalism in the West (e.g., Long's 1968 study of Zambian Jehovah's Witnesses). Others explore social attributes (e.g., ethnic status or gender), addressing the social recruitment of entrepreneurs by investigating what characteristics in their social backgrounds might favour their emergence. It is often suggested that they are in some senses marginal members of their societies whose lack of

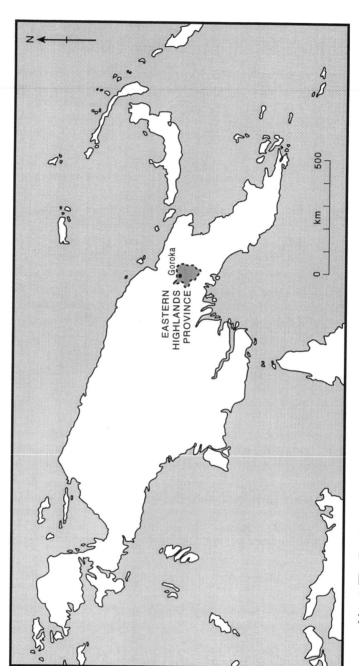

Map 6 The Goroka region of the Eastern Highlands

standing and sense of dissatisfaction spur them to innovate (e.g., Geertz's 1963 study of two Indonesian towns). The thrust of these studies is to explain why in some development contexts individuals with certain ideological and social backgrounds are apparently better placed strategically to seize upon new economic opportunities.

The Goroka region in the Eastern Highlands Province of Papua New Guinea is one of the most changed in the highlands. The burgeoning of capitalist-like developments here has been attributed in part to the dynamic innovations of individuals modelling themselves on the traditional big man role. 'In Weberian terms, it can be said that the Gorokans already had their own analogue of the spirit of capitalism [in their traditional status system] and needed only linkage with the cash economy to express it' (Finney 1973:122). Several language groups live around Goroka, the largest township in the Eastern Highlands, from the Siane in the west to the Bena Bena in the east. They are typical central highlanders with sweet potato staple, pigs, big men, extensive sociopolitical exchange, ancestor beliefs, and so on.

The landscape, except in the rugged west and north, is one of gentle grassy hills, rolling across a large basin through which the Asaro and Bena Bena Rivers flow. The climate is mild, almost temperate, and the soils are good. This was a region agreeable to European planters, who were attracted to it after World War II. The climate and soils particularly suited it to the cultivation of coffee, the cash crop upon which the startlingly rapid economic development of the area came to depend. Besides these environmental considerations there were several other factors making coffee a particularly suitable cash crop for the Goroka people. They could quickly learn how to grow it, especially given their extensive traditional horticultural knowledge, and once established the bushes required relatively little attention to yield a reasonable return, thus not interfering with subsistence cultivation. The Gorokans could also earn reasonable cash returns with only a few bushes; they did not have to give up considerable areas of land from their subsistence holdings or expend hard labour in clearing large areas of natural vegetation to establish coffee plantings. The very high price received for coffee on the international market in the 1950s, when these people were starting to grow it as a cash crop, was also of some importance here. The inordinately high monetary returns were a powerful incentive. On top of this, coffee was a crop which individuals could grow alone, and this suited it to the egoistic social organisation of these highlanders. Nor did it require considerable investment in capital equipment to process it for sale.

The Europeans attracted to the region, with many of whom the local people had good relations, were happy to cooperate with the Gorokans and assist them in establishing their own coffee holdings. The highlanders were fortunate: 'colonised' only after World War II, they found the expatriates who settled among them willing to cooperate with them in advancing their region rather than merely to exploit them as a pool of cheap labour. The expatriates supplied the processing capital required in the region and purchased the locals' sun-dried coffee beans for processing with theirs for export. They also stimulated both the upgrading of transport services (initially by air and later by road) to move the crop out at the most economical rates and the establishment of support services and other commercial developments which led to the rapid growth of Goroka town. And their plantations also served as examples of what to do to earn money by growing coffee. The administration adopted a benign policy, on the whole, actively encouraging people to grow their own cash crops. It followed up the opportunities and developments fostered by the planters, for instance, with agricultural officers patrolling the region to encourage and demonstrate cash crop cultivation. In short, the incentives were very favourable to the development of cash-cropping in the Goroka region.

Big man businessmen

The responses were also favourable to this development; in particular, the values that surrounded the traditional big man role predisposed ambitious Gorokans to commercial activity. The achievement of big man status, it is argued, was an ideal model for those aspiring to the role of successful businessman. 'Modern business leaders follow the style of traditional big-men in seeking and achieving eminence. They, like their predecessors, are ambitious and opportunistic men . . . [their] exploitation of modern opportunities is not opposed to traditional achievement behaviour but combines with it' (Finney 1973:90).

A big man is a person of repute and influence in Melanesian society. He achieves the status, it is not ascribed through inheritance, although in some regions sons of big men are reckoned to be in a better position to make the grade than others. It is an informal standing, not an instituted office, and it carries no authority. Any man endowed with the requisite qualities can aspire to it. These vary from one society to another: from an above-average ability to transact wealth in sociopolitical exchange, to a reputation for fearlessness backed by an aggressive temperament and from a capacity to speak and persuade others in argument to specialised ritual knowledge which may extend to renown as a sorcerer. A big man's reputation and status decline as these qualities wane with age; the position depends on current ability, not previous glories. The influence that accrues to it varies from one region to another. In some places, big men reportedly exert considerable political control over the activities of small local groups, directing them by force of character, proven ability and putting others in their debt. In others, while some influence accrues to them as first among equals, they cannot be said to achieve positions of political leadership.

The proposition is not that traditional big men become modern business leaders but that they have similarly motivated careers which depend on personal achievement. We cannot know if the same men would have achieved renown under traditional conditions. If ambition and motivation to achieve success are the sole criteria for achieving both positions, then presumably today's business leaders would have been their generation's big men if Europeans had not intruded into their lives. This is what the highlands entrepreneurial argument suggests, but there is considerably more at issue here than motivation and opportunity to achieve.

The evidence suggests that chance historical encounters have played a significant part in the careers of Goroka's business leaders. They have had extensive associations with Europeans, having gone away early to school or to work elsewhere and learned a great deal about the commercial society encroaching on their own valleys. These experiences may indicate that they are adventurous personalities, risk-takers who are likely to experiment and foment change. And these are qualities that could perhaps break rather than make a big man, who is pre-eminently a reliable sort who inspires confidence rather than a gambler. Many of these associations developed out of chance meetings, albeit involving individuals who had the qualities to seize opportunities that subsequently proved crucial to their business success. Furthermore, in seizing these opportunities and making something of them, these successful local businessmen acted in a distinctly aberrant fashion. They worked to earn money capital which they saved to invest in commercial enterprises, in coffee planting and, when they had secured this productive base, in ventures such as local trade stores and trucks. They obtained much of their productive capital through their own hard labour, whereas the big man depends on relatives to supply him with his transactional capital, receiving valuables from them which he in turn gives away again. The traditional system depends on the continual and repeated distribution rather than the hoarding of wealth capital. The up-and-coming businessmen were acting antithetically to big men by saving and then investing in their own commercial enterprises and were, at least initially, in no way achieving high social standing for themselves. It would appear that Goroka's first entrepreneurs were somewhat like those disenchanted innovators characterised by others elsewhere, who are likely to foment change if social conditions favour them.

Plate 6.1 A man prunes a coffee bush in the Goroka region.

Plate 6.2 A buyer weighs sun-dried smallholder-grown coffee beans before purchasing them.

Individual entrepreneurs

Today's new businessmen build up their commercial and cash-cropping enterprises largely through their own individual efforts, and this is a salient point given the premium placed by the traditional stateless and fiercely egalitarian societies of the highlands on individual action. It is also an attitude more conducive to capitalistic economic development than expectations of concerted action and rights of kin-groups, which respond to changes and seize on opportunities less readily than the unencumbered individual. The scope allowed individual social and political action by traditional highland culture is equally important in promoting commercial development as the big man role of which it is an integral part. The development incentives favour active individuals, not the slowly rallying kin-group with no Western legal identity. The capitalist system can respond to them and readily promote their endeavours, given its own supposedly individual competitive market ethos. It can enter into contracts with individuals, lend them money, and extend them credit against produce, whereas performing these operations with traditional kin-groups is beyond its competence. But there are problems with this individualistic ethos; not all the responses to commercial opportunities and changes are positive.

Some cooperation between individuals is necessary to organise business ventures and to raise some of the capital they require. It is erroneous to think of the social groups that cooperate in various enterprises as organised bodies rallied by successful business leaders – an interpretation invited by some ethnographic reports on the place of these groups in the region's traditional societies. They are loose associations of kin that are liable to have problems organising themselves. 'Enterprises with significant levels of group participation, dictated by high capital or land requirements, seem particularly prone to organisational difficulties. Participants who donate their money or pledge their land may not necessarily work harmoniously together to operate the resulting enterprises efficiently' (Finney 1973:172). The fractious social groups that characterise the acephalous polities of highlanders are contextual, coming into focus in times of exchange and warfare, and have problems organising themselves to pursue short-term goals, let alone the long-term ones presupposed in development contexts.

Business leaders do not rally and organise these groups to follow them actively for any period. It is mistaken to suggest that they coordinate their labour to some joint end of equal mutual benefit to the group and all of its members. They are out for themselves and everyone knows it, and this does not engender committed cooperation. These business ventures centre on, indeed depend on, opportunistic individuals with a certain commercial flair; when these individuals die or their talents fade their little empires tend to collapse and disappear. They are not founded on any permanent social grouping such as the landholding corporations of Goroka society, and without such a corporate structure to ensure their survival they are short-lived.

The business big men may on occasion be able to encourage relatives and friends to assist them with their labour – planting coffee or picking it – but they receive this help from them and are expected to reward them individually. Relatives and friends may bask in the success of a business venture not because it promotes the status of their kin-group *vis-à-vis* others but because it improves the place where they live, the land and community with which they identify. The major return they expect is some material reward or service of commensurate value to the one they have invested. In short, business cooperation depends on the ethic of reciprocity which is crucial to the structuring of Melanesian society.

Exchange investment

What business big men are particularly effective at is mobilising the investment potential of their relatives and friends, which is of considerable significance in the initial stage of their careers. The talent they show for raising capital from their kinsmen derives directly from the reciprocity ethic as it relates to traditional exchange and the big man complex. When an indigenous business leader has worked hard and saved a considerable sum to contribute to some business project he has in mind and his relatives have faith in his ability to make it a success, these people are likely to invest in the venture. The experience that business leaders have of the Europeans' monetary economic system, gained by working for them or attending their schools or both, and the ability they demonstrate to operate within this system and amass considerable funds to invest themselves, inspire confidence in their relatives, who, feeling inadequate to invest their little money on their own and see a return, hand it over to them to use and earn an anticipated profit on their behalf. This capacity to act as foci of investment is significant in a region where per capita cash earnings are small but the population large and considerable sums can be raised when people pool their resources. It allows the business leaders to accumulate capital for investment in trucks, processing plants, and so on. But mobilising investment above labour leads to problems over returns.

The logic behind the contributions parallels that underpinning gifts made in sociopolitical exchange contexts: that there will be a return payment to match the investment. If this repayment were made in the form of a manageable dividend from profits, with a percentage ploughed back into the enterprise to maintain stock, capital and so forth, the enterprise would thrive, but this is not the case. The investors expect not only to share in the fruits of the enterprise – to ride on the truck free, have extended credit at the store, and so on – but also to receive a handsome return payment, often in some traditional context such as a contribution to bridewealth or some pigs to kill at a feast.

[A businessman] must keep his following of contributors and other supporters happy by means of direct cash payments and gifts . . . there is a danger that if a man pays too much attention to the management of his enterprises and to his bank balance, he may neglect to reward his followers [i.e., investors] sufficiently, or, conversely, that if he devotes most of his time and resources to keeping his followers [investors] happy, then his enterprises and financial position are apt to run down. (Finney 1973:173)

Those contributing to ventures hand over cash as individuals as they do wealth in sociopolitical exchange rather than to further the interests of or support any social group. When they make a financial contribution to a business big man's enterprise they expect to receive a return, each individually according to what he has put in, not as a group with other investors.

The exchange ethos that pervades highland society has proved highly effective in financing commercial ventures, allowing those with business acumen to raise considerably larger sums than they could alone. But the exchange obligations entailed by the acceptance of these contributions hamper further commercial developments. The business big man has to disburse a considerable part of any profit he makes and sometimes part of the initial capital to his contributors, if not in sociopolitical exchange contexts then prompted by the obligations of reciprocity upon which they are predicated. The effect of these reciprocal expectations is to move one step forward and then one step back. People pool their resources with a business big man, who is obliged later to return them from his profits or his capital. They may also expect some further share of any profits that he has made (assuming that the enterprise shows a profit). We have seen how this sharing phenomenon affects returning migrant labourers among the Siane. Obliged to share out the goods and money they have brought back with them they are left with little to show that they have been away, let alone sufficient to finance any business enterprise. They are the normal ones according to the expectations of their culture; the few who save their earnings to finance commercial developments are behaving oddly or innovating.

The innovating behaviour of the aspiring highland businessman in amassing a considerable part of his capital personally takes on added significance in the context of the reciprocal obligations to which he is subject. The more he can finance his enterprise alone, the more secure it will be in the long run. The most successful and enduring commercial ventures are those in which the business big man manages to buy out other contributors by making whatever return payments to them they expect without depleting his operating capital and rendering his enterprise unprofitable. The most successful business big men of the Goroka region all achieve this to varying degrees and in so doing are acting according to one of the tenets of their culture while flouting another. They are vigorously pursuing their own individual interests while ignoring any obligations to share the fruits of their commercial success with kin.

Women and development

A glaring shortcoming of the big-man-to-business-man entrepreneurial model is that it omits half of the population, namely, women. The unwritten suggestion is that women do not become entrepreneurs, which is untrue. There are several reports of enterprising women participating in coffee processing, operating local bus services and managing successful stores. Nonetheless, considerably fewer women than men are commercially active and successful. The overlooking of women in development contexts is epitomised in Papua New Guinea as elsewhere in the world in the preponderance of men in agricultural research and extension work – the *didiman* agricultural officers – and their overwhelming concern for male-dominated crops such as coffee, tea, copra and rubber. Women, however, play a major part in farming activities, sometimes earning a sizeable part of their families' incomes from the sale of their garden produce in local markets.

Some people attribute the overlooking of women in development in Melanesia to traditional values which led to their occupying subordinate positions in their societies. While there is no doubt that they lived in markedly gender-differentiated societies, frequently occupying separate living spaces and engaging in different but complementary activities, it is questionable to conclude from this that women were inferior in status. These commentators seem to have observed the dominance of men in public events and assumed that women, whose lives centre on the more private domestic sphere, must have occupied subordinate social positions. This is an assessment founded on the judgment of Western intellectuals, who value public politics highly and consider the domestic sphere less important. A closer look at Melanesian social relations suggests an alternative interpretation in which women and men complement one another with no necessary imputation of a hierarchical relationship. The household, the *locus* of domestic activities, is embedded in, not isolated from, the wider political economy. All the members of a household, not just its male ones, have relationships outside it (women are equally sisters, wives and daughters, as men are brothers, husbands and sons), and around these relationships articulate sociopolitical exchanges. The accumulation and production of the wealth distributed in these transactions are household activities, albeit assigning women and men different responsibilities. Success in public events reflects on the entire household. All Gorokans know that the pigs men exchange are available to them only because of the combined efforts of their female relatives. The household has two faces, a public one facing outwards and a domestic one facing inwards, represented respectively by men and women, and is itself embedded in an egalitarian society. The activities of women and men complement one another, with no necessary evaluation of one as superior to the other. Both are necessary to the orderly flow of social life. Both women and men have influence, and the household does not function without cooperation between them.

According to this revised version of Melanesian gender relations, it is the so-called modernisation process itself that introduces the notion of a sexual status hierarchy. Missionaries have often started this process by eroding the influence of kin on the family – discouraging women from paying attention to their relatives' demands and encouraging them to be loyal and submissive wives, thus interfering with the affinal conduit central to exchange relations. Furthermore, while sociopolitical exchanges with affinal and other kin continue, the wealth involved is increasingly amassed less by the joint efforts of the household than by wage labour undertaken outside it. This emphasis on money and purchased commodities is further undermining the position of women. A concurrent change is occurring in the balance of power with the increasing separation of the household's domestic activities from its public ones; women are finding it difficult to exercise influence within their households if they earn no cash income outside it. And on top of this, Western intellectuals have heaped ignominy on the household, judging mere housewives and mothers subjugated, unfulfilled and inferior.

From this perspective, the less prominent role women often play in capitalist-driven economic development takes on a different hue. Many Melanesian women continue to believe in the equal importance of their role as mothers and household managers and are struggling to forge a new ideology that can encompass it now that the relations that once ensured its dignity and centrality to society have been shattered. This helps to explain why many females drop out of higher education when enrolments at the primary school level approach gender parity. While

Plate 6.3 Two workers inspect a coffee-grading and bagging machine in a Goroka factory.

education is widely perceived as an important vehicle for the advancement of women towards the Western ideal of equal opportunity in employment and the public domain, many women turn their backs on it, sensing that it may lead to conflict, and willingly accede to family pressure to comply with kin expectations. This domestic worldview may also explain the reluctance that women evidence to enter the political fray, which many argue is the other major vehicle for their advancement. There is also the complementary male view that politics is not really an appropriate female activity. The increasingly aggressive and violent character of politics may further deter women. Fewer than 2 per cent of the candidates in any of Papua New Guinea's national elections have been female, and consequently parliaments are overwhelmingly male-dominated. But there is nothing in its constitution that prevents females from competing with males in politics and the workplace; there are even some ennobled female politicians, such as Lady Abaijah and Lady Kidu. Some observers, subscribing to the view that Papua New Guinean society is male-dominated, were surprised during the negotiations for independence when the male politicians readily accepted as one of their eight aims for development 'a rapid increase in the equal and active participation of women in all forms of economic and social activity'.

Plate 6.4 Vegetables for sale at Gordons in Port Moresby: women dominate the marketing of local produce.

The evidence again points to the need to search for culturally appropriate avenues of development and not be overly troubled by the fact that few women display any inclination for big-man-like business advancement. Regardless of development consultants' gender recommendations, the women of Papua New Guinea are going their own way. Where they are able to manage the changes in their household role and continue to perform their highly valued domestic duties while engaging with the increasingly market-dominated world, they do so with energy and flair. Women dominate the small-scale marketing of local produce – vegetables, eggs, fish, cooked food, fruit and handicrafts. Some enterprising individuals have taken out loans to cover capital costs such as the purchase of sewing machines to make and repair clothes, freezers to manage wholesale produce, bales of second-hand clothes to break up and sell, and produce to stock stores. In their modest way many have been highly successful. And some women, for various reasons, enter waged employment, making up about 15 percent of the formal workforce (although some of these are young unmarried women who will drop out after marriage). A few of these eventually achieve highly paid and very senior positions. These women come from households with two incomes; men with well-paid jobs tend to have wives in paid employment too. These households are becoming increasingly wealthy – running two cars, sending their children to fee-paying schools, employing domestic servants, and so on – while others remain desperately poor. The outcome for a national society whose myriad cultures place a premium on equality is unclear, but social division and conflict are possible as kin and tribal loyalties are further eroded.

Flagging development

Even the commercially successful men, those apparently less susceptible to their society's demands to share and exchange with kin, seem to go only so far in developing their cash-earning concerns. The never-ending-growth mentality assumed by capitalist economics is apparently absent. One of the reasons for this is the nature of status in the egalitarian societies of the highlands. A powerful motive behind the struggles of business leaders to succeed in commercial ventures is to achieve renown and social standing in their regions, and once they have done so there is little incentive for them to expand their enterprise further. Even if they could manage the conflicting pressures acting upon them (notably the demands of contributing relatives for exchange equity), their uneasiness at over-stepping the accepted bounds of inequality would make them chary of more than modest expansion. If they became too successful they would offend against their society's militant egalitarian ethic, which stresses the equal standing of all, and would not only lose the goodwill and respect of their relatives but also risk revenge on the part of those they had offended – if not violence then sorcery. One outstanding business big man said of his enterprises: '[They] do not belong to me, they belong to all the people who pooled their money – I manage them that's all. I don't brag to the people; it would be no good to say they belong to me . . . or the people would like to injure me or something' (Finney 1973:115).

Another significant force restricting commercial growth beyond rather modest levels is that local consumption patterns and material demands have not changed much since contact. The Goroka people desire only a limited range of manufactured goods and relatively few processed foods. They continue to practise subsistence agriculture and grow most of the food they need, they build their own houses, largely from local materials. Until they demand more of the things that money can buy they are unlikely to become further involved in the outside monetary economy by increasing their cash-cropping or other business activities. They can soon satisfy their relatively modest demands with a modicum of cash-earning work. The vast majority are content to go little beyond tending a few coffee bushes to earn sufficient money to meet these demands. A potent force spurring a few on, as we have seen, is a wish to achieve social renown, not to improve their standard of living. This, taken together with their relatively small consumer demands, explains why Gorokans have invested a considerable part of their earnings in productive capital instead of consuming them.

The other direction in which cash has flowed, besides financing consumption and investment, is into sociopolitical exchange. The highlanders accept money as an item of wealth for exchange, and considerable sums circulate today in this sphere. This removes money from the economy, making it inaccessible for financing productive ventures, and acts as a further drag on sustained economic growth. We might anticipate that, under these circumstances, men would be eager to earn as much money as possible to finance their exchange commitments. Yet, strangely, this is not so. Initially men may respond in this manner to opportunities to earn cash, giving the appearance of enthusiastically entering into the monetary economy, but their enthusiasm is short-lived. They soon realise that as they earn more money and pump it into the sociopolitical exchange sphere, payments increase and even threaten to become unmanageable. All having about the same opportunities to earn cash, they find themselves working to stay where they are. It would only be worth it for an individual to devote himself to cash earning if he alone could do so, thus gaining an advantage over his fellows. But even if it were possible this avenue would be extremely dangerous, flouting the tenets of equality. Furthermore, these people sense that using cash subverts the essence and meaning of sociopolitical exchange events. The object is to receive gifts from others and pass them on again, not to earn or produce the objects required. The Tolai, for instance, who have had considerably more commercial experience than highlanders, reserve their *tambu* shell wealth for use in traditional social exchanges. They can also buy it, but in amounts too small to finance sociopolitical exchange commitments. It is through social exchange receipts that they largely finance their obligations, and this is right and proper.

It appears that Eastern Highlands society, rather than promoting a sustained positive response to development opportunities, reacted favourably at first, spurring apparent rapid growth, only to stall. The local cash-earning economy advanced and then retreated, and the same social forces were involved in both phases. The traditional egalitarian exchange-focused values of the local people were not solely responsible. Just as a series of fortuitous outside factors had come together in the Goroka region in the 1950s and, combined with the initially favourable indigenous response to commercial opportunities, promoted rapid market take-off, so by chance outside conditions, notably regarding the cultivation of coffee as a cash crop, became less auspicious and, combined with resistance to capitalist economic growth, caused development to flag.

The decline of the very high world price of coffee has been a significant factor in stalling commercial development in the highlands. Although people have tried alternative cash crops, none can match the early returns earned by coffee or its suitability, both environmentally and socially, to the Goroka situation. The fluctuating world price for coffee, like that for many other tropical primary products, discourages sustained economic growth. People continue to expect high returns for their efforts, which are improbable in most of the ventures open to them in the future, and so withdraw to some extent from the monetary sector.

In addition to these changes in economic circumstances, the political situation has changed. Papua New Guinea has gained independence since the Gorokans first entered the cash economy, and the expatriate European population has declined dramatically, taking away many of the services that made cash-cropping so cost-effective and profitable. The original expatriate settlers, for instance, have sold out to large plantation companies under contract managers who do not have the same interest in assisting local development, and they left before they had passed on sufficient of their experience and knowledge to the local people for them to maintain their own commercial development. The highlanders do not manage their cash crops as they ought to, for instance, to ensure top-grade marketable quality – neglecting to prune their coffee bushes correctly, to fertilise them appropriately, and so on – or maintain their capital equipment in proper working order.

This pinpoints one of the major issues at the root of current problems. The people of the Goroka region became intensely involved in the market before they had the education and technical knowledge necessary to sustain the changes put in train. Economic change and technological development of the magnitude they experienced, leaving aside the question of their social desirability and cultural consequences, demand a solid foundation of knowledge, and education takes years, even generations, to have effect. Changes in technology and economic organisation need to be introduced at a pace that allows people to adjust and cope with them. It is no surprise that the Goroka people have apparently been moving back towards their cultural roots. The rapid material change they experienced, however dramatic, was only a material veneer, a short-lived phenomenon resulting from the fortuitous combination of favourable circumstances at a certain time in the region's history.

The flexible Eastern Highlands society stretched only as far as it comfortably could without doing violence to itself and then contracted. This violent swinging response to change is common; the trend with economic change is less a growth curve than a series of swings like those of the familiar boom-and-bust economic cycle. The local cash-earning economy of the Goroka region is currently in this fluctuating state. A steady long-term shift founded on education might seem more advantageous and less wasteful, but that would demand considerable time, which is one thing the modern world seems to lack. While local entrepreneurs are a significant force in fomenting commercial growth and consequent social change, they can only have a limited impact on their societies if their members are not prepared to tolerate activities that conflict with traditional expectations.

FURTHER READING

On big man entrepreneurship see:
B. R. Finney 1973 *Big-men and business* Honolulu: University of Hawaii Press
B. R. Finney 1969 *New Guinean entrepreneurs* Canberra: Australian National University New Guinea Research Bulletin No. 27
A. J. Strathern 1972 The entrepreneurial model of social change: from Norway to New Guinea *Ethnology* 11:368–79

On entrepreneurship in the context of social change see:
F. Barth 1963 *The role of the entrepreneur in social change in northern Norway* Bergen: Universitetsforlaget
B. I. Belasco 1980 *The entrepreneur as culture hero* New York: Praeger
W. G. Broehl 1978 *The village entrepreneur: change agents in India's rural development* Cambridge, MA: Harvard University Press
F. Cancian 1979 *The innovator's situation* Stanford: Stanford University Press
P. Kilby (ed.) 1971 *Entrepreneurship and economic development* New York: Free Press
N. Long and B. Roberts 1984 *Miners, peasants, and entrepreneurs* Cambridge: Cambridge University Press
P. Marris and A. Somerset 1971 *African businessmen* London: Routledge
M. Weber 1976 *The Protestant ethic and the spirit of capitalism* London: Allen and Unwin

On women in development see:
R. Clelland 1996 *Grassroots to independence and beyond: the contribution of women in Papua New Guinea 1951–1991* Claremont (Western Australia): R. Clelland
C. V. Scott 1995 *Gender and development: rethinking modernization and dependency theory* London: Lynne Rienner
N. Visvanathan, L. Duggan and N. Wiegersma (eds.) 1997 *The women, gender, and development reader* London: Zed Books
K. Young 1994 *Planning development with women* London: Macmillan

Also see:

C. Geertz 1963 *Peddlers and princes* Chicago: University of Chicago Press

N. Long 1968 *Social change and the individual* Manchester: Manchester University
Press

FILMS

A man without pigs Pacific Video-Cassette Series No. 23

7   From tribespeople to peasants

The capitalist commercial developments and associated social changes affecting Melanesia are said to be turning its population from tribespeople into peasants. What this change of status implies is that where previously there was an egalitarian society a hierarchical one is now emerging. The successful business big men are emerging as a class, and those gaining access to national political and bureaucratic positions are evolving into an élite class. The marxist argument assumes a social hierarchy in which certain classes control access to capital and resources and thereby dominate and exploit others, obliging them to sell their labour on unfair terms to secure their livelihoods and expropriating their surplus to their benefit.

Melanesian peasants

Both 'peasants' and 'tribespeople' are ill-defined, writers having used the terms as catch-alls in referring to people throughout the world whose lifestyles have some features in common, but who differ widely in cultural traditions. Broadly speaking tribespeople live in small-scale societies in which kinship figures importantly in the structuring of social relations. They are economically and politically independent. They are subsistence cultivators throughout Melanesia who produce sufficient both to ensure their survival and to support their social commitments, and their stateless polities maintain relatively stable and orderly social environments. The members of these societies, allowing for differences in roles, are relatively independent too, being more or less equal in economic and political terms. Peasants, in contrast, are dependent in some regards on economic and political institutions beyond their local society. They supply their own subsistence needs but beyond this they produce a surplus to market for cash. They use this money to purchase goods manufactured elsewhere, and to pay the taxes levied on them by the colonial/national governments to which they are subject. Peasants are incorporated into larger political formations which rule significant aspects of their lives and may supply them with certain services. They are part of a hierarchical order in which they occupy a low and frequently exploited position. What they receive financially in return for their surplus produce is unfair; the élite, controlling access to imperfect factor markets and the arrangements for the marketing of produce, make a sizeable profit that supports their privileged position and lifestyle.

As Melanesians shift from tribespeople to peasants they remain, in terms of subsistence, self-sufficient. The Eastern Highlanders, for instance, 'are not wholly dependent on the cash economy for meeting their needs; a man and his wife, or wives, can still easily grow most of the food they eat . . . Although a modest amount of cash comes in handy . . . most Gorokan men are not so tightly bound to the cash economy that a shortage or lack of cash would spell disaster' (Finney 1973:148). The subsistence swidden cultivation regime continues to underpin life throughout the highlands and beyond, and it is crucial that it not be undermined before there is a viable economic arrangement to replace it.

We can appreciate the importance of this when we recall the manner in which cash-earning developments burgeon only to collapse under shifting pressures. There is no regular progression as some development planners assume. While the gross trend may be depicted in the abstract as a series of steps from one level of monetary production and consumption to another, in reality change proceeds in unpredictable and irregular swings. If on an upswing people become dependent to some extent on outside-supplied processed food that a subsequent downswing makes it difficult to finance, they may find themselves in serious trouble. And such disastrous turnabouts are particularly likely where people rely on a single crop – coffee, copra, cocoa – to earn their cash, as is the situation throughout nearly all of Melanesia. A drop in the international price of that commodity or the advent of some disease seriously affecting yields or some other disaster can cut the income people earn dramatically, and if they are too reliant on it this may be a disaster.

The tenacity with which peasants hang on to their subsistence self-sufficiency suggests that they are aware of the danger of becoming overly dependent on the monetary commodity market, over which they have no control and which on occasion deals with them harshly. Many commentators interpret their reluctance to commit themselves to more extensive cash-crop cultivation as evidence of a negative, fatalistic and demoralised outlook, suspicious of innovation and resistant to change. This may be partly correct, given the unfortunate experiences of many peasants, but it is important that, in maintaining their subsistence independence, they are ensuring their security in an unpredictable and uncontrollable world. Whatever happens on the commodity markets, they have the means to

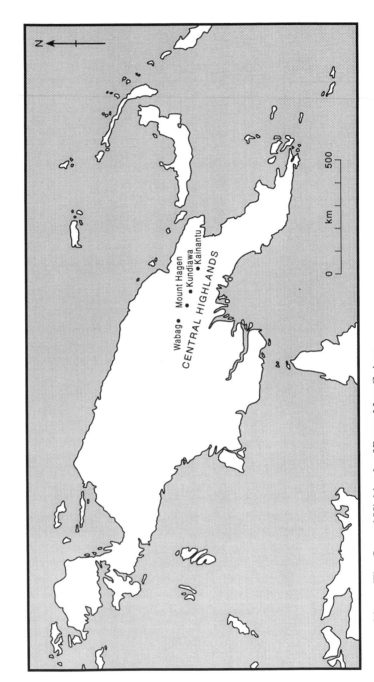

Map 7 The Central Highlands of Papua New Guinea

survive. This is not evidence of an inveterate traditional mentality adverse to any development but is sensible and prudent.

Subsistence development

The difficulties experienced in integrating peasant producers into the monetary economy beyond a certain limited participation are almost legendary. Indeed, the problems encountered in encouraging people to rely on the sale of their produce to earn money to buy the necessities of life from others, have proved so intractable as to prompt some observers to argue that the peasant condition may prove a terminal stage of development in Melanesia. Whether or not this view proves accurate in the long run, the partiality which Melanesians show for maintaining their subsistence capacity indicates that those involved in promoting development should give this important sphere of the Melanesian economy more attention. Its maintenance is important to people, serving to ensure their tribal identity

To date agricultural research has concentrated heavily on improving the cultivation and yields of cash crops, whereas current conditions point to the need for a close look at traditional agricultural practices and crops too. If the livelihood of Melanesians is going to continue to depend in large part on subsistence cultivation, then to ensure sustained and firmly founded change planners need to give some attention to improving the traditional cultivation system. This will become more urgent as the population of Melanesia expands and the pressure on land resources increases.

If the productivity of the traditional subsistence regime is not improved to keep pace with the growing numbers demanding food, people will take back into subsistence cultivation the land they are using for cash crops, thus further withdrawing from commercial activity instead of becoming more market involved. It is unlikely that Melanesians, as tribespeople-peasants, with their heritage of subsistence self-sufficiency, would maintain their cash crops at the expense of food gardens and thus become dependent on money incomes for their survival. If, however, there is a possibility that people in any region will shift from peasants to market farmers under demographic duress, it gives added urgency to the need to develop the full potential of their agricultural regime. Otherwise they will find themselves in a precarious position, dependent on a fragile cash crop economy with an expanding population.

While the urge to remain self-sufficient is probably too deeply ingrained in Melanesians for them to make such changes, the imperative to develop traditional cultivation regimes remains. If Melanesians are going to continue to depend upon them, then the more efficient these

Plate 7.1 An aspiring highlander business big man sits at the wheel of his four-wheel-drive truck, which he uses to ferry passengers and cargo, having learnt to drive on a tractor used to pull a roller on the local airstrip.

systems are the more resources will be available for other activities such as cash-cropping, and the higher and more secure will be their standards of living. Various colonial and national governments in the region have acknowledged the need for improvements in subsistence agriculture for some years. The Annual Report for Papua New Guinea (1967–8:55) noted, for instance, that 'the advancement of indigenous agriculture to improve food supplies, to bring about a more efficient use of village land and increase the production of cash crops, is given a high priority'. And the Papua New Guinea government has recently expressed this as a central policy objective.

Intervention in shifting cultivation systems has, however, proved notoriously difficult throughout the tropical world. There are various ways in which the productivity and efficiency of swidden systems might possibly be improved. By experimenting with new crop cultivars yields might be increased and disease-resistant varieties developed. Erosion control and the use of fertilisers might increase productivity. A shift to fast-growing fallow species could speed up and perhaps improve soil regeneration, and the possibility of commercially exploitable fallow plants might be investigated. Attempts could be made to regulate and rationalise the pattern of movement so that land is used optimally, and opportunities for combining subsistence and cash-cropping into a single integrated system could be explored.

Peasants and dependency

The introduction of cash crops leads not only to changes in people's subsistence arrangements and livelihoods but also to changes in the ordering of their societies. Simultaneously, their stateless and egalitarian tribal orders become subsumed under a hierarchically organised state, relegated to the bottom of the political structure. Occupying the lowest socioeconomic position, they may eventually find their cash-earning capacities exploited by those who control their nation's economic and political structures. A hierarchy may simultaneously evolve in the local peasant community as some individuals, imbued with the traditional ethic of competitively achieved status, come to recognise the potential of cash-cropping and other business opportunities and earn more money than others.

According to dependency theory, less developed countries are sharply divided between a wealthy minority monopolising resources and power and an impoverished majority, largely peasants and urban poor. These markedly divided nations are linked by dependency relationships to industrial powers; they are satellites of these metropolises, which expropriate a considerable proportion of their economic surpluses. They are unable to exercise much influence over capital investment, world markets or international politics and cannot achieve autonomous development; their economic growth depends upon more powerful nations. A chain of domination and dependency relations that extends from the metropolis to the satellite nation and on down to the peasant village perpetuates underdevelopment. The argument is that the economic growth assumed by modernisation and manipulated by outside powers has led to the impoverishment of the majority of people in less developed nations and improvement for a small élite and that this indigenous bourgeoisie has a vested interest in maintaining the exploitative structures based on differential control of economic and political resources.

A problem with dependency theory, which it shares with modernisation theory, is that it assumes that when capitalism intrudes into other societies it eliminates traditional socioeconomic arrangements. This is not so. While the traditional system may undergo considerable modification, it may come to coexist with the new capitalist arrangements. The anthropological study of different modes of production and the processes whereby they reproduce themselves has explored the interconnections between traditional and capitalist systems. It attempts to account for the persistence of some traditional socioeconomic arrangements following penetration by the outside monetary market, for example, viewing the continuance of subsistence cultivation among Melanesian peasants as suiting the capitalist sector by supplying people's subsistence needs and thus reducing the amounts it needs to pay in wages. Dependency theory also sees underdevelopment almost exclusively in terms of vertical relations of domination. Any relationship assumes, however, that the two parties are dependent on each other to some degree and that cooperation exists both between and within opposed interest groups. It is incorrect to argue that metropolitan centres set the agenda for change which the national élite oversees; local communities have connections too, and can play a part in determining the allocation of regional if not national resources.

Dependency theory, again like modernisation theory, overlooks the specific sociohistorical circumstances of different cultures and the interaction of unique internal social factors in influencing the direction of any change. Individuals who recognise and seize upon the opportunities presented by change may gain a competitive edge, as we have seen in the Papua New Guinea highlands, and promote successful cash-earning enterprises. This is a new status which bears some resemblance to the old position of renown achieved by socially ambitious men, except that, whereas the traditional big men occupied no permanent hierarchy or enduring, inheritable social positions, the new business big men have the potential to do so. Indeed, some writers claim that their emergence is currently giving rise to a class structure, with some tribespeople-peasants increasing their productive capacity over others and becoming rich and dominant:

the changing agricultural policies of the colonial Government and the subsequent strategies adopted by administration and extension field officers encouraged some tendencies already apparent within pre-colonial societies, so that we can now identify new and powerful rural classes, namely the rich peasantry and rural capitalists. (Donaldson and Good, n.d.:143)

A change along these lines and of this magnitude would represent the virtual overthrow of the traditional social order, with its emphasis on individual autonomy and equality. In short, it would be a revolution the effects of which would go well beyond those experienced at first contact. The evidence is that these marxist interpretations are somewhat wide of the mark. They fail to allow for the resilience of Melanesian society and its ability to subvert such tendencies. For a class structure to emerge it will be necessary for those who achieve superior productive and social positions in the evolving hierarchy to hand on what they accumulate to their heirs and thus establish wealthy and powerful families. Otherwise their positions will amount to grandiose versions of the traditional transitory big-man status.

Classes subverted

There are a number of features of traditional Melanesian social organisation which militate against the formation of a class structure. The customary system of land tenure is one crucial variable here. As we have seen, all Melanesians have a right to sufficient land to meet their needs. They may claim rights to use land wherever they are related in the customarily prescribed manner to those who collectively claim custodial rights to it. No person controls access to land under this system, and all have equal access to what they require. So long as this land tenure system continues, there is no chance of the emergence of a landless proletariat forced to rent at exploitative rates from landlords or enter into unfair sharecropping contracts with them or to provide labour on their estates to earn a meagre livelihood.

Legislation encouraging individuals to claim fee-simple title to land will undermine this equitable situation and promote the exploitative developments that the marxists predict. This tenure-conversion legislation recalls the English Enclosure Acts, which allowed persons to enclose common land to which they had no exclusive rights. Judging by the resis-

Plate 7.2 Sociopolitical exchange in the 1990s: two highlanders inspect
the valuables offered in a bridewealth transaction.

tance they are showing to tenure conversion, Melanesians appear to sense
the threat. As long as individuals cannot own and sell land, they cannot
permanently separate themselves from their birthright by selling their
rights to others who are commercially more successful and, coming to
own more and more land, will become a landlord class. Furthermore, as
land rights are currently constituted, whatever cash-crop holdings and
other commercial developments a man builds up on his land will be dispersed at his death, several kin customarily having a justifiable claim to a
share. Even with individual title this would apply unless governments
drafted legislation stipulating a single person – such as the eldest son – as
sole heir, which would be extremely unlikely to find any favour. In its
absence, whatever estate and commercial enterprises the energetic and
money-wise manage to build up in their lives will be distributed among
several persons when they die, which works against the establishment of a
formal and enduring class structure favouring some by birth over others.
    The dependence of business success on personal achievement, cen-

tring profitable ventures on single individuals, is another important feature preventing the evolution of a class structure. Where business concerns depend exclusively on the enterprise and management flair of single dynamic individuals, they are liable to fail when the entrepreneurs' talents and energy decline with age, as successors equal to them are unlikely to emerge from among their kin and associates. This tendency is evident in the Eastern Highlands:

The commercial structures that Gorokan entrepreneurs erect have what appears to be a basic flaw: they are fragile organisations which, with a few exceptions, revolve around single men . . . egocentrically organised and operated, when an entrepreneur dies the businesses are liable to collapse from the lack of a firm and continuous leadership. (Finney 1973:177)

These enterprises are doomed to remain small-scale ventures of the kind that a single man can build up in his lifetime, and their instability undermines the formation of an élite business class with economic resources and power concentrated in a few hands and passed on from one generation to another. The intergenerational fragility of enterprises reflects the absence of any legally instituted means of converting kin entities to companies.

Although the context is radically different, the situation parallels closely that which obtains traditionally with big men, who similarly build up exchange networks which fall apart with their demise. Both contribute to an egalitarian social environment in which a formal class structure is unimaginable. The demands of sociopolitical exchange operate in a similar manner to thwart any classlike developments while a successful entrepreneur is alive. They promote a trend towards equality by encouraging the social consumption of profits instead of their investment in productive capital. It is not sufficient for renown and high social standing that a man excel in commercial enterprises alone: he must also shine in traditional sociopolitical exchange. But today's entrepreneur finances many of his exchange commitments through production – from the profits he earns in his business ventures – whereas the orthodox big man finances his by the assiduous management and manipulation of exchange obligations. This is a fundamental change that can be expected in the long run to undermine tribal egalitarian relationships and promote the evolution of a class structure predicted by dependency theorists if the other obstacles to its development are simultaneously eroded away. For the time being, however, the value placed on sociopolitical exchange prevents the concentration of wealth in the hands of a few. Successful entrepreneurs, like traditional big men, live much the same as everyone else; there is little of the conspicuous consumption of the wealthy in class-structured societies. Furthermore, the sociopolitical-exchange-like demands of those who invest in commercial ventures for a fair return on what they contribute also has the effect of cutting entrepreneurs down to size.

Another feature of traditional Melanesian society that is thwarting the evolution of a class structure is the persistence of so-called tribal warfare. This is not, as one marxist commentator suggests, evidence of 'inchoate, unorganized action against rich peasants' (Amarshi, Good and Mortimer 1979:120). It is the customary way of dealing with intractable disputes and homicides. Whatever the reason for the periodic resurgence of warfare – and this poses a considerable and embarrassing problem to the national government of Papua New Guinea – it militates against the emergence of have and have-not classes in at least two ways. First, it makes the successful wary of offending against their fellows' sense of equality. A man who attempted to control others' actions and live markedly better off than they would foment resentment and find himself embroiled in disputes that could easily end in violence. The remark of a Hagen big man illustrates this wariness: 'We shall make money-moka, buy vehicles, build stores, do all these things, and stay ahead, so that people will be envious and angry with us. Be careful, then, as I have often told you, for they may kill us' (Strathern 1982:157). Secondly, whether or not their actions contribute to an outbreak of armed hostilities, business big men, having more fixed capital, stand to lose more than others. In warfare it is usual for each side to try to destroy as many as possible of the enemy's assets – chopping down coffee bushes, looting and burning buildings, and so forth. If an entrepreneur is unfortunate enough to find himself involved in a war, he may lose a good deal of his capital. This is effective at bringing the successful back down to the level of everyman.

Classes promoted

The dependency theorists' interpretation of the social consequences of capitalist development in Melanesia, suggesting the rise of a rural class system dominated by so-called rich peasants, does not fit the current situation. Entrenched traditional values and persistent features of the pre-contact acephalous tribal social order are sufficient to subvert the formation of rigid classes along capitalist lines. These elements of the traditional order are, however, subject to a sustained onslaught from those bent on modernisation at the national level.

The formation of classes depends not just on economic issues, such as monopolising certain resources and capital, but on a political system which facilitates the control of the various relations of production and wields the accruing power. A significant legacy of the colonial era in this

Plate 7.3 A Southern Highlander brandishing a home-made shotgun increasingly used in tribal warfare and 'rascalism', comprising a length of plumbers' pipe with an inner-tube strip and sharpened nail firing mechanism.

regard is central government where previously there were countless autonomous acephalous tribal orders. The governmental systems of the various newly independent Melanesian nations differ in detail, but they are all constituted on the Westminster parliamentary model, with democratically elected legislative bodies supporting executive bureaucracies and independent judiciaries. And they currently show every sign of remaining healthily democratic. These national governments are antithetical to the existence of stateless polities, and so are the remaining colonially administered countries of Melanesia. The evolution of social classes is an aspect of these states' elimination of acephalous orders.

Regarding the formation of a class structure, it is of considerable moment that those who are particularly successful commercially in their local regions are the ones involving themselves in national and provincial politics. Business big men are running for election to political office with notable success. Consequently, we are witnessing here the emergence not of a local rural capitalist class but of a national ruling one the members of which are in the process of consolidating for themselves powerful home economic bases. It is these people who have a vested interest in seeing the

Plate 7.4 A disturbing street scene in Boroko suggestive of an emergent class structure: have-nots loot a shop during the 1997 disturbances over the hiring of mercenaries to 'solve' the Bougainville problem.

overthrow of the traditional values and behaviour which are preventing them from consolidating their commercial enterprises. Once elected to political office, they have access to the governmental levers they need to accomplish this. Many politicians stand explicitly on a platform which pledges them to exactly this end, promising to *kirapim ples* (Pidgin for 'promote economic development') even though it is doubtful that either they or their electorates have any clear idea of its probable social consequences.

It is these individuals – members of the nascent élite class – who are enacting legislation to break down the barriers that are currently hindering their emergence, albeit with no hidden agenda for their own advancement but in the belief that this will promote economic growth for the good of all citizens. It is they who authorise the conversion of landholding into individual fee-simple title, amending legislation to that effect and encouraging people (so far with marked lack of success) to take advantage of it. It is they who administer the considerable sums received in aid from industrial nations, particularly from Australia, disbursing it via development banks and agencies which encourage the formation and financing of companies instead of individual enterprises. It is these that are a major source of capital for the buying up of expatriate-owned plantations by indigenous corporations that has been happening since independence.

National governments are also legislating to clamp down on tribal warfare, and extending to the police extraordinary powers to stamp it out; some politicians are urging draconian measures which if imposed by any colonial power would be internationally condemned. And finally, eroding away the last bastion of the traditional egalitarian order, they are promoting in every way possible the assimilation of their nation's citizens into a monetary market economy and the devaluation of their customary wealth arrangements. When and if individual men come literally to buy wives with cash or forgo bridewealth transactions altogether, they will have succeeded in rendering sociopolitical exchange meaningless, and establishing commercial success and class as the prerequisites for social renown.

It would be foolhardy to predict how far and how soon the emerging élite will succeed in these endeavours. Undoubtedly their societies are undergoing a tremendous transformation, and the emergence of some kind of class order seems unavoidable on current evidence. Whether we applaud or abhor such changes depends on how much we consider it justifiable for people to give up for a certain level of technological and economic development, but, given the current structure of international politics and the worldwide dominance of the capitalist economic order, development seems to entail them.

FURTHER READING

On emerging inequality and social stratification in Melanesia see:

A. Amarshi, K. Good and R. Mortimer 1979 *Development and independency* Oxford: Oxford University Press

M. Donaldson and K. Good n.d. The Eastern Highlands: coffee and class. In D. Denoon and C. Snowden (eds.) *A time to plant and a time to uproot* Boroko: Institute of Papua New Guinea Studies

D. Gewertz and F. Errington 1999 *Emerging class in Papua New Guinea: the telling of difference* Cambridge: Cambridge University Press

K. Good 1986 *Papua New Guinea: a false economy* London: Anti-Slavery Society, Indigenous Peoples and Development Series Report No. 3

R. Gorden and M. Meggitt 1985 *Law and order in the New Guinea highlands* Hanover: University Press of New England

D. Howlett 1973 Terminal development: from tribalism to peasantry. In H. Brookfield (ed.) *The Pacific in transition* London: Edward Arnold

R. J. May (ed.) 1984 *Social stratification in Papua New Guinea* Canberra: Australian National University Political and Social Change Department Working Paper No. 5

M. Meggitt 1971 From tribesmen to peasants: the case of the Mae Enga of New Guinea. In L. R. Hiatt and C. Jayawardena (eds.) *Anthropology in Oceania* Sydney: Angus and Robertson

M. F. Smith 1994 *Hard times on Kairiru Island: poverty, development, and morality in a Papua New Guinea village* Honolulu: University of Hawaii Press
A. J. Strathern (ed.) 1982 *Inequality in New Guinea highland societies* Cambridge: Cambridge University Press
A. J. Strathern 1984 *A line of power* London: Tavistock
M. Turner 1990 *Papua New Guinea: the challenge of independence* Ringwood: Penguin

On dependency theory in development see:
W. Hout 1993 *Capitalism and the Third World: development, dependence, and the world system* Aldershot: Elgar
J. Larrain 1989 *Theories of development: capitalism, colonialism, and dependency* Cambridge: Polity Press
P. N. Mathur 1991 *Why developing countries fail to develop* New York: St Martin's Press
R. A. Packenham 1992 *The dependency movement: scholarship and politics in development studies* Cambridge, MA: Harvard University Press
T. Spybey 1992 *Social change, development, and dependency: modernity, colonialism and the development of the West* Cambridge: Polity Press

FILMS

Black harvest Australian Film Commission, Arundel Productions
Joe Leahy's neighbours Pacific Video-Cassette Series No. 19
Tinpis run Mondo Cinema

8　Mining, misunderstanding and insurrection

The activities of small-scale local entrepreneurs may cumulatively have a notable impact on their country's economies and foment considerable social change, but singly their activities are minuscule and of only parochial interest. There are other agencies of development, involving international development funds and multinational companies, which by themselves can have massive economic and social impacts and cause extensive change. In Melanesia these developments largely involve primary extractive industries established to exploit the region's rich mineral reserves, and examining them calls for a change of focus from the local to the national and international arenas. So far we have been considering economic development and its effects largely from the perspective of the grass roots, investigating the consequences of and the local response to the intrusion of Western society. In considering the likelihood of class formation we began to shift our attention from the local rural to the national level, where policy decisions have profound effects on the course of change.

This chapter continues this shift of perspective. It considers how national governments and their supporting bureaucracies manage economic growth and the cross-cutting forces that impinge on centrally planned development without losing sight of the consequences at the rural 'periphery'. Centrally planned development concerns issues and projects far beyond the level and capacity of any rural entrepreneur, involving colossal sums of money and capital investment in massive ventures which individually have a marked impact on the financial standing and balance of payments of nations. These projects invariably depend on multinational corporations and consortia. They are not initiated locally but proceed from outside enterprise, and control of them passes in some regards beyond the countries in which they are situated not simply to the companies involved but to the international economic marketplace that dictates their profit-motivated decisions. The consequent distancing of these projects from the local populations that they intrude upon and from their national governments unavoidably gives rise to tensions.

In the early days large-scale developments in Melanesia predominantly concerned the establishment of plantations, with associated processing plant and service infrastructure to facilitate export of their produce. By today's standards, even where investment was high the sums involved and the technological inputs were small. These enterprises are now passing increasingly into indigenous ownership, albeit often retaining European managers and sanctioning the near-continuance of the colonial regime with regard to labour and working conditions. Although plantations continue to contribute significantly to the export earnings of Melanesian nations and provide the greater part of the foreign earnings of some, such as Fiji, the Solomons and Vanuatu, the big investment concerns with associated highly sophisticated technology centre on mining. The Melanesian islands, situated on the Pacific 'ring of fire', have been subject to massive tectonic activity that has resulted in the formation of valuable ore-bearing rocks.

Gold prospecting

The idea that Melanesia should prove to be a Pacific El Dorado has held the European imagination from the earliest times and some countries in the region have proved to be so but only through massive capital investment and startling engineering projects for large-scale mining that make it profitable to extract relatively low-grade ores. Initial interest in minerals centred largely on gold. Small strikes and gold rushes have occurred in the Melanesian region from the late nineteenth century to the present, the majority in eastern New Guinea and the adjacent islands. As have gold rushes around the world, they have attracted a motley collection of tough and resourceful characters with dreams of the big strike and a life of affluence. Few have been this lucky.

Time and again, the pursuit of gold has stimulated men to explore unknown parts of the Melanesian region. The prospectors, with their hearts set on gold, have paid scant attention to the local populations, and their contacts with them have often been violent. Ruthless miners on occasion gunned down those who reacted aggressively to their intrusion; for many of these people this was their first contact with Europeans. Many Melanesians believe that this set a pattern of callous exploitation of their mineral resources that continues to this day. In gold prospecting this has often been so; not only have the local populations been treated as if they had no rights but Melanesians from elsewhere have been employed virtually as slaves. Someone recalling a visit to a goldfield described, for instance, how some of the prospectors solved the transport problem in their roadless region (probably, I suspect, after a heavy bout of drinking): 'it sounds dreadful now, but every man who had his own boy had given him the name of a car, "Buick" or "Ford." When they wanted to go home, they would call for their "car," and the boy would piggy-back them' (Nelson 1982:145). It is small wonder that many Melanesians resented the colonial order. Besides enduring such degrading and humiliating treatment, the indentured – almost forced – labourers employed by prospectors received paltry 'wages' and their diets were often grossly inadequate; the death rate among them was high.

Many of the miners fared little better, washing up paltry returns for the risks and the hard life. It would be offensive to refer to their activities as promoting development, although their intrusion into often uncontacted cultures did produce certain social changes. It revolutionised people's perceptions of life, informing them of the outside world's existence and setting in train the events that led to their conquest. The prospecting was done by individuals, working their 'boys' with pan and sluice to wash up gold and financing their operations on slender budgets that precluded generosity to labourers. They gambled, unsuccessfully by and large, on lining their own pockets, regardless of the traumatic effects of their activities on local people unfortunate enough to come into contact with them. This style of prospecting has continued up to the present day, and indigenous people now take part in gold rushes, as at Mount Kare in the late 1980s. And today large-scale mining ventures are reworking some of the locations of early gold strikes, such as Lakekamu in the Gulf and Misima Island in the Louisiades.

This pattern of gold exploitation was altered in the early 1930s with the big strike on Edie Creek in the Morobe region of New Guinea. Prospectors flocked to the area and some made rich claims and went on to explore considerable parts of the highlands. What distinguished this strike from others was that it led to a large dredging venture, the precursor of mining developments to come. The silt of the Bulolo Valley contained gold too thin for individual prospectors to work but sufficient for a profitable commercial venture using dredges. The company airlifted into this remote mountain region the parts for eight massive barge-fitted dredges (the heaviest weighing almost 4,000 tons) and a construction team to assemble them (many of them riveters who had previously worked on the Sydney Harbour Bridge). They also built a town with associated mining plant to support the venture and staff. We can imagine the shock to the local Anga-speaking population. Confronted by the rush of gold-seeking prospectors, followed by the numerous employees of a mining company which constructed gigantic dinosaur-like dredges that literally tore up the floor of one of their valleys, they were at a loss to know how to deal with the invaders except by attacking them, and this brought down punitive government patrols and earned them a fearsome reputation. This

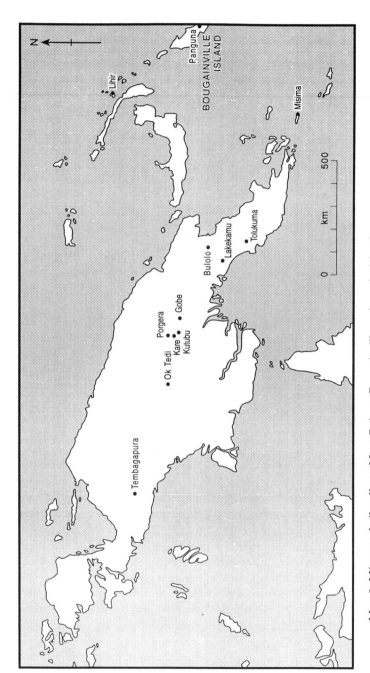

Map 8 Mines and oil wells on New Guinea, Bougainville and nearby islands

response has parallels up to the present day, when people are familiar with European ways and the political climate is quite different from the colonial one. The reactions of local populations to more recent mining ventures have ranged from loud protest to violent and bloody confrontation.

National incomes

While few individual prospectors have ever struck it rich, their returns have been cumulatively significant in some years and gold has on occasion made up a significant proportion of the exports of some countries. This was notably so for the Territory of New Guinea shortly after the establishment of the dredging company, when gold made up over 80 per cent of the colony's export earnings. The Bulolo Company had made a profit of US$32 million during its first decade of operation. The early high returns from the mining of gold again foreshadowed a trend that continues in parts of Melanesia up to the present day, where some nations depend heavily on mineral extraction to finance their international trade and development. The sums involved now are colossal. Gold continues to feature as a mineral export, frequently as a by-product of the mining of copper, which is the ore on which subsequent large-scale mineral extraction developments have particularly centred. Large mines have been established in Papua New Guinea, on Bougainville Island, at Ok Tedi in the Star Mountains, at Porgera in Enga Province, and on the small island of Lihir, with others under development, and in Irian Jaya at Tembagapura (Ertsberg). The other major mineral mined in Melanesia is nickel, in the French colony of New Caledonia. Oil and gas are increasingly important, particularly in Papua New Guinea, with the Hides gas field and oil wells at Gobe and Lake Kutubu, and oilfield developments in Irian Jaya.

These minerals contribute significantly to the export earnings of the countries that produce them. Although the percentage varies from one year to another, given the dramatic fluctuations in the international prices paid for these and the other primary products on which these countries' economies depend, the following statistics give some idea of their importance. In New Caledonia, nickel regularly makes up something like 90 per cent of the value of the colony's exports. Copper and gold provided between 40 per cent and 60 per cent of Papua New Guinea's export earnings before the closure of the Bougainville mine, and copper and oil make up an estimated 95 per cent of Irian Jaya's exports. These translate into substantial foreign earnings – comfortably in excess of US$1,000 million per annum, for instance, for Papua New Guinea, during the early 1990s, rising to over US$2,000 million by the middle of the decade – and through royalties and taxes on ensuing profits the nations involved derive from them a substantial part of their revenues. The government of Papua New Guinea raised an average of US$60 million through the 1970s, increasing to some US$200 million during the 1980s when Ok Tedi (estimated to bring in US$10 billion total profit) came into production and climbing to over US$250 million by the mid-1990s, with further increases in prospect as other new ventures come into production. These figures will probably average out over several decades at about one-third of the nation's foreign revenues. It is predictable that the governments of the countries involved should take considerable interest in promoting mineral extraction, facilitating and overseeing these developments directly from the centre.

A major incentive to governments in promoting these primary extractive industries is to reduce their reliance on aid from overseas, the ongoing supply of which they do not control (the Australian government, for instance, threatened to curtail its aid to Papua New Guinea when it recklessly invited a mercenary force into the region: see page 137 below). Papua New Guinea depended on Australian grants for about two-thirds of its total revenue before independence, but this figure has subsequently fallen to about one-quarter as local revenues, largely from minerals, have increased. The extraction of these minerals depends, however, on enormous capital investments and engineering capabilities far beyond the means of these Third World countries. The three enormous open-cast copper mines established in the region illustrate the magnitude of these costs: Tembagapura, possibly the largest base-metal outcrop in the world, demanded a capital investment of US$163 million before it was operational; Bougainville required A $400 million investment (A $20 million of which was expended exploring the feasibility of the project) and Ok Tedi called for US$1,300 million of capital investment (situated almost in the centre of the island of New Guinea, in remote and rugged mountains, it demanded very costly construction work, including an enormous slurry pipeline, to bring it into production).

The governments involved have had to turn to multinational mining companies to supply finance and technical skill of this order. At Tembagapura (also called Freeport) the multinational is Freeport of America, on Bougainville Conzinc Riotinto of England, and at Ok Tedi an international consortium led by Broken Hill Proprietary of Australia. The nations involved are not consequently breaking their dependence on foreign industrial powers; rather, the nature of their dependency has shifted, becoming more indirect. They are partners in some senses. They perceive a need for multimillion-dollar mining ventures to finance their advancement independently of direct aid and need to attract considerable foreign investment to do so. They walk a political and economic tightrope in attracting it. They wish to ensure that their countries benefit maximally from the exploitation of their resources, but they have to offer prospects of good profits and stable political conditions to induce companies to sink the enormous sums needed into these high-risk ventures. The Ok Tedi mine agreement, for instance, allocated nearly one-third of the projected US$5.8 billion net profit to the mining companies involved.

Both parties are there to make a profit: the multinational companies for their overseas shareholders and the national governments to finance their countries' development. The local populations caught between these two monolithic interest groups feature only marginally, if at all, in the negotiations and decision-making about such projects, although they are increasingly subject to short-term research and consultation (following high-level decisions to proceed) in an attempt to minimise costly local conflict over land rights, royalty distributions, and so on. The enormous sums at stake, which can make or break the national budgets of the countries concerned, make the implementation of projects that exploit these resources the high-level affair of central governments.

The developments, being crucial for national economic growth, may proceed on terms unfavourable to and even against the wishes of the traditional owners of the land, following John Stuart Mill's democratic political philosophy that what is of the greatest good for the greatest number is the best policy. The intervention of central governments and their imposition of projects on local people predictably give rise to social and political tensions with which they have to contend. The massive localised technological developments involved in the establishment of mining ventures can both benefit and distress those living in the vicinity. The mine that has most starkly revealed these conflicting pressures is the enormous open-cast one at Panguna on the island of Bougainville, adjacent to a former goldfield.

The local population is fairly dense and has long had extensive contact with Europeans, making it familiar with how central governments and large companies operate and therefore not at a loss as to how to express its wishes and discontents. In this it contrasts with people elsewhere who have had to contend with mines, where thin populations, particularly of relatively recently contacted people (e.g., Ok Tedi) or colonially overwhelmed people (e.g., New Caledonia) or both (e.g., Tembagapura), have muted the expression of local feeling and inhibited international notice. Companies have recently begun making more effort early on to inform and consult local populations, especially where they are dense and potentially disruptive of mining activities (e.g., Porgera) or well informed about their rights and the consequences of mining (e.g., Lihir). The

Plate 8.1 The huge opencast mine of Panguna, looking from Moroni across the pit.

Plate 8.2 An electric shovel loads a truck with rock ore in the pit at Panguna mine.

Bougainvillians, for all their noisy protests, were not thought seriously to threaten the Panguna mine until fairly recently, when a bloody rebellion resulted in the virtual destruction of both the island's infrastructure and its administration and closed the mine.

Benefits and costs

Besides the enormous income flowing to national governments from these projects, they obviously bring rapid technological advances, usually to otherwise relatively undeveloped regions – advances not restricted to mine construction but extending to improvements in support facilities. These include the construction of roads, townships, and the like which will serve the local population too. But these construction programmes, engaged in to facilitate mining and only incidentally benefiting the local people, are confined to small areas. In these areas (for example, the town of Arawa, which catered for Panguna) services may improve immeasurably – with new hospitals and schools, electric power and well-stocked shops – but this may lead to a reduction of these services in adjacent rural areas, to the detriment of people living there.

The incomes of people living in the vicinity of the mine increase dramatically with its establishment. They receive considerable cash sums in compensation and royalties. These payments, although only a tiny percentage of the profits, are astronomically higher than anything the people could have earned without mine development (on Bougainville, for instance, they exceeded US$30 million, about 1 per cent of profits). These payments are made not only in cash, to indemnify people for the loss of garden land, tree crops, settlement sites, and so forth, but also in durable goods. The company may construct new houses of permanent materials with modern fittings to replace the traditional dwellings of bush materials destroyed by the mine development. This material recompense is just as well where people have little use for cash and 'some of the money received may simply be buried in the ground as were traditional shell valuables in the old days' (Momis and Ogan 1972:112). On Misima Island two brothers are allegedly searching for the royalties their father received from the new gold mine, money which he buried and then died without telling them where.

Besides receiving payments as traditional landowners, people also have the opportunity of earning a regular wage by working for the mine company, but the fluctuating demands for labour at different stages of the development can cause problems. The construction phase of a project requires a considerably larger workforce than that demanded later to operate the mine, and employment decreases with the completion of its infrastructure needs. The fall-off in work can affect people who have become accustomed to a certain monetary income but no longer have the chance to earn it. In Papua New Guinea companies have tried to ameliorate this inevitable decline in employment with a policy of replacing expatriate employees with indigenous ones when they have mastered the necessary skills.

The training and education opportunities that become available range from learning simple skills such as driving to training in the operation of modern technology. The learning of technical skills may prove one of the most enduring consequences of massive primary industry developments. Skilled manpower and management are any country's most valuable resources, determining the course and extent of its future development. In addition to training in mining-related skills the company on Bougainville offered advice and assistance to people regarding agricultural production and the running of small businesses so that they could avail themselves of opportunities to earn cash by selling crops and supplying services (such as transport and vehicle repairs) for which the mine stimulated local demand.

The stimulation of demand for local goods and services is another positive economic aspect of mine development, although it is greatly attenuated where companies resort to a fly-in, fly-out policy for their personnel (a policy intended to reduce friction with the local population). If managed properly the multiplier effect could promote long-term self-sustaining growth, but if people remain dependent on mine rather than local demand for their goods and services it will contribute to the trauma of the region's economic collapse when the mine closes down. Whatever the future may hold, in the short term the establishment of a mine considerably increases people's material standard of living, bringing them both considerable sums of money and the goods and services to spend it on.

The incentives seem significant and we might anticipate rapid economic growth, but events on Bougainville demonstrate how critical the local response is to subsequent developments. Furthermore, these general observations on the benefits of mine development apply fully only to the newly emerged democratic nations of Melanesia, where governments have made some effort to include local populations in their prosperity. They do not apply to Irian Jaya, where Indonesians and their American partners reportedly pay little attention to the wishes and advancement of the Melanesian population, or to New Caledonia, where the strictures against colonial exploitation apply (amidst growing unrest and ominous demands for autonomy in both regions). The local populations in these countries have to swallow the bitter costs of mine development with hardly any of the benefits.

The loss of their land figures as a considerable cost to local people, predictably given their great emotional attachment to it. This loss amounts not to the mere alienation of some of their territory but to its literal removal and destruction. The opencast mine on Bougainville, for instance, has resulted in one of the largest human-made holes in the world, a crater six miles in diameter, and the destruction is not confined to the mine site alone. The surrounding landscape has been transfigured and contaminated by the disposal of the vast rock waste – both rocks removed as overburden to expose the ore-bearing strata and a mudlike slurry called tailings, the waste from the crushing and processing of the ore-bearing rock. On Bougainville they dumped the rock overburden in an adjacent valley, raising the level of the floor and diverting the course of a river, and pumped the tailings into a river that is depositing this inert sediment in its lower reaches as it flows through a swamp, building up a delta. The total area affected maybe only 0.8 per cent of Bougainville Island, which is nonetheless a considerable geographical area on an island 120 miles long by 30 miles wide, and the mining company may have intended, as it asserted, to leave the region inhabitable, albeit physically transformed (it conducted experiments, for example, to turn the tailings into cultivable land, bringing unusable swamp into agricultural production), but this does not diminish the shock of these changes for the contemporary population. Monetary compensation does little to make up for the loss they feel, as several have demonstrated by refusing to accept payments: 'to an indigenous owner unaccustomed to evaluating land in monetary terms, such standards have little or no meaning . . . for people whose ties to residence are deeply sentimental and even religious, the costs of moving involve much more than money' (Oliver 1973:164).

On top of seeing their cherished land ravaged, local people experience difficulty in adjusting to the social and economic change that inevitably follows the establishment of a mine. The rapid transformation of the local economy demands considerable adjustment and many other social problems stem from the influx of workers, both Europeans and others from elsewhere in the country. Some of the unattached males may prey on local women out of frustration, to the consternation of some of their menfolk; others may turn to pimping to earn money. The availability of liquor increases dramatically and some local people may turn to it for escape from the heartbreaking events over which they have no control. This is a common response of those dispossessed and experiencing traumatic change the world over.

The scene is set, with social disruption of this order, for a breakdown in law and order. This has occurred on Bougainville both within traditional communities and between the local population and immigrant workers from elsewhere, and latterly between Bougainvillians and the Papua New Guinea government. The racial strife occurred not just between Europeans and Melanesians but between Papua New Guineans from different parts of the country, such as highlanders and Solomon Islanders. Confrontations between black and white, though less frequent, were potentially more dangerous to the company; these were implicated in the rebellion that closed the mine. The company may have done what it could to discourage these conflicts, instantly dismissing any European employee involved in a fracas and issuing warnings in handbooks distributed with contracts of employment such as: 'The people of Bougainville are proud . . . unless invited, you should keep away from village areas and certainly in no way interfere with their affairs.' Unfortunately, some locals actively encouraged and solicited visits to wheedle money, and in the unstable social environment these sometimes turned nasty.

The people of Bougainville regularly called for secession from Papua New Guinea, being dissatisfied with their returns from the copper mine given the disruption they had to endure and objecting to the use of the money earned to develop other regions of Papua New Guinea. They maintained that they should benefit from it as they would if they were independent. The combination of two decades of social disruption and massive environmental destruction came to a head in the late 1980s when Bougainvillean claims for massive compensation and part ownership of the mine were dismissed by the mining company and the Papua New Guinea government. Some islanders, led by a one-time mine surveyor called Francis Ona, obtained some explosives and sabotaged the power line to the mine, closing it. The Papua New Guinea government called out its riot police and army to restore order, and out of the bloody ensuing turmoil emerged the Bougainville Revolutionary Army (BRA) and its associated political wing the Bougainville Interim Government (BIG). The BRA drove the Papua New Guinea forces, covertly assisted by the Australian military, from much of the island. A blockade and conflict followed. The details are unclear with Bougainville effectively shut off from the rest of the world, but stories regularly emerge of barbarity on both sides – of captives hurled from helicopters or bound at the low tide mark to drown or savagely beaten with rifle butts.

The mine is closed and the island's material prosperity has come to an end, with little medicine and few manufactured goods arriving and no state-enforced law and order. Whatever details finally emerge about this unhappy episode, it is directly linked to development without adequate local participation, which the people violently rejected, and parallel disintegration of their local communities. Successive Papua New Guinea governments made several abortive attempts to end the rebellion; from peace delegations which had some limited success to military operations, one of which brought the nation to the verge of chaos in early 1997 for hiring a foreign mercenary contingent. But the intransigence of the BIG and the BRA, which insist on independence for Bougainville, combined with their suspicions, which the policy shifts of thwarted Papua New Guinea governments reinforced, worked to frustrate any settlement, and the situation became increasingly complex as various factions emerged on the island. Those opposed to the BRA, confusingly called 'the resistance', resorted to armed counteraction in their turn with the connivance of the Papua New Guinea Defence Force. However, a United Nations-monitored peace agreement signed in May 1998, known as the Burnham Peace Accords, led to an uneasy stand-off.

Who is responsible?

Some maintain that the costs of massive mining developments are too high and that they should not be allowed to proceed. Others argue that the minerals should be left in the ground until Melanesians are able to mine and benefit more from them without having to share the profits with multinationals overseas. As a chairman of the Bougainville mine has commented, however, 'without projects of this magnitude an emerging nation would be very slow to stand on its feet economically' (Espie 1974:336). If

Plate 8.3 A burnt-out helicopter on Bougainville after violence in
January 1990 which the *Post Courier* headlined as 'a night of terror'.

Plate 8.4 Men cultivate a garden in the forest on Bougainville while an armed colleague stands guard.

these resources were left until Melanesians were ready to exploit them, it would mean waiting decades or even centuries – by which time the world would be a different place, perhaps with no use for these raw materials. Furthermore, where would the money come from now to finance development, to educate people to a level where they could exploit these resources and others?

This points to the dilemma facing those responsible for making decisions about such investments. The answers to these issues are not black and white. In some areas national governments, not colonial powers, are proceeding with ventures at the expense of their citizens, and on Bougainville the government was even at war with them. Those who subscribe to dependency theory maintain that the decision-making of national governments is manipulated by outside powers via neocolonial arrangements. But if the emerging governments of the region desire economic independence while maintaining their nations' services and material standard of living built upon aid and inherited from colonial times, then they must earn money in the world marketplace to finance it. This is a hard fact of life.

The nations of the South-West Pacific can scarcely expect industrial nations to finance their advancement beyond a minimal level or imagine that this aid will not create a certain dependence on the donor nation. Nor can they opt to be left alone and avoid the traumas of change, for whether they like it or not they are inevitably members of the modern global community. The opt-out option, even if feasible, would mean defencelessness and probable colonial re-annexation by some nearby Asian nation which, if the recent experience of Indonesia in Irian Jaya is any guide, would be more repressive than the recently departed European colonial regimes. There is no alternative. These nations are obliged to participate in the world economy to finance their development. It would appear that economic development and social change are inevitable, and the question remains who has the right to make the decisions about them.

Advocates of participatory development argue that the local people to be affected by proposed large-scale developments should have a say in the decisions about them, but in all probability they will be uninformed about the alternatives facing them and their consequences. If tribal people unfamiliar with large-scale industrial developments were approached, for example, about establishing an open-cast mine in their region, they would probably express enthusiasm about the project because of the benefits they think it will bring them. If previous experience is anything to go by, however, they would eventually come to resent the intrusion, aware too late of its enormous costs. People need educating first to make intelligent and considered decisions not merely on the alternatives and consequences facing them over a single project but about the outside world to which such developments relate. This level of awareness cannot be generated in a brief space of time; it will demand education over several generations. The real world will not wait; it demands decisions and action now. And in any case the education itself requires money which has first to be earned to finance it.

Some argue that we need not worry about the fate of small local populations when the massive industrial developments involved are for the benefit of entire nations and their economic growth. They consider the adjustment agonies of today's traditionally oriented adults the unavoidable if not easily accepted price to pay for developments that will improve their descendants' material standard of living. Besides being callous, this attitude can impede the development of large capital projects. It costs less in hard economic terms to keep the local population on one's side so far as possible. Decision-making that disregards it is likely to lead to apathy and alienation or to violence.

Today's adults are responsible for socialising the next generation and will pass on many of their traditional values and aspirations and their dislike of and even inability to cope with rapid change. It is impossible to transform attitudes in a generation. Where this has been tried, the results have been devastating. When people are effectively robbed of their cultural identity and pride and their ability to determine the course of their own lives within customary expectations, they become disillusioned and apathetic. Alternatively, a sense of invasion may lead to violence, and the sentiments of tribalism that may arise in this context are a potent source of tension that could seriously disrupt economic advance. The bloody rebellion on Bougainville demonstrates that the threat of disorder is no imaginary one.

The dilemmas of development are legion. Given the structure of international economics and politics, somebody has to make decisions. Although we may cavil at this, arguing that no outside body should have the right to decide the fates of other human beings, this is as inevitable as it is in our own centrally governed lives. It is a conundrum over which philosophers have argued for centuries and one which traditional stateless Melanesian polities had effectively resolved. This accounts in part for the trauma they experience when others' decisions are imposed on them. And the moral issues, even if unresolvable, are at least addressed in liberal independent political contexts concerned to minimise trauma and share out some of the profits. What anthropologists are obliged to do is not question the validity of such decision-making, which is pointless because it is unavoidable, but defend the interests of those who cannot understand the consequences of planned developments and advise the decision-makers in such a way that they make the wisest and least damaging choices for all involved. We cannot stop 'progress' any more than we can stop history; we can only help ameliorate its worst effects.

FURTHER READING

On Bougainville mine and mining in general in Melanesia see:

Bougainville Copper Ltd n.d. *About Bougainville: an introduction* Arawa

J. Connell and R. Howitt (eds.) 1991 *Mining and indigenous peoples in Australia* Sydney: Sydney University Press

P. Donigi 1994 *Indigenous or aboriginal rights to property: a Papua New Guinea perspective* Utrecht: International Books

F. F. Espie 1974 Bougainville copper: difficult development decisions. In R. J. May (ed.) *Priorities in Melanesian development* 6th Waigani seminar, Canberra: Australian National University Press, pp. 335–42

R. Jackson 1982 *Ok Tedi: the pot of gold* Waigani: University of Papua New Guinea Word Publishing

Y. A. Lira 1993 *Bougainville campaign diary* Eltham North (Victoria): Indira Publishing

R. J. May and M. Spriggs (eds.) 1990 *The Bougainville crisis* Bathurst: Crawford House Press

J. Momis and E. Ogan 1972 A view from Bougainville. In M. W. Ward (ed.) *Change and development in rural Melanesia* 5th Waigani seminar, Canberra: Allans Printers, pp. 106–18

H. Nelson 1976 *Black, white and gold: goldmining in Papua New Guinea 1878–1930* Canberra: Australian National University Press

D. Oliver 1973 *Bougainville: a personal history* Melbourne: Melbourne University Press

D. Oliver 1991 *Black islanders: a personal perspective of Bougainville 1937–1991* Melbourne: Hyland House

W. Pintz 1984 *Ok Tedi: evolution of a Third World mining project* London: Mining Journal Books

P. Quodling 1991 *Bougainville: the mine and the people* St Leonards and Auckland: Centre for Independent Studies

P. Ryan 1991 *Black bonanza: a landslide of gold* Melbourne: Hyland House

M. Spriggs and D. Denoon (eds.) 1992 *The Bougainville crisis, 1991 up-date* Bathurst: Crawford House Press

J. Sinclair (ed.) 1979 *Up from south: Jack O'Neill a prospector in New Guinea 1931–37* Melbourne: Oxford University Press

F. Wilson 1981 *The conquest of copper mountain* Melbourne: Athenaeum

Also see:
H. Nelson 1982 *Taim bilong masta* Sydney: Australian Broadcasting Commission

FILMS

Hell in the Pacific British Broadcasting Commission

9　Forestry and local knowledge

The idea of applying anthropology in a practical sense, like applying engineering in constructing roads or agriculture in breeding crops, may be inappropriate in development contexts, but this is not to say that anthropology has nothing to contribute to the development process. The discipline should be at the heart of attempts to assist other nations. Anyone who pursues work in development overseas should have some background in anthropology as well as in an applied technical discipline. The more we know about the history, social order and cultural heritage, the better will be our understanding of rapidly changing contemporary society. And the more informed our understanding of all the circumstances, the more likely any development initiatives are to comply with cultural expectations and to meet with success.

Regarding forestry in Melanesia, for example, an appreciation of the way people see forests can further interventions to exploit their timber appropriately. The islands of the South-West Pacific support large areas of primary rainforest containing commercially valuable tropical hardwoods such as mahogany, but the people who live there see the forest not merely as a collection of trees and other vegetation but as a lived landscape, a part of their cultural inheritance. The forest embodies social relations, past and present, having witnessed events that have contributed to today's community: by that tree there, So-and-So was ambushed and killed; under that foliage-covered overhang are the mortal remains of my kin; in that sago stand our sister was born; these fruiting trees attracting the birds that I am snaring are the regrowth of my last swidden; and so on. They may include the locales from which people believe they originated, tracing their origins in myths which may cite stretches of forest as the places where the ancestors came up in some epic event perhaps involving totemic species. And these significances are not mere sentimental expressions but real statements about belonging, infusing the forest with spiritual presence, of ancestral ghosts and intangible forces perhaps manifest as arboreal demons. Clearly these ideas and beliefs engender attitudes to forests which must be appreciated in promoting logging or conservation.

Anthropology and development

Forestry falls into the sphere of natural resources exploitation and management, where anthropology is currently making a long overdue contribution to development practice by furthering understanding of indigenous knowledge (sometimes called local knowledge), and advocating a place for it in development programmes. A focus on indigenous knowledge in development contexts puts the local perspective on the agenda, attempting to give some voice to the knowledge and ideas of those subject to development initiatives. It acknowledges that they already have views and aspirations and that these need to be accommodated in the development process not only for interventions to be appropriate but also on grounds of equity. The contribution of research on indigenous knowledge is a part of the broader participation movement in development, a mid-range response to the grand theories of modernisation and dependency which, lacking grass-roots practical perspectives, are seen as having failed the poor.

A participation or joint-enterprise approach to development is currently gaining ground. It comes out of the new discourse of the emerging global state, which argues that all parties (local people, donor agencies, national bureaucrats and others) that have a stake in any initiative should have a voice in its formulation and execution. It poses some of the most challenging and stimulating problems in the field today. One major problem is how to facilitate meaningful participation. Some commentators suggest that all we need to do is to allow local populations access to the technological alternatives we can offer and they will sort things out for themselves. If it were only this straightforward a great deal of overseas development work would be superfluous. The problems are, first, knowing what technological alternatives might be culturally and environmentally appropriate, which demands research; and, secondly, informing the local population about these and their possible social, ecological and other consequences, which demands effective public education. Anthropology can and should play a key role in both stages.

An anthropological perspective helps to create a meaningful awareness of cultural relativity and its implications by encouraging a real regard for what others have achieved in land management, health care, or whatever the field of interest. Without genuine respect for the accomplishments of other cultures, talk of local participation is no more than hot air. Respect is the first step. While it is common today to meet people who pay lip service to respecting others' ways, this unfortunately often appears to be more because they think it politically correct than out of conviction. Underneath the tolerant veneer is the assumption that we are superior because of our awesome technology. After all, the idea is that 'we' have to assist 'them' to develop. It is not easy from our nuclear-missile moon-walking computer-chip perspective to admit that others have equally effective and perhaps even better ways of managing their natural and social environments. No matter how outwardly liberal, we all seem to have a chauvinistic and even a dark xenophobic side. Anthropology helps us to confront and come to terms with it. It is one of the discipline's major achievements.

That technical competence is needed in development contexts goes without saying, but it should be harnessed to the cultural awareness which an anthropological background promotes. If it is not, it can all too easily become technical arrogance, which is likely to do great damage. While it is beyond doubt that our culture has evolved a staggering techni-cal capacity, others have made equally impressive technological adapta-tions to their environments, often sufficient to meet their needs. We should agree that development, for those of us who wish to assist the poor (as opposed to playing macropolitical games in which they may feature as pawns) is not imposing our 'superior' technical solutions to their prob-lems as we perceive them, but engaging in a joint enterprise in which we all seek to further their food security, health and well-being. The partici-pation movement seeks to empower the disadvantaged.

Once our minds are opened to this idea, the next step ought to be to achieve some understanding of how others manage their natural or other resources before we interfere. This is indigenous knowledge research, and it is no easy or short-term task. The time required for anthropological research is considerable, and this often presents a problem in develop-ment contexts with their short-term project orientation and politically driven demand for immediate returns. It can take several years, not months or weeks, for someone unacquainted with a region to achieve meaningful anthropological insight into local knowledge and practices and from this perspective to throw some light on technical and other development-related problems. While in some development contexts there may be a place for 'rapid rural appraisal', a currently popular approach to collecting information relevant to some problems usually involving a few days' survey work, and anthropologists already familiar with a region may be able to undertake such work with a fairly reliable return on their efforts, this is not and cannot substitute for anthropologi-cal research.

Perhaps more important than what anthropological methods are or are not used, is that in pursuing this work we see things somewhat anew. We are all imbued with the expectations and values of our own culture, and it is extremely difficult to cultivate a sympathetic awareness of others' ways.

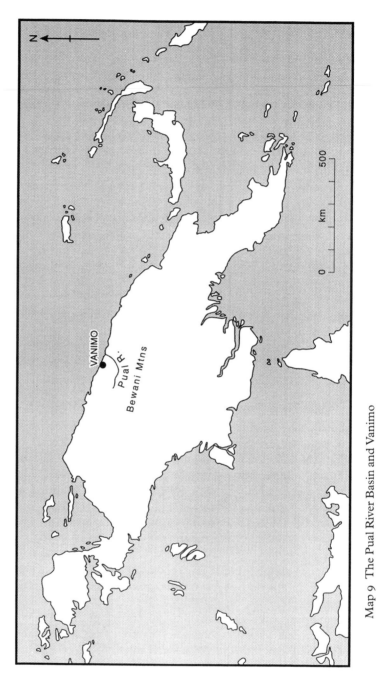

Map 9   The Pual River Basin and Vanimo

By exposing us to a range of ethnographic evidence, anthropology can help promote an open and more flexible attitude of mind more alive to alternatives and more likely to appreciate the health, economic, agricultural and other arrangements of other cultures. If we already have an awareness of the fascinating array of solutions that humans have come up with to secure their lives in a range of environments around the world, we are more likely to see, hear and appreciate what others are doing, perhaps against our expectations, somewhere else.

Anthropology can also assist in the critical appraisal of development goals. Its culturally relative stance helps it pose thought-provoking and sometimes awkward questions. Many people around the world live environmentally and socially sound and sustainable lives and have done so for millennia. We may well have something to learn from them. The rate at which we are polluting our environment, using up non-renewable resources and leading ever more alienated social lives would seem to indicate that our way of doing things may prove harmful in the long run. We in the West should perhaps be learning from tribal people such as those who inhabit the islands of Melanesia about how we might develop a better way of doing things – about egalitarian government, fair economic reforms, and so on. Anthropology should play a central role in development, promoting a genuinely beneficial two-way flow of ideas and practices.

Logging and the local community

The Vanimo region of the West Sepik has a long history of commercial logging, starting in the early 1960s with the Goldore Timber Company and continuing today with Vanimo Forest Products, a subsidiary of a large Malaysian logging enterprise. The Timber Rights Purchase area in Vanimo, declared in 1967 and valid for forty years, covers 340,190 hectares of lowland rainforest and has recently seen extensive logging in the Pual River Basin north of the Bewani Mountains. The logging operations have been fraught with environmental and other problems and have provoked protests from local people, including a blockade of roads that has forced the Department of Forests to impose cease-work orders for varying periods.

The Pual River Basin has a highly mobile population. The people occupy villages, some of them sizeable, clustered along logging roads, particularly where there are schools and aid posts. They also occupy isolated camps in the forest where they have traditionally gone for varying periods (usually longer in the past than today) to process sago, collect tree fruits, and hunt. They are unusual for New Guineans in not herding pigs but relying on the hunting of wild ones, which are plentiful in the forest, to supply them with pork. They also clear small gardens in which they cultivate a range of crops (including yams, taro, sugarcane, cucurbits and pawpaw). The Pual River Basin people not only live very intimately with their forest in a physical sense, securing a goodly part of their subsistence requirements and living in it in kin-based groups, but also emotionally and spiritually. Several myths give particular forest locations, often on mountains, as the places where named clans had their origins, and there are locales in the forest considered efficacious in curing illness, usually featuring water sources with believed medicinal properties. The forest is home to many supernatural forces and spirits, and when hunting men perform rituals to ensure their help in attracting game.

Unlike loggers who are interested in only a few commercial species – among them *ypno* (kwila (*Intsija bijuga*)), *yepus* (walnut (*Draconotomelon* sp.)), *torou* (rosewood (*Pterocarpus indicus*)), *tiniya* (taun (*Pometia pinnata*)) and *naragag* (ebony (*Diospyros* sp.)) – the Pual River Basin people have a sophisticated understanding of the plants and animals of their rainforest. They cultivate a variety of trees, including stands of *su* (sago (*Metroxylon rumphii*)) in low-lying swampy areas, *sou* (coconut palms (*Cocos nucifera*)) on dry ridges, *wi* (bananas (*Musa* sp.)) across old reforesting garden clearings, sometimes together with *sau* (pandans (*Pandanus conoideus*)) and *fu* (betel nut palms (*Areca catechu*)), and several tree species scattered across slopes, including *dei* (breadfruit (*Artocarpus* sp.)), *sauwe* (mango (*Mangifera* sp.)), *irriyau* (galip nut (*Canarium* sp.)), *dandan* (an unidentified fruit tree) and *wesia* (tulip (*Gnetum gnemon*)). Consulting this ethnobotanical and ethnozoological store of knowledge would be helpful in assessing the damage inflicted on the forest by logging. The logging company has reneged on a commitment to establish reafforestation trials and an FAO research project to study sustainable logging methods was ruined because the designated experimental area was logged recklessly using very heavy equipment. Investigating local understandings and expectations would also assist in making timber harvesting more culturally acceptable and less destructive (see chapter 13). A central issue here is ownership, and ideas of ownership revolve around access to land.

As we have seen, in Melanesia it is rights to specific tracts of land that give substance to residential groups. Pual kin-groups lay claim to certain territories on which their members reside and across which they hunt and collect wild plants and cultivate small plots. Uncultivated areas are held in common by the group as a whole, whereas once any area has been cultivated prior rights to it and anything growing on it subsequently reside with the gardener and his nearest relatives. Likewise, cultivated trees belong to those who plant and tend them. Individuals cannot permanently alienate land; if they do not use it, it automatically returns to the kin-group pool. The idea of a landowner is alien.

These landholding groups, based on kinship rather than a corporate ideology present conceptual problems for promoters of development from the centre. They fail to comprehend the essential individual component in the constitution of these groups and are disappointed when they do not perform as corporate bodies. This becomes evident when trying to negotiate logging contracts because no one can represent a non-existent resource-owning group; it requires a network of related individuals to reach some consensus, which can be a protracted and difficult affair. The intruding capitalist economic system assumes cooperation among large numbers of people (employed in specialised tasks to produce goods and supply services which they transact, using the medium of money, in the marketplace for goods and services produced by others). This economic system is alien to rural Melanesians. We can anticipate conflict when they confront the capitalist system over the purchase of rights to fell commercially valuable trees.

When economists, agronomists, planners and others talk about developing a region such as Vanimo, what they are contemplating is drastically modifying the traditional social order – transforming it to conform with the centralised capitalist-like system. The traditional order must of necessity give way because its premises are antithetical to the aims of the intruding culture regarding economic progress. This raises enormous ethical issues: it assumes that one economic and social system is superior and should be promoted to replace the other. 'Development' implies progress and change for the better. While change is inevitable, especially when one of the cultures in contact is technologically considerably more powerful than the other, whether it will be advancement is questionable.

The emphasis which acephalous social orders place on the autonomy of the individual has tremendous implications for involvement in a monetary economy. Their subsistence economy depends almost exclusively on cooperation among the members of a single household: a man, his wife or wives, and any unmarried adolescent children and perhaps a widowed parent or other relative. The cooperation that takes place among household members depends largely on the sexual division of labour; only men can perform certain tasks such as hunting and women others such as processing sago. Consequently, men and women of necessity cooperate in households. While the members of a household share their produce equally when consuming it themselves and even freely share it with others outside the household, when they sell it, they do not necessarily share the proceeds. A woman may sell the food which she processes and keep the money, and a man may do likewise; individuals need not share the

Plate 9.1 A hunter from Krisa near Vanimo departs for the forest
armed with machete and shotgun.

Plate 9.2 A woman pounds sago pith to extract starch in the forest of the Pual River basin adjacent to the village of Isi while loggers work one hundred metres away.

proceeds with those with whom they cooperate. This is not to imply that the members of different households do not cooperate occasionally in various productive tasks. But when persons from different households do cooperate, they behave in a manner which indicates that they perceive their actions as a series of coordinated individual acts. For instance, two or three male relatives may sometimes work together to establish a new garden, but when they have finished they will divide the area up among themselves into clearly marked plots from which their households alone will benefit. The area is not held in common, and neither are rights to it.

Development projects that focus on the individual or the household as the domestic unit of production are more likely to meet with success than those that treat people as the members of vaguely defined larger groups cooperating in a productive venture (as intimated previously in the discussion of business ventures in the Central Highlands: see page 98 above). This will demand some rethinking of the capitalist approach, where the trend has been towards larger and larger groups cooperating in large-scale productive enterprises with an elaborate division and specialisation of labour to increase efficiency. This specialised productive system evolved slowly in Europe, and it is only reasonable to expect people like Papua New Guineans to adapt to it gradually and to formulate development projects accordingly.

The decentralised organisation not only leads to protracted negotiations over access to natural resources such as hardwood timber or mineraliferous rock but also to ongoing disputes. These occur both between 'landowners', who have a processual attitude to negotiations and not a once-and-for-all contractual one, and outside agencies, and among the resource owners themselves as they try to sort out the sharing of royalties obtained for leasing areas of land which they have previously never had to evaluate and divide. These confrontations over rights to natural resources can stop commercial operations, with local people demanding ever higher payments for the damage done to their land until they price themselves out of the market. Perhaps the most effective protection for the forest is in fact the customary land-tenure system rather than any innate conservation ethic whereby people live close to and in harmony with nature. When approached, resource owners seem more interested in extracting rent than in protecting the environment, at least initially. In their minds the money equates with longed-for development. As Colin Filer (in Sekhran and Miller 1996:198) puts it:

When a nation of gardeners becomes a nation of customary landlords, it is perhaps understandable that many people begin to believe that the royal road to 'development' is found in the collection of natural resource rents from foreign operators . . . [but these] local gatekeepers sometimes contribute to the conservation of their resources by raising the entry fees to the point which deters all potential customers, either because their expectations of 'development' begin to exceed what can feasibly be realised from some particular economic activity, or because they are pricing themselves out of the market in order to achieve non-market objectives. Chief amongst these objectives is the maintenance or restoration of social and economic equality between individuals or communities. The local version of the 'tall poppy syndrome' explains much of the resentment and many of the accusations which are directed at those who demonstrate unusual success in the acquisition of wealth.

It is only later, when they witness the extent of the environmental destruction that they may come to rue their decision. Where logging has occurred in the Pual River Basin people now express regret over the damage done to the forest – saying that they had not realised that it would scare animals away, change the range of fruiting trees available for marsupials and birds to feed in, and so on. The Barnett Commission of Inquiry into the timber industry catalogued extensive environmental destruction in the Vanimo region, including logging on steep slopes and adjacent to streams, sometimes obstructing these and resulting in turbid conditions and pollution with toxic saponins leached from bark, snigging (hauling logs along the ground) in wet conditions and across slopes, causing excessive soil damage and erosion, and the use of excessively heavy equipment that destroys vegetation and produces massive soil compaction.

If disputes among those claiming rights to resources, over who owns which tracts and should receive what moneys, interfere with operations, conservationists worried about environmental destruction and loss of biodiversity may welcome them. The *Financial Times* (25 August 1995), reporting on the compensation being offered for the environmental damage done to the Fly River region by the Ok Tedi mine, reported that 'according to mining companies operating there, negotiations with landowners for access for development of land are often so detailed that there is payment for individual trees'. Traditional land tenure arrangements may be more effective in protecting the natural environment than any legislation or other intervention and will be supported by those who advocate protecting biodiversity against the modernisation onslaught. People are torn between a wish to cash in on the rent that they can obtain for permitting exploitation of natural resources on their land, which for them is synonymous with development, and worries over the ensuing destruction of their environment.

A review of the responses to a survey sponsored by the International Institute for Environment and Development and conducted by the National Research Institute at Waigani suggests that attitudes towards and understanding of issues pertaining to the sustainable exploitation and conservation of forest resources vary along two principal axes. One is the extent to which communities have direct or indirect experience of logging activities on their land; and the other is the extent to which they have been exposed to debates about commercial forestry development, primarily through some of their members having acquired formal higher education or employment experience that has raised their awareness of these issues. There are communities with little or no exposure to commercial forestry, which largely subscribe to traditional views of forest resource use and conservation. These traditional views remain pertinent even where people have had exposure to market-driven exploitation of forest resources, for they make up the cultural background that continues to inform their responses.

The survey responses uniformly report the absence of any traditional notion of forest conservation. The idea of sustainable development and implied concepts such as not compromising the opportunities of future generations elicit scant recognition. This does not mean, however, that

Plate 9.3 A logging access road tears a gash in the forest. Logs in the foreground await transportation to a holding point.

Plate 9.4 Loading logs onto a transporter at a logging camp on the Vanimo–Aitape road to carry them to the shipping yard in Vanimo.

people are reckless in their exploitation of forest resources (clearing forest for food gardens, hunting and gathering wild animals and plants, collecting raw materials for making artifacts and constructing houses). A regard for the sustainable use of resources can be seen in various customary expressions, referring to saving, taking care of, and setting aside. A respect for sustainability can also be seen in resource-use practices. Shifting cultivation is the norm throughout Papua New Guinea for subsistence crop production, and there are many references to people's practising this agricultural regime in a manner that ensures the rapid re-establishment of forest cover upon abandonment. Also notable are references to beliefs in supernatural denizens of forests and sacred sites, which may prompt people to act with some circumspection but may equally prompt a desire to keep the forest and its spirits at bay, encouraging its destruction as population expands.

Several respondents referred to local peoples' willingness to see logging developments in their regions. People are eager to encourage timber companies to log in their regions, expecting high monetary returns, but once such developments come we move to the opposite end of the continuum regarding perceptions of sustainability and conservation. People predictably are acutely aware of the benefits and costs of logging and the possible meaning of 'sustainable development'. They rue the destruction of forest and worry that when logging companies have cut all the trees they will no longer have access to large sums of royalty money; therefore they express interest in reforestation and sustainable development not for aesthetic but for commercial reasons. The survey evidence suggests that education about conservation and sustainable development has a limited impact, being restricted largely to those who have received formal education and have a predisposition to internalise it (perhaps manifest in their selection of courses with a conservation component). Otherwise the indications are that people learn only from direct experience of logging. They are suspicious of awareness campaigns, which they interpret as attempts to trick them out of earning royalties.

Compensation and individual action

It is common to hear people refer to all moneys received for rights to resources, whether royalties, profit shares or payments for damages, as compensation. While the former two are negotiated at the time of leasing and probably renegotiated subsequently to quell landowner frustration, the latter is subject to ongoing negotiation. People go around behind the loggers to inspect the destruction and submit claims for any damaged food-producing plants, such as breadfruit trees or sago palms, to which households stake individual claims. A kind of payment has burgeoned in the past two decades that has its roots in customary exchanges made largely to indemnify persons and their kin for bodily injury or death. The exchange ethic conditions a considerable amount of behaviour, including responses to money-earning opportunities such as development projects. It accounts for the clash between landowners and companies over what compensation implies. The local people's generalised reciprocity mindset, which accommodates the flexibility of shifting personal relationships and social events and is essentially ongoing without end, is inconsistent with the logging companies' notion of fixed legal contracts binding both parties to an agreed course of action.

Exchange is not confined to institutionalised events such as marriage and death but ramifies throughout Melanesian social life. For instance, although food production is largely a household affair, the consumption of its produce is not confined to the household. While Pual River households secure most of their food from their own efforts, they share a considerable amount of it with others. The effect is to spread out the food produced, levelling disparities between households. This is particularly apparent when people consume game. The meat from slaughtered animals is distributed to and consumed by a large number of people. The redistribution effected largely evens out differences between households, the more successful ones with able adult male hunters consume about the same amounts. It is through success in hunting and generosity with meat that men bolster their reputations.

The levelling effected by this sharing is expectable in an egalitarian society, where the individual basis of production could give rise to marked inequalities between households. The exchange ethic so deeply ingrained into the Melanesian character ensures that no family markedly outstrips any other. Those who produce more willingly part with it to achieve renown and a marginal degree of influence, with no idea of hoarding it in the capitalist spirit and using it to improve their own standard of living. It is those who give away the most who are reckoned to be successful. Subsistence production is largely an individual affair, rarely involving more than a single household, and the social obligation to share is engrained to such an extent that any differences in individual enterprise are largely erased.

Two issues emerge as critical with regard to development planning for the exploitation of natural resources: the predominantly domestic nature of productive enterprises and the enormous social pressures on individuals to share what comes into their possession. Planners should try to exploit the potential of the traditional individualistic approach to production rather than entertain unreasonable expectations requiring extensive cooperation. Instead of thinking of a group cooperating for the benefit of the individual, sharing the profits earned through their joint labour, they should think of individuals working more or less alone and subsequently sharing the products of their labour within the group or network of relatives. This reverses the accepted economic order: while individuals and their domestic units will work separately, they will distribute their profits widely. The social forces compelling individuals to distribute both what they produce and what they receive in various transactions raise issues unique to Papua New Guinea which developers need to tackle imaginatively if they are to stimulate self-sustaining economic growth.

The sums demanded in compensation, previously in traditional wealth such as seashell valuables and now in cash, have reached previously unimaginable levels and now regularly cover not only bodily injury (often in new contexts such as vehicle accidents) but also material damages (as in logging operations). Indeed, these latter demands for compensation have come to represent in some people's minds the road to development, with rural populations waiting hopefully for the gold/copper find, oil strike or timber contract that will fund their desired increase in material living standards. While the revenue from logging or some other enterprise is fondly thought to advance development, from the perspective of the development planner it is largely squandered. The recipients put some cash into sociopolitical exchange, and they spend some on desired durable consumables such as clothing, domestic utensils and occasionally vehicles (which if not wrecked are literally driven until beyond repair and left to rust). Furthermore, the sharing of the spoils can give rise to social tensions; women frequently feel that the sudden flood of money is being ill-used.

Development planners need to give some thought to ways of encouraging projects that cause those who earn money from them to use it for capital investment rather than dispersing it among their relatives and, to this end, ways of discouraging the use of money in sociopolitical exchange. It would be unwise if not unethical to tamper with people's sharing practices and exchange customs; planners should take cognisance of them with a view to avoiding unnecessary conflict. The use of cash in sociopolitical exchange is transmogrifying that exchange; in bridewealth, for example, it is promoting the idea that men literally buy women, a perversion of the sociality of customary marriage practices. Money is also contributing to the excesses of the compensation boom, in which some behaviour now verges on extortion. As Colin Filer expresses it (in Toft 1997:172–3, 180–1):

There is less reason for developers to hope that landowners demanding compensation are on their way to becoming petty landlords collecting a reasonable rent, and more reason for them to suspect that 'compensation' is another name for extortion, and thus a form of theft rather than a form of rent, whose collection is hardly to be distinguished from the 'gate-keeping' practices of the hold-up merchants along the Okuk Highway. In that case, we may not be contemplating the forward march of a market economy, but regression towards the state of affairs which existed at the time of 'first contact,' when mutual hostility or 'negative reciprocity' was the characteristic form of economic relationship outside of the community within which reproduction payments were organised. This we may call the developer's nightmare.

And he goes on to relate this behaviour to customary values of equality:

Landowners are not interested in a 'fair price' for their resources, or a reasonable 'trade-off' between financial and political rewards, but seek instead to do away with every form of wealth and power which makes them seem to be dependent or inferior in their relationship with 'their' developers . . . landowners may be less interested in achieving the correct 'balance of power' between themselves and their developers than in demonstrating that the latter are as powerless as decent people ought to be . . . an 'excessive compensation demand' may no longer represent a bid to achieve or restore some notional condition of 'balanced reciprocity' between landowners and developers, but may only count as an act of outright hostility, like a spear hurled at an enemy.

These are manifestations of traumatic change, customary exchange ideology gone awry. Perhaps governments could think of ways to discourage the use of money in sociopolitical exchange through some sort of public awareness campaign, as is already happening in some regions (see chapters 6 and 14), to release money for productive investment.

There is a need to conceive of projects that allow for individualistic production, exploiting the household as the productive unit, and prevent the profits from seeping away in exchange. The growing reliance of Papua New Guinea's national economy on natural resources rent income portends problems to come which will compound those of the country's long-time dependency on foreign aid. It is not only environmentally but also economically unsustainable in terms of current living standards, let alone improved ones.

Several schemes could be devised which might accommodate to this individualistic exchange-founded society. One possibility would be for agencies to sponsor cooperative ventures in which productive effort is organised around individuals and the cooperative controls marketing and cash flow, keeping back a certain percentage of the profit earned for corporate investment and distributing the remainder to the producers according to the amounts they contribute. Trends evident in the highlands region suggest that the recipients would share their dividends with others, spend them on a few material possessions and manufactured foods (shared with others too), and use the remainder in sociopolitical exchange. Projects demanding considerable cooperation have foundered time and again; for instance, efforts to develop cattle-herding ventures, which demand cooperation to muster the initial capital required and to maintain the long runs of fencing necessary, have proved short-lived; those involved have soon killed and eaten the animals, often distributing the meat in sociopolitical exchange (the small amount of land available suitable for grazing cattle is another factor limiting the development of cattle projects). Projects that have depended upon individuals' working alone to their own ends and directly earning the profit that accrues to their efforts have proved more successful and enduring; this explains the success of coffee throughout the highlands (see chapter 6).

Planners need to recognise that their projects may contribute to the slow erosion of Melanesians' egalitarian social order as individuals see the possibilities in the new situation and start to corner resources for themselves rather than share with others. The result will be the development of an all-too-familiar peasant society manipulated by a small elite class (see chapter 7). The least objectionable course to follow is to allow the people involved the maximum scope for participation in planning and implementing development to control the direction of change. Indeed, in reality, this is inevitably what will happen: they will select the alternatives that appeal to them and reject the others. Consequently, those responsible for planning should present people with alternatives and opportunities that comply with their cultural expectations and may appeal to them and not waste valuable resources on schemes that assault their values and are unlikely to meet with their approval. Local people want the fruits of development rooted in custom; the problem is uniting the roots with the fruits.

This implies some knowledge of the society one intends to change. While prediction is notoriously difficult concerning social factors, at least it should be possible to avoid the squandering of resources on projects that are unlikely to succeed. By pointing out some of the disjunctions between the local social order and the assumptions of the intruding one, particularly in matters relating to the operationalisation of indigenous knowledge, the observations made here suggest ways in which those responsible for implementing development projects could formulate plans that are more likely to meet with success and make sounder judgments as to what may be possible and practical.

The key is clearly education not only of planners and developers but also, through effective extension services, of those who are to be subjected to the change. People can assume joint responsibility for planning and implementing changes only when they have some understanding of what is at stake from the other's perspective. While Melanesians will adapt their social and economic system to suit themselves in the face of technological change, they require education to understand the implications of their absorption into the Western capitalist economic system. This places a considerable responsibility on the shoulders of those implementing development plans to inform both themselves and the people subject to the change about what it might entail.

FURTHER READING

On development issues see:
H. Brookfield (ed.) 1973 *The Pacific in transition* London: Edward Arnold
R. Crittenden and D. A. M. Lea 1989 *Integrated rural development programmes in Papua New Guinea* Waigani: Institute for Applied Social and Economic Research Monograph No. 28
E. K. Fisk (ed.) 1966 *New Guinea on the threshold* Canberra: Australian National University Press
J. Pottier (ed.) 1992 *Practising development* London: Routledge

On the Vanimo region see:

T. M. Boyce 1992 *Infrastructure and security: problems of development in the West Sepik Province of Papua New Guinea* Canberra: Australian National University Strategic Defence Studies Centre

B. Juillerat, 1996 *Children of the blood: society, reproduction and cosmology in New Guinea* Oxford: Berg

R. Kameata and F. Topni 1999 'we have no problems but just people. People just want money': The local politics of landowning entities of the Vanimo Timber Rights Purchase (TRP) area in Sandown Province of Papua New Guinea. In D. Bley, H. Pagezy and N. Vernazza-Licht (eds.) *L'homme et la forêt tropicale* Travaux de la Societe d'Ecologie Humaine, Grasse: Editions du Bergier

R. Kara 1996 *Krisa local group study, Kilimeri census division, Sandaun Province* Waigani: National Research Institute Report

J. Simet and J. Ketan 1992 *Trans-Pual study: Vanimo local group structures and territorial claims* Waigani: National Research Institute Report

On compensation see:

R. Scaglion (ed.) 1981 *Homicide compensation in Papua New Guinea* Boroko: Law Reform Commission Monograph No. 1

S. Toft (ed.) 1997 *Compensation and resource development* Boroko: Law Reform Commission Monograph No. 6 and Canberra: Australian National University National Centre for Development Studies Pacific Policy Paper No. 24

On natural resources and conservation see:

R. C. Duncan 1994 *Melanesian forestry sector study* Canberra: Australian International Development Assistance Bureau

C. Filer (ed.) 1997 *The political economy of forest management in Papua New Guinea* Waigani: National Research Institute Monograph

C. Filer with N. Sekhran 1998 *Loggers, donors and resource owners. Policy that works for forests and people series No. 2: Papua New Guinea* Port Moresby and London: National Research Institute and International Institute for Environment and Development

S. Henningham and R. J. May (eds.) 1992 *Resources, development and politics in the Pacific islands* Bathurst: Crawford House

R. Howitt with J. Connell and P. Hirsch (eds.) 1996 *Resources, nations and indigenous peoples: case studies from Australasia, Melanesia, and Southeast Asia* Melbourne: Oxford University Press

N. Sekhran and S. Miller (eds.) 1996 *Papua New Guinea country study on biological diversity* Waigani: Conservation Resource Centre, Department of Environment and Conservation

On participatory development and indigenous knowledge see:

S. Burkey 1994 *People first: a guide to self-reliant participatory rural development* London: Zed Books

R. Chambers 1996 *Whose reality counts? Putting the first last* London: Intermediate Technology Publications

J. Farrington and A. Martin 1988 *Farmer participation in agricultural research: a review of concepts and practices* Overseas Development Agency Agricultural Administration Unit Occasional Paper No. 9

N. Nelson and S. Wright (eds.) 1995 *Power and participatory development: theory and practice* London: Intermediate Technology Publications

D. Posey and G. Dutfield 1996 *Beyond intellectual property: toward traditional resource rights for indigenous peoples and local communities* Ottawa: IDRC Books

P. Richards 1985 *Indigenous agricultural revolution* London: Hutchinson

I. Scoones, J. Thompson and R. Chambers (eds.) 1994 *Beyond farmer first* London: Intermediate Technology Publications

A. J. Strathern 1993 Compensation: What does it mean? *Taimlain* 1:57–62

D. M. Warren, L. J. Slikkerveer and D. Brokensha 1995 *The cultural dimensions of development: indigenous knowledge systems* London: Intermediate Technology Publications

FILMS

Un jardin à Iafar 1977 CNRS Audio-visuel
Le sang du sagou 1983 CNRS Audio-visuel

10   Migration and urbanisation

Large-scale commercial developments such as plantations and mines attract people in search of waged employment to the regions in which they are located. Indeed, they depend on people's moving to them to supply them with a goodly proportion of their labour force, for local populations are usually too small to meet their requirements. This movement of people, predominantly young men in the first instance, gives rise to a phenomenon common to many Third World developing countries – migrant labour. The movement of people has also contributed significantly in Melanesia, particularly in recent decades, to the growth of urban centres, both those directly servicing plantations and/or mines and, through the casual drift set in motion by the labour migration experience, those elsewhere. This movement, though currently affecting a small percentage of the population in most Melanesian countries (New Caledonia and Fiji excepted), is a belated parallel of trends throughout the world with industrialisation – urbanisation – and poses considerable social and economic problems for Melanesian nations.

Labour migration

Migrant labourers leave their home areas for elsewhere to work for a time on plantations, in mines or in towns or cities. They intend to return home again, and their absences are usually fairly brief – two or three years is about average. Although their relatives back home may not hear from them during this time, migrants remain firmly connected there socially, affectively and culturally. It is where they belong. Going off to work somewhere else is merely an episode in their lives. They do not usually go with the intention of its leading to a long-term or permanent change of status to an urban-dwelling wage-earner, although some individuals do repeatedly leave home to work elsewhere or drift willy-nilly into urban areas without returning home. Most continue to maintain relations with kin at home throughout their stays, however long, with a view to returning home eventually.

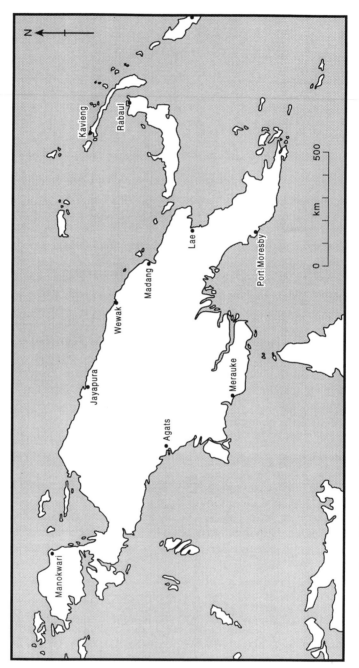

Map 10 Some Melanesian urban centres

In some regards we can view the virtual kidnapping in the last century by blackbirders of able-bodied natives to work on plantations as a crude precursor of labour migration. Labour recruiters resorted to similar tactics well into the twentieth century to recruit workers for the goldfields, for instance, and the war effort: 'Some of the more unscrupulous recruiters used dog chains and padlocks. Every night they'd chain the boys up because the further they got from home, the more homesick they'd get, and they'd try to break back' (Nelson 1982:143). Some justified this treatment of the people as ensuring their safety, maintaining that if they ran off in a foreign place enemies there would kill them. On the whole, though, employers realised that it was not in their long-term interest for labourers to be recruited under duress and managed badly. One of the economic attractions of Melanesia has been its cheap labour; if labourers are forced or tricked into leaving home, overworked, abused and poorly paid they will soon inform others on their return home, and no one will want to go away to work. There are reports of people in the past even running off when recruiters arrived in their community.

Migrant labourers did, however, work under difficult conditions by our standards, although there was progressive improvement over the years. They were issued a few basic items such as a blanket and a mug, and herded together in cramped accommodations, commonly called barracks. They worked very long hours, usually on monotonous, repetitive and sometimes physically demanding tasks. They were commonly subject to rigorous discipline in an attempt to curb their otherwise relaxed attitude to work and attendance. And their pay was low; they usually received a percentage of their pay as pocket money (their employers often supplying them with food) and the remainder as a lump sum when their contract expired.

It was not only enlightened self-interest on the part of employers that was responsible for the gradual improvement in the migrant labourers' circumstances. Governments have also intervened to protect them, legislating on conditions, wages, hours, and so on. The colonial administrations enacted codes early on, and labour laws have subsequently been revised and updated a number of times with the introduction of various labour schemes to control migration. This legislation was intended to protect not only indigenous labourers but also employers, both parties being required to enter into formal legally binding contracts. The Melanesian Pidgin term *mekim pepa* became the name for the system of migratory indentured labour, the non-literate employees signing on or 'making paper' by touching a pen as a clerk signed for them or making a mark themselves on the indenture contract. If workers broke the contract

– absconded or refused to work – they were subject to legal sanctions the threat of which ensured their compliance on the whole.

Although conditions have improved, worker motivation remains a problem. Labour may be cheap in Melanesia, but its productivity is low, often having little technical assistance. The work is boring and pointless to many labourers, who are frequently involved in the preliminary stages of preparing primary products for export and have little understanding of what they are used to produce. The conditions are often uncongenial and irksome, and workers come to resent the regime and become homesick. They lack the incentive to work harder. In capitalist regimes this problem is usually addressed by offering to pay employees more to increase their efforts, but plantations in Melanesia can ill afford this, for it is cheap labour that contributes significantly to their profitability. Furthermore, it is argued that if the mines, which are in fact capable of paying more competitive wages, were to do so they would seriously disrupt the employment market and bankrupt many marginal economic concerns (besides embarrassing governments as employees left for highly paid jobs elsewhere).

In an attempt to maintain respectable levels of productivity, some managers have established paternalistic relationships with their employees, encouraging them to work well in return for small perks and favours, building up personal relations of sorts with them in an attempt to oblige them to work effectively. Others have veered in the opposite direction, resorting to intimidation and violence to maintain order in their labour lines. This was particularly common in the past: 'Two planters (not Englishmen) had been in the habit of flogging their natives (Fijian), and rubbing the juice of the Chilli pepper into their backs afterwards; sometimes they would use nettles for this purpose' (Palmer 1871:78). As one planter bluntly put it: 'It was well known that we caught them a swift clout across the ear if they did something wrong. We also applied the boot to the area where it did most good' (Nelson 1982:79).

In addition to trying to protect migrant workers from barbaric and unfair treatment, governments have also intervened to protect the interests of those remaining behind at home. They have had to guard against the deleterious effects of overzealous labour recruitment, denuding rural areas of able-bodied males to the point where their subsistence regimes have been put in jeopardy and their women, children and old and infirm have suffered deprivation and hardship through food shortage. Administrations sometimes had to declare regions out of bounds for labour recruitment to allow local populations to recover and stabilise after experiencing heavy out-migration (the Germans, for instance, declared the entire island of New Ireland such a closed region in the late nineteenth century).

Today such dramatic undermining of local subsistence is unlikely. The labour recruiters who were responsible for it are a thing of the past. People now leave voluntarily to search for work, and this results in a more staggered exodus roughly matched by returning migrants. Nevertheless, this can amount to a considerable number of the able-bodied men from remote and underdeveloped regions, who lack the opportunity to earn cash near home and are obliged to leave and seek work elsewhere. While their absence is unlikely to upset their families' subsistence regime unduly, the same cannot be said for their communities' social arrangements. If several men are away from a community for an extended period, social relations within it are inevitably disturbed. Their absence not only has a detrimental effect on family life but also upsets the entire community's social existence. In the absence of many persons of a certain status, some events and institutions may pass into disuse. Equally significant or possibly even more so as a force for change is the effect of migration on the attitudes of the migrants. Going away to work teaches men about Western ways, the new order and the outside world, and this knowledge changes their aspirations and their attitudes to traditional customs and expectations.

Migrant workers return home different men who question and challenge village standards and practices. They query the validity and significance of their traditional culture in the light of their radically changed view of the world. It is common, for instance, for young men to depart to work before their initiation and on their return as mature and travelled adults to refuse to take part in these rituals. In some places it has even become the practice for young men to go off as migrant workers to prove their manhood and achieve some knowledge of the new world instead of that passed on during initiation. Migration thus, in some senses, replaces traditional initiation ceremonies, and they fall into disuse.

Tribespeople as townspeople

Some of the migrant labourers develop such an antipathy for traditional rural life that they do not return home or, having returned, leave again for extended periods. These people constitute a considerable proportion of the urban populations in Melanesia, particularly of first-generation townsmen. In their minds they have left home not permanently but indefinitely while they work for a money income. Their ties to their home communities remain important to them, and they maintain them by sending home gifts and periodically returning on visits, sometimes to participate in neighbourhood events (notably those featuring sociopolitical

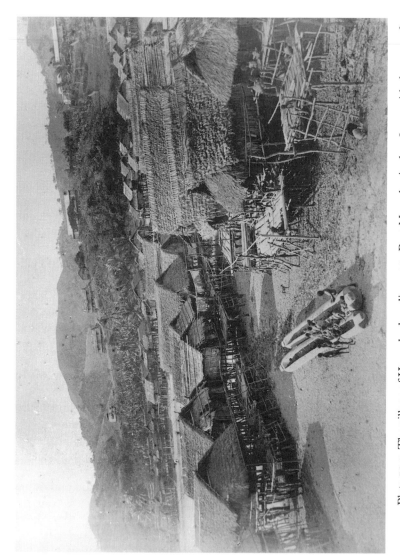

Plate 10.1 The village of Hanuabada, adjacent to Port Moresby, in the 1890s, with the start of European settlement on the hill behind.

exchange). They are absentee members of their home communities, actively maintaining meaningful links there especially by keeping up with exchange commitments that socially validate their connections.

The attitude of the majority of urban residents to their stay and work in *taun* (Pidgin for 'town', which is what Melanesians commonly call urban areas) makes their position, in some senses, like an extended period of migrant labour. Recently there has been an increasing tendency for women to move to urban areas, frequently raising families there. The rural focus carries over into second and subsequent town-born generations too. These people maintain home ties not just for the sake of emotional security (although preserving affectively important links with kin and culture is significant, particularly for first-generation town dwellers) but also as insurance against unemployment or old age. Many town dwellers intend to return home anyway, ideally before they are forced to by straitened circumstances, to start some business venture with the money they have earned. They maintain healthy social relations to ensure that others recognise their rights when they return home to claim garden land and live in the neighbourhood. If they do not maintain these ties to place they become disinherited and landless.

Roots in the home area are also important in structuring relations in urban contexts. Those who live and work in town tend to congregate with those who come from the same region of the country as themselves, who speak the same language and share a cultural tradition. These people live clustered together in the same neighbourhoods, commonly work side by side in the same occupations, and interact intensively with one another socially and at work, having relatively little to do with others. This is predictable: a new arrival in town will seek out those already there from home, some of whom he will know and will probably even be related to. These people make up a security circle in the somewhat hostile urban environment, extending assistance to one another when needed and support if unemployed and looking for work. Besides, they are convivial and comfortable company, people who understand the same cultural idioms and behave according to the same social code.

The urban areas of Melanesia tend, as a consequence, to consist of numerous ethnic enclaves relatively isolated socially one from another. They attract many people from different cultural backgrounds, giving rise to what are called pluralistic social situations, but instead of resulting in a cosmopolitan mix this pluralism has produced many relatively independent and unconnected ethnic blocks. This sticking together of people from the same cultural and linguistic background is common in Third World urban contexts. Known as **tribalism** it has in Papua New Guinea given rise to what they call the *wantok* system. A *wantok* (literally, 'one

Plate 10.2 The village of Hanuabada 100 years later, the pile houses extending into the sea, overlooked by the office tower blocks of downtown Port Moresby.

talk') is someone who speaks the same language as oneself and shares one's cultural heritage. The social category *wantok* displays the general flexibility and fuzzy boundedness characteristic of Melanesian categories. In urban contexts it may be broad; people refer to both kinsmen, real or classificatory, and good friends as *wantok* and may extend the term to acquaintances on occasion and even use it as a casual and friendly greeting. But it is properly understood to refer to those with whom one interacts frequently and has a close, trusting relationship. When asked what made people *wantok*, individuals consistently replied: 'They stick together, converse frequently and eat together . . . *wantok* come from the "same place," a reference to their having a common village, province or (occasionally) region of origin. The farther one is from home, the wider the spatial referent' (Levine and Levine 1979:71).

The evolution of the *wantok* system was perhaps inevitable with the growth of urban areas in Papua New Guinea and the coming together of culturally different tribespeople. While it has doubtless facilitated the adaptation of these people to this radically different social environment, it has resulted in awkward situations which militate against the development of stable conurbations. The rural focus and mobility of the majority of their populations exacerbate this instability. The *wantok* system splinters urban areas into many relatively isolated residential enclaves on which centre social networks that scarcely connect in any socially meaningful sense. The result is a brittle and overall poorly integrated social environment, even more faceless, daunting and potentially hostile than many Western urban jungles.

People feel safe in their quarter of town, where informal social constraints founded on shared traditional cultural expectations and trust between relatives ensure an orderly and secure social haven. When they have dealings with people from elsewhere they feel insecure, even threatened, and with good cause; not only is sorcery an ever-present threat but civil order is ineffectively maintained in urban areas throughout Papua New Guinea and violence, almost unchecked, is a common nasty feature of urban life. It is a vicious circle: the lack of integration of tribally based neighbourhoods promotes stiff and potentially violent interaction between their members, but without these *wantok* enclaves people would be unable to cope with the threats and insecurity of urban life at all.

The social fragmentation of towns carries over into the workplace, where the *wantok* system promotes blatant nepotism. Individuals like to work with people of the same cultural background for the same reasons as they choose to live with them. Consequently, when a vacancy occurs at the place where they work, they try to ensure that a relative or friend secures the job, informing that person of the opening and recommending him strongly to their employer, who may well be ethnically one of them and require no persuading. Many experienced employers are aware that employees of the same cultural background tend to work more harmoniously and reliably than an ethnic hotchpotch and so promote the perpetuation of the *wantok* system as their most profitable course. The result is that in some towns a single ethnic group may have cornered a particular occupation (for example, as the Goilala people have rubbish collection in Port Moresby and Southern Highlanders the taxi service).

Tribalism versus class

The *wantok* system also makes it difficult for individuals to amass any considerable personal capital, which is one of the principal motivating factors for many in moving to towns to work. The obligations of *wantok* relationships serve to redistribute the earnings of those who work, supporting the unemployed and those on low wages. This acts as a drain on the resources of the working and better-paid but they see it as an unavoidable social obligation. An individual cannot deny his or her less fortunate

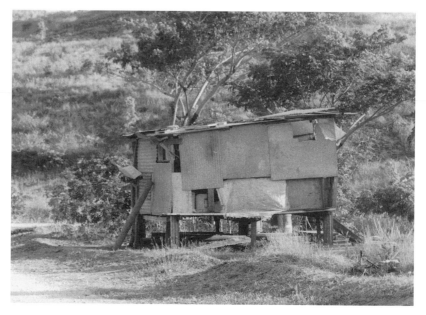

Plate 10.3 Self-help housing of the poor: a homestead in a squatter
settlement on the outskirts of Hohola suburb, Port Moresby.

kin assistance, because to do so is to repudiate social relations, to deny
oneself acceptance in one's social circle. Giving assistance is also part of a
system of mutual insurance, an investment against hard times guarantee-
ing one support if in turn one becomes unemployed or is in need.

The *wantok*-based redistribution of wealth parallels the sharing of business venture profits in rural areas and similarly serves to inhibit the emergence of social classes. Nevertheless, there is evidence of a nascent class
consciousness emerging in towns between members of different cultural
groups. What interaction there is between people from different cultural
backgrounds tends to follow class-like lines, depending primarily on
occupation and income. While these social interactions across tribal and
cultural boundaries are relatively few, it is those in similar jobs and
earning comparable incomes who tend to mix with one another at work
and in private life. There is an increasing tendency for men and women
from different cultural regions to marry. Those concerned are mainly at
the apex of the evolving class pyramid, being the small emerging élite who
control the bureaucracy, dominate politics and manage major commercial enterprises.

The demands of tribalism prevent any rapid efflorescence of social
interaction along class lines, keeping relations largely within ethnically

Plate 10.4 Urban entertainment: score any double or treble on the dart board to win a bottle of South Pacific beer.

defined networks where traditional expectations and obligations apply. These obligations centre on the ethic of exchange, a structure of reciprocal relations. In towns people continue to admire the generous and accord social standing to those who liberally distribute what they have rather than save it. A marked ethos of egalitarianism continues to characterise social relationships. The continuance of these cultural values promotes the sharing of resources between members of the same urban ethnic networks, reducing income differences which would be central to the development of a class system. Again, fear of offending their fellows' sense of equality, fomenting jealousy and possible revengeful action, either physical violence or sorcery, encourages people to share and prompts them to play down their success rather than highlight it with ostentatious material display.

Furthermore, the majority of townspeople intend to return home eventually or at least work assiduously to maintain their social links there for affective and insurance reasons. They cannot slough off obligations to their *wantok* in town because their heinous behaviour would become known at home and might lead to their rejection when and if they returned. The urban and rural networks are not separate: the former has grown out of and is closely related to the latter. No one who wishes to keep up meaningful relations with his home can become an independent townsman looking out for his interests alone. He is inevitably a tribesman-townsman. The maintenance of relations back home further effects a levelling of income. The financing of periodic visits and the sending of gifts and money to kin there may act as a significant drain on an individual's resources.

The behaviour of highlander migrant labourers or urban dwellers or visitors returning from the coast or more commercially developed highlands regions clearly illustrates the strength of these social forces. They distribute what they return with (both money and material objects purchased with their earnings) to a wide circle of relatives, and within a few weeks it is common for them to possess little more than anyone else. Some friends staying with me while working in Port Moresby brought home to me the strength of these expectations when their requests for cash, clothing and other possessions to take home verged on the fantastic, although it turned out that they were treating me no differently from their other *wantoks*, from whom they expected cash handouts. Although a recent phenomenon, this distribution rests on age-old traditional principles: there is tremendous social pressure on individuals to redistribute whatever comes into their possession; their social standing depends on it. They are shamed if they fail to return with adequate gifts for their expectant kinsfolk; an inability to find work in Port Moresby prompted some of my Wola friends to return home after a few weeks, before their relatives' expectations had reached very high levels. When asked why they give away much of what they return with, returnees say that they find the requests of their relatives for things undeniable. It is what everyone expects of them and generosity inclines people to think well of them (a not inconsiderable factor for persons who have been absent from a community for some years and need to reintegrate themselves). The strength of these reciprocal forces is further illustrated by the belief that those who feel they have not received their rightful share may call on supernatural forces to attack and bring illness to the offending individual or one of his relatives. Several men returning from contract labour told me that fear of this traditional sanction had prompted them to distribute more of their earnings than they intended.

While these social forces promote an egalitarian social environment, they may adversely affect economic development by inhibiting the accumulation of capital. This would not matter if those who received from others put what they received to some productive use, but this infrequently happens. Instead they in turn pass it on to others, who give it away again, and so on in an interminable series of transactions. The introduction of money and opportunities to earn it has not resulted in any noticeable capital investment in an effort to increase productive capacity (except for steel tools, some clothing, a few culinary implements, etc.). Instead, money has been added to the traditional items of wealth used in sociopolitical exchange. One consequence is that, whereas previously there was relatively little scope for people to increase their pool of valuables to any marked extent, today they have the opportunity to earn considerable sums of money, much of which passes into the exchange system as wealth. The result has been a dramatic inflation in the amounts of wealth exchanged and especially their cash component.

While these considerations serve to mute the emergence of a class-like hierarchy within societies, there are indications of such differences emerging between them. In Melanesia, tribalism substitutes for class in more than one sense. There are considerable variations in the development of different regions and consequently the affluence and opportunities of the different cultural groups that inhabit them. These differences are largely attributable to Melanesia's colonial history. Those living in accessible regions, around the coasts of the larger islands and on the smaller ones, were contacted and 'pacified' first, and they have had a head start and advanced farther along the road of capitalist-oriented market development. The difference between some places amounts to three or more generations' more experience of waged work, evangelism and education. Those living in places contacted early on have a considerably more sophisticated awareness of the new order than those contacted later. They monopolise the well-paid and powerful jobs, being better educated and more experienced, and their home regions tend to support more cash-earning ventures.

Those from less advanced regions see themselves as disadvantaged as a result of this uneven development and even exploited by those living elsewhere. In the highlands of Papua New Guinea, for instance, those living in the Western Highlands Province, who have taken over the ownership of many of the expatriate-founded coffee and tea plantations established in their region in the 1950s, are employing considerable numbers of migrant labourers from the less developed Southern Highlands Province on quite unfair terms. It is on a regional and ethnic level that we have exploitation emerging and can perhaps talk of a marxist proletariat, with one tribe as the employer and poorer less-developed surrounding ones supplying the disadvantaged workers. This threatens to become a major problem throughout Melanesia, one that will be very difficult to rectify as differences which evolved from chance historical events deepen and the exceedingly rugged physical terrain continues to hinder the advancement of remote regions.

This is a problem to which governments urgently need to direct attention, for these differences in opportunity that face those from divergent regions and dissimilar cultural backgrounds are predictably the source of considerable tension. They exacerbate antagonisms between people from previously isolated cultures thrown together by modern events, whose reactions might be expected to be partisan even with equal opportunities. The differences in cultural background and experience promote suspicion and uneasiness which can easily flare into violence. Aggressive confrontations between different ethnic groups, so-called tribal fighting, are common in urban areas. The social fragmentation of towns, with the gathering together of people into relatively impervious ethnic *wantok* blocks, promotes hostility.

From forest to urban jungles

Violence is perhaps unavoidable to some extent where many people from different linguistic and cultural groups are gathered together and have little tolerance for the differences revealed in their strange new pluralistic situations. This is particularly so in urban areas (which, as volatile poorly integrated social environments, encourage polarisation, suspicion and aggression) and on plantations and in other such workplaces where people are engaged in boring and tiresome work. In these brittle social milieus, men are liable to resort readily to aggression to settle differences, as the following case illustrates.

A young Wola man from a neighbourhood adjacent to the one that I know in the Southern Highlands, while working as a migrant labourer on a plantation in New Britain, became embroiled in a dispute during a card game that developed into a fight in which his Chimbu adversary hit him on the head with a stone, killing him. When a relative of the Wola man from the same neighbourhood – they had gone away together to find work – heard of his murder, he rushed out to find a Chimbu, any Chimbu, to kill in revenge. Unfortunately, he mistook a man from Madang sitting outside his barrack block for a Chimbu man and axed him. When he realised his mistake, he stormed on until he met someone he knew was a Chimbu and axed him too. The result was a bloody three-cornered confrontation – Southern Highlanders versus Chimbu versus people from Madang – which turned the plantation into a battleground until the riot police intervened. Many men subsequently deserted the plantation in fear. When we heard about the fatal fracas in the Southern Highlands, I commiserated with the dead boy's relatives and expressed concern over his kinsman's revengeful action. An elderly relative rebuked me, saying that he had acted well and properly in avenging his brother's death.

The response of the dead boy's elderly relative points to another difficulty facing those trying to contain urban and plantation violence between ethnic groups: the persistence of traditional war-like values, particularly the revenge ethic. Someone who commits an assault may set in train a chain of tit-for-tat violent encounters, dragging in people uninvolved in the original offence, and this spreading involvement can result in the opposition of monolithic blocs and embroil a substantial part of any urban or plantation population in conflict. In Papua New Guinea, for instance, it can result in some situations in pitting highlanders against coastal dwellers or islanders – these categories and groups expanding or contracting to include different people depending on the context. This antagonism between tribally defined groups, amalgamating into large new cultural categories, and the resulting violence and destruction constitute a major problem hindering economic development in Melanesia, and there is no easy solution. While planned economic and social development may gradually reduce the problem, the considerable sociocultural differences between people will, for the foreseeable future, promote the continuance of destructive tribalism and aggression as people defend what they perceive as their rights in the ways they believe proper – ways inherited from their forebears and an entirely different sociohistorical context.

The inhabitants of urban centres do not identify positively with these places, their allegiances are far narrower and in significant regards tribally conditioned. Partly as a result of this, the urban areas of Melanesia are hollow, artificial and alienating. Their character can also be partly attributed to their peculiar history. They were established as colonial centres in which until relatively recently few indigenes were permitted to reside and those who were (domestics, labourers, and so on) had to live in certain insalubrious locales, observe a curfew and avoid white-only areas (such as some beaches). These restrictions were not conducive to the formation of an urban identification. Furthermore, these places grew up largely as administrative centres, not around industrial developments. In this Melanesian towns are the reverse of many European ones, where industrialisation led to urban growth. In Melanesia we find urban centres desperately searching with little success for industrial developments to sustain their rapid growth. This is urbanisation back to front, giving rise to ever-deepening problems.

The populations of towns are expanding rapidly. Now that they are established, people are flocking to them and to likely unemployment, becoming a drain on the probably slender resources of relatives who work. People come to town from rural areas for various reasons: to earn money, probably to finance some business enterprise back home; for adventure and to prove themselves; to escape an irksome or embarrassing social situation (perhaps the ignominy of having committed a serious wrong); to try the new life and not miss out; to prolong the freedom of adolescence and avoid the responsibilities of married life; and to find work in which they can use any education they may have received. The inability of society to match educated individuals' aspirations is becoming a serious problem. The school system gives individuals unrealistic ambitions, leading them to expect far more than either rural or urban life can offer them. Their disillusionment is thought to have contributed, among other things, to the alarming rise in *raskol* (Pidgin for 'rascal' or violent criminal) behaviour. The phenomenon of armed gangs preying on towns and sometimes rural communities has recently emerged as a major social issue. Added to the ethnic and other tensions that characterise urban areas, they contribute to the violent atmosphere of these places.

The urban areas of Papua New Guinea are perceived as increasingly lawless. The alarming tendency for people to riot when some issue arises to give a focus to their frustrations reinforces the impression that order is precarious. The riots in Lae city in September 1989 intimately touched my Wola friends and show how customary political expectations can inform contemporary political expressions. They were sparked off when Ibne Wala, a young Wola man and policeman in Lae, was murdered by an armed gang which, breaking into a house in which he and his wife's relatives were staying, tried to drag away a young woman and shot him and another member of the family as they struggled to protect her. A prominent Morobe politician interfered in the subsequent investigations, accusing the police of behaving like hooligans. The indignation sparked in the Lae highlander population, who sympathised with Wala's relatives in their search for revenge, led to two days of rioting in the city and the looting of premises owned by associates of the politician. Violent outbursts like this one increasingly involve a political dimension of protest. The 1997 disturbances in Port Moresby and elsewhere, ignited by the government's ill-advised and dubiously funded attempt to hire mercenaries to solve the Bougainville crisis with a 'surgical military strike', suggest that this protest dimension may be becoming more clearly defined, finding a political forum in the press and in politically active non-governmental organisations. The disenchanted urban populations are seeking ways to make their frustrations known and provoke some action to assist them to find better lives.

Whatever their motivation for migrating to towns, people are coming in considerable numbers, and many of them perforce become permanent townspeople. The obligations attendant on living there and their low incomes and frequent periods of unemployment prevent them from amassing the sums of money they aspire to return home with to invest in the business ventures of their dreams. The lifting of colonial restrictions that prohibited migrants from bringing their families with them to town has encouraged this trend. When only single men could migrate to work, this and the restrictions on their urban activities obstructed the emergence of stable and settled indigenous urban populations. The rapid growth of shantytowns is one consequence of these changes. Areas of makeshift housing lacking any amenities are springing up not only because governments are unable to construct new houses to accommodate the increasing numbers of urban arrivals but also because, like colonial administrations before them, they are refusing to acknowledge the substantial urban drift and face the considerable problems to which it is increasingly giving rise.

The towns of Melanesia are rapidly expanding but have little industrial or other employment to absorb their ever-increasing populations. This suggests mounting unemployment and unrest as living standards in urban areas decline and no welfare net is available to catch the disadvantaged, who will have to rely on fortunate relatives to support them. The situation becomes explosive when combined with the splintering of urban populations into potentially hostile interest groups based on tribalism. Throughout Melanesia people refer to urban centres as bad places, with good reason. They are not places people wish to call home. It is unfortunate that they cannot be persuaded to act on their convictions and stem the flow to towns. Governments should perhaps encourage this by promoting the sustainable development of rural areas, to make them more attractive places to stay. By focusing equally on rural economic development they might do something to arrest the ominous urban drift.

FURTHER READING

On urbanisation in Melanesia see:

C. S. Belshaw 1957 *The great village* London: Routledge

S. Bergendorff 1994 *Faingu city: a modern Mekeo clan in Papua New Guinea* Lund: Lund University Press

S. Dinnan 1991 Big men, small men – some comments on urban crime and inequality in Papua New Guinea *Melanesian Law Journal* 19:79–100

N. Hitchcock and N. D. Oram 1967 *Rabia camp: a Port Moresby migrant settlement* Canberra: Australian National University New Guinea Research Bulletin No. 14

H. B. Levine and M. W. Levine 1979 *Urbanisation in Papua New Guinea* Cambridge: Cambridge University Press

J. V. Longmore and N. D. Oram 1970 *Port Moresby urban development* Canberra: Australian National University New Guinea Research Bulletin No. 37

N. D. Oram 1976 *Colonial town to Melanesian city* Canberra: Australian National University Press

A. Rew 1974 *Social images and process in urban New Guinea* St Paul: West

M. Strathern 1975 *No money on our skins* Canberra: Australian National University New Guinea Research Bulletin No. 61

On migration in Melanesia see:
R. D. Bedford 1973 *New Hebridean mobility* Canberra: Australian National University Press
M. Chapman and R. M. Prothero (eds.) 1985 *Circulation in population movement* London: Routledge
R. J. May (ed.) 1977 *Change and movement* Port Moresby: Institute of Applied and Social Research
C. D. Rowley 1972 *The New Guinea villager* Melbourne: Cheshire

Also referred to:
H. Nelson 1982 *Taim bilong masta* Sydney: Australian Broadcasting Commission
G. Palmer 1871 *Kidnapping in the South Seas* Edinburgh: Edmonston and Douglas

FILMS

Cowboy and Maria town Pacific Video-Cassette Series No. 24

11   Cargo cults and millennial politics

So far we have looked largely at technological and economic aspects of development, according to the capitalist model, and social reactions to change. This chapter considers the intellectual responses of Melanesians to these cataclysmic events – how they explain them. The cargo cult is one of these expository reactions.

A letter from a man who played a prophet-like role in one cargo cult reads in part as follows (Giuart 1952:177):

> john the great
> my brother here is joe: my name is karaperamun
> everything is near to me
> see us two joe captain cockle shell.

I am joe. I am saying to you two brothers and father that this spirit writing speaks to you these four lines only which you see. See how his writing has not capital letters. He says cockle shell. The meaning of this is that we two fit like the two halves of a cockle shell. Everything will come from Sidni [village on Tanna] Jonfrum wants you to answer this letter by the Morinda.

The cult in question was the John Frum movement, which emerged on the Vanuatuan island of Tanna. The passage does not make much sense out of context, and the confusion we feel in reading it may give us some insight into the bafflement experienced by people confronted by invading foreigners with astounding technological know-how, material goods and an apparently irresistible political order.

Cargo cults

Cargo cults are movements which anticipate the imminent arrival of the millennium. Those who follow the ritual manipulations and observances specified to promote it are to receive material rewards, notably an abundance of manufactured goods, and a better, even paradisiacal, life. The term 'cargo cult' originates in the participants' frequent use of the Pidgin word *kago*, which derives from the English word 'cargo', to describe the returns they intend their activities to bring.

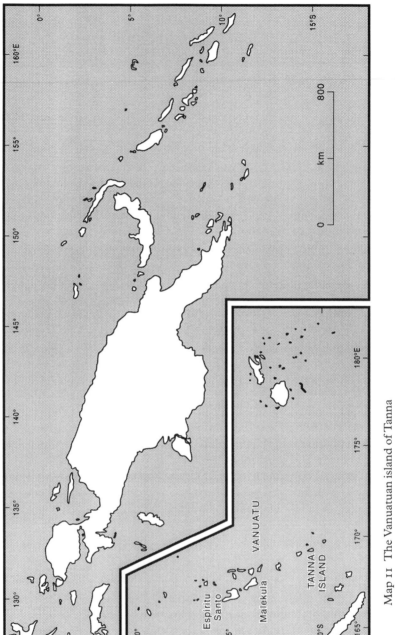

Map II The Vanuatuan island of Tanna

Cargo cults are small-scale and short-lived affairs, but similar ones may recur time and again in the same region, each new one rising from the ashes of previous ones whose millennial promises came to naught. During their brief existences cargo cults give rise to intense and frenetic activity which is often highly disturbing to orderly life. They usually feature messianic leaders who play a significant role in sparking them off, rising up to direct their activities, recasting what people have apprehended of European ideas (in which mission-taught Christianity usually features prominently) in the light of traditional belief and moral expectations, reinterpreting myths and manipulating the associated symbols to promulgate an appealing message. The activities inspired and directed by these 'prophets' frequently disrupt everyday life, as they divert people from subsistence tasks and encourage the pursuit of preparations for the coming millennium. This response is understandable as these persons are predicting the end of the known world, perhaps in a cataclysm and this makes continuing with such everyday activities appear pointless. Out of the upheaval a new order, perhaps ushered in by the return of the participants' ancestors, will emerge and there will be sufficient goods for all and eternal prosperity.

The newcomers have material wealth and technical capabilities beyond Melanesians' wildest dreams and irresistible political and military power. They apparently do no physical work to produce their fabulous goods, and they do not share their wealth. Clearly, Europeans know something, and the problem for Melanesians is how to gain access to this knowledge. Unable to understand Western society from their traditional perspective or to comprehend the worldwide capitalist economic system, they turn to millenarian cults.

A recurring feature of cargo cults is a belief that the ancestors of the Europeans tricked those of the Melanesians and are withholding from them their rightful share of material goods. Cargo movements attempt to reverse this situation – to discover the ritual formula that will facilitate access to their misappropriated manufactured possessions. They conclude that material goods come from some spirit world and that the wealthy outsiders are stealing their share, making it a matter of manipulating rituals to reverse the situation. An oft-repeated claim of these movements is that they will secure for people the cargo of their ancestors, who some cultists believe will return at the millennium to right the injustices currently manifest. Some cults also take on a disturbing racist tone, probably a response to the attitudes of some European newcomers. Blacks will become whites and the whites turn black with the coming of the millennium. In a nutshell: when the cargo comes, outside domination

Plate 11.1 A homestead on Tanna at the beginning of the twentieth century, with two European visitors.

will go and the good life will start for today's *kanaka* (Pidgin for 'native') underdogs.

The John Frum cult movement of Tanna and neighbouring islands in Vanuatu started in the late 1930s and has subsequently recurred several times in modified form. Tannese society has a graded system of chiefly offices reminiscent of nearby Polynesia. These positions have ritual encumbrances, and succeeding to one involves considerable ceremony in which pig kills feature centrally. Their responsibilities include tending supernaturally charged stones called *kapiel* that are believed to influence fertility and rain. The people continue to place great store by sociopolitical exchange, with bridewealth and mortuary payments persisting to this day. They talk about their hamlets, which comprise clans, as being linked together by a network of *suatu* (roads) along which wealth, food and wives travel. Overlying this is a moiety structure with divisions called Koiamata and Numrukuen, important previously in warfare and today in politics.

The people of Tanna also present giant decorated yams to one another in certain ceremonial contexts, cultivating the tubers in special mounds in their gardens. Yams, taro and bananas are prominent subsistence crops in

Plate 11.2 Custom revived: after their circumcision, boys in Central Tanna stand surrounded by the various exchange goods (yams, sugar cane, kava etc.) distributed by their relatives as their period of seclusion ends.

swidden gardens. The people also cultivate a range of cash crops, of which the most important is the coconut for copra. They produce the intoxicating drink kava, which they drink on ceremonial occasions and also casually, from crushed roots of the *Piper* shrub. The Vanuatuan islands produce distinctive anthropomorphic carvings and slit gongs, some of which feature in secret men's societies which involve initiation rituals and circumcision of young men. The people of Tanna have had missionary teaching of Christianity for several generations. Their traditional beliefs centred on spirit forces, many associated with natural features such as rock outcrops, rivers, mountains and banyan trees. An active volcano called Yasur, which dominates the island, is believed to house one such powerful spirit and regularly covers areas with ash that enhances soil fertility.

The John Frum movement

The John Frum movement came to the attention of Europeans in the early 1940s, when there was clear evidence of agitation and unrest on the island of Tanna. The islanders deserted the Christian mission churches and schools, and many of them abandoned official settlements and moved inland to establish hamlets beyond European influence. They made menacing suggestions to outsiders, notably foreign traders, that they should leave the island. Behind all of this was a hazy messiah-like figure called John Frum. The name Frum derives from 'broom', to sweep foreigners off the island, and John comes from connections with John the Baptist, oracle of Christ's coming. It was rumoured that someone calling himself John Frum had been appearing to men in a certain village at night. His audience, it was said, was under the influence of kava, and his appearance was carefully managed to conceal his identity. He spoke in an unrecognisable falsetto voice and could be seen only by the faint light of a fire. Some of those who said they saw him described a man with bleached hair who wore a coat with shining buttons and spoke in a squeaky voice; others saw a white-suited man with a walking stick and a book under one arm.

The apparition claimed that he was the earthly representation of Karaperamun, spirit of the island's volcano, and that at the time of Noah and the flood he had floated up into the clouds – saved then to come and help the islanders now. He made exciting promises and encouraged the revival of traditional customs. At first his speeches seem to have been conservative and not threatening to the missions and the administration, but the messages gradually developed into a strong attack on Christianity and government. John Frum prophesied a cataclysm: Tanna would become flat, mountains falling to fill in the valleys or, alternatively, would turn right over. When this happened he would reveal himself to all, and from then on there would be no more sickness and no need to work, for there would be abundant cargo for all and all foreigners (notably whites) would go and leave them to live without interference in their new island paradise.

The islanders were incited to revive the customs of their ancestors, which the missions had banned, to promote this millennial event. Many willingly complied not because of any misguided romantic wish to return to their 'primitive' past but because they were thoroughly disillusioned with the way in which missionaries were trying to suppress many aspects of their traditional life without offering any acceptable alternative. The outsiders were not allowing them any significant place in the new order and were not passing on much of their highly effective technical knowledge so that they could improve their lot and control their own destinies. The islanders said that with the missions it was 'pray, pray, pray and sing, sing, sing, all the time' (Guiart 1952:172), and they had soon discovered that this was no way to produce the Europeans' manufactured goods or match their political power.

The John Frum cult also encouraged people to stop using the outsiders' money. This promoted mad rushes on trade stores, with adherents spending all the money they had in their possession. It even prompted some zealots to cast money into the sea. They reasoned that the traders would leave when they had no money left, and when John Frum came they would receive more than adequate recompense, for he promised to issue his own new currency with a coconut motif struck on it. Furthermore, worked up to a high anticipatory pitch, cult followers staged lavish feasts, using up considerable supplies of food with reckless abandon because they expected plenty of everything soon. They indulged in a certain licence during these events, defying existing mission and government imposed conventions and thus breaking with the irksome recent past in anticipation of the paradisiacal future.

The authorities predictably reacted to these events in a heavy-handed way, interpreting them as dangerous subversion. They started by arresting a dull-witted man who was said to be John Frum's impersonator. They forced a confession from him and then tied him to a tree for all to see as an impostor. Few believed he was John Frum except the white expatriates. He was a scapegoat put forward by the non-Christians fomenting the cult in a challenge to the mission's authority. The movement continued, indeed flourished, regardless of this and many subsequent imprisonments of individuals believed to be implicated in it, and even spread to neighbouring islands.

People received their messages from John Frum in different ways. Soon after his reported appearance in person to kava-influenced audiences, for example, John Frum's three half-caste sons, dressed in long robes, were said to appear regularly near a certain banyan tree, relaying instructions and prophecies to everyone through a twelve-year-old girl. Then a person somewhere else declared that he was John Frum, 'King of America and Tanna', and incited people to clear an airstrip on which cargo-laden aircraft sent by his father from America could land. They erected huts to store the anticipated goods, put up an aerial and landing lights of bamboo in imitation of a regular airfield, and so on. Before landing, it was predicted, the aircraft would bomb those who had refused to help in these preparations. They never showed up, and that John Frum ended up in a mental hospital.

But around this time large numbers of aircraft did appear in the Vanuatuan sky as part of the Allied campaign in the Pacific during World War II. It was now that the cult developed a fixation that persists to this day on the United States of America as the place from which the millennium would come – as John Frum's homeland and the source of the coming cargo. The arrival of American aeroplanes, ships and troops inflamed the movement. The US forces recruited many willing labourers from Tanna and rewarded them generously. One American in particular, who became known as 'Tom Navy' (a navy man called Thomas Beatty, who was responsible for labour recruitment), came to symbolise US generosity for the Tannese with his open-handed Frum-like behaviour. He paid well from their perspective and gave away quantities of material goods. The Americans were doubtless less severe taskmasters than Europeans and markedly wealthier and freer in giving things away (as they were in Europe too at the time). The islanders saw astounding quantities of cargo arrive, exceeding their wildest imaginations, and, to cap these revelatory events, they met American black troops: dark-skinned people like themselves with apparently the same access to all this incredible cargo as fair-skinned soldiers.

The result of these experiences was a fervent identification with the United States, as the place from which Tanna's salvation would come that makes it today one of the few places on earth where people, ignorant of America's dubious world power record, would welcome US intervention. According to some rumours, the volcano with which John Frum is identified houses marines who will emerge to fight when the millennium comes to rid the island of foreign influences. In a similar vein, men have paraded with mock rifles and 'USA' painted in red on their chests to promote the return of GIs and cargo-laden ships. And across the island they have erected numerous red crosses to symbolise their faith in John Frum's return, as Christians do Jesus Christ's – although the cross apparently owes less to spurned mission teaching than to American troops, deriving from the red cross of the US military medical corps, which was probably particularly generous in dispensing medicine and helping the sick in the manner of true John Frum representatives.

Messages and directions have continued sporadically to come from John Frum via various prophets who claim that he communicates with them. He has spoken to one man regularly, for instance, at dusk on Thursday evenings at a particular remote spot. The people of Tanna have patiently awaited his return with their cargo. This is not so fantastic or unusual; we can recognise a likeness here to the genesis of many world religions, such as Christianity, which started in similar chiliastic ways among the discontented.

Explaining cargo cults

The bizarre quality of some of the behaviour associated with cargo movements has predictably attracted considerable attention, and attempts have been made to make sense of what people are doing in them. Commentators have advanced a variety of explanations to account for and detail the effects of cargo cults. In keeping with social science writing in general, it is not the case that some interpretations are right and others wrong; they all have probably had some relevance at some time regarding some movements. In this chapter we shall divide them into five categories: (1) stress, (2) material concerns, (3) conservation of custom, (4) status, and (5) nationalism.

Early reports interpreted cargo movements as indications of **stress** and anomie in local populations unable to cope with the rapid social change thrust upon them. It was argued that the failure of customary lore to provide satisfactory explanations of the dramatically changing world gave rise to confusion and feelings of acute insecurity. In anxiety and frustration people responded hysterically with movements that amounted to temporary delusions, even manifestations of collective madness. The reactions were indeed sometimes extreme, inviting such conclusions: recklessly flouting social conventions, wilfully defying the proprieties, indulging in wanton sexual abandon, and so on.

Later writers have, on the whole, played down these aspects of cults, understandably not wishing to encourage the dismissive interpretations of 'wild savage' behaviour to which many people too readily subscribe. But some observers have interpreted these frenetic responses positively, as promoting rapid adjustment to the changed world. They maintain that ecstasy and mass hysteria not only are significant psychological coping mechanisms but also promote essential rapid changes in the traditional ideological system. They break with the pre-contact past and swiftly establish a new ontological system that can cope with the greatly changed circumstances by flouting and openly sweeping away traditional customs and expectations. They make way for the new by revealing ritual secrets to the uninitiated, breaking hallowed objects, copulating incestuously with clan mates, and so forth, in a frenzy of destruction of the old order.

Others have focused on the **material** emphasis of these movements as distinctive. The argument is that coming into contact with the technologically superior outside world engendered feelings of material deprivation and inferiority. Before, people had been unaware of their material 'poverty' and content with their standard of living. Now they have less than they desire materially, realising how Spartan their technical assemblage is in comparison with that of the industrial world. The cults express their desires and according to some are even a manifestation of envy. These commentators point out that the people are in a hopeless position, being ignorant of how Europeans manufacture the goods they covet. Unable to obtain what they desire, they turn to fantasy. The cults are an example of escapism, of retreat from unpleasant and unchangeable reality.

Plate 11.3 Allied transport ships unload equipment on the Green Islands.

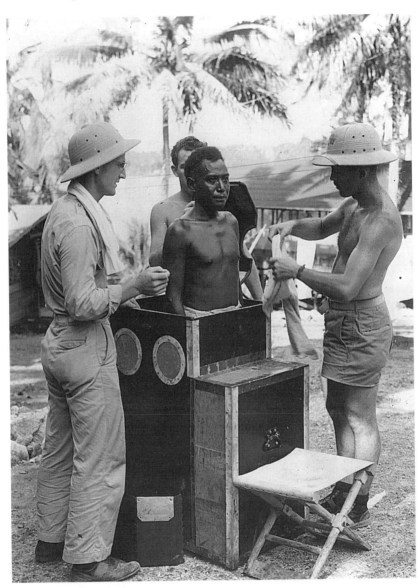

Plate 11.4 US Navy doctors treat a New Georgia Islander suffering from ringworm.

Others have interpreted cargo cults the other way round, arguing that what they express is not the desire to embrace European ways but the reverse – their wish to ward off the corrosive and disruptive effects of contact with outsiders. Here the argument is that people turn to these movements to promote the **preservation** of traditional customs and behaviour. Some observers have even gone so far as to suggest that in millenarian cults people are attempting to return to some idealised vision of the pre-contact past – that these are 'nativistic' movements. A crude early version of this point of view was that the missionaries and administrators, in forbidding many traditional practices, had deprived people of customary means of social fulfilment and stimulation and cargo cults filled the resulting void. If this is so, however, it is unclear why people did not simply revive versions of their repressed customs instead of inventing entirely new cults – except that they perceived that their old practices would not bring them the manufactured goods they desired. Like all these explanations, this one is partial.

A subsequent version of the cultural preservation argument concerns the sociopolitical exchange activities which are central to the structuring of polities throughout Melanesia. According to this view, in some places people even had too much 'cargo' and resorted to millenarian movements to deal with the problems that arose in their traditional exchange systems when the arrival of Europeans dramatically increased the supply of imported wealth objects. The cults were a response to inflation, an attempt to accommodate a major perturbation to customary arrangements. People turned to cargo movements in the hope of improving their access to the markedly increased supplies of wealth and thus increasing their chances of becoming politically dominant by excelling at exchange, and this promoted the rapid absorption of these goods into their traditional sociopolitical exchange systems. Alternatively, it is argued that cargo cults united people in opposition and protest in places where missionaries and others had severely disrupted exchange arrangements. They signalled a challenge to these changes and promoted a return to customary transactional ways through, among other things, the reinstatement of bridewealth payments.

Although the extent to which cults represent a wish to maintain customary arrangements is open to question, given the desire expressed in them to acquire manufactured goods and embrace European ways, it is undeniable that they have their roots in traditional culture and beliefs. These movements have even been described as typical Melanesian religions paralleling the fashion cycles that characterised customary rites. We should hardly expect anything else but attempts to account for change in familiar terms. It is understandable, for instance, that people commonly revise certain myths in an attempt to explain what they cannot otherwise understand as the Wola have their myth of the fair- and dark-skinned brothers. The Tangu people, who live near Madang in Papua New Guinea and have experienced cargo activity, have a similar myth which they have likewise modified to explain the changes that have come with Europeans and to justify their cargo cult movements. In their myth, the two brothers who part company, one to found the black-skinned Melanesian race and the other the white-skinned materially inventive European one, are separated by a tidal wave and flood caused by one's having killed a large fish that had emerged from the decomposing corpse of a child belonging to the other, which the child's father had warned him not to kill. The arrival of Europeans marks the return of the wronged sibling, leading to the cargo movements (Burridge 1960:155–65).

The realisation that cargo cults inevitably have a traditional component to them prevents us from mistakenly dismissing them as irrational. They are eminently rational from the viewpoint of the participants, given their limited knowledge and experience of the forces responsible for the traumatic changes with which they are struggling to cope. They cannot understand the source of manufactured goods and try (erroneously, from a Western viewpoint) to account for them in cargo cult ideologies. Movements inevitably have a traditional focus and logic; people turn to customary beliefs and idioms to cope with the bewildering events that have engulfed them. While these movements may be inappropriate, perhaps even comical, in their misunderstanding of industrial society, they are not illogical.

Whatever the appropriateness or otherwise of the traditional element in cargo cults, it is fused with an aspiration for alien material wealth and power – but not at any price. In these movements Melanesians are indicating clearly that they desire these things on their own terms, within a cultural context that they understand. This is by no means the same thing as a wish to return to the primitive past. Other commentators have developed this theme, linking participants' wishes to maintain their cultural order relatively intact with efforts to oblige the powerful outsiders to recognise their society and so restore their **status** and their self-respect. They stress, as do those taking the cultural preservation line, the role of cargo cults as symbolic acts in addition to supposedly instrumental ones believed literally to lead to material gains.

In these movements Melanesians are expressing their discontent with the newly imposed order. It is not merely that they desire material goods but that they want to receive these in the context of what they perceive as a fair, moral relationship with outsiders. In short, cargo is a symbol of their wish for equal status with them. While they admire European goods and power, Melanesians abhor their selfishness, racism and domineering attitudes. Europeans are immoral, to their minds, in not sharing their goods and knowledge. What Melanesians are expressing in cargo movements, according to this argument, is a wish somehow to oblige Europeans to cooperate and share fairly.

The wish of Melanesians is to achieve the equality among all human beings that characterises their traditional polities:

It is perhaps in the very relationship with the Europeans that the Melanesians' ideology of reciprocity and exchange should be assessed in connection with the cargo cult . . . The Melanesians have shown willingness to enter into reciprocal relations, but have been obstructed in this because the Europeans have up to now refused to accept their place in the system. Therefore the Melanesians have to try to find a way whereby they can become the equals of the Europeans. (Christiansen 1969:112–13)

The transactional focus of cults further helps to account for the material emphasis on cargo, which is unexceptional in this context. After all, the region's sociopolitical exchange systems focus on the continual passage of material objects between persons. Equality is a value that Melanesians cherish, but Europeans apparently do not. Their resort to cargo movements is a protest against their deprivation of status. They are showing the outsiders the proper way to behave – how to share and enter into exchange relationships. Some argue that the big-man ideology is also significant in generating cults, which depend on the emergence of charismatic personalities who, if not big men, model themselves on this role. These often prophet-like figures mobilise people's dissatisfactions, claiming that some supernatural power has revealed to them the knowledge they need to ensure success in their endeavours, which include recognition for all and equal standing with the invaders.

Some commentators have expanded on the status deprivation explanation of cults, maintaining that these movements represent the first stirrings of Melanesian **nationalism**. This is the line usually taken by those who subscribe to a marxist perspective and dependency theory, and the argument is that cargo cults are evidence of a wish to throw off the exploitive colonial yoke. Although at this early stage in the development of a nationalistic sentiment this wish is poorly articulated, we can see here the beginnings of the struggle by Melanesians to emerge from the shadow of European domination. And cargo cults are not mere impotent yearnings in this regard. By breaking down the barriers between independent and perhaps hostile stateless political groups, they promote unity among people otherwise too fractiously organised to protest effectively.

The cults give peoples' protests considerably more weight and effect by presenting a united front to the invaders. One way in which cargo movements achieve this is by flagrantly violating convention, disposing of the old divisive order to achieve a new united one more effective in meeting the challenges of the changed world. While the marxist view of colonial repression and exploitation is perhaps somewhat extreme for most of Melanesia, it is nonetheless the case that some cults have evolved into more clearly defined nationalistic and more effective political move-ments. On Tanna Island, for example, the John Frum movement has become a political force. The seeds of political awareness that it con-tained germinated during the later stages of the colonial condominium, when large differences between the British and French partners emerged, the former negotiating for independence while the latter manoeuvred to maintain colonial rule.

The French colonial authorities supplied services such as schools and clinics free, whereas the British charged a fee and levied a head tax. The generosity of the French impressed the followers of John Frum, waiting for cargo to come, and they became increasingly dependent on their ser-vices. When independence, as advocated by the Vanua'aku Pati (the pro-independence political party) and supported by the British, appeared on the agenda, they started to worry that they would lose their services and have to pay a tax to boot. They also feared that the Presbyterian church, prominent in the Vanua'aku Pati, would once again dominate their lives. The French capitalised on these fears by encouraging a movement called Kapiel (its name deriving from the *kapiel* stones believed to contain supernatural powers), which subsequently became a political party closely allied to the John Frum. The conservatives who supported these two parties and a third called Kastom were largely unaware of the wider issues at stake regarding independence and hence the political significance of their opposition to the Vanua'aku Pati.

The result was that the people of Tanna were split almost equally over the issue of independence. In the 1979 elections the conservative parties won 49 per cent of the vote and Vanua'aku Pati 51 per cent, and in the 1983 elections leading up to independence (when the conservative John Frum, Kapiel and Kastom parties had amalgamated into the Union of Moderate Parties (UMP)) the percentage distribution was reversed, with the UMP just winning a majority of the votes. The political tensions erupted into violence on Tanna. The conservatives, led by the John Frum representative elected to the Representative Assembly (who was subse-quently shot dead in a struggle at Isangel, the district headquarters, to free some arrested political colleagues), maintained that Tanna should break away from Vanuatu and invite France and the United States to govern them. Subsequently incorporated into the new independent nation of Vanuatu, Tanna continues to display the same divisions. The

UMP pursues campaigns that rest on the old cargo cult ideas, promising to supply free services such as education and health, and won the most votes in subsequent elections in the late 1980s and 1990s. People today continue to interpret politics in the light of John Frum's prophecies.

In their expression of tensions, cargo cults lend themselves to a variety of sociological and psychological interpretations, and their appeal will depend in part on one's temperament and in part on the particular move-ment to which one attempts to apply them. The relatively frequent pan-Melanesian occurrence of cargo cults in a wide range of disparate cultures, and their recurrence time and again in the same region testify to their importance. Although frenetic, short-lived and, to outsiders, disrup-tive, they allow Melanesians who find themselves in a confusing and inex-plicable situation to cope with it and even manipulate it to their advantage. When we consider that these people have rocketed from the stone age to the space age these cults lose their bizarre quality; it is a wonder that all Melanesians did not go insane. Cargo cults are testimony to human resilience and adaptability.

FURTHER READING

On the John Frum cult see:
J. Guiart 1952 The John Frum movement in Tanna *Oceania* 22:165–77
J. Guiart 1956 *Un siècle et demi des contacts culturels à Tanna* Paris: Publications de la Société des Océanistes No. 5
E. Rice 1974 *John Frum he come* New York: Doubleday

See also:
M. Allen (ed.) 1981 *Vanuatu: politics, economics, and ritual in island Melanesia* Sydney: Academic Press
R. Brunton 1989 *The abandoned narcotic* Cambridge: Cambridge University Press
L. Lindstrom 1990 *Knowledge and power in a South Pacific society* Washington, DC: Smithsonian Institution Press
H. Van (ed.) 1995 *Melanesian politics: stael blong Vanuatu* Suva: University of the South Pacific and Canterbury University

On other cargo cult movements elsewhere in Melanesia see:
K. O. L. Burridge 1960 *Mambu* London: Methuen
M. Kaplan 1995 *Neither cargo nor cult: ritual politics and the colonial imagination in Fiji* Durham, NC: Duke University Press
P. Lawrence 1964 *Road belong cargo* Manchester: Manchester University Press
L. Lindstrom 1993 *Cargo cult* Honolulu: University of Hawaii Press
T. Schwartz 1962 The Palian movement in the Admiralty Islands 1946–1954 *Anthropological Papers of the American Museum of Natural History* 49:211-421
H. Whitehouse 1995 *Inside the cult: religious innovation and transmission in Papua New Guinea* Oxford: Oxford University Press

On cargo cults and millenarian movements in general see

K. O. L. Burridge 1969 *New heaven, new earth* Oxford: Blackwell

P. Christiansen 1969 *The Melanesian cargo cult* Copenhagen: Akademisk Forlag

G. Cochrane 1970 *Big men and cargo cults* Oxford: Clarendon Press

J. C. Jarvie 1964 *The revolution in anthropology* London: Routledge

F. Steinbauer 1979 *Melanesian cargo cults* St Lucia: Queensland University Press

P. Worsley 1968 *The trumpet shall sound* London: Macgibbon and Kee

FILMS

The fantastic invasion Nigel Evans Production for British Broadcasting Corporation (Everyman)

12   Missionaries and social change

The Christian religion widely promoted by missionaries in Melanesia coincides at several points with cargo cults, particularly with its early markedly chiliastic history and a prophet figure, the Son of God, and beliefs in a paradisiacal afterlife. Throughout Melanesia an increase in millenarian talk and activity marked the approach of the start of the third millennium since Christ's death. It was widely believed that when the Christian calendar's year 2000 began the known world would come to a cataclysmic end and believers would be saved and transported to a heavenly world of plenty while unbelievers would be cast into the eternal fires of damnation. Such beliefs have a powerful effect on people's imaginations and are fuelled in considerable measure by evangelical missionaries, many connected to the US Midwest, whose churches subscribe to similar beliefs. In some parts of Melanesia it was being predicted that people would come into possession of credit cards and be tattooed with the personal identification number 666 (after the Revelations reference to the devil's works) and as a consequence would have access to unlimited wealth from certain holes in walls.

Mission motives

Missionaries have long played a prominent part in the changes that have occurred in Melanesian societies with the intrusion of the outside world. They are sent by churches to proclaim the 'good word' of the Bible to unbelievers – to teach the Gospel and persuade people to convert to the faith and live as Christians. While this common aim informs most mission work, the motives of different missionaries vary from the breathtakingly selfless to the downright selfish. The pioneer Methodist George Brown (1908:18–19) wrote about his call:

I cannot call to mind any particular day on which I first realised the pardoning love of God. I had long experienced the throbbings of a new life, new thoughts, new desires, and a new purpose in life . . . I fully realised my acceptance through faith in the Lord Jesus Christ, and determined to live in accordance with His will, and to labour for His sake, that some might be the better for my life . . . I was willing to offer myself exclusively for foreign mission work, and that, if accepted, my desire was to go to Fiji.

And at the end of his long career he spoke (1908:398) of:

the people amongst whom we had lived and laboured, to whom it had been our privilege to proclaim for the first time the blessed Gospel of the Lord Jesus Christ, to tell them of their privileges as the children of God, and by God's blessing to lead some of them to that peace and joy which is given to men and women the wide world over who, being justified by faith in Him who came to seek and to save that which is lost, have peace with God through our Lord Jesus Christ.

This attitude contrasts starkly with that of certain missionaries known to me in the Papua New Guinea highlands in the 1970s, who had built themselves a home with many modern conveniences (cooker, refrigerator, washing machine, three-piece suites, luxury shower, and so on) surrounded by beautifully landscaped gardens and a carefully tended kitchen garden that produced such exotic luxuries as strawberries, which were served with fresh cream from the cows they kept. This remarkable estate was surrounded by a high chain-link fence topped with barbed wire, and only a few local people were admitted. This isolation reflected the occupants' attitude to the local people for they believed that black-skinned people could never be saved and admitted to heaven. Asked what they were doing in the highlands if they believed the local souls were unsavable, they would reply that informing them about the existence of Jesus and his infinite love ensured their own places in paradise. This again raises starkly the issue of racist attitudes colouring some of the interaction between Melanesians and others, predisposing people to certain conclusions and encouraging negative attitudes on both sides, which as we shall see has been common, if often implicit, in a deal of missionary work.

Whatever the missionaries' motives there is a gulf between their work and the lives of the people they settle among, and they rarely attempt to bridge that gulf. They live in large houses, usually at some distance from local settlements and, even if by our standards in basic conditions, in luxury relative to their neighbours. Furthermore, unlike anthropologists, they presume to interfere directly in people's lives, seeking to impart their ideas of morality, disapproving of certain social relations and non-Christian ritual practices, and promoting their notions of proper behaviour, cleanliness, dress, and so on. They even enter sacred sites, places of dangerous local spirits, and upset sacra, sometimes then building churches on the sites to underline their displacement. Indeed, missionaries measure their success to some extent by the outward changes they effect in people's lives. The romantic notion of finding truly 'benighted

Plate 12.1 A chapel built of bush materials after a traditional architectural design at the Roman Catholic seminary on the coast at Lote in West Sepik Province.

pagans' and converting them to Christianity, which has some parallels with the anthropological romanticism of studying 'untouched natives', has driven missionaries to enter new areas and establish missions sometimes before the arrival of any administration; George Brown, for example, established a mission on tiny Duke of York Island (between New Ireland and New Britain) a decade before the German colonial authorities arrived there. Different churches have tended to stake out territories and jealously guard their own flocks there from approaches by others in a market-like competition for converts and the associated financial support from home.

Missionary impacts

Missionaries have preached to the people of New Ireland and New Britain for well over a century and to those living in Fiji for longer still. A shared feature of their histories was the Methodist Overseas Mission whose staff included the redoubtable George Brown. Brought up in County Durham, Brown had run away to sea as a youth and spent several years before the mast, visiting North America and New Zealand among other places. It was while he was living with missionary relatives in New

Plate 12.2 A Sunday-morning service at Hohola Christian church in a
Port Moresby squatter settlement.

Zealand that he had received the call. When he first visited the Bismarck
Archipelago, few people had had direct experience of Europeans:

Of this fine group but little was known before the year 1875, when we landed
there. (1908:97)

They cultivate large quantities of yams, taro, sweet potatoes, and bananas.
(1908:100)

Their large fish traps were anchored far out at sea, in deep blue water, with a tall
ornamented pole attached to them as a beacon. The traps float a few feet below
the surface, and large quantities of fish are caught in them. (1908:149)

There are no large villages here. Every family seemed to have a separate enclosure
containing five or six houses, and these are scattered all about the bush.
(1908:114)

[The] house was built without eaves, the rafters reaching from the ground to the
ridge pole and, meeting those from the other side, form a semicircle. Along the
sides and down the centre of the house were raised wooden benches, which form
seats by day and beds by night. These large houses are occupied at night by the
unmarried men only, those who are married having separate houses in the village.
A string of pigs' claws [tusks?] ornamented one end of the house, and spears, etc.,
were hung all about the roof. Some human skulls were suspended from a tree
outside. (1908:110–11)

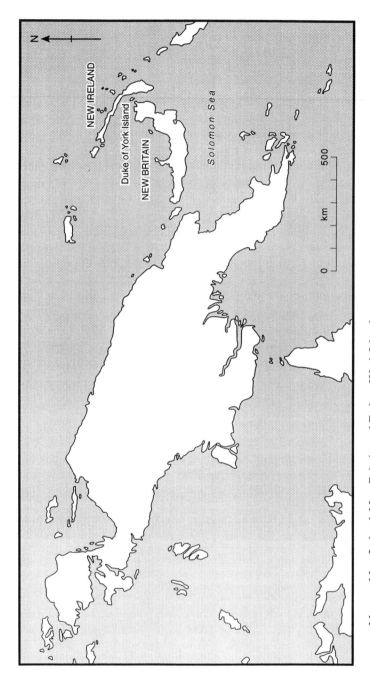

Map 12 New Ireland, New Britain and Duke of York Island

There was no doubt at all about the cannibalism of the people, in fact, they made no secret at all about it. Most of the spears had a human leg- or arm-bone on one end, and when I asked by interpreter where all these bones came from, he replied, 'Oh man belong salt water he fight man belong bush. He kaikai (eat) him. He catch him bone he go belong spear. All same this fellow place,' which last sentence means, such is the custom here. [1908:125]

At one end of the enclosure there was a large house containing two large chalk images, one of which, representing a man, was much larger than the other, which represented a woman ... they evidently view them with some superstitious regard, as they dance to them, and strictly forbid all women and children to go near the place where they are kept. (1908:127)

We had the inevitable Dukduk or dancing mask affair again. I noticed here that all people outside kept clear of the masked figures, as they have the privilege of beating or stoning any who came their way. (1908:111)

The impact of missionaries on people's lives was predictably considerable. Relations started off suspiciously, combined with curiosity about these strange-looking, pale-skinned, weirdly attired newcomers with their extraordinary technology, exemplified at first in impressive ships and later in aircraft. Over time relations became more complex as the representatives of these different cultures interacted and became aware of the others' differing values and expectations. Some conflicting beliefs and aspirations soon became evident, on occasion expressing themselves in physical violence, and from the early days the question was asked, as it is by some today, on what grounds outsiders presumed to interfere unbidden in others' lives. In 1878, for example, *The Australasian* asked, in criticism of a punitive expedition in which George Brown had participated against a Blanche Bay community that had killed and eaten some of his Pacific islander colleagues (for which unmissionary act preliminary investigations were started for a possible court trial and he was disciplined by his Mission Board):

If missionary enterprise in such an island as this leads to wars of vengeance, which may readily develop into wars of extermination, the question may be asked whether it may not be better to withdraw the Mission from savages who show so little appreciation of its benefits.

Together with others involved in the bloody expedition, Brown consistently argued that the action was necessary to prevent a massacre of all newcomers, which he believed likely if the native population thought that they were weak and defenceless. And, not surprisingly, he was alive to the vexed question of the extent to which outsiders should interfere in the lives of others. Discussing his intervention in a dispute in which a man had purportedly intended to kill and eat one of his wives, he wrote (1908:193):

I have often wondered since whether we were wise in the action which we took, and I have always come to the conclusion that we did right. We knew that the woman would certainly be killed the moment her head was outside our door, and I cannot imagine any man looking at that poor bleeding woman lying on the floor of our house listening, as she did, to the demand made for her to be taken out and killed for a cannibal feast, and allowing such a foul act to take place. Had we been killed, we should no doubt have been blamed for our folly, but fortunately the affair ended happily, and so we were not blamed. But the question still remains, apart from success or failure: Was it right to interfere and to take the risk? And I certainly believe that it was. I know of no sermon which we preached during that year which had such an effect upon the minds of the people. They realised as they had never done before that we were there not for our own good or profit, but for theirs.

This is a graphic illustration of the clash of cultural values. Whatever one's views on the comparative moral issue, it is unrealistic to think that no foreigner would intrude into the lives of Pacific islanders once the technology was available to travel safely to the region and confront those living there; for example, Brown refers to traders who had preceded his mission into the Bismarcks. It was inevitable, and missionaries were among the more benign of these intruders.

Regarding the islanders' view of these events, we can only guess at the cannibalistic New Irelanders' ideas at this distance in time. But of one thing we can be sure: they were not merely passive and thankful recipients of the word as they are sometimes portrayed in the accounts of European missionaries. The following passage from Brown's autobiography (1908:475) makes this clear:

It was on an old shed in which they worshipped; there was no light except that of the moon outside and the flickering gleam from a small fire inside the shed; the people were but very scantily dressed; the language used was an unknown one to us, and probably the speaker knew only the very rudiments of the Christian faith; but I felt that God, the Great Father of all, was there, and the feeble utterances of the old New Guinea chief brought hope and strength to one who could catch only a word or two occasionally, not sufficient indeed to indicate the tenor of the remarks, but quite enough to show that Iakopo in his own way was teaching his people the same great truths which are preached to all.

The people obviously made their own interpretations of what they heard and incorporated it to varying degrees into their own cultures. The Christian message was mediated by their own experiences, interpreted in terms of local ideas.

A pressing issue for the region is the working through of a satisfying relationship between indigenous worldviews and traditions and Christianity in its several denominational guises. It is increasingly evident that the creativity of Melanesians is finding expression, from the highlands pig kills at which Catholic fathers say mass and bless the event before the dancing begins to the church murals depicting Christ with a black skin and Pontius Pilate as a slouch-hatted *kiap* patrol officer. Many customary beliefs persist interdigitated with local Christian practices. People still entertain notions of spirits, commonly of ancestors, which can potentially interfere in the affairs of the living, and among others malevolent bush spirits which they may equate with Old Testament demons. They may manage these different sets of beliefs by juxtaposing them; New Guinea highlanders I know, for example, believe that the spirits of the dead frequent some riverside caves which they may now pass through on their way to heaven or hell. And fears of sorcery remain prominent in Melanesia, people frequently turn to church rites and prayer to protect or rid themselves of this supernatural menace.

In everyday life people strive continually to make sense of a world populated by the ghosts of the dead, other spirit forces, and the Holy Trinity. The theological outcomes are extremely varied, not only because of the kaleidoscopic variation in cultures and beliefs across the region but also because of the great variation between different churches in their ministries. The tendency for missions to compete for proselytising control over regions and divide them up into acknowledged spheres of influence has implications for this blending of religious beliefs, the response of people to the Christian message is predictably conditioned by the version preached to them. Catholics, for instance, have long had a reputation for being relatively liberal in their attitudes to pre-existing beliefs and practices, the idea being that they hide some primordial understanding of the divine which awaits awakening and mission-led recovery. Protestants of various denominations are sometimes harder on local customs, some considering them evidence of Satanic beliefs which must be swept away. George Brown illustrates attitudes to spheres of influence in his comments about the founding of missions in the Massim region (1908:467):

I soon found that there was some misunderstanding about the proposed field of our mission . . . From inquiries made, it was clear that the Louisiade, with other groups, had been offered, or rather suggested, to the Anglican Church as a suitable field, and that they had been for some time preparing to act upon that suggestion, and to undertake the work . . . and the announcement that it had been offered to and accepted by us was a great surprise to all, and a great disappointment to one of the missionaries who was preparing to visit that particular district. It will thus be seen that there were complications of no little difficulty to be dealt with, but these were happily overcome by the strong determination of all concerned, that the respective districts of the societies should be so arranged that all chances of collision or interference would be entirely prevented.

If the aim was to avoid confusing the 'poor natives' this was probably fruitless, there being several instances on record to suggest that they fully realised what was at stake and played one mission off against another to maximise their benefits.

Melanesians not only predictably interpreted the good word when they heard it according to their culturally conditioned prior understanding of the world but since the earliest mission days also supplied from their ranks a large number of missionaries who went on to preach the Gospel themselves. Like the indigenous reinterpretation of the Christian message, the contribution of these Melanesian missionaries to its spread has long been overlooked, another consequence of the Western bias and implicit racism of the region's recorded history. It is only now that historical narratives are catching up with the significant indigenous contribution to the spread of the Gospel and the social changes consequent upon its arrival. It is undeniable that these indigenous pastors and teachers greatly improved the effectiveness with which the message was taught, more readily rephrasing it in local idioms and relating it to indigenous concerns. George Brown, who relied heavily on a cadre of Fijian catechists, wrote (1908:229):

Another point which I noticed as affording valuable testimony to the wisdom of our plan of carrying out this evangelistic work principally by native teachers, was the testimony which our teachers gave me, that the natives often considered them as belonging to them, and forming part of their own community, and that they did not thieve so much from them as they formerly did, and were also very much ashamed if they were caught doing so.

Missions have long relied on faithful men and women to establish and maintain amicable relations with people, preaching and promoting their conversion to the faith. And they have always relied on local evangelists to spread the Gospel in remote, inhospitable and sometimes turbulent regions, from large numbers of Pacific islanders that the London Missionary Society stationed along the south coast of Papua in the 1870s to today's itinerant preachers appearing irregularly among sparse populations such as the Bogaia of the Strickland River.

The Melanesian missionaries not only considerably increased the rate at which Christianity spread and was adopted but also served to protect their European counterparts from the folly of some of their actions, again furthering the effectiveness of their ministries. This too has been evident from the first days. Missionaries were dependent on their assistants to guide them in very foreign environments, probably sometimes saving their lives, as Brown records (1908:133–4):

It was not until after we landed at Kalil that I learnt that the chief I scolded for being so inattentive had killed a man the day before we arrived, and at the very time I was scolding him was interested in some culinary operations which were being carried on in a house close to where we were sitting. Kaplen, one of our lads, went into a house, and saw the women engaged in roasting the thigh and leg of a man on some hot stones. He was so frightened that he would not sit down all the time we were there. I noticed this at the time, but did not know then the reason for his conduct, as I was quite unconscious of the horrible affair, though the house was only a few yards distant, and, in fact, I passed quite close to the door. I asked Kaplen why he did not tell me at the time, but I could get no reply from him. He afterwards, however, told some of the others, and they told me. He said: 'I did not tell the missionary, because I know he was such a fool that he would try and get it (the thigh and leg) away from them. Then they would be angry, and would probably kill him.'

It would not have been easy for islanders to heed the mission's work and give themselves to its service. In the early days they risked outright rejection by their communities. The Europeans, worried that they might quickly revert to their heathen ways if they remained in their home communities, often moved the most committed to proselytise elsewhere, hence the presence of Fijians in New Ireland and New Britain (where initially they were also necessary because there were no local converts to act as catechists).

The faith of indigenous missionaries is remarkable, for they have found themselves in the unenviable position of standing between and being distanced from both the European outsiders, who sometimes rather arrogantly treated them as apprentices or inferiorly trained, and the local insiders, who considered them different from themselves. It required no less bravery and fortitude to serve what they had come to believe in than it did of their European counterparts, as Brown (1908:78–80) warmly acknowledged in the following report on the address of the British Administrator to Fiji to nine volunteer teachers:

He then told them about the people – that they were great cannibals and very fierce; that the islands were very unhealthy, so that almost every one that went there suffered much from fever and ague; that food might be very scarce, and that although we might take food with us, yet it was not the food to which Fijians were accustomed. He told them that they would be left alone, without protection or support, for some months, and asked them to consider the matter, and if after hearing what had been told them they still wished to go, he would not prevent them, but would wish them Godspeed. I confess that after hearing the address by His Honour the Administrator, I felt some degree of alarm . . . Aminio Bale stood up, and with deep feeling thanked His Honour for the remarks which he had made to them . . . 'We wish also to thank Your Excellency for telling us that we are British subjects, and that you take such an interest in us, and that if we wish to remain you will take care that we are not taken from our homes in Fiji. But, sir, we have fully considered this matter in our hearts; no one has pressed us in any way; we have given ourselves up to God's work, and our mind today, sir, is to go with Mr. Brown. If we die, we die; if we live, we live.'

This is not, of course, to deny the Europeans' own courage, faith and personal sacrifice, heart-rendingly evidenced, for example, in the account of the deaths of two of the Browns' children. Considerable numbers of missionaries lost their lives violently, and many more died of tropical diseases. The historical record is clear, however, that we have to replace the image of a few courageous preachers' being responsible for the conversion of the Pacific region to Christianity with one in which they served as catalysts in a dramatic sequence of events in which Melanesians came to play a prominent part – vigorously promoting religious change, deciding according to traditional canons what to adopt, reject and modify to meet their spiritual needs in a rapidly changing world. It is evident that the spread of Christianity across the Pacific, while initiated by Europeans, was largely the result of indigenous dissemination, both formal through mission-trained personnel and informal by word of mouth among kin and friends, and that during this process various local interpretations combined to produce what is becoming a distinctive Melanesian version of Christianity.

Education and health

Although in some regards missionaries are easy targets for criticism for their sometimes high-handed interference in others' lives, we need to remember that the majority were not hypocrites but by their own lights doing good work. Many of them learnt local languages, a sign of deep commitment, and some stayed and served in Melanesia all their lives; George Brown, for instance, resided in the region for forty-eight years. Also, compared with many other newcomers they were benign and sympathetic to many local sensibilities, and people's recognition of this doubtless contributed to the rate of conversion. What one makes of their good works will vary with personal outlook and values, but in the fields of education and health they are widely believed to have done good service.

Education

Until the mid-twentieth century, education throughout Melanesia was almost exclusively the province of missions; in the 1920s an overwhelming 99.85 per cent of schools in New Guinea were mission-run. The contribution of missions to the education of new generations probably more than anything else promoted them as agents of social change. Today states run nationwide education systems, from primary through to tertiary levels, overseen by ministries of education, but many of the problems remain the same. Progressive mission teachers early questioned the appropriateness of the formal Western-modelled elementary schooling they were trying to give Pacific islanders. They asked if the teaching of skills more appropriate to everyday village life would not be more appropriate and supply a better foundation for subsequent development; in 1900, for example, the progressive Charles Abel of the London Missionary Society established in Milne Bay a school devoted to the teaching of 'industrial' skills such as furniture making and house construction. The tug-of-war between academic and applied educations continues unabated.

In Papua New Guinea, the pre-independence National Development Strategy continues to inform government education policy, which advocates the widest access to education and its redirection away from formal schooling, in the sense of awarding qualifications necessary for securing public/private sector wage-paying jobs, to equipping individuals to work in their own communities and promote local advancement. But the population does not agree with this policy, which is also strangely at odds with the nation's needs to train a skilled labour force for the national commercial economy. So long as there are opportunities to work for cash incomes people will compete, often ferociously, for the kind of education that will qualify their children for this work. It is for this reason that largely subsistence-farming families I know struggle to raise the cash to pay what for them are astronomical school fees (the 450-kina high school fee in 1997, for example, was more than many rural families' annual earned income). The parents anticipate that if their children are successful they will have increased access to the products of the capitalist marketplace and escape some of the heavy physical burdens of a subsistence-farming lifestyle.

The pressures on children, knowing the trouble to which their parents go to fund their education and seeing the demands made on the successful for payback by kin who have contributed to their fees, are enormous and here we find for the first time the alien idea of failure. I recall being told by a young lad who was in the first cohort from his community to attend primary school: 'I'm a failure, I'm an inadequate, I'm finished eh.' Children have to take daunting, unfamiliar examinations, and a proportion of them fail every year (only about 20 per cent of those who attend primary school enter secondary school). This breeds resentment of a kind that it is difficult to comprehend, given our resignation to the idea of winners and losers in a game rigged in favour of more privileged echelons of society. The anger and bitterness engendered by this 'failure' has contributed significantly to the upsurge in 'rascal' crime and violence and, increasingly, drugs abuse. We see here in sharp relief what Western educators are beginning to recognise – that it is not students who fail but the education system that fails them and society.

The education system, funded by and inevitably serving the needs of the nation-state, is contributing to the emergence of social stratification. Many of the growing pains of the new nations of Melanesia have to do with coming to terms with these changes. An intriguing question is whether they will be able to forge a fair social system. The response of those who have well-paid jobs bodes ill in this regard, for they are increasingly sending their offspring if they can afford it to the expensive international schools originally established to serve expatriate children, which are becoming their nations' Etons and Marlboroughs. They are already attempting to reproduce themselves in the next generation by ensuring their children a privileged education; the playing field is already tilted to the advantage of a few. The head start is reinforced by differences in home environments, the more advantaged having electricity, books, informed parents, and so on, which encourage educational success whereas the less advantaged live in squatter settlements or traditional bush houses and drop out of the race in large numbers at every stage. The tragedy is that these latter have not been prepared for anything, either waged work or rural life. The governments find themselves in the unenviable dilemma of having to devise an education system that both serves the demands of an emerging modern economy and a large rural population largely dependent on subsistence farming, and that is perceived to be fair. The social consequences of error could be dire.

Despite valiant government attempts to increase educational opportunities and build new schools, the high levels of population growth mean that in percentage terms they are scarcely holding their ground, let alone increasing participation. The participation rates give the education problem a further twist, with, for example in Papua New Guinea, only an estimated 70 per cent of primary-school-aged children and 15 per cent of secondary-school-aged ones attending school. Not all children even get to start the race. Levels of illiteracy are high with such non-attendance and drop-out rates, and many people are thus prevented from participating effectively in national life. The translation work on religious and other texts undertaken by missionaries and continued today by organisations such as the Summer Institute of Linguistics has from the beginning contributed significantly to the attainment of literacy by many people outside formal schools, as George Brown (1908:406–7) observed:

As soon as we were settled I began the work of translating one of the Gospels into the Duke of York language . . . It was a great joy to me when this translation work of the Gospel of St Mark, the first one which had ever been made into any of the languages or dialects of New Britain, was in the hands of the natives, and it was also a great joy to me to receive from teachers and others testimonies as to its value. Some years afterwards when I revisited New Britain I was delighted to hear

Plate 12.3 Children look up to their teacher in a rural community school (the imbalance of boys and girls is evident).

men and women and boys and girls reading the wondrous story of God's love contained in that Gospel as fluently as we ourselves can read our own Bibles. I gratefully remembered that only a few years before the alphabet of that language had never been written, nor had the Gospel ever been preached amongst those people.

This focus on literacy in local vernaculars remains a hotly debated issue in education today. Some argue that communication skills learnt in *tokples* (mother tongue) are superior to those learnt in a foreign language and that students readily transfer these skills when they start to read and write in English. But local people have not appreciated pilots of this policy when conducted in their children's community schools, believing that they represent an inferior education. This again pertains to the problem facing education of the gap between governments' policy initiatives and what the populace desires of the system.

The need for some urgent policy initiatives to address the problems of an educational system perceived to be in crisis and failing the nation is widely acknowledged. Expansion, even without serious rethinking of education provision the better to meet the country's varied needs (which implies, among other things, teacher-retraining programmes), is expensive. Funding further expansion and perhaps making changes demands

Plate 12.4 Medical services: an infant welfare clinic at Mumini village
in the then Northern District of Papua.

an increase in national income which itself requires an increasingly skilled and educated workforce. The teachers themselves are part of this salaried labour market, and increasing their numbers not only places an increased burden on public-sector financial requirements but also perpetuates the current system. Persuading them to become a cadre of subsistence producer/teachers tailoring the education they give more appropriately to the rural population implies an improbable revolution in education provision, and there is currently no evidence of the political will to push it through or of the voters' endorsing it. The country could ill afford to increase spending on its education system even if the returns in national economic terms were to suggest that it would be a good long-term investment. The assumption that the standard of education is sufficient to meet national demands for a skilled workforce in the waged sector is dubious: evidence suggests that it may be seriously declining, leaving Papua New Guinea with one of the most inefficient and expensive education systems in the world. This may supply further, eventually irresistible pressure for root-and-branch reforms of the education system to serve the entire nation's needs.

Health

The other field in which missions have long been prominent is health. Again, until the mid-twentieth century they dominated provision of health services, supplying 85 per cent of Papua New Guinea's medical facilities and training the majority of health personnel. The clinics and hospitals they established had undisputed impacts on the health of people suffering from indigenous diseases such as malaria and introduced ones such as tuberculosis, and also significantly buttressed their influence and evangelical success. Today their role is considerably less, given state-run health services extending from rural aid posts to urban hospitals controlled by ministries of health, although missions are still significant in operating clinics and hospitals across the region. Many problems stubbornly persist, however, and some have even worsened. Visitors to the region will be aware of the ominous increase in malaria with the evolution of drug-resistant strains. Respiratory disease remains frequent, with pneumonia manifesting penicillin-resistant strains, and asthma, previously unknown, is evident. Diarrhoeal diseases, which together with respiratory diseases such as tuberculosis are attributed to poor living conditions, also remain prevalent. Even the AIDS virus is now present, a banner headline in the *Post Courier* newspaper in February 1997 predicting 5,000 deaths from this source in Papua New Guinea by the year 2000.

Governments are acutely aware of these health issues and tackling them with varying success. In Papua New Guinea the aims of the National Development Strategy continue to inform health policy, the equity principles underlying it closely paralleling those behind education. But again, emergent social stratification is working against these goals, not only through an increase in expensive private health care but also through differences in education and knowledge. The issue of water supply illustrates this: few formally educated persons are unaware of the importance of clean water to health, whereas many uneducated persons are ignorant of this and therefore indifferent to attempts to improve water supplies such as the installation of drinking-water pumps. Regarding preventive medicine, where a few inexpensive steps could dramatically improve the nation's health, the problem is again lack of education; aid post orderlies give little health extension advice. It is, however, through efficiency gains at this level that governments are most likely to improve health in the future, lacking the funds to make significant inroads in alleviating sickness in other ways.

Despite the disturbing trends regarding some diseases, the health of Melanesians has improved dramatically throughout the twentieth century, the mission-initiated improvements of the colonial era continuing to the present. But this success may have sown the seeds for problems in the future by contributing to a staggering increase in population growth. In Papua New Guinea the average annual rate of population growth is estimated to be 2.8 per cent, which means a doubling of the population every twenty-five years. Currently, this is not widely perceived as a problem. The large areas still under rainforest suggest ample land for expansion, and – leaving aside biodiversity conservation issues –this might be reasonable if the population were willing to maintain a largely subsistence lifestyle. But people wish to participate in the cash economy, preferably through paid employment. It is the realisation that the economy cannot possibly supply jobs even for the majority of school-leavers, least of all for everyone, together with the association of disillusioned out-of-work youth with growing law-and-order problems, that has raised interest in the population issue. Family-planning programmes have so far met with limited success. Some of the problems originate with some missions' religious objections to birth control; others relate to conflict with cultural mores, a health care system that focuses on motherhood, scarcely any extension services on reproduction, too many male staff at a local level, and so on. All this returns us to the issue of meddling in others' lives. Assuming that medical interventions that save and extend life are benign while conceding that the demographic issue complicates matters, does it follow that this sanctions a birth-control policy to save communities from projected future problems, or is this undue interference?

Christianity and change

Christianity is the dominant world religion in Melansia, though not the only one. There are many Muslims in Irian Jaya, Islam being the official religion of Indonesia, and in 1994 the government expelled 200 largely Christian missionaries to allow other faiths to expand. In Fiji, with its large Indian population, there are many Hindus, although they too have suffered discrimination when the Melanesian led military coups of the 1980s encouraged a more vigorous imposition of Christian ways. The incorporation of Christianity into Melanesian life has contributed inestimably to change in people's world outlooks, and its association with technology's originating socioeconomic tradition has doubtless played a part in its ready adoption. How could people ignore the 'real God' when his emissaries possessed such extraordinary powers?

It is arguable that the adoption of one religion has promoted nationhood, contributing to an emergent shared identity by bringing together cultures that previously had multifarious beliefs. The reverse might also be argued – that the existence of competing missions jealously guarding their geographical spheres of influence has worked against nation building, promoting a sort of neotribalism by dividing people along denominational lines. Whatever the balance between these countervailing tendencies, missionaries' language work has contributed to the development of nationhood by building first on trade languages and subsequently on emergent *lingua franca* to promote interregional communication (for example, Frank Mihalic's founding of Word Publications and his well-known *Dictionary and Grammar of Melanesian Pidgin*). The missionaries were attentive to this possibility from the start. George Brown (1908:136) observed:

I believe that our principal difficulties in the future will arise from the great difference between the dialects, the constant feuds between the villages, and the want of authority amongst the chiefs. But as our knowledge of the language increases, we shall no doubt be able to decrease very much the number of dialects as we introduce the use of books in our schools; and the reception of the religion of Jesus will soon produce peace and order where now all is discord and confusion.

While the historical contribution of missions to nation building may be open to debate, not so the prominent part that the Christian religion has come to play in national politics. Many politicians received mission-school educations and frequently resort to religious rhetoric in their public addresses. Throughout Melanesia people use theology to give moral legitimacy to their political demands, their arguments at times being reminiscent of Latin American revolutionary theology. These trends are marked in colonial New Caledonia. The Catholic priest Apollinaise Ataba was a founder of the Kanak independence movement, preaching the equality of humankind in opposition to the French colonial regime's racist sociopolitical arrangements. The radical Father Jean-Marie Tjibaou, heir to Ataba, preached social justice and a multiracial society and resigned his priesthood when the church equivocated over decolonisation, but a more revolutionary Kanak wing assassinated him in the belief that his non-violent stance was inhibiting progress towards independence. The Protestant *Eglise Evangelique*, overwhelmingly Melanesian, has strongly supported Kanak independence since its 1979 general synod's unanimous endorsement of it, advocating non-violent action in the name of justice. In Vanuatu, the Anglican minister Walter Lini's Vanua'aku party, which subsequently formed the first independent government, invoked the Bible and Christian values in its struggle against the British and French New Hebrides' condominium administration. The party's subsequent handling of political opponents, up until its defeat in 1991, resorting to impeachment before courts and imprisonment, showed less Christian charity though typical political cynicism and opportunism. In Papua New Guinea, the evocation of Christian values played a prominent part in what was arguably the most serious political crisis yet faced by the country, the insurrection on Bougainville, besides featuring regularly in comments on the nation's many other social problems. Several prominent churchmen tried to intercede in the Bougainville crisis, including John Momis, a one-time Catholic priest turned politician, and Bishop Gregory Singkai, who though sympathetic to fellow Bougainvilleans' demands for independence abhorred the violence and payback killing provoked by the secessionists and counselled reconciliation and a peaceful solution founded on Christian tolerance and equality.

The influence of the church in politics is part of a broader trend discernible in Melanesia from the earliest missionary efforts of people's creating the version of Christianity that best meets their needs in a rapidly changing modern world. An identifiable mainstream Melanesian theology began to flower when some missions became less repressive of local beliefs and rituals originally seen as 'false' pagan religions keeping people in lives of sin. A more mature exploration of the relationship between customary beliefs and Christian faith is now evident, and the former, so long as they are not compromising of Christian principles, are sometimes represented as Melanesia's Old Testament and acquire new associations in this context. This has proceeded concurrently with Pacific churches'

acquiring greater autonomy and localising their clergy, indigenous ministers now outnumbering expatriate ones. This efflorescence of Melanesian
theology and the move from evangelical missions to islander churches is
clearly evident in the non-established churches. Cargo cults are not the
region's only home-grown response to rapid change. Well known among
the separatist churches is the Paliau movement of Manus, which teaches a
Christianity reformulated according to indigenous precepts, featuring the
theology of *wing* (breath or life-force), *wang* (the Son of God guiding from
within), and *wong* (the Holy Spirit or supernatural forces around us).
Other independent churches include the Hehela church of Buka, Abel's
Kwato church in Milne Bay, Lotu ni Dravudravua on Fiji, and the Peli
Association of the Sepik.

Perhaps, as they forge their own version of Christianity, Melanesians
will evolve something spiritual for the wider world. Focusing on disrupted
social relations' leading to sorcery, immoral behaviour's bringing down
the wrath of an ancestor spirit, or inappropriate propitiation's raising a
bush spirit's ire allows people readily to go beyond the empirical. The
spirituality which these perspectives nourish contrasts strongly with the
secularity of the West. There is a widespread perception that the so-called
First World is sinking in a self-centred materialistic mire and urgently
needs some sense of spirituality to pull it out. Perhaps there is something
to the quip that as Melanesia is now more Christian than Europe, with an
estimated 95 per cent of its population being church members, it should
redress history and send missionaries there. One area where Melanesia is
taking the lead within the world of churches is in its ecumenical movement, bringing different denominations together in a common forum
(the Melanesian Council of Churches), which is offsetting the divisive-
ness of the regional spheres of influence established by missions across
the Pacific. This healthy ecumenism reflects a central Melanesian trait
rooted in the region's rich and varied cultural heritage – the ready acceptance of diversity without the need of dominance captured in the slogan
'unity in diversity'.

Is this idea of a Pacific blossoming of spirituality a romantic miscon-
ception? There seems to be some evidence of increasing secularity,
perhaps, ironically, initiated by missionaries in replacing the cyclical
time-frame of traditional societies, in which the generations followed the
same life course, with the linear one of modern development thinking, in
which no two generations expect to share many of the same life experiences. There are Melanesian 'hollow men' and 'bigheads', alienated by
formal education from their rural roots, who pursue self-centred worldly
goals in urban areas and spurn their obligations to relatives, and there are
drop-outs who turn to 'rascalism' to pay back society and gain access to

otherwise unobtainable consumer goods. The spiritual and the secular both have something to offer in advancing our understanding of contemporary Melanesian society, and it is undeniable that the church and religion have helped people to come to terms with the social, emotional and psychological problems flowing from rapid change.

FURTHER READING

On Melanesian churches and missions see:

J. Boutilier, D. Hughes and S. Tiffany 1978 *Mission church and sect in Oceania* Ann Arbor: University of Michigan Press

G. Delbos 1985 *The mustard seed: from a French mission to a Papuan church 1885–1985*. Port Moresby: Institute of Papua New Guinea Studies

N. Gunsen 1978 *Messengers of grace: evangelical missionaries in the South Seas 1797–1860* Melbourne: Oxford University Press

D. Hilliard 1978 *God's gentlemen: a history of the Melanesian mission 1849–1942* Brisbane: Queensland University Press

C. Loeliger andf G. Trompf (eds.) 1985 *New religious movements in Melanesia* Suva: University of the South Pacific

T. Swain and G. Trompf 1995 *The religions of Oceania London*: Routledge

G. W. Trompf 1991 *Melanesian religion* Cambridge: Cambridge University Press

On missionaries see:

G. Brown 1908 *George Brown, DD: pioneer missionary and explorer, an autobiography* London: Charles Kelly

D. Langmore, 1989 *Missionary lives: Papua 1874–1914*. Honolulu: University of Hawaii Press

W. Robson 1933 *James Chalmers of New Guinea* London: Pickering and Inglis

On Melanesian Christian theology see:

J. Barker (ed.) 1990 *Christianity in Oceania: ethnographic perspectives* Association for Social Anthropology in Oceania Monograph No. 12.

C.W. Forman 1982 *The island churches of the South Pacific: emergence in the twentieth century* Maryknoll, NY: Orbis

G. Trompf (ed.) 1987 *The Gospel is not Western: black theologies from the Southwest Pacific* Maryknoll, NY: Orbis

On Duke of York Islands ethnography see:

G. Aijmer 1997 *Ritual dramas in the Duke of York Islands: an exploration of cultural imagery* Göteborg: Institute for Advanced Studies in Social Anthropology

13   From tribal to state politics

Headlines in the press regularly tell of tribal warfare in the Papua New Guinea highlands, increasingly with the devastating firepower of assault rifles, in which the police are powerless bystanders if present at all. It is an image that sits uneasily with that of an independent democratic state participating in the global political community. Papuan freedom fighters in the mountain jungles of Irian Jaya are reported to have hacked hostages to death as Indonesian troops closed in to rescue them. It is an image that distresses the Indonesian government, portraying it internationally as a repressive colonial regime. The evidence from Melanesia suggests that the transition from tribe to state is difficult, and this is expectable, for it involves accommodation to a political order based on hierarchy, centralised power and contract relations rather than equality, diffused power and kin obligations.

The emergence of nation-states where previously there were myriad stateless societies is obviously an enormous change. The nationalistic aspirations of people, initially expressed inchoately in cargo cult activity, may continue to have a parochial and bizarre side to them following their achievement of independence. But the democracies left in Melanesia by the departing colonial administrations depend critically on the understanding that their populations have of the role of central government. The ideas that some Melanesians entertain about centralised political systems and their role as voters may occasionally be somewhat inapposite. After the Australian government had granted Papua New Guinea self-government as a prelude to independence, some Southern Highlanders associated *selfguvman*, as they called it, with *developman*, thinking that both were somehow going to involve *men* arriving in their region to effect changes. The production of sophisticated electorates able to participate meaningfully in the political system will probably require generations of experience of the new order. In the meantime, people participate for unclear reasons sometimes with unrealistic objectives.

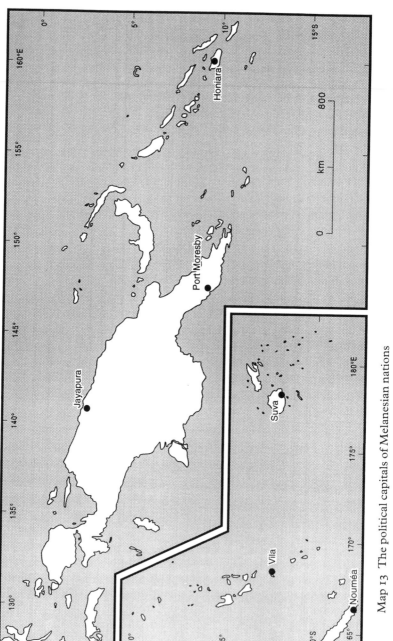

Map 13 The political capitals of Melanesian nations

Institutional barriers

The conflict between customary values, many of them carried over from tribal society, and state systems of governance may give rise to behaviours that aid donor agencies identify as institutional barriers to development. What they intend by this is obstacles to the implementation and administration of development programmes originating with governments and bureaucracies in the countries they are trying to assist. These obstacles include local practices resulting in inefficiency in the use of funds, ranging from slack accounting procedures through administrative confusion, wasted opportunities and inappropriate training of personnel, through to outright corruption and embezzlement. In an attempt to eliminate these practices, donor agencies sponsor what they call institutional-strengthening projects, which are designed to retrain national personnel and review the organisation of ministries and other public agencies with a view to restructuring them so as to improve their efficiency. These projects come under the larger objective of promoting good governance according to the values and standards of Western democracies – part of a social development agenda which includes promoting women's participation and targeting the poorest.

On one level this is expectable: when outside agencies identify shortcomings in tribally informed responses to central government – for example, when they hand over large sums of money and a considerable proportion is wasted if not stolen – they are likely to conclude that something must be done about them. On another level, however, 'institutional strengthening' might be taken as a euphemism for interference in the governmental structures of independent nations. The notion of modernisation is prominent, given the aim of making administrative structures more efficient, accountable and transparent, and some projects are but a step away from social engineering in the degree of restructuring they call for. The national staff may predictably resent the intrusion and attempt to thwart the reorganisation efforts. Some interference and restructuring is inevitable, however, if other countries' (bilateral) or international (multilateral) aid agencies are pledging large sums of money which they consider the recipient governments incapable of using effectively. The citizens of the countries donating the funds, raised via taxation, oblige them to act in this way; there is nothing more likely to raise the ire of taxpayers than news of Third World élites' siphoning off well-intentioned aid into their already fat bank accounts. If lesser developed countries' governments wish to accept assistance, they must also accept the possibility of some restructuring of their administrative arrangements.

The problems go far deeper than mere administrative arrangements, however, extending to the values and expectations according to which people arrange their lives. No amount of restructuring may stop them from figuring out ways of circumventing irksome procedures, particularly if they see no moral wrongdoing. This has promoted another donor response: increasing support for the work of non-governmental organisations (NGOs), which are considered less corrupt and more efficient than government ministries and agencies and frequently include some expatriates on their staffs to oversee the work and ensure some observance of Western ethics of accountability. In Papua New Guinea, for example, there are several NGOs working on forest conservation and biodiversity issues, combining these concerns with development initiatives and thus promoting sustainable exploitation of forest resources far more effectively than the Ministry of Forests. In the Collingwood Bay region Greenpeace is organising the production of barkcloth decorated with indigenous designs for sale commercially. The Research and Conservation Foundation in the Crater Mountain region is experimenting with the production of a variety of traditional artifacts made from forest materials, from war shields to net bags, for the market. And the Individual and Community Rights Advocacy Forum concerns itself with human rights in various fields including logging policy. A possible long-term problem, if current trends in South Asia are any guide, is the promotion of well-funded and influential but unelected bureaucracies within nominally democratically elected but, from the perspective of the average citizen's welfare, highly inefficient nation-states. This use of donor moneys not only bypasses government rigidities and inefficiencies but also may undermine democracy itself.

There are currently two principal kinds of polity in Melanesia – the colonies, Irian Jaya and New Caledonia, and the newly independent states, which range from the volatile democracies of Papua New Guinea, Vanuatu and the Solomons to Fiji's previous military regime. It is illuminating to compare and contrast the problems each experiences as they struggle to govern their tribal populations.

Independence movements – the Kanaks in New Caledonia and the Organsasi Papua Merdeka (OPM) in Irian Jaya – predictably characterise the colonies. Neither is particularly effective in the face of firm state control with vigorous policing and a strong military presence. The colonial administrations have so far proved very efficient at maintaining social order and containing any protest, attributing unrest to a few dissidents. In independent Papua New Guinea, in contrast, unrest is all too evident. Politics, while democratically regulated, is no longer a matter of competing ideologies (right-wing colonial versus left-wing independence) but a game of opportunism in which politicians vie for office by supporting

Plate 13.1 In the capital: the Papua New Guinea Parliament building at Waigani, designed to reflect the country's traditional architectural heritage.

whatever coalition of interests within Parliament seems most likely to offer them ministerial or other prizes and access to a large budget – some of which they may proceed to use to bolster their standing with their supporters. Those left out will struggle to bring down governments in votes of no confidence, hoping to secure something for themselves as a new coalition that can command a majority emerges phoenix-like from the ashes on the floor of the House. This is a traditional response to the new political system and the opportunities it offers. Meanwhile, the people, who see little of the largesse, become increasingly sceptical of the political system and its merits.

Corruption

Bribery is commonplace in Indonesia at almost every level of society. It is so pervasive that it is almost institutionalised as an aspect of people's incomes; indeed, to call it corruption seems inappropriate, for it is expected and accepted. At the higher echelons of society it is more concealed and difficult to assess, but one of the charges of the OPM is that a large proportion of the profits from the Tembagapura mine is finding its

Plate 13.2 In the provinces: the West Sepik Provincial Government offices largely occupying the dilapidated buildings of the departed Australian colonial administration.

way to Jakarta, some of it going into the bank accounts of ruling families. Bribes have also come to feature in the Indonesian government's dealings with Papua New Guinea, with politicians sympathetic to the regime receiving gifts and money to fund their political activities. Acceptance of these bribes reflects the explosion of corrupt activity in Papua New Guinea. The country is reckoned to be an accountable democracy accepting overseas aid on these terms, and corruption is seen as a major perverter of assistance. Here bribery is not an accepted part of the social fabric, but gift giving is, and the way in which some corrupt activities divert resources into kin networks and local communities resonates with exchange behaviour.

The provincial government initiative has foundered on the rocks of gross incompetence which allowed corruption to flourish. The provincial governments were established to accommodate the centralised political system better to the enormous sociocultural variety of Papua New Guinea by delegating several government responsibilities and functions to the provinces, in line with the call for 'unity in diversity'. It was argued that extending some autonomy to the provinces would help contain and offset demands for secession – no mere imaginary worry, as the events in Bougainville attested. One consequence was a large increase in the number of politicians making demands on the public purse to defray both constitutionally legitimate expenses and others, although, as Dorney (1993:179) observes: 'In a country that speaks 700 languages, perhaps 700 politicians is not such a bad answer.' During the 1980s something like half of the provincial governments were suspended for financial mismanagement and misappropriation.

The Sandaun (West Sepik) provincial government was suspended in 1987 when investigations by the Auditor-General's Office revealed accumulated debts of millions of kina. Illegal financial transactions were uncovered in the appallingly kept accounts, including illicit loans to members of the Provincial Assembly and transactions that financed the leisure activities of politicians and their staff. A safe in the provincial government's offices in Vanimo even contained rifled pay packets. Not all the losses were due to corruption; some of them were the result of incompetence. The provincial government's development corporation Westdeco not only lost everything invested in it but also was sued by an Australian company for more than A$1 million for breach of contract as guarantor of an agreement to lease logging equipment. Having retained the services of its former legal officer as a private defence lawyer for a fee nearly five times his public servant's salary, the provincial government strangely failed to file any defence. The Clifford Report of the mid-1980s suggested that some lack of accountability might be attributable to cultural barriers, people being used to marking obligations in public events such as ceremonial exchanges rather than keeping private written records.

The logging business is notorious for promoting corruption. In more colourful language than one normally associates with dry government investigations, the Barnett Report's (Asia-Pacific Action Group 1990:5) findings are damning:

It would be fair to say, of some of the companies, that they are now roaming the countryside with the self-assurance of robber barons; bribing politicians and leaders, creating social disharmony and ignoring laws in order to gain access to, rip out, and export the last remnants of the province's valuable timber. These companies are fooling the landowners and making use of corrupt, gullible, and unthinking politicians. It downgrades Papua New Guinea's sovereign status that such rapacious foreign exploitation has been allowed to continue with such devastating effects to the social and physical environment, and with so few positive benefits.

The investigation catalogues corruption and environmental despoliation on a grand scale. In the space of a decade the forests of New Ireland, for example, had been so damaged by reckless logging that the commission warned of the resource's total destruction and recommended a moratorium on timber exports:

The New Ireland timber industry is out of control and has blighted the hopes of landowners and devastated a valuable timber resource for very little gain to the people or government of Papua New Guinea . . . bribery, corruption, and the buying of support have become so widespread that they have become a major social sickness. (1990:19)

The corruption encouraged by the Asian loggers, some of them working for subsidiaries of well-known multinational companies, fills many pages of the report (which runs to twenty volumes). One of the more bizarre cases catalogued concerns former New Ireland provincial premier Robert Seeto, who wrote letters to the Malaysian Sia brothers in a strange code requesting numbers of 'cabbages' and 'apples' for himself and others to fund personal jaunts and election expenses in return for releasing logging concessions and other political favours. It transpired that a 'cabbage' was 1,000 kina and an 'apple' 100 kina. Barnett observed: 'Political leaders who have become aware that timber companies were making secret profits by transfer pricing should have taken steps to expose and stop these abuses. Instead, however, some latched on like leeches to get a share for themselves' (1990:22).

Transfer pricing is one of the illegal ways in which logging companies conspire to increase their profits at the expense of local people's royalties and Papua New Guinea's tax revenues. It involves declaring a sale price for exported logs far lower than the real market price and subsequently recouping the difference via a subsidiary company farther along the marketing chain and thus secretly transferring profits offshore. Another practice to disguise real profits is listing highly valuable species as less valuable ones or classifying them under the cheaper catch-all 'mixed species'. The rogue logging companies and their national politician partners conspired to cheat local landowners out of an estimated A$10 per cubic metre of timber exported, taking illegal profits in excess of 10 million kina. As Barnett puts it: 'A combination of natural greed and dire domestic financial necessity drove them to cut into landowner company's profits by unlawful deductions involving fraud and forgery in such an unrestrained way as to be actually obscene.'

The damage to the natural environment has been extensive, with over-cutting to such an extent that in places it has virtually removed the forest canopy, clear-felling of slopes, with dramatic loss of soil, the deforesting of the margins of streams which therefore dry or silt up, and the destruction of ecological communities. This resource destruction is accompanied by social problems as communities try to come to terms with the pillage of their territories, for which they have received little in return compared with the benefits they had imagined (see chapter 9). 'An elderly New Ireland landowner discussing a "timber war" between land-owner groups backed by rival foreign contractors warned that, when the foreigners had departed with the logs, the rival and now hostile land-owner groups would be left still trying to live together – because they had nowhere else to go' (1990:18). Elsewhere Barnett observed 'disillusioned and bewildered people pondering over how their expectations of development had failed to be realised and squabbling over money "leaking" from trust accounts' (1990:23).

Since the investigation scarcely anything has changed. The findings of massive abuse of power clearly shook the government, and some members of the cabinet tried to suppress them. Judge Barnett was stabbed, almost fatally, outside his Port Moresby home. Many of those named in the report continue to hold office, and no politicians have been prosecuted. In fact, much of the evidence uncovered against them was destroyed in a suspicious fire at the Anti-Corruption Squad's offices or allegedly stolen in a burglary at the Ombudsman's Commission. According to the Asia-Pacific Action Group (1990:58):

The Commission of Inquiry shows clearly that the timber industry in Papua New Guinea is effectively unpoliceable, inherently corrupt and beyond reform. As in so many other countries, the government gives the appearance of controlling what is effectively out of control; forestry policy amounts to no more than window dress-ing for free market anarchy. It is vital that those endorsing and encouraging the timber industry, in particular the multilateral aid agencies, realise that the prob-lems cannot be solved through more monitoring, administrative restructuring and incentives to companies. The problems arise from the huge sums of money to be made from the 'once only cut' and from the system based on tendering conces-sions to competing companies. Destroyed lives, social disintegration, and cultural and biological extinction, are, by any value system, too high a cost for having one's country plundered by foreign companies.

The Asia-Pacific Action Group is one of several NGOs seeking action to curb the practices so vividly documented in the Barnett Report. In Papua New Guinea, the National Alliance of Non-Government Organisations, which includes all the major development and environ-ment groups and the Melanesian Council of Churches, is pressing for a ban on all log exports given the continuation of the abuses revealed by the Barnett inquiry. It is one of the first instances of NGOs' combining to take on a government that is failing to represent the people who elected it to office.

The forestry business can only be described as development run amok, and clearly no amount of participatory rural appraisal and research into indigenous knowledge relating to forest use and conservation or any other such techniques are going to have any impact on such pervasive corruption and fraud. And yet to label the behaviour of some Papua New Guinean politicians greed-motivated fraud seems to miss something about it; the use to which these people put their ill-gotten gains has a customary side to it. In his bizarre letters, Premier Seeto also regularly requested donations to 'Lucy', which turned out to be the People's Progress party, demanding several vehicles and tens of thousands of kina. It is the fate of such payments that is intriguing: a considerable proportion of them find their way back into local communities as politicians like Seeto seek to convince voters that they should be returned to office. These *grisim* (grease) payments to electorates are a common feature of Papua New Guinea political life, to such an extent that governments talk openly about 'slush funds', allowances made to the Members of Parliament under special budgetary appropriations such as the Village Economic Development Fund for the express purpose of funding local development initiatives. The impetus behind them is illustrated in the comments of one MP during a debate on politicians' salaries:

When people elect me to Parliament, they think I own the Bank of PNG. People demand you buy them motor vehicles or give them money because they have been your campaign managers or cast their votes in your favour. They demand you produce K10,000 and buy them a car . . . People have this kind of mentality that when we become MPs, we inherit wealth. (Dorney 1993:54–5)

One of the more extravagant 'greasing' displays was made by the late deputy prime minister Iambakey Okuk, who before the 1982 national elections staged a distribution of beer in Kundiawa to his Simbu Highlands electorate. Decked out in traditional bird-of-paradise headdress and standing on a platform of beer cartons, he gave away 4,000 cases of lager, but he lost the election nevertheless.

Elections

The issue which dominates the thinking of voters during an election is the development of their region. This was so in the 1977 and 1997 Papua New Guinea elections, and comparison of the two campaigns reveals some intriguing trends and underlines the conflict which attends the change from tribal to state polity. Many people have only the haziest idea of what they are doing in an election or why. When asked what they think an MP does, a disconcerting number of people reply that they do not really know except that he has some responsibility for encouraging economic development. It is often women who reply in this vein, and this accords with the realities of everyday life; women play a small role in politics and, because their influence is indirect, express less open interest. But haziness on this subject is not restricted to ordinary people. Constitutional lawyers have also been unable to keep up with the torrent of reforms enacted by legislators, with the result that no one is certain of the legality of the 1997 elections (which some think should have been preceded by a national census to compile electoral rolls). The cynical suggest that this confusion was a deliberate political ploy – that it was the aim of incumbents, more than half of whom expected to lose their seats, to have the elections declared invalid. Many voters think that in an election they are 'marking' someone to promote their interests with the powers that be in Port Moresby. The person 'marked' goes to meetings to persuade those with the knowledge, resources and money to initiate development projects in their home region so that their constituents can earn money and spend it to improve their standard of living. When explaining what an MP does, people sometimes draw an explicit parallel with sociopolitical exchange, in which a man needs to speak out strongly and argue well to secure the wealth he wants.

The ideas which candidates hold about the duties of an MP mirror those of the electorate; they think that their job is to encourage economic development in their home regions. While the candidates' backgrounds vary in detail, they tend to have some particulars in common. By the standards of their home regions, they are those most experienced in Western ways; they are the best educated, the most experienced in salaried occupations, and the most experienced in government and in projects of economic development. This experience seems a prerequisite for standing in a national election not only because without it a person would be unlikely to venture into such an enterprise but also because the electorate considers persons having it best qualified for the job. People say that they need to 'mark' someone who is not intimidated by strangers and therefore will not be afraid to speak out strongly in meetings and so win the best for those he represents.

It is usual for large numbers of candidates to nominate themselves. They give a variety of reasons for this, depending on their political sophistication, but in the opinion of many voters it is the lure of an astronomical income that prompts so many to stand for election. News of corruption is giving rise to cynicism at the grass roots; many people are coming to believe that an election is a lottery and all candidates are self-interested and greedy. When asked why they bother to vote, some people in rural areas reply that it is out of fear of imprisonment if they do not have a good excuse such as illness or incapacity. While the money is important to candidates, it would be incorrect to think that that was all. Ambition is important too, although given the egalitarian ethos of traditional tribal polities, candidates attempt to avoid the appearance of seeking personal advancement. It is interesting that at this interface between the old and the new, an elected official may spend his income on sociopolitical exchange rather than personal consumption (for example, buying pigs or beer and distributing widely).

In election campaigns politicians try to hide their ambition behind a facade of concern for improving the lives of those they represent. But nearly everyone realises that candidates stand for election to further their own advancement by gaining access to Western ways and goods, and their efforts to appear altruistic strike many as not only ridiculous but also infuriating. Candidates rarely try to appeal to their electorates on ideological grounds by expressing support for policies which would promote some persons' interests over those of others. There are currently no such clearly defined interest groups, but there is evidence of nascent political ideologies centring on the issue of corruption; for example, the Melanesian Alliance campaigned heavily on the theme of honest politics in 1997. Without these ideological concerns the need to campaign all but evaporates. While all candidates refer to the need for economic development and clean politics, no one has a radically different agenda. Furthermore, people are generally so ill-informed about Papua New Guinea's political parties that any campaign along these lines would be a waste of time.

Candidates travel around their districts to let people, as they say, 'see their faces', on the assumption that if they are 'happy' with what they see and hear they will 'mark' them in the election. If they push themselves forward with too much talk about what they plan to do this can make a poor impression; it is considered unseemly for a successful man to sing his own praises. They may appeal to this egalitarian ethic in their campaign speeches by stressing the need for equal shares in the fruits of development for all. Some MPs attempt to continue to live according to these egalitarian ideals, distributing resources far and wide, and point out in their campaigns that they have not spent their incomes on themselves but distributed it. This approach to electoral politics is interesting for the way it attempts to blend traditional requirements with those of an elected representative, manipulating the office to many people's advantage. Sitting MPs also try to promote themselves by referring to recent developments in their districts as evidence of their success, although frequently they have played no part in these projects. If they make any extravagant promises (*tok gris* in Pidgin) they are likely to appear to be trying to hoodwink voters.

Seeing faces and forming opinions about character are important when

Plate 13.3 An Anga woman casts her vote at one of the many mobile
booths used in Papua New Guinea's national elections.

there is little else on which people can make a reasoned choice. Without
radically different views to present, the candidates face a difficult task if
they are to win a considerable percentage of the votes. The faces of candidates are well known in the areas where they live, and rivals are hard
pressed to usurp their votes; people calculate that the nearer to their home
the MP lives the more likely it is that any distribution of his largesse will
reach them, and they expect him to favour his home area in pushing for
development projects. Aspiring politicians concentrate on places where
their support is ensured by virtue of residence or, where several candidates live close to one another, trespass into one another's strongholds in
the hope of swinging the vote. The parochial nature of campaigning and
voting, clear in the 1977 election, had twenty years later taken an
unhealthy turn. Candidates may urge their supporters to see that no one
in their home areas defects to someone else, and many people fear that if
they do not support their nearest local candidate they will be found out
when the votes are counted and threatened with violence. An editorial in
the *Post Courier* commenting on the 1997 election lamented: 'Violence
stems from political rivalry that is often encouraged by those running for
public office . . . In the country today, there is this sad situation where
aspiring public office holders, in their bid to secure support, use muscle

Plate 13.4 Armed men involved in the insurrection on Bougainville, where central government authority collapsed.

and encourage their followers to ensure by force that no one else enters their area of support.' The prizes if elected are so desirable that violence is becoming a commonplace feature of politics; several politicians now employ armed bodyguards.

Whatever the campaign strategy, the proportion of votes won by a successful candidate tends to be small, partly because of the large number of candidates standing in any election. The primary consideration for voters is to support the candidate who lives nearest to them, provided that the person seems to have the required knowledge and experience. The distribution of voting returns confirms this parochialism.

The relatively even distribution of votes between candidates in many districts results in some close races, and with only a fraction of the votes those elected cannot say that they have the confidence of the majority. A proper understanding of the role of government in the nation and of elections in the democratic process will only come slowly as future generations receive formal education, but even if voters were better informed it is doubtful they would vote any differently. They ask themselves who is going to help them most and, having no other yardstick, settle for the nearest neighbour. In this they follow to some extent their traditional way of doing things, judging others on the basis of personal knowledge, and some decline to vote because they do not know any of the candidates. Voters behave in the only way which makes sense to them, given the scant political differences between candidates and limited knowledge of the governmental process. Parochialism can work against everyone's interests. Serious outbreaks of violence have occurred following elections in Papua New Guinea, for example, with people starting fights when their candidates have lost. Yet a country is fortunate if it has no more serious divisions than this.

Law and order

The dramatic upsurge in violence since independence adds further to the perception that the state is in crisis. The events on Bougainville feed the international image of a nation on the edge of anarchy. The burgeoning of violent criminal activity under the catch-all term 'rascalism' is taken as evidence of the inability of the state to maintain order and suggests that a sizeable percentage of the population is contemptuous of government and its laws. People's perception of politicians as rogues feeds this contempt for state institutions and fuels voters' demands for benefits in return for their continued support. Some criminals are described as Melanesian Robin Hoods for targeting the wealthy and the banks – a romantic image that misrepresents their activities but reflects the expectation of equality central to a stateless polity. The violence too is consistent with acephalous politics, a feature of which is the physical conflict epitomised by incessant tribal warfare.

Another common reason for violence is 'payback', or revenge, which is common in stateless societies around the world. Here people believe that if someone injures or kills a relative, they have a moral right to seek vengeance on that person or his kin unless they receive adequate compensation for the wrong. Punishing killers, rapists, and the like with prison sentences and then allowing them to go free is unacceptable. The persistence of payback killing reflects dissatisfaction with the new, alien legal regime rather than a reaction to the new economic order.

The countrys' legal codes rest on Western ideas of jurisprudence inherited from the colonial authorities, and these may be inappropriate to Melanesian nations. The passage of legislation outlawing sorcery in Papua New Guinea illustrates well the gulf between Western and Melanesian notions of justice. The Sorcery Act is part of a body of legislation enacted since independence to modify the legal code in ways thought by politicians more appropriate to Papua New Guinea society. Another change is the restoration of the death penalty, and during the debate over the bill several prominent politicians, including the first prime minister,

Michael Somare, who had recently lost a close relative in a violent incident, argued passionately that exacting a life for a life was the Melanesian
way. A Law Reform Commission conducts research to assist the government in the formulation of legal policy, but the changes so far have
amounted to little more than tinkering with the inherited English legal
model with all of its cultural assumptions. The one-time Supreme Court
judge Bernard Narokobi observed: 'While some significant reforms have
already taken place, the legal system is still essentially a (British) common
law one, with some legislative, and to a lesser degree some judicial recognition of customary law . . . law embodies the natural law perceptions of
Englishmen, via Queensland and imposed upon Melanesians in Papua
New Guinea' (1989:7 and 12). But is it realistic to expect anything more
than tinkering? Is a fundamental Melanesian-informed restructuring of
the legal system feasible? Could a modern nation-state encompass tribal
notions of dispute management, or are today's law-and-order problems
part of the painful process of assimilation of small decentralised societies
into the nation-state, a transitory phase of adjustment as opposed to the
evolution of some entirely new sociopolitical order?

Whatever answers the future holds to these questions, criminal violence poses considerable problems for contemporary society. The political and social contrast could hardly be greater than between the
independent democracies of the South-West Pacific, where we find
rampant corruption, lawlessness and violence, and the remaining colonies, where we find reassuring order and everyday security, albeit with
underlying political unrest. This poses what until recently would have
been an unthinkable proposition for liberal intellectuals and democratic
politicians – that the colonial state may have some redeeming features.
This is a suggestion supported by the turmoil experienced in several
former colonial states around the world, and it is a view voiced by several
of my Wola friends, who frequently comment that when the Australian
colonial officers were in authority those were the 'good times'.

Tribal and state politics, as we have seen, are based on antithetical principles, but the assumption is that the state, preferably democratic, is the
better or at any rate the inevitable way forward. We have consequently
forced the centralised state onto tribal people from colonial times to the
present. Some conflict is inevitable as the two systems collide. In hindsight, would it be better to admit that, as the state has to be imposed, it
would be more in the interests of the majority of citizens for this to be
done by those with the necessary experience of central government political and bureaucratic traditions until the emerging nation is firmly
embedded in one of the evolving global mega-states? Is it racist to suggest
that people with tribal heritages have trouble adapting to state regimes, or

is it a pragmatic appraisal of current events? It would seem that some nations in Melanesia and elsewhere have been encouraged, even obliged, to rush into independence before they were appropriately and adequately prepared to handle the stresses of the tribal-to-state transformation. Some argue that the 1970s Labour Government in Australia, in a fit of conscience – colonialism being ideologically incompatible with its liberal socialism – promoted a rapid and ill-considered withdrawal from Papua New Guinea and transfer of power before the country was adequately prepared to govern itself centrally through a state bureaucracy (up until that time the intention had been to grant independence over a longer period and there had consequently been no long-term preparations for the transfer). This set a precedent, and the politically active in the Solomon Islands and the New Hebrides pressed for independence too and likewise found a compliant Labour Government in the United Kingdom only too willing to relinquish the ignominy of colonialism; the French were somewhat reluctant in Vanuatu, and their attitude contributed to the instigation of a rebellion on the island of Espiritu Santo, said to have been supported by foreigners, which was put down with the assistance of troops from newly independent Papua New Guinea in an act of Melanesian brotherhood.

These contentious observations do not obviate the problems and injustices that attend colonial regimes; they simply put them in a different perspective. Similar problems plague both Irian Jaya and New Caledonia, the South-West Pacific's two remaining colonies. In both, the colonial authorities have overseen massive immigration that has reduced the indigenous populations to minorities with diminished voices. The French authorities have promoted immigration into New Caledonia for over a century, starting with penal colony deportations and continuing today to welcome new European settlers, and Asians and other Pacific peoples, notably Wallis Islanders, to the point that immigrants make up nearly three-fifths of the population. The Indonesian authorities have changed the composition of Irian Jaya's population through their transmigration programme – moving many landless peasants, predominantly Javanese, to migrant settlements, where they are given farm land, until they make up nearly one-half of the population. Both colonies also have large mines which contribute significantly to their gross domestic products, copper in Irian Jaya and nickel in New Caledonia. The local Melanesian populations find little employment in them – indeed, little employment anywhere in the formal sector except as menial domestic servants and labourers – the majority of them live as subsistence farmers, selling a little produce or occasional labour. The resentment they feel, particularly in New Caledonia, is considerable, but being outnumbered in their own countries puts them at a substantial disadvantage. The only independent Melanesian nation to inherit a similar situation was Fiji, where it led to military coup and imposition of unrepresentative rule as the indigenous Melanesian population sought to assert its birthright over the more numerous Asians.

In Irian Jaya, the threat of Javanese numerical dominance is recent and many Melanesians continue to live isolated tribal lives largely unaware of its political implications. A small proportion are politically aware, among them many of those living around the massive Tembagapura copper mine and those living in urban areas like Jayapura, who have received some formal education and resent Indonesian political domination. Some of these people are active members of the OPM, the only prominent organ-isation opposing Indonesian colonial rule in the country, although as an illegal organisation it is very restricted in its activities and the military quickly extinguishes any overt armed resistance. If the Indonesian regime continues to pursue its present policies, of which it gives every sign, the OPM is unlikely to have any significant political impact in the foreseeable future, lacking substantial international support. The newly arrived Javanese immigrants are a largely docile population, as are the majority of Melanesian tribals, and while there are some racial tensions these show no signs of becoming serious as yet.

The situation on New Caledonia is quite different, with serious racial differences and aggression, particularly between the indigenous Kanak population and French immigrants. The struggle against the colonial authorities has a considerable history with opposition organisations ranging from the early movements such as the Union Calédonnienne, campaigning for autonomy from France, to political parties such as the Front de Libération Nationale Kanak et Socialiste, campaigning for an independent Kanaky nation. The French metropolitan authorities have tried various ploys to reduce demands for independence, among them a programme to return some alienated land to Kanak reservations and the promise of a referendum on self-determination, which the Kanak minor-ity is unlikely to win in the near future. These offers have invariably been too little too late, however, reflecting the French authorities' largely inflexible position regarding New Caledonia as an overseas territory, which it intends to continue to govern as evidence of its world-power status further signalled by its deeply unpopular Polynesian nuclear bomb testing programme. The position is further complicated by the demo-graphic composition of New Caledonia. On one side, the European set-tlers are threatening violence if there is any move towards independence; this is the position, for example, of the right-wing Rassemblement pour la Calédonie dans la République party, and it is reinforced by the arrival of settlers from other former French colonies, who see New Caledonia as their last chance to maintain the *colon* lifestyle somewhere on the globe and are organising militias to fight for it. On the other side, the Kanaks are threatening violence if there is no move towards independence; increasingly frustrated at being treated as second-class citizens in their own country, pushed onto marginal land and excluded from full participation in society, they are increasingly advocating violence to drive the foreigners, including the *caldoche* French families of several generations, off their island and reclaim their rightful heritage.

The people of Melanesia have governed themselves adequately for thousands of years according to tribally instituted political conventions, but many today are critical of the centralised political systems that have usurped them. The thoughtful worry about the future. They realise that they cannot turn the clock back to pre-contact tribal times, but where, they ask, are they going? It is hazardous to predict, but two opposing scenarios have been mooted.

In the first scenario, the internal situation in newly independent nations such as Papua New Guinea will continue to worsen and they will slide towards chaos, anarchy and political fragmentation. In desperation some politicians will call on an outside power to help them restore order. The neighbour likely to oblige, having the military capacity and political will to intervene decisively, is expansionist Indonesia, so long as the international climate, and notably the United States, allows it to do so. Some senior politicians and military officers already have personal relationships with their opposite numbers in Indonesia; that they might seek assistance there if they perceived that their country was out of their control is not unrealistic. The Papua New Guinea government hired an internationally recruited mercenary army in early 1997 to assist in putting down the insurrection in Bougainville, amid strong international condemnation. An appeal for military assistance would be the country's equivalent of a military coup, which its own armed forces, demoralised, ill-equipped and undisciplined, and ideologically disinclined to try to govern the country, are unlikely to mount. The events of March 1997, which brought the country to the brink of political chaos, confirm this view. Popular anger, expressed in rioting and looting, at the government's spending millions on mercenaries resulted in some ministers stepping down. Once an outside power had re-established order it would find it difficult to extricate itself, certainly in the short term, without further chaos and would be tempted to stay. The upshot would be the reinstatement of a colonial regime with all its implications.

In the second scenario, the independent states pass through who knows what stages of turmoil and civil dislocation until they develop some notion of central government which incorporates values from their tribal political heritage well enough to be acceptable to their populations. In this view, the states need their independence, however chaotic life may appear, to experiment and evolve their own tribal democratic state. This represents entirely new ground for political theory and practice. It is debatable whether such a synthesis is feasible. If it is, these Melanesian political adjustments may have something profound to teach the world about fairness and equality within democracies. It is perhaps not fanciful to suggest that those imbued with tribal values of equality and political power for all will evolve something unique as they struggle to accommodate to the global world order.

FURTHER READING

On electoral politics in Papua New Guinea see:

D. G. Bettison, C. A. Hughes and P. W. van der Veur 1965 *The Papua New Guinea elections, 1964* Canberra: Australian National University Press

A. L. Epstein, R. S. Parker and M. Reay (eds.) 1971 *The politics of independence* Canberra: Australian National University Press

D. Hegarty (ed.) 1983 *Electoral politics in Papua New Guinea* Port Moresby: University of Papua New Guinea Press

P. King (ed.) 1989 *Pangu returns to power: the 1982 elections in Papua New Guinea* Canberra: Australian National University

M. Oliver (ed.) 1989 *Eleksin: the 1987 national election in Papua New Guinea* Port Moresby: University of Papua New Guinea Press

Y. Saffu (ed.) 1996 *The 1992 PNG election* Canberra: Australian National University

D. Stone (ed.) 1976 *Prelude to self-government* Canberra: Australian National University Press

M. Turner and D. Hegarty 1987 *The 1987 national elections in Papua New Guinea* Australian Institute of International Affairs Occasional Paper No. 6

E. Wolfers and A. Regan 1988 *The electoral process in Papua New Guinea: a handbook of issues and options* Waigani: Institute of Applied Social and Economic Research

Also see:

W. A. Axline 1993 *Governance in Papua New Guinea: approaches to institutional reform* Waigani: NRI/INA Discussion Paper

A. Clunies Ross and J. Langmore (eds.) 1973 *Alternative strategies for Papua New Guinea* Oxford: Oxford University Press

S. Dorney 1993 *Papua New Guinea: people, politics, and history since 1975* Sydney: Random House

P. Fitzpatrick 1980 *Law and state in Papua New Guinea* London: Academic Press

C. Moore and M. Kooyman (eds.) 1998 *Papua New Guinea political chronicle 1967–91* Bathurst: Crawford House Publishing

H. Nelson 1974 *Papua New Guinea: black unity or black chaos?* Ringwood: Penguin

M. Spencer, A. Ward and J. Connel (eds.) 1988 *New Caledonia: essays in nationalism and dependency* St Lucia: University of Queensland Press

M. Turner 1990 *Papua New Guinea: the challenge of independence* Ringwood: Penguin

A. Wanek 1996 *The state and its enemies in Papua New Guinea* Richmond: Curzon Press

On corruption and forestry see:

Asia-Pacific Action Group 1990 *The Barnett report: a summary of the report of the commission of inquiry into aspects of the timber industry in Papua New Guinea* Hobart, Tasmania

FILMS

Ileksen Pacific Video-Cassette Series No. 6
Tukana: Husat I asua Pacific Video-Cassette Series No. 8

14 Custom and identity

The speed of social change in the South-West Pacific produces a certain apprehension in its people. Increasingly perplexed about who they are and where they are going, they tend to cling to certain traditional ways or even sometimes to rediscover or reinvent them. It is common to hear people describing this trend in terms of *kastom*, which, while it derives from the English word 'custom', like many other Pidgin terms has its own distinctive Melanesian meaning and connotations. Indeed, the word highlights some of the ambiguities that characterise modern Melanesia's accommodation to the global imperative, being a claim to cultural continuity expressed in a *lingua franca* which testifies historically to the magnitude of the cultural intrusions that have prompted its very emergence. In the precolonial era, the Melanesians' ancestors had no awareness of 'custom', the category that is used today to capture something of that past, externalising and objectifying culture as never before. While *kastom* appears to exemplify persistence, it is in fact a response to enormous social change, it relates the old to the new and is a paradoxical blend of convention and invention.

When people talk about *kastom*, they have in mind something which we can gloss as traditional lore, that is, practices that originate in their own cultural tradition and are rooted in their value system as opposed to deriving from elsewhere. It is understandably an ambiguous notion, given the cultural variability that characterises the Melanesian region and the differing historical experiences of connection with the outside world; like Melanesian ideas in general it evades any straightforward exegesis and demands sympathetic, sometimes multilayered and even contradictory contextual interpretation. People want the best of both worlds – access to cash and material prosperity without the loss of culture and customary rights – and therefore *kastom* is riddled with contradictions. Sometimes it is used locally, sometimes regionally, and occasionally at the national level to differentiate neighbours and strangers (ranging from speakers of the same language living in adjacent communities to one-time enemies and from expatriate workers to tourists), to demarcate boundaries, to lay claim to rights and to assert cultural autonomy. It often features cultural revivalism and reclamation and sometimes involves idealisation of the pre-colonial past (see chapter 11). Here it finds parallels in the ideas of cultural revival that have featured in Asian and African nationalist struggles and likewise invites interpretation as symbolic discourse expressing anti-colonial and more recently, anti-state sentiments. It contrasts with and may be defined in opposition to other alien Pidgin-labelled categories such as *gavman* (government), *loa* (law), *lotu* (church) and *bisnis* (business).

Identity and *kastom*

The pursuit of *kastom* is part of the search for identity in the contemporary world. Similar pursuits seem to occupy many populations today, and research into identity is a prominent anthropological theme. This marks a shift of theoretical focus over the past two decades or so away from theories centring on social structure, featuring the documentation of normatively conditioned behaviour contributing to the orderly continuance of society, to theories involving social process, attempting to incorporate individual actors' behaviours and ideas into social models as these make up the abstraction we call society. In the Melanesian region the emergence of the concept of personhood has marked this shift. It asserts that the members of any society, born and socialised into a predominantly kinship defined social network, create and constantly redefine their social identities through their interactions within this set of moral relationships – contributing to sociopolitical exchange, participating in disputes, assisting with productive tasks. According to this view persons are situated within a kin web which conditions the behaviour that contributes to their social identity, particularly, in Melanesia, as informed by the morality of the gift between relatives. The Melanesian person contrasts with the Western individual, who interacts more frequently with strangers in terms of the profit morality of the marketplace. There is nothing exceptionable in this view of persons versus individuals, which is largely a restatement of a long-held anthropological position dating back to Maine's distinction between status (kinship) and contract (market).

An intriguing point of further difference is that in stateless societies such as the tribal polities of Melanesia, persons have a large degree of individual autonomy within the broad and fluid constraints of their predominantly kin-constructed social environments. This autonomy facilitates a Melanesian sociopolitical individualism involving the exchange of gifts within a markedly egalitarian social order, in sharp contrast to the socioeconomic individualism of the West, where strangers meet in market contexts and trade commodities within a markedly hierarchical social

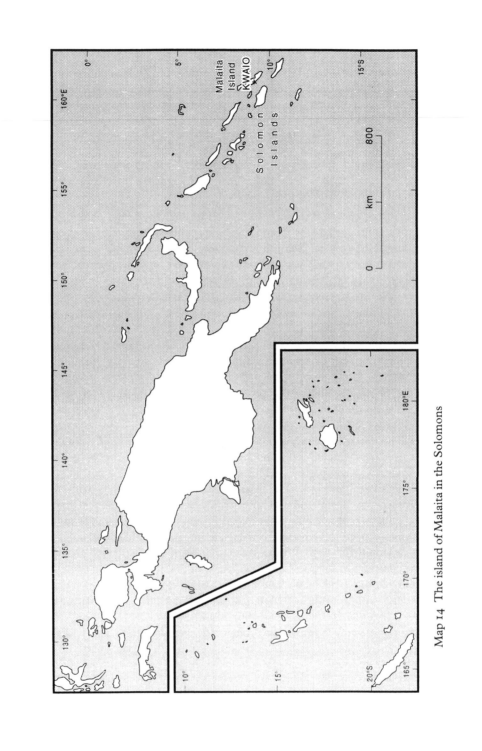

Map 14   The island of Malaita in the Solomons

system that concentrates power in a relatively few wealthy hands. The contrast affords a comparative vantage point from which to view the contested relationship between individuals and groups. Just as the electron behaves as both a particle and a wave but cannot be observed simultaneously behaving as both, so we cannot conceive of an unsocialised human being or a social collectivity uninfluenced by the calculations of individual humans. These abstract intellectual issues are central to understanding social change, for they have to do with the forces that produce it. To what extent does change originate with discontented individuals, and why are they not content with current social arrangements? To what extent does any social entity exist in a state of constant unresolvable tension, predicated on irreconcilable contradictions and opposed values, that inevitably gives rise to dynamic flux? The phenomenon of *kastom* addresses these issues from a Melanesian perspective. In representing attempts to maintain individual identity in contexts of rapid social change it underlines the intriguing coexistence of change with continuity.

The Kwaio people who live on the island of Malaita have a long-standing involvement with *kastom*. Their population ranges from those who have embraced Christianity and avidly pursue development opportunities and commercial openings, largely along the coast, to those who are more conservative and attempt to follow their ancestors' ways in the interior. The customary life features swidden cultivation with taro and yams as staple crops, the exchange at important social events like weddings and funerals of shell valuables called *bata* (strings of ground and polished *Conus* shell discs), adherence to rules that enjoin the separation of the sexes because women are believed to endanger men's health, and the regular performance of elaborate rituals which include offerings to *adalo* ancestor spirits whom they believe continue to interfere in the lives of their descendants. According to Roger Keesing, the history of the Kwaio since the outside world's intrusion into their lives falls into three broad phases: violent confrontation, retreat into supernatural cults when armed resistance proved futile (the Kwaio having suffered brutal reprisals after the murder of a tax-collecting colonial officer in the 1920s), and finally political confrontation and negotiation with the central authorities.

Kwaio *kastom*

The Kwaio interest in *kastom* is complex and invites a range of complementary interpretations. On one level it reflects a concern over the loss of cultural identity, a response to feeling overwhelmed by the outside world. In the words of one Malaitan man:

All our customs are going to break down. It's not the same for us as it is for Europeans. They write things down in books. We see in their Bible how everything is recorded: the generations, the passing of the years. But we pass our custom down from generation to generation, and unless we preserve it, it will break down and eventually disappear as the elders die. We have to raise it up and make it strong, and we have to write it down so it won't be lost. (Keesing 1992:123)

But the capture of *kastom* for posterity is not a straightforward matter of pride in one's cultural heritage – of seeking to establish a history and culture comparable to others to anchor one's identity in the world and give a sense of dignity and respect. Any attempt at formal recognition of *kastom* is constantly open to negotiation and challenge as different parties attempt to manipulate events to their perceived advantage. In societies where previously there was no cultural self-awareness there is the initial problem of deciding what constitutes *kastom*, the content of this category being subject to varying interpretations depending on one's life experiences and aspirations. Anthropologists can even find themselves dragged into these debates as supposed authorities on issues relating to custom, sometimes seeing their work cited as a definitive source of knowledge and even used to arbitrate in disputes over details of custom. This is perplexing for anthropologists, particularly in the light of the postmodernist argument that the outside academic's view is unavoidably a theory-driven distortion of the indigenous perspective. This conflict of interpretations can become evident when people pursuing *kastom* try to enlist the assistance of an anthropologist. The Kwaio, for example, became exasperated at anthropologist Roger Keesing's interest in sociological issues and community interaction and his apparent unwillingness to comply with their views about how they should document Kwaio culture:

My hosts were happy when I documented what fell squarely into their category of *kastomu*. I wanted to know, too, how people went about their daily lives. Who slept where? Who chopped the firewood? Where this could be cast rhetorically in terms of taboos or women's virtues, the Kwaio ideologues were satisfied; but often, my interest in the mundane was in their eyes a waste of time.

The Kwaio wanted an Old-Testament-like genealogical record of previous generations, detailed historical documentation about who used what areas of land and for what purposes, and the legalistic formulation of taboos and practices associated with listed shrines to serve as 'law' to guide behaviour. This clash of views over what *kastom* is not only highlights the partial nature of the anthropological record but also puts the discipline in an ironic position as regards its own identity. The irony is that as the discipline struggles to encompass contemporary homogenis-

Plate 14.1 Malaitan women grinding the small shell discs that, threaded onto lengths of string, make up the 'currency' exchanged at important social events.

ing global trends without losing its intellectual integrity, so Melanesians are seeking to present themselves in all their cultural heterogeneity and distinctiveness, sometimes even reinventing traditions with the assistance of ethnographic texts. Anthropology is transfixed by the intriguing contradiction that is increasingly manifesting itself around the world – that as people become swept up by the global community they struggle to reassert their local cultural heritage and difference.

The struggle for *kastom* may also take on a local political aspect as part of people's attempts to come to terms with and to some extent manage and manipulate the intrusion of the outside world. This is evident when people are exposed to the predatory capitalist market, where production arrangements and associated commodity transactions for profit not only contrast markedly with but also threaten to subvert the sociopolitical exchange that is so prominent in Melanesian social life. A Kwaio man expressed the problem as follows (Keesing 1992:149–50):

My shell valuables – that's the foundation on which I stand. That's what's been passed down to us. If there was a fight, if something bad happened, it would be straightened out with valuables [as compensation], as has always been our way, for twenty or thirty generations . . . From olden times, whatever bad things happened, we straightened them out with our own [shell] money, our own Kwaio money. Nothing is left in a mess after it is fixed up. The hostility doesn't keep spreading like vines on a trellis. But the law [loa] you've brought doesn't fit our living here in Kwaio . . . That's the kind of freedom for the Kwaio. That's the real kind of government for Kwaio. Resolving things – quarrels, fights – with the exchange of valuables. It's shell money that settles things.

When Kwaio men marry, they and their relatives amass wealth to present to the bride's kin to legitimate their union, and when someone dies the kin who bury the corpse receive a mortuary prestation. These transactions set up reciprocal obligations which balance equally over time. It is by excelling in these events that one achieves high standing and renown. It is significant from the point of view of *kastom* that the Kwaio restrict the wealth acceptable in these transactions to strings of shell discs and locally reared pigs. It is as if they were attempting to compartmentalise their lives, to insulate these aspects of them from corrosive contact with outside forces – the monetary economy and state government (see chapters 6 and 9). The distinction between *kastom* and *bisnis* is notable in this regard: one features shell wealth and the other cash, and, critically, the two differ in the form and duration of the social and political relations they entail. If money were to feature in sociopolitical exchange, it would alter these relationships and give those who could earn more money the opportunity to dominate sociopolitical exchange and destroy the egalitarian basis of local communities of which this exchange is an integral part. Alternatively, young men returning from migrant labour might use cash to finance their own marriages and other exchange commitments, thus buying themselves out of dependence on their kin for assistance and short-circuiting the logic of the exchange system. The autonomy of the Melanesian sociopolitical individual is enshrined in *kastom* that stipulates that only customary shell wealth is acceptable in exchange. The threat of *bisnis* is subordination.

On another level *kastom* may take on a national political aspect, expressing resistance to incorporation into the nation-state. Both aversion to the stealthy progress of capitalism, with its unequal relations of production, and noisy confrontation with the state have contributed to the emergence of *kastom*. Before the Europeans arrived, Melanesians

Plate 14.2 Two young Malaitan men discuss the shell wealth to be
contributed to a bridewealth, spread out on the linoleum floor of a
house in Honiara, capital of the Solomon Islands.

lived in sovereign social orders, albeit small-scale acephalous tribal ones, the polar opposite of the large-scale nation-states that came to dominate them. While initially in awe of the technological capacity of the outsiders and eager to acquire the material advantages of the industrial world without fully appreciating their political-economic and sociological implications, they have come to resent the invasion of their lands and lives and their defeat at the hands of the newcomers. A Kwaio man expressed these feelings as follows (Keesing 1992:149):

> I want to live on the land that has been passed down from my ancestors, down to my grandfathers. I want to live there in freedom . . . What I envision is that kind of freedom that came down from ancient times. Who are you, the government of the Solomon Islands, to come here and mess up my living? . . . What have I transgressed, that you can come here and say I've done something wrong? When I'm following the ways that have come down to me from ancient times! . . . You, the government in Honiara – what right have you to seize control of us here in Kwaio? None. We have always been free, responsible for ourselves. But you, the government, have just come and messed us up!

The emergence of *kastom* challenges the state's claim to be benevolently bringing the rule of law to uncivilised and anarchic tribespeople who will be grateful once they recognise its benefits.

The Kwaio, like people everywhere, are reluctant to pay taxes, but, given their cultural heritage, in which reciprocity is a moral imperative, their resistance takes on a uniquely Melanesian aspect. It seems to Kwaio that the government exact taxes without giving anything in return and it is therefore understandable that resistance to paying taxes should relate to cultural identity and to their attempts to secure political autonomy. The problem has been how to resist effectively. Early encounters demonstrated the futility of armed resistance, and it has gradually become evident that one effective way to oppose domination is to adopt and turn to one's own ends some of the outsiders' discourse. An early example of this concerns a man who smashed a valuable consecrated pearl-shell chest pendant, ground a piece down to the size and shape of a coin, carved a likeness on it, and presented it together with four shillings to a tax-collecting district officer, saying: 'The other four have your King on them; this one has my ancestor on it' (Keesing 1992:232). The following year, unfortunately, the same Kwaio man led a violent assault on the tax-collecting patrol, killing all of its members, and this brought retributory patrols to burn down houses, smash ancestral shrines, and kill Kwaio. The desecration and murder still haunt them to this day.

The formulation of opposition to cultural domination in terms of *kastom* has itself emerged from the adoption of outsiders' categories to resist it, for, as we have seen, people entertained no such conceptions in pre-contact times. Today people present customary practice as an alternative to Western-derived law. A desire to establish the legitimacy of customary law in opposition to the alien laws of the Solomon Islands state in part drives the Kwaio wish to codify *kastom* by writing it down. Coming from a non-literate cultural tradition, people actually sense that writing imparts power, even mystery, to words and by using the same medium of communication they hope to empower themselves. For decades the Kwaio have been imprisoned and even sometimes hanged for following precepts that were culturally legitimate, such as exacting violent revenge on those who had harmed or wronged their kin, and they have had to contain their rage at seeing wrongdoers who have committed serious offences, such as adultery, treated leniently by the state's judiciary. The aggrieved parties gain no satisfaction either through appropriate retaliation or through adequate compensation in a relationship-repairing exchange. In the words of a Kwaio man (Keesing 1992:195–6):

In the old days we used to meet all the time to discuss what's happening and straighten out whatever is going wrong. But now we just all go our separate ways. We don't work together anymore. We just are wandering around lost . . . We need to start working to straighten out our customs. We don't want to hide what we're doing from the Government. We want our customs to be recognised as if they were laws, so that people in our area have to follow them. We want to be able to settle disputes according to custom.

It is not only economic and political changes that people are questioning through *kastom* but religious ones too. An intriguing refiguring of relations is occurring between *kastom* and church. Whereas previously custom was associated by missionaries with savage pagans, ignorance and immoral behaviour, and church with civilised belief, enlightenment and propriety, today's Melanesians question this dichotomy. The positive reassessment of indigenous ideology and praxis with the emergence of *kastom* has given people the confidence to question trends in the wider modern world. At a time when internal contradictions are mounting in Western society, it makes sense to them to hark back to a time of self-sufficiency and independence. While Pacific nations are now caught up in the global consumer culture, they are also experiencing the problems of unemployment, rising living costs to meet rising material expectations and the associated increase in poverty, economies that are weak and prone to fiscal shock, mounting social problems, particularly in urban areas, and lawlessness. It is understandable that some people are questioning the way ahead, their relations with the wider world, and the identity they project to it.

Tourism and *kastom*

The governments of the South-West Pacific see their countries' cultures as potentially significant revenue earners if promoted as destinations for cultural tourism. A recent headline in the *Post Courier* (16 October 1996), quotes the minister of culture and tourism as saying, 'Cultures of PNG are a gold mine', and urging members of his audience at the Simbu Cultural Show to maintain their traditions with pride. He was reiterating a well-established government policy, regularly reflected in the promotional materials of the Papua New Guinea Tourism Promotion Authority with advertisements such as: 'If you think our scenery is impressive, wait until you meet our people.' The result is that increasingly local people are being exposed to tourists, and tourism in a sense consequently informs identity according to outsiders' conceptions of indigenous culture. What this means is that people have to maintain an image that complies with the tourists' expectations – one of exotic, even primitive cultures largely unsullied by the outside world. The Tourism Promotion Authority's brochure *Papua New Guinea Paradise Live* claims that:

Papua New Guinea is, in the truest sense, the last frontier on earth . . . It was barely more than a century ago that the first Europeans really explored this diverse and fascinating country, and there are still many areas that remain virtually untouched by western influences . . . This dramatic setting is home to an extraordinary array of cultures, unique to PNG. Travellers setting out on an adventure through this amazing country will be exposed to some of the most ancient traditions in the world.

One region promoted as a popular destination for culture-hungry tourists is the mighty Sepik River, with its renowned artistic tradition and its cults and elaborately decorated ceremonial houses. Others include the highlands, with its warriors sporting colourful self-decoration, elaborate wigs and feather headdresses, including the mudmen of the Asaro Valley. Also the world's original bungee jumpers on Pentecost Island, whose dramatic initiatory land dives are now performed to entertain visitors. On the Sepik River, tour companies operate specially designed cruise ships which, according to the promotional literature, offer air-conditioned deluxe accommodation, while providing 'intimate exposure to the area without the mass tourism often experienced elsewhere'. The Sepik is described as 'an area where the river banks are dotted with many large traditional villages. Each village features its own unique "*haus tambaran*" or spirit house decorated with ancestral figures, massive garamut drums and secretive ancient ritual flutes.' Among the tours that are on offer, 'every Monday, the *Sepik Spirit* cruises the remote and seldom visited Blackwater Lakes area. Here passengers can mingle with the friendly local people and experience a culture that encounters few outsiders each year.' Few, that is, other than those in the regular Monday stopovers, when the tour company encourages some of the local people to perform some appropriate cultural activity for the tourists. One such activity is a *singsing* dance, preferably with some associated ritual in or around the *haus tambaran* or even some initiation rite. The impact on tourists, to judge from their comments, is generally favourable, as is shown by the following extract from an account published in Air Niugini's in-flight magazine, *Paradise* (March–April 1996:20):

After walking along a carefully tended path, through a rainforest filled with tropical birds, lush ferns, brightly coloured butterflies and flowers, we rounded the last bend and were taken by surprise at the *haus tambaran* which resembled a 'cathedral' . . . In front of the stairway, a semi-circle of elders were grouped, ready to begin singing-in the spirits . . . The elders began to chant to the beat of hand drums. One by one, they called out the names of the long deceased warriors, famous for their valiant deeds . . . there was a sudden burst of sound from within the house: hand drums, bull roarer, blasts on bamboo horns and beating of the floor barring the spirits from escape . . . from the farthest end of the *haus tambaran* came the deep notes of five old garamut drums which together with the notes from the *haus* signified the spirits were again in residence. The chanting swelled, giving thanks to the spirits for their return. The atmosphere was spell bounding! Passengers sat in silence for some time after the ceremony. No one understood what they had felt, but for each it was a moving experience. I had goose bumps!

In addition to witnessing some exotic tribal activity and capturing it on film, tourists are also usually eager to obtain mementos of their visit and men's houses have been turned into virtual art galleries to meet this demand, displaying various carvings of figures, masks, weapons and other ritual paraphernalia for sale to visitors. The impact on artifact production has been considerable, with men competing to produce things that sell well to tourists, appealing to their sense of the primitive without being too gaudy and of suitcase dimensions – sometimes scaled-down and sometimes made to be disassembled. Makers of these objects do not imbue them with supernatural power by chanting secret totemic names over them. They produce them to earn cash, and the objects therefore function as commodities in ephemeral social transactions which entail no further obligations or relations – the antithesis of the reciprocal exchanges that feature so prominently in Melanesian society. The social interaction with tourists, brief and vacuous and founded on cash, is one manifestation of the commercialisation of relations that comes with the capitalist market.

The identity implications for those dwelling along the Sepik River are profound. The initiation of young men, involving painful scarification of the back and weeks of torment and ritual indoctrination by their seniors, was previously an important stage in the formulation of personhood, but today the rites are staged as tourist attractions for which admission is charged 'as a mark of respect for tradition'. These rituals and other 'traditional' practices which attract the tourists will, like the manufacture of carved objects, inevitably change through being staged for outside audiences. In other words, perceptions of what the outsiders want will mould the identities people present to them. The irony is that the tourists are increasingly witnessing not what the local people live as their culture but a distorted-mirror-like reflection of their ancestral ways. The local people are giving the visitors what they believe is a privileged glimpse of the last of the 'primitives' before they change irrevocably in confrontation with the outside world of which the tourists themselves are a part. The irony for the Sepik people is that what makes them do this is the desire to earn cash that will allow them access to the products of the market – clothes, outboards, Coca-Cola – but success in this will undermine their capacity to continue earning because their attraction is as 'unchanged' and 'primitive'.

Melanesian ways

Few Melanesians wish to promote the image of themselves as primitive; they are eager to formulate their own identities in the emerging global society. This development of a national, even regional identity is less a conscious endeavour than an evolving experience, symbolised by the burgeoning of support for national sports teams like the PNG Pukpuks in regional and global international events. But some people are debating these issues and trying to formulate more clearly what it means to be a Solomon Islander, a Papua New Guinean or a Melanesian today. At this level concerns with identity are opposed in some regards to those with *kastom*, for whereas the latter revels in the differences between cultural and linguistic groups and may even be interpreted as a rejection of the state, the former wrestles to identify commonalties and to bind groups together – to forge national identities from the region's disparate cultures.

The problem is promoting a consensus view of what will comprise this shared national and regional identity. Some people are encouraging its emergence through the arts with theatre groups, dance troupes, and string bands all evolving distinctive Melanesian styles, as are artists like painters and sculptors experimenting with new media. These vibrant contemporary expressions of 'Melanesianness' stand in stark contrast to tourist-demand primitive art, which stifles creativity and free expression of ideas. Perhaps the nearest these two come to converging is at the various annual cultural shows, such as the Hiri Moale Festival in Port Moresby and the Highlands Shows in Mount Hagen, Goroka and else-

Plate 14.3 Artists experiment with Papua New Guinea's identity using new materials and traditional designs at the Waigani National Arts School.

where. These colourful events attract large tourist audiences with their displays of traditional finery and dances interspersed with contemporary innovations. They celebrate the region's cultural variety while simultaneously bringing people together, and it is this capacity to accommodate diversity without animosity, a genuine cosmopolitan tolerance, which some cite as characteristic of what in the 1980s came to be dubbed the 'Melanesian way'. Others cite the level of violence between members of different sociocultural groups, particularly in urban settings, as evidence to the contrary.

These issues are under incessant debate by intellectuals, politicians, writers and others in novels, autobiographies, newspaper articles and academic reflections. The well-known Papua New Guinean thinker Bernard Narokobi, who has frequently advocated the 'Melanesian way' as the path to the future, writes (1980:9–11):

I see a new vision and a new hope for Melanesians. I see ourselves holding fast to the worthy customs of our people. I see Melanesians accepting principles of Christianity. I see Melanesians as a people who have patience and time for every person. I see Melanesians giving their highest regard to the spirituality of the human dignity and the proper but insignificant role to the building up of status

Plate 14.4 Cultural performances increasingly cater to tourism, a
Manus Island troupe plays on slit-gongs.

through materialism . . . Our vision sees the human person in his totality with the
spirit world as well as the animal and plant world. Human person is not an absolute master of the universe but an important perhaps the most important component in a world of interdependence of the person with the animal, the plant and
the spiritual worlds . . . We should spring from our cultural values to forge ahead
in a world that is moving more and more towards a confused uniformity, monot-
ony and insensitivity to the fine, subtle and sublime beauty of diversity. It is the
simplistic imperialist who seeks uniformity as a technique to command obedience
. . . Papua New Guinea has been portrayed as a land of division, of disunity, of 700
languages and thousands of cultures. Some have even dared to call it a land of
chaos . . . More and more I travel throughout these rich and beautiful lands of
ours, and listen to the old and young, I am convinced, Melanesians are guided by
a common cultural and spiritual unity, though diverse in many cultural practices,
including languages, still we are united, and are different from Asians or
Europeans . . . Our common unity has been at work thousands of years ago. We
are a united people because of our common vision.

It is intriguing to reflect on what the world has to learn from Melanesia.
There is a clear message in Narokobi's definition of the 'Melanesian
way' for those who believe in conservation of the natural environment
and advocate sustainable development and use of natural resources.
Elsewhere (1989:34–6), on sociopolitical issues, he has written:

Now that we are in international contact with the rest of humankind, where do we go from here? This moves us to ask: What kind of society do we want for ourselves and our people? These questions are often answered in ideological terms such as, do we want capitalism or socialism or a mixture of both; do we want Western, African, Eastern or other models? We must categorically reject any brand of 'ism.' All too often, leaders get caught in the great 'isms' of their flags and deny or suppress the basic needs of their people. An over-simplistic description of the predominant 'ism' in the world would place the concepts of 'individualism' and 'collectivism,' at opposite ends of a continuum. The proponents of each consider theirs to be the more scientific, rational and 'freeing,' and the other, more irrational, emotive and 'oppressive.' We are not alone in cautioning against blind adoption of one or the other . . . [It is] almost impossible to draw the rigid distinction between actions which merely concern a man himself and actions which also concern society . . . In my view Melanesian communities had reached a scientifically advanced stage of progress and had no need to pass through any Marxist mill! At the same time, the very nature of Melanesian communities afforded flexibility which is adequate to adjust the old orders to new institutional phenomena. Marxists assume that through class struggle, there was an 'excluded majority,' controlled and dominated by an all powerful minority . . . Melanesian societies, on the whole, did not have an 'excluded majority,' for even where there was a paramount chief, he rarely issued orders without consultation with lesser chiefs and elders. Participation in the processes of decision making was reasonably high . . . absence of any claim to 'rationalism,' 'scientific approach' or 'supremacy,' and indeed its absence of any claim that the law was given by a Divine Being to 'uphold the cosmic order,' makes it singularly open to develop principles that will best meet its needs.

It is fascinating to contemplate what state systems, whether democratic or totalitarian, capitalist or communist, might have to learn from Melanesian tribal orders as they struggle to adapt to incorporation within nations, particularly for those who believe in individual liberty, equality and fairness. Maybe they will evolve something new – come to some new accommodation of right and left.

In promoting this view of Melanesian distinctiveness, Narokobi and others have been criticised for promoting external intolerance of non-Melanesian cultures. They hotly deny the charge. The struggle for a Melanesian identity can, however, be seen in part as a reaction to Occidental racism experienced over two or three generations of colonial rule (Narokobi 1980:13 and 15):

Over the centuries, Melanesians have come to see themselves as they are understood and written up by foreigners. Melanesians are walking in the shadows of their Western thinkers and analysts. . . . I am merely exposing the ugly mask of racism practised in Melanesia. PNG must develop its own institutions to meet its changing needs. To cling on to foreign systems as if they are divinely conceived and given birth to, is not only racist, but inhuman, for it denies us our right to be creative, to make mistakes and to learn from these mistakes.

This is a theme alluded to by Michael Somare, who as the first prime minister of independent Papua New Guinea contributed significantly to the political emancipation of his country: 'We do not wish to become a nation of black Australians. Only if we learn to understand the values of our traditional cultures will we be able to bring to the task of modern nation building that special touch that will allow us to build a unique country' (Somare 1975:14). It is in this spirit that he talks of his initiation: the 'ceremony meant that I had again struck roots at home. Rather than remaining a floating city dweller I had been reintegrated with my clan, my family and my village. The wisdom of Sana, my grandfather, had been passed on to me together with his strength and his fighting spirit' (Somare 1975:37).

It would be imprudent, if not impertinent, for an outsider to presume to predict future trends. But it is likely that the Papua New Guinea Tourism Promotion Authority's slogan inviting us to visit 'the land of the unexpected' will continue to have some resonance, at least for foreigners, as Melanesians surprise us with their responses to global pressures. Change is occurring very rapidly, and those caught up in it have diverse interests and agendas, informed by very different cultural heritages and histories. It appears that the way ahead will be both exciting and painful, rewarding and perplexing, as these Pacific islanders struggle with their own destinies in an increasingly complex and integrated global community. The novelist Michael Yake Meli captures the mood in his prize winning novel *The Call of the Land* (1993:47–9):

'Watinga, that's exactly what I mean. You and I, regardless, have to accept the way our people see and define things, from their point of view. It is so very easy for you and me, who are sitting on the threshold of change, to almost ignore their predicament. However, we are the ones going through the experience. Our ways will grow less traditional and hard to follow while the white man's ways will be easier to us,' explained Bulda.

Watinga said doubtfully, concern on his face, 'Bulda, I agree with what you just said. All this time I have been asking myself, what am I going to be upon completion of my schooling? What kind of life will I lead in the town – a way of life our people are not used to? What does this whole experience mean to me and my people? I ask this question all the time.'

Smiling his usual friendly smile, Watinga spoke again. 'Bro, I feel grateful for the conversation we've just had. Now that you've opened my mind to the effects of such a dual system and the effects the traditional and the foreign have on you and me, and our peoples, I am greatly relieved. But there is more. Something else.'

'Let's hear it, Watinga?' Bulda asked, as he turned and peered through the window, but still listening.

'Yeah, the traditional and the modern. How can one live, accepting the new but still holding onto what is good of the old ways?'

'Brother, this is one of the fundamental questions most citizens of our country are asking themselves today. Personally, I'd prefer to accept both systems but apply them to suit the circumstances. I'd rather be flexible because we've already accepted the white man's ways and the fact that it is too late to return to our traditional ways.'

Watinga spoke, 'Brother, what you say is true. Today, if we compare ourselves with the elders, we find they are completely different because they have missed out on the formal education process.'

'What is the difference?' Bulda asked.

'I mean our grandparents were brought up under our traditional code of conduct. You and I seem like victims of the introduction of the European ways. We are like the sacrificial lamb, having to pay the price and be torn apart by the demands of the two different cultures.'

'You're right, but not exactly,' said Bulda. 'There are both advantages and disadvantages to the question of introduction of foreign values. As we are all aware, our country is composed of many tribes and a few hundred different languages. We have diverse cultures ranging from those of the flat coastal areas up to those of the rugged mountains, such as ours. Today, however, the thousand independent mini-governments or tribes have all united and are under one umbrella, making ours one of the most unique nations in the world. We have a National Parliament which is a parliament of a thousand tribes. The negative side may be the cost involved in changing to the foreign way as you have suggested.'

FURTHER READING

On *kastom* and identity see:

R. J. Foster 1995 *Social reproduction and history in Melanesia* Cambridge: Cambridge University Press

R. J. Foster (ed.) 1995 *Nation making: emergent identities in postcolonial Melanesia* Ann Arbor: University of Michigan Press

R. M. Keesing 1992 *Custom and confrontation: the Kwaio struggle for cultural autonomy* Chicago: University of Chicago Press

R. M. Keesing and R. Tonkinson (eds.) 1982 Reinventing traditional culture: the politics of *kastom* in island Melanesia *Mankind* 13(4)

M. Kwa'ioloa with Ben Burt 1997 *Living tradition: a changing life in the Solomon Islands* London: British Museum Press

C. Moore 1985 *Kanaka: a history of Melanesian Mackay* Port Moresby: Institute of Papua New Guinea Studies

G. White 1991 *Identity through history: living stories in a Solomon Islands society* Cambridge: Cambridge University Press

On tourism see:

D. B. Gewertz and F. K. Errington 1991 *Twisted histories, altered contexts* Cambridge: Cambridge University Press

Also see:

B. Narokobi 1980 *The Melanesian way* Port Moresby: Institute of Papua New Guinea Studies

B. Narokobi 1983 *Life and leadership in Melanesia* Suva: Institute of Pacific Studies, University of the South Pacific

B. Narokobi 1989 *Lo bilong yumi yet: law and custom in Melanesia* Suva: Institute of Pacific Studies, University of the South Pacific

T. Otto and N. Thomas (eds.) 1997 *Narratives of nation in the South Pacific* Amsterdam: Harwood Academic

U. Samana 1988 *Papua New Guinea: which way?* Melbourne: Arena Publications

M. Somare 1975 Sana: *an autobiography of Michael Somare* Port Moresby: Niugini Press

FILMS

Cannibal tours Institute of Papua New Guinea Studies Video-Cassette Series

Wokabout bilong tonten Institute of Papua New Guinea Studies Video-Cassette Series

Marab Institute of Papua New Guinea Studies Video-Cassette Series

Gogodala. A cultural revival? Pacific Video-Cassette Series No. 2

Malangan labadama: a tribute to Buk Buk Pacific Video-Cassette Series No. 10

Index